THE HUGO WINNERS

VOLUME THREE

Science Fiction Anthologies
edited by Isaac Asimov

VOLUME THREE

THE HUGO WINNERS

Edited by Isaac Asimov

Doubleday & Company, Inc., Garden City, New York

In "Adrift Just Off the Islets of Langerhans: Latitude 38° 54′ N, Longitude
77° 00′ 13″ W" by Harlan Ellison, excerpt from "Little Gidding" in *Four
Quartets* by T. S. Eliot, copyright © 1943, by T. S. Eliot; copyright ©
1971, by Esme Valerie Eliot. Reprinted by permission of Harcourt Brace
Jovanovich, Inc., and Faber and Faber, Ltd.
"Ship of Shadows," by Fritz Leiber, copyright © 1969 by Mercury Press,
Inc. Reprinted by permission of the author and the author's agent, Robert P.
Mills, Ltd.
"Ill Met in Lankhmar," by Fritz Leiber, copyright © 1969 by Mercury
Press, Inc. Reprinted by permission of the author and the author's agent,
Robert P. Mills, Ltd.
"Slow Sculpture," by Theodore Sturgeon, copyright © 1970 by Universal
Publishing and Distributing Corp. Reprinted by permission of the author
and the author's agent, Kirby McCauley.
"The Queen of Air and Darkness," by Poul Anderson, copyright © 1971 by
Mercury Press, Inc. Reprinted by permission of the author and the author's
agent, Scott Meredith Literary Agency, Inc.
"Inconstant Moon," by Larry Niven, copyright © 1971 by Larry Niven. Re-
printed by permission of the author and the author's agent, Robert P. Mills,
Inc.
"The Word for World Is Forest," by Ursula K. Le Guin, copyright © 1972
by Ursula K. Le Guin. Reprinted by permission of Berkley Publishing Cor-
poration.

To Sharon Jarvis and to Cathleen Jordan
for helping, but mostly for being around

Contents

THIRD TIME AROUND
by Isaac Asimov

Back in 1962, I edited an anthology of Hugo winners—that is, those stories that had won those awards called Hugos, in honor of Hugo Gernsback, the founder of magazine science fiction, which are voted annually by those attending the World Science Fiction Conventions.

Through a stroke of inspired brilliance, I called this anthology of Hugo winners *The Hugo Winners*.

The Hugo Winners covered the conventions from the thirteenth at Cleveland in 1955 (at which Hugos in all categories were first awarded) to the nineteenth at Seattle in 1961.

I recall feeling at the time that once the Hugo-awarding activities of these conventions had reached a fitting climax through the appearance of an anthology devoted to them, and edited by a person of note, sane and rational, fearless and intrepid, witty and forceful, and, above all, devilishly handsome, the conventions would heave a sigh of relief and stop the practice. (I even wanted them to do so since they all showed a distressing tendency to overlook my own work when the time came to hand out the awards.)

To my confusion, however, they did not. Conventions continued to award Hugos year after year; and for year after year new Hugo winners spewed forth in such profusion that even I was absent-mindedly handed a couple.

Finally, there was nothing left to do but to put out a new anthology on the subject, covering the conventions from the twentieth at Chicago in 1962 to the twenty-eighth at Heidelberg in 1970. I drew on my vivid imagination for a new title for this new anthology and came up with a real sparkler: *The Hugo Winners, Volume Two*. It was published in 1971.

But that didn't halt things, either. Indeed, there seems to have developed a tendency to make stories longer and to increase the incidence of ties. The second volume was twice as long as the first, for instance, though the second covered nine years compared to the first's six. And though this third volume has gone back to covering only six years, it is as thick as the second.

In fact, although the book is being published in 1977, there was only room for the conventions from the twenty-ninth in Boston in 1971 to the thirty-third in Melbourne in 1975. The thirty-fourth convention in Kansas City in 1976, though now history, will have to wait for the fourth volume.

Now that I've gone through the convention statistics, let me explain a couple of things about these anthologies, taking the Gentle Readers into my confidence (as is my wont) and hiding nothing from them. You will notice that these volumes of Hugo winners are published at long intervals. Why are there not annual volumes, as there are, for instance, annual volumes of the Nebula winners?° There are several reasons for this.

1. Neither Doubleday nor I thought of doing this. We didn't dream, back in 1916, that the readers' appetite for anthologies was such that we could stick them with one every year, especially since, in order to flesh out the volume, we would have had to include also-rans—as is true in the annual Nebula volumes.

2. The Nebula volumes are edited each year by a different editor. (I edited the eighth volume in 1973.) This means that no one editor need be intellectually maimed and shattered oftener than once. (Have you any idea how difficult it is dealing with prize-winning authors? Not one of them is as sweet and delightful as I am.) For the Hugo winner anthologies, however, any other editor but myself is unthinkable—at least, I can't think of any—and I have to be carefully rationed. Since I am (despite appearances) not superhuman, I can only do the editing once in a long while.

° The Nebula awards are given out annually by the Science Fiction Writers of America. They are writers' awards while the Hugos are readers' awards.

3. And besides, it works out. Since these Hugo winners volumes appear only at long intervals, the crazed public, parched and maddened for them, buys them in large quantities over an indefinitely long period of time. Neither Doubleday nor myself, nor the authors represented in these volumes, for that matter, are interested in financial rewards—we are above such things—but we do obtain deep spiritual pleasure in satisfying the Gentle Reader.

Now for a second point. When I did the first volume, it was necessary for me to write introductions to the stories and to the volume as a whole. The usual pattern in such introductions had always been to write a philosophical piece as general intro and a slavishly sycophantic piece, praising each story, as special intros.

I couldn't do that. For one thing, I didn't select the stories, the readers did—so that it is not my place to praise the stories. This is especially true if I should happen to disagree with the readers' decisions, as when one of my own stories loses out. I have to be sportsmanlike in such cases and pretend I don't have the deepest contempt for the resultant miscarriage of justice, and I can do that only if I don't talk about the story at all.

Then, too, I didn't feel like praising the authors, since when this whole thing started I had never won a Hugo myself and I was filled with righteous indignation against all those who had perpetuated this injustice by accepting the awards. Instead, then, I seized the opportunity in the general introductions to denounce the Establishment and used the story introductions as an opportunity to insult the author.

It worked out fine. It made me feel a lot better.

I continued this in the second volume, but with a great deal more difficulty.

You see, in the old days, I was totally immersed in science fiction and it was a rather small field. This meant that I knew all the authors personally; we were all Convention buddies; we were all drunk together (no, I don't drink because I don't have to; I was born drunk). Therefore, when it came time to introduce a story by one of these dearest of all dear friends, I was primed with vicious jabs and degrading anecdotes about them.

Ah, how things have changed.

For one thing, while I have maintained my connection with science fiction, while I write stories and articles for the magazines and have even initiated a new magazine entitled *Isaac Asimov's Science Fiction Magazine* (published by Davis Publications and edited by George Scithers, who was mentioned in the introduction to the second volume), I must admit that manifold other activities have filled much of my time. For another, the number of bright new talented writers increases yearly and most of them are almost unknown to me on a personal basis.

I can't jibe savagely at strangers. That's what *friends* are for.

I am afraid, therefore, that in some cases you will find me unaccustomedly gentle with an author. I may have to find some other subject to talk about. I may even, in sheer desperation, have to violate my well-known modesty and talk about myself.

1970
28th *CONVENTION*
HEIDELBERG

Fritz Leiber

This story made it, as you see, at the twenty-eighth convention in Heidelberg in 1970. Naturally, *I* didn't make it. I don't fly and I've got a thing about traveling, because it takes me away from my typewriter. (Don't sneer. How would you like to be away from *your* typewriter?)

Consequently, when I looked at a map of the world and found that Heidelberg was seven full inches from New York, I turned pale and had to sit down at the typewriter and type seven full pages before I recovered. Heck, I have to steel myself to drive to New Haven and that's only a quarter of an inch from New York.

Anyway, the point is that I wasn't around when "Ship of Shadows" won the Hugo at Heidelberg. It therefore didn't burn itself into my brain, as it certainly would have had I been there, since Fritz had won a Hugo only two years earlier at the twenty-sixth convention in San Francisco and I despise greedy people.

Consequently, when I sat down to put together Volume Two of this series, which covered the conventions from 1962 to 1970 inclusive, I made a small error. I knew that there had been two winners in the shorter-than-novel categories which are included in these volumes and when I listed Samuel R. Delany's "Time Considered as a Helix of Semi-Precious Stones," the title was so long that I thought it covered both of them. I looked no further and "Ship of Shadows" was therefore inadvertently omitted.

I found out about it, of course, as soon as Volume Two was published. For one thing, in the appendix, in which all the Hugo winners in every category are listed, there, under the twenty-eighth convention, is to be found "Ship of Shadows" by Fritz Leiber as the Hugo-winning novella.

Naturally, many a shrewd and sharp-eyed reader noted the discrepancy and I received a volley of letters from those of them who had searched the volume minutely (some of them looking under the chair, too, in case it had dropped out) and in vain for the story. I was accused of having been paid off by the notorious anti-Leiber faction at the Science Fiction Writers of America.

(This is not so. There is no anti-Leiber faction. Everybody loves Fritz. It is true I *have* accepted bribes to leave out Harlan Ellison, but I always tell him about it and he doubles the bribe to have me leave him in.)

I promised everyone, of course, that I would place the story in an anthology at the first available opportunity and this is the opportunity. I am sorry, Fritz. I know that you should have been collecting royalties for six years on this story, and I am only grateful that you happen to be the kind of guy who has always donated all your royalties to charity anyway.

1

SHIP OF SHADOWS

"Issiot! Fffool! Lushshsh!" hissed the cat and bit Spar some-where.

The fourfold sting of the eye teeth balanced the gut-wretchedness of his looming hangover, so that Spar's mind floated as free as his body in the blackness of Windrush, in which shone only a couple of running lights dim as churning dream-glow and infinitely distant as the Bridge or the Stern.

The vision came of a ship with all sails set creaming through blue, wind-ruffled sea against a blue sky. The last two nouns were not obscene now. He could hear the whistle of the salty wind through shrouds and stays, its drumming against the taut sails, and the creak of the three masts and all the rest of the ship's wood.

What was wood? From somewhere came the answer: plastic alive-o.

And what force flattened the water and kept it from breaking up into great globules and the ship from spinning away, keel over masts, in the wind?

Instead of being blurred and rounded like reality, the vision was sharp-edged and bright—the sort Spar never told, for fear of being accused of second sight and so of witchcraft.

Windrush was a ship too, was often called the Ship. But it was a strange sort of ship, in which the sailors lived forever in the shrouds inside cabins of all shapes made of translucent sails welded together. And it was a ship that was not sailing any-where, because it had everywhere in it—it was all there was.

The only other things the two ships shared were the wind and the unending creaking. As the vision faded, Spar began to hear the winds of Windrush softly moaning through the long passageways, while he felt the creaking in the vibrant shroud to which he was clipped wrist and ankle to keep him from floating around in the Bat Rack.

Sleepday's dreams had begun good, with Spar having Crown's three girls at once. But Sleepday night he had been half-waked by the distant grinding of Hold Three's big chewer. Then werewolves and vampires had attacked him, solid shadows diving in from all six corners, while witches and their familiars tittered in the black shadowy background. Somehow he had been protected by the cat, familiar of a slim witch whose bared teeth had been an ivory blur in the larger silver blur of her wild hair. Spar pressed his rubbery gums together. The cat had been the last of the supernatural creatures to fade. Then had come the beautiful vision of the ship.

His hangover hit him suddenly and mercilessly. Sweat shook off him until he must be surrounded by a cloud of it. Without warning his gut reversed. His free hand found a floating waste tube in time to press its small trumpet to his face. He could hear his acrid vomit gurgling away, urged by a light suction.

His gut reversed again, quick as the flap of a safety hatch when a gale blows up in the corridors. He thrust the waste tube inside the leg of his short, loose slopsuit and caught the dark stuff, almost as watery and quite as explosive as his vomit. Then he had the burning urge to make water.

Afterwards, feeling blessedly weak, Spar curled up in the equally blessed dark and prepared to snooze until Keeper woke him.

"Sssot!" hissed the cat. "Sssleep no more! Sssee! Sssee shshsharply!"

In his left shoulder, through the worn fabric of his slopsuit, Spar could feel four sets of prickles, like the touch of small thorn clusters in the Gardens of Apollo or Diana. He froze.

"Sspar," the cat hissed more softly, quitting to prickle. "I wishsh you all besst. Mosst ashshuredly."

Spar warily reached his right hand across his chest, touched short fur softer than Suzy's, and stroked gingerly.

The cat hissed very softly, almost purring, "Ssturdy Sspar! Ssee ffar! Ssee fforever! Fforessee! Afftssee!"

Spar felt a surge of irritation at this constant talk of seeing—

bad manners in the cat!—followed by an irrational surge of hope about his eyes. He decided that this was no witch cat left over from his dream, but a stray which had wormed its way through a wind tube into the Bat Rack, setting off his dream. There were quite a few animal strays in these days of the witch panic and the depopulation of the Ship, or at least of Hold Three.

Dawn struck the Bow then, for the violet fore-corner of the Bat Rack began to glow. The running lights were drowned in a growing white blaze. Within twenty heartbeats Windrush was bright as it ever would be on Workday or any other morning.

Out along Spar's arm moved the cat, a black blur to his squinting eyes. In teeth Spar could not see, it held a smaller gray blur. Spar touched the latter. It was even shorter furred, but cold.

As if irked, the cat took off from his bare forearm with a strong push of hind legs. It landed expertly on the next shroud a wavery line of gray that vanished in either direction before reaching a wall.

Spar unclipped himself, curled his toes round his own pencil-thin shroud, and squinted at the cat.

The cat stared back with eyes that were green blurs which almost coalesced in the black blur of its outsize head.

Spar asked, "Your child? Dead?"

The cat loosed its gray burden, which floated beside its head.

"Chchchchild!" All the former scorn and more were back in the sibilant voice. "It izzzz a rat I sssslew her, issssiot!"

Spar's lips puckered in a smile. "I like you, cat. I will call you Kim."

"Kim-shlim!" the cat spat. "I'll call you Lushshsh! Or Sssot!"

The creaking increased, as it always did after dayspring and noon. Shrouds twanged. Walls crackled.

Spar swiftly swiveled his head. Though reality was by its nature a blur, he could unerringly spot movement.

Keeper was slowly floating straight at him. On the round of his russet body was mounted the great, pale round of his face, its bright pink target-center drawing attention from the tiny, wide-set, brown blurs of his eyes. One of his fat arms ended in the bright gleam of pliofilm, the other in the dark gleam of steel. Far beyond him was the dark red aft corner of the Bat Rack, with the great gleaming torus, or doughnut, of the bar midway between.

"Lazy, pampered he-slut," Keeper greeted. "All Sleepday you snored while I stood guard, and now I bring your morning pouch of moonmist to your sleeping shroud.

"A bad night, Spar," he went on, his voice growing sententious. "Werewolves, vampires, and witches loose in the corridors. But I stood them off, not to mention rats and mice. I heard through the tubes that the vamps got Girlie and Sweetheart, the silly sluts! Vigilance, Spar! Now suck your moonmist and start sweeping. The place stinks."

He stretched out the pliofilm-gleaming hand.

His mind hissing with Kim's contemptuous words, Spar said, "I don't think I'll drink this morning, Keeper. Corn gruel and moonbrew only. No, water."

"What, Spar?" Keeper demanded. "I don't believe I can allow that. We don't want you having convulsions in front of the customers. Earth strangle me!—what's that?"

Spar instantly launched himself at Keeper's steel-gleaming hand. Behind him his shroud twanged. With one hand he twisted a cold, thick barrel. With the other he pried a plump finger from a trigger.

"He's not a witch cat, only a stray," he said as they tumbled over and kept slowly rotating.

"Unhand me, underling!" Keeper blustered. "I'll have you in irons. I'll tell Crown."

"Shooting weapons are as much against the law as knives or needles," Spar countered boldly, though he already was feeling dizzy and sick. "It's you should fear the brig." He recognized beneath the bullying voice the awe Keeper always had of his ability to move swiftly and surely, though half-blind.

They bounced to rest against a swarm of shrouds. "Loose me, I say," Keeper demanded, struggling weakly. "Crown gave me this pistol. And I have a permit for it from the Bridge." The last at least, Spar guessed, was a lie. Keeper continued, "Besides, it's only a line-shooting gun reworked for heavy, elastic ball. Not enough to rupture a wall, yet sufficient to knock out drunks—or knock in the head of a witch cat!"

"Not a witch cat, Keeper," Spar repeated, although he was

having to swallow hard to keep from spewing. "Only a well-behaved stray, who has already proved his use to us by killing one of the rats that have been stealing our food. His name is Kim. He'll be a good worker."

The distant blur of Kim lengthened and showed thin blurs of legs and tail, as if he were standing out rampant from his line. "Assset izz I," he boasted. "Ssanitary. Uzze wasste tubes. Sslay ratss, micece! Sspy out witchchess, vampss ffor you!"

"He speaks!" Keeper gasped. "Witchcraft!"

"Crown has a dog who talks," Spar answered with finality. "A talking animal's no proof of anything."

All this while he had kept firm hold of barrel and finger. Now he felt through their grappled bodies a change in Keeper, as though inside his blubber the master of the Bat Rack were transforming from stocky muscle and bone into a very thick, sweet syrup that could conform to and flow around anything.

"Sorry, Spar," he whispered unctuously. "It was a bad night and Kim startled me. He's black like a witch cat. An easy mistake on my part. We'll try him out at catcher. He must earn his keep! Now take your drink."

The pliant double pouch filling Spar's palm felt like the philosopher's stone. He lifted it toward his lips, but at the same time his toes unwittingly found a shroud, and he dove swiftly toward the shining torus, which had a hole big enough to accommodate four barmen at a pinch.

Spar collapsed against the opposite inside of the hole. With a straining of its shrouds, the torus absorbed his impact. He had the pouch to his lips, its cap unscrewed, but had not squeezed. He shut his eyes and with a tiny sob blindly thrust the pouch back into the moonmist cage.

Working chiefly by touch, he took a pouch of corn gruel from the hot closet, snitching at the same time a pouch of coffee and thrusting it into an inside pocket. Then he took a pouch of water, opened it, shoved in five salt tablets, closed it, and shook and squeezed it vigorously.

Keeper, having drifted behind him, said into his ear, "So you drink anyhow. Moonmist not good enough, you make yourself a cocktail. I should dock it from your scrip. But all drunks are liars, or become so."

Unable to ignore the taunt, Spar explained, "No, only salt water to harden my gums."

"Poor Spar, what'll you ever need hard gums for? Planning to share rats with your new friend? Don't let me catch you roasting them in my grill! I should dock you for the salt. To sweeping, Spar!" Then turning his head toward the violet fore-corner and speaking loudly, "And you! Catch mice!"

Kim had already found the small chewer tube and thrust the dead rat into it, gripping tube with foreclaws and pushing rat with aft. At the touch of the rat's cadaver against the solid wrist of the tube, a grinding began there which would continue until the rat was macerated and slowly swallowed away toward the great cloaca which fed the Gardens of Diana.

Three times Spar manfully swished salt water against his gums and spat into a waste tube, vomiting a little after the first gargle. Then facing away from Keeper as he gently squeezed the pouches, he forced into his throat the coffee—dearer than moonmist, the drink distilled from moonbrew—and some of the corn gruel.

He apologetically offered the rest to Kim, who shook his head. "Jusst had a mousse."

Hastily Spar made his way to the green starboard corner. Outside the hatch he heard some drunks calling with weary and mournful anger, "Unzip!"

Grasping the heads of two long waste tubes, Spar began to sweep the air, working out from the green corner in a spiral, quite like an orb spider building her web.

From the torus, where he was idly polishing its thin titanium, Keeper upped the suction on the two tubes, so that reaction sped Spar in his spiral. He need use his body only to steer course and to avoid shrouds in such a way that his tubes didn't tangle.

Soon Keeper glanced at his wrist and called, "Spar, can't you keep track of the time? Open up!" He threw a ring of keys which Spar caught, though he could see only the last half of their flight. As soon as he was well headed toward the green door, Keeper called again and pointed aft and aloft. Spar obediently unlocked and unzipped the dark and also the blue hatch, though there was no one at either, before opening the green. In each case he avoided the hatch's gummy margin and the sticky emergency hatch hinged close beside.

In tumbled three brewos, old customers, snatching at shrouds and pushing off from each other's bodies in their haste to reach the torus, and meanwhile cursing Spar.

"Sky strangle you!"

"Earth bury you!"

"Seas sear you!"

"Language, boys!" Keeper reproved. "Though I'll agree my helper's stupidity and sloth tempt a man to talk foul."

Spar threw the keys back. The brewos lined up elbow to elbow around the torus, three grayish blobs with heads pointing toward the blue corner.

Keeper faced them. "Below, below!" he ordered indignantly. "You think you're gents?"

"But you're serving no one aloft yet."

"There's only us three."

"No matter," Keeper replied. "Propriety, suckers! Unless you mean to buy by the pouch, invert."

With low grumbles the brewos reversed their bodies so that their heads pointed toward the black corner.

Himself not bothering to invert, Keeper tossed them a slim and twisty faint red blur with three branches. Each grabbed a branch and stuck it in his face.

The pudge of his fat hand on glint of valve, Keeper said, "Let's see your scrip first."

With angry mumbles each unwadded something too small for Spar to see clearly, and handed it over. Keeper studied each item before feeding it to the cashbox. Then he decreed, "Six seconds of moonbrew. Suck fast," and looked at his wrist and moved the other hand.

One of the brewos seemed to be strangling, but he blew out through his nose and kept sucking bravely.

Keeper closed the valve.

Instantly one brewo splutteringly accused, "You cut us off too soon. That wasn't six."

The treacle back in his voice, Keeper explained, "I'm squirting it to you four and two. Don't want you to drown. Ready again?"

The brewos greedily took their second squirt and then, at

times wistfully sucking their tubes for remnant drops, began to shoot the breeze. In his distant circling, Spar's keen ears heard most of it.

"A dirty Sleepday, Keeper."

"No, a good one, brewo—for a drunken sucker to get his blood sucked by a lust-tickling vamp."

"I was dossed safe at Pete's, you fat ghoul."

"Pete's safe? That's news!"

"Dirty Atoms to you! But vamps did get Girlie and Sweetheart. Right in the starboard main drag, if you can believe it. By Cobalt Ninety, Windrush is getting lonely! Third Hold, anyhow. You can swim a whole passageway by day without meeting a soul."

"How do you know that about the girls?" the second brewo demanded. "Maybe they've gone to another hold to change their luck."

"Their luck's run out. Suzy saw them snatched."

"Not Suzy," Keeper corrected, now playing umpire. "But Mabel did. A proper fate for drunken sluts."

"You've got no heart, Keeper."

"True enough. That's why the vamps pass me by. But speaking serious, boys, the werethings and witches are running too free in Three. I was awake all Sleepday guarding. I'm sending a complaint to the Bridge."

"You're kidding."

"You wouldn't."

Keeper solemnly nodded his head and crossed his left chest. The brewos were impressed.

Spar spiraled back toward the green corner, sweeping farther from the wall. On his way he overtook the black blob of Kim, who was circling the periphery himself, industriously leaping from shroud to shroud and occasionally making dashes along them.

A fair-skinned, plump shape twice circled by blue—bra and culottes—swam in through the green hatch.

"Morning, Spar," a soft voice greeted. "How's it going?"

"Fair and foul," Spar replied. The golden cloud of blonde hair floating loose touched his face. "I'm quitting moonmist, Suzy."

"Don't be too hard on yourself, Spar. Work a day, loaf a day, play a day, sleep a day—that way it's best."

"I know. Workday, Loafday, Playday, Sleepday. Ten days make a terranth, twelve terranths make a sunth, twelve sunths make a starth, and so on, to the end of time. With corrections, some tell me. I wish I knew what all those names mean."

"You're too serious. You should— Oh, a kitten! How darling!"

"Kitten-shmitten!" the big-headed black blur hissed as it leapt past them. "Izzz cat. IZZZ Kim."

"Kim's our new catcher," Spar explained. "He's serious too."

"Quit wasting time on old Toothless Eyeless, Suzy," Keeper called, "and come all the way in."

As Suzy complied with a sigh, taking the easy route of the ratlines, her soft taper fingers brushed Spar's crumpled cheek. "Dear Spar . . ." she murmured. As her feet passed his face, there was a jingle of her charm-anklet—all gold-washed hearts, Spar knew.

"Hear about Girlie and Sweetheart?" a brewo greeted ghoulishly. "How'd you like your carotid or outside iliac sliced, your—?"

"Shut up, sucker!" Suzy wearily cut him off. "Gimme a drink, Keeper."

"Your tab's long, Suzy. How you going to pay?"

"Don't play games, Keeper, please. Not in the morning, anyhow. You know all the answers, especially to that one. For now, a pouch of moonbrew, dark. And a little quiet."

"Pouches are for ladies, Suzy. I'll serve you aloft, you got to meet your marks, but—"

There was a shrill snarl which swiftly mounted to a scream of rage. Just inside the aft hatch, a pale figure in vermilion culottes and bra—no, wider than that, jacket or short coat—was struggling madly, somersaulting and kicking.

Entering carelessly, likely too swiftly, the slim girl had got parts of herself and her clothes stuck to the hatch's inside margin and the emergency hatch.

Breaking loose by frantic main force while Spar dove toward her and the brewos shouted advice, she streaked toward the torus, jerking at the ratlines, black hair streaming behind her.

Coming up with a *bong* of hip against titanium, she grabbed together her vermilion—yes, clutch coat with one hand and thrust the other across the rocking bar.

Drifting in close behind, Spar heard her say, "Double pouch of moonmist, Keeper. Make it fast."

"The best of mornings to you, Rixende," Keeper greeted. "I would gladly serve you goldwater, except, well—" The fat arms spread "—Crown doesn't like his girls coming to the Bat Rack by themselves. Last time he gave me strict orders to—"

"What the smoke! It's on Crown's account I came here, to find something he lost. Meanwhile, moonmist. Double!" She pounded on the bar until reaction started her aloft, and she pulled back into place with Spar's unthanked help.

"Softly, softly, lady," Keeper gentled, the tiny brown blurs of his eyes vanishing with his grinning. "What if Crown comes in while you're squeezing?"

"He won't!" Rixende denied vehemently, though glancing past Spar quickly—black blur, blur of pale face, black blur again. "He's got a new girl. I don't mean Phanette or Doucette, but a girl you've never seen. Name of Almodie. He'll be busy with the skinny bitch all morning. And now uncage that double moonmist, you dirty devil!"

"Softly, Rixie. All in good time. What is it Crown lost?"

"A little black bag. About so big." She extended her slender hand, fingers merged. "He lost it here last Playday night, or had it lifted."

"Hear that, Spar?" Keeper said.

"No little black bags," Spar said very quickly. "But you did leave your big orange one here last night, Rixende. I'll get it." He swung inside the torus.

"Oh, damn both bags. Gimme that double!" the black-haired girl demanded frantically. "Earth Mother!"

Even the brewos gasped. Touching hands to the side of his head, Keeper begged. "No big obscenities, please. They sound worse from a dainty girl, gentle Rixende."

"Earth Mother, I said! Now cut the fancy, Keeper, and give, before I scratch your face off and rummage your cages!"

"Very well, very well. At once, at once. But how will you pay? Crown told me he'd get my license revoked if I ever put you on his tab again. Have you scrip? Or . . . . coins?"

"Use your eyes! Or you think this coat's got inside pockets?" She spread it wide, flashing her upper body, then clutched it tight again. "Earth Mother! Earth Mother! Earth Mother!" The brewos babbled scandalized. Suzy snorted mildly in boredom.

With one fat hand-blob Keeper touched Rixende's wrist where a yellow blur circled it closely. "You've got gold," he said in hushed tones, his eyes vanishing again, this time in greed.

"You know damn well they're welded on. My anklets too."

"But these?" His hand went to a golden blur close beside her head.

"Welded too. Crown had my ears pierced."

"But . . ."

"Oh, you atom-dirty devil! I get you, all right. Well, then, *all right!*" The last words ended in a scream more of anger than pain as she grabbed a gold blur and jerked. Blood swiftly blobbed out. She thrust forward her fisted hand. "Now *give!* Gold for a double moonmist."

Keeper breathed hard but said nothing as he scrabbled in the moonmist cage, as if knowing he had gone too far. The brewos were silent too. Suzy sounded completely unimpressed as she said, "*And* my dark." Spar found a fresh dry sponge and expertly caught up the floating scarlet blobs with it before pressing it to Rixende's torn ear.

Keeper studied the heavy gold pendant, which he held close to his face. Rixende milked the double pouch pressed to her lips and her eyes vanished as she sucked blissfully. Spar guided Rixende's free hand to the sponge, and she automatically took over the task of holding it to her ear. Suzy gave a hopeless sigh, then reached her whole plump body across the bar, dipped her hand into a cool cage, and helped herself to a double of dark.

A long, wiry, very dark brown figure in skintight dark violet jumpers mottled with silver arrowed in from the dark red hatch at a speed half again as great as Spar ever dared and without brushing a single shroud by accident or intent. Midway the newcomer did a half somersault as he passed Spar, his long, narrow bare feet hit the titanium next to Rixende. He accordioned up so expertly that the torus hardly swayed.

One very dark brown arm snaked around her. The other

plucked the pouch from her mouth, and there was a snap as he spun the cap shut.

A lazy musical voice inquired, "What'd we tell you would happen, baby, if you ever again took a drink on your own?"

The Bat Rack held very still. Keeper was backed against the opposite side of the hole, one hand behind him. Spar had his arm in his lost-and-found nook behind the moonbrew and moonmist cages and kept it there. He felt fear-sweat beading on him. Suzy kept her dark close to her face.

A brewo burst into violent coughing, choked it to a wheezing end, and gasped subserviently, "Excuse me, coroner. Salutations."

Keeper chimed dully, "Morning . . . Crown."

Crown gently pulled the clutch coat off Rixende's far shoulder and began to stroke her. "Why, you're all gooseflesh, honey, and rigid as a corpse. What frightened you? Smooth down, skin. Ease up, muscles. Relax, Rix, and we'll give you a squirt."

His hand found the sponge, stopped, investigated, found the wet part, then went toward the middle of his face. He sniffed.

"Well, boys, at least we know none of you are vamps," he observed softly. "Else we'd found you sucking at her ear."

Rixende said very rapidly in a monotone, "I didn't come for a drink, I swear to you. I came to get that little bag you lost. Then I was tempted. I didn't know I would be. I tried to resist, but Keeper led me on. I—"

"Shut up," Crown said quietly. "We were just wondering how you paid him. Now we know. How were you planning to buy your third double? Cut off a hand or a foot? Keeper . . . show me your other hand. We said show it. That's right. Now unfist."

Crown plucked the pendant from Keeper's opened hand-blob. His yellow-brown eye-blurs on Keeper all the while, he wagged the precious bauble back and forth, then tossed it slowly aloft.

As the golden blur moved toward the open blue hatch at unchanging pace, Keeper opened and shut his mouth twice, then babbled, "I didn't tempt her, Crown, honest I didn't. I didn't know she was going to hurt her ear. I tried to stop her, but—"

"We're not interested," Crown said. "Put the double on our tab." His face never leaving Keeper's, he extended his arm aloft and pinched the pendant just before it straight-lined out of reach.

"Why's this home of jollity so dead?" Snaking a long leg across the bar as easily as an arm, Crown pinched Spar's ear between his big and smaller toes, pulled him close and turned him round. "How're you coming along with the saline, baby? Gums hardening? Only one way to test it." Gripping Spar's jaw and lip with his other toes, he thrust the big one into Spar's mouth. "Come on, bite me, baby."

Spar bit. It was the only way not to vomit. Crown chuckled. Spar bit hard. Energy flooded his shaking frame. His face grew hot and his forehead throbbed under its drenching of fear-sweat. He was sure he was hurting Crown, but the Coroner of Hold Three only kept up his low, delighted chuckle and when Spar gasped, withdrew his foot.

"My, my, you're getting strong, baby. We almost felt that. Have a drink on us."

Spar ducked his stupidly wide-open mouth away from the thin jet of moonmist. The jet struck him in his eye and stung so that he had to knot his fists and clamp his aching gums together to keep from crying out.

"Why's this place so dead, I ask again? No applause for baby and now baby's gone temperance on us. Can't you give us just one tiny laugh?" Crown faced each in turn. "What's the matter? Cat got your tongues?"

"Cat? We have a cat, a new cat, came just last night, working as catcher," Keeper suddenly babbled. "It can talk a little. Not as well as Hellhound, but it talks. It's very funny. It caught a rat."

"What'd you do with the rat's body, Keeper?"

"Fed it to the chewer. That is, Spar did. Or the cat."

"You mean to tell us that you disposed of a corpse without notifying us? Oh, don't go pale on us, Keeper. That's nothing. Why, we could accuse you of harboring a witch cat. You say he came last night, and that was a wicked night for witches. Now don't go green on us too. We were only putting you on. We were only looking for a small laugh."

"Spar! Call your cat! Make him say something funny."

Before Spar could call, or even decide whether he'd call Kim or not, the black blur appeared on a shroud near Crown, green eye-blurs fixed on the yellow-brown ones.

"So you're the joker, eh? Well . . . joke."

Kim increased in size. Spar realized it was his fur standing on end.

"Go ahead, joke . . . like they tell us you can. Keeper, you wouldn't be kidding us about this cat being able to talk?"

"Spar! Make your cat joke!"

"Don't bother. We believe he's got his own tongue too. That the matter, Blackie?" He reached out his hand. Kim lashed at it and sprang away. Crown only gave another of his low chuckles.

Rixende began to shake uncontrollably. Crown examined her solicitously yet leisurely, using his outstretched hand to turn her head toward him, so that any blood that might have been coming from it from the cat's slash would have gone into the sponge.

"Spar swore the cat could talk," Keeper babbled. "I'll—"

"Quiet," Crown said. He put the pouch to Rixende's lips, squeezed until her shaking subsided and it was empty, then flicked the crumpled pliofilm toward Spar.

"And now about that little black bag, Keeper," Crown said flatly.

"Spar!"

The latter dipped into his lost-and-found nook, saying quickly, "No little black bags, coroner, but we did find this one the lady Rixende forgot last Playday night," and he turned back holding out something big, round, gleamingly orange, and closed with draw strings.

Crown took and swung it slowly in a circle. For Spar, who couldn't see the strings, it was like magic. "Bit too big, and a mite the wrong shade. We're certain we lost the little black bag here, or had it lifted. You making the Bat Rack a tent for dips, Keeper?"

"Spar—?"

"We're asking *you*, Keeper."

Shoving Spar aside, Keeper groped frantically in the nook, pulling aside the cages of moonmist and moonbrew pouches. He produced many small objects. Spar could distinguish the largest —an electric hand-fan and a bright red footglove. They hung around Keeper in a jumble.

Keeper was panting and had scrabbled his hands for a full minute in the nook without bringing out anything more, when Crown said, his voice lazy again, "That's enough. The little black bag was of no importance to us in any case."

Keeper emerged with a face doubly blurred. It must be surrounded by a haze of sweat. He pointed an arm at the orange bag.

"It might be inside that one!"

Crown opened the bag, began to search through it, changed his mind, and gave the whole bag a flick. Its remarkably numerous contents came out and moved slowly aloft at equal speeds, like an army on the march in irregular order. Crown scanned them as they went past.

"No, not there." He pushed the bag toward Keeper. "Return Rix's stuff to it and have it ready for us the next time we dive in—"

Putting his arm around Rixende, so that it was his hand that held the sponge to her ear, he turned and kicked off powerfully for the aft hatch. After he had been out of sight for several seconds, there was a general sigh, the three brewos put out new scrip-wads to pay for another squirt. Suzy asked for a second double dark, which Spar handed her quickly, while Keeper shook off his daze and ordered Spar, "Gather up all the floating trash, especially Rixie's, and get that back in her purse. On the jump, lubber!" Then he used the electric hand-fan to cool and dry himself.

It was a mean task Keeper had set Spar, but Kim came to help, darting after objects too small for Spar to see. Once he had them in his hands, Spar could readily finger or sniff which was which.

When his impotent rage at Crown had faded, Spar's thoughts went back to Sleepday night. Had his vision of vamps and werewolves been dream only?—now that he knew the werethings had been abroad in force. If only he had better eyes to distinguish illusion from reality! Kim's "Sssee! Sssee shshsharply!" hissed in his memory. What would it be like to see sharply? Everything brighter? Or closer?

After a weary time the scattered objects were gathered and he went back to sweeping and Kim to his mouse hunt. As Workday morning progressed, the Bat Rack gradually grew less bright, though so gradually it was hard to tell.

A few more customers came in, but all for quick drinks, which Keeper served them glumly; Suzy judged none of them worth cottoning up to.

As time slowly passed, Keeper grew steadily more fretfully angry, as Spar had known he would after groveling before Crown. He tried to throw out the three brewos, but they produced more crumpled scrip, which closest scrutiny couldn't prove counterfeit. In revenge he short-squirted them and there were arguments. He called Spar off his sweeping to ask him nervously, "That cat of yours—he scratched Crown, didn't he? We'll have to get rid of him; Crown said he might be a witch cat, remember?" Spar made no answer. Keeper set him renewing the glue of the emergency hatches, claiming that Rixende's tearing free from the aft one had shown it must be drying out. He gobbled appetizers and drank moonmist with tomato juice. He sprayed the Bat Rack with some abominable synthetic scent. He started counting the boxed scrip and coins but gave up the job with a slam of self-locking drawer almost before he'd begun. His grimace fixed on Suzy.

"Spar!" he called. "Take over! And over-squirt the brewos on your peril!"

Then he locked the cash box, and giving Suzy a meaningful jerk of his head toward the scarlet starboard hatch, he pulled himself toward it. With an unhappy shrug toward Spar, she wearily followed.

As soon as the pair were gone, Spar gave the brewos an eight-second squirt, waving back their scrip, and placed two small serving cages—of fritos and yeast balls—before them. They grunted their thanks and fell to. The light changed from healthy bright to corpse white. There was a faint, distant roar, followed some seconds later by a brief crescendo of creakings. The new light made Spar uneasy. He served two more suck-and-dives and sold a pouch of moonmist at double purser's prices. He started to eat an appetizer, but just then Kim swam in to show him proudly a mouse. He conquered his nausea, but began to dread the onset of real withdrawal symptoms.

A pot-bellied figure clad in sober black dragged itself along the ratlines from the green hatch. On the aloft side of the bar there appeared a visage in which the blur of white hair and beard almost hid leather-brown flesh, though accentuating the blurs of gray eyes.

"Doc!" Spar greeted, his misery and unease gone, and instantly handed out a chill pouch of three-star moonbrew. Yet all he could think to say in his excitement was the banal, "A bad Sleep-day night, eh, Doc? Vamps and—"

"—And other doltish superstitions, which wax every sunth, but never wane," an amiable, cynical old voice cut in. "Yet, I suppose I shouldn't rob you of your illusions, Spar, even the terrifying ones. You've little enough to live by, as it is. And there *is* viciousness astir in Windrush. Ah, that smacks good against my tonsils."

Then Spar remembered the important thing. Reaching deep inside his slopsuit, he brought out, in such a way as to hide it from the brewos below, a small flat narrow black bag.

"Here, Doc," he whispered, "you lost it last Playday. I kept it safe for you."

"Dammit, I'd lose my jumpers, if I ever took them off," Doc commented, hushing his voice when Spar put finger to lips. "I suppose I started mixing moonmist with my moonbrew—again?"

"You did, Doc. But you didn't lose your bag. Crown or one of his girls lifted it, or snagged it when it sat loose beside you. And then I . . . I, Doc, lifted it from Crown's hip pocket. Yes, and kept that secret when Rixende and Crown came in demanding it this morning."

"Spar, my boy, I am deeply in your debt," Doc said. "More than you can know. Another three-star, please. Ah, nectar. Spar, ask any reward of me, and if it lies merely within the realm of the first transfinite infinity, I will grant it."

To his own surprise, Spar began to shake—with excitement. Pulling himself forward halfway across the bar, he whispered hoarsely, "Give me good eyes, Doc!" adding impulsively, "and teeth!"

After what seemed a long while, Doc said in a dreamy, sorrowful voice, "In the Old Days, that would have been easy. They'd perfected eye transplants. They could regenerate cranial nerves, and sometimes restore scanning power to an injured cerebrum. While transplanting tooth buds from a stillborn was intern's play. But now . . . Oh, I might be able to do what you ask in an uncomfortable, antique, inorganic fashion, but . . ." He broke off on a note that spoke of the misery of life and the uselessness of all effort.

"The Old Days," one brewo said from the corner of his mouth to the brewo next to him. "Witch talk!"

"Witch-smitch!" the second brewo replied in like fashion. "The flesh mechanic's only senile. He dreams all four days, not just Sleepday."

The third brewo whistled against the evil eye a tune like the wind.

Spar tugged at the long-armed sleeve of Doc's black jumper. "Doc, you promised. I want to see sharp, bite sharp!"

Doc laid his shrunken hand commiseratingly on Spar's forearm. "Spar," he said softly, "seeing sharply would only make you very unhappy. Believe me, I *know*. Life's easier to bear when things are blurred, just as it's best when thoughts are blurred by brew or mist. And while there are people in Windrush who yearn to bite sharply, you are not their kind. Another three-star, if you please."

"I quit moonmist this morning, Doc," Spar said somewhat proudly as he handed over the fresh pouch.

Doc answered with sad smile, "Many quit moonmist every Workday morning and change their minds when Playday comes around."

"Not me, Doc! Besides," Spar argued, "Keeper and Crown and his girls and even Suzy all see sharply, and they aren't unhappy."

"I'll tell you a secret, Spar," Doc replied. "Keeper and Crown and the girls are all zombies. Yes, even Crown with his cunning and power. To them Windrush is the universe."

"It isn't, Doc?"

Ignoring the interruption, Doc continued, "But you wouldn't be like that, Spar. You'd want to know more. And that would make you far unhappier than you are."

"I don't care, Doc," Spar said. He repeated accusingly, "You promised."

The gray blurs of Doc's eyes almost vanished as he frowned in thought. Then he said, "How would this be, Spar? I know moonmist brings pains and sufferings as well as easings and joys. But suppose that every Workday morning and Loafday noon I should bring you a tiny pill that would give you all the good effects of moonmist and none of the bad. I've one in this bag. Try it now and see. And every Playday night I would bring you without fail another sort of pill that would make you sleep soundly with never a nightmare. Much better than eyes and teeth. Think it over."

As Spar considered that, Kim drifted up. He eyed Doc with his close-set green blurs. "Resspectfful greetingss, ssir," he hissed. "Name izz Kim."

Doc answered, "The same to you, sir. May mice be ever abundant." He softly stroked the cat, beginning with Kim's chin and chest. The dreaminess returned to his voice. "In the Old Days, all cats talked, not just a few sports. The entire feline tribe. And many dogs, too—pardon me, Kim. While as for dolphins and whales and apes . . ."

Spar said eagerly, "Answer me one question, Doc. If your pills give happiness without hangover, why do you always drink moonbrew yourself and sometimes spike it with moonmist?"

"Because for me—" Doc began and then broke off with a grin. "You've trapped me, Spar. I never thought you used your mind. Very well, on your own mind be it. Come to my office this Loafday—you know the way? Good!—and we'll see what we can do about your eyes and teeth. And now a double pouch for the corridor."

He paid in bright coins, thrust the big squunchy three-star in a big pocket, said, "See you, Spar. So long, Kim," and tugged himself toward the green hatch, zig-zagging.

"Ffarewell, ssir," Kim hissed after him.

Spar held out the small black bag. "You forgot it again, Doc."

As Doc returned with a weary curse and pocketed it, the scarlet hatch unzipped and Keeper swam out. He looked in a good humor now and whistled the tune of "I'll Marry the Man on the Bridge" as he began to study certain rounds on scrip-till and moonbrew valves, but when Doc was gone he asked Spar suspiciously, "What was that you handed the old geezer?"

"His purse," Spar replied easily. "He just forgot it now." He shook his loosely fisted hand and it chinked. "Doc paid in coins, Keeper." Keeper took them eagerly. "Back to sweeping, Spar."

As Spar dove toward the scarlet hatch to take up larboard tubes, Suzy emerged and passed him with face averted. She sidled up to the bar and unsmilingly snatched the pouch of moonmist Keeper offered her with mock courtliness.

Spar felt a brief rage on her behalf, but it was hard for him to keep his mind on anything but his coming appointment with Doc. When Workday night fell swiftly as a hurled knife, he was hardly aware of it and felt none of his customary unease. Keeper turned on full all of the lights in the Bat Rack. They shone brightly while beyond the translucent walls there was a milky churning.

Business picked up a little. Suzy made off with the first likely mark. Keeper called Spar to take over the torus, while he himself got a much-erased sheet of paper and holding it to a clipboard held against his bent knees, wrote on it laboriously, as if he were thinking out each word, perhaps each letter, often wetting his pencil in his mouth. He became so absorbed in his difficult task that without realizing he drifted off toward the black below hatch, rotating over and over. The paper got dirtier and dirtier with his scrawlings and smudgings, new erasures, saliva and sweat.

The short night passed more swiftly than Spar dared hope, so that the sudden glare of Loafday dawn startled him. Most of the customers made off to take their siestas.

Spar wondered what excuse to give Keeper for leaving the Bat Rack, but the problem was solved for him. Keeper folded the grimy sheet, and sealed it with hot tape. "Take this to the Bridge, loafer, to the Exec. Wait." He took the repacked, orange bag from its nook and pulled on the cords to make sure they were drawn tight. "On your way deliver this at Crown's Hole. With all courtesy and subservience, Spar! Now, on the jump!"

Spar slid the sealed message into his only pocket with working zipper and drew that tight. Then he dove slowly toward the aft hatch, where he almost collided with Kim. Recalling Keeper's talk of getting rid of the cat, he caught hold of him around the slim furry chest under the forelegs and gently thrust him inside his slopsuit, whispering, "You'll take a trip with me, little Kim." The cat set his claws in the thin material and steadied himself.

For Spar, the corridor was a narrow cylinder ending in mist either way and decorated by lengthwise blurs of green and red. He guided himself chiefly by touch and memory, this time remembering that he must pull himself against the light wind hand-over-hand along the centerline. After curving past the larger cylinders of the fore-and-aft gangways, the corridor straightened. Twice he worked his way around centrally slung fans whirring so softly that he recognized them chiefly by the increase in breeze before passing them and the slight suction after.

Soon he began to smell soil and green stuff growing. With a shiver he passed a black round that was the elastic-curtained door to Hold Three's big chewer. He met no one—odd even for Loafday. Finally he saw the green of the Gardens of Apollo and beyond it a huge black screen, in which hovered toward the aft side a small, smoky-orange circle that always filled Spar with inexplicable sadness and fear. He wondered in how many black screens that doleful circle was portrayed, especially in the starboard end of Windrush. He had seen it in several.

So close to the gardens that he could make out wavering green shoots and the silhouette of a floating farmer, the corridor right-angled below. Two dozen pulls along the line and he floated by an open hatch, which both memory for distance and the strong scent of musky, mixed perfumes told him was the entry to Crown's Hole. Peering in, he could see the intermelting black and silver spirals of the decor of the great globular room. Directly opposite the hatch was another large black screen with the red-mottled dun disk placed similarly off center.

From under Spar's chin, Kim hissed very softly, but urgently, "Sstop! Ssilencce, on your liffe!" The cat had poked his head out of the slopsuit's neck. His ears tickled Spar's throat. Spar was getting used to Kim's melodrama, and in any case the warning was hardly needed. He had just seen the half-dozen floating naked bodies and would have held still if only from embarrassment. Not that Spar could see genitals any more than ears at the distance. But he could see that save for hair, each body was of one texture: one very dark brown and the other five—or was it four? no, five—fair. He didn't recognize the two with platinum and golden hair, who also happened to be the two palest. He wondered which was Crown's new girl, name of Almodie. He was relieved that none of the bodies were touching.

There was the glint of metal by the golden-haired girl, and he could just discern the red blur of a slender, five-forked tube which went from the metal to the five other faces. It seemed strange that even with a girl to play bartender, Crown should have moonbrew served in such plebeian fashion in his palatial Hole. Of course the tube might carry moonwine, or even moonmist.

Or was Crown planning to open a rival bar to the Bat Rack? A poor time, these days, and a worse location, he mused as he tried to think of what to do with the orange bag.

"Sslink offf!" Kim urged still more softly.

Spar's fingers found a snap-ring by the hatch. With the faintest of clicks he secured it around the draw-cords of the pouch and then pulled back the way he had come.

But faint as the click had been, there was a response from Crown's Hole—a very deep, long growl.

Spar pulled faster at the centerline. As he rounded the corner leading inboard, he looked back.

Jutting out from Crown's hatch was a big, prick-eared head narrower than a man's and darker even than Crown's.

The growl was repeated.

It was ridiculous he should be so frightened of Hellhound, Spar told himself as he jerked himself and his passenger along. Why, Crown sometimes even brought the big dog to the Bat Rack.

Perhaps it was that Hellhound never growled in the Bat Rack, only talked in a hundred or so monosyllables.

Besides, the dog couldn't pull himself along the centerline at any speed. He lacked sharp claws. Though he might be able to bound forward, caroming from one side of the corridor to another.

This time the center-slit black curtains of the big chewer made Spar veer violently. He was a fine one—going to get new eyes today and frightened as a child!

"Why did you try to scare me back there, Kim?" he asked angrily.

"I ssaw shsheer evil, isssiot!"

"You saw five folk sucking moonbrew. And a harmless dog. This time you're the fool, Kim, you're the idiot!"

Kim shut up, drawing in his head, and refused to say another word. Spar remembered about the vanity and touchiness of all cats. But by now he had other worries. What if the orange bag were stolen by a passerby before Crown noticed it? And if Crown did find it, wouldn't he know Spar, forever Keeper's errandboy, had been peeping? That all this should happen on the most important day of his life! His verbal victory over Kim was small consolation.

Also, although the platinum-haired girl had interested him most of the two strange ones, something began to bother him about the girl who'd been playing bartender, the one with golden hair like Suzy's, but much slimmer and paler—he had the feeling he'd seen her before. And something about her had frightened him.

When he reached the central gangways, he was tempted to go to Doc's office before the Bridge. But he wanted to be able to relax at Doc's and take as much time as needed, knowing all errands were done.

Reluctantly he entered the windy violet gangway and dove at a fore angle for the first empty space on the central gang-line, so that his palms were only burned a little before he had firm hold of it and was being sped fore at about the same speed as the wind. Keeper was a miser, not to buy him handgloves, let alone footgloves!—but he had to pay sharp attention to passing the shroud-slung roller bearings that kept the thick, moving line centered in the big corridor. It was an easy trick to catch hold of the line ahead of the bearing and then get one's other hand out of the way, but it demanded watchfulness.

There were few figures traveling on the line and fewer still being blown along the corridor. He overtook a doubled up one tumbling over and over and crying out in an old cracked voice, "Jacob's Ladder, Tree of Life, Marriage Lines . . ."

He passed the squeeze in the gangway marking the division between the Third and Second Holds without being stopped by the guard there and then he almost missed the big blue corridor leading aloft. Again he slightly burned his palms making the transfer from one moving gang-line to another. His fretfulness increased.

"Sspar, you isssiot—!" Kim began.

"Ssh!—we're in officers' territory," Spar cut him off, glad to have that excuse for once more putting down the impudent cat. And true enough, the blue spaces of Windrush always did fill him with awe and dread.

Almost too soon to suit him, he found himself swinging from the gang-line to a stationary monkey jungle of tubular metal just below the deck of the Bridge. He worked his way to the aloft-most bars and floated there, waiting to be spoken to.

Much metal, in many strange shapes, gleamed in the Bridge, and there were irregularly pulsing rainbow surfaces, the closest of which sometimes seemed ranks of files of tiny lights going on and off—red, green, all colors. Aloft of everything was an endless velvet-black expanse very faintly blotched by churning, milky glintings.

Among the metal objects and the rainbows floated figures all clad in the midnight blue of officers. They sometimes gestured to each other, but never spoke a word. To Spar, each of their movements was freighted with profound significance. These were the gods of Windrush, who guided everything, if there were gods at all. He felt reduced in importance to a mouse, which would be chased off chittering if it once broke silence.

After a particularly tense flurry of gestures, there came a brief distant roar and a familiar creaking and crackling. Spar was amazed, yet at the same time realized he should have known that the Captain, the Navigator, and the rest were responsible for the familiar diurnal phenomena.

It also marked Loafday noon. Spar began to fret. His errands were taking too long. He began to lift his hand tentatively toward each passing figure in midnight blue. None took the least note of him.

Finally he whispered, "Kim—?"

The cat did not reply. He could hear a purring that might be a snore. He gently shook the cat. "Kim, let's talk."

"Shshut offf! I ssleep! Ssh!" Kim resettled himself and his

claws and recommenced his purring snore—whether natural or feigned, Spar could not tell. He felt very despondent.

The lunths crept by. He grew desperate and weary. He must not miss his appointment with Doc! He was nerving himself to move farther aloft and speak, when a pleasant, young voice said, "Hello, grandpa, what's on your mind?"

Spar realized that he had been raising his hand automatically and that a person as dark-skinned as Crown, but clad in midnight blue, had at last taken notice. He unzipped the note and handed it over. "For the Exec."

"That's my department." A trilled crackle—fingernail slitting the note? A larger crackle—note being opened. A brief wait. Then, "Who's Keeper?"

"Owner of the Bat Rack, sir. I work there."

"Bat Rack?"

"A moonbrew mansion. Once called the Happy Torus, I've been told. In the Old Days, Wine Mess Three, Doc told me."

"Hmm. Well, what's all this mean, gramps? And what's your name?"

Spar stared miserably at the dark-mottled gray square. "I can't read, sir. Name's Spar."

"Hmm. Seen any . . . er . . . supernatural beings in the Bat Rack?"

"Only in my dreams, sir."

"Mmm. Well, we'll have a look in. If you recognize me, don't let on. I'm Ensign Drake, by the way. Who's your passenger, grandpa?"

"Only my cat, Ensign," Spar breathed in alarm.

"Well, take the black shaft down." Spar began to move across the monkey jungle in the direction pointed out by the blue armblur.

"And next time remember animals aren't allowed on the Bridge."

As Spar traveled below, his warm relief that Ensign Drake had seemed quite human and compassionate was mixed with anxiety as to whether he still had time to visit Doc. He almost missed the shift to the gang-line grinding aft in the dark red main drag. The corpse-light brightening into the false dawn of late afternoon bothered him. Once more he passed the tumbling bent figure, this time croaking, "Trinity, Trellis, Wheat Ear . . ."

He was fighting down the urge to give up his visit to Doc and pull home to the Bat Rack, when he noticed he had passed the second squeeze and was in Hold Four with the passageway to Doc's coming up. He dove off, checked himself on a shroud and began the hand-drag to Doc's office, as far larboard as Crown's Hole was starboard.

He passed two figures clumsy on the line, their breaths malty in anticipation of Playday. Spar worried that Doc might have closed his office. He smelled soil and greenery again, from the Gardens of Diana.

The hatch was shut, but when Spar pressed the bulb, it unzipped after three honks, and the white-haloed gray-eyed face peered out.

"I'd just about give up on you, Spar."

"I'm sorry, Doc. I had to—"

"No matter. Come in, come in. Hello, Kim—take a look around if you want."

Kim crawled out, pushed off from Spar's chest, and soon was engaged in a typical cat's tour of inspection.

And there was a great deal to inspect, as even Spar could see. Every shroud in Doc's office seemed to have objects clipped along its entire length. There were blobs large and small, gleaming and dull, light and dark, translucent and solid. They were silhouetted against a wall of the corpse-light Spar feared, but had no time to think of now. At one end was a band of even brighter light.

"Careful Kim!" Spar called to the cat as he landed against a shroud and began to paw his way from blob to blob.

"He's all right," Doc said. "Let's have a look at you, Spar. Keep your eyes open."

Doc's hands held Spar's head. The gray eyes and leathery face came so close they were one blur.

"Keep them open, I said. Yes, I know you have to blink them, that's all right. Just as I thought. The lenses are dissolved. You've suffered the side-effect which one in ten do who are infected with the Lethean rickettsia."

"Styx ricks, Doc?"

"That's right, though the mob's got hold of the wrong river in the Underworld. But we've all had it. We've all drunk the water of Lethe. Though sometimes when we grow very old we begin to remember the beginning. Don't squirm."

"Hey, Doc, is it because I've had the Styx ricks I can't remember anything back before the Bat Rack?"

"It could be. How long have you been at the Rack?"

"I don't know, Doc. Forever."

"Before I found the place, anyhow. When the Rumdum closed here in Four. But that's only a starth ago."

"But I'm awful old, Doc. Why don't I start remembering?"

"You're not old, Spar. You're just bald and toothless and etched by moonmist and your muscles have shriveled. Yes, and your mind has shriveled too. Now open your mouth."

One of Doc's hands went to the back of Spar's neck. The other probed. "Your gums are tough, anyhow. That'll make it easier."

Spar wanted to tell about the salt water, but when Doc finally took his hand out of Spar's mouth, it was to say, "Now open wide as you can."

Doc pushed into his mouth something big as a handbag and hot. "Now bite down hard."

Spar felt as if he had bitten fire. He tried to open his mouth, but hands on his head and jaw held it closed. Involuntarily he kicked and clawed air. His eyes filled with tears.

"Stop writhing! Breathe through your nose. It's not that hot. Not hot enough to blister, anyhow."

Spar doubted that, but after a bit decided it wasn't quite hot enough to bake his brain through the roof of his mouth. Besides, he didn't want to show Doc his cowardice. He held still. He blinked several times and the general blur became the blurs of Doc's face and the cluttered room silhouetted by the corpse-glare. He tried to smile, but his lips were already stretched wider than their muscles could ever have done. That hurt too; he realized now that the heat was abating a little.

Doc was grinning for him. "Well, you would ask an old drunkard to use techniques he'd only read about. To make it up to you, I'll give you teeth sharp enough to sever shrouds. Kim, please get away from that bag."

The black blur of the cat was pushing off from a black blur

twice his length. Spar mumbled disapprovingly at Kim through his nose and made motions. The larger blur was shaped like Doc's little bag, but bigger than a hundred of them. It must be massive too, for in reaction to Kim's push it had bent the shroud to which it was attached and—the point—the shroud was very slow in straightening.

"That bag contains my treasure, Spar," Doc explained, and when Spar lifted his eyebrows twice to signal another question, went on, "No, not coin and gold and jewels, but a second transfinite infinitude—sleep and dreams and nightmares for every soul in a thousand Windrushes." He glanced at his wrist. "Time enough now. Open your mouth." Spar obeyed, though it cost him new pain.

Doc withdrew what Spar had bitten on, wrapped it in gleam, and clipped it to the nearest shroud. Then he looked in Spar's mouth again.

"I guess I did make it a bit too hot," he said. He found a small pouch, set it to Spar's lips, and squeezed it. A mist filled Spar's mouth and all pain vanished.

Doc tucked the pouch in Spar's pocket. "If the pain returns, use it again."

But before Spar could thank Doc, the latter had pressed a tube to his eye. "Look, Spar, what do you see?"

Spar cried out, he couldn't help it, and jerked his eye away.

"What's wrong, Spar?"

"Doc you gave me a dream," Spar said hoarsely. "You won't tell anyone, will you? And it tickled."

"What was the dream like?" Doc asked eagerly.

"Just a picture, Doc. The picture of a goat with the tail of a fish. Doc, I saw the fish's . . ." His mind groped, ". . . scales! Everything had . . . edges! Doc, is *that* what they mean when they talk about seeing sharply?"

"Of course, Spar. This is good. It means there's no cerebral or retinal damage. I'll have no trouble making up field glasses—that is, if there's nothing seriously wrong with my antique pair. So you still see things sharp-edged in dreams—that's natural enough. But why were you afraid of me telling?"

"Afraid of being accused of witchcraft, Doc. I thought seeing

things like that was clairvoyance. The tube tickled my eye a little."

"Isotopes and insanity! It's supposed to tickle. That's the field.
Let's try the other eye."

Again Spar wanted to cry out, but he restrained himself, and
this time he had no impulse to jerk his eye away, although there
was again the faint tickling. The picture was that of a slim girl.
He could tell she was female because of her general shape. But
he could see her edges. He could see . . . details. For instances,
her eyes weren't mist-bounded colored ovals. They had points at
both ends, which were china-white . . . triangles. And the pale
violet round between the triangles had a tiny black round at its
center.

She had silvery hair, yet she looked young, he thought, though
it was hard to judge such matters when you could see edges. She
made him think of the platinum-haired girl he'd glimpsed in
Crown's Hole.

She wore a long, gleaming white dress, which left her shoulders bare, but either art or some unknown force had drawn her
hair and her dress toward her feet. In her dress it made . . .
folds.

"What's her name, Doc? Almodie?"

"No. Virgo. The Virgin. You can see her edges?"

"Yes, Doc. Sharp. I get it!—like a knife. And the goat-fish?"

"Capricorn," Doc answered, removing the tube from Spar's
eye.

"Doc, I know Capricorn and Virgo are the names of lunths,
terranths, sunths, and starths, but I never knew they had pictures. I never knew they *were* anything."

"You— Of course, you've never seen watches, or stars, let alone
the constellations of the zodiac."

Spar was about to ask what all *those* were, but then he saw
that the corpse-light was all gone, although the ribbon of
brighter light had grown very wide.

"At least in this stretch of your memory," Doc added. "I should
have your new eyes and teeth ready next Loafday. Come earlier
if you can manage. I may see you before that at the Bat Rack,
Playday night or earlier."

"Great, Doc, but now I've got to haul. Come on, Kim! Sometimes business heavies up Loafday night, Doc, like it was Playday night come at the wrong end. Jump in, Kim."

"Sure you can make it back to the Bat Rack all right, Spar? It'll be dark before you get there."

"Course I can, Doc."

But when night fell, like a heavy hood jerked down over his head, halfway down the first passageway, he would have gone back to ask Doc to guide him, except he feared Kim's contempt, even though the cat still wasn't talking. He pulled ahead rapidly, though the few running lights hardly let him see the centerline.

The fore gangway was even worse—completely empty and its lights dim and flickering. Seeing by blurs bothered him now that he knew what seeing sharp was like. He was beginning to sweat and shake and cramp from his withdrawal from alcohol and his thoughts were a tumult. He wondered if *any* of the weird things that had happened since meeting Kim were real or dream. Kim's refusal—or inability?—to talk any more was disquieting. He began seeing the misty rims of blurs that vanished when he looked straight toward them. He remembered Keeper and the brewos talking about vamps and witches.

Then instead of waiting for the Bat Rack's green hatch, he dove off into the passageway leading to the aft one. This passageway had no lights at all. Out of it he thought he could hear Hellhound growling, but couldn't be sure because the big chewer was grinding. He was scrabbling with panic when he entered the Bat Rack through the dark red hatch, remembering barely in time to avoid the new glue.

The place was jumping with light and excitement and dancing figures, and Keeper at once began to shout abuse at him. He dove into the torus and began taking orders and serving automatically, working entirely by touch and voice, because withdrawal now had his vision swimming—a spinning blur of blurs.

After a while that got better, but his nerves got worse. Only the unceasing work kept him going—and shut out Keeper's abuse—but he was getting too tired to work at all. As Playday dawned, with the crowd around the torus getting thicker all the while, he snatched a pouch of moonmist and set it to his lips.

Claws dug his chest. "Isssiot! Sssot! Ssslave of fffear!"

Spar almost went into convulsions, but put back the moonmist.

Kim came out of the slopsuit and pushed off contemptuously, circled the bar and talked to various of the drinkers, soon became a conversation piece. Keeper started to boast about him and quit serving. Spar worked on and on and on through sobriety more nightmarish than any drunk he could recall. And far, far longer.

Suzy came in with a mark and touched Spar's hand when he served her dark to her. It helped.

He thought he recognized a voice from below. It came from a kinky-haired, slopsuited brewo he didn't know. But then he heard the man again and thought he was Ensign Drake. There were several brewos he didn't recognize.

The place started really jumping. Keeper upped the music. Singly or in pairs, somersaulting dancers bounded back and forth between shrouds. Others toed a shroud and shimmied. A girl in black did splits on one. A girl in white dove through the torus. Keeper put it on her boyfriend's check. Brewos tried to sing.

Spar heard Kim recite:

"Izz a cat.
Killzz a rat.
Greetss each guy.
Thin or ffat.
Saay dolls, hi!"

Playday night fell. The place got hotter. Doc didn't come. But Crown did. Dancers parted and a whole section of drinkers made way aloft for him and his girls and Hellhound, so that they had a third of the torus to themselves, with no one below in that third either. To Spar's surprise they all took coffee except the dog, who when asked by Crown, responded, "Bloody Mary," drawing out the words in such deep tones that they were little more than a low "Bluh-Muh" growl.

"Iss that sspeech, I assk you?" Kim commented from the other side of the torus. Drunks around him choked down chuckles.

Spar served the pouched coffee piping hot with felt holders and mixed Hellhound's drink in a self-squeezing syringe with sipping tube. He was very groggy and for the moment more afraid for Kim than himself. The face blurs tended to swim, but he could distinguish Rixende by her black hair, Phanette and Doucette by their matching red-blonde hair and oddly red-mottled fair skins, while Almodie *was* the platinum-haired pale one, yet she looked horribly right between the dark brown, purple-vested blur to one side of her and the blacked, narrower, prick-eared silhouette to the other.

Spar heard Crown whisper to her, "Ask Keeper to show you the talking cat." The whisper was very low and Spar wouldn't have heard it except that Crown's voice had a strange excited vibrancy Spar had never known in it before.

"But won't they fight then?—I mean Hellhound," she answered in a voice that sent silvery tendrils around Spar's heart. He yearned to see her face through Doc's tube. She would look like Virgo, only more beautiful. Yet, Crown's girl, she could be no virgin. It was a strange and horrible world. Her eyes *were* violet. But he was sick of blurs. Almodie sounded very frightened, yet she continued, "Please don't, Crown." Spar's heart was captured.

"But that's the whole idea, baby. And nobody dont's us. We thought we'd schooled you to that. We'd teach you another lesson here, except tonight we smell high fuzz—lots of it, Keeper!—our new lady wishes to hear your cat talk. Bring it over."

"I really don't . . ." Almodie began and went no further.

Kim came floating across the torus while Keeper was shouting in the opposite direction. The cat checked himself against a slender shroud and looked straight at Crown. "Yesss?"

"Keeper, shut that junk off." The music died abruptly. Voices rose, then died abruptly too. "Well, cat, talk."

"Shshall ssing insstead," Kim announced and began an eerie caterwauling that had a pattern but was not Spar's idea of music.

"It's an abstraction," Almodie breathed delightedly. "Listen, Crown, that was a diminished seventh."

"A demented third, I'd say," Phanette commented from the other side.

Crown signed them to be quiet.

Kim finished with a high trill. He slowly looked around at his baffled audience and then began to groom his shoulder.

Crown gripped a ridge of the torus with his left hand and said evenly, "Since you will not talk to us, will you talk to our dog?"

Kim stared at Hellhound sucking his Bloody Mary. His eyes

widened, their pupils slitted, his lips writhed back from needle-like fangs.

He hissed, "Schschweinhund!"

Hellhound launched himself, hind paws against the palm of Crown's left hand, which threw him forward toward the left, where Kim was dodging. But the cat switched directions, rebounding hindwards from the next shroud. The dog's white-jagged jaws snapped sideways a foot from their mark as his great-chested black body hurtled past.

Hellhound landed with four paws in the middle of a fat drunk, who puffed out his wind barely before his swallow, but the dog took off instantly on reverse course. Kim bounced back and forth between shrouds. This time hair flew when jaws snapped, but also a rigidly spread paw slashed.

Crown grabbed Hellhound by his studded collar, restraining him from another dive. He touched the dog below the eye and smelled his fingers. "That'll be enough, boy," he said. "Can't go around killing musical geniuses." His hand dropped from his nose to below the torus and came up loosely fisted. "Well, cat, you've talked with our dog. Have you a word for us?"

"Yesss!" Kim drifted to the shroud nearest Crown's face. Spar pushed off to grab him back, while Almodie gazed at Crown's fist and edged a hand toward it.

Kim loudly hissed, "Hellzzz ssspawn! Fffiend!"

Both Spar and Almodie were too late. From between two of Crown's fisted fingers a needle-stream jetted and struck Kim in the open mouth.

After what seemed to Spar a long time, his hand interrupted the stream. Its back burned acutely.

Kim seemed to collapse into himself, then launched himself away from Crown, toward the dark, open-jawed.

Crown said, "That's mace, an antique weapon like Greek fire, but well-known to our folk. The perfect answer to a witch cat."

Spar sprang at Crown, grappled his chest, tried to butt his jaw. They moved away from the torus at half the speed with which Spar had sprung.

Crown got his head aside. Spar closed his gums on Crown's throat. There was a *snick*. Spar felt wind on his bare back. Then a cold triangle pressed his flesh over his kidneys. Spar opened his jaws and floated limp. Crown chuckled.

A blue fuzz-glare, held by a brewo, made everyone in the Bat Rack look more corpse-like than larboard light. A voice commanded, "Okay, folks, break it up. Go home. We're closing the place."

Sleepday dawned, drowning the fuzz-glare. The cold triangle left Spar's back. There was another *snick*. Saying, "Bye-bye, baby," Crown pushed off through the white glare toward four women's faces and one dog's. Phanette's and Doucette's faintly red-mottled ones were close beside Hellhound's, as if they might be holding his collar.

Spar sobbed and began to hunt for Kim. After a while Suzy came to help him. The Bat Rack emptied. Spar and Suzy cornered Kim. Spar grasped the cat around the chest. Kim's forelegs embraced his wrist, claws pricking. Spar got out the pouch Doc had given him and shoved its mouth between Kim's jaws. The claws dug deep. Taking no note of that, Spar gently sprayed. Gradually the claws came out and Kim relaxed. Spar hugged him gently. Suzy bound up Spar's wounded wrist.

Keeper came up followed by two brewos, one of them Ensign Drake, who said, "My partner and I will watch today by the aft and starboard hatches." Beyond them the Bat Rack was empty.

Spar said, "Crown has a knife." Drake nodded.

Suzy touched Spar's hand and said, "Keeper, I want to stay here tonight. I'm scared."

Keeper said, "I can offer you a shroud."

Drake and his mate dove slowly toward their posts.

Suzy squeezed Spar's hand. He said, rather heavily, "I can offer you my shroud, Suzy."

Keeper laughed and after looking toward the Bridge men, whispered, "I can offer you mine, which, unlike Spar, I own. And moonmist. Otherwise, the passageways."

Suzy sighed, paused, then went off with him.

Spar miserably made his way to the fore corner. Had Suzy expected him to fight Keeper? The sad thing was that he no longer wanted her, except as a friend. He loved Crown's new girl. Which was sad too.

He was very tired. Even the thought of new eyes tomorrow

didn't interest him. He clipped his ankle to a shroud and tied a rag over his eyes. He gently clasped Kim, who had not spoken. He was asleep at once.

He dreamed of Almodie. She looked like Virgo, even to the white dress. She held Kim, who looked sleek as polished black leather. She was coming toward him smiling. She kept coming without getting closer.

Much later—he thought—he woke in the grip of withdrawal. He sweated and shook, but those were minor. His nerves were jumping. Any moment, he was sure, they would twitch all his muscles into a stabbing spasm of sinew-snapping agony. His thoughts were moving so fast he could hardly begin to understand one in ten. It was like speeding through a curving, ill-lit passageway ten times faster than the main drag. If he touched a wall, he would forget even what little Spar knew, forget he was Spar. All around him black shrouds whipped in perpetual sine curves.

Kim was no longer by him. He tore the rag from his eyes. It was dark as before. Sleepday night. But his body stopped speeding and his thoughts slowed. His nerves still crackled, and he still saw the black snakes whipping, but he knew them for illusion. He even made out the dim glows of three running lights.

Then he saw two figures floating toward him. He could barely make out their eye-blurs, green in the smaller, violet in the other, whose face was spreadingly haloed by silvery glints. She was pale and whiteness floated around her. And instead of a smile, he could see the white horizontal blur of bared teeth. Kim's teeth too were bared.

Suddenly he remembered the golden-haired girl who he'd thought was playing bartender in Crown's Hole. She was Suzy's one-time friend Sweetheart, snatched last Sleepday by vamps.

He screamed, which in Spar was a hoarse, retching bellow, and scrabbled at his clipped ankle.

The figures vanished. Below, he thought.

Lights came on. Someone dove and shook Spar's shoulder. "What happened, gramps?"

Spar gibbered while he thought what to tell Drake. He loved Almodie and Kim. He said, "Had a nightmare. Vamps attacked me."

"Description?"

"An old lady and a . . . a . . . little dog."

The other officer dove in. "The black hatch is open."

Drake said, "Keeper told us that was always locked. Follow through, Fenner." As the other dove below, "You're sure this was a nightmare, gramps? A *little* dog? And an *old* woman?"

Spar said, "Yes," and Drake dove after his comrade, out through the black hatch.

Workday dawned. Spar felt sick and confused, but he set about his usual routine. He tried to talk to Kim, but the cat was as silent as yesterday afternoon. Keeper bullied and found many tasks—the place was a mess from Playday. Suzy got away quickly. She didn't want to talk about Sweetheart or anything else. Drake and Fenner didn't come back.

Spar swept and Kim patrolled, out of touch. In the afternoon Crown came in and talked with Keeper while Spar and Kim were out of earshot. They mightn't have been there for all notice Crown took of them.

Spar wondered about what he had seen last night. It might really have been a dream, he decided. He was no longer impressed by his memory-identification of Sweetheart. Stupid of him to have thought that Almodie and Kim, dream or reality, were vamps. Doc had said vamps were superstitions. But he didn't think much. He still had withdrawal symptoms, only less violent.

When Loafday dawned, Keeper gave Spar permission to leave the Bat Rack without his usual prying questions. Spar looked around for Kim, but couldn't see his black blob. Besides, he didn't really want to take the cat.

He went straight to Doc's office. The passageways weren't as lonely as last Loafday. For a third time he passed the bent figure croaking, "Seagull, Kestrel, Cathedral . . ."

Doc's hatch was unzipped, but Doc wasn't there. Kim waited a long while, uneasy in the corpse-light. It wasn't like Doc to leave his office unzipped and unattended. And he hadn't turned up at the Bat Rack last night, as he'd half promised.

Finally Spar began to look around. One of the first things he noticed was that the big black bag, which Doc had said contained his treasure, was missing.

Then he noticed that the gleaming pliofilm bag in which Doc

had put the mold of Spar's gums, now held something different. He unclipped it from its shroud. There were two items in it.

He cut a finger on the first, which was half circle, half pink and half gleaming. He felt out its shape more cautiously then, ignoring the tiny red blobs welling from his finger. It had irregular depressions in its pink top and bottom. He put it in his mouth. His gums mated with the depressions. He opened his mouth; then closed it, careful to keep his tongue back. There was a *snick* and a dull *click*. He had teeth!

His hands were shaking, not just from withdrawal, as he felt the second item.

It was two thick rounds joined by a short bar and with a thicker long bar ending in a semicircle going back from each.

He thrust a finger into one of the rounds. It tickled, just as the tube had tickled his eyes, only more intensely, almost painfully.

Hands shaking worse than ever, he fitted the contraption to his face. The semicircles went around his ears, the rounds circled his eyes, not closely enough to tickle.

He could see sharply! *Everything* had edges, even his spread-fingered hands and the . . . clot of blood on one finger. He cried out—a low, wondering wail—and scanned the office. At first the scores and dozens of sharp-edged objects, each as distinct as the pictures of Capricorn and Virgo had been, were too much for him. He closed his eyes.

When his breathing was a little evener and his shaking less, he opened them cautiously and began to inspect the objects clipped to the shrouds. Each one was a wonder. He didn't know the purpose of half of them. Some of them with which he was familiar by use or blurred sight startled him greatly in their appearance —a comb, a brush, a book with pages (that infinitude of ranked black marks), a wrist watch (the tiny pictures around the circular margin of Capricorn and Virgo, and of the Bull and the Fishes, and so on, and the narrow bars radiating from the center and swinging swiftly or slowly or not at all—and pointing to the signs of the zodiac).

Before he knew it, he was at the corpse-glow wall. He faced it with a new courage, though it forced from his lips another wondering wail.

The corpse-glow didn't come from everywhere, though it took

up the central quarter of his field of vision. His fingers touched taut, transparent pliofilm. What he saw beyond—a great way beyond, he began to think—was utter blackness with a great many tiny . . . points of bright light in it. Points were even harder to believe in than edges, but he had to believe what he saw.

But centrally, looking much bigger than all the blackness, was a vast corpse-white round pocked with faint circles and scored by bright lines and mottled with slightly darker areas.

It didn't look as if it were wired for electricity, and it certainly didn't look afire. After a while Spar got the weird idea that its light was reflected from something much brighter *behind* Windrush.

It was infinitely strange to think of so much *space* around Windrush. Like thinking of a reality containing reality.

And if Windrush were between the hypothetical brighter light and the pocked white round, its shadow ought to be on the latter. Unless Windrush were almost infinitely small. Really these speculations were utterly too fantastic to deal with.

Yet could anything be too fantastic? Werewolves, witches, points, edges, size and space beyond any but the most insane belief.

When he had first looked at the corpse-white object, it had been round. And he had heard and felt the creakings of Loafday noon, without being conscious of it at the time. But now the round had its fore edge evenly sliced off, so that it was lopsided. Spar wondered if the hypothetical incandescence behind Windrush were moving, or the white round rotating, or Windrush itself revolving around the white round. Such thoughts, especially the last, were dizzying almost beyond endurance.

He made for the open door, wondering if he should zip it behind him, decided not to. The passageway was another amazement, going off and off and off, and narrowing as it went. Its walls bore . . . arrows, the red pointing to larboard, the way from which he'd come, the green pointing starboard, the way he was going. The arrows were what he'd always seen as dash-shaped blurs. As he pulled himself along the strangely definite drag-line, the passageway stayed the same diameter, all the way to the violet main-drag.

He wanted to jerk himself as fast as the green arrows to the starboard end of Windrush to verify the hypothetical incandescence and see the details of the orange-dun round that always depressed him.

But he decided he ought first to report Doc's disappearance to the Bridge. He might find Drake there. And report the loss of Doc's treasure too, he reminded himself.

Passing faces fascinated him. Such a welter of noses and ears! He overtook the croaking, bent shape. It was that of an old woman whose nose almost met her chin. She was doing something twitchy with her fingers to two narrow sticks and a roll of slender, fuzzy line. He impulsively dove off the drag-line and caught hold of her, whirling them around.

"What are you doing, grandma?" he asked.

She puffed with anger. "Knitting," she answered indignantly.

"What are the words you keep saying?"

"Names of knitting patterns," she replied, jerking loose from him and blowing on. "Sand Dunes, Lightning, Soldiers Marching . . ."

He started to swim for the drag-line, then saw he was already at the blue shaft leading aloft. He grabbed hold of its speeding centerline, not minding the burn, and speeded to the Bridge.

When he got there, he saw there was a multitude of stars aloft. The oblong rainbows were all banks of multi-colored lights winking on and off. But the silent officers—they looked very old, their faces stared as if they were sleep-swimming, their gestured orders were mechanical, he wondered if they knew where Windrush was going—or anything at all, beyond the Bridge of Windrush.

A dark, young officer with tightly curly hair floated to him. It wasn't until he spoke that Spar knew he was Ensign Drake.

"Hello, gramps. Say, you look younger. What are those things around your eyes?"

"Field glasses. They help me see sharp."

"But field glasses have tubes. They're a sort of binocular telescope."

Spar shrugged and told about the disappearance of Doc and his big, black treasure bag.

"But you say he drank a lot and he told you his treasures were dreams? Sounds like he was wacky and wandered off to do his drinking somewhere else."

"But Doc was a regular drinker. He always came to the Bat Rack."

"Well, I'll do what I can. Say, I've been pulled off the Bat Rack investigation. I think that character Crown got at someone higher up. The old ones are easy to get at—not so much greed as going by custom, taking the easiest course. Fenner and I never did find the old woman and the little dog, or any female and animal . . . or anything."

Spar told about Crown's earlier attempt to steal Doc's little black bag.

"So you think the two cases might be connected. Well, as I say, I'll do what I can."

Spar went back to the Bat Rack. It was very strange to see Keeper's face in detail. It looked old and its pink target center was a big red nose criss-crossed by veins. His brown eyes were not so much curious as avid. He asked about the things around Spar's eyes. Spar decided it wouldn't be wise to tell Keeper about seeing sharply.

"They're a new kind of costume jewelry, Keeper. Blasted Earth, I don't have any hair on my head, ought to have something."

"Language, Spar! It's like a drunk to spend precious scrip on such a grotesque bauble."

Spar neither reminded Keeper that all the scrip he'd earned at the Bat Rack amounted to no more than a wad as big as his thumb-joint, nor that he'd quit drinking. Nor did he tell him about his teeth, but kept them hidden behind his lips.

Kim was nowhere in sight. Keeper shrugged. "Gone off somewhere. You know the way of strays, Spar."

Yes, thought Spar, this one's stayed put too long.

He kept being amazed that he could see *all* of the Bat Rack sharply. It was an octahedron criss-crossed by shrouds and made up of two pyramids put together square base to square base. The apexes of the pyramids were the violet fore and dark red aft corners. The four other corners were the starboard green, the black below, the larboard scarlet, and the blue aloft, if you named them from aft in the way the hands of a watch move.

Suzy drifted in early Playday. Spar was shocked by her blowzy appearance and bloodshot eyes. But he was touched by her signs of affection and he felt the strong friendship between them. Twice when Keeper wasn't looking he switched her nearly empty pouch of dark for a full one. She told him that, yes, she'd once known Sweetheart and that, yes, she'd heard people say Mabel had seen Sweetheart snatched by vamps.

Business was slow for Playday. There were no strange brewos. Hoping against fearful, gut-level certainty, Spar kept waiting for Doc to come in zig-zagging along the ratlines and comment on the new gadgets he'd given Spar and spout about the Old Days and his strange philosophy.

Playday night Crown came in with his girls, all except Almodie. Doucette said she'd had a headache and stayed at the Hole. Once again, all of them ordered coffee, though to Spar all of them seemed high.

Spar covertly studied their faces. Though nervous and alive, they all had something in their stares akin to those he'd seen in most of the officers on the Bridge. Doc had said they were all zombies. It was interesting to find out that Phanette's and Doucette's red-mottled appearance was due to . . . freckles, tiny reddish star-clusters on their white skins.

"Where's that famous talking cat?" Crown asked Spar.

Spar shrugged. Keeper said, "Strayed. For which I'm glad. Don't want a little feline who makes fights like last night."

Keeping his yellow-brown irised eyes on Spar, Crown said, "We believe it was that fight last Playday gave Almodie her headache, so she didn't want to come back tonight. We'll tell her you got rid of the witch cat."

"I'd have got rid of the beast if Spar hadn't," Keeper put in. "So you think it was a witch cat, coroner?"

"We're certain. What's that stuff on Spar's face?"

"A new sort of cheap eye-jewelry, coroner, such as attracts drunks."

Spar got the feeling that this conversation had been prearranged, that there was a new agreement between Crown and Keeper. But he just shrugged again. Suzy was looking angry, but she said nothing.

Yet she stayed behind again after the Bat Rack closed. Keeper put no claim on her, though he leered knowingly before disappearing with a yawn and a stretch through the scarlet hatch. Spar checked that all six hatches were locked and shut off the lights, though that made no difference in the morning glare, before returning to Suzy, who had gone to his sleeping shroud.

Suzy asked, "You didn't get rid of Kim?"

Spar answered, "No, he just strayed, as Keeper said at first. I don't know where Kim is."

Suzy smiled and put her arms around him. "I think your new eye-things are beautiful," she said.

Spar said, "Suzy, did you know that Windrush isn't the Universe? That's it's a ship going through space around a white round marked with circles, a round much bigger than all Windrush?"

Suzy replied, "I know Windrush is sometimes called the Ship. I've seen that round—in pictures. Forget all wild thoughts, Spar, and lose yourself in me."

Spar did so, chiefly from friendship. He forgot to clip his ankle to the shroud. Suzy's body didn't attract him. He was thinking of Almodie.

When it was over, Suzy slept. Spar put the rag around his eyes and tried to do the same. He was troubled by withdrawal symptoms only a little less bad than last Sleepday's. Because of that little, he didn't go to the torus for a pouch of moonmist. But then there was a sharp jab in his back, as if a muscle had spasmed there, and the symptoms got much worse. He convulsed, once, twice, then just as the agony became unbearable, blanked out.

Spar woke, his head throbbing, to discover that he was not only clipped, but lashed to his shroud, his wrists stretched in one direction, his ankles in the other, his hands and his feet both numb. His nose rubbed the shroud.

Light made his eyelids red. He opened them a little at a time and saw Hellhound poised with bent hind legs against the next shroud. He could see Hellhound's great stabbing teeth very clearly. If he had opened his eyes a little more swiftly, Hellhound would have dived at his throat.

He rubbed his sharp metal teeth together. At least he had more than gums to meet an attack on his face.

Beyond Hellhound he saw black and transparent spirals. He

realized he was in Crown's Hole. Evidently the last jab in his back had been the injection of a drug.

But Crown had not taken away his eye jewelry, nor noted his teeth. He had thought of Spar as old Eyeless Toothless.

Between Hellhound and the spirals, he saw Doc lashed to a shroud and his big black bag clipped next to him. Doc was gagged. Evidently he had tried to cry out. Spar decided not to. Doc's gray eyes were open and Spar thought Doc was looking at him.

Very slowly Spar moved his numb fingers on top of the knot lashing his wrists to the shroud and slowly contracted all his muscles and pulled. The knot slid down the shroud a millimeter. So long as he did something slowly enough, Hellhound could not see it. He repeated this action at intervals.

Even more slowly he swung his face to the left. He saw nothing more than that the hatch to the corridor was zipped shut, and that beyond the dog and Doc, between the black spirals, was an empty and unfurnished cabin whose whole starboard side was stars. The hatch to that cabin was open, with its black-striped emergency hatch wavering beside it.

With equal slowness he swung his face to the right, past Doc and past Hellhound, who was eagerly watching him for signs of life or waking. He had pulled down the knot on his wrists two centimeters.

The first thing he saw was a transparent oblong. In it were more stars and, by its aft edge, the smoky orange round. At last he could see the latter more clearly. The smoke was on top, the orange underneath and irregularly placed. The whole was about as big as Spar's palm could have covered, if he had been able to stretch out his arm to full length. As he watched, he saw a bright flash in one of the orange areas. The flash was short, then it turned to a tiny black round pushing out through the smoke. More than ever, Spar felt sadness.

Below the transparency, Spar saw a horrible tableau. Suzy was strapped to a bright metal rack guyed by shrouds. She was very pale and her eyes were closed. From the side of her neck went a red sipping-tube which forked into five branches. Four of the branches went into the red mouths of Crown, Rixende, Phanette, and Doucette. The fifth was shut by a small metal clip, and beyond it Almodie floated cowering, hands over her eyes.

Crown said softly, "We want it all. Strip her, Rixie."

Rixende clipped shut the end of her tube and swam to Suzy. Spar expected her to remove the blue culottes and bra, but instead she simply began to massage one of Suzy's legs, pressing always from ankle toward waist, driving her remaining blood nearer her neck.

Crown removed his sipping tube from his lips long enough to say, "Ahhh, good to the last drop." Then he had mouthed the blood that had spurted out in the interval and had the tube in place again.

Phanette and Doucette convulsed with soundless giggles.

Almodie peered between her parted fingers, out of her mass of platinum hair, then scissored them shut again.

After a while Crown said, "That's all we'll get. Phan and Doucie, feed her to the big chewer. If you meet anyone in the passageway, pretend she's drunk. Afterwards we'll get Doc to dose us high, and give him a little brew if he behaves, then we'll drink Spar."

Spar had his wrist knot more than halfway to his teeth. Hellhound kept watching eagerly for movement, unable to see movement that slow. Slaver made tiny gray globes beside his fangs.

Phanette and Doucette opened the hatch and steered Suzy's dead body through it.

Embracing Rixende, Crown said expansively toward Doc, "Well, isn't it the right thing, old man? Nature bloody in tooth and claw, a wise one said. They've poisoned everything there." He pointed toward the smoky orange round sliding out of sight. "They're still fighting, but they'll soon all be dead. So death should be the rule too for this gimcrack, so-called survival ship. Remember they are aboard her. When we've drunk the blood of everyone aboard Windrush, including their blood, we'll drink our own, if our own isn't theirs."

Spar thought, Crown thinks too much in they's. The knot was close to his teeth. He heard the big chewer start to grind.

In the empty next cabin, Spar saw Drake and Fenner, clad once more as brewos, swimming toward the open hatch.

But Crown saw them too. "Get 'em, Hellhound," he directed, pointing. "It's our command."

The big black dog bulleted from his shroud through the open hatch. Drake pointed something at him. The dog went limp.

Chuckling softly, Crown took by one tip a swastika with curved, gleaming, razor-sharp blades and sent it off spinning. It curved past Spar and Doc, went through the open hatch, missed Drake and Fenner—and Hellhound—and struck the wall of stars.

There was a rush of wind, then the emergency hatch smacked shut. Spar saw Drake, Fenner, and Hellhound, wavery through the transparent pliofilm, spew blood, bloat, burst bloodily open. The empty cabin they had been in disappeared. Windrush had a new wall and Crown's Hole was distorted.

Far beyond, growing ever tinier, the swastika spun toward the stars.

Phanette and Doucette came back. "We buried Suzy. Someone was coming, so we beat it." The big chewer stopped grinding.

Spar bit cleanly through his wrist lashings and immediately doubled over to bite his ankles loose.

Crown dove at him. Pausing to draw knives, the four girls did the same.

Phanette, Doucette, and Rixende went limp. Spar had the impression that small black balls had glanced from their skulls.

There wasn't time to bite his feet loose, so he straightened. Crown hit his chest as Almodie hit his feet.

Crown and Spar giant-swung around the shroud. Then Almodie had cut Spar's ankles loose. As they spun off along the tangent, Spar tried to knee Crown in the groin, but Crown twisted and evaded the blow as they moved toward the inboard wall.

There was the *snick* of Crown's knife unfolding. Spar saw the dark wrist and grabbed it. He butted at Crown's jaw. Crown evaded. Spar set his teeth in Crown's neck and bit.

Blood covered Spar's face, spurted over it. He spat out a hunk of flesh. Crown convulsed. Spar fought off the knife. Crown went limp. That the pressure in a man should work against him.

Spar shook the blood from his face. Through its beads, he saw Keeper and Kim side by side. Almodie was clutching his ankles. Phanette, Doucette, Rixende floated.

Keeper said proudly, "I shot them with my gun for drunks. I knocked them out. Now I'll cut their throats, if you wish."

Spar said, "No more throat-cutting. No more blood." Shaking off Almodie's hands, he took off for Doc, picking up Doucette's floating knife by the way.

He slashed Doc's lashings and cut the gag from his face.

Meanwhile Kim hissed, "Sstole and ssecreted Keeper's sscrip from the boxx. Ashshured him you sstole it, Sspar. You and Ssuzzy. Sso he came. Keeper izz a shshlemiel."

Keeper said, "I saw Suzy's foot going into the big chewer. I knew it by its anklet of hearts. After that I had the courage to kill Crown or anyone. I loved Suzy."

Doc cleared his throat and croaked, "Moonmist." Spar found a triple pouch and Doc sucked it all. Doc said, "Crown spoke the truth. Windrush is a plastic survival ship from Earth. Earth—" He motioned toward the dull orange round disappearing aft in the window "—poisoned herself with smog pollution and with nuclear war. She spent gold for war, plastic for survival. Best forgotten. Windrush went mad. Understandably. Even without the Lethean rickettsia, or Styx ricks, as you call it. Thought Windrush was the cosmos. Crown kidnapped me to get my drugs, kept me alive to know the doses."

Spar looked at Keeper. "Clean up here," he ordered. "Feed Crown to the big chewer."

Almodie pulled herself from Spar's ankles to his waist. "There was a second survival ship. Circumluna. When Windrush went mad, my father and mother—and you—were sent here, to investigate and cure. But my father died and you got Styx ricks. My mother died just before I was given to Crown. She sent you Kim."

Kim hissed, "My fforebear came from Circumluna to Windrush, too. Great grandmother. Taught me the ffigures for Windrushsh . . . Radiuss from moon-ccenter, 2,500 miles. Period, ssixx hours—sso, the sshort dayss. A terranth izz the time it takess Earth to move through a consstellation, and sso on."

Doc said, "So, Spar, you're the only one who remembers without cynicism. You'll have to take over. It's all yours, Spar."

Spar had to agree.

1971
29th CONVENTION
BOSTON

Fritz Leiber

I take it back. I take it back. I'm *glad* I omitted Fritz's "Ship of Shadows" from Volume Two.

Can you imagine all I have suffered over these years; the misery I have had over the financial loss Fritz had experienced. To such extremes of unhappiness and contrition have I been driven that I was even considering, with some seriousness, the possibility of perhaps sending Fritz a sum of money to make up for those losses—money out of my own pocket—five, maybe even ten, dollars.

But not any more. Not a penny does that miserable rascal get.

Surely you've noticed. Surely you're not surprised at my honest indignation. Having won the Hugo in the novella category in 1970, do you see how he actually proceeded to win the Hugo in the novella category in 1971 also? The twenty-eight and twenty-ninth conventions each suffered from his depredations, the only time in the history of the award that any writer took two novella Hugos back to back. No one but a blackhearted scoundrel would do such a thing.

Where was his pity? Did he think of all the virginal young authors waiting for their chance, standing in the wings and biting their thumbnails, with pretty little blushes mantling their downy cheeks as they waited for the winner to be announced?

So here they are. Two Leiber stories with a combined wordage of forty thousand starting off Volume Three. People will read the length of more than half a novel, wondering if anyone writes Hugo-winning stories besides good old Fritz.

Incidentally, since this convention was held in Boston I attended. I had just, a few months before, made a permanent move to New York, but I can handle the trip to Boston with very little in the way of apprehensive fainting at the prospect of travel. The twenty-ninth was the most efficiently run convention I have ever attended and Robert Silverberg, as I recall, was the toastmaster.

He was terrific. He has this solemn and Satanic look and scowls out upon the world. Nor does his expression change as he makes his satirically humorous remarks, and the contrast between expression and words slays the audience.

It also slays me and riddles me with envy, for I don't have his natural advantages. My frank, open, and ingenuous countenance sparkles so continually with good humor that people *expect* me to be funny, and I lose the advantage of surprise. I *know* they expect me to be funny because on frequent occasions, as I rise to address the audience, they start laughing at once, even before I say a word.

2

ILL MET IN LANKHMAR

Silent as specters, the tall and the fat thief edged past the dead, noose-strangled watch-leopard, out the thick, lock-picked door of Jengao the Gem Merchant, and strolled east on Cash Street through the thin black night-smog of Lankhmar, City of Sevenscore Thousand Smokes.

East on Cash it had to be, for west at the intersection of Cash and Silver was a police post with unbribed guardsmen in browned-iron cuirasses and helms, restlessly grounding and rattling their pikes, while Jengao's place had no alley entrance or even window in its stone walls three spans thick and the roof and floor almost as strong and without trap doors.

But tall, tight-lipped Slevyas, master thief candidate, and fat, darting-eyed Fissif, thief second class, brevetted first class for this operation, with a rating of talented in double-dealing, were not in the least worried. Everything was proceeding according to plan. Each carried thonged in his pouch a much smaller pouch of jewels of the first water only, for Jengao, now breathing stentoriously inside and senseless from the slugging he'd suffered, must be allowed, nay, nursed and encouraged, to build up his business again and so ripen it for another plucking. Almost the first law of the Thieves' Guild was never kill the hen that laid brown eggs with a ruby in the yolk, or white eggs with a diamond in the white.

The two thieves also had the relief of knowing that, with the satisfaction of a job well done, they were going straight home now, not to a wife, Aarth forbid!—or to parents and children, all gods forfend!—but to Thieves' House, headquarters and barracks of the all-mighty Guild which was father to them both and

mother too, though no woman was allowed inside its ever-open
portal on Cheap Street.

In addition there was the comforting knowledge that although
each was armed only with his regulation silver-hilted thief's
knife, a weapon seldom used except in rare intramural duels and
brawls, in fact more a membership token than a weapon, they
were nevertheless most strongly convoyed by three reliable and
lethal bravos hired for the evening from the Slayers' Brotherhood, one moving well ahead of them as point, the other two
well behind as rear guard and chief striking force, in fact almost
out of sight—for it is never wise that such convoying be obvious,
or so believed Krovas, Grandmaster of the Thieves' Guild.

And if all that were not enough to make Slevyas and Fissif feel
safe and serene, there danced along soundlessly beside them in
the shadow of the north curb a small, malformed or at any rate
somewhat large-headed shape that might have been a small dog,
a somewhat undersized cat, or a very big rat. Occasionally it
scuttled familiarly and even encouragingly a little way toward
their snugly felt-slippered feet, though it always scurried swiftly
back into the darker dark.

True, this last guard was not an absolutely unalloyed reassurance. At that very moment, scarcely twoscore paces yet from
Jengao's, Fissif tautly walked for a bit on tiptoe and strained his
pudgy lips upward to whisper softly in Slevyas' long-lobed ear,
"Damned if I like being dogged by that Familiar of Hristomilo,
no matter what security he's supposed to afford us. Bad enough
that Krovas employs or lets himself be cowed into employing a
sorcerer of most dubious, if dire, reputation and aspect, but
that—"

"Shut your trap!" Slevyas hissed still more softly.

Fissif obeyed with a shrug and occupied himself even more
restlessly and keenly than was his wont in darting his gaze this
way and that, but chiefly ahead.

Some distance in that direction, in fact just short of the Gold
Street intersection, Cash was bridged by an enclosed second-
story passageway connecting the two buildings which made up
the premises of the famous stone-masons and sculptors Rokkermas and Slaarg. The firm's buildings themselves were fronted
by very shallow porticos supported by unnecessarily large pillars

of varied shape and decoration, advertisements more than structural members.

From just beyond the bridge there came two low, brief whistles, signal from the point bravo that he had inspected that area for ambushes and discovered nothing suspicious and that Gold Street was clear.

Fissif was by no means entirely satisfied by the safety signal. To tell the truth, the fat thief rather enjoyed being apprehensive and even fearful, at least up to a point. A sense of strident panic overlaid with writhing calm made him feel more excitingly alive than the occasional woman he enjoyed. So he scanned most closely through the thin, sooty smog the frontages and overhangs of Rokkermas and Slaarg as his and Slevyas' leisurely seeming yet unslow pace brought them steadily closer.

On this side the bridge was pierced by four small windows, between which were three large niches in which stood—another advertisement—three life-size plaster statues, somewhat eroded by years of weather and dyed varyingly tones of dark gray by as many years of smog. Approaching Jengao's before the burglary, Fissif had noted them with a swift but comprehensive over-shoulder glance. Now it seemed to him that the statue to the right had indefinably changed. It was that of a man of medium height wearing cloak and hood, who gazed down with crossed arms and brooding aspect. No, not indefinably quite—the statue was a more uniform dark gray now, he fancied, cloak, hood, and face; it seemed somewhat sharper featured, less eroded; and he would almost swear it had grown shorter!

Just below the niche, moreover, there was in the street a scattering of gray and raw white rubble which he didn't recall having been there earlier. He strained to remember if during the excitement of the burglary, with its lively leopard-slaying and slugging and all, the unsleeping watch-corner of his mind had recorded a distant crash, and now he believed it had. His quick imagination pictured the possibility of a hole or even door behind each statue, through which it might be given a strong push and so tumbled onto passersby, himself and Slevyas specifically, the right-hand statue having been crashed to test the device and then replaced with a near twin.

He would keep close watch on all three statues as he and

Slevyas walked under. It would be easy to dodge if he saw one start to overbalance. Should he yank Slevyas out of harm's way when that happened? It was something to think about.

Without pause his restless attention fixed next on the porticos and pillars. The latter, thick and almost three yards tall, were placed at irregular intervals as well as being irregularly shaped and fluted, for Rokkermas and Slaarg were most modern and emphasized the unfinished look, randomness, and the unexpected.

Nevertheless it seemed to Fissif, his wariness wide awake now, that there was an intensification of unexpectedness, specifically that there was one more pillar under the porticos than when he had last passed by. He couldn't be sure which pillar was the newcomer, but he was almost certain there was one.

Share his suspicions with Slevyas? Yes, and get another hissed reproof and flash of contempt from the small, dull-seeming eyes.

The enclosed bridge was close now. Fissif glanced up at the right-hand statue and noted other differences from the one he'd recalled. Although shorter, it seemed to hold itself more strainingly erect, while the frown carved in its dark gray face was not so much one of philosophic brooding as sneering contempt, self-conscious cleverness, and conceit.

Still, none of the three statues toppled forward as he and Slevyas walked under the bridge. However, something else happened to Fissif at that moment.

One of the pillars winked at him.

The Gray Mouser—for so Mouse now named himself to himself and his beloved Ivrian—turned around in the right-hand niche, leaped up and caught hold of the cornice, silently vaulted to the flat roof, and crossed it precisely in time to see the two thieves emerge below.

Without hesitation he leaped forward and down, his body straight as a crossbow bolt, the soles of his ratskin boots aimed at the shorter thief's fat-buried shoulder blades, though leading him a little to allow for the yard he'd walk while the Mouser hurtled toward him.

In the instant that he leaped, the tall thief glanced up overshoulder and whipped out a knife, though making no move to push or pull Fissif out of the way of the human projectile speeding toward him. The Mouser shrugged in full flight. He'd just have to deal with the tall thief faster after knocking down the fat one.

More swiftly than one would have thought he could manage, Fissif whirled around then and thinly screamed, "Slivikin!"

The ratskin boots took him high in the belly. It was like landing on a big cushion. Writhing aside from Slevyas' first thrust, the Mouser somersaulted forward, turning feet over head, and as the fat thief's skull hit a cobble with a dull *bong* he came to his feet with dirk in hand, ready to take on the tall one.

But there was no need. Slevyas, his small eyes glazed, was toppling too.

One of the pillars had sprung forward, trailing a voluminous robe. A big hood had fallen back from a youthful face and long-haired head. Brawny arms had emerged from the long, loose sleeves that had been the pillar's topmost section, while the big fist ending one of the arms had dealt Slevyas a shrewd knockout punch on the chin.

Fafhrd and the Gray Mouser faced each other across the two thieves sprawled senseless. They were poised for attack, yet for the moment neither moved.

Each discerned something inexplicably familiar in the other.

Fafhrd said, "Our motives for being here seem identical."

"Seem? Surely must be!" the Mouser answered curtly, fiercely eyeing this potential new foe, who was taller by a head than the tall thief.

"You said?"

"I said, 'Seem? Surely must be!'"

"How civilized of you!" Fafhrd commented in pleased tones.

"Civilized?" the Mouser demanded suspiciously, gripping his dirk tighter.

"To care, in the eye of action, exactly what's said," Fafhrd explained. Without letting the Mouser out of his vision, he glanced down. His gaze traveled from the belt and pouch of one fallen thief to those of the other. Then he looked up at the Mouser with a broad, ingenuous smile.

"Sixty-sixty?" he suggested.

The Mouser hesitated, sheathed his dirk, and rapped out, "A deal!" He knelt abruptly, his fingers on the drawstrings of Fissif's pouch. "Loot your Slivikin," he directed.

It was natural to suppose that the fat thief had been crying his companion's name at the end.

Without looking up from where he knelt, Fafhrd remarked, "That . . . ferret they had with them. Where did it go?"

"Ferret?" the Mouser answered briefly. "It was a marmoset!"

"Marmoset," Fafhrd mused. "That's a small tropical monkey, isn't it? Well, might have been, but I got the strange impression that—"

The silent, two-pronged rush which almost overwhelmed them at that instant really surprised neither of them. Each had been expecting it, but the expectation had dropped out of conscious thought with the startlement of their encounter.

The three bravos racing down upon them in concerted attack, two from the west and one from the east, all with swords poised to thrust, had assumed that the two highjackers would be armed at most with knives and as timid or at least cautious in weapons-combat as the general run of thieves and counter-thieves. So it was they who were surprised and thrown into confusion when with the lightning speed of youth the Mouser and Fafhrd sprang up, whipped out fearsomely long swords, and faced them back to back.

The Mouser made a very small parry in carte so that the thrust of the bravo from the east went past his left side by only a hair's breath. He instantly riposted. His adversary, desperately springing back, parried in turn in carte. Hardly slowing, the tip of the Mouser's long, slim sword dropped under that parry with the delicacy of a princess curtsying and then leaped forward and a little upward, the Mouser making an impossibly long-looking lunge for one so small, and went between two scales of the bravo's armored jerkin and between his ribs and through his heart and out his back as if all were angelfood cake.

Meanwhile Fafhrd, facing the two bravos from the west, swept aside their low thrusts with somewhat larger, down-sweeping parries in seconde and low prime, then flipped up his sword, long as the Mouser's but heavier, so that it slashed through the neck of his right-hand adversary, half decapitating him. Then he, dropping back a swift step, readied a thrust for the other.

But there was no need. A narrow ribbon of bloodied steel,

followed by a gray glove and arm, flashed past him from behind and transfixed the last bravo with the identical thrust the Mouser had used on the first.

The two young men wiped and sheathed their swords. Fafhrd brushed the palm of his open right hand down his robe and held it out. The Mouser pulled off right-hand gray glove and shook the other's big hand in his sinewy one. Without word exchanged, they knelt and finished looting the two unconscious thieves, securing the small bags of jewels. With an oily towel and then a dry one, the Mouser sketchily wiped from his face the greasy ash-soot mixture which had darkened it, next swiftly rolled up both towels and returned them to his own pouch. Then, after only a questioning eye-twitch east on the Mouser's part and a nod from Fafhrd, they swiftly walked on in the direction Slevyas and Fissif and their escort had been going.

After reconnoitering Gold Street, they crossed it and continued east on Cash at Fafhrd's gestured proposal.

"My woman's at the Golden Lamprey," he explained.

"Let's pick her up and take her home to meet my girl," the Mouser suggested.

"Home?" Fafhrd inquired politely, only the barest hint of question in his voice.

"Dim Lane," the Mouser volunteered.

"Silver Eel?"

"Behind it. We'll have some drinks."

"I'll pick up a jug. Never have too much juice."

"True. I'll let you."

Several squares farther on Fafhrd, after stealing a number of looks at his new comrade, said with conviction, "We've met before."

The Mouser grinned at him. "Beach by the Mountains of Hunger?"

"Right! When I was a pirate's ship-boy."

"And I was a wizard's apprentice."

Fafhrd stopped, again wiped right hand on robe, and held it out. "Name's Fafhrd. Ef ay ef aitch ar dee."

Again the Mouser shook it. "Gray Mouser," he said a touch defiantly, as if challenging anyone to laugh at the sobriquet. "Excuse me, but how exactly do you pronounce that? Faf-hrud?"

"Just Faf-erd."

"Thank you." They walked on.

"Gray Mouser, eh?" Fafhrd remarked. "Well, you killed your-self a couple of rats tonight."

"That I did." The Mouser's chest swelled and he threw back his head. Then with a comic twitch of his nose and a sidewise half-grin he admitted, "You'd have got your second man easily enough. I stole him from you to demonstrate my speed. Besides, I was excited."

Fafhrd chuckled. "You're telling me? How do you suppose I was feeling?"

Later, as they were crossing Pimp Street, he asked, "Learn much magic from your wizard?"

Once more the Mouser threw back his head. He flared his nos-trils and drew down the corners of his lips, preparing his mouth for boastful, mystifying speech. But once more he found himself twitching his nose and half grinning. What the deuce did this big fellow have that kept him from putting on his usual acts? "Enough to tell me it's damned dangerous stuff. Though I still fool with it now and then."

Fafhrd was asking himself a similar question. All his life he'd mistrusted small men, knowing his height awakened their instant jealousy. But this clever little chap was somehow an exception. Quick thinker and brilliant swordsman too, no argument. He prayed to Kos that Vlana would like him.

On the northeast corner of Cash and Whore a slow-burning torch shaded by a broad gilded hoop cast a cone of light up into the thickening black night-smog and another cone down on the cobbles before the tavern door. Out of the shadows into the sec-ond cone stepped Vlana, handsome in a narrow black velvet dress and red stockings, her only ornaments a silver-sheathed and -hilted dagger and a silver-worked black pouch, both on a plain black belt.

Fafhrd introduced the Gray Mouser, who behaved with an al-most fawning courtesy, obsequiously gallant. Vlana studied him boldly, then gave him a tentative smile.

Fafhrd opened under the torch the small pouch he'd taken off the tall thief. Vlana looked down into it. She put her arms around Fafhrd, hugged him tight, and kissed him soundly. Then she thrust the jewels into the pouch on her belt.

When that was done, he said, "Look, I'm going to buy a jug. You tell her what happened, Mouser."

When he came out of the Golden Lamprey he was carrying four jugs in the crook of his left arm and wiping his lips on the back of his right hand. Vlana was frowning. He grinned at her. The Mouser smacked his lips at the jugs. They continued east on Cash. Fafhrd realized that the frown was for more than the jugs and the prospect of stupidly drunken male revelry. The Mouser tactfully walked ahead, ostensibly to lead the way.

When his figure was little more than a blob in the thickening smog, Vlana whispered harshly, "You had two members of the Thieves' Guild knocked out cold and you didn't cut their throats?"

"We slew three bravos," Fafhrd protested by way of excuse.

"My quarrel is not with the Slayers' Brotherhood, but that abominable Guild. You swore to me that whenever you had the chance—"

"Vlana! I couldn't have the Gray Mouser thinking I was an amateur counter-thief consumed by hysteria and blood lust."

"You already set great store by him, don't you?"

"He possibly saved my life tonight."

"Well, he told me that *he'd* have slit their throats in a wink, if he'd known I wanted it that way."

"He was only playing up to you from courtesy."

"Perhaps and perhaps not. But *you* knew and you didn't—"

"Vlana, shut up!"

Her frown became a rageful glare, then suddenly she laughed wildly, smiled twitchingly as if she were about to cry, mastered herself and smiled more lovingly. "Pardon me, darling," she said. "Sometimes you must think I'm going mad and sometimes I believe I am."

"Well, don't," he told her shortly. "Think of the jewels we've won instead. And behave yourself with our new friends. Get some wine inside you and relax. I mean to enjoy myself tonight. I've earned it."

She nodded and clutched his arm in agreement and for comfort and sanity. They hurried to catch up with the dim figure ahead.

The Mouser, turning left, led them a half square north on Cheap Street to where a narrower way went east again. The black mist in it looked solid.

"Dim Lane," the Mouser explained.

Fafhrd nodded that he knew.

Vlana said, "Dim's too weak—too *transparent* a word for it tonight," with an uneven laugh in which there were still traces of hysteria and which ended in a fit of strangled coughing. When she could swallow again, she gasped out, "Damn Lankhmar's night-smog! What a hell of a city!"

"It's the nearness here of the Great Salt Marsh," Fafhrd explained.

And he did indeed have part of the answer. Lying low betwixt the Marsh, the Inner Sea, the River Hlal, and the flat southern grainfields watered by canals fed by the Hlal, Lankhmar with its innumerable smokes was the prey of fogs and sooty smogs. No wonder the citizens had adopted the black toga as their formal garb. Some averred the toga had originally been white or pale brown, but so swiftly soot-blackened, necessitating endless laundering, that a thrifty overlord had ratified and made official what nature or civilization's arts decreed.

About halfway to Carter Street, a tavern on the north side of the lane emerged from the murk. A gape-jawed serpentine shape of pale metal crested with soot hung high for a sign. Beneath it they passed a door curtained with begrimed leather, the slit in which spilled out noise, pulsing torchlight, and the reek of liquor.

Just beyond the Silver Eel the Mouser led them through an inky passageway outside the tavern's east wall. They had to go single file, feeling their way along rough, slimily bemisted brick and keeping close together.

"Mind the puddle," the Mouser warned. "It's deep as the Outer Sea."

The passageway widened. Reflected torchlight filtering down through the dark mist allowed them to make out only the most general shape of their surroundings. To the right was more windowless, high wall. To the left, crowding close to the back of the Silver Eel, rose a dismal, rickety building of darkened brick and blackened, ancient wood. It looked utterly deserted to Fafhrd and Vlana until they had craned back their heads to gaze at the fourth-story attic under the ragged-guttered roof. There faint lines and points of yellow light shone around and through three tightly-latticed windows. Beyond, crossing the T of the space they were in, was a narrow alley.

"Bones Alley," the Mouser told them in somewhat lofty tones. "I call it Ordure Boulevard."

"I can smell that," Vlana said.

By now she and Fafhrd could see a long, narrow wooden outside stairway, steep yet sagging and without a rail, leading up to the lighted attic. The Mouser relieved Fafhrd of the jugs and went up it quite swiftly.

"Follow me when I've reached the top," he called back. "I think it'll take your weight, Fafhrd, but best one of you at a time."

Fafhrd gently pushed Vlana ahead. With another hysteria-tinged laugh and a pause midway up for another fit of choked coughing, she mounted to the Mouser where he now stood in an open doorway, from which streamed yellow light that died swiftly in the night-smog. He was lightly resting a hand on a big, empty, wrought-iron lamp-hook firmly set in a stone section of the outside wall. He bowed aside, and she went in.

Fafhrd followed, placing his feet as close as he could to the wall, his hands ready to grab for support. The whole stairs creaked ominously and each step gave a little as he shifted his weight onto it. Near the top, one gave way with the muted crack of half-rotted wood. Gently as he could, he sprawled himself hand and knee on as many steps as he could reach, to distribute his weight, and cursed sulphurously.

"Don't fret, the jugs are safe," the Mouser called down gayly.

Fafhrd crawled the rest of the way, a somewhat sour look on his face, and did not get to his feet until he was inside the door-way. When he had done so, he almost gasped with surprise.

It was like rubbing the verdigris from a cheap brass ring and finding a rainbow-fired diamond of the first water set in it. Rich drapes, some twinkling with embroidery of silver and gold, covered the walls except where the shuttered windows were— and the shutters of those were gilded. Similar but darker fabrics hid the low ceiling, making a gorgeous canopy in which the flecks of gold and silver were like stars. Scattered about were plump cushions and low tables, on which burned a multitude of candles. On shelves against the walls were neatly stacked like small logs a vast reserve of candles, numerous scrolls, jugs, bottles, and enameled boxes. A low vanity table was backed by a mirror of honed silver and thickly scattered over with jewels and cosmetics. In a large fireplace was set a small metal stove, neatly blacked, with an ornate fire-pot. Also set beside the stove were a tidy pyramid of thin, resinous torches with frayed ends—fire-kindlers—and other pyramids of short-handled brooms and mops, small, short logs, and gleamingly black coal.

On a low dais by the fireplace was a wide, short-legged, high-backed couch covered with cloth of gold. On it sat a thin, pale-faced, delicately handsome girl clad in a dress of thick violet silk worked with silver and belted with a silver chain. Her slippers were of white snow-serpent fur. Silver pins headed with amethysts held in place her high-piled black hair. Around her shoulders was drawn a white ermine wrap. She was leaning forward with uneasy-seeming graciousness and extending a narrow, white hand which shook a little to Vlana, who knelt before her and now gently took the proffered hand and bowed her head over it, her own glossy, straight, dark-brown hair making a canopy, and pressed the other girl's hand's back to her lips.

Fafhrd was happy to see his woman playing up properly to this definitely odd though delightful situation. Then looking at Vlana's long, red-stockinged leg stretched far behind her as she knelt on the other, he noted that the floor was everywhere strewn —to the point of double, treble, and quadruple overlaps—with thick-piled, close-woven, many-hued rugs of the finest imported from the Eastern Lands. Before he knew it, his thumb had shot toward the Gray Mouser.

"You're the Rug Robber!" he proclaimed. "You're the Carpet Crimp!—and the Candle Corsair too!" he continued, referring to two series of unsolved thefts which had been on the lips of all Lankhmar when he and Vlana had arrived a moon ago.

The Mouser shrugged impassive-faced at Fafhrd, then suddenly grinned, his slitted eyes a-twinkle, and broke into an impromptu dance which carried him whirling and jigging around the room and left him behind Fafhrd, where he deftly reached down the hooded and long-sleeved huge robe from the latter's stooping shoulders, shook it out, carefully folded it, and set it on a pillow.

After a long, uncertain pause, the girl in violet nervously patted with her free hand the cloth of gold beside her and Vlana seated herself there, carefully not too close, and the two women spoke together in low voices, Vlana taking the lead, though not obviously.

The Mouser took off his own gray, hooded cloak, folded it almost fussily, and laid it beside Fafhrd's. Then they unbelted their swords, and the Mouser set them atop folded robe and cloak.

Without those weapons and bulking garments, the two men looked suddenly like youths, both with clear, close-shaven faces, both slender despite the swelling muscles of Fafhrd's arms and calves, he with long red-gold hair falling down his back and about his shoulders, the Mouser with dark hair cut in bangs, the one in brown leather tunic worked with copper wire, the other in jerkin of coarsely woven gray silk.

They smiled at each other. The feeling each had of having turned boy all at once made their smiles for the first time a bit embarrassed. The Mouser cleared his throat and, bowing a little, but looking still at Fafhrd, extended a loosely spread-fingered arm toward the golden couch and said with a preliminary stammer, though otherwise smoothly enough, "Fafhrd, my good friend, permit me to introduce you to my princess. Ivrian, my dear, receive Fafhrd graciously if you please, for tonight he and I fought back to back against three and we conquered."

Fafhrd advanced, stooping a little, the crown of his red-gold hair brushing the bestarred canopy, and knelt before Ivrian exactly as Vlana had. The slender hand extended to him looked steady now, but was still quiveringly a-tremble, he discovered as soon as he touched it. He handled it as if it were silk woven of the white spider's gossamer, barely brushing it with his lips, and still felt nervous as he mumbled some compliments.

He did not sense, at least at the moment, that the Mouser was quite as nervous as he, if not more so, praying hard that Ivrian would not overdo her princess part and snub their guests, or collapse in trembling or tears or run to him or into the next room, for Fafhrd and Vlana were literally the first beings, human or animal, noble, freeman, or slave, that he had brought or allowed into the luxurious nest he had created for his aristocratic beloved —save the two love birds that twittered in a silver cage hanging to the other side of the fireplace from the dais.

Despite his shrewdness and new-found cynicism it never occurred to the Mouser that it was chiefly his charming but preposterous coddling of Ivrian that was keeping doll-like and even making more so the potentially brave and realistic girl who had fled with him from her father's torture chamber four moons ago.

But now as Ivrian smiled at last and Fafhrd gently returned her her hand and cautiously backed off, the Mouser relaxed with relief, fetched two silver cups and two silver mugs, wiped them needlessly with a silken towel, carefully selected a bottle of violet wine, then with a grin at Fafhrd uncorked instead one of the jugs the Northerner had brought, and near-brimmed the four gleaming vessels and served them all four.

With another preliminary clearing of throat, but no trace of stammer this time, he toasted, "To my greatest theft to date in Lankhmar, which willy-nilly I must share sixty-sixty with"—he couldn't resist the sudden impulse—"with this great, longhaired, barbarian lout here!" And he downed a quarter of his mug of pleasantly burning wine fortified with brandy.

Fafhrd quaffed off half of his, then toasted back, "To the most boastful and finical little civilized chap I've ever deigned to share loot with," quaffed off the rest, and with a great smile that showed white teeth held out his empty mug.

The Mouser gave him a refill, topped off his own, then set that down to go to Ivrian and pour into her lap from their small pouch the gems he'd filched from Fissif. They gleamed in their new, enviable location like a small puddle of rainbow-hued quicksilver.

Ivrian jerked back a-tremble, almost spilling them, but Vlana gently caught her arm, steadying it, and leaned in over the jewels with a throaty gasp of wonder and admiration, slowly turned an envious gaze on the pale girl, and began rather urgently but smilingly to whisper to her. Fafhrd realized that Vlana was acting now, but acting well and effectively, since Ivrian was soon nodding eagerly and not long after that beginning to whisper back. At her direction, Vlana fetched a blue-enameled box inlaid with silver, and the two of them transferred the jewels from Ivrian's lap into its blue velvet interior. Then Ivrian placed the box close beside her and they chatted on.

As he worked through his second mug in smaller gulps, Fafhrd relaxed and began to get a deeper feeling of his surroundings. The dazzling wonder of the first glimpse of this throne room in a slum, its colorful luxury intensified by contrast with the dark and mud and slime and rotten stairs and Ordure Boulevard just outside, faded, and he began to note the rickettiness and rot under the grand overlay.

Black, rotten wood and dry, cracked wood too showed here and there between the drapes and also loosed their sick, ancient stinks. The whole floor sagged under the rugs, as much as a span at the center of the room. A large cockroach was climbing down a gold-worked drape, another toward the couch. Threads of night-smog were coming through the shutters, making evanescent black arabesques against the gilt. The stones of the large fireplace had been scrubbed and varnished, yet most of the mortar was gone from between them; some sagged, others were missing altogether.

The Mouser had been building a fire there in the stove. Now he pushed in all the way the yellow-flaring kindler he'd lit from the fire-pot, hooked the little black door shut over the mounting flames, and turned back into the room. As if he'd read Fafhrd's mind, he took up several cones of incense, set their peaks a-smolder at the fire-pot, and placed them about the room in gleaming, shallow, brass bowls—stepping hard on the one cockroach by the way and surreptitiously catching and crushing the other in the base of his flicked fist. Then he stuffed silken rags in the widest shutter-cracks, took up his silver mug again, and for a moment gave Fafhrd a very hard look, as if daring him to say just one word against the delightful yet faintly ridiculous doll's house he'd prepared for his princess.

Next moment he was smiling and lifting his mug to Fafhrd, who was doing the same. Need of refills brought them close together. Hardly moving his lips, the Mouser explained *sotto voce*, "Ivrian's father was a duke. I slew him, by black magic, I believe, while he was having me done to death on the torture rack. A most cruel man, cruel to his daughter too, yet a duke, so that Ivrian is wholly unused to fending or caring for herself. I pride myself that I maintain her in grander state than ever her father did with all his serving men and maids."

Suppressing the instant criticisms he felt of this attitude and program, Fafhrd nodded and said amiably, "Surely you've thieved together a most charming little palace, quite worthy of Lankhmar's overlord Karstak Ovartamortes, or the King of Kings at Tisilinilit."

From the couch Vlana called in her husky contralto, "Gray Mouser, your princess would hear an account of tonight's adventure. And might we have more wine?"

Ivrian called, "Yes, please, Mouse."

Wincing almost imperceptibly at that earlier nickname, the Mouser looked to Fafhrd for the go-ahead, got the nod, and launched into his story. But first he served the girls wine. There wasn't enough for their cups, so he opened another jug and after a moment of thought uncorked all three, setting one by the couch, one by Fafhrd where he sprawled now on the pillowy carpets, and reserving one for himself. Ivrian looked wide-eyed apprehensive at this signal of heavy drinking ahead, Vlana cynical with a touch of anger, but neither voiced their criticism.

The Mouser told the tale of counter-thievery well, acting it out in part, and with only the most artistic of embellishments—the ferret-marmoset before escaping ran up his back and tried to scratch out his eyes—and he was interrupted only twice.

When he said, "And so with a whish and a snick I bared Scalpel—" Fafhrd remarked, "Oh, so you've nicknamed your sword as well as yourself?"

The Mouser drew himself up. "Yes, and I call my dirk Cat's Claw. Any objections? Seem childish to you?"

"Not at all. I call my own sword Graywand. All weapons are in a fashion alive, civilized and nameworthy. Pray continue."

And when he mentioned the beastie of uncertain nature that had gamboled along with the thieves (and attacked his eyes!), Ivrian paled and said with a shudder, "Mouse! That sounds like a witch's familiar!"

"Wizard's," Vlana corrected. "Those gutless Guild-villains have no truck with women, except as fee'd or forced vehicles for their lust. But Krovas, their current king, though superstitious, is noted for taking *all* precautions, and might well have a warlock in his service."

"That seems most likely; it harrows me with dread," the Mouser agreed with ominous gaze and sinister voice. He really didn't believe or feel what he said—he was about as harrowed as virgin prairie—in the least, but he eagerly accepted any and all atmospheric enhancements of his performance.

When he was done, the girls, eyes flashing and fond, toasted him and Fafhrd for their cunning and bravery. The Mouser bowed and eye-twinklingly smiled about, then sprawled him down with a weary sigh, wiping his forehead with a silken cloth and downing a large drink.

After asking Vlana's leave, Fafhrd told the adventurous tale of their escape from Cold Corner—he from his clan, she from an acting troupe—and of their progress to Lankhmar, where they lodged now in an actors' tenement near the Plaza of Dark Delights. Ivrian hugged herself to Vlana and shivered large-eyed at the witchy parts—at least as much in delight as fear of Fafhrd's tale, he thought. He told himself it was natural that a doll-girl should love ghost stories, though he wondered if her pleasure would have been as great if she had known that his ghost stories were truly true. She seemed to live in worlds of imagination—once more at least half the Mouser's doing, he was sure.

The only proper matter he omitted from his account was Vlana's fixed intent to get a monstrous revenge on the Thieves' Guild for torturing to death her accomplices and harrying her out of Lankhmar when she'd tried free-lance thieving in the city, with miming as a cover. Nor of course did he mention his own promise—foolish, he thought now—to help her in this bloody business.

After he'd done and got his applause, he found his throat dry despite his skald's training, but when he sought to wet it, he discovered that his mug was empty and his jug too, though he didn't feel in the least drunk; he had talked all the liquor out of him, he told himself, a little of the stuff escaping in each glowing word he'd spoken.

The Mouser was in like plight and not drunk either—though inclined to pause mysteriously and peer toward infinity before answering question or making remark. This time he suggested, after a particularly long infinity-gaze, that Fafhrd accompany him to the Eel while he purchased a fresh supply.

"But we've a lot of wine left in *our* jug," Ivrian protested. "Or at least a little," she amended. It did sound empty when Vlana shook it. "Besides, you've wine of all sorts here."

"Not this sort, dearest, and first rule is never mix 'em," the Mouser explained, wagging a finger. "That way lies unhealth, aye, and madness."

"My dear," Vlana said, sympathetically patting Ivrian's wrist, "at some time in any good party all the men who are really men simply have to go out. It's extremely stupid, but it's their nature and can't be dodged, believe me."

"But, Mouse, I'm scared. Fafhrd's tale frightened me. So did yours—I'll hear that big-headed, black, ratty familiar a-scratch at the shutters when you're gone, I know I will!"

It seemed to Fafhrd she was not afraid at all, only taking pleasure in frightening herself and in demonstrating her power over her beloved.

"Darlingest," the Mouser said with a small hiccup, "there is all the Inner Sea, all the Land of the Eight Cities, and to boot all the Trollstep Mountains in their sky-scraping grandeur between you and Fafhrd's frigid specters or—pardon me, my comrade, but it could be—hallucinations admixed with coincidences. As for familiars, pish! They've never in the world been anything but the loathy, all-too-natural pets of stinking old women and womanish old men."

"The Eel's but a step, Lady Ivrian," Fafhrd said, "and you'll have beside you my dear Vlana, who slew my chiefest enemy with a single cast of that dagger she now wears."

With a glare at Fafhrd that lasted no longer than a wink, but conveyed "What a way to reassure a frightened girl!" Vlana said merrily, "Let the sillies go, my dear. 'Twill give us chance for a private chat, during which we'll take 'em apart from wine-fumey head to restless foot."

So Ivrian let herself be persuaded and the Mouser and Fafhrd slipped off, quickly shutting the door behind them to keep out the night-smog. Their rather rapid steps down the stairs could clearly be heard from within. There were faint creakings and groanings of the ancient wood outside the wall, but no sound of another tread breaking or other mishap.

Waiting for the four jugs to be brought up from the cellar, the two newly met comrades ordered a mug each of the same fortified wine, or one near enough, and ensconced themselves at the least noisy end of the long serving counter in the tumultuous tavern. The Mouser deftly kicked a rat that thrust black head and shoulders from his hole.

After each had enthusiastically complimented the other on his girl, Fafhrd said diffidently, "Just between ourselves, do you think there might be anything to your sweet Ivrian's notion that the small dark creature with Slivikin and the other Guild-thief was a wizard's familiar, or at any rate the cunning pet of a sorcerer, trained to act as go-between and report disasters to his master or to Krovas or to both?"

The Mouser laughed lightly. "You're building bug-bears— formless baby ones unlicked by logic—out of nothing, dear barbarian brother, if I may say so. *Imprimis*, we don't really know the beastie was connected with the Guild-thieves at all. May well have been a stray catling or a big bold rat—like this damned one!" He kicked again. "But, *secundus*, granting it to be the creature of a wizard employed by Krovas, how could it make useful report? I don't believe in animals that talk—except for parrots and such birds, which only . . . parrot—or ones having an elaborate sign language men can share. Or perhaps you envisage the beastie dipping its paddy paw in a jug of ink and writing its report in big on a floor-spread parchment?

"Ho, there, you back of the counter! Where are my jugs? Rats eaten the boy who went for them days ago? Or he simply starved to death while on his cellar quest? Well, tell him to get a swifter move on and meanwhile brim us again!

"No, Fafhrd, even granting the beastie to be directly or indirectly a creature of Krovas, and that it raced back to Thieves' House after our affray, what could it tell them there? Only that something had gone wrong with the burglary at Jengao's. Which they'd soon suspect in any case from the delay in the thieves' and bravos' return."

Fafhrd frowned and muttered stubbornly, "The furry slinker might, nevertheless, convey our appearances to the Guild masters, and they might recognize us and come after us and attack us in our homes. Or Slivikin and his fat pal, revived from their bumps, might do likewise."

"My dear friend," the Mouser said condolingly, "once more begging your indulgence, I fear this potent wine is addling your wits. If the Guild knew our looks or where we lodge, they'd have been nastily on our necks days, weeks, nay, months ago. Or conceivably you don't know that their penalty for free-lance or even unassigned thieving within the walls of Lankhmar and for three leagues outside them is nothing less than death, after torture if happily that can be achieved."

"I know all about that and my plight is worse even than yours," Fafhrd retorted, and after pledging the Mouser to secrecy told him the tale of Vlana's vendetta against the Guild and her deadly serious dreams of an all-encompassing revenge.

During his story the four jugs came up from the cellar, but the Mouser only ordered that their earthenware mugs be refilled.

Fafhrd finished, "And so, in consequence of a promise given by an infatuated and unschooled boy in a southern angle of the Cold Waste, I find myself now as a sober—well, at other times—man being constantly asked to make war on a power as great as that of Karstak Ovartamortes, for as you may know, the Guild has locals in all other cities and major towns of this land, not to mention agreements including powers of extradition with robber and bandit organizations in other countries. I love Vlana dearly, make no mistake about that, and she is an experienced thief herself, without whose guidance I'd hardly have survived my first week in Lankhmar, but on this one topic she has a kink in her brains, a hard knot neither logic nor persuasion can even begin to loosen. And I, well, in the month I've been here I've learned that the only way to survive in civilization is to abide by its unwritten rules—far more important than its laws chiseled in stone —and break them only at peril, in deepest secrecy, and taking all precautions. As I did tonight—not my first hijacking, by the by."

"Certes t'would be insanity to assault the Guild direct, your wisdom's perfect there," the Mouser commented. "If you cannot break your most handsome girl of this mad notion, or coax her from it—and I can see she's a fearless, self-willed one—then you must stoutly refuse e'en her least request in that direction."

"Certes I must," Fafhrd agreed, adding somewhat accusingly, "though I gather you told her you'd have willingly slit the throats of the two we struck senseless."

"Courtesy merely, man! Would you have had me behave ungraciously to your girl? 'Tis measure of the value I was already setting then on your goodwill. But only a woman's man may cross her. As you must, in this instance."

"Certes I must," Fafhrd repeated with great emphasis and conviction. "I'd be an idiot taking on the Guild. Of course if they should catch me they'd kill me in any case for free-lancing and highjacking. But wantonly to assault the Guild direct, kill one Guild-thief needlessly, only behave as if I might—lunacy entire!"

"You'd not only be a drunken, drooling idiot, you'd questionless be stinking in three nights at most from that emperor of diseases, Death. Malicious attacks on her person, blows directed at the organization, the Guild requites tenfold what she does other rule-breakings. All planned robberies and other thefts would be called off and the entire power of the Guild and its allies mobilized against you alone. I'd count your chances better to take on single-handed the host of the King of Kings rather than the Thieves' Guild's subtle minions. In view of your size, might, and wit you're a squad perhaps, or even a company, but hardly an army. So, no least givings-in to Vlana in this one matter."

"Agreed!" Fafhrd said loudly, shaking the Mouser's iron-thewed hand in a near crusher grip.

"And now we should be getting back to the girls," the Mouser said.

"After one more drink while we settle the score. Ho, boy!"

"Suits." The Mouser dug into his pouch to pay, but Fafhrd protested vehemently. In the end they tossed coin for it, and Fafhrd won and with great satisfaction clinked out his silver smerduks on the stained and dented counter, also marked with an infinitude of mug circles, as if it had been once the desk of a mad geometer. They pushed themselves to their feet, the Mouser giving the rathole one last light kick for luck.

At this, Fafhrd's thoughts looped back and he said, "Grant the beastie can't paw-write, or talk by mouth or paw, it still could have followed us at distance, marked down your dwelling, and then returned to Thieves' House to lead its masters down on us like a hound!"

"Now you're speaking shrewd sense again," the Mouser said. "Ho, boy, a bucket of small beer to go! On the instant!" Noting Fafhrd's blank look, he explained, "I'll spill it outside the Eel to kill our scent and all the way down the passageway. Yes, and splash it high on the walls too."

Fafhrd nodded wisely. "I thought I'd drunk my way past the addled point."

Vlana and Ivrian, deep in excited talk, both started at the pounding rush of footsteps up the stairs. Racing behemoths could hardly have made more noise. The creaking and groaning were prodigious and there were the crashes of two treads breaking, yet the pounding footsteps never faltered. The door flew open and their two men rushed in through a great mushroom top of night-smog which was neatly sliced off its black stem by the slam of the door.

"I told you we'd be back in a wink," the Mouser cried gayly to Ivrian, while Fafhrd strode forward, unmindful of the creaking floor, crying, "Dearest heart, I've missed you sorely," and caught up Vlana despite her voiced protests and pushings-off and kissed and hugged her soundly before setting her back on the couch again.

Oddly, it was Ivrian who appeared to be angry at Fafhrd then, rather than Vlana, who was smiling fondly if somewhat dazedly.

"Fafhrd, sir," she said boldly, her little fists set on her narrow hips, her tapered chin held high, her dark eyes blazing, "my beloved Vlana has been telling me about the unspeakably atrocious things the Thieves' Guild did to her and to her dearest friends. Pardon my frank speaking to one I've only met, but I think it quite unmanly of you to refuse her the just revenge she desires and fully deserves. And that goes for you too, Mouse, who boasted to Vlana of what you would have done had you but known, who in like case did not scruple to slay my very own father—or reputed father—for his cruelties!"

It was clear to Fafhrd that while he and the Gray Mouser had idly boozed in the Eel, Vlana had been giving Ivrian a doubtless empurpled account of her grievances against the Guild and playing mercilessly on the naïve girl's bookish, romantic sympathies and high concept of knightly honor. It was also clear to him that Ivrian was more than a little drunk. A three-quarters empty flask of violet wine of far Kiraay sat on the low table next them.

Yet he could think of nothing to do but spread his big hands helplessly and bow his head, more than the low ceiling made necessary, under Ivrian's glare, now reinforced by that of Vlana. After all, they *were* in the right. He *had* promised.

So it was the Mouser who first tried to rebut.

"Come now, pet," he cried lightly as he danced about the room, silk-stuffing more cracks against the thickening night-smog and stirring up and feeding the fire in the stove, "and you too, beauteous Lady Vlana. For the past month Fafhrd has been hitting the Guild-thieves where it hurts them most—in their purses a-dangle between their legs. His highjackings of the loot of their robberies have been like so many fierce kicks in their groins. Hurts worse, believe me, than robbing them of life with a swift, near painless sword slash or thrust. And tonight I helped him in his worthy purpose—and will eagerly do so again. Come, drink we up all." Under his handling, one of the new jugs came uncorked with a pop and he darted about brimming silver cups and mugs.

"A merchant's revenge!" Ivrian retorted with scorn, not one whit appeased, but rather angered anew. "Ye both are at heart true and gentle knights, I know, despite all current backsliding. At the least you must bring Vlana the head of Krovas!"

"What would she *do* with it? What *good* would it be except to spot the carpets?" the Mouser plaintively inquired, while Fafhrd, gathering his wits at last and going down on one knee, said slowly, "Most respected Lady Ivrian, it is true I solemnly promised my beloved Vlana I would help her in her revenge, but that was while I was still in barbarous Cold Corner, where blood-feud is a commonplace, sanctioned by custom and accepted by all the clans and tribes and brotherhoods of the savage Northerners of the Cold Waste. In my naïveté I thought of Vlana's revenge as being of that sort. But here in civilization's midst. I discover all's different and rules and customs turned upside-down. Yet—Lankhmar or Cold Corner—one must seem to observe rule and custom to survive. Here cash is all-powerful, the idol placed

highest, whether one sweat, thieve, grind others down, or scheme
for it. Here feud and revenge are outside all rules and punished
worse than violent lunacy. Think, Lady Ivrian, if Mouse and I
should bring Vlana the head of Krovas, she and I would have to
flee Lankhmar on the instant, every man's hand against us; while
you infallibly would lose this fairyland Mouse has created for
love of you and be forced to do likewise, be with him a beggar
on the run for the rest of your natural lives."

It was beautifully reasoned and put . . . and no good whatsoever. While Fafhrd spoke, Ivrian snatched up her new-filled cup
and drained it. Now she stood up straight as a soldier, her pale
face flushed, and said scathingly to Fafhrd kneeling before her,
"*You count the cost!* You speak to me of *things*"—she waved at
the many-hued splendor around her—"of mere property, however costly, when *honor* is at stake. You gave Vlana *your word*.
Oh, is knighthood wholly dead? And that applies to you, too,
Mouse, who swore you'd slit the miserable throats of two
noisome Guild-thieves."

"I didn't swear *to*," the Mouser objected feebly, downing a big
drink. "I merely said I *would have*," while Fafhrd could only
shrug again and writhe inside and gulp a little easement from his
silver mug. For Ivrian was speaking in the same guilt-showering
tones and using the same unfair yet heart-cleaving womanly arguments as Mor his mother might have, or Mara, his deserted
Snow Clan sweetheart and avowed wife, big-bellied by now with
his child.

In a master stroke, Vlana tried gently to draw Ivrian down to
her golden seat again. "Softly, dearest," she pleaded. "You have
spoken nobly for me and my cause, and believe me, I am most
grateful. Your words revived in me great, fine feelings dead these
many years. But of us here, only you are truly an aristocrat at-
tuned to the highest proprieties. We other three are naught but
thieves. Is it any wonder some of us put safety above honor and
word-keeping, and most prudently avoid risking our lives? Yes,
we are three thieves and I am outvoted. So please speak no more
of honor and rash, dauntless bravery, but sit you down and—"

"You mean they're both *afraid* to challenge the Thieves' Guild,
don't you?" Ivrian said, eyes wide and face twisted by loathing.
"I always thought my Mouse was a nobleman first and a thief

second. Thieving's nothing. My father lived by cruel thievery done on rich wayfarers and neighbors less powerful than he, yet he was an aristocrat. Oh, you're *cowards*, both of you! *Poltroons!*" she finished, turning her eyes flashing with cold scorn first on the Mouser, then on Fafhrd.

The latter could stand it no longer. He sprang to his feet, face flushed, fists clenched at his sides, quite unmindful of his down-clattered mug and the ominous creak his sudden action drew from the sagging floor.

"*I am not a coward!*" he cried. "I'll dare Thieves' House and fetch you Krovas' head and toss it with blood a-drip at Vlana's feet. I swear that, witness me, Kos the god of Dooms, by the brown bones of Nalgron my father and by his sword Graywand here at my side!"

He slapped his left hip, found nothing there but his tunic, and had to content himself with pointing tremble-armed at his belt and scabbarded sword where they lay atop his neatly folded robe—and then picking up, refilling splashily, and draining his mug.

The Gray Mouser began to laugh in high, delighted, tuneful peals. All stared at him. He came dancing up beside Fafhrd, and still smiling widely, asked, "*Why not?* Who speaks of fearing the Guild-thieves? Who becomes upset at the prospect of this ridiculously easy exploit, when all of us know that all of them, even Krovas and his ruling clique, are but pygmies in mind and skill compared to me or Fafhrd here? A wondrously simple, foolproof scheme has just occurred to me for penetrating Thieves' House, every closet and cranny. Stout Fafhrd and I will put it into effect at once. Are you with me, Northerner?"

"Of course I am," Fafhrd responded gruffly, at the same time frantically wondering what madness had gripped the little fellow.

"Give me a few heartbeats to gather needed props, and we're off!" the Mouser cried. He snatched from a shelf and unfolded a stout sack, then raced about, thrusting into it coiled ropes, bandage rolls, rags, jars of ointment and unction and unguent, and other oddments.

"But you can't go *tonight*," Ivrian protested, suddenly grown pale and uncertain-voiced. "You're both . . . in no condition to."

"You're both *drunk*," Vlana said harshly. "Silly drunk—and that way you'll get naught in Thieves' House but your deaths. Fafhrd, where's that heartless reason you employed to slay or ice-veined see slain a clutch of mighty rivals and win me at Cold Corner and in the chilly, sorcery-webbed depths of Trollstep Canyon? Revive it! And infuse some into your skipping gray friend."

"Oh, no," Fafhrd told her as he buckled on his sword. "You wanted the head of Krovas heaved at your feet in a great splatter of blood, and that's what you're going to get, like it or not!"

"Softly, Fafhrd," the Mouser interjected, coming to a sudden stop and drawing tight the sack's mouth by its strings. "And softly you too, Lady Vlana, and my dear princess. Tonight I intend but a scouting expedition. No risks run, only the information gained needful for planning our murderous strike tomorrow or the day after. So no head-choppings whatsoever tonight, Fafhrd, you hear me? Whatever may hap, hist's the word. And don your hooded robe."

Fafhrd shrugged, nodded, and obeyed.

Ivrian seemed somewhat relieved. Vlana too, though she said, "Just the same you're both drunk."

"All to the good!" the Mouser assured her with a mad smile. "Drink may slow a man's sword-arm and soften his blows a bit, but it sets his wits ablaze and fires his imagination, and those are the qualities we'll need tonight. Besides," he hurried on, cutting off some doubt Ivrian was about to voice, "drunken men are supremely cautious! Have you ever seen a staggering sot pull himself together at sight of the guard and walk circumspectly and softly past?"

"Yes," Vlana said, "and fall flat on his face just as he comes abreast 'em."

"Pish!" the Mouser retorted and, throwing back his head, grandly walked toward her along an imaginary straight line. Instantly he tripped over his own foot, plunged forward, suddenly without touching floor did an incredible forward flip, heels over head, and landed erect and quite softly—toes, ankles, and knees bending just at the right moment to soak up impact—directly in front of the girls. The floor barely complained.

"You see?" he said, straightening up and unexpectedly reeling backward. He tripped over the pillow on which lay his cloak and sword, but by a wrenching twist and a lurch stayed upright and begain rapidly to accouter himself.

Under cover of this action Fafhrd made quietly yet swiftly to fill once more his and the Mouser's mugs, but Vlana noted it and gave him such a glare that he set down mugs and uncorked jug so swiftly his robe swirled, then stepped back from the drinks table with a shrug of resignation and toward Vlana a grimacing nod.

The Mouser shouldered his sack and drew open the door. With a casual wave at the girls, but no word spoken, Fafhrd stepped out on the tiny porch. The night-smog had grown so thick he was almost lost to view. The Mouser waved four fingers at Ivrian, softly called, "Bye-bye, Misling," then followed Fafhrd.

"Good fortune go with you," Vlana called heartily.

"Oh, be careful, Mouse," Ivrian gasped.

The Mouser, his figure slight against the loom of Fafhrd's, silently drew shut the door.

Their arms automatically gone around each other, the girls waited for the inevitable creaking and groaning of the stairs. It delayed and delayed. The night-smog that had entered the room dissipated and still the silence was unbroken.

"What can they be doing out there?" Ivrian whispered. "Plotting their course?"

Vlana, scowling, impatiently shook her head, then disentangled herself, tiptoed to the door, opened it, descended softly a few steps, which creaked most dolefully, then returned, shutting the door behind her.

"They're gone," she said in wonder, her eyes wide, her hands spread a little to either side, palms up.

"I'm frightened!" Ivrian breathed and sped across the room to embrace the taller girl.

Vlana hugged her tight, then disengaged an arm to shoot the door's three heavy bolts.

In Bones Alley the Mouser returned to his pouch the knotted line by which they'd descended from the lamp hook. He suggested, "How about stopping at the Silver Eel?"

"You mean and just *tell* the girls we've been to Thieves' House?" Fafhrd asked, not too indignantly.

"Oh, no," the Mouser protested. "But you missed your stirrup cup upstairs and so did I."

At the word "stirrup" he looked down at his ratskin boots and then crouching began a little gallop in one place, his boot-soles clopping softly on the cobbles. He flapped imaginary reins— "Giddap!"—and quickened his gallop, but leaning sharply back pulled to a stop—"Whoa!"—when with a crafty smile Fafhrd drew from his robe two full jugs.

"Palmed 'em, as 'twere, when I set down the mugs. Vlana sees a lot, but not all."

"You're a prudent, far-sighted fellow, in addition to having some skill at sword taps," the Mouser said admiringly. "I'm proud to call you comrade."

Each uncorked and drank a hearty slug. Then the Mouser led them west, they veering and stumbling only a little. Not so far as Cheap Street, however, but turning north into an even narrower and more noisome alley.

"Plague Court," the Mouser said. Fafhrd nodded.

After several preliminary peepings and peerings, they staggered swiftly across wide, empty Crafts Street and into Plague Court again. For a wonder it was growing a little lighter. Looking upward, they saw stars. Yet there was no wind blowing from the north. The air was deathly still.

In their drunken preoccupation with the project at hand and mere locomotion, they did not look behind them. There the night-smog was thicker than ever. A high-circling nighthawk would have seen the stuff converging from all sections of Lankhmar, north, east, south, west—from the Inner Sea, from the Great Salt Marsh, from the many-ditched grainlands, from the River Hlal—in swift-moving black rivers and rivulets, heaping, eddying, swirling, dark and reeking essence of Lankhmar from its branding irons, braziers, bonfires, bonefires, kitchen fires and warmth fires, kilns, forges, breweries, distilleries, junk and garbage fires innumerable, sweating alchemists' and sorcerers' dens, crematoriums, charcoal burners' turfed mounds, all those and many more . . . converging purposefully on Dim Lane and particularly on the Silver Eel and perhaps especially on the ricketty house behind it, untenanted except for attic. The closer to that center it got, the more substantial the smog became, eddy-strands and swirl-tatters tearing off and clinging to rough stone corners and scraggly-surfaced brick like black cobwebs.

But the Mouser and Fafhrd merely exclaimed in mild, muted amazement at the stars, muggily mused as to how much the improved visibility would increase the risk of their quest, and cautiously crossing the Street of the Thinkers, called Atheist Avenue by moralists, continued to Plague Court until it forked.

The Mouser chose the left branch, which trended northwest.

"Death Alley."

Fafhrd nodded.

After a curve and recurve, Cheap Street swung into sight about thirty paces ahead. The Mouser stopped at once and lightly threw his arm against Fafhrd's chest.

Clearly in view across Cheap Street was a wide, low, open doorway, framed by grimy stone blocks. There led up to it two steps hollowed by the treadings of centuries. Orange-yellow light spilled out from bracketed torches inside. They couldn't see very far in because of Death Alley's angle. Yet as far as they *could* see, there was no porter or guard in sight, nor anyone at all, not even a watchdog on a chain. The effect was ominous.

"Now how do we get into the damn place?" Fafhrd demanded in a hoarse whisper. "Scout Murder Alley for a back window that can be forced. You've pries in that sack, I trow. Or try the roof? You're a roof man, I know already. Teach me the art. I know trees and mountains, snow, ice, and bare rock. See this wall here?" He backed off from it, preparing to go up it in a rush.

"Steady on, Fafhrd," the Mouser said, keeping his hand against the big young man's chest. "We'll hold the roof in reserve. Likewise all walls. And I'll take it on trust you're a master climber. As to how we get in, we walk straight through that doorway." He frowned. "Tap and hobble, rather. Come on, while I prepare us."

As he drew the skeptically grimacing Fafhrd back down Death Alley until all Cheap Street was again cut off from view, he explained, "We'll pretend to be beggars, members of *their* guild, which is but a branch of the Thieves' Guild and houses with it, or at any rate reports in to the Beggarmasters at Thieves' House. We'll be new members, who've gone out by day, so it'll not be expected that the Night Beggarmaster and any night watchmen know our looks."

"But we don't look like beggars," Fafhrd protested. "Beggars have awful sores and limbs all atwist or lacking altogether."

"That's just what I'm going to take care of now," the Mouser chuckled, drawing Scalpel. Ignoring Fafhrd's backward step and wary glance, the Mouser gazed puzzledly at the long tapering strip of steel he'd bared, then with a happy nod unclipped from his belt Scalpel's scabbard furbished with ratskin, sheathed the sword and swiftly wrapped it up, hilt and all, in a spiral, with the wide ribbon of a bandage roll dug from his sack.

"There!" he said, knotting the bandage ends. "Now I've a tapping cane."

"What's that?" Fafhrd demanded. "And why?"

"Because I'll be blind, that's why." He took a few shuffling steps, tapping the cobbles ahead with wrapped sword—gripping it by the quillons, or crossguard, so that the grip and pommel were up his sleeve—and groping ahead with his other hand. "That look all right to you?" he asked Fafhrd as he turned back. "Feels perfect to me. Bat-blind, eh? Oh, don't fret, Fafhrd—the rag's but gauze. I can see through it fairly well. Besides, I don't have to convince anyone inside Thieves' House I'm actually blind. Most Guild-beggars fake it, as you must know. Now what to do with you? Can't have you blind also—too obvious, might wake suspicion." He uncorked his jug and sucked inspiration. Fafhrd copied this action, on principle.

The Mouser smacked his lips and said, "I've got it! Fafhrd, stand on your right leg and double up your left behind you at the knee. Hold! Don't fall on me! Avaunt! But steady yourself by my shoulder. That's right. Now get that left foot higher. We'll disguise your sword like mine, for a crutch cane—it's thicker and'll look just right. You can also steady yourself with your other hand on my shoulder as you hop—the halt leading the blind, always good for a tear, always good theater! But higher with that left foot! No, it just doesn't come off—I'll have to rope it. But first unclip your scabbard."

Soon the Mouser had Graywand and its scabbard in the same state as Scalpel and was tying Fafhrd's left ankle to his thigh, drawing the rope cruelly tight, though Fafhrd's wine-anesthetized nerves hardly registered it. Balancing himself with his steel-cored crutch cane as the Mouser worked, he swigged from his jug and pondered deeply. Ever since joining forces with Vlana, he'd been interested in the theater, and the atmosphere of the actors' tenement had fired that interest further, so that he was delighted at the prospect of acting a part in real life. Yet brilliant as the Mouser's plan undoubtedly was, there did seem to be drawbacks to it. He tried to formulate them.

"Mouser," he said, "I don't know as I like having our swords tied up, so we can't draw 'em in emergency."

"We can still use 'em as clubs." the Mouser countered, his breath hissing between his teeth as he drew the last knot hard. "Besides, we'll have our knives. Say, pull your belt around until yours is behind your back, so your robe will hide it sure. I'll do the same with Cat's Claw. Beggars don't carry weapons, at least in view, and we must maintain dramatic consistency in every detail. Stop drinking now; you've had enough. I myself need only a couple swallows more to reach my finest pitch."

"And I don't know as I like going hobbled into that den of cutthroats. I can hop amazingly fast, it's true, but not as fast as I can run. Is it really wise, think you?"

"You can slash yourself loose in an instant," the Mouser hissed with a touch of impatience and anger. "Aren't you willing to make the least sacrifice for art's sake?"

"Oh, very well," Fafhrd said, draining his jug and tossing it aside. "Yes, of course I am."

"Your complexion's too hale," the Mouser said, inspecting him critically. He touched up Fafhrd's features and hands with pale gray greasepaint, then added wrinkles with dark. "And your garb's too tidy." He scooped dirt from between the cobbles and smeared it on Fafhrd's robe, then tried to put a rip in it, but the material resisted. He shrugged and tucked his lightened sack under his belt.

"So's yours," Fafhrd observed, and stooping on his right leg got a good handful of muck himself, ordure in it by its feel and stink. Heaving himself up with a mighty effort, he wiped the stuff off on the Mouser's cloak and gray silken jerkin too.

The small man got the odor and cursed, but, "Dramatic consistency," Fafhrd reminded him. "It's well we stink. Beggars do—

that's one reason folk give 'em coins: to get rid of 'em. And no one at Thieves' House will be eager to inspect us close. Now come on, while our fires are still high." And grasping hold of the Mouser's shoulder, he propelled himself rapidly toward Cheap Street, setting his bandaged sword between cobbles well ahead and taking mighty hops.

"Slow down, idiot," the Mouser cried softly, shuffling along with the speed almost of a skater to keep up, while tapping his (sword) cane like mad. "A cripple's supposed to be *feeble*— that's what draws the sympathy."

Fafhrd nodded wisely and slowed somewhat. The ominous empty doorway slid again into view. The Mouser tilted his jug to get the last of his wine, swallowed awhile, then choked sputteringly. Fafhrd snatched and drained the jug, then tossed it over shoulder to shatter noisily.

They hop-shuffled into Cheap Street, halting almost at once for a richly clad man and woman to pass. The richness of the man's garb was sober and he was on the fat and oldish side, though hard-featured. A merchant doubtless, and with money in the Thieves' Guild—protection money, at least—to take this route at this hour.

The richness of the woman's garb was garish though not tawdry and she was beautiful and young, and looked still younger. A competent courtesan, almost certainly.

The man started to veer around the noisome and filthy pair, his face averted, but the girl swung toward the Mouser, concern growing in her eyes with hothouse swiftness. "Oh, you poor boy! Blind. What tragedy," she said. "Give us a gift for him, lover."

"Keep away from those stinkards, Misra, and come along," he retorted, the last of his speech vibrantly muffled, for he was holding his nose.

She made him no reply, but thrust white hand into his ermine pouch and swiftly pressed a coin against the Mouser's palm and closed his fingers on it, then took his head between her palms and kissed him sweetly on the lips before letting herself be dragged on.

"Take good care of the little fellow, old man," she called fondly back to Fafhrd while her companion grumbled muffled reproaches at her, of which only "perverted bitch" was intelligible.

The Mouser stared at the coin in his palm, then sneaked a long look after his benefactress. There was a dazed wonder in his voice as he whispered to Fafhrd, "Look. *Gold.* A golden coin and a beautiful woman's sympathy. Think you we should give over this rash project and for a profession take up beggary?"

"Buggery even, rather!" Fafhrd answered harsh and low. That "old man" rankled. "Onward we, bravely!"

They upped the two worn steps and went through the doorway, noting the exceptional thickness of the wall. Ahead was a long, straight, high-ceilinged corridor ending in a stairs and with doors spilling light at intervals and wall-set torches adding their flare, but empty all its length.

They had just got through the doorway when cold steel chilled the neck and pricked a shoulder of each of them. From just above, two voices commanded in unison, "Halt!"

Although fired—and fuddled—by fortified wine, they each had wit enough to freeze and then very cautiously look upward.

Two gaunt, scarred, exceptionally ugly faces, each topped by a gaudy scarf binding back hair, looked down at them from a big, deep niche just above the doorway and helping explain its lowness. Two bent, gnarly arms thrust down the swords that still pricked them.

"Gone out with the noon beggar-batch, eh?" one of them observed. "Well, you'd better have a high take to justify your tardy return. The Night Beggarmaster's on a Whore Street furlough. Report above to Krovas. Gods, you stink! Better clean up first, or Krovas will have you bathed in live steam. Begone!"

The Mouser and Fafhrd shuffled and hobbled forward at their most authentic. One niche-guard cried after them, "Relax, boys! You don't have to put it on here."

"Practice makes perfect," the Mouser called back in a quavering voice. Fafhrd's finger-ends dug his shoulder warningly. They moved along somewhat more naturally, so far as Fafhrd's tied-up leg allowed.

"Gods, what an easy life the Guild-beggars have," the other niche-guard observed to his mate. "What slack discipline and

low standards of skill! Perfect, my sacred butt! You'd think a
child could see through those disguises."

"Doubtless some children do," his mate retorted. "But their
dear mothers and fathers only drop a tear and a coin or give a
kick. Grown folk go blind, lost in their toil and dreams, unless
they have a profession such as thieving which keeps them mindful of things as they really are."

Resisting the impulse to ponder this sage philosophy, and
glad they would not have to undergo a Beggarmaster's shrewd
inspection—truly, thought Fafhrd, Kos of the Dooms seemed to
be leading him direct to Krovas and perhaps head-chopping
would be the order of the night—he and the Mouser went
watchfully and slowly on. And now they began to hear voices,
mostly curt and clipped ones, and other noises.

They passed some doorways they'd liked to have paused at, to
study the activities inside, yet the most they dared do was slow
down a bit more. Fortunately most of the doorways were wide,
permitting a fairly long view.

Very interesting were some of those activities. In one room
young boys were being trained to pick pouches and slit purses.
They'd approach from behind an instructor, and if he heard scuff
of bare foot or felt touch of dipping hand—or, worst, heard
clunk of dropped leaden mock-coin—that boy would be
thwacked. Others seemed to be getting training in group-tactics:
the jostle in front, the snatch from behind, the swift passing of
lifted items from youthful thief to confederate.

In a second room, from which pushed air heavy with the reeks
of metal and oil, older student thieves were doing laboratory
work in lock picking. One group was being lectured by a grimy-
handed graybeard, who was taking apart a most complex lock
piece by weighty piece. Others appeared to be having their skill,
speed, and ability to work soundlessly tested—they were probing
with slender picks the keyholes in a half dozen doors set side-by-
side in an otherwise purposeless partition, while a supervisor
holding a sandglass watched them keenly.

In a third, thieves were eating at long tables. The odors were
tempting, even to men full of booze. The Guild did well by its
members.

In a fourth, the floor was padded in part and instruction was

going on in slipping, dodging, ducking, tumbling, tripping, and
otherwise foiling pursuit. These students were older too. A voice
like a sergeant-major's rasped, "Nah, nah, nah! You couldn't give
your crippled grandmother the slip. I said duck, not genuflect to
holy Aarth. Now this time—"

"Grif's used grease," an instructor called.

"He has, eh? To the front, Grif!" the rasping voice replied as
the Mouser and Fafhrd moved somewhat regretfully out of sight,
for they realized much was to be learned here: tricks that might
stand them in good stead even tonight. "Listen, all of you!" the
rasping voice continued, so far-carrying it followed them a surprisingly long way. "Grease may be very well on a night job—by
day its glisten shouts its user's profession to all Nehwon! But
in any case it makes a thief overconfident. He comes to depend
on it and then in a pinch he finds he's forgot to apply it. Also its
aroma can betray him. Here we work always dry-skinned—save
for natural sweat!—as all of you were told first night. Bend over,
Grif. Grasp your ankles. Straighten your knees."

More thwacks, followed by yelps of pain, distant now, since
the Mouser and Fafhrd were halfway up the end-stairs, Fafhrd
vaulting somewhat laboriously as he grasped curving banister
and swaddled sword.

The second floor duplicated the first, but was as luxurious as
the other had been bare. Down the long corridor lamps and
filagreed incense pots pendant from the ceiling alternated, diffus-
ing a mild light and spicy smell. The walls were richly draped,
the floor thick-carpeted. Yet this corridor was empty too and,
moreover, *completely* silent. After a glance at each other, they
started off boldly.

The first door, wide open, showed an untenanted room full of
racks of garments, rich and plain, spotless and filthy, also wig
stands, shelves of beards and such, and several wall mirrors
faced by small tables crowded with cosmetics and with stools before them. A disguising room, clearly.

After a look and listen either way, the Mouser darted in and
out to snatch up a large green flask from the nearest table. He
unstoppered and sniffed it. A rotten-sweet gardenia-reek con-
tended with the nose-sting of spirits of wine. The Mouser sloshed
his and Fafhrd's fronts with this dubious perfume.

"Antidote to ordure," he explained with the pomp of a physician, stoppering the flask. "Don't want to be parboiled by Krovas. No, no, no."

Two figures appeared at the far end of the corridor and came toward them. The Mouser hid the flask under his cloak, holding it between elbow and side, and he and Fafhrd continued onward —to turn back would look suspicious, both drunkenly judged.

The next three doorways they passed were shut by heavy doors. As they neared the fifth, the two approaching figures, coming on arm-in-arm, yet taking long strides, moving more swiftly than the hobble-shuffle, became distinct. Their clothing was that of noblemen, but their faces those of thieves. They were frowning with indignation and suspicion too at the Mouser and Fafhrd.

Just then—from somewhere between the two man-pairs, it sounded—a voice began to speak words in a strange tongue, using the rapid monotone priests employ in a routine service, or some sorcerers in their incantations.

The two richly clad thieves slowed at the seventh doorway and looked in. Their progress ceased altogether. Their necks strained, their eyes widened. They visibly paled. Then of a sudden they hastened onward, almost running, and bypassed Fafhrd and the Mouser as if they were furniture. The incantatory voice drummed on without missing a beat.

The fifth doorway was shut, but the sixth was open. The Mouser peeked in with one eye, his nose brushing the jamb. Then he stepped forward and gazed inside with entranced expression, pushing the black rag up onto his forehead for better vision. Fafhrd joined him.

It was a large room, empty so far as could be told of human and animal life, but filled with most interesting things. From knee-height up, the entire far wall was a map of the city of Lankhmar and its immediate surrounds. Every building and street seemed depicted, down to the meanest hovel and narrowest court. There were signs of recent erasure and redrawing at many spots, and here and there little colored hieroglyphs of mysterious import.

The floor was marble, the ceiling blue as lapis lazuli. The side walls were thickly hung, by ring and padlock. One was covered with all manner of thieves' tools, from a huge thick pry-bar that looked as if it could unseat the universe, or at least the door of the overlord's treasure-vault, to a rod so slim it might be an elf-queen's wand and seemingly designed to telescope out and fish from distance for precious gauds on milady's spindle-legged, ivory-topped vanity table; the other wall had on it all sorts of quaint, gold-gleaming and jewel-flashing objects, evidently mementos chosen for their oddity from the spoils of memorable burglaries, from a female mask of thin gold, breathlessly beautiful in its features and contours, but thickly set with rubies simulating the spots of the pox in its fever-stage, to a knife whose blade was wedge-shaped diamonds set side by side and this diamond cutting-edge looking razor-sharp.

All about were tables set chiefly with models of dwelling houses and other buildings, accurate to the last minutia, it looked, of ventilation hole under roof gutter and ground-level drain hole, of creviced wall and smooth. Many were cut away in partial or entire section to show the layout of rooms, closets, strongrooms, doorways, corridors, secret passages, smoke-ways, and air-ways in equal detail.

In the center of the room was a bare round-table of ebony and ivory squares. About it were set seven straight-backed but well-padded chairs, the one facing the map and away from the Mouser and Fafhrd being higher backed and wider armed than the others—a chief's chair, likely that of Krovas.

The Mouser tiptoed forward, irresistibly drawn, but Fafhrd's left hand clamped down on his shoulder like the iron mitten of a Mingol cataphract and drew him irresistibly back.

Scowling his disapproval, the Northerner brushed down the black rag over the Mouser's eyes again, and with his crutch-hand thumbed ahead; then set off in that direction in most carefully calculated, silent hops. With a shrug of disappointment the Mouser followed.

As soon as they had turned away from the doorway, but before they were out of sight, a neatly black-bearded, crop-haired head came like a serpent's around the side of the highest-backed chair and gazed after them from deep-sunken yet glinting eyes. Next a snake-supple, long hand followed the head out, crossed thin lips with ophidian forefinger for silence, and then finger-beckoned the two pairs of dark-tunicked men who were standing to either side of the doorway, their backs to the corridor wall, each of the four gripping a curvy knife in one hand and a dark leather, lead-weighted bludgeon in the other.

When Fafhrd was halfway to the seventh doorway, from which the monotonous yet sinister recitation continued to well, there shot out through it a slender, whey-faced youth, his narrow hands clapped over his mouth, under terror-wide eyes, as if to shut in screams or vomit, and with a broom clamped in an arm-pit, so that he seemed a bit like a young warlock about to take to the air. He dashed past Fafhrd and the Mouser and away, his racing footsteps sounding rapid-dull on the carpeting and hollow-sharp on the stairs before dying away.

Fafhrd gazed back at the Mouser with a grimace and shrug, then squatting one-legged until the knee of his bound-up leg touched the floor, advanced half his face past the doorjamb. After a bit, without otherwise changing position, he beckoned the Mouser to approach. The latter slowly thrust half his face past the jamb, just above Fafhrd's.

What they saw was a room somewhat smaller than that of the great map and lit by central lamps that burned blue-white instead of customary yellow. The floor was marble, darkly colorful and complexly whorled. The dark walls were hung with astrological and anthropomantic charts and instruments of magic and shelved with cryptically labeled porcelain jars and also with vitreous flasks and glass pipes of the oddest shapes, some filled with colored fluids, but many gleamingly empty. At the foot of the walls, where the shadows were thickest, broken and discarded stuff was irregularly heaped, as if swept out of the way and forgot, and here and there opened a large rathole.

In the center of the room and brightly illuminated by contrast was a long table with thick top and many stout legs. The Mouser thought fleetingly of a centipede and then of the bar at the Eel, for the tabletop was densely stained and scarred by many a spilled elixir and many a deep black burn by fire or acid or both.

In the midst of the table an alembic was working. The lamp's flame—deep blue, this one—kept a-boil in the large crystal cucurbit a dark, viscid fluid with here and there diamond glints. From out of the thick, seething stuff, strands of a darker vapor streamed upward to crowd through the cucurbit's narrow mouth and stain—oddly, with bright scarlet—the transparent head and then, dead black now, flow down the narrow pipe from the head into a spherical crystal receiver, larger even than the cucurbit, and there curl and weave about like so many coils of living black cord—an endless, skinny, ebon serpent.

Behind the left end of the table stood a tall, yet hunchbacked man in black robe and hood, which shadowed more than hid a face of which the most prominent features were a long, thick, pointed nose with out-jutting, almost chinless mouth just below. His complexion was sallow-gray like clay and a short-haired, bristly, gray beard grew high on his wide cheeks. From under a receding forehead and bushy gray brows, wide-set eyes looked intently down at an age-browned scroll, which his disgustingly small clubhands, knuckles big, short backs gray-bristled, cease-lessly unrolled and rolled up again. The only move his eyes ever made, besides the short side-to-side one as he read the lines he was rapidly intoning, was an occasional farther sidewise glance at the alembic.

On the other end of the table, beady eyes darting from the sor-cerer to the alembic and back again, crouched a small black beast, the first glimpse of which made Fafhrd dig fingers pain-fully into the Mouser's shoulder and the latter almost gasp, not from the pain. It was most like a rat, yet it had a higher forehead and closer-set eyes than either had ever seen in a rat, while its forepaws, which it constantly rubbed together in what seemed restless glee, looked like tiny copies of the sorcerer's clubhands.

Simultaneously yet independently, Fafhrd and the Mouser each became certain it was the beast which had gutter-escorted Slivikin and his mate, then fled, and each recalled what Ivrian had said about a witch's familiar and Vlana about the likelihood of Krovas employing a warlock.

What with the ugliness of the clubhanded man and beast and between them the ropy black vapor coiling and twisting in the great receiver and head, like a black umbilical cord, it was a most horrid sight. And the similarities, save for size, between the two creatures were even more disquieting in their implications.

The tempo of the incantation quickened, the blue-white flames brightened and hissed audibly, the fluid in the cucurbit grew thick as lava, great bubbles formed and loudly broke, the black rope in the receiver writhed like a nest of snakes; there was an increasing sense of invisible presences, the supernatural tension grew almost unendurable, and Fafhrd and the Mouser were hard put to keep silent the open-mouthed gasps by which they now breathed, and each feared his heartbeat could be heard cubits away.

Abruptly the incantation peaked and broke off, like a drum struck very hard, then instantly silenced by palm and fingers outspread against the head. With a bright flash and dull explosion, cracks innumerable appeared in the cucurbit; its crystal became white and opaque, yet it did not shatter or drip. The head lifted a span, hung there, fell back. While two black nooses appeared among the coils in the receiver and suddenly narrowed until they were only two big black knots.

The sorcerer grinned, rolling up the end of the parchment with a snap, and shifted his gaze from the receiver to his familiar, while the latter chittered shrilly and bounded up and down in rapture.

"Silence, Slivikin! Comes now your time to race and strain and sweat," the sorcerer cried, speaking pidgin Lankhamarese now, but so rapidly and in so squeakingly high-pitched a voice that Fafhrd and the Mouser could barely follow him. They did, however, both realize they had been completely mistaken as to the identity of Slivikin. In moment of disaster, the fat thief had called to the witchbeast for help rather than to his human comrade.

"Yes, master," Slivikin squealed back no less clearly, in an instant revising the Mouser's opinions about talking animals. He continued in the same fifelike, fawning tones, "Harkening in obedience, Hristomilo."

Now they knew the sorcerer's name too.

Hristomilo ordered in whiplash pipings, "To your appointed work! See to it you summon an ample sufficiency of feasters! I want the bodies stripped to skeletons, so the bruises of the enchanted smog and all evidence of death by suffocation will be vanished utterly. But forget not the loot! On your mission, now—depart!"

Slivikin, who at every command had bobbed his head in manner reminiscent of his bouncing, now squealed, "I'll see it done!" and gray-lightninglike leaped a long leap to the floor and down an inky rathole.

Hristomilo, rubbing together his disgusting clubhands much as Slivikin had his, cried chucklingly, "What Slevyas lost, my magic has rewon!"

Fafhrd and the Mouser drew back out of the doorway, partly with the thought that since neither his incantation and his alembic, nor his familiar now required his unblinking attention, Hristomilo would surely look up and spot them; partly in revulsion from what they had seen and heard; and in poignant if useless pity for Slevyas, whoever he might be, and for the other unknown victims of the ratlike and conceivably rat-related sorcerer's deathspells, poor strangers already dead and due to have their flesh eaten from their bones.

Fafhrd wrested the green bottle from the Mouser and, though almost gagging on the rotten-flowery reek, gulped a large, stinging mouthful. The Mouser couldn't quite bring himself to do the same, but was comforted by the spirits of wine he inhaled during this byplay.

Then he saw, beyond Fafhrd, standing before the doorway to the map room, a richly clad man with gold-hilted knife jewel-scabbarded at his side. His sunken-eyed face was prematurely wrinkled by responsibility, overwork, and authority, and framed by neatly cropped black hair and beard. Smiling, he silently beckoned them.

The Mouser and Fafhrd obeyed, the latter returning the green bottle to the former, who recapped it and thrust it under his left elbow with well-concealed irritation.

Each guessed their summoner was Krovas, the Guild's Grandmaster. Once again Fafhrd marveled, as he hobbledehoyed along, reeling and belching, how Kos or the Fates were guiding him to his target tonight. The Mouser, more alert and more apprehensive too, was reminding himself that they had been directed by the niche-guards to report to Krovas, so that the situation, if not developing quite in accord with his own misty plans, was still not deviating disastrously.

Yet not even his alertness, nor Fafhrd's primeval instincts, gave him forewarning as they followed Krovas into the map room.

Two steps inside, each of them was shoulder-grabbed and bludgeon-menaced by a pair of ruffians further armed with knives tucked in their belts.

They judged it wise to make no resistance, on this one occasion at least bearing out the Mouser's mouthings about the supreme caution of drunken men.

"All secure, Grandmaster," one of the ruffians rapped out.

Krovas swung the highest-backed chair around and sat down, eyeing them coolly yet searchingly.

"What brings two stinking, drunken beggar-Guildsmen into the top-restricted precincts of the masters?" he asked quietly.

The Mouser felt the sweat of relief bead his forehead. The disguises he had brilliantly conceived were still working, taking in even the head man, though he had spotted Fafhrd's tipsiness. Resuming his blind-man manner, he quavered, "We were directed by the guard above the Cheap Street door to report to you in person, great Krovas, the Night Beggarmaster being on furlough for reasons of sexual hygiene. Tonight we've made good haul!" And fumbling in his purse, ignoring as far as possible the tightened grip on his shoulders, he brought out the golden coin given him by the sentimental courtesan and displayed it tremble-handed.

"Spare me your inexpert acting," Krovas said sharply. "I'm not one of your marks. And take that rag off your eyes."

The Mouser obeyed and stood to attention again insofar as his pinioning would permit, and smiling the more seeming carefree because of his reawakening uncertainties. Conceivably he wasn't doing quite as brilliantly as he'd thought.

Krovas leaned forward and said placidly yet piercingly, "Granted you were so ordered—and most improperly so; that door-guard will suffer for his stupidity!—why were you spying into a room beyond this one when I spotted you?"

"We saw brave thieves flee from that room," the Mouser answered pat. "Fearing that some danger threatened the Guild, my comrade and I investigated, ready to scotch it."

"But what we saw and heard only perplexed us, great sir," Fafhrd appended quite smoothly.

"I didn't ask you, sot. Speak when you're spoken to," Krovas snapped at him. Then, to the Mouser, "You're an overweening rogue, most presumptuous for your rank."

In a flash the Mouser decided that further insolence, rather than fawning, was what the situation required. "That I am, sir," he said smugly. "For example, I have a master plan whereby you and the Guild might gain more wealth and power in three months than your predecessors have in three millennia."

Krovas' face darkened. "Boy!" he called. Through the curtains of an inner doorway, a youth with dark complexion of a Kleshite and clad only in a black loincloth sprang to kneel before Krovas, who ordered, "Summon first my sorcerer, next the thieves Slevyas and Fissif," whereupon the dark youth dashed into the corridor.

Then Krovas, his face its normal pale again, leaned back in his great chair, lightly rested his sinewy arms on its great padded ones, and smilingly directed the Mouser, "Speak your piece. Reveal to us this master plan."

Forcing his mind *not* to work on the surprising news that Slevyas was not victim but thief and not sorcery-slain but alive and available—why did Krovas want him *now?*—the Mouser threw back his head and, shaping his lips in a faint sneer, began, "You may laugh merrily at me, Grandmaster, but I'll warrant that in less than a score of heartbeats you'll be straining sober-faced to hear my least word. Like lightning, wit can strike anywhere, and the best of you in Lankhmar have age-honored blind spots for things obvious to us of outland birth. My master plan is but this: let Thieves' Guild under your iron autocracy seize supreme power in Lankhmar City, then in Lankhmar Land, next over all Nehwon, after which who knows what realms undreamt will know your suzerainty!"

The Mouser had spoken true in one respect: Krovas was no longer smiling. He was leaning forward a little and his face was darkening again, but whether from interest or anger it was too soon to say.

The Mouser continued, "For centuries the Guild's had more than the force and intelligence needed to make a *coup d'état* a nine-finger certainty; today there's not one hair's chance in a bushy head of failure. It is the proper state of things that thieves rule other men. All Nature cries out for it. No need slay old Kar-

stak Ovartamortes, merely overmaster, control, and so rule
through him. You've already fee'd informers in every noble or
wealthy house. Your post's better than the King of Kings'. You've
a mercenary striking force permanently mobilized, should you
have need of it, in the Slayers' Brotherhood. We Guild-beggars
are your foragers. O great Krovas, the multitudes know that
thievery rules Nehwon, nay, the universe, nay, more, the highest
gods' abode! And the multitudes accept this, they balk only at
the hypocrisy of the present arrangement, at the pretense that
things are otherwise. Oh, give them their decent desire, great
Krovas! Make it all open, honest and aboveboard, with thieves
ruling in name as well as fact."

The Mouser spoke with passion, for the moment believing all
he said, even the contradictions. The four ruffians gaped at him
with wonder and not a little awe. They slackened their holds on
him and on Fafhrd too.

But leaning back in his great chair again and smiling thinly
and ominously, Krovas said coolly, "In *our* Guild intoxication is
no excuse for folly, rather grounds for the extremest penalty. But
I'm well aware your organized beggars operate under a laxer discipline. So I'll deign to explain to you, you wee drunken
dreamer, that we thieves know well that, behind the scenes, we
already rule Lankhmar, Nehwon, all life in sooth—for what is
life but greed in action? But to make this an open thing would
not only force us to take on ten thousand sorts of weary work
others now do for us, it would also go against another of life's
deep laws: illusion. Does the sweetmeats hawker show you his
kitchen? Does a whore let average client watch her enamel-over
her wrinkles and hoist her sagging breasts in cunning gauzy
slings? Does a conjuror turn out for you his hidden pockets? Nature works by subtle, secret means—man's invisible seed, spider
bite, the viewless spores of madness and of death, rocks that are
born in earth's unknown bowels, the silent stars a-creep across
the sky—and we thieves copy her."

"That's good enough poetry, sir," Fafhrd responded with undertone of angry derision, for he had himself been considerably
impressed by the Mouser's master plan and was irked that
Krovas should do insult to his new friend by disposing of it so
lightly. "Closet kingship may work well enough in easy times.

But"—he paused histrionically—"will it serve when Thieves' Guild is faced with an enemy determined to obliterate it forever, a plot to wipe it entirely from the earth?"

"What drunken babble's this?" Krovas demanded, sitting up straight. *"What* plot?"

" 'Tis a most *secret* one," Fafhrd responded grinning, delighted to pay this haughty man in his own coin and thinking it quite just that the thief-king sweat a little before his head was removed for conveyance to Vlana. "I know naught of it, except that many a master thief is marked down for the knife—and your head doomed to fall!"

Fafhrd merely sneered his face and folded his arms, the still slack grip of his captors readily permitting it, his (sword) crutch hanging against his body from his lightly gripping hand. Then he scowled as there came a sudden shooting pain in his numbed, bound-up left leg, which he had forgotten for a space.

Krovas raised a clenched fist and himself half out of his chair, in prelude to some fearsome command—likely that Fafhrd be tortured. The Mouser cut in hurriedly with, "The Secret Seven, they're called, are its leaders. None in the outer circles of the conspiracy know their names, though rumor has it that they're secret Guild-thief renegades representing, one for each, the cities of Oool Hrusp, Kvarch Nar, Ilthmar, Horborixen, Tisilinilit, far Kiraay and Lankhmar's very self. It's thought they're moneyed by the merchants of the East, the priests of Wan, the sorcerers of the Steppes and half the Mingol leadership too, legended Quarmall, Aarth's Assassins in Sarheenmar, and also no lesser man than the King of Kings."

Despite Krovas' contemptuous and then angry remarks, the ruffians holding the Mouser continued to harken to their captive with interest and respect, and they did not retighten their grip on him. His colorful revelations and melodramatic delivery held them, while Krovas' dry, cynical, philosophic observations largely went over their heads.

Hristomilo came gliding into the room then, his feet presumably taking swift, but very short steps, at any rate his black robe hung undisturbed to the marble floor despite his slithering speed.

There was a shock at his entrance. All eyes in the map room

followed him, breaths were held, and the Mouser and Fafhrd felt
the horny hands that gripped them shake just a little. Even
Krovas' all-confident, world-weary expression became tense and
guardedly uneasy. Clearly the sorcerer of the Thieves' Guild
was more feared than loved by his chief employer and by the
beneficiaries of his skills.

Outwardly oblivious to this reaction to his appearance, Hristomilo, smiling thin-lipped, halted close to one side of Krovas'
chair and inclined his hood-shadowed rodent face in the ghost of
a bow.

Krovas held palm toward the Mouser for silence. Then, wetting his lips, he asked Hristomilo sharply yet nervously, "Do you
know these two?"

Hristomilo nodded decisively. "They just now peered a befud-
dled eye each at me," he said, "whilst I was about that business
we spoke of. I'd have shooed them off, reported them, save such
action might have broken my spell, put my words out of time
with the alembic's workings. The one's a Northerner, the other's
features have a southern cast—from Tovilyis or near, most like.
Both younger than their now-looks. Free-lance bravos, I'd judge
'em, the sort the Brotherhood hires as extras when they get at
once several big guard and escort jobs. Clumsily disguised now,
of course, as beggars."

Fafhrd by yawning, the Mouser by pitying headshake tried to
convey that all this was so much poor guesswork.

"That's all I can tell you without reading their minds," Hristomilo concluded. "Shall I fetch my lights and mirrors?"

"Not yet." Krovas turned face and shot a finger at the Mouser.
"How do you know these things you rant about?—Secret Seven
and all. Straight simplest answer now—no rodomontades."

The Mouser replied most glibly: "There's a new courtesan
dwells on Pimp Street—Tyarya her name, tall, beauteous, but
hunchbacked, which oddly delights many of her clients. Now
Tyarya loves me 'cause my maimed eyes match her twisted
spine, or from simple pity of my blindness—*she* believes it!—and
youth, or from some odd itch, like her clients' for her, which that
combination arouses in her flesh.

"Now one of her patrons, a trader newly come from Klelg Nar
—Mourph, he's called—was impressed by my intelligence,

strength, boldness, and closemouthed tact, and those same qualities in my comrade too. Mourph sounded us out, finally asking if we hated the Thieves' Guild for its control of the Beggars' Guild. Sensing a chance to aid the Guild, we played up, and a week ago he recruited us into a cell of three in the outermost strands of the conspiracy web of the Seven."

"You presumed to do all of this on your own?" Krovas demanded in freezing tones, sitting up straight and gripping hard the chair arms.

"Oh, no," the Mouser denied guilelessly. "We reported our every act to the Day Beggarmaster and he approved them, told us to spy our best and gather every scrap of fact and rumor we could about the Sevens' conspiracy."

"And he told me not a word about it!" Krovas rapped out. "If true, I'll have Bannat's head for this! But you're lying, aren't you?"

As the Mouser gazed with wounded eyes at Krovas, meanwhile preparing a most virtuous denial, a portly man limped past the doorway with help of a gilded staff. He moved with silence and aplomb.

But Krovas saw him. "Night Beggarmaster!" he called sharply. The limping man stopped, turned, came crippling majestically through the door. Krovas stabbed finger at the Mouser, then Fafhrd. "Do you know these two, Flim?"

The Night Beggarmaster unhurriedly studied each for a space, then shook his head with its turban of cloth of gold. "Never seen either before. What are they? Fink beggars?"

"But Flim wouldn't know us," the Mouser explained desperately, feeling everything collapsing in on him and Fafhrd. "All our contacts were with Bannat alone."

Flim said quietly, "Bannat's been abed with the swamp ague this past ten-day. Meanwhile *I* have been Day Beggarmaster as well as Night."

At that moment Slevyas and Fissif came hurrying in behind Flim. The tall thief bore on his jaw a bluish lump. The fat thief's head was bandaged above his darting eyes. He pointed quickly at Fafhrd and the Mouser and cried, "There are the two that slugged us, took our Jengao loot, and slew our escort."

The Mouser lifted his elbow and the green bottle crashed to

shards at his feet on the hard marble. Gardenia-reek sprang swiftly through the air.

But more swiftly still the Mouser, shaking off the careless hold of his startled guards, sprang toward Krovas, clubbing his wrapped-up sword. If he could only overpower the King of Thieves and hold Cat's Claw at his throat, he'd be able to bargain for his and Fafhrd's lives. That is, unless the other thieves wanted their master killed, which wouldn't surprise him at all.

With startling speed Flim thrust out his gilded staff, tripping the Mouser, who went heels over head, midway seeking to change his involuntary somersault into a voluntary one.

Meanwhile Fafhrd lurched heavily against his left-hand captor, at the same time swinging bandaged Graywand strongly upward to strike his right-hand captor under the jaw. Regaining his one-legged balance with a mighty contortion, he hopped for the loot-wall behind him.

Slevyas made for the wall of thieves' tools, and with a muscle-cracking effort wrenched the great pry-bar from its padlocked ring.

Scrambling to his feet after a poor landing in front of Krovas' chair, the Mouser found it empty and the Thief King in a half-crouch behind it, gold-hilted dagger drawn, deep-sunk eyes coldly battle-wild. Spinning around, he saw Fafhrd's guards on the floor, the one sprawled senseless, the other starting to scramble up, while the great Northerner, his back against the wall of weird jewelry, menaced the whole room with wrapped-up Graywand and with his long knife, jerked from its scabbard behind him.

Likewise drawing Cat's Claw, the Mouser cried in trumpet voice of battle, "Stand aside, all! He's gone mad! I'll hamstring his good leg for you!" And racing through the press and between his own two guards, who still appeared to hold him in some awe, he launched himself with flashing dirk at Fafhrd, praying that the Northerner, drunk now with battle as well as wine and poisonous perfume, would recognize him and guess his stratagem.

Graywand slashed well above his ducking head. His new friend not only guessed, but was playing up—and not just missing by accident, the Mouser hoped. Stooping low by the wall, he cut the lashings on Fafhrd's left leg. Graywand and Fafhrd's long knife continued to spare him. Springing up, he headed for the corridor, crying overshoulder to Fafhrd, "Come on!"

Hristomilo stood well out of his way, quietly observing. Fissif scuttled toward safety. Krovas stayed behind his chair, shouting, "Stop them! Head them off!"

The three remaining ruffian guards, at last beginning to recover their fighting-wits, gathered to oppose the Mouser. But menacing them with swift feints of his dirk, he slowed them and darted between—and then just in the nick of time knocked aside with a downsweep of wrapped-up Scalpel Flim's gilded staff, thrust once again to trip him.

All this gave Slevyas time to return from the tools-wall and aim at the Mouser a great swinging blow with the massive pry-bar. But even as that blow started, a very long, bandaged sword on a very long arm thrust over the Mouser's shoulder and solidly and heavily poked Slevyas high on the chest, jolting him backward, so that the pry-bar's swing was short and whistled past harmlessly.

Then the Mouser found himself in the corridor and Fafhrd beside him, though for some weird reason still only hopping. The Mouser pointed toward the stairs. Fafhrd nodded, but delayed to reach high, still on one leg only, and rip off the nearest wall a dozen cubits of heavy drapes, which he threw across the corridor to baffle pursuit.

They reached the stairs and started up the next flight, the Mouser in advance. There were cries behind, some muffled.

"Stop hopping, Fafhrd!" the Mouser ordered querulously. "You've got two legs again."

"Yes, and the other's still dead," Fafhrd complained. "Ahh! Now feeling begins to return to it."

A thrown knife whisked between them and dully clinked as it hit the wall point-first and stone-power flew. Then they were around the bend.

Two more empty corridors, two more curving flights, and then they saw above them on the last landing a stout ladder mounting to a dark, square hole in the roof. A thief with hair bound back by a colorful handkerchief—it appeared to be a door-guards' identification—menaced the Mouser with drawn sword, but when he saw that there were two of them, both charging him de-

terminedly with shining knives and strange staves or clubs, he
turned and ran down the last empty corridor.

The Mouser, followed closely by Fafhrd, rapidly mounted the
ladder and without pause vaulted up through the hatch into the
star-crusted night.

He found himself near the unrailed edge of a slate roof which
slanted enough to have made it look most fearsome to a novice
roof-walker, but safe as houses to a veteran.

Crouched on the long peak of the roof was another kerchiefed
thief holding a dark lantern. He was rapidly covering and un-
covering, presumably in some code, the lantern's bull's eye,
whence shot a faint green beam north to where a red point of
light winked dimly in reply—as far away as the sea wall, it
looked, or perhaps the masthead of a ship beyond, riding in the
Inner Sea. Smuggler?

Seeing the Mouser, this one instantly drew sword and, swinging the lantern a little in his other hand, advanced menacingly.
The Mouser eyed him warily—the dark lantern with its hot
metal, concealed flame, and store of oil would be a tricky
weapon.

But then Fafhrd had clambered out and was standing beside
the Mouser, on both feet again at last. Their adversary backed
slowly away toward the north end of the roof ridge. Fleetingly
the Mouser wondered if there was another hatch there.

Turning back at a bumping sound, he saw Fafhrd prudently
hoisting the ladder. Just as he got it free, a knife flashed up close
past him out of the hatch. While following its flight, the Mouser
frowned, involuntarily admiring the skill required to hurl a knife
vertically with any accuracy.

It clattered down near them and slid off the roof. The Mouser
loped south across the slates and was halfway from the hatch to
that end of the roof when the faint chink came to the knife
striking the cobbles of Murder Alley.

Fafhrd followed more slowly, in part perhaps from a lesser experience of roofs, in part because he still limped a bit to favor
his left leg, and in part because he was carrying the heavy ladder
balanced on his right shoulder.

"We won't need that," the Mouser called back.

Without hesitation Fafhrd heaved it joyously over the edge.

By the time it crashed in Murder Alley, the Mouser was leaping down two yards and across a gap of one to the next roof, of opposite and lesser pitch. Fafhrd landed beside him.

The Mouser led them at almost a run through a sooty forest of chimneys, chimney pots, ventilators with tails that made them always face the wind, black-legged cisterns, hatch covers, bird houses, and pigeon traps across five roofs, four progressively a little lower, the fifth regaining a yard of the altitude they'd lost—the spaces between the buildings easy to leap, none more than three yards, no ladder-bridge required, and only one roof with a somewhat greater pitch than that of Thieves' House—until they reached the Street of the Thinkers at a point where it was crossed by a roofed passageway much like the one at Rokkermas and Slaarg's.

While they crossed it at a crouching lope, something hissed close past them and clattered ahead. As they leaped down from the roof of the bridge, three more somethings hissed over their heads to clatter beyond. One rebounded from a square chimney almost to the Mouser's feet. He picked it up, expecting a stone, and was surprised by the greater weight of a leaden ball big as two doubled-up fingers.

"They," he said, jerking thumb overshoulder, "lost no time in getting slingers on the roof. When roused, they're good."

Southeast then through another black chimney-forest to a point on Cheap Street where upper stories overhung the street so much on either side that it was easy to leap the gap. During this roof-traverse, an advancing front of night-smog, dense enough to make them cough and wheeze, had engulfed them and for perhaps sixty heartbeats the Mouser had had to slow to a shuffle and feel his way, Fafhrd's hand on his shoulder. Just short of Cheap Street they had come abruptly and completely out of the smog and seen the stars again, while the black front had rolled off northward behind them.

"Now what the devil was that?" Fafhrd had asked and the Mouser had shrugged.

A nighthawk would have seen a vast thick hoop of black night-smog blowing out in all directions from a center near the Silver Eel, growing ever greater and greater in diameter and circumference.

East of Cheap Street the two comrades soon made their way to the ground, landing back in Plague Court behind the narrow premises of Nattick Nimblefingers the Tailor.

Then at last they looked at each other and their trammeled swords and their filthy faces and clothing made dirtier still by roof-soot, and they laughed and laughed and laughed, Fafhrd roaring still as he bent over to massage his left leg above and below knee. This hooting and wholly unaffected self-mockery continued while they unwrapped their swords—the Mouser as if his were a surprise package—and clipped their scabbards once more to their belts. Their exertions had burned out of them the last mote and atomy of strong wine and even stronger stenchful perfume, but they felt no desire whatever for more drink, only the urge to get home and eat hugely and guzzle hot, bitter gahveh, and tell their lovely girls at length the tale of their mad adventure.

They loped on side by side, at intervals glancing at each other and chuckling, though keeping a normally wary eye behind and before for pursuit or interception, despite their expecting neither.

Free of night-smog and drizzled with starlight, their cramped surroundings seemed much less stinking and oppressive than when they had set out. Even Ordure Boulevard had a freshness to it.

Only once for a brief space did they grow serious.

Fafhrd said, "You were drunken idiot-genius indeed tonight, even if I was a drunken clodhopper. Lashing up my leg! Tying up our swords so we couldn't use 'em save as clubs!"

The Mouser shrugged. "Yet that sword-tying doubtless saved us from committing a number of murders tonight."

Fafhrd retorted, a little hotly, "Killing in fight isn't murder."

Again the Mouser shrugged. "Killing is murder, no matter what nice names you give. Just as eating is devouring, and drinking guzzling. Gods, I'm dry, famished, and fatigued! Come on, soft cushions, food, and steaming gahveh!"

They hastened up the long, creaking, broken treaded stairs with an easy carefulness and when they were both on the porch, the Mouser shoved at the door to open it with surprise-swiftness.

It did not budge.

"Bolted," he said to Fafhrd shortly. He noted now there was hardly any light at all coming through the cracks around the door, or noticeable through the lattices—at most, a faint orange-red glow. Then with sentimental grin and in a fond voice in which only the ghost of uneasiness lurked, he said, "They've gone to sleep, the unworrying wenches!" He knocked loudly thrice and then cupping his lips shouted softly at the door crack, "Hola, Ivrian! I'm home safe. Hail, Vlana! Your man's done you proud, felling Guild-thieves innumerable with one foot tied behind his back!"

There was no sound whatever from inside—that is, if one discounted a rustling so faint it was impossible to be sure of it.

Fafhrd was wrinkling his nostrils. "I smell smoke."

The Mouser banged on the door again. Still no response.

Fafhrd motioned him out of the way, hunching his big shoulder to crash the portal.

The Mouser shook his head and with a deft tap, slide, and tug removed a brick that a moment before had looked a firm-set part of the wall beside the door. He reached in all his arm. There was the scrape of a bolt being withdrawn, then another, then a third. He swiftly recovered his arm and the door swung fully inward at a touch.

But neither he nor Fafhrd rushed in at once, as both had intended to, for the indefinable scent of danger and the unknown came puffing out along with an increased reek of smoke and a slight sickening sweet scent that though female was no decent female perfume, and a musty-sour animal odor.

They could see the room faintly by the orange glow coming from the small oblong of the open door of the little, well-blacked stove. Yet the oblong did not sit properly upright but was unnaturally a-tilt; clearly the stove had been half overset and now leaned against a side wall of the fireplace, its small door fallen open in that direction.

By itself alone, that unnatural angle conveyed the entire impact of a universe overturned.

The orange glow showed the carpets oddly rucked up with here and there black circles a palm's breadth across, the neatly stacked candles scattered about below their shelves along with some of the jars and enameled boxes, and, above all, two black, low, irregular, longish heaps, the one by the fireplace, the other half on the golden couch, half at its foot.

From each heap there stared at the Mouser and Fafhrd innumerable pairs of tiny, rather widely set, furnace-red eyes.

On the thickly carpeted floor on the other side of the fireplace was a silver cobweb—a fallen silver cage, but no love birds sang from it.

There was a faint scrape of metal as Fafhrd made sure Graywand was loose in his scabbard.

As if that tiny sound had beforehand been chosen as the signal for attack, each instantly whipped out sword and they advanced side by side into the room, warily at first, testing the floor with each step.

At the screech of the swords being drawn, the tiny furnace-red eyes had winked and shifted restlessly, and now with the two men's approach they swiftly scattered pattering, pair by red pair, each pair at the forward end of a small, low, slender, hairless-tailed black body, and each making for one of the black circles in the rugs, where they vanished.

Indubitably the black circles were ratholes newly gnawed up through the floor and rugs, while the red-eyed creatures were black rats.

Fafhrd and the Mouser sprang forward, slashing and chopping at them in a frenzy, cursing and human-snarling besides.

They sundered few. The rats fled with preternatural swiftness, most of them disappearing down holes near the walls and the fireplace.

Also Fafhrd's first frantic chop went through the floor and on his third step with an ominous crack and splintering his leg plunged through the floor to his hip. The Mouser darted past him, unmindful of further crackings.

Fafhrd heaved out his trapped leg, not even noting the splinter-scratches it got and as unmindful as the Mouser of the continuing creakings. The rats were gone. He lunged after his comrade, who had thrust a bunch of kindlers into the stove, to make more light.

The horror was that, although the rats were all gone, the two longish heaps remained, although considerably diminished and, as now shown clearly by the yellow flames leaping from the tilted black door, changed in hue, no longer were the heaps red-beaded black, but a mixture of gleaming black and dark brown, a sickening purple-blue, violet and velvet black and ermine white, and the reds of stockings and blood and bloody flesh and bone.

Although hands and feet had been gnawed bone-naked, and bodies tunneled heart-deep, the two faces had been spared. That was not good, for they were the parts purple-blue from death by strangulation, lips drawn back, eyes bulging, all features contorted in agony. Only the black and very dark brown hair gleamed unchanged—that and the white, white teeth.

As each man stared down at his love, unable to look away despite the waves of horror and grief and rage washing higher and higher in him, each saw a tiny black strand uncurl from the black depression ringing each throat and drift off, dissipating, toward the open door behind them—two strands of night-smog.

With a crescendo of crackings the floor sagged fully three spans more in the center before arriving at a new temporary stability.

Edges of centrally tortured minds noted details: that Vlana's silver-hilted dagger skewered to the floor a rat, which, likely enough, overeager had approached too closely before the night-smog had done its magic work. That her belt and pouch were gone. That the blue-enameled box inlaid with silver, in which Ivrian had put the Mouser's share of the highjacked jewels, was gone too.

The Mouser and Fafhrd lifted to each other white, drawn faces which were quite mad, yet completely joined in understanding and purpose. No need to tell each other what must have happened here when the two nooses of black vapor had jerked tight in Hristomilo's receiver, or why Slivikin had bounced and squeaked in glee, or the significance of such phrases as "an ample sufficiency of feasters," or "forget not the loot," or "that business we spoke of." No need for Fafhrd to explain why he now stripped off his robe and hood, or why he jerked up Vlana's dagger, snapped the rat off it with a wrist-flick, and thrust it in his belt. No need for the Mouser to tell why he searched out a half dozen jars of oil and after smashing three of them in front of the flaming stove, paused, thought, and stuck

the other three in the sack at his waist, adding to them the
remaining kindlers and the fire-pot, brimmed with red coals, its
top lashed down tight.

Then, still without word exchanged, the Mouser muffled his
hand with a small rug and reaching into the fireplace deliberately tipped the flaming stove forward, so that it fell door-down
on oil-soaked rugs. Yellow flames sprang up around him.

They turned and raced for the door. With louder crackings
than any before, the floor collapsed. They desperately scrambled
their way up a steep hill of sliding carpets and reached door and
porch just before all behind them gave way and the flaming rugs
and stove and all the firewood and candles and the golden couch
and all the little tables and boxes and jars—and the unthinkably
mutilated bodies of their first loves—cascaded into the dry,
dusty, cobweb-choked room below, and the great flames of a
cleansing or at least obliterating cremation began to flare upward.

They plunged down the stairs, which tore away from the wall
and collapsed and dully crashed in the dark just as they reached
the ground. They had to fight their way over the wreckage to get
to Bones Alley.

By then flames were darting their bright lizard-tongues out of
the shuttered attic windows and the boarded-up ones in the
story just below. By the time they reached Plague Court, running
side by side at top speed, the Silver Eel's fire-alarm was clanging cacophonously behind them.

They were still sprinting when they took the Death Alley fork.
Then the Mouser grappled Fafhrd and forced him to a halt. The
big man struck out, cursing insanely, and only desisted—his
white face still a lunatic's—when the Mouser cried, panting,
"Only ten heartbeats to arm us!"

He pulled the sack from his belt and, keeping tight hold of its
neck, crashed it on the cobbles—hard enough to smash not only
the bottles of oil, but also the fire-pot, for the sack was soon
flaming a little at its base.

Then he drew gleaming Scalpel and Fafhrd Graywand and
they raced on, the Mouser swinging his sack in a great circle beside him to fan its flames. It was a veritable ball of fire burning
his left hand as they dashed across Cheap Street and into

Thieves' House, and the Mouser, leaping high, swung it up into the great niche above the doorway and let go of it.

The niche-guards screeched in surprise and pain at the fiery invader of their hidey-hole and had no time to do anything with their swords, or whatever weapons else they had, against the other two invaders.

Student thieves poured out of the doors ahead at the screeching and foot-pounding, and then poured back as they saw the fierce point of flames and the two demon-faced oncomers brandishing their long, shining swords.

One skinny little apprentice—he could hardly have been ten years old—lingered too long. Graywand thrust him pitilessly through as his big eyes bulged and his small mouth gaped in horror and plea to Fafhrd for mercy.

Now from ahead of them there came a weird, wailing call, hollow and hair-raising, and doors began to thus shut instead of spewing forth the armed guards they almost prayed would appear to be skewered by their swords. Also, despite the long, bracketed torches looking newly released, the corridor was dark.

The reason for this last became clear as they plunged up the stairs. Strands of night-smog were appearing in the well, materializing from nothing or the air.

The strands grew longer and more numerous and tangible. They touched and clung nastily. In the corridor above they were forming from wall to wall and from ceiling to floor, like a gigantic cobweb, and were becoming so substantial that the Mouser and Fafhrd had to slash them to get through, or so their two maniac minds believed. The black web muffled a little a repetition of the eerie, wailing call, which came from the seventh door ahead and this time ended in a gleeful chittering and cackling insane as the emotions of the two attackers.

Here too doors were thudding shut. In an ephemeral flash of rationality, it occurred to the Mouser that it was not he and Fafhrd the thieves feared, for they had not been seen yet, but rather Hristomilo and his magic, even though working in defense of Thieves' House.

Even the map room, whence counter-attack would most likely erupt, was closed off by a huge oaken, iron-studded door.

They were now twice slashing back, clinging rope-thick

spiderweb for every single step they drove themselves forward. Midway between the map and magic rooms, there was forming on the inky web, ghostly at first but swiftly growing more substantial, a black spider big as a wolf.

The Mouser slashed heavy cobweb before it, dropped back two steps, then hurled himself at it in a high leap. Scalpel thrust through it, striking amidst its eight new-formed jet eyes, and it collapsed like a daggered bladder, loosing a vile stink.

Then he and Fafhrd were looking into the magic room, the alchemist's chamber. It was much as they had seen it before, except some things were doubled, or multiplied even further.

On the long table two blue-boiled cucurbits bubbled and roiled, their heads shooting out a solid, writhing rope more swiftly than moves the black swamp-cobra, which can run down a man—and not into twin receivers, but into the open air of the room (if any of the air in Thieves' House could have been called open then) to weave a barrier between their swords and Hristomilo, who once more stood tall though hunchbacked over his sorcerous, brown parchment, though this time his exultant gaze was chiefly fixed on Fafhrd and the Mouser, with only an occasional downward glance at the text of the spell he drummingly intoned.

At the other end of the table, in the web-free space, there bounced not only Slivikin, but also a huge rat matching him in size in all members except the head.

From the ratholes at the foot of the walls, red eyes glittered and gleamed in pairs.

With a bellow of rage Fafhrd began slashing at the black barrier, but the ropes were replaced from the cucurbit heads as swiftly as he sliced them, while the cut ends, instead of drooping slackly, now began to strain hungrily toward him like constrictive snakes or strangle-vines.

He suddenly shifted Graywand to his left hand, drew his long knife and hurled it at the sorcerer. Flashing toward its mark, it cut through three strands, was deflected and slowed by a fourth and fifth, almost halted by a sixth, and ended hanging futilely in the curled grip of a seventh.

Hristomilo laughed cacklingly and grinned, showing his huge

upper incisors, while Slivikin chittered in ecstasy and bounded the higher.

The Mouser hurled Cat's Claw with no better result—worse, indeed, since his action gave two darting smog-strands time to curl hamperingly around his sword-hand and stranglingly around his neck. Black rats came racing out of the big holes at the cluttered base of the walls.

Meanwhile other strands snaked around Fafhrd's ankles, knees and left arm, almost toppling him. But even as he fought for balance, he jerked Vlana's dagger from his belt and raised it over his shoulder, its silver hilt glowing, its blade brown with dried rat's-blood.

The grin left Hristomilo's face as he saw it. The sorcerer screamed strangely and importuningly then and drew back from his parchment and the table, and raised clawed clubhands to ward off doom.

Vlana's dagger sped unimpeded through the black web—its strands even seemed to part for it—and betwixt the sorcerer's warding hands, to bury itself to the hilt in his right eye.

He screamed thinly in dire agony and clawed at his face.

The black web writhed as if in death spasm.

The cucurbits shattered as one, spilling their lava on the scarred table, putting out the blue flames even as the thick wood of the table began to smoke a little at the lava's edge. Lava dropped with *plops* on the dark marble floor.

With a faint, final scream Hristomilo pitched forward, hands still clutched to his eyes above his jutting nose, silver dagger-hilt still protruding between his fingers.

The web grew faint, like wet ink washed with a gush of clear water.

The Mouser raced forward and transfixed Slivikin and the huge rat with one thrust of Scalpel before the beasts knew what was happening. They too died swiftly with thin screams, while all the other rats turned tail and fled back down their holes swift almost as black lightning.

Then the last trace of night-smog or sorcery-smoke vanished and Fafhrd and the Mouser found themselves standing alone with three dead bodies and a profound silence that seemed to fill not only this room but all Thieves' House. Even the cucurbit-lava had ceased to move, was hardening, and the wood of the table no longer smoked.

Their madness was gone and all their rage too—vented to the last red atomy and glutted to more than satiety. They had no more urge to kill Krovas or any other of the thieves than to swat flies. With horrified inner eye Fafhrd saw the pitiful face of the child-thief he'd skewered in his lunatic anger.

Only their grief remained with them, diminished not one whit, but rather growing greater—that and an ever more swiftly growing revulsion from all that was around them: the dead, the disordered magic room, all Thieves' House, all of the city of Lankhmar to its last stinking alleyway and smog-wreathed spire.

With a hiss of disgust the Mouser jerked Scalpel from the rodent cadavers, wiped it on the nearest cloth, and returned it to its scabbard. Fafhrd likewise sketchily cleansed and sheathed Graywand. Then the two men picked up their knife and dirk from where they'd dropped to the floor when the web had dematerialized, though neither so much as glanced at Vlana's dagger where it was buried. But on the sorcerer's table they did notice Vlana's black velvet, silver-worked pouch and belt, the latter half overrun by the hardened black lava, and Ivrian's blue-enameled box inlaid with silver. From these they took the gems of Jengao.

With no more word than they had exchanged back at the Mouser's burned nest behind the Eel, but with a continuing sense of their unity of purpose, their identity of intent, and of their comradeship, they made their way with shoulders bowed and with slow, weary steps which only very gradually quickened out of the magic room and down the thick-carpeted corridor, past the map room's wide door still barred with oak and iron, and past all the other shut, silent doors—clearly the entire Guild was terrified of Hristomilo, his spells, and his rats; down the echoing stairs, their footsteps speeding a little; down the bare-floored lower corridor past its closed, quiet doors, their footsteps resounding loudly no matter how softly they sought to tread; under the deserted, black-scorched guardniche, and so out into Cheap Street, turning left and north because that was the nearest way to the Street of the Gods, and there turning right and east—not a waking soul in the wide street except for one skinny, bent-backed apprentice lad unhappily swabbing the flagstones in front of a wine shop in the dim pink light beginning to seep from the east, although there were many forms asleep, a-snore and a-dream in the gutters and under the dark porticos— yes, turning right and east down the Street of the Gods, for that way was the Marsh Gate, leading to Causey Road across the Great Salt Marsh, and the Marsh Gate was the nearest way out of the great and glamorous city that was now loathsome to them, indeed, not to be endured for one more stabbing, leaden heart-beat than was necessary—a city of beloved, unfaceable ghosts.

Theodore Sturgeon

I met Ted for the first time about a third of a century ago, when he was young and boyish and as pretty as a picture and I was much the same age I still am now. I saw him more recently on the good ship *Statendam* in the first half of December 1972.

We were all going down to the coast of Florida to watch Apollo 17 take off for the Moon in the last of the man-to-Moon ventures. It was a night launch and it was beautiful, but for me the trip was beautiful from the start because on the dock, as I was waiting to board, who should I see but Ted in a buckskin costume, with his young son and his wife.

I remember Weena, his wife, very well as being young and girlish and as pretty as a picture, but what I remember most is that she was interested in natural foods and lectured me about it severely on board the ship. (I haven't the foggiest idea why people are always lecturing me on diet. I know all about diet. Why just to make sure I don't miss out on important vitamins and trace minerals, I routinely eat everything in sight.) Then, when she was all through, she lit up a cigarette.

I said, "If you're so concerned about my health, be concerned about your own," and I tore the cigarette out of her mouth (along with a piece of lip, I think), and threw it on the ground and stamped on it.

Later, she told me that she had been so impressed by the subtle logic of my argument that she had given up smoking. (I hope she has stuck to this resolve.)

One more thing about the twenty-ninth convention before I leave it. Bob Silverberg in his toastmasterish remarks had, as a running gag, references to "donating it to Clarion." This arose out of an incident at the twenty-seventh convention in St. Louis in 1969, when Harlan Ellison, having collected some money in a good cause, found there was a surplus and donated that surplus to a science fiction writers conference named for Clarion College. That too was a good cause, but Harlan, carried away by his benevolent heart, had neglected to go through the formality of asking the approval of the people whose money it had been. There was a public fight between Harlan and the rest of the convention, with the rest of the convention badly outnumbered, of course.

So toward the end of Bob's speech, I scrawled out a limerick and, when it was my turn to say a few words, I sang it to the audience and got the biggest laugh of the evening. I have recently published books entitled *Lecherous Limericks* (Walker, 1975) and *More Lecherous Limericks* (Walker, 1976), each containing a hundred limericks of my own composing, and the one I recited at the convention, being reasonably unlecherous, is not included. I don't want to lose it for posterity so here it is:

> *There was a young stripper named Marion*
> *Who did bump, and did grind, and did carry on.*
> > *The result of her joy*
> > *Was a fine bastard boy*
> *Which she promptly donated to Clarion.*

3

SLOW SCULPTURE

She didn't know who he was when she met him; well, not many
people did. He was in the high orchard doing something under a
pear tree. The land smelled of late summer and wind: bronze, it
smelled bronze. He looked up at a compact girl in her mid-twenties, with a fearless face and eyes the same color as her hair,
which was extraordinary because her hair was red-gold. She
looked down at a leather-skinned man in his forties with a gold-
leaf electroscope in his hand, and felt she was an intruder. She
said, "Oh," in what was apparently the right way, because he
nodded once and said, "Hold this," and there could then be no
thought of intrusion. She knelt down by him and took the instrument, holding it just where he positioned her hand, and then he
moved a little away and struck a tuning fork against his kneecap.
"What's it doing?" He had a good voice, the kind of voice
strangers notice and listen to.

She looked at the delicate leaves of gold in the glass shield of
the electroscope. "They're moving apart."

He struck the tuning fork again and the leaves pressed away
from one another. "Much?"

"About forty-five degrees when you hit the fork."

"Good—that's about the most we'll get." From a pocket of his
bush jacket he drew a sack of chalk-dust and dropped a small
handful on the ground. "I'll move now. You stay right there and
tell me how much the leaves separate."

He traveled around the pear tree in a zigzag course, striking
his tuning fork while she called out numbers—ten degrees,
thirty, five, twenty, nothing. Whenever the gold foil pressed
apart to maximum, forty degrees or more, he dropped more
chalk. When he was finished the tree was surrounded, in a rough

oval, by the white dots of chalk. He took out a notebook and diagrammed them and the tree, and put away the book, and took the electroscope out of her hands. "Were you looking for something?" he asked her.

"No," she said. "Yes."

He could smile. Though it did not last long, she found it very surprising in a face like that. "That's not what is called, in a court of law, a responsive answer."

She glanced across the hillside, metallic in that late light. There wasn't much on it—rocks, weeds the summer was done with, a tree or so, and then the orchard. Anyone present had come a long way to get here. "It wasn't a simple question," she said, tried to smile, and burst into tears.

She was sorry and said so.

"Why?" he asked. This was the first time she was to experience this ask-the-next-question thing of his. It was unsettling. It always would be—never less, sometimes a great deal more. "Well —one doesn't have emotional explosions in public."

"*You* do. I don't know this 'one' you're talking about."

"I—guess I don't either, now that you mention it."

"Tell the truth then. No sense in going round and round about it, 'he'll think that I—' and the like. I'll think what I think, whatever you say. Or—go on down the mountain and just don't say any more." She did not turn to go, so he added, "Try the truth, then. If it's important, it's simple, and if it's simple it's easy to say."

"I'm going to die!" she cried.

"So am I."

"I have a lump in my breast."

"Come up to the house and I'll fix it."

Without another word he turned away and started through the orchard. Startled half out of her wits, indignant and full of insane hope, experiencing, even, a quick curl of astonished laughter, she stood for a moment watching him go, and then found herself (at what point did I decide?) running after him.

She caught up with him on the uphill margin of the orchard. "Are you a doctor?"

He appeared not to notice that she had waited, had run. "No," he said, and, walking on, appeared not to see her stand again pulling at her lower lip, then run again to catch up.

"I must be out of my mind," she said, joining him on a garden path. She said it to herself, which he must have known because he did not answer. The garden was alive with defiant chrysanthemums and a pond in which she saw the flicker of a pair of redcap imperials—silver, not gold fish—which were the largest she had ever seen. Then—the house.

First it was part of the garden, with its colonnaded terrace, and then, with its rock walls (too big to be called fieldstone) part of the mountain. It was on and in the hillside, and its roofs paralleled the skylines, front and sides, and part of it was backed against an outjutting cliff face. The door, beamed and studded and with two archers' slits, was opened for them (but there was no one there) and when it closed it was silent, a far more solid exclusion of things outside than any click or clang of latch or bolt. She stood with her back against it watching him cross what seemed to be the central well of the house, or at least this part of it. It was a kind of small court in the center of which was an atrium, glazed on all of its five sides and open to the sky at the top. In it was a tree, a cypress or juniper, gnarled and twisted and with the turned-back, paralleled, sculptured appearance of what the Japanese call bonsai.

"Aren't you coming?" he called, holding open a door behind the atrium.

"Bonsai just aren't fifteen feet tall," she said.

"This one is."

She came by it slowly, looking. "How long have you had it?"

His tone of voice said he was immensely pleased. It is a clumsiness to ask the owner of a bonsai how old it is; you are then demanding to know if it is his work or if he has acquired and continued the concept of another; you are tempting him to claim for his own the concept and the meticulous labor of someone else, and it becomes rude to tell a man he is being tested. Hence "How long have you had it?" is polite, forbearing, profoundly courteous. He answered, "Half my life." She looked at the tree. Trees can be found, sometimes, not quite discarded, not quite forgotten, potted in rusty gallon cans in not quite successful nurseries, unsold because they are shaped oddly or have dead branches here and there, or because they have grown too slowly in whole or part. These are the ones which develop interesting trunks and a resistance to misfortune that makes them flourish if given the least excuse for living. This one was far older than half this man's life, or all of it. Looking at it, she was terrified by the unbidden thought that a fire, a family of squirrels, some subterranean worm or termite could end this beauty—something working outside any concept of rightness or justice or . . . or respect. She looked at the tree. She looked at the man.

"Coming?"

"Yes," she said and went with him into his laboratory. "Sit down over there and relax," he told her. "This might take a little while."

"Over there" was a big leather chair by the bookcase. The books were right across the spectrum—reference works in medicine and engineering, nuclear physics, chemistry, biology, psychiatry. Also tennis, gymnastics, chess, the oriental war game Go, and golf. And then drama, the techniques of fiction, *Modern English Usage, The American Language* and supplement, Wood's and Walker's rhyming dictionaries and an array of other dictionaries and encyclopedias. A whole long shelf of biographies. "You have quite a library."

He answered her rather shortly: clearly he did not want to talk just now, for he was very busy. He said only, "Yes I have— perhaps you'll see it some time," which left her to pick away at his words to find out what on earth he meant by them. He could only have meant, she decided, that the books beside her chair were what he kept handy for his work—that his real library was elsewhere. She looked at him with a certain awe.

And she watched him. She liked the way he moved—swiftly, decisively. Clearly he knew what he was doing. He used some equipment that she recognized—a glass still, titration equipment, a centrifuge. There were two refrigerators, one of which was not a refrigerator at all, for she could see the large indicator on the door: it stood at 70° F. It came to her that a modern refrigerator is perfectly adaptable to the demand for controlled environment, even a warm one.

But all that, and the equipment she did not recognize, was only furniture. It was the man who was worth watching, the man who kept her occupied so that not once in all the long time she sat there was she tempted toward the bookshelves.

At last he finished a long sequence at the bench, threw some switches, picked up a tall stool and came over to her. He perched on the stool, hung his heels on the cross-spoke, and laid a pair of long brown hands over his knees. "Scared?"

"I s'pose I am."

"You don't have to stay."

"Considering the alternative," she began bravely, but the courage-sound somehow oozed out, "it can't matter much."

"Very sound," he said, almost cheerfully. "I remember when I was a kid there was a fire scare in the apartment house where we lived. It was a wild scramble to get out, and my ten-year-old brother found himself outside in the street with an alarm clock in his hand. It was an old one and it didn't work—but of all the things in the place he might have snatched up at a time like that, it turned out to be the clock. He's never been able to figure out why."

"Have you?"

"Not why he picked that particular thing, no. But I think I know why he did something obviously irrational. You see, panic is a very special state. Like fear and flight, or fury and attack, it's a pretty primitive reaction to extreme danger. It's one of the expressions of the will to survive. What makes it so special is that it's irrational. Now, why would the abandonment of reason be a survival mechanism?"

She thought about this seriously. There was that about this man which made serious thought imperative. "I can't imagine," she said finally. "Unless it's because, in some situations, reason just doesn't work."

"You *can* imagine," he said, again radiating that huge approval, making her glow. "And you just did. If you are in danger and you try reason, and reason doesn't work, you abandon it. You can't say it's unintelligent to abandon what doesn't work, right? So then you are in panic; then you start to perform random acts. Most of them—far and away most—will be useless; some might even be dangerous, but that doesn't matter—you're in danger already. Where the survival factor comes in is that away down deep you know that one chance in a million is better than no chance at all. So—here you sit—you're scared and you could run; something says you should run; but you won't."

She nodded.

He went on: "You found a lump. You went to a doctor and he made some tests and gave you the bad news. Maybe you went to another doctor and he confirmed it. You then did some research and found out what was to happen next—the exploratory, the radical, the questionable recovery, the whole long agonizing procedure of being what they call a terminal case. You then flipped out. Did some things you hope I won't ask you about. Took a trip somewhere, anywhere, wound up in my orchard for no reason." He spread the good hands and let them go back to their kind of sleep. "Panic. The reason for little boys in their pajamas standing at midnight with a broken alarm clock in their arms, and for the existence of quacks." Something chimed over on the bench and he gave her a quick smile and went back to work, saying over his shoulder: "I'm not a quack, by the way. To qualify as a quack you have to claim to be a doctor. I don't."

She watched him switch off, switch on, stir, measure and calculate. A little orchestra of equipment chorused and soloed around him as he conducted, whirring, hissing, clicking, flickering. She wanted to laugh, to cry, and to scream. She did no one of these things for fear of not stopping, ever.

When he came over again, the conflict was not raging within her, but exerting steady and opposed tensions; the result was a terrible stasis, and all she could do when she saw the instrument in his hand was to widen her eyes. She quite forgot to breathe.

"Yes, it's a needle," he said, his tone almost bantering. "A long shiny sharp needle. Don't tell me you are one of those needle-shy people." He flipped the long power-cord which trailed from the black housing around the hypodermic, to get some slack, and straddled the stool. "Want something to steady your nerves?"

She was afraid to speak; the membrane containing her sane self was very thin, stretched very tight.

He said, "I'd rather you didn't, because this pharmaceutical stew is complex enough as it is. But if you need it . . ."

She managed to shake her head a little, and again she felt the wave of approval from him. There were a thousand questions she wanted to ask—had meant to ask—needed to ask: What was in the needle? How many treatments must she have? What would they be like? How long must she stay, and where? And most of all—oh, could she live, could she live?

He seemed concerned with the answer to only one of these. "It's mostly built around an isotope of potassium. If I told you all I know about it and how I came on it in the first place, it would take—well, more time than we've got. But here's the general idea: Theoretically, every atom is electrically balanced (never mind ordinary exceptions). Likewise all electrical charges in the molecule are supposed to be balanced—so much plus, so much minus, total zero. I happened on the fact that the balance of charges in a wild cell is not zero—not quite. It's as if there was a submicroscopic thunderstorm going on at the molecular level, with little lightning bolts flashing back and forth and changing the signs. Interfering with communications—static—and that," he said, gesturing with the shielded hypo in his hand, "is what this is all about. When something interferes with communications—especially the RNA mechanism, which says, Read this blueprint and build accordingly, and stop when it's done—when that message gets garbled, lopsided things get built, off-balance things, things which do almost what they should, do it almost right: they're wild cells, and the messages they pass on are even worse.

"Okay: Whether these thunderstorms are caused by viruses or chemicals or radiation or physical trauma or even anxiety—and don't think anxiety can't do it—that's secondary. The important thing is to fix it so the thunderstorm can't happen. If you can do that, the cells have plenty of ability all by themselves to repair and replace what's gone wrong. And biological systems aren't like ping-pong balls with static charges waiting for the charge to leak away or to discharge into a grounded wire. They have a kind of resilience—I call it forgiveness—which enables them to take on a little more charge, or a little less, and do all right. Well then: Say a certain clump of cells is wild and say it carries an aggregate of a hundred units extra on the positive side. Cells immediately around it are affected, but not the next layer or the next.

"If they could be opened to the extra charge, if they could help to drain it off, they would, well, *cure* the wild cells of the surplus, you see what I mean? And they would be able to handle that little overage themselves, or pass it on to other cells and still others who could deal with it. In other words, if I can flood your body with some medium which can drain off and distribute a concentration of this unbalanced charge, the ordinary bodily processes will be free to move in and clear up the wild-cell damage. And that's what I have here."

He held the shielded needle between his knees and from a side pocket of his lab coat he took a plastic box, opened it and drew out an alcohol swab. Still cheerfully talking, he took her terror-numbed arm and scrubbed at the inside of her elbow. "I am not for one second implying that nuclear charges in the atom are the same thing as static electricity. They're in a different league altogether. But the analogy holds. I could use another analogy. I could liken the charge on the wild cells to accumulations of fat, and this gunk of mine to a detergent, which would break it up and spread it so far it couldn't be detected any more. But I'm led to the static analogy by an odd side effect—organisms injected with this stuff do build up one hell of a static charge. It's a by-product, and for reasons I can only theorize about at the moment, it seems to be keyed to the audio spectrum. Tuning forks and the like. That's what I was playing with when I met you. That tree is drenched with this stuff. It used to have a whorl of wild-cell growth. It hasn't any more." He gave her the quick surprising smile and let it click away as he held the needle point upward and squirted it. With his other hand wrapped around her left biceps, he squeezed gently and firmly. The needle was lowered and placed and slid into the big vein so deftly that she gasped—not because it hurt, but because it did not. Attentively he watched the bit of glass barrel protruding from a black housing as he withdrew the plunger a fraction and saw the puff of red into the colorless fluid inside, and then he bore steadily on the plunger again.

"Please don't move . . . I'm sorry; this will take a little time. I have to get quite a lot of this into you. Which is fine, you know," he said, resuming the tone of his previous remarks about audio spectra, "because side effect or no, it's consistent. Healthy bio systems develop a strong electrostatic field, unhealthy ones a weak one or none at all. With an instrument as primitive and simple as that little electroscope you can tell if any part of the organism has a community of wild cells, and if so, where it is and how big and how wild." Deftly he shifted his grip on the encased hypodermic without moving the point or varying the amount of plunger pressure. It was beginning to be uncomfortable, an ache turning into a bruise. "And if you're wondering why this mosquito has a housing on it with a wire attached (although I'll bet you're not and that you know as well as I do that I'm doing all this talking just to keep your mind occupied!) I'll tell you. It's nothing but a coil carrying a high-frequency alternating current. The alternating field sees to it that the fluid is magnetically and electrostatically neutral right from the start." He withdrew the needle suddenly and smoothly, bent her arm, and trapped in the inside of her elbow a cotton swab.

"Nobody ever told me that before after a treatment," she said.

"What?"

"No charge," she said.

Again that wave of approval, this time with words: "I like your style. How do you feel?"

She cast about for accurate phrases. "Like the owner of a large sleeping hysteria begging someone not to wake it up."

He laughed. "In a little while you are going to feel so weird you won't have time for hysteria." He got up and returned the needle to the bench, looping up the cable as he went. He turned off the AC field and returned with a large glass bowl and a square of plywood. He inverted the bowl on the floor near her and placed the wood on its broad base.

"I remember something like that," she said. "When I was in—in junior high school. They were generating artificial lightning with a . . . let me see . . . well, it had a long endless belt running over pulleys and some little wires scraping on it and a big copper ball on top."

"Van de Graaf generator."

"Right! And they did all sorts of things with it, but what I specially remember is standing on a piece of wood on a bowl like that and they charged me up with the generator, and I didn't feel much of anything except all my hair stood out from my head. Everyone laughed. I looked like a golliwog. They said I was carrying forty thousand volts."

"Good! I'm glad you remember that. This'll be a little different, though. By roughly another forty thousand."

"Oh!"

"Don't worry. Long as you're insulated, and as long as grounded, or comparatively grounded objects—me, for example —stay well away from you, there won't be any fireworks."

"Are you going to use a generator like that?"

"Not like that, and I already did. You're the generator."

"I'm—*oh!*" She had raised her hand from the upholstered chair arm and there was a crackle of sparks and the faint smell of ozone.

"Oh you sure are, and more than I thought, and quicker. Get up!"

She started up slowly; she finished the maneuver with speed. As her body separated from the chair she was, for a fractional second, seated in a tangle of spitting blue-white threads. They, or she, propelled her a yard and a half away, standing. Literally shocked half out of her wits, she almost fell.

"Stay on your feet!" he snapped, and she recovered, gasping. He stepped back a pace. "Get up on the board. Quick, now!"

She did as she was told, leaving, for the two paces she traveled, two brief footprints of fire. She teetered on the board. Visibly, her hair began to stir. "What's happening to me?" she cried.

"You're getting charged after all," he said jovially, but at this point she failed to appreciate the extension of even her own witticism. She cried again, "What's happening to me?"

"It's all right," he said consolingly. He went to the bench and turned on a tone generator. It moaned deep in the one to three hundred cycle range. He increased the volume and turned the pitch control. It howled upward and as it did so her red-gold hair shivered and swept up and out, each hair attempting frantically to get away from all the others. He ran the tone up above ten thousand cycles and all the way back to a belly-bumping inaudible eleven; at the extremes her hair slumped, but at around eleven hundred it stood out in (as she had described it) golliwog style.

He turned down the gain to a more or less bearable level and picked up the electroscope. He came toward her, smiling. "You

are an electroscope, you know that? And a living Van de Graaf
generator as well. And a golliwog."

"Let me down," was all she could say.

"Not yet. Please hang tight. The differential between you and
everything else here is so high that if you got near any of it you'd
discharge into it. It wouldn't harm you—it isn't current electricity
—but you might get a burn and a nervous shock out of it." He
held out the electroscope; even at that distance, and in her distress, she could see the gold leaves writhe apart. He circled her,
watching the leaves attentively, moving the instrument forward
and back and from side to side. Once he went to the tone generator and turned it down some more. "You're sending such a
strong field I can't pick up the variations," he explained, and returned to her, closer now.

"I can't, much more . . . I can't," she murmured; he did not
hear, or he did not care. He moved the electroscope near her ab-
domen, up and from side to side.

"Yup. There you are!" he said cheerfully, moving the instrument close to her right breast.

"What?" she whimpered.

"Your cancer. Right breast, low, around toward the ampit." He
whistled. "A mean one, too. Malignant as hell."

She swayed and then collapsed forward and down. A sick
blackness swept down on her, receded explosively in a glare of
agonizing blue-white, and then crashed down on her like a
mountain falling.

Place where wall meets ceiling. Another wall, another ceiling.
Hadn't seen it before. Didn't matter. Don't care.

Sleep.

Place where wall meets ceiling. Something in the way. His
face, close, drawn, tired; eyes awake though and penetrating.
Doesn't matter. Don't care.

Sleep.

Place where wall meets ceiling. Down a bit, late sunlight.
Over a little, rusty-gold chrysanthemums in a goldgreen glass
cornucopia. Something in the way again: his face.

"Can you hear me?"

Yes, but don't answer. Don't move. Don't speak.

Sleep.

It's a room, a wall, a table, a man pacing; a nighttime window and mums you'd think were alive, but don't you know they're cut right off and dying?

Do they know that?

"*How are you?*" Urgent, urgent.

"Thirsty."

Cold and a bite to it that aches the hinges of the jaws. Grapefruit juice. Lying back on his arm while he holds the glass in the other hand, oh no, that's not . . . "Thank you. Thanks very—" Try to sit up, the sheet—*my clothes!*

"Sorry about that," he said, the mind-reader-almost. "Some things that have to be done just aren't consistent with panty-hose and a mini-dress. All washed and dried and ready for you, though—any time. Over there."

The brown wool and the panty-hose and the shoes, on the chair. He's respectful, standing back, putting the glass next to an insulated carafe on the night-table.

"What things?"

"Throwing up. Bedpans," he said candidly.

Protective with the sheet, which can hide bodies but oh not embarrassment. "Oh I'm sorry . . . Oh. I must've—" Shake head and he slides back and forth in the vision.

"You went into shock, and then you just didn't come out of it." He hesitated. It was the first time she had ever seen him hesitate over anything. She became for a moment an almost-mind-reader: *Should I tell her what's in my mind?* Sure he should, and he did: "You didn't *want* to come out of it."

"It's all gone out of my head."

"The pear tree, the electroscope. The injection, the electrostatic response."

"No," she said, not knowing, then, knowing: "*No!*"

"Hang on!" he rapped, and next thing she knew he was by the bed, over her, his two hands hard on her cheeks. "Don't slip off again. You can handle it. You can handle it because it's all right now, do you understand that? You're all right!"

"You told me I had cancer." It sounded pouty, accusing. He laughed at her, actually laughed.

"You told *me* you had it."

"Oh, but I didn't *know*."

"That explains it, then," he said in a load-off-my-back tone. "There wasn't anything in what I did that could cause a three-day withdrawal like that; it had to be something in you."

"Three *days!*"

He simply nodded in response to that and went on with what he was saying. "I get a little pompous once in a while," he said engagingly. "Comes from being right so much of the time. Took a bit more for granted than I should have, didn't I? when I assumed you'd been to a doctor, maybe even had a biopsy. You didn't, did you?"

"I was afraid," she admitted. She looked at him. "My mother died of it, and my aunt, and my sister had a radical mastectomy. I couldn't bear it. And when you—"

"When I told you what you already knew, and what you never wanted to hear, you couldn't take it. You blacked right out, you know. Fainted away, and it had nothing to do with the seventy-odd thousand volts of static you were carrying. I caught you." He put out his arms and instinctively she shrank back, but he held the arms where they were, on display, until she looked at them and saw the angry red scorch marks on his forearms and the heavy biceps, as much of them as she could see from under his short-sleeved shirt. "About nine-tenths knocked me out too," he said, "but a least you didn't crack your head or anything."

"Thank you," she said reflexively, and then began to cry. "What am I going to *do?*"

"Do? Go back home, wherever that is—pick up your life again, whatever that might mean."

"But you said—"

"When are you going to get it into your head that what I did was not a diagnostic?"

"Are you—did you—you mean you cured it?"

"I mean you're curing it right now. I explained it all to you before—you remember that now, don't you?"

"Not altogether, but—yes." Surreptitiously (but not enough, because he saw her) she felt under the sheet for the lump. "It's still there."

"If I bopped you over the head with a bat," he said with slightly exaggerated simplicity, "there would be a lump on it. It would be there tomorrow and the next day. The day after that it might be smaller, and in a week you'd still be able to feel it, but it would be gone. Same thing here."

At last she let the enormity of it touch her. "A one-shot cure for cancer . . ."

"Oh God," he said harshly, "I can tell by looking at you that I am going to have to listen to that speech *again*. Well, I won't."

Startled, she said, "What speech?"

"The one about my duty to humanity. It comes in two phases and many textures. Phase one has to do with my duty to humanity and really means we could make a classic buck with it. Phase two deals solely with my duty to humanity, and I don't hear that one very often. Phase two utterly overlooks the reluctance humanity has to accept good things unless they arrive from accepted and respectable sources. Phase one is fully aware of this but gets very rat-shrewd in figuring ways around it."

She said, "I don't—" but could get no farther.

"The textures," he overrode her, "are accompanied by the light of revelation, with or without religion and/or mysticism; or they are cast sternly in the ethical-philosophy mold and aim to force me to surrender through guilt mixed, to some degree all the way up to total, with compassion."

"But I only—"

"You," he said, aiming a long index finger at her, "have robbed yourself of the choicest example of everything I have just said. If my assumptions had been right and you had gone to your friendly local sawbones, and he had diagnosed cancer and referred you to a specialist, and he had done likewise and sent you to a colleague for consultation, and in random panic you had fallen into my hands and been cured, and had gone back to your various doctors to report a miracle, do you know what you'd have gotten from them? 'Spontaneous remission,' that's what you'd have gotten. And it wouldn't be only doctors," he went on with a sudden renewal of passion, under which she quailed in her bed. "Everybody has his own commercial. Your nutritionist would have nodded over his wheat germ or his macrobiotic rice cakes, your priest would have dropped to his knees and looked at the sky, your geneticist would have a pet theory about generation skipping and would assure you that your grandparents probably had spontaneous remissions too and never knew it."

"Please!" she cried, but he shouted at her: "Do you know what I am? I am an engineer twice over, mechanical and electrical, and I have a law degree. If you were foolish enough to tell anyone about what has happened here (which I hope you aren't, but if you are I know how to protect myself) I could be jailed for practicing medicine without a license, you could have me up for assault because I stuck a needle into you and even for kidnapping if you could prove I carried you in here from the lab. Nobody would give a damn that I had cured your cancer. You don't know who I am, do you?"

"No, I don't even know your name."

"And I won't tell you. I don't know your name, either—"

"Oh! It's—"

"Don't tell me! Don't tell me! I don't want to hear it! I wanted to be involved with your lump and I was. I want it and you to be gone as soon as you're both up to it. Have I made myself absolutely clear?"

"Just let me get dressed," she said tightly, "and I'll leave right now!"

"Without making a speech?"

"Without making a speech." And in a flash her anger turned to misery and she added, "I was going to say I was grateful. Would that have been all right?"

And his anger underwent a change too, for he came close to the bed and sat down on his heel, bringing their faces to a level, and said quite gently, "That would be fine. Although . . . you won't really be grateful for another ten days, when you get your 'spontaneous remission' reports, or maybe for six months or a year or two or five, when examinations keep on testing out negative."

She detected such a wealth of sadness behind this that she found herself reaching for the hand with which he steadied himself against the edge of the bed. He did not recoil, but he didn't seem to welcome it either. "Why can't I be grateful right now?"

"That would be an act of faith," he said bitterly, "and that just doesn't happen any more—if it ever did." He rose and went toward the door. "Please don't go tonight," he said. "It's dark and you don't know the way. I'll see you in the morning."

When he came back in the morning the door was open. The bed was made and the sheets were folded neatly on the chair, together with the pillow slips and the towels she had used. She wasn't there.

He came out into the entrance court and contemplated his bonsai.

Early sun gold-frosted the horizontal upper foliage of the old tree and brought its gnarled limbs into sharp relief, tough brown-gray and crevices of velvet. Only the companion of a bonsai (there are owners of bonsai, but they are a lesser breed) fully understands the relationship. There is an exclusive and individual treeness to the tree because it is a living thing, and living things change, and there are definite ways in which the tree desires to change. A man sees the tree and in his mind makes certain extensions and extrapolations of what he sees, and sets about making them happen. The tree in turn will do only what a tree can do, will resist to the death any attempt to do what it cannot do, or to do it in less time than it needs. The shaping of a bonsai is therefore always a compromise and always a cooperation. A man cannot create bonsai, nor can a tree; it takes both, and they must understand each other. It takes a long time to do that. One memorizes one's bonsai, every twig, the angle of every crevice and needle, and, lying awake at night or in a pause a thousand miles away, one recalls this or that line or mass, one makes one's plans. With wire and water and light, with tilting and with the planting of water-robbing weeds or heavy root-shading ground cover, one explains to the tree what one wants, and if the explanation is well enough made, and there is great enough understanding, the tree will respond and obey—almost. Always there will be its own self-respecting, highly individual variation: *Very well, I shall do what you want, but I will do it my way.* And for these variations, the tree is always willing to present a clear and logical explanation, and more often than not (almost smiling) it will make clear to the man that he could have avoided it if his understanding had been better.

It is the slowest sculpture in the world, and there is, at times, doubt as to which is being sculpted, man or tree.

So he stood for perhaps ten minutes watching the flow of gold over the upper branches, and then went to a carved wooden chest, opened it, shook out a length of disreputable cotton duck, opened the hinged glass at one side of the atrium, and spread the canvas over the roots and all the earth to one side of the trunk, leaving the rest open to wind and water. Perhaps in a while—a month or two—a certain shoot in the topmost branch would take the hint, and the uneven flow of moisture up through the cambium layer would nudge it away from that upward reach and persuade it to continue the horizontal passage. And perhaps not, and it would need the harsher language of binding and wire. But then it might have something to say, too, about the rightness of an upward trend, and would perhaps say it persuasively enough to convince the man; altogether, a patient, meaningful, and rewarding dialogue.

"Good morning."

"Oh goddam!" he barked, "you made me bite my tongue. I thought you'd gone."

"I did." She knelt in the shadows with her back against the inner wall, facing the atrium. "But then I stopped to be with the tree for a while."

"Then what?"

"I thought a lot."

"What about?"

"You."

"Did you now!"

"Look," she said firmly, "I'm not going to any doctor to get this thing checked out. I didn't want to leave until I had told you that, and until I was sure you believed me."

"Come on in and we'll get something to eat."

Foolishly, she giggled. "I can't. My feet are asleep."

Without hesitation he scooped her up in his arms and carried her around the atrium. She said, her arm around his shoulders and their faces close, "Do you believe me?"

He continued around until they reached the wooden chest, then stopped and looked into her eyes. "I believe you. I don't know why you decided that, but I'm willing to believe you." He set her down on the chest and stood back.

"It's that act of faith you mentioned," she said gravely. "I thought you ought to have it, at least once in your life, so you can never say such a thing again." She tapped her heels gingerly against the slate floor. "Ow." She made a pained smile. "Pins and needles."

"You must have been thinking for a long time."

"Yes. Want more?"

"Sure."

"You are an angry, frightened man."

He seemed delighted. "Tell me about all that!"

"No," she said quietly, "you tell me. I'm very serious about this. Why are you angry?"

"I'm not!"

"Why are you so angry?"

"I tell you I'm not! Although," he added good-naturedly, "You're pushing me in that direction."

"Well then, why?"

He gazed at her for what, to her, seemed a very long time indeed. "You really want to know, don't you?"

She nodded.

He waved a sudden hand, up and out. "Where do you suppose all this came from—the house, the land, the equipment?"

She waited.

"An exhaust system," he said, with a thickening of the voice she was coming to know. "A way of guiding exhaust gases out of internal-combustion engines in such a way that they are given a spin. Unburned solids are embedded in the walls of the muffler in a glass-wool liner that slips out in one piece and can be replaced by a clean one every couple of thousand miles. The rest of the exhaust is fired by its own spark plug and what will burn, burns. The heat is used to preheat the fuel; the rest is spun again through a five-thousand-mile cartridge. What finally gets out is, by today's standards at least, pretty clean; and because of the preheating, it actually gets better mileage out of the engine."

"So you've made a lot of money."

"I made a lot of money," he echoed. "But not because the thing is being used to cut down air pollution. I got the money because an automobile company bought it and buried it in a lock-box. They don't like it because it costs something to install in new cars. Some friends of theirs in the refining business don't like it because it gets high performance out of crude fuels. Well all right—I didn't know any better and I won't make the same mistake again. But yes—I'm angry. I was angry when I was a kid on a tankship and we were set to washing down bulkhead with chipped brown-soap and canvas, and I went ashore and bought a detergent and tried it and it was better, faster and cheaper so I took it to the bos'n, who gave me a punch in the mouth for pretending to know his job better than he did . . . well, he was drunk at the time, but the rough part was when the old shellbacks in the crew got wind of it and ganged up on me for being what they called a 'company man'—that's a dirty name in a ship. I just couldn't understand why people got in the way of something better.

"I've been up against that all my life. I have something in my head that just won't quit: it's a way I have of asking the next question: Why is so-and-so the way it is? Why can't it be such-and-such instead? There is always another question to be asked about any thing or any situation; especially you shouldn't quit when you like an answer because there's always another one after it. And we live in a world where people just don't want to ask the next question!

"I've been paid all my stomach will take for things people won't use, and if I'm mad all the time it's really my fault—I admit it; because I just can't stop asking that next question and coming up with answers. There's a half-dozen real blockbusters in that lab that nobody will ever see, and half a hundred more in my head; but what can you do in a world where people would rather kill each other in a desert even when they're shown it can turn green and bloom, where they'll fall all over themselves to pour billions into developing a new oil strike when it's been proved over and over again that the fossil fuels will kill us all?

"Yes. I'm angry. Shouldn't I be?"

She let the echoes of his voice swirl around the court and out through the hole in the top of the atrium, and waited a little longer to let him know he was here with her and not beside himself and his fury. He grinned at her sheepishly when he came to this, and she said:

"Maybe you're asking the next question instead of asking the right question. I think people who live by wise old sayings are trying not to think, but I know one worth paying some attention to. It's this: If you ask a question the right way, you've just given the answer." She paused to see if he was paying real attention. He was. She went on, "I mean, if you put your hand on a hot stove you might ask yourself, how can I stop my hand from burning? And the answer is pretty clear, isn't it? If the world keeps rejecting what you have to give, there's some way of asking why that contains the answer."

"It's a simple answer," he said shortly. "People are stupid."

"That isn't the answer and you know it," she said.

"What is?"

"Oh, I can't tell you that! All I know is that the way you do something, when people are concerned, is more important than what you do, if you want results. I mean . . . you already know how to get what you want with the tree, don't you?"

"I'll be damned."

"People are living growing things too. I don't know a hundredth part of what you do about bonsai, but I do know this: when you start one, it isn't often the strong straight healthy ones you take. It's the twisted sick ones that can be made the most beautiful. When you get to shaping humanity, you might remember that."

"Of all the—I don't know whether to laugh in your face or punch you right in the mouth!"

She rose. He hadn't realized she was quite this tall. "I'd better go."

"Come on now. You know a figure of speech when you hear one."

"Oh, I didn't feel threatened. But—I'd better go, all the same."

Shrewdly, he asked her, "Are you afraid to ask the next question?"

"Terrified."

"Ask it anyway."

"No!"

"Then I'll do it for you. You said I was angry—and afraid. You want to know what I'm afraid of."

"Yes."

"You. I am scared to death of you."

"Are you really?"

"You have a way of provoking honesty," he said with some difficulty. "I'll say what I know you're thinking: I'm afraid of any close human relationship. I'm afraid of something I can't take apart with a screwdriver or a mass spectroscope or a table of cosines and tangents." His voice was jocular but his hands were shaking.

"You do it by watering one side," she said softly, "or by turning it just so in the sun. You handle it as if it were a living thing, like a species or a woman or a bonsai. It will be what you want it to be if you let it be itself and take the time and the care."

"I think," he said, "that you are making me some kind of offer. Why?"

"Sitting there most of the night," she said, "I had a crazy kind of image. Do you think two sick twisted trees ever made bonsai out of one another?"

"What's your name?" he asked her.

1972
30th CONVENTION
LOS ANGELES

Poul Anderson

Let me tell you the kind of guy that Poul is.

Back in 1971, I published a book called *Isaac Asimov's Treasury of Humor* (Houghton Mifflin).* I liked it very much and ever since then I have been planning to do a second book to be called *Isaac Asimov Laughs Again*. I've got part of it done, but like so many of the books I plan, it keeps getting bogged down because other commitments keep getting in the way.

Poul knows, however, that I've been planning it, and keeps sending me pages and pages of jokes he's heard—free of charge, and not a word about giving him any credit. That's the kind of guy he is.

Naturally, I wouldn't dream of hurting Poul's feelings. He wants me to take them free of charge? Okay, I wouldn't spoil that splendid gesture by offering to pay. He wants no credit? Never would I thwart so reasonable a desire.

Except this time. I've told the following joke with considerable success and I heard it from him first. Here it is (in my own words):

An Englishman, a Frenchman, and a Russian are debating the meaning of true happiness.

The Englishman says, "My friends, let me give you the meaning by example. Imagine being astride a tall horse in the early dawn of a crisp fall morning; of galloping over the fields, leaping the brooks and bushes, with hounds baying, and all in full

---

* I suspect that there may be some people in the audience who think I keep mentioning my own books in these introductions and on other such occasions in an attempt at self-promotion. If you really think so little of me, then let me explain. —Yes, I do.

pursuit of the fox. Imagine riding home with the tail, and then sitting in triumph before a roaring fire with a glass of fine whiskey in your hand. *That* is true happiness."

"Bah," says the Frenchman. "That, my friend, if I may say so without offense, is but animal pleasure. If *I* may give you an example, imagine dinner in a cosy restaurant on the left bank, where the finest foods can be washed down with a splendid champagne in the company of a beautiful woman. Then, after dinner is done, you take your companion to your apartment—or hers—and make magnificent love to her all night. *That* is true happiness."

And the Russian laughs throatily and says, "Ah, my friend, that is merely having a good time. Let *me* give you an example. Imagine you have come home from a hard day's work at the tractor factory, and have just seated yourself in your best armchair—the one with the shaky leg. You have placed your little son, Mikhail, on your knee and have opened your copy of *Pravda,* when there is a loud knock at the door. You open the door and three men in ill-fitting brown suits enter, look at you accusingly, and demand, 'Ivan Mikhailovich Federov?' and you answer, 'No, gentlemen, he lives two flights up.' *That* is true happiness."

4

THE QUEEN OF AIR
AND DARKNESS

The last glow of the last sunset would linger almost until mid-winter. But there would be no more day, and the northlands rejoiced. Blossoms opened, flamboyance on firethorn trees, steelflowers rising blue from the brok and rainplant that cloaked all hills, shy whiteness of kiss-me-never down in the dales. Flitteries darted among them on iridescent wings; a crownbuck shook his horns and bugled through warmth and flower odors. Between horizons the sky deepened from purple to sable. Both moons were aloft, nearly full, shining frosty on leaves and molten on waters. The shadows they made were blurred by an aurora, a great blowing curtain of light across half heaven. Behind it the earliest stars had come out.

A boy and a girl sat on Wolund's Barrow just under the dolmen it upbore. Their hair, which streamed halfway down their backs, showed startlingly forth, bleached as it was by summer. Their bodies, still dark from that season, merged with earth and bush and rock; for they wore only garlands. He played on a bone flute and she sang. They had lately become lovers. Their age was about sixteen, but they did not know this, considering themselves Outlings and thus indifferent to time, remembering little or nothing of how they had once dwelt in the lands of men.

His notes piped cold around her voice:

"Cast a spell,
weave it well
of dust and dew
and night and you."

A brook by the grave-mound, carrying moonlight down to a hill-hidden river, answered with its rapids. A flock of hellbats passed black beneath the aurora.

A shape came bounding over Cloudmoor. It had two arms and two legs, but the legs were long and claw-footed and feathers covered it to the end of a tail and broad wings. The face was half-human, dominated by its eyes. Had Ayoch been able to stand wholly erect, he would have reached to the boy's shoulder.

The girl rose. "He carries a burden," she said. Her vision was not meant for twilight like that of a northland creature born, but she had learned how to use every sign her senses gave her. Besides the fact that ordinarily a pook would fly, there was a heaviness to his haste.

"And he comes from the south." Excitement jumped in the boy, sudden as a green flame that went across the constellation Lyrth. He sped down the mound. "Ohoi, Ayoch!" he called. "Me here, Mistherd!"

"And Shadow-of-a-Dream," the girl laughed, following.

The pook halted. He breathed louder than the soughing in the growth around him. A smell of bruised yerba lifted where he stood.

"Well met in winterbirth," he whistled. "You can help me bring this to Carheddin."

He held out what he bore. His eyes were yellow lanterns above. It moved and whimpered.

"Why, a child," Mistherd said.

"Even as you were, my son, even as you were. Ho, ho, what a snatch!" Ayoch boasted. "They were a score in yon camp by Fallowwood, armed, and besides watcher engines they had big ugly dogs aprowl while they slept. I came from above, however, having spied on them till I knew that a handful of dazedust—"

"The poor thing." Shadow-of-a-Dream took the boy and held him to her small breasts. "So full of sleep yet, aren't you, littleboo?" Blindly, he sought a nipple. She smiled through the veil of her hair. "No, I am still too young, and you already too old. But come, when you wake in Carheddin under the mountain you shall feast."

"Yo-ah," said Ayoch very softly. "She is abroad and has heard and seen. She comes." He crouched down, wings folded. After a moment Mistherd knelt, and then Shadow-of-a-Dream, though she did not let go the child.

The Queen's tall form blocked off the moons. For a while she regarded the three and their booty. Hill and moor sounds withdrew from their awareness until it seemed they could hear the northlights hiss.

At last Ayoch whispered, "Have I done well, Starmother?"

"If you stole a babe from a camp full of engines," said the beautiful voice, "then they were folk out of the far south who may not endure it as meekly as yeomen."

"But what can they do, Snowmaker?" the pook asked. "How can they track us?"

Mistherd lifted his head and spoke in pride. "Also, now they too have felt the awe of us."

"And he is a cuddly dear," Shadow-of-a-Dream said. "And we need more like him, do we not, Lady Sky?"

"It had to happen in some twilight," agreed she who stood above. "Take him onward and care for him. By this sign," which she made, "is he claimed for the Dwellers."

Their joy was freed. Ayoch cartwheeled over the ground till he reached a shiverleaf. There he swarmed up the trunk and out on a limb, perched half-hidden by unrestful pale foliage, and crowed. Boy and girl bore the child toward Carheddin at an easy distance-devouring lope which let him pipe and her sing:

"Wahaii, wahaii

Wayala, laii!

Wing on the wind

high over heaven,

shrilly shrieking,

rush with the rainspears,

tumble through tumult,

drift to the moonhoar trees and the dream-heavy shadows beneath them,

and rock in, be one with the clinking wavelets of lakes where the starbeams drown."

As she entered, Barbro Cullen felt, through all grief and fury, stabbed by dismay. The room was unkempt. Journals, tapes, reels, codices, file boxes, bescribbled papers were piled on every

table. Dust filmed most shelves and corners. Against one wall
stood a laboratory setup, microscope and analytical equipment.
She recognized it as compact and efficient, but it was not what
you would expect in an office, and it gave the air a faint chemical reek. The rug was threadbare, the furniture shabby.

This was her final chance?

Then Eric Sherrinford approached. "Good day, Mrs. Cullen,"
he said. His tone was crisp, his handclasp firm. His faded
gripsuit didn't bother her. She wasn't inclined to fuss about her
own appearance except on special occasions. (And would she
ever again have one, unless she got back Jimmy?) What she observed was a cat's personal neatness.

A smile radiated in crow's feet from his eyes. "Forgive my
bachelor housekeeping. On Beowulf we have—we had, at any
rate, machines for that, so I never acquired the habit myself, and
I don't want a hireling disarranging my tools. More convenient
to work out of my apartment than keep a separate office. Won't
you be seated?"

"No, thanks. I couldn't," she mumbled.

"I understand. But if you'll excuse me, I function best in a
relaxed position."

He jackknifed into a lounger. One long shank crossed the
other knee. He drew forth a pipe and stuffed it from a pouch.
Barbro wondered why he took tobacco in so ancient a way.
Wasn't Beowulf supposed to have the up-to-date equipment that
they still couldn't afford to build on Roland? Well, of course old
customs might survive anyhow. They generally did in colonies,
she remembered reading. People had moved starward in the
hope of preserving such outmoded things as their mother
tongues or constitutional government or rational-technological
civilization . . .

Sherrinford pulled her up from the confusion of her weariness:
"You must give me the details of your case, Mrs. Cullen. You've
simply told me that your son was kidnapped and your local constabulary did nothing. Otherwise I know just a few obvious
facts, such as your being widowed rather than divorced; and
you're the daughter of outwayers in Olga Ivanoff Land who,
nevertheless, kept in close telecommunication with Christmas
Landing; and you're trained in one of the biological professions;

and you had several years' hiatus in field work until recently you started again."

She gaped at the high-cheeked, beak-nosed, black-haired and gray-eyed countenance. His lighter made a *scrit* and a flare which seemed to fill the room. Quietness dwelt on this height above the city, and winter dusk was seeping in through the windows. "How in cosmos do you know that?" she heard herself exclaim.

He shrugged and fell into the lecturer's manner for which he was notorious. "My work depends on noticing details and fitting them together. In more than a hundred years on Roland, tending to cluster according to their origins and thought-habits, people have developed regional accents. You have a trace of the Olgan burr, but you nasalize your vowels in the style of this area, though you live in Portolondon. That suggests steady childhood exposure to metropolitan speech. You were part of Matsuyama's expedition, you told me, and took your boy along. They wouldn't have allowed any ordinary technician to do that; hence you had to be valuable enough to get away with it; the team was conducting ecological research; therefore you must be in the life sciences. For the same reason, you must have had previous field experience. But your skin is fair, showing none of the leatheriness one gets from prolonged exposure to this sun. Accordingly, you must have been mostly indoors for a good while before you went on your ill-fated trip. As for widowhood—you never mentioned a husband to me, but you have had a man whom you thought so highly of that you still wear both the wedding and the engagement ring he gave you."

Her sight blurred and stung. The last of those words had brought Tim back, huge, ruddy, laughterful and gentle. She must turn from this other person and stare outward. "Yes," she achieved saying, "you're right."

The apartment occupied a hilltop above Christmas Landing. Beneath it the city dropped away in walls, roofs, archaistic chimneys and lamplit streets, goblin lights of human-piloted vehicles, to the harbor, the sweep of Venture Bay, ships bound to and from the Sunward Islands and remoter regions of the Boreal Ocean, which glimmered like mercury in the afterglow of Charlemagne. Oliver was swinging rapidly higher, a mottled orange disc a full degree wide; closer to the zenith which it could never reach, it would shine the color of ice. Alde, half the seeming size, was a thin slow crescent near Sirius, which she remembered was near Sol, but you couldn't see Sol without a telescope—

"Yes," she said around the pain in her throat, "my husband is about four years dead. I was carrying our first child when he was killed by a stampeding monocerus. We'd been married three years before. Met while we were both at the University—'casts from School Centra can only supply a basic education, you know —we founded our own team to do ecological studies under contract—you know, can a certain area be settled while maintaining a balance of nature, what crops will grow, what hazards, that sort of question—Well, afterward I did lab work for a fisher co-op in Portolondon. But the monotony, the . . . shut-in-ness . . . was eating me away. Professor Matsuyama offered me a position on the team he was organizing to examine Commissioner Hauch Land. I thought, God help me, I thought Jimmy—Tim wanted him named James, once the tests showed it'd be a boy, after his own father and because of 'Timmy and Jimmy' and—Oh, I thought Jimmy could safely come along. I couldn't bear to leave him behind for months, not at his age. We could make sure he'd never wander out of camp. What could hurt him inside it? *I* had never believed those stories about the Outlings stealing human children. I supposed parents were trying to hide from themselves the fact they'd been careless, they'd let a kid get lost in the woods or attacked by a pack of satans or— Well, I learned better, Mr. Sherrinford. The guard robots were evaded and the dogs were drugged and when I woke, Jimmy was gone."

He regarded her through the smoke from his pipe. Barbro Engdahl Cullen was a big woman of thirty or so (Rolandic years, he reminded himself, ninety-five percent of Terrestrial, not the same as Beowulfan years), broad-shouldered, long-legged, full-breasted, supple of stride; her face was wide, straight nose, straightforward hazel eyes, heavy but mobile mouth; her hair was reddish-brown, cropped below the ears, her voice husky, her garment a plain street robe. To still the writhing of her fingers, he asked skeptically, "Do you now believe in the Outlings?"

"No. I'm just not so sure as I was." She swung about with half a glare for him. "And we have found traces."

"Bits of fossils," he nodded. "A few artifacts of a neolithic sort. But apparently ancient, as if the makers died ages ago. Intensive search has failed to turn up any real evidence for their survival."

"How intensive can search be, in a summer-stormy, winter-gloomy wilderness around the North Pole?" she demanded. "When we are, how many, a million people on an entire planet, half of us crowded into this one city?"

"And the rest crowding this one habitable continent," he pointed out.

"Arctica covers five million square kilometers," she flung back. "The Arctic Zone proper covers a fourth of it. We haven't the industrial base to establish satellite monitor stations, build aircraft we can trust in those parts, drive roads through the damned darklands and establish permanent bases and get to know them and tame them. Good Christ, generations of lonely outwayment told stories about Greymantle, and the beast was never seen by a proper scientist till last year!"

"Still, you continue to doubt the reality of the Outlings?"

"Well, what about a secret cult among humans, born of isolation and ignorance, lairing in the wilderness, stealing children when they can for—" She swallowed. Her head drooped. "But you're supposed to be the expert."

"From what you told me over the visiphone, the Portolondon constabulary questions the accuracy of the report your group made, thinks the lot of you were hysterical, claims you must have omitted a due precaution and the child toddled away and was lost beyond your finding."

His dry words pried the horror out of her. Flushing, she snapped: "Like any settler's kid? No. I didn't simply yell. I consulted Data Retrieval. A few too many such cases are recorded for accident to be a very plausible explanation. And shall we totally ignore the frightened stories about reappearances? But when I went back to the constabulary with my facts, they brushed me off. I suspect that was not entirely because they're undermanned. I think they're afraid too. They're recruited from country boys; and Portolondon lies near the edge of the unknown."

Her energy faded. "Roland hasn't got any central police force," she finished drably. "You're my last hope."

The man puffed smoke into twilight, with which it blent, before he said in a kindlier voice than hitherto: "Please don't make it a high hope, Mrs. Cullen. I'm the solitary private investigator on this world, having no resources beyond myself, and a newcomer to boot."

"How long have you been here?"

"Twelve years. Barely time to get a little familiarity with the relatively civilized coastlands. You settlers of a century or more —what do you, even, know about Arctica's interior?"

Sherrinford sighed. "I'll take the case, charging no more than I must, mainly for the sake of the experience," he said. "But only if you'll be my guide and assistant, however painful it will be for you."

"Of course! I dreaded waiting idle. Why me, though?"

"Hiring someone else as well qualified would be prohibitively expensive, on a pioneer planet where every hand has a thousand urgent tasks to do. Besides, you have motive. And I'll need that. I, who was born on another world altogether strange to this one, itself altogether strange to Mother Earth, I am too dauntingly aware of how handicapped we are."

Night gathered upon Christmas Landing. The air stayed mild, but glimmer-lit tendrils of fog, sneaking through the streets, had a cold look, and colder yet was the aurora where it shuddered between the moons. The woman drew closer to the man in this darkening room, surely not aware that she did, until he switched on a fluoropanel. The same knowledge of Roland's aloneness was in both of them.

One light-year is not much as galactic distances go. You could walk it in about 270 million years, beginning at the middle of the Permian Era, when dinosaurs belonged to the remote future, and continuing to the present day when spaceships cross even greater reaches. But stars in our neighborhood average some nine light-years apart; and barely one percent of them have planets which are man-habitable; and speeds are limited to less than that of radiation. Scant help is given by relativistic time contraction and suspended animation en route. These make the journeys seem short; but history meanwhile does not stop at home.

Thus voyages from sun to sun will always be few. Colonists

will be those who have extremely special reasons for going. They will take along germ plasm for exogenetic cultivation of domestic plants and animals—and of human infants, in order that population can grow fast enough to escape death through genetic drift. After all, they cannot rely on further immigration. Two or three times a century, a ship may call from some other colony. (Not from Earth. Earth has long ago sunk into alien concerns.) Its place of origin will be an old settlement. The young ones are in no position to build and man interstellar vessels.

Their very survival, let alone their eventual modernization, is in doubt. The founding fathers have had to take what they could get, in a universe not especially designed for man.

Consider, for example, Roland. It is among the rare happy finds, a world where humans can live, breathe, eat the food, drink the water, walk unclad if they choose, sow their crops, pasture their beasts, dig their mines, erect their homes, raise their children and grandchildren. It is worth crossing three quarters of a light-century to preserve certain dear values and strike new roots into the soil of Roland.

But the star Charlemagne is of type F9, forty percent brighter than Sol, brighter still in the treacherous ultraviolet and wilder still in the wind of charged particles that seethes from it. The planet has an eccentric orbit. In the middle of the short but furious northern summer, which includes periastron, total insolation is more than double what Earth gets; in the depth of the long northern winter, it is barely less than Terrestrial average.

Native life is abundant everywhere. But lacking elaborate machinery, not economically possible to construct for more than a few specialists, man can only endure the high latitudes. A ten-degree axial tilt, together with the orbit, means that the northern part of the Arctican continent spends half its year in unbroken sunlessness. Around the South Pole lies an empty ocean.

Other differences from Earth might superficially seem more important. Roland has two moons, small but close, to evoke clashing tides. It rotates once in thirty-two hours, which is endlessly, subtly disturbing to organisms evolved through gigayears of a quicker rhythm. The weather patterns are altogether unterrestrial. The globe is a mere 9,500 kilometers in diameter; its surface gravity is 0.42×980 cm/sec^2; the sea level air pressure is slightly above one Earth atmosphere. (For actually Earth is the freak, and man exists because a cosmic accident blew away most of the gas that a body its size ought to have kept, as Venus has done.)

However, Homo can truly be called Sapiens when he practices his specialty of being unspecialized. His repeated attempts to freeze himself into an all-answering pattern or culture or ideology or whatever he has named it, have repeatedly brought ruin. Give him the pragmatic business of making his living and he will usually do rather well. He adapts, within broad limits.

These limits are set by such factors as his need for sunlight and his being, necessarily and forever, a part of the life that surrounds him and a creature of the spirit within.

Portolondon thrust docks, boats, machinery, warehouses into the Gulf of Polaris. Behind them huddled the dwellings of its five thousand permanent inhabitants; concrete walls, storm shutters, high-peaked tile roofs. The gaiety of their paint looked forlorn amidst lamps; this town lay past the Arctic Circle.

Nevertheless Sherrinford remarked, "Cheerful place, eh? The kind of thing I came to Roland looking for."

Barbro made no reply. The days in Christmas Landing, while he made his preparations, had drained her. Gazing out the dome of the taxi that was whirring them downtown from the hydrofoil that brought them, she supposed he meant the lushness of forest and meadows along the road, brilliant hues and phosphorescence of flowers in gardens, clamor of wings overhead. Unlike Terrestrial flora in cold climates, Arctican vegetation spends every daylit hour in frantic growth and energy storage. Not till summer's fever gives place to gentle winter does it bloom and fruit; and estivating animals rise from their dens and migratory birds come home.

The view was lovely, she had to admit: beyond the trees, a spaciousness climbing toward remote heights, silvery-gray under a moon, an aurora, the diffuse radiance from a sun just below the horizon.

Beautiful as a hunting satan, she thought, and as terrible. That wilderness had stolen Jimmy. She wondered if she would at least be given to find his little bones and take them to his father.

Abruptly she realized that she and Sherrinford were at their hotel and that he had been speaking of the town. Since it was next in size after the capital, he must have visited here often before. The streets were crowded and noisy; signs flickered, music blared from shops, taverns, restaurants, sports centers, dance halls; vehicles were jammed down to molasses speed; the several-stories-high office buildings stood aglow. Portolondon linked an enormous hinterland to the outside world. Down the Gloria River came timber rafts, ores, harvest of farms whose owners were slowly making Rolandic life serve them, meat and ivory and furs gathered by rangers in the mountains beyond Troll Scarp. In from the sea came coastwise freighters, the fishing fleet, produce of the Sunward Islands, plunder of whole continents farther south where bold men adventured. It clanged in Portolondon, laughed, blustered, swaggered, connived, robbed, preached, guzzled, swilled, toiled, dreamed, lusted, built, destroyed, died, was born, was happy, angry, sorrowful, greedy, vulgar, loving, ambitious, human. Neither the sun's blaze elsewhere nor the half-year's twilight here—wholly night around midwinter—was going to stay man's hand.

Or so everybody said.

Everybody except those who had settled in the darklands. Barbro used to take for granted that they were evolving curious customs, legends, and superstitions, which would die when the outway had been completely mapped and controlled. Of late, she had wondered. Perhaps Sherrinford's hints, about a change in his own attitude brought about by his preliminary research, were responsible.

Or perhaps she just needed something to think about besides how Jimmy, the day before he went, when she asked him whether he wanted rye or French bread for a sandwich, answered in great solemnity—he was becoming interested in the alphabet—"I'll have a slice of what we people call the F bread."

She scarcely noticed getting out of the taxi, registering, being conducted to a primitively furnished room. But after she unpacked she remembered Sherrinford had suggested a confidential conference. She went down the hall and knocked on his door. Her knuckles sounded less loud than her heart.

He opened the door, finger on lips, and gestured her toward a corner. Her temper bristled until she saw the image of Chief Constable Dawson in the visiphone. Sherrinford must have chimed him up and must have a reason to keep her out of scanner range. She found a chair and watched, nails digging into knees.

The detective's lean length refolded itself. "Pardon the interruption," he said. "A man mistook the number. Drunk, by the indications."

Dawson chuckled. "We get plenty of those." Barbro recalled his fondness for gabbing. He tugged the beard which he affected, as if he were an outwayer instead of a townsman. "No harm in them as a rule. They only have a lot of voltage to discharge, after weeks or months in the backlands."

"I've gathered that that environment—foreign in a million major and minor ways to the one that created man—I've gathered that it does do odd things to the personality." Sherrinford tamped his pipe. "Of course, you know my practice has been confined to urban and suburban areas. Isolated garths seldom need private investigators. Now that situation appears to have changed. I called to ask you for advice."

"Glad to help," Dawson said. "I've not forgotten what you did for us in the de Tahoe murder case." Cautiously: "Better explain your problem first."

Sherrinford struck fire. The smoke that followed cut through the green odors—even here, a paved pair of kilometers from the nearest woods—that drifted past traffic rumble through a crepuscular window. "This is more a scientific mission than a search for an absconding debtor or an industrial spy," he drawled. "I'm looking into two possibilities: that an organization, criminal or religious or whatever, has long been active and steals infants; or that the Outlings of folklore are real."

"Huh?" On Dawson's face Barbro read as much dismay as surprise. "You can't be serious!"

"Can't I?" Sherrinford smiled. "Several generations' worth of reports shouldn't be dismissed out of hand. Especially not when they become more frequent and consistent in the course of time, not less. Nor can we ignore the documented loss of babies and small children, amounting by now to over a hundred, and never a trace found afterward. Nor the finds which demonstrate that an intelligent species one inhabited Arctica and may still haunt the interior."

Dawson leaned forward as if to climb out of the screen. "Who engaged you?" he demanded. "That Cullen woman? We were sorry for her, naturally, but she wasn't making sense and when she got downright abusive—"

"Didn't her companions, reputable scientists, confirm her story?"

"No story to confirm. Look, they had the place ringed with detectors and alarms, and they kept mastiffs. Standard procedure in a country where a hungry sauroid or whatever might happen by. Nothing could've entered unbeknownst."

"On the ground. How about a flyer landing in the middle of camp?"

"A man in a copter rig would've roused everybody."

"A winged being might be quieter."

"A living flyer that could lift a three-year-old boy? Doesn't exist."

"Isn't in the scientific literature, you mean, Constable. Remember Graymantle; remember how little we know about Roland, a planet, and entire world. Such birds do exist on Beowulf —and on Rustum, I've read. I made a calculation from the local ratio of air density to gravity and, yes, it's marginally possible here too. The child could have been carried off for a short distance before wing muscles were exhausted and the creature must descend."

Dawson snorted. "First it landed and walked into the tent where mother and boy were asleep. Then it walked away, toting him, after it couldn't fly further. Does that sound like a bird of prey? And the victim didn't cry out, the dogs didn't bark, nothing!"

"As a matter of fact," Sherrinford said, "those inconsistencies are the most interesting and convincing feature of the whole account. You're right, it's hard to see how a human kidnapper could get in undetected, and an eagle type of creature wouldn't operate in that fashion. But none of this applies to a winged intelligent being. The boy could have been drugged. Certainly the dogs showed signs of having been."

"The dogs showed signs of having overslept. Nothing had dis-

turbed them. The kid wandering by wouldn't do so. We don't
need to assume one damn thing except, first, that he got restless
and, second, that the alarms were a bit sloppily rigged—seeing
as how no danger was expected from inside camp—and let him
pass out. And, third, I hate to speak this way, but we must assume the poor tyke starved or was killed."

Dawson paused before adding: "If we had more staff, we
could have given the affair more time. And would have, of
course. We did make an aerial sweep, which risked the lives of
the pilots, using instruments which would've spotted the kid anywhere in a fifty-kilometer radius, unless he was dead. You know
how sensitive thermal analyzers are. We drew complete blank.
We have more important jobs than to hunt for the scattered
pieces of a corpse."

He finished brusquely, "If Mrs. Cullen's hired you, my advice
is you find an excuse to quit. Better for her, too. She's got to
come to terms with reality."

Barbro checked a shout by biting her tongue.

"Oh, this is merely the latest disappearance of the series,"
Sherrinford said. She didn't understand how he could maintain
his easy tone when Jimmy was lost. "More thoroughly recorded
than any before, thus more suggestive. Usually an outwayer family has given a tearful but undetailed account of their child who
vanished and must have been stolen by the Old Folk. Sometimes,
years later, they'd tell about glimpses of what they swore must
have been the grown child, not really human any longer, flitting
past in murk or peering through a window or working mischief
upon them. As you say, neither the authorities nor the scientists
have had personnel or resources to mount a proper investigation.
But as I say, the matter appears to be worth investigating.
Maybe a private party like myself can contribute."

"Listen, most of us constables grew up in the outway. We
don't just ride patrol and answer emergency calls, we go back
there for holidays and reunions. If any gang of . . . of human
sacrificers was around, we'd know."

"I realize that. I also realize that the people you came from
have a widespread and deep-seated belief in nonhuman beings
with supernatural powers. Many actually go through rites and
make offerings to propitiate them."

"I know what you're leading up to," Dawson fleered. "I've heard it before, from a hundred sensationalists. The aborigines are the Outlings. I thought better of you. Surely you've visited a museum or three, surely you've read literature from planets which do have natives—or damn and blast, haven't you ever applied that logic of yours?"

He wagged a finger. "Think," he said. "What have we in fact discovered? A few pieces of worked stone; a few megaliths that might be artificial; scratchings on rock that seem to show plants and animals, though not the way any human culture would ever have shown them; traces of fires and broken bones; other fragments of bone that seem as if they might've belonged to thinking creatures, as if they might've been inside fingers or around big brains. If so, however, the owners looked nothing like men. Or angels, for that matter. Nothing! The most anthropoid reconstruction I've seen shows a kind of a two-legged crocagator.

"Wait, let me finish. The stories about the Outlings—oh, I've heard them too, plenty of them; I believed them when I was a kid—the stories tell how there're different kinds, some winged, some not, some half-human, some completely human except maybe for being too handsome—it's fairyland from ancient Earth all over again. Isn't it? I got interested once and dug into the Heritage Library microfiles, and be damned if I didn't find almost the identical yarns, told by peasants centuries before spaceflight.

"None of it squares with the scanty relics we have, if they are relics, or with the fact that no area the size of Arctica could spawn a dozen different intelligent species, or . . . hellfire, man, with the way your common sense tells you aborigines would behave when humans arrived!"

Sherrinford nodded. "Yes, yes," he said. "I'm less sure than you that the common sense of nonhuman beings is precisely like our own. I've seen so much variation within mankind. But, granted, your arguments are strong. Roland's too few scientists have more pressing tasks than tracking down the origins of what is, as you put it, a revived medieval superstition."

He cradled his pipe bowl in both hands and peered into the tiny hearth of it. "Perhaps what interests me most," he said softly, "is why—across that gap of centuries, across a barrier of machine civilization and its utterly antagonistic world-view—no continuity of tradition whatsoever—why have hardheaded, technologically organized, reasonably well-educated colonists here brought back from its grave a belief in the Old Folk?"

"I suppose eventually, if the University ever does develop the psychology department they keep talking about, I suppose eventually somebody will get a thesis out of that question." Dawson spoke in a jagged voice, and he gulped when Sherrinford replied:

"I propose to begin now. In Commissioner Hauch Land, since that's where the latest incident occurred. Where can I rent a vehicle?"

"Uh, might be hard to do—"

"Come, come. Tenderfoot or not, I know better. In an economy of scarcity, few people own heavy equipment. But since it's needed, it can always be rented. I want a camper bus with a ground-effect drive suitable for every kind of terrain. And I want certain equipment installed which I've brought along, and the top canopy section replaced by a gun turret controllable from the driver's seat. But I'll supply the weapons. Besides rifles and pistols of my own, I've arranged to borrow some artillery from Christmas Landing's police arsenal."

"Hoy? Are you genuinely intending to make ready for . . . a war . . . against a myth?"

"Let's say I'm taking out insurance, which isn't terribly expensive, against a remote possibility. Now, besides the bus, what about a light aircraft carried piggyback for use in surveys?"

"No." Dawson sounded more positive than hitherto. "That's asking for disaster. We can have you flown to a base camp in a large plane when the weather report's exactly right. But the pilot will have to fly back at once, before the weather turns wrong again. Meteorology's underdeveloped on Roland, the air's especially treacherous this time of year, and we're not tooled up to produce aircraft that can outlive every surprise." He drew breath. "Have you no idea of how fast a whirly-whirly can hit, or what size hailstones might strike from a clear sky, or—? Once you're there, man, you stick to the ground." He hesitated. "That's an important reason our information is so scanty about the outway and its settlers are so isolated."

Sherrinford laughed ruefully. "Well, I suppose if details are what I'm after, I must creep along anyway."

"You'll waste a lot of time," Dawson said. "Not to mention your client's money. Listen, I can't forbid you to chase shadows, but—"

The discussion went on for almost an hour. When the screen finally blanked, Sherrinford rose, stretched, and walked toward Barbro. She noticed anew his peculiar gait. He had come from a planet with a fourth again Earth's gravitational drag, to one where weight was less than half Terrestrial. She wondered if he had flying dreams.

"I apologize for shuffling you off like that," he said. "I didn't expect to reach him at once. He was quite truthful about how busy he is. But having made contact, I didn't want to remind him overmuch of you. He can dismiss my project as a futile fantasy which I'll soon give up. But he might have frozen completely, might even have put up obstacles before us, if he'd realized through you how determined we are."

"Why should he care?" she asked in her bitterness.

"Fear of consequences, the worse because it is unadmitted—fear of consequences, the more terrifying because they are unguessable." Sherrinford's gaze went to the screen, and thence out the window to the aurora pulsing in glacial blue and white immensely far overhead. "I suppose you saw I was talking to a frightened man. Down underneath his conventionality and scoffing, he believes in the Outlings—oh, yes, he believes."

The feet of Mistherd flew over yerba and outpaced windblown driftweed. Beside him, black and misshapen, hulked Nagrim the nicor, whose earthquake weight left a swathe of crushed plants. Behind, luminous blossoms of a firethorn shone through the twining, trailing outlines of Morgarel the wraith.

Here Cloudmoor rose in a surf of hills and thickets. The air lay quiet, now and then carrying the distance-muted howl of a beast. It was darker than usual at winterbirth, the moons being down and aurora a wan flicker above mountains on the northern worldedge. But this made the stars keen, and their numbers crowded heaven, and Ghost Road shone among them as if it, like the leafage beneath, were paved with dew.

"Yonder!" bawled Nagrim. All four of his arms pointed. The party had topped a ridge. Far off glimmered a spark. "Hoah, hoah! 'Ull we right off stamp dem flat, or pluck dem apart slow?"

We shall do nothing of the sort, bonebrain, Morgarel's answer slid through their heads. *Not unless they attack us, and they will not unless we make them aware of us, and her command is that we spy out their purposes.*

"Gr-r-rum-m-m. I know deir aim. Out down trees, stick plows in land, sow deir cursed seed in de clods and in deir shes. 'Less we drive dem into de bitterwater, and soon, soon, dey'll wax too strong for us."

"Not too strong for the Queen!" Mistherd protested, shocked.

Yet they do have new powers, it seems, Morgarel reminded him. *Carefully must we probe them.*

"Den carefully can we step on dem?" asked Nagrim.

The question woke a grin out of Mistherd's own uneasiness. He slapped the scaly back. "Don't talk, you," he said. "It hurts my ears. Nor think; that hurts your head. Come, run!"

Ease yourself, Morgarel scolded. *You have too much life in you, human-born.*

Mistherd made a face at the wraith, but obeyed to the extent of slowing down and picking his way through what cover the country afforded. For he traveled on behalf of the Fairest, to learn what had brought a pair of mortals guesting hither.

Did they seek that boy whom Ayoch stole? (He continued to weep for his mother, though less and less often as the marvels of Carheddin entered him.) Perhaps. A birdcraft had left them and their car at the now abandoned campsite, from which they had followed an outward spiral. But when no trace of the cub had appeared inside a reasonable distance, they did not call to be flown home. And this wasn't because weather forbade the farspeaker waves to travel, as was frequently the case. No, instead the couple set off toward the mountains of Moonhorn. Their course would take them past a few outlying invader steadings and on into realms untrodden by their race.

So this was no ordinary survey. Then what was it?

Mistherd understood now why she who reigned had made her adopted mortal children learn, or retain, the clumsy language of their forebears. He had hated that drill, wholly foreign to

Dweller ways. Of course, you obeyed her, and in time you saw how wise she had been . . .

Presently he left Nagrim behind a rock—the nicor would only be useful in a fight—and crawled from bush to bush until he lay within man-lengths of the humans. A rainplant drooped over him, leaves soft on his bare skin, and clothed him in darkness. Morgarel floated to the crown of a shiverleaf, whose unrest would better conceal his flimsy shape. He'd not be much help either. And that was the most troublous, the almost appalling thing here. Wraiths were among those who could not just sense and send thoughts, but cast illusions. Morgarel had reported that this time his power seemed to rebound off an invisible cold wall around the car.

Otherwise the male and female had set up no guardian engines and kept no dogs. Belike they supposed none would be needed, since they slept in the long vehicle which bore them. But such contempt of the Queen's strength could not be tolerated, could it?

Metal sheened faintly by the light of their campfire. They sat on either side, wrapped in coats against a coolness that Mistherd, naked, found mild. The male drank smoke. The female stared past him into a dusk which her flame-dazzled eyes must see as thick gloom. The dancing glow brought her vividly forth. Yes, to judge from Ayoch's tale, she was the dam of the new cub.

Ayoch had wanted to come too, but the Wonderful One forbade. Pooks couldn't hold still long enough for such a mission.

The man sucked on his pipe. His cheeks thus pulled into shadow while the light flickered across nose and brow, he looked disquietingly like a shearbill about to stoop on prey.

"—No, I tell you again, Barbro, I have no theories," he was saying. "When facts are insufficient, theorizing is ridiculous at best, misleading at worst."

"Still, you must have some idea of what you're doing," she said. It was plain that they had threshed this out often before. No Dweller could be as persistent as she or as patient as he was. "That gear you packed—that generator you keep running—"

"I have a working hypothesis or two, which suggested what equipment I ought to take."

"Why won't you tell me what the hypotheses are?"

"They themselves indicate that that might be inadvisable at the present time. I'm still feeling my way into the labyrinth. And I haven't had a chance yet to hook everything up. In fact, we're really only protected against so-called telepathic influence—"

"What?" She started. "Do you mean . . . those legends about how they can read minds too . . ." Her words trailed off and her gaze sought the darkness beyond his shoulders.

He leaned forward. His tone lost its clipped rapidity, grew earnest and soft. "Barbro, you're racking yourself to pieces. Which is no help to Jimmy if he's alive, the more so when you may well be badly needed later on. We've a long trek before us, and you'd better settle into it."

She nodded jerkily and caught her lip between her teeth for a moment before she answered, "I'm trying."

He smiled around his pipe. "I expect you'll succeed. You don't strike me as a quitter or a whiner or an enjoyer of misery."

She dropped a hand to the pistol at her belt. Her voice changed; it came out of her throat like knife from sheath. "When we find them, they'll know what I am. What humans are."

"Put anger aside also," the man urged. "We can't afford emotions. If the Outlings are real, as I told you I'm provisionally assuming, they're fighting for their homes." After a short stillness he added: "I like to think that if the first explorers had found live natives, men would not have colonized Roland. But too late now. We can't go back if we wanted to. It's a bitter-end struggle, against an enemy so crafty that he's even hidden from us the fact that he is waging war."

"Is he? I mean, skulking, kidnapping an occasional child—"

"That's part of my hypothesis. I suspect those aren't harassments, they're tactics employed in a chillingly subtle strategy."

The fire sputtered and sparked. The man smoked a while, brooding, until he went on:

"I didn't want to raise your hopes or excite you unduly while you had to wait on me, first in Christmas Landing, then in Portolondon. Afterward we were busy satisfying ourselves Jimmy had been taken farther from camp than he could have wandered before collapsing. So I'm only telling you now how thoroughly I studied available material on the . . . Old Folk. Besides, at first I did it on the principle of eliminating every imaginable possibility, however absurd. I expected no result other than final disproof. But I went through everything, relics, analyses, histories, journalistic accounts, monographs; I talked to outwayers who happened to be in town and to what scientists we have who've taken any interest in the matter. I'm a quick study. I flatter myself I became as expert as anyone—though God knows there's little to be expert on. Furthermore, I, a comparative stranger, maybe looked on the problem with fresh eyes. And a pattern emerged for me.

"If the aborigines became extinct, why didn't they leave more remnants? Arctica isn't enormous; and it's fertile for Rolandic life. It ought to have supported a population whose artifacts ought to have accumulated over millennia. I've read that on Earth literally tens of thousands of paleolithic hand axes were found, more by chance than archaeology.

"Very well. Suppose the relics and fossils were deliberately removed, between the time the last survey party left and the first colonizing ships arrived. I did find some support for that idea in the diaries of the original explorers. They were too preoccupied with checking the habitability of the planet to make catalogues of primitive monuments. However, the remarks they wrote down indicate they saw much more than later arrivals did. Suppose what we have found is just what the removers overlooked or didn't get around to.

"That argues a sophisticated mentality, thinking in long-range terms, doesn't it? Which in turn argues that the Old Folk were not mere hunters or neolithic farmers."

"But nobody ever saw buildings or machines or any such thing?" Barbro protested.

"No. Most likely the natives didn't go through our kind of metallurgic-industrial evolution. I can conceive of other paths to take. Their full-fledged civilization might have begun, rather than ended, in biological science and technology. It might have developed potentialities of the nervous system, which might be greater in their species than in man. We have those abilities to some degree ourselves, you realize. A dowser, for instance, actually senses variations in the local magnetic field caused by a water table. However, in us, these talents are maddeningly rare and tricky. So we took our business elsewhere. Who needs to be a telepath, say, when he has a visiphone? The Old Folk may have seen it the other way around. The artifacts of their civilization may have been, may still be unrecognizable to men."

"They could have identified themselves to the men, though," Barbro said. "Why didn't they?"

"I can imagine any number of reasons. As, they could have had a bad experience with interstellar visitors earlier in their history. Ours is scarcely the sole race that has spaceships. However, I told you I don't theorize in advance of the facts. Let's say no more than that the Old Folk, if they exist, are alien to us."

"For a rigorous thinker, you're spinning a mighty thin thread."

"I've admitted this is entirely provisional." He squinted at her through a roil of campfire smoke. "You came to me, Barbro, insisting in the teeth of officialdom your boy had been stolen; but your own talk about cultist kidnappers was ridiculous. Why are you reluctant to admit the reality of nonhumans?"

"In spite of the fact that Jimmy's being alive probably depends on it," she sighed. "I know." A shudder: "Maybe I don't dare admit it."

"I've said nothing thus far that hasn't been speculated about in print," he told her. "A disreputable speculation, true. In a hundred years, nobody has found valid evidence for the Outlings being more than a superstition. Still, a few people have declared it's at least possible intelligent natives are at large in the wilderness."

"I know," she repeated. "I'm not sure, though, what has made you, overnight, take those arguments seriously."

"Well, once you got me started thinking, it occurred to me that Roland's outwayers are not utterly isolated medieval crofters. They have books, telecommunications, power tools, motor vehicles, above all they have a modern science-oriented education. Why *should* they turn superstitious? Something must be causing it." He stopped. "I'd better not continue. My ideas go further than this; but if they're correct, it's dangerous to speak them aloud."

Mistherd's belly muscles tensed. There was danger for fair, in that shearbill head. The Garland Bearer must be warned. For a minute he wondered about summoning Nagrim to kill these two. If the nicor jumped them fast, their firearms might avail them naught. But no. They might have left word at home, or— He came back to his ears. The talk had changed course. Barbro was murmuring, "—why you stayed on Roland."

The man smiled his gaunt smile. "Well, life on Beowulf held no challenge for me. Heorot is—or was; this was decades past, remember—Heorot was densely populated, smoothly organized, boringly uniform. That was partly due to the lowland frontier, a safety valve that bled off the dissatisfied. But I lack the carbon dioxide tolerance necessary to live healthily down there. An expedition was being readied to make a swing around a number of colony worlds, especially those which didn't have the equipment to keep in laser contact. You'll recall its announced purpose, to seek out new ideas in science, arts, sociology, philosophy, whatever might prove valuable. I'm afraid they found little on Roland relevant to Beowulf. But I, who had wangled a berth, I saw opportunities for myself and decided to make my home here."

"Were you a detective back there, too?"

"Yes, in the official police. We had a tradition of such work in our family. Some of that may have come from the Cherokee side of it, if the name means anything to you. However, we also claimed collateral descent from one of the first private inquiry agents on record, back on Earth before spaceflight. Regardless of how true that may be, I found him a useful model. You see, an archetype—"

The man broke off. Unease crossed his features. "Best we go to sleep," he said. "We've a long distance to cover in the morning."

She looked outward. "Here is no morning."

They retired. Mistherd rose and cautiously flexed limberness back into his muscles. Before returning to the Sister of Lyrth, he risked a glance through a pane in the car. Bunks were made up, side by side, and the humans lay in them. Yet the man had not touched her, though hers was a bonny body, and nothing that had passed between them suggested he meant to do so.

Eldritch, humans. Cold and claylike. And they would overrun the beautiful wild world? Mistherd spat in disgust. It must not happen. It would not happen. She who reigned had vowed that.

The lands of William Irons were immense. But this was because a barony was required to support him, his kin and cattle, on native crops whose cultivation was still poorly understood. He raised some Terrestrial plants as well, by summerlight and in conservatories. However, these were a luxury. The true conquest of northern Arctica lay in yerba hay, in bathyrhiza wood, in pericoup and glycophyllon and eventually, when the market had expanded with population and industry, in chalcanthemum for city florists and pelts of cage-bred rover for city furriers.

That was in a tomorrow Irons did not expect he would live to see. Sherrinford wondered if the man really expected anyone ever would.

The room was warm and bright. Cheerfulness crackled in the fireplace. Light from fluoropanels gleamed off handcarven chests and chairs and tables, off colorful draperies and shelved dishes. The outwayer sat solid in his highseat, stoutly clad, beard flowing down his chest. His wife and daughters brought coffee, whose fragrance joined the remnant odors of a hearty supper, to him, his guests, and his sons.

But outside, wind hooted, lightning flared, thunder bawled, rain crashed on roof and walls and roared down to swirl among the courtyard cobblestones. Sheds and barns crouched against hugeness beyond. Trees groaned; and did a wicked undertone of laughter run beneath the lowing of a frightened cow? A burst of hailstones hit the tiles like knocking knuckles.

You could feel how distant your neighbors were, Sherrinford thought. And nonetheless they were the people whom you saw oftenest, did daily business with by visiphone (when a solar storm didn't make gibberish of their voices and chaos of their faces) or in the flesh, partied with, gossiped and intrigued with, intermarried with; in the end, they were the people who would bury you. The lights and machinery of the coastal towns were monstrously farther away.

William Irons was a strong man. Yet when now he spoke, fear was in his tone. "You'd truly go over Troll Scarp?"

"Do you mean Hanstein Palisades?" Sherrinford responded, more challenge than question.

"No outwayer calls it anything but Troll Scarp," Barbro said.

And how had a name like that been reborn, light-years and centuries from Earth's dark ages?

"Hunters, trappers, prospectors—rangers, you call them—travel in those mountains," Sherrinford declared.

"In certain parts," Irons said. "That's allowed, by a pact once made 'tween a man and the Queen after he'd done well by a jack-o'-the-hill that a satan had hurt. Wherever the plumablanca grows, men may fare, if they leave man-goods on the altar boulders in payment for what they take out of the land. Elsewhere"—one fist clenched on a chair arm and went slack again—"'s not wise to go."

"It's been done, hasn't it?"

"Oh, yes. And some came back all right, or so they claimed, though I've heard they were never lucky afterward. And some didn't, they vanished. And some who returned babbled of wonders and horrors, and stayed witlings the rest of their lives. Not for a long time has anybody been rash enough to break the pact and overtread the bounds." Irons looked at Barbro almost entreatingly. His woman and children stared likewise, grown still. Wind hooted beyond the walls and rattled the storm shutters. "Don't you."

"I've reason to believe my son is there," she answered.

"Yes, yes, you've told and I'm sorry. Maybe something can be done. I don't know what, but I'd be glad to, oh, lay a double offering on Unvar's Barrow this midwinter, and a prayer drawn in the turf by a flint knife. Maybe they'll return him." Irons sighed. "They've not done such a thing in man's memory, though. And he could have a worse lot. I've glimpsed them myself, speeding madcap through twilight. They seem happier than we are. Might be no kindness, sending your boy home again."

"Like in the Arvid song," said his wife.

Irons nodded. "M-hm. Or others, come to think of it."

"What's this?" Sherrinford asked. More sharply than before, he felt himself a stranger. He was a child of cities and technics, above all a child of the skeptical intelligence. This family *believed*. It was disquieting to see more than a touch of their acceptance in Barbro's slow nod.

"We have the same ballad in Olga Ivanoff Land," she told him, her voice less calm than the words. "It's one of the traditional ones, nobody knows who composed them, that are sung to set the measure of a ring-dance in a meadow."

"I noticed a multilyre in your baggage, Mrs. Cullen," said the wife of Irons. She was obviously eager to get off the explosive topic of a venture in defiance of the Old Folk. A songfest could help. "Would you like to entertain us?"

Barbro shook her head, white around the nostrils. The oldest boy said quickly, rather importantly, "Well, sure, I can, if our guests would like to hear."

"I'd enjoy that, thank you." Sherrinford leaned back in his seat and stroked his pipe. If this had not happened spontaneously, he would have guided the conversation toward a similiar outcome.

In the past he had had no incentive to study the folklore of the outway, and not much chance to read the scanty references on it since Barbro brought him her trouble. Yet more and more he was becoming convinced he must get an understanding—not an anthropological study; a feel from the inside out—of the relationship between Roland's frontiersmen and those beings which haunted them.

A bustling followed, rearrangement, settling down to listen, coffee cups refilled and brandy offered on the side. The boy explained, "The last line is the chorus. Everybody join in, right?" Clearly he too hoped thus to bleed off some of the tension. Catharsis through music? Sherrinford wondered, and added to himself: No, exorcism.

A girl strummed a guitar. The boy sang, to a melody which beat across the storm-noise:

> "It was the ranger Arvid
> rode homeward through the hills
> among the shadowy shiverleafs,
> along the chiming hills.
> 　　　The dance weaves under the firethorn.

> "The night wind whispered around him
> with scent of brok and rue.
> Both moons rose high above him
> and hills aflash with dew.
> 　　　The dance weaves under the firethorn.

> "And dreaming of that woman
> who waited in the sun,

> he stopped, amazed by starlight,
> and so he was undone.
> > The dance weaves under the firethorn.

"For there beneath a barrow
> that bulked athwart a moon,
> the Outling folk were dancing
> in glass and golden shoon.
> > The dance weaves under the firethorn.

"The Outling folk were dancing
> like water, wind, and fire
> to frosty-ringing harpstrings,
> and never did they tire.
> > The dance weaves under the firethorn.

"To Arvid came she striding
> from where she watched the dance,
> the Queen of Air and Darkness,
> with starlight in her glance.
> > The dance weaves under the firethorn.

"With starlight, love, and terror
> in her immortal eye,
> the Queen of Air and Darkness—"

"No!" Barbro leaped from her chair. Her fists were clenched
and tears flogged her cheekbones. "You can't—pretend that—
about the things that stole Jimmy!"

She fled from the chamber, upstairs to her guest bedroom.

But she finished the song herself. That was about seventy
hours later, camped in the steeps where rangers dared not fare.

She and Sherrinford had not said much to the Irons family
after refusing repeated pleas to leave the forbidden country
alone. Nor had they exchanged many remarks at first as they
drove north. Slowly, however, he began to draw her out about
her own life. After a while she almost forgot to mourn, in her
remembering of home and old neighbors. Somehow this led to
discoveries—that he beneath his professorial manner was a gour-
met and a lover of opera and appreciated her femaleness; that

she could still laugh and find beauty in the wild land around her —and she realized, half guiltily, that life held more hopes than even the recovery of the son Tim gave her.

"I've convinced myself he's alive," the detective said. He scowled. "Frankly, it makes me regret having taken you along. I expected this would be only a fact-gathering trip, but it's turning out to be more. If we're dealing with real creatures who stole him, they can do real harm. I ought to turn back to the nearest garth and call for a plane to fetch you."

"Like bottommost hell you will, mister," she said. "You need somebody who knows outway conditions; and I'm a better shot than average."

"M-m-m . . . it would involve considerable delay too, wouldn't it? Besides the added distance, I can't put a signal through to any airport before this current burst of solar interference has calmed down."

Next "night" he broke out his remaining equipment and set it up. She recognized some of it, such as the thermal detector. Other items were strange to her, copied to his order from the advanced apparatus of his birthworld. He would tell her little about them. "I've explained my suspicion that the ones we're after have telepathic capabilities," he said in apology.

Her eyes widened. "You mean it could be true, the Queen and her people can read minds?"

"That's part of the dread which surrounds their legend, isn't it? Actually there's nothing spooky about the phenomenon. It was studied and fairly well defined centuries ago, on Earth. I daresay the facts are available in the scientific microfiles and Christmas Landing. You Rolanders have simply had no occasion to seek them out, any more than you've yet had occasion to look up how to build power beamcasters or spacecraft."

"Well, how does telepathy work, then?"

Sherrinford recognized that her query asked for comfort as much as it did for facts, and spoke with deliberate dryness: "The organism generates extremely long-wave radiation which can, in principle, be modulated by the nervous system. In practice, the feebleness of the signals and their low rate of information transmission make them elusive, hard to detect and measure. Our prehuman ancestors went in for more reliable senses, like vision and hearing. What telepathic transceiving we do is marginal at best. But explorers have found extraterrestrial species that got an evolutionary advantage from developing the system further, in their particular environments. I imagine such species could include one which gets comparatively little direct sunlight—in fact, appears to hide from broad day. It could even become so able in this regard that, at short range, it can pick up man's weak emissions and make man's primitive sensitivities resonate to its own strong sendings."

"That would account for a lot, wouldn't it?" Barbro asked faintly.

"I've now screened our car by a jamming field," Sherrinford told her, "but it reaches only a few meters past the chassis. Beyond, a scout of theirs might get a warning from your thoughts, if you knew precisely what I'm trying to do. I have a well-trained subconscious which sees to it that I think about this in French when I'm outside. Communication has to be structured to be intelligible, you see, and that's a different enough structure from English. But English is the only human language on Roland, and surely the Old Folk have learned it."

She nodded. He had told her his general plan, which was too obvious to conceal. The problem was to make contact with the aliens, if they existed. Hitherto they had only revealed themselves, at rare intervals, to one or a few backwoodsmen at a time. An ability to generate hallucinations would help them in that. They would stay clear of any large, perhaps unmanageable expedition which might pass through their territory. But two people, braving all prohibitions, shouldn't look too formidable to approach. And . . . this would be the first human team which not only worked on the assumption that the Outlings were real but possessed the resources of modern, off-planet police technology.

Nothing happened at that camp. Sherrinford said he hadn't expected it would. The Old Folk seemed cautious this near to any settlement. In their own lands they must be bolder.

And by the following "night," the vehicle had gone well into yonder country. When Sherrinford stopped the engine in a meadow and the car settled down, silence rolled in like a wave.

They stepped out. She cooked a meal on the glower while he gathered wood, that they might later cheer themselves with a campfire. Frequently he glanced at his wrist. It bore no watch—instead, a radio-controlled dial, to tell what the instruments in the bus might register.

Who needed a watch here? Slow constellations wheeled beyond glimmering aurora. The moon Alde stood above a snowpeak, turning it argent, though this place lay at a goodly height. The rest of the mountains were hidden by the forest that crowded around. Its trees were mostly shiverleaf and feathery white plumablanca, ghostly amid their shadows. A few firethorns glowed, clustered dim lanterns, and the underbrush was heavy and smelled sweet. You could see surprisingly far through the blue dusk. Somewhere nearby a brook sang and a bird fluted.

"Lovely here," Sherrinford said. They had risen from their supper and not yet sat down or kindled their fire.

"But strange," Barbro answered as low. "I wonder if it's really meant for us. If we can really hope to possess it."

His pipestem gestured at the stars. "Man's gone to stranger places than this."

"Has he? I . . . oh, I suppose it's just something left over from my outway childhood, but do you know, when I'm under them I can't think of the stars as balls of gas, whose energies have been measured, whose planets have been walked on by prosaic feet. No, they're small and cold and magical; our lives are bound to them; after we die, they whisper to us in our graves." Barbro glanced downward. "I realize that's nonsense."

She could see in the twilight how his face grew tight. "Not at all," he said. "Emotionally, physics may be a worse nonsense. And in the end, you know, after a sufficient number of generations, thought follows feeling. Man is not at heart rational. He could stop believing the stories of science if those no longer felt right."

He paused. "That ballad which didn't get finished in the house," he said, not looking at her. "Why did it affect you so?"

"I was overwrought. I couldn't stand hearing *them,* well, praised. Or that's how it seemed. My apologies for the fuss."

"I gather the ballad is typical of a large class."

"Well, I never thought to add them up. Cultural anthropology is something we don't have time for on Roland, or more likely it hasn't occurred to us, with everything else there is to do. But—

now you mention it, yes, I'm surprised at how many songs and stories have the Arvid motif in them."

"Could you bear to recite it for me?"

She mustered the will to laugh. "Why, I can do better than that if you want. Let me get my multilyre and I'll perform."

She omitted the hypnotic chorus line, though, when the notes rang out, except at the end. He watched her where she stood against moon and aurora.

> *"—the Queen of Air and Darkness*
> *cried softly under sky:*
>
> *"'Light down, you ranger Arvid,*
> *and join the Outling folk.*
> *You need no more be human,*
> *which is a heavy yoke.'*
>
> *"He dared to give her answer:*
> *'I may do naught but run.*
> *A maiden waits me, dreaming*
> *in lands beneath the sun.*
>
> *"'And likewise wait me comrades*
> *and tasks I would not shirk,*
> *for what is Ranger Arvid*
> *if he lays down his work?*
>
> *"'So wreak your spells, you Outling,*
> *and cast your wrath on me.*
> *Though maybe you can slay me,*
> *you'll not make me unfree.'*
>
> *"The Queen of Air and Darkness*
> *stood wrapped about with fear*
> *and northlight-flares and beauty*
> *he dared not look too near.*
>
> *"Until she laughed like harpsong*
> *and said to him in scorn:*
> *'I do not need a magic*
> *to make you always mourn.*

> "'I send you home with nothing
>   except your memory
>   of moonlight, Outling music,
>   night breezes, dew, and me.
>
> "'And that will run behind you,
>   and shadow on the sun,
>   and that will lie beside you
>   when every day is done.
>
> "'In work and play and friendship
>   your grief will strike you dumb
>   for thinking what you are—and—
>   what you might have become.
>
> "'Your dull and foolish woman
>   treat kindly as you can.
>   Go home now, Ranger Arvid,
>   set free to be a man!'
>
> "In flickering and laughter
>   the Outling folk were gone.
>   He stood alone by moonlight
>   and wept until the dawn.
>   The dance weaves under the firethorn."

She laid the lyre aside. A wind rustled leaves. After a long quietness Sherrinford said, "And tales of this kind are part of everyone's life in the outway?"

"Well, you could put it thus," Barbro replied. "Though they're not all full of supernatural doings. Some are about love or heroism. Traditional themes."

"I don't think your particular tradition has arisen of itself." His tone was bleak. "In fact, I think many of your songs and stories were not composed by humans."

He snapped his lips shut and would say no more on the subject. They went early to bed.

Hours later, an alarm roused them.

The buzzing was soft, but it brought them instantly alert. They slept in gripsuits, to be prepared for emergencies. Sky-glow lit them through the canopy. Sherrinford swung out of his bunk, slipped shoes on feet and clipped gun holster to belt. "Stay inside," he commanded.

"What's there?" Her pulse thudded.

He squinted at the dials of his instruments and checked them against the luminous telltale on his wrist. "Three animals," he counted. "Not wild ones happening by. A large one, homeothermic, to judge from the infrared, holding still a short ways off. Another . . . hm, low temperature, diffuse and unstable emission, as if it were more like a . . . a swarm of cells coordinated somehow . . . pheromonally? . . . hovering, also at a distance. But the third's practically next to us, moving around in the brush; and that pattern looks human."

She saw him quiver with eagerness, no longer seeming a professor. "I'm going to try to make a capture," he said. "When we have a subject for interrogation, stand ready to let me back in again fast. But don't risk yourself, whatever happens. And keep this cocked." He handed her a loaded big-game rifle.

His tall frame poised by the door, opened it a crack. Air blew in, cool, damp, full of fragrances and murmurings. The moon Oliver saw was now also aloft, the radiance of both unreally brilliant, and the aurora seethed in whiteness and ice-blue.

Sherrinford peered afresh at his telltale. It must indicate the directions of the watchers, among those dappled leaves. Abruptly he sprang out. He sprinted past the ashes of the campfire and vanished under trees. Barbro's hand strained on the butt of her weapon.

Racket exploded. Two in combat burst onto the meadow. Sherrinford had clapped a grip on a smaller human figure. She could make out by streaming silver and rainbow flicker that the other was nude, male, long-haired, lithe, and young. He fought demoniacally, seeking to use teeth and feet and raking nails, and meanwhile he ululated like a satan.

The identification shot through her: a changeling, stolen in babyhood and raised by the Old Folk. This creature was what they would make Jimmy into.

"Ha!" Sherrinford forced his opponent around and drove stiffened fingers into the solar plexus. The boy gasped and sagged. Sherrinford manhandled him toward the car.

Out from the woods came a giant. It might itself have been a tree, black and rugose, bearing four great gnarly boughs; but earth quivered and boomed beneath its leg-roots, and its hoarse bellowing filled sky and skulls.

Barbro shrieked. Sherrinford whirled. He yanked out his pistol, fired and fired, flat whipcracks through the half-light. His free arm kept a lock on the youth. The troll shape lurched under those blows. It recovered and came on, more slowly, more carefully, circling around to cut him off from the bus. He couldn't move fast enough to evade unless he released his prisoner—who was his sole possible guide to Jimmy—

Barbro leaped forth. "Don't!" Sherrinford shouted. "For God's sake, stay inside!" The monster rumbled and made snatching motions at her. She pulled trigger. Recoil slammed her in the shoulder. The colossus rocked and fell. Somehow it got its feet back and lumbered toward her. She retreated. Again she shot and again. The creature snarled. Blood began to drip from it and gleam oilily amidst dewdrops. It turned and went off, breaking branches, into the darkness that laired beneath the woods.

"Get to shelter!" Sherrinford yelled. "You're out of the jammer field!"

A mistiness drifted by overhead. She barely glimpsed it before she saw the new shape at the meadow edge. "Jimmy!" tore from her.

"Mother." He held out his arms. Moonlight coursed in his tears. She dropped her weapon and ran to him.

Sherrinford plunged in pursuit. Jimmy flitted away into the brush. Barbro crashed after, through clawing twigs. Then she was seized and borne away.

Standing over his captive, Sherrinford strengthened the fluoro output until vision of the wilderness was blocked off from within the bus. The boy squirmed beneath that colorless glare.

"You are going to talk," the man said. Despite the haggardness in his features, he spoke quietly.

The boy glowered through tangled locks. A bruise was purpling on his jaw. He'd almost recovered ability to flee while Sherrinford chased and lost the woman. Returning, the detective had barely caught him. Time was lacking to be gentle, when

Outling reinforcements might arrive at any moment. Sherrinford had knocked him out and dragged him inside. Now he sat lashed into a swivel seat.

He spat. "Talk to you, man-clod?" But sweat stood on his skin and his eyes flickered unceasingly around the metal which caged him.

"Give me a name to call you by."

"And have you work a spell on me?"

"Mine's Eric. If you don't give me another choice, I'll have to call you . . . m-m-m . . . Wuddikins."

"What?" However eldritch, the bound one remained a human adolescent. "Mistherd, then." The lilting accent of his English somehow emphasized its sullenness. "That's not the sound, only what it means. Anyway, it's my spoken name, naught else."

"Ah, you keep a secret name you consider to be real?"

"She does. I don't know myself what it is. She knows the real names of everybody."

Sherrinford raised his brows. "She?"

"Who reigns. May she forgive me, I can't make the reverent sign when my arms are tied. Some invaders call her the Queen of Air and Darkness."

"So." Sherrinford got pipe and tobacco. He let silence wax while he started the fire. At length he said:

"I'll confess the Old Folk took me by surprise. I didn't expect so formidable a member of your gang. Everything I could learn had seemed to show they work on my race—and yours, lad—by stealth, trickery, and illusion."

Mistherd jerked a truculent nod. "She created the first nicors not long ago. Don't think she has naught but dazzlements at her beck."

"I don't. However, a steel-jacketed bullet works pretty well too, doesn't it?"

Sherrinford talked on, softly, mostly to himself: "I do still believe the, ah, nicors—all your half-humanlike breeds—are intended in the main to be seen, not used. The power of projecting mirages must surely be quite limited in range and scope as well as in the number of individuals who possess it. Otherwise she wouldn't have needed to work as slowly and craftily as she has. Even outside our mind-shield, Barbro—my companion—could

have resisted, could have remained aware that whatever she saw
was unreal . . . if she'd been less shaken, less frantic, less driven
by need."

Sherrinford wreathed his head in smoke. "Never mind what I
experienced," he said. "It couldn't have been the same as for her.
I think the command was simply given us, 'You will see what
you most desire in the world, running away from you into the
forest.' Of course, she didn't travel many meters before the nicor
waylaid her. I'd no hope of trailing them; I'm no Arctican woods-
man, and besides, it'd have been too easy to ambush me. I came
back to you." Grimly: "You're my link to your overlady."

"You think I'll guide you to Starhaven or Carheddin? Try
making me, clod-man."

"I want to bargain."

"I s'pect you intend more'n that." Mistherd's answer held surprising shrewdness. "What'll you tell after you come home?"

"Yes, that does pose a problem, doesn't it? Barbro Cullen and I
are not terrified outwayers. We're of the city. We brought
recording instruments. We'd be the first of our kind to report an
encounter with the Old Folk, and that report would be detailed
and plausible. It would produce action."

"So you see I'm not afraid to die," Mistherd declared, though
his lips trembled a bit. "If I let you come in and do your man-
things to my people, I'd have naught left worth living for."

"Have no immediate fears," Sherrinford said. "You're merely
bait." He sat down and regarded the boy through a visor of
calm. (Within, it wept in him: *Barbro, Barbro!*) "Consider. Your
Queen can't very well let me go back, bringing my prisoner and
telling about hers. She has to stop that somehow. I could try
fighting my way through—this car is better armed than you
know—but that wouldn't free anybody. Instead, I'm staying put.
New forces of hers will get here as fast as they can. I assume
they won't blindly throw themselves against a machine gun, a
howitzer, a fulgurator. They'll parley first, whether their inten-
tions are honest or not. Thus I make the contact I'm after."

"What d' you plan?" The mumble held anguish.

"First, this, as a sort of invitation." Sherrinford reached out to
flick a switch. "There. I've lowered my shield against mind-read-

ing and shape-casting. I daresay the leaders, at least, will be able to sense that it's gone. That should give them confidence."

"And next?"

"Why, next we wait. Would you like something to eat or drink?"

During the time which followed, Sherrinford tried to jolly Mistherd along, find out something of his life. What answers he got were curt. He dimmed the interior lights and settled down to peer outward. That was a long few hours.

They ended at a shout of gladness, half a sob, from the boy. Out of the woods came a band of the Old Folk.

Some of them stood forth more clearly than moons and stars and northlights should have caused. He in the van rode a white crownbuck whose horns were garlanded. His form was manlike but unearthly beautiful, silver-blond hair falling from beneath the antlered helmet, around the proud cold face. The cloak fluttered on his back like living wings. His frost-colored mail rang as he fared.

Behind him, to right and left, rode two who bore swords whereon small flames gleamed and flickered. Above, a flying flock laughed and trilled and tumbled in the breezes. Near them drifted a half-transparent mistiness. Those others who passed among trees after their chieftain were harder to make out. But they moved in quicksilver grace, and as it were to a sound of harps and trumpets.

"Lord Luighaid." Glory overflowed in Mistherd's tone. "Her master Knower—himself."

Sherrinford had never done a harder thing than to sit at the main control panel, finger near the button of the shield generator, and not touch it. He rolled down a section of canopy to let voices travel. A gust of wind struck him in the face, bearing odors of the roses in his mother's garden. At his back, in the main body of the vehicle, Mistherd strained against his bonds till he could see the incoming troop.

"Call to them," Sherrinford said. "Ask if they will talk with me."

Unknown, flutingly sweet words flew back and forth. "Yes," the boy interpreted. "He will, the Lord Luighaid. But I can tell you, you'll never be let go. Don't fight them Yield. Come away.

You don't know what 'tis to be alive till you've dwelt in Carheddin under the mountain."

The Outlings drew nigh.

Jimmy glimmered and was gone. Barbro lay in strong arms,
against a broad breast, and felt the horse move beneath her. It
had to be a horse, though only a few were kept any longer on
the steadings, and they for special uses or love. She could feel
the rippling beneath its hide, hear a rush of parted leafage and
the thud when a hoof struck stone; warmth and living scent
welled up around her through the darkness.

He who carried her said mildly, "Don't be afraid, darling. It
was a vision. But he's waiting for us and we're bound for him."

She was aware in a vague way that she ought to feel terror or
despair or something. But her memories lay behind her—she
wasn't sure just how she had come to be here—she was borne
along in a knowledge of being loved. At peace, at peace, rest in
the calm expectation of joy . . .

After a while the forest opened. They crossed a lea where
boulders stood gray-white under the moons, their shadows shift-
ing in the dim hues which the aurora threw across them. Flitteries danced, tiny comets, above the flowers between. Ahead
gleamed a peak whose top was crowned in clouds.

Barbro's eyes happened to be turned forward. She saw the
horse's head and thought, with quiet surprise: Why, this is
Sambo, who was mine when I was a girl. She looked upward at
the man. He wore a black tunic and a cowled cape, which made
his face hard to see. She could not cry aloud, here. "Tim," she
whispered.

"Yes, Barbro."

"I buried you—"

His smile was endlessly tender. "Did you think we're no more
than what's laid back into the ground? Poor torn sweetheart. She
who's called us is the All Healer. Now rest and dream."

"Dream," she said, and for a space she struggled to rouse herself. But the effort was weak. Why should she believe ashen tales
about . . . atoms and energies, nothing else to fill a gape of emptiness . . . tales she could not bring to mind . . . when Tim and
the horse her father gave her carried her on to Jimmy? Had the

other thing not been the evil dream, and this her first drowsy awakening from it?

As if he heard her thoughts, he murmured, "They have a song in Outling lands. The Song of the Men:

> *"The world sails*
> *to an unseen wind.*
> *Light swirls by the bows.*
> *The wake is night.*

But the Dwellers have no such sadness."

"I don't understand," she said.

He nodded. "There's much you'll have to understand, darling, and I can't see you again until you've learned those truths. But meanwhile you'll be with our son."

She tried to lift her head and kiss him. He held her down. "Not yet," he said. "You've not been received among the Queen's people. I shouldn't have come for you, except that she was too merciful to forbid. Lie back, lie back."

Time blew past. The horse galloped tireless, never stumbling, up the mountain. Once she glimpsed a troop riding down it and thought they were bound for a last weird battle in the west against . . . who? . . . one who lay cased in iron and sorrow . . . Later she would ask herself the name of him who had brought her into the land of the Old Truth.

Finally spires lifted splendid among the stars, which are small and magical and whose whisperings comfort us after we are dead. They rode into a courtyard where candles burned unwavering, fountains splashed and birds sang. The air bore fragrance of brok and pericoup, of rue and roses; for not everything that man brought was horrible. The Dwellers waited in beauty to welcome her. Beyond their stateliness, pooks cavorted through the gloaming; among the trees darted children; merriment caroled across music more solemn.

"We have come—" Tim's voice was suddenly, inexplicably a croak. Barbro was not sure how he dismounted, bearing her. She stood before him and saw him sway on his feet.

Fear caught her. "Are you well?" She seized both his hands. They felt cold and rough. Where had Sambo gone? Her eyes searched beneath the cowl. In this brighter illumination, she ought to have seen her man's face clearly. But it was blurred, it kept changing. "What's wrong, oh, what's happened?"

He smiled. Was that the smile she had cherished? She couldn't completely remember. "I, I must go," he stammered, so low she could scarcely hear. "Our time is not ready." He drew free of her grasp and leaned on a robed form which had appeared at his side. A haziness swirled over both their heads. "Don't watch me go . . . back into the earth," he pleaded. "That's death for you. Till our time returns . . . There, our son!"

She had to fling her gaze around. Kneeling, she spread wide her arms. Jimmy struck her like a warm, solid cannonball. She rumpled his hair, she kissed the hollow of his neck, she laughed and wept and babbled foolishness; and this was no ghost, no memory that had stolen off when she wasn't looking. Now and again, as she turned her attention to yet another hurt which might have come upon him—hunger, sickness, fear—and found none, she would glimpse their surroundings. The gardens were gone. It didn't matter.

"I misted you so, Mother. Stay?"

"I'll take you home, dearest."

"Stay. Here's fun. I'll show. But you stay."

A sighing went through the twilight. Barbro rose. Jimmy clung to her hand. They confronted the Queen.

Very tall she was in her robes woven of northlights, and her starry crown and her garlands of kiss-me-never. Her countenance recalled Aphrodite of Milos, whose picture Barbro had often seen in the realms of men, save that the Queen's was more fair, and more majesty dwelt upon it and in the night-blue eyes. Around her the gardens woke to new reality, the court of the Dwellers and the heaven-climbing spires.

"Be welcome," she spoke, her speaking a song, "forever."

Against the awe of her, Barbro said, "Moonmother, let us go home."

"That may not be."

"To our world, little and beloved," Barbro dreamed she begged, "which we build for ourselves and cherish for our children."

"To prison days, angry nights, works that crumble in the

fingers, loves that turn to rot or stone or driftweed, loss, grief, and the only sureness that of the final nothingness. No. You too, Wanderfoot, who is to be, will jubilate when the banners of the Outworld come flying into the last of the cities and man is made wholly alive. Now go with those who will teach you."

The Queen of Air and Darkness lifted an arm in summons. It halted, and none came to answer.

For over the fountains and melodies lifted a gruesome growling. Fires leaped, thunders crashed. Her hosts scattered screaming before the steel thing which boomed up the mountainside. The pooks were gone in a whirl of frightened wings. The nicors flung their bodies against the unalive invader and were consumed, until their Mother cried to them to retreat.

Barbro cast Jimmy down and herself over him. Towers wavered and smoked away. The mountain stood bare under icy moons, save for rocks, crags, and farther off a glacier in whose depths the auroral light pulsed blue. A cave mouth darkened a cliff. Thither folk streamed, seeking refuge underground. Some were human of blood, some grotesques like the pooks and nicors and wraiths; but most were lean, scaly, long-tailed, long-beaked, not remotely men or Outlings.

For an instant, even as Jimmy wailed at her breast—perhaps as much because the enchantment had been wrecked as because he was afraid—Barbro pitied the Queen who stood alone in her nakedness. Then that one also had fled, and Barbro's world shivered apart.

The guns fell silent, the vehicle whirred to a halt. From it sprang a boy who called wildly, "Shadow-of-a-Dream, where are you? It's me, Mistherd, oh, come, come!"—before he remembered that the language they had been raised in was not man's. He shouted in that until a girl crept out of a thicket where she had hidden. They stared at each other through dust, smoke, and moon-glow. She ran to him.

A new voice barked from the car, "Barbro, hurry!"

Christmas Landing knew day: short at this time of year, but sunlight, blue skies, white clouds, glittering water, salt breezes in busy streets, and the sane disorder of Eric Sherrinford's living room.

He crossed and uncrossed his legs where he sat, puffed on his pipe as if to make a veil, and said, "Are you certain you're recovered? You mustn't risk overstrain."

"I'm fine," Barbro Cullen replied, though her tone was flat. "Still tired, yes, and showing it, no doubt. One doesn't go through such an experience and bounce back in a week. But I'm up and about. And to be frank, I must know what's happened, what's going on, before I can settle down to regain my full strength. Not a word of news anywhere."

"Have you spoken to others about the matter?"

"No. I've simply told visitors I was too exhausted to talk. Not much of a lie. I assumed there's a reason for censorship."

Sherrinford looked relieved. "Good girl. It's at my urging. You can imagine the sensation when this is made public. The authorities agreed they need time to study the facts, think and debate in a calm atmosphere, have a decent policy ready to offer voters who're bound to become rather hysterical at first." His mouth quirked slightly upward. "Furthermore, your nerves and Jimmy's get their chance to heal before the journalistic storm breaks over you. How is he?"

"Quite well. He continues pestering me for leave to go play with his friends in the Wonderful Place. But at his age, he'll recover—he'll forget."

"He may meet them later anyhow."

"What? We didn't—" Barbro shifted in her chair. "I've forgotten too. I hardly recall a thing from our last hours. Did you bring back any kidnapped humans?"

"No. The shock was savage, as it was, without throwing them straight into an . . . an institution. Mistherd, who's basically a sensible young fellow, assured me they'd get along, at any rate as regards survival necessities, till arrangements can be made." Sherrinford hesitated. "I'm not sure what the arrangements will be. Nobody is, at our present stage. But obviously they include those people—or many of them, especially those who aren't full-grown—rejoining the human race. Though they may never feel at home in civilization. Perhaps in a way that's best, since we will need some kind of mutually acceptable liaison with the Dwellers."

His impersonality soothed them both. Barbro became able to

say: "Was I too big a fool? I do remember how I yowled and beat my head on the floor."

"Why, no." He considered the big woman and her pride for a few seconds before he rose, walked over and laid a hand on her shoulder. "You'd been lured and trapped by a skillful play on your deepest instincts, at a moment of sheer nightmare. Afterward, as that wounded monster carried you off, evidently another type of being came along, one that could saturate you with close-range neuropsychic forces. On top of this, my arrival, the sudden brutal abolishment of every hallucination, must have been shattering. No wonder if you cried out in pain. Before you did, you competently got Jimmy and yourself into the bus, and you never interfered with me."

"What did you do?"

"Why, I drove off as fast as possible. After several hours, the atmospherics let up sufficiently for me to call Portolondon and insist on an emergency airlift. Not that that was vital. What chance had the enemy to stop us? They didn't even try. But quick transportation was certainly helpful."

"I figured that's what must have gone on." Barbro caught his glance. "No, what I meant was, how did you find us in the backlands?"

Sherrinford moved a little off from her. "My prisoner was my guide. I don't think I actually killed any of the Dwellers who'd come to deal with me. I hope not. The car simply broke through them, after a couple of warning shots, and afterward outpaced them. Steel and fuel against flesh wasn't really fair. At the cave entrance, I did have to shoot down a few of those troll creatures. I'm not proud of it."

He stood silent. Presently: "But you were a captive," he said. "I couldn't be sure what they might do to you, who had first claim on me." After another pause: "I don't look for any more violence."

"How did you make . . . the boy . . . cooperate?"

Sherrinford paced from her, to the window, where he stood staring out at the Boreal Ocean. "I turned off the mind shield," he said. "I let their band get close, in full splendor of illusion. Then I turned the shield back on and we both saw them in their true shapes. As we went northward I explained to Mistherd how he and his kind had been hoodwinked, used, made to live in a world that was never really there. I asked him if he wanted himself and whoever he cared about to go on till they died as domestic animals—yes, running in limited freedom on solid hills, but always called back to the dream-kennel." His pipe fumed furiously. "May I never see such bitterness again. He had been taught to believe he was free."

Quiet returned, above the hectic traffic. Charlemagne drew nearer to setting; already the east darkened.

Finally Barbro asked, "Do you know why?"

"Why children were taken and raised like that? Partly because it was in the pattern the Dwellers were creating; partly in order to study and experiment on members of our species—minds, that is, not bodies; partly because humans have special strengths which are helpful, like being able to endure full daylight."

"But what was the final purpose of it all?"

Sherrinford paced the floor. "Well," he said, "of course the ultimate motives of the aborigines are obscure. We can't do more than guess at how they think, let alone how they feel. But our ideas do seem to fit the data.

"Why did they hide from man? I suspect they, or rather their ancestors—for they aren't glittering elves, you know; they're mortal and fallible too—I suspect the natives were only being cautious at first, more cautious than human primitives, though certain of those on Earth were also slow to reveal themselves to strangers. Spying, mentally eavesdropping, Roland's Dwellers must have picked up enough language to get some idea of how different man was from them, and how powerful; and they gathered that more ships would be arriving, bringing settlers. It didn't occur to them that they might be conceded the right to keep their lands. Perhaps they're still more fiercely territorial than us. They determined to fight, in their own way. I daresay, once we begin to get insight into that mentality, our psychological science will go through its Copernican revolution."

Enthusiasm kindled in him. "That's not the sole thing we'll learn, either," he went on. "They must have science of their own, a nonhuman science born on a planet that isn't Earth. Because they did observe us as profoundly as we've ever observed ourselves; they did mount a plan against us, that would have taken another century or more to complete. Well, what else do they know? How do they support their civilization without visible agriculture or aboveground buildings or mines or anything? How can they breed whole new intelligent species to order? A million questions, ten million answers!"

"*Can* we learn from them?" Barbro asked softly. "Or can we only overrun them as you say they fear?"

Sherrinford halted, leaned elbow on mantel, hugged his pipe and replied: "I hope we'll show more charity than that to a defeated enemy. It's what they are. They tried to conquer us, and failed, and now in a sense we are bound to conquer them, since they'll have to make their peace with the civilization of the machine rather than see it rust away as they strove for. Still, they never did us any harm as atrocious as what we've inflicted on our fellow man in the past. And, I repeat, they could teach us marvelous things; and we could teach them, too, once they've learned to be less intolerant of a different way of life."

"I suppose we can give them a reservation," she said, and didn't know why he grimaced and answered so roughly:

"Let's leave them the honor they've earned! They fought to save the world they'd always known from that"—he made a chopping gesture at the city—"and just possibly we'd be better off ourselves with less of it."

He sagged a trifle and sighed, "However, I suppose if Elfland had won, man on Roland would at last—peacefully, even happily—have died away. We live with our archetypes, but can we live in them?"

Barbro shook her head. "Sorry, I don't understand."

"What?" He looked at her in a surprise that drove out melancholy. After a laugh: "Stupid of me. I've explained this to so many politicians and scientists and commissioners and Lord knows what, these past days, I forgot I'd never explained to you. It was a rather vague idea of mine, most of the time we were traveling, and I don't like to discuss ideas prematurely. Now that we've met the Outlings and watched how they work, I do feel sure."

He tamped down his tobacco. "In limited measure," he said, "I've used an archetype throughout my own working life. The rational detective. It hasn't been a conscious pose—much—it's simply been an image which fitted my personality and professional style. But it draws an appropriate response from most people, whether or not they've ever heard of the original. The phenomenon is not uncommon. We meet persons who, in varying degrees, suggest Christ or Buddha or the Earth Mother or, say, on a less exalted plane, Hamlet or d'Artagnan. Historical, fictional, and mythical, such figures crystallize basic aspects of the human psyche, and when we meet them in our real experience, our reaction goes deeper than consciousness."

He grew grave again: "Man also creates archetypes that are not individuals. The Ani, the Shadow—and, it seems, the Outworld. The world of magic, of glamour—which originally meant enchantment—of half-human beings, some like Ariel and some like Caliban, but each free of mortal frailties and sorrows—therefore, perhaps, a little carelessly cruel, more than a little tricksy; dwellers in dusk and moonlight, not truly gods but obedient to rulers who are enigmatic and powerful enough to be—Yes, our Queen of Air and Darkness knew well what sights to let lonely people see, what illusions to spin around them from time to time, what songs and legends to set going among them. I wonder how much she and her underlings gleaned from human fairy tales, how much they made up themselves, and how much men created all over again, all unwittingly, as the sense of living on the edge of the world entered them."

Shadows stole across the room. It grew cooler and the traffic noises dwindled. Barbro asked mutedly: "But what could this do?"

"In many ways," Sherrinford answered, "the outwayer *is* back in the dark ages. He has few neighbors, hears scanty news from beyond his horizon, toils to survive in a land he only partly understands, that may any night raise unforeseeable disasters against him and is bounded by enormous wildernesses. The machine civilization which brought his ancestors here is frail at best. He could lose it as the dark age nations had lost Greece and Rome, as the whole of Earth seems to have lost it. Let him be worked on, long, strongly, cunningly, by the archetypical Outworld, until he has come to believe in his bones that the magic of the Queen of Air and Darkness is greater than the energy of engines; and first his faith, finally his deeds will follow her. Oh, it wouldn't happen fast. Ideally, it would happen too slowly to be noticed, especially by self-satisfied city people. But when in the end a hinterland gone back to the ancient way turned from them, how could they keep alive?"

Barbro breathed, "She said to me, when their banners flew in the last of our cities, we would rejoice."

"I think we would have, by then," Sherrinford admitted. "Nevertheless, I believe in choosing one's own destiny."

He shook himself, as if casting off a burden. He knocked the dottle from his pipe and stretched, muscle by muscle. "Well," he said, "it isn't going to happen."

She looked straight at him. "Thanks to you."

A flush went up his thin cheeks. "In time, I'm sure, somebody else would have— Anyhow, what matters is what we do next, and that's too big a decision for one individual or one generation to make."

She rose. "Unless the decision is personal, Eric," she suggested, feeling heat in her own face.

It was curious to see him shy. "I was hoping we might meet again."

"We will."

Ayoch sat on Wolund's Barrow, Aurora shuddered so brilliant, in such vast sheafs of light, as almost to hide the waning moons. Firethorn blooms had fallen; a few still glowed around the tree roots, amidst dry brok which crackled underfoot and smelled like woodsmoke. The air remained warm but no gleam was left on the sunset horizon.

"Farewell, fare lucky," the pook called. Mistherd and Shadow-of-a-Dream never looked back. It was as if they didn't dare. They trudged on out of sight, toward the human camp whose lights made a harsh new star in the south.

Ayoch lingered. He felt he should also offer goodbye to her who had lately joined him that slept in the dolmen. Likely none would meet here again for loving or magic. But he could only think of one old verse that might do. He stood and trilled:

"Out of her breast
A blossom ascended.
The summer burned it.
The song is ended."

Then he spread his wings for the long flight away.

Larry Niven

In Volume Two, in connection with Larry's story there ("Neutron Star"), I mentioned that he had a "clean-shaven square countenance."

Well, unless he has changed again, he now has a beard: a neat, well-kept beard that seems to improve his looks. (I say "seems" because I have no expertise in men's looks. In general, I don't see them. I have been known to walk into a room full of men, walk up to the only woman, look around blankly and ask her, "Where is everybody?" It's a peculiarity, but I'm resigned to it and have refused all treatment.)

Anyway, what we have to thank the sixties for most of all, I think, is the first real recrudescence in men's facial hair since the Gibson man popularized the style of leaving a man's face utterly blank back in the first decade of the twentieth century.

I took advantage of the new look myself. Starting in 1970, I let my hair grow long and was very delighted at saving the time I would otherwise spend at the barber's and very relieved at not being arrested as soon as I appeared in the street.

My hair now falls gracefully to my shoulders in many a wave and curl and it is my ambition to have it fall in additional waves and curls all the way to the small of my back. That, however, is not the ambition of my wife, Janet. Every now and then she persuades me, in her soft and gentle way, to allow her to cut my hair. Kneeling on my back, with scissors in hand and razor at my throat, she cuts—and cuts—and cuts—

I also grew sideburns which I gradually allowed to grow longer and longer and bushier and bushier in the intervals when Janet wasn't looking. But then it turned out she liked them. I don't know why. Women are mysterious.

And Larry's wife (who, as an MIT undergraduate was known as Fuzzy Pink—possibly for her sweaters) seems indecently fond of Larry, beard and all.

I also mentioned in Volume Two that Larry speculates on the sex life of Superman. I wondered then, and I wonder now, whether I ought to tell you the sort of details he considers; the hydraulic force, for instance, of—

But no, I couldn't do it as well as Larry. It's always these quiet, blushing, nether-lip-biting fellows who are the real erotomaniacs.

5

INCONSTANT MOON

I

I was watching the news when the change came, like a flicker of motion at the corner of my eye. I turned toward the balcony window. Whatever it was, I was too late to catch it.

The moon was very bright tonight.

I saw that, and smiled, and turned back. Johnny Carson was just starting his monologue.

When the first commercials came on I got up to reheat some coffee. Commercials came in strings of three and four, going on midnight. I'd have time.

The moonlight caught me coming back. If it had been bright before, it was brighter now. Hypnotic. I opened the sliding glass door and stepped out onto the balcony.

The balcony wasn't much more than a railed ledge, with standing room for a man and a woman and a portable barbecue set. These past months the view had been lovely, especially around sunset. The Power and Light Company had been putting up a glass-slab-style office building. So far it was only a steel framework of open girders. Shadow-blackened against a red sunset sky, it tended to look stark and surrealistic and hellishly impressive.

Tonight . . .

I had never seen the moon so bright, not even in the desert. *Bright enough to read by,* I thought, and immediately, *but that's an illusion.* The moon was never bigger (I had read somewhere) than a quarter held nine feet away. It couldn't possibly be bright enough to read by.

It was only three-quarters full!

But, glowing high over the San Diego Freeway to the west, the moon seemed to dim even the streaming automobile headlights. I blinked against its light, and thought of men walking on the moon, leaving corrugated footprints. Once, for the sake of an article I was writing, I had been allowed to pick up a bone-dry moon rock and hold it in my hand . . .

I heard the show starting again, and I stepped inside. But, glancing once behind me, I caught the moon growing even brighter—as if it had come from behind a wisp of scudding cloud.

Now its light was brain-searing, lunatic.

The phone rang five times before she answered.

"Hi," I said. "Listen—"

"Hi," Leslie said sleepily, complainingly. Damn. I'd hoped she was watching television, like me.

I said, "Don't scream and shout, because I had a reason for calling. You're in bed, right? Get up and— Can you get up?"

"What time is it?"

"Quarter of twelve."

"Oh, Lord."

"Go out on your balcony and look around."

"Okay."

The phone clunked. I waited. Leslie's balcony faced north and west, like mine, but it was ten stories higher, with a correspondingly better view.

Through my own window, the moon burned like a textured spotlight.

"Stan? You there?"

"Yah. What do you think of it?"

"It's gorgeous. I've never seen anything like it. What could make the moon light up like that?"

"I don't know, but isn't it gorgeous?"

"You're supposed to be the native." Leslie had only moved out here a year ago.

"Listen, I've *never* seen it like this. But there's an old legend," I said. "Once every hundred years the Los Angeles smog rolls away for a single night, leaving the air as clear as interstellar space. That way the gods can see if Los Angeles is still there. If it is, they roll the smog back so they won't have to look at it."

"I used to know all that stuff. Well, listen, I'm glad you woke me up to see it, but I've got to get to work tomorrow."

"Poor baby."

"That's life. 'Night."

"'Night."

Afterward I sat in the dark, trying to think of someone else to call. Call a girl at midnight, invite her to step outside and look at the moonlight . . . and she may think it's romantic or she may be furious, but she won't assume you called six others.

So I thought of some names. But the girls who belonged to them had all dropped away over the past year or so, after I started spending all my time with Leslie. One could hardly blame them. And now Joan was in Texas and Hildy was getting married, and if I called Louise I'd probably get Gordie too. The English girl? But I couldn't remember her number. Or her last name.

Besides, everyone I knew punched a time clock of one kind or another. Me, I worked for a living, but as a freelance writer I picked my hours. Anyone I woke up tonight, I'd be ruining her morning. Ah, well . . .

The Johnny Carson show was a swirl of gray and a roar of static when I got back to the living room. I turned the set off and went back out on the balcony.

The moon was brighter than the flow of headlights on the freeway, brighter than Westwood Village off to the right. The Santa Monica Mountains had a magical pearly glow. There were no stars near the moon. Stars could not survive that glare.

I wrote science and how-to articles for a living. I ought to be able to figure out what was making the moon do that. Could the moon be suddenly larger? Inflating like a balloon? No.

Closer, maybe. The moon falling?

Tides! Waves fifty feet high . . . and earthquakes! San Andreas Fault splitting apart like the Grand Canyon! Jump in my car, head for the hills . . . no, too late already . . .

Nonsense. The moon was brighter, not bigger. I could see that. And what could possibly drop the moon on our heads like that?

I blinked, and the moon left an afterimage on my retinae. It was *that* bright.

A million people must be watching the moon right now, and wondering, like me. An article on the subject would sell big . . . if I wrote it before anyone else did . . .

There must be some simple, obvious explanation.

Well, how could the moon grow brighter? Moonlight was reflected sunlight. Could the sun have gotten brighter? It must have happened after sunset, then, or it would have been noticed . . .

I didn't like that idea.

Besides, half the Earth was in direct sunlight. A thousand correspondents for *Life* and *Time* and *Newsweek* and Associated Press would all be calling in from Europe, Asia, Africa . . . unless they were all hiding in cellars. Or dead. Or voiceless, because the sun was blanketing everything with static, radio and phone systems and televisions . . . Television. Oh my God.

I was just barely beginning to be afraid.

All right, start over. The moon had become very much brighter. Moonlight, well, moonlight was reflected sunlight; any idiot knew that. Then . . . something had happened to the sun.

II

"Hello?"

"Hi. Me," I said, and then my throat froze solid. Panic! What was I going to *tell* her?

"I've been watching the moon," she said dreamily. "It's wonderful. I even tried to use my telescope, but I couldn't see a thing; it was too bright. It lights up the whole city. The hills are all silver."

That's right, she kept a telescope on her balcony. I'd forgotten.

"I haven't tried to go back to sleep," she said. "Too much light."

I got my throat working again. "Listen, Leslie love, I started thinking about how I woke you up and how you probably couldn't get back to sleep, what with all this light. So let's go out for a midnight snack."

"Are you out of your mind?"

"No, I'm serious. I mean it. Tonight isn't a night for sleeping. We may never have a night like this again. To hell with your diet. Let's celebrate. Hot fudge sundaes, Irish coffee—"

"That's different. I'll get dressed."

"I'll be right over."

Leslie lived on the fourteenth floor of Building C of the Barrington Plaza. I rapped for admission, and waited.

And waiting, I wondered without any sense of urgency: Why Leslie?

There must be other ways to spend my last night on Earth than with one particular girl. I could have picked a different particular girl, or even several not too particular girls, except that that didn't really apply to me, did it? Or I could have called my brother, or either set of parents . . .

Well, but brother Mike would have wanted a good reason for being hauled out of bed at midnight. "But, Mike, the moon is so beautiful . . ." Hardly. Any of my parents would have reacted similarly. Well, I had a good reason, but would they believe me?

And if they did, what then? I would have arranged a kind of wake. Let 'em sleep through it. What I wanted was someone who would join my . . . farewell party without asking the wrong questions.

What I wanted was Leslie. I knocked again.

She opened the door just a crack for me. She was in her underwear. A stiff, misshapen girdle in one hand brushed my back as she came into my arms. "I was about to put this on."

"I came just in time, then." I took the girdle away from her and dropped it. I stooped to get my arms under her ribs, straightened up with effort, and walked us to the bedroom with her feet dangling against my ankles.

Her skin was cold. She must have been outside.

"So!" she demanded. "You think you can compete with a hot fudge sundae, do you?"

"Certainly. My pride demands it." We were both somewhat out of breath. Once in our lives I had tried to lift her cradled in my arms, in conventional movie style. I'd damn near broken my back. Leslie was a big girl, my height, and almost too heavy around the hips.

I dropped us on the bed, side by side. I reached around her from both sides to scratch her back, knowing it would leave her helpless to resist me, *ah* ha hahahaha. She made sounds of pleasure to tell me where to scratch. She pulled my shirt up around my shoulders and began scratching my back.

We pulled pieces of clothing from ourselves and each other, at random, dropping them over the edges of the bed. Leslie's skin was warm now, almost hot . . .

All right, now *that's* why I couldn't have picked another girl. I'd have had to teach her how to scratch. And there just wasn't time.

Some nights I had a nervous tendency to hurry our lovemaking. Tonight we were performing a ritual, a rite of passage. I tried to slow it down, to make it last. I tried to make Leslie like it more. It paid off incredibly. I forgot the moon and the future when Leslie put her heels against the backs of my knees and we moved into the ancient rhythm.

But the image that came to me at the climax was vivid and frightening. We were in a ring of blue-hot fire that closed like a noose. If I moaned in terror and ecstasy, then she must have thought it was ecstasy alone.

We lay side by side, drowsy, torpid, clinging together. I was minded to go back to sleep then, renege on my promise, sleep and let Leslie sleep . . . but instead I whispered into her ear: "Hot fudge sundae." She smiled and stirred and presently rolled off the bed.

I wouldn't let her wear the girdle. "It's past midnight. Nobody's going to pick you up, because I'd thrash the blackguard, right? So why not be comfortable?" She laughed and gave in. We hugged each other once, hard, in the elevator. It felt much better without the girdle.

III

The gray-haired counter waitress was cheerful and excited. Her eyes glowed. She spoke as if confiding a secret. "Have you noticed the moonlight?"

Ship's was fairly crowded, this time of night and this close to UCLA. Half the customers were university students. Tonight they talked in hushed voices, turning to look out through the glass walls of the twenty-four-hour restaurant. The moon was low in the west, low enough to compete with the street globes.

"We noticed," I said. "We're celebrating. Get us two hot fudge sundaes, will you?" When she turned her back I slid a ten-dollar bill under the paper place mat. Not that she'd ever spend it, but at least she'd have the pleasure of finding it. I'd never spend it either.

I felt loose, casual. A lot of problems seemed suddenly to have solved themselves.

Who would have believed that peace could come to Vietnam and Cambodia in a single night?

This thing had started around eleven-thirty, here in California. That would have put the noon sun just over the Arabian Sea, with all but a few fringes of Asia, Europe, Africa, and Australia in direct sunlight.

Already Germany was reunited, the Wall melted or smashed by shock waves. Israelis and Arabs had laid down their arms. Apartheid was dead in Africa.

And I was free. For me there were no more consequences. Tonight I could satisfy all my dark urges, rob, kill, cheat on my income tax, throw bricks at plate-glass windows, burn my credit cards. I could forget the article on explosive metal forming, due Thursday. Tonight I could substitute cinnamon candy for Leslie's Pills. Tonight—

"Think I'll have a cigarette."

Leslie looked at me oddly. "I thought you'd given that up."

"You remember. I told myself if I got any overpowering urges, I'd have a cigarette. I did that because I couldn't stand the thought of never smoking again."

She laughed. "But it's been months!"

"But they keep putting cigarette ads in my magazines!"

"It's a plot. All right, go have a cigarette."

I put coins in the machine, hesitated over the choice, finally picked a mild filter. It wasn't that I wanted a cigarette. But certain events call for champagne, and others for cigarettes. There is the traditional last cigarette before a firing squad . . .

I lit up. *Here's to lung cancer.*

It tasted just as good as I remembered; though there was a faint stale undertaste, like a mouthful of old cigarette butts. The third lungful hit me oddly. My eyes unfocused and everything went very calm. My heart pulsed loudly in my throat.

"How does it taste?"

"Strange. I'm buzzed," I said.

Buzzed! I hadn't even heard the word in fifteen years. In high school we'd smoked to get that buzz, that quasi-drunkenness produced by capillaries constricting in the brain. The buzz had stopped coming after the first few times, but we'd kept smoking, most of us . . .

I put it out. The waitress was picking up our sundaes.

Hot and cold, sweet and bitter; there is no taste quite like that of a hot fudge sundae. To die without tasting it again would have been a crying shame. But with Leslie it was a *thing*, a symbol of all rich living. Watching her eat was more fun than eating myself.

Besides . . . I'd killed the cigarette to taste the ice cream. Now, instead of savoring the ice cream, I was anticipating Irish coffee.

Too little time.

Leslie's dish was empty. She stage-whispered, "Aahh!" and patted herself over the navel.

A customer at one of the small tables began to go mad.

I'd noticed him coming in. A lean scholarly type wearing sideburns and steel-rimmed glasses, he had been continually twisting around to look out at the moon. Like others at other tables, he seemed high on a rare and lovely natural phenomenon.

Then he got it. I saw his face changing, showing suspicion, then disbelief, then horror, horror and helplessness.

"Let's go," I told Leslie. I dropped quarters on the counter and stood up.

"Don't you want to finish yours?"

"Nope. We've got things to do. How about some Irish coffee?"

"And a Pink Lady for me? Oh, look!" She turned full around.

The scholar was climbing up on a table. He balanced, spread wide his arms and bellowed, "Look out your windows!"

"You get down from there!" a waitress demanded, jerking emphatically at his pants leg.

"The world is coming to an end! Far away on the other side of the sea, death and hellfire—"

But we were out the door, laughing as we ran. Leslie panted, "We may have—escaped a religious—riot in there!"

I thought of the ten I'd left under my plate. Now it would please nobody. Inside, a prophet was shouting his message of doom to all who would hear. The gray-haired woman with the glowing eyes would find the money and think: They knew it too.

Buildings blocked the moon from the Red Barn's parking lot. The street lights and the indirect moonglare were pretty much the same color. The night only seemed a bit brighter than usual.

I didn't understand why Leslie stopped suddenly in the driveway. But I followed her gaze, straight up to where a star burned very brightly just south of the zenith.

"Pretty," I said.

She gave me a very odd look.

There were no windows in the Red Barn. Dim artificial lighting, far dimmer than the queer cold light outside, showed on dark wood and quietly cheerful customers. Nobody seemed aware that tonight was different from other nights.

The sparse Tuesday night crowd was gathered mostly around the piano bar. A customer had the mike. He was singing some half-familiar song in a wavering weak voice, while the black pianist grinned and played a schmaltzy background.

I ordered two Irish coffees and a Pink Lady. At Leslie's questioning look I only smiled mysteriously.

How ordinary the Red Barn felt. How relaxed; how happy. We held hands across the table, and I smiled and was afraid to speak. If I broke the spell, if I said the wrong thing . . .

The drinks arrived. I raised an Irish coffee glass by the stem. Sugar, Irish whiskey, and strong black coffee, with thick whipped cream floating on top. It coursed through me like a magical potion of strength, dark and hot and powerful.

The waitress waved back my money. "See that man in the turtleneck, there at the end of the piano bar? He's buying," she said with relish. "He came in two hours ago and handed the bartender a hundred-dollar bill."

So that was where all the happiness was coming from. Free drinks! I looked over, wondering what the guy was celebrating.

A thick-necked, wide-shouldered man in a turtleneck and sports coat, he sat hunched over into himself, with a wide bar glass clutched tight in one hand. The pianist offered him the mike, and he waved it by, the gesture giving me a good look at his face. A square, strong face, now drunk and miserable and scared. He was ready to cry from fear.

So I knew what he was celebrating.

Leslie made a face. "They didn't make the Pink Lady right."

There's one bar in the world that makes a Pink Lady the way Leslie likes it, and it isn't in Los Angeles. I passed her the other Irish coffee, grinning an I-told-you-so grin. Forcing it. The other man's fear was contagious. She smiled back, lifted her glass and said, "To the blue moonlight."

I lifted my glass to her, and drank. But it wasn't the toast I would have chosen.

The man in the turtleneck slid down from his stool. He moved carefully toward the door, his course slow and straight as an ocean liner cruising into dock. He pulled the door wide, and turned around, holding it open, so that the weird blue-white light streamed past his broad black silhouette.

Bastard. He was waiting for someone to figure it out, to shout out the truth to the rest. *Fire and doom—*

"Shut the door!" someone bellowed.

"Time to go," I said softly.

"What's the hurry?"

The hurry? He might *speak!* But I couldn't say that . . .

Leslie put her hand over mine. "I know. I *know.* But we can't run away from it, can we?"

A fist closed hard on my heart. She'd known, and I hadn't noticed?

The door closed, leaving the Red Barn in reddish dusk. The man who had been buying drinks was gone.

"Oh, God. When did you figure it out?"

"Before you came over," she said. "But when I tried to check it out, it didn't work."

"Check it out?"

"I went out on the balcony and turned the telescope on Jupiter. Mars is below the horizon these nights. If the sun's gone nova, all the planets ought to be lit up like the moon, right?"

"Right. Damn." I should have thought of that myself. But Leslie was the stargazer. I knew some astrophysics, but I couldn't have found Jupiter to save my life.

"But Jupiter wasn't any brighter than usual. So then I didn't know *what* to think."

"But then—" I felt hope dawning fiery hot. Then I remembered. "That star, just overhead. The one you stared at."

"Jupiter."

"All lit up like a fucking neon sign. Well, that tears it."

"Keep your voice down."

I *had* been keeping my voice down. But for a wild moment I wanted to stand up on a table and scream! *Fire and doom—* What right had they to be ignorant?

Leslie's hand closed tight on mine. The urge passed. It left me shuddering. "Let's get out of here. Let 'em think there's going to be a dawn."

"There is." Leslie laughed a bitter, barking laugh like nothing I'd ever heard from her. She walked out while I was reaching for my wallet—and remembering that there was no need.

Poor Leslie. Finding Jupiter its normal self must have looked like a reprieve—until the white spark flared to shining glory an hour and a half late. An hour and a half, for sunlight to reach Earth by the way of Jupiter.

When I reached the door Leslie was half-running down Westwood toward Santa Monica. I cursed and ran to catch up, wondering if she'd suddenly gone crazy.

Then I noticed the shadows ahead of us. All along the other side of Santa Monica Boulevard: moon shadows, in horizontal patterns of dark and blue-white bands.

I caught her at the corner.

The moon was setting.

A setting moon always looks tremendous. Tonight it glared at us through the gap of sky beneath the freeway, terribly bright, casting an incredible complexity of lines and shadows. Even the unlighted crescent glowed pearly bright with earthshine.

Which told me all I wanted to know about what was happening on the lighted side of Earth.

And on the moon? The men of Apollo 19 must have died in the first few minutes of nova sunlight. Trapped out on a lunar plain, hiding perhaps behind a melting boulder . . . Or were they on the night side? I couldn't remember. Hell, they could outlive us all. I felt a stab of envy and hatred.

And pride. We'd put them there. We reached the moon before the nova came. A little longer, we'd have reached the stars.

The disc changed oddly as it set. A dome, a flying saucer, a lens, a line . . .

Gone.

Gone. Well, that was that. Now we could forget it; now we could walk around outside without being constantly reminded that something was *wrong*. Moonset had taken all the queer shadows out of the city.

But the clouds had an odd glow to them. As clouds glow after sunset, tonight the clouds shone livid white at their western edges. And they streamed too quickly across the sky. As if they tried to run . . .

When I turned to Leslie, there were big tears rolling down her cheeks.

"Oh, damn." I took her arm. "Now stop it. Stop it."

"I can't. You know I can't stop crying once I get started."

"This wasn't what I had in mind. I thought we'd do things we've been putting off, things we like. It's our last chance. Is this the way you want to die, crying on a street corner?"

"I don't want to die at all!"

"Tough shit!"

"Thanks a lot." Her face was all red and twisted. Leslie was crying as a baby cries, without regard for dignity or appearance. I felt awful. I felt guilty, and I *knew* the nova wasn't my fault, and it made me angry.

"I don't want to die either!" I snarled at her. "You show me a way out and I'll take it. Where would we go? The South Pole? It'd just take longer. The moon must be molten all across its day side. Mars? When this is over Mars will be part of the sun, like the Earth. Alpha Centauri? The acceleration we'd need, we'd be spread across a wall like peanut butter and jelly—"

"Oh, shut up."

"Right."

"Hawaii. Stan, we could get to the airport in twenty minutes. We'd get two hours extra, going west! Two hours more before sunrise!"

She had something there. Two hours was worth any price! But I'd worked this out before, staring at the moon from my balcony. "No. We'd die sooner. Listen, love, we saw the moon go bright about midnight. That means California was at the back of the Earth when the sun went nova."

"Yes, that's right."

"Then we must be farthest from the shock wave."

She blinked. "I don't understand."

"Look at it this way. First the sun explodes. That heats the air and the oceans, all in a flash, all across the day side. The steam and superheated air expand *fast*. A flaming shock wave comes roaring over into the night side. It's closing on us right now. Like a noose. But it'll reach Hawaii first. Hawaii is two hours closer to the sunset line."

"Then we won't see the dawn. We won't live even that long."

"No."

"You explain things so well," she said bitterly. "A flaming shock wave. So graphic."

"Sorry. I've been thinking about it too much. Wondering what it will be like."

"Well, stop it." She came to me and put her face in my shoulder. She cried quietly. I held her with one arm and used the other to rub her neck, and I watched the streaming clouds, and I didn't think about what it would be like.

Didn't think about the ring of fire closing on us.

It was the wrong picture anyway.

I thought of how the oceans must have boiled on the day side, so that the shock wave had been mostly steam to start with. I thought of the millions of square miles of ocean it had to cross. It would be cooler and wetter when it reached us. And the Earth's rotation would spin it like the whirlpool in a bathtub.

Two counterrotating hurricanes of live steam, one north, one south. That was how it would come. We were lucky. California would be near the eye of the northern one.

A hurricane wind of live steam. It would pick a man up and cook him in the air, strip the steamed flesh from him and cast him aside. It was going to hurt like hell.

We would never see the sunrise. In a way that was a pity. It would be spectacular.

Thick parallel streamers of cloud were drifting across the stars, too fast, their bellies white by city light. Jupiter dimmed, then went out. Could it be starting already? Heat lightning jumped—

"Aurora," I said.

"What?"

"There's a shock wave from the sun, too. There should be an aurora like nothing anybody's ever seen before."

Leslie laughed suddenly, jarringly. "It seems so strange, standing on a street corner talking like this! Stan, are we dreaming it?"

"We could pretend—"

"No. Most of the human race must be dead already."

"Yah."

"And there's nowhere to go."

"Damn it, you figured that out long ago, all by yourself. Why bring it up now?"

"You could have let me sleep," she said bitterly. "I was dropping off to sleep when you whispered in my ear."

I didn't answer. It was true.

" 'Hot fudge sundae,' " she quoted. Then, "It wasn't a bad idea, actually. Breaking my diet."

I started to giggle.

"Stop that."

"We could go back to your place now. Or my place. To sleep."

"I suppose. But we couldn't sleep, could we? No, don't say it. We take sleeping pills, and five hours from now we wake up screaming. I'd rather stay awake. At least we'll know what's happening."

But if we took all the pills . . . but I didn't say it. I said, "Then how about a picnic?"

"Where?"

"The beach, maybe. Who cares? We can decide later."

IV

All the markets were closed. But the liquor store next to the Red Barn was one I'd been using for years. They sold us foie gras, crackers, a couple of bottles of chilled champagne, six kinds of cheese and a hell of a lot of nuts—I took one of everything— more crackers, a bag of ice, frozen rumaki hors d'oeuvres, a fifth of an ancient brandy that cost twenty-five bucks, a matching fifth of Cherry Heering for Leslie, six-packs of beer and Bitter Orange . . .

By the time we had piled all that into a dinky store cart, it was raining. Big fat drops spattered in flurries across the acre of plate glass that fronted the store. Wind howled around the corners.

The salesman was in a fey mood, bursting with energy. He'd been watching the moon all night. "And now this!" he exclaimed as he packed our loot into bags. He was a small, muscular old man with thick arms and shoulders. "It *never* rains like this in California. It comes down straight and heavy, when it comes at all. Takes days to build up."

"I know." I wrote him a check, feeling guilty about it. He'd known me long enough to trust me. But the check was good. There were funds to cover it. Before opening hours the check would be ash, and all the banks in the world would be bubbling in the heat of the sun. But that was hardly my fault.

He piled our bags in the cart, set himself at the door. "Now when the rain lets up, we'll run these out. Ready?" I got ready to open the door. The rain came like someone had thrown a bucket of water at the window. In a moment it had stopped, though water still streamed down the glass. "Now!" cried the salesman, and I threw the door open and we were off. We reached the car laughing like maniacs. The wind howled around us, sweeping up spray and hurling it at us.

"We picked a good break. You know what this weather reminds me of? Kansas," said the salesman. "During a tornado."

Then suddenly the sky was full of gravel! We yelped and ducked, and the car rang to a million tiny concussions, and I got the car door unlocked and pulled Leslie and the salesman in after me. We rubbed our bruised heads and looked out at white gravel bouncing everywhere.

The salesman picked a small white pebble out of his collar. He put it in Leslie's hand, and she gave a startled squeak and handed it to me, and it was cold.

"Hail," said the salesman. "Now I really don't get it."

Neither did I. I could only think that it had something to do with the nova. But what? How?

"I've got to get back," said the salesman. The hail had expended itself in one brief flurry. He braced himself, then went out of the car like a marine taking a hill. We never saw him again.

The clouds were churning up there, forming and disappearing, sliding past each other faster than I'd ever seen clouds move; their bellies glowing by city light.

"It must be the nova," Leslie said shivering.

"But how? If the shock wave were here already, we'd be *dead* —or at least deaf. Hail?"

"Who cares? Stan, we don't have *time!*"

I shook myself. "All right. What would you like to do most, right now?"

"Watch a baseball game."

"It's two in the morning," I pointed out.

"That lets out a lot of things, doesn't it?"

"Right. We've hopped our last bar. We've seen our last play, and our last clean movie. What's left?"

"Looking in jewelry store windows."

"Seriously? Your last night on Earth?"

She considered, then answered. "Yes."

By damn, she meant it. I couldn't think of anything duller. "Westwood or Beverly Hills?"

"Both."

"Now, *look—*"

"Beverly Hills, then."

We drove through another spatter of rain and hail—a capsule tempest. We parked half a block from the Tiffany salesroom.

The sidewalk was one continuous puddle. Secondhand rain dripped on us from various levels of the buildings overhead. Leslie said, "This is great. There must be half a dozen jewelry stores in walking distance."

"I was thinking of driving."

"No no no, you don't have the proper attitude. One must window-shop on foot. It's in the rules."

"But the rain!"

"You won't die of pneumonia. You won't have time," she said, too grimly.

Tiffany's had a small branch office in Beverly Hills, but they didn't put expensive things in the windows at night. There were a few fascinating toys, that was all.

We turned up Rodeo Drive—and struck it rich. Tibor showed an infinite selection of rings, ornate and modern, large and small, in all kinds of precious and semiprecious stones. Across the street, Van Cleef & Arpels showed brooches, men's wristwatches of elegant design, bracelets with tiny watches in them, and one window that was all diamonds.

"Oh, lovely," Leslie breathed, caught by the flashing diamonds. "What they must look like in daylight! . . . Wups—"

"No, that's a good thought. Imagine them at dawn, flaming with nova light, while the windows shatter to let the raw daylight in. Want one? The necklace?"

"Oh, *may* I? Hey, hey, I was kidding! Put that down, you idiot, there must be alarms in the glass."

"Look, nobody's going to be wearing any of that stuff between now and morning. Why shouldn't we get some good out of it?"

"We'd be caught!"

"Well, you *said* you wanted to window-shop . . ."

"I don't want to spend my last hour in a cell. If you'd brought the car we'd have *some* chance—"

"Of getting away. Right. I *wanted* to bring the car—" But at that point we both cracked up entirely, and had to stagger away holding onto each other for balance.

There were a good half-dozen jewelry stores on Rodeo. But there was more. Toys, books, shirts and ties in odd and advanced styling. In Francis Orr, a huge plastic cube full of new pennies. A couple of damn strange clocks farther on. There was an extra kick in window shopping, knowing that we could break a window and take anything we wanted badly enough.

We walked hand in hand, swinging our arms. The sidewalks were ours alone; all others had fled the mad weather. The clouds still churned overhead.

"I wish I'd known it was coming," Leslie said suddenly. "I spent the whole day fixing a mistake in a program. Now we'll never run it."

"What would you have done with the time? A baseball game?"

"Maybe. No. The standings don't matter now." She frowned at dresses in a store window. "What would you have done?"

"Gone to the Blue Sphere for cocktails," I said promptly. "It's a topless place. I used to go there all the time. I hear they've gone full nude now."

"I've never been to one of those. How late are they open?"

"Forget it. It's almost two-thirty."

Leslie mused, looking at giant stuffed animals in a toy store window. "Isn't there someone you would have murdered, if you'd had the time?"

"Now, you *know* my agent lives in New York."

"Why him?"

"My child, why would any writer want to murder his agent? For the manuscripts he loses under other manuscripts. For his ill-gotten ten percent, and the remaining ninety percent that he sends me grudgingly and late. For—"

Suddenly the wind roared and rose up against us. Leslie pointed, and we ran for a deep doorway that turned out to be Gucci's. We huddled against the glass.

The wind was suddenly choked with hail the size of marbles. Glass broke somewhere, and alarms lifted thin, frail voices into the wind. There was more than hail in the wind! There were rocks!

I caught the smell and taste of sea water.

We clung together in the expensively wasted space in front of Gucci's. I coined a short-lived phrase and screamed, "Nova weather! How the blazes did it—" But I couldn't hear myself, and Leslie didn't even know I was shouting.

Nova weather. How did it get here so fast? Coming over the

pole, the nova shock wave would have to travel about four thousand miles—at least a five-hour trip.

No. The shock wave would travel in the stratosphere, where the speed of sound was higher, then propagate down. Three hours was plenty of time. Still, I thought, it should not have come as a rising wind. On the other side of the world, the exploding sun was tearing our atmosphere away and hurling it at the stars. The shock should have come as a single vast thunderclap.

For an instant the wind gentled, and I ran down the sidewalk pulling Leslie after me. We found another doorway as the wind picked up again. I thought I heard a siren coming to answer the alarm.

At the next break we splashed across Wilshire and reached the car. We sat there panting, waiting for the heater to warm up. My shoes felt squishy. The wet clothes stuck to my skin.

Leslie shouted, "How much longer?"

"I don't know! We ought to have *some* time."

"We'll have to spend our picnic indoors!"

"Your place or mine? Yours," I decided, and pulled away from the curb.

V

Wilshire Boulevard was flooded to the hubcaps in spots. The spurts of hail and sleet had become a steady, pounding rain. Fog lay flat and waist-deep ahead of us, broke swirling over our hood, churned in a wake behind us. Weird weather.

Nova weather. The shock wave of scalding superheated steam hadn't happened. Instead, a mere hot wind roaring through the stratosphere, the turbulence eddying down to form strange storms at ground level.

We parked illegally on the upper parking level. My one glimpse of the lower level showed it to be flooded. I opened the trunk and lifted two heavy paper bags.

"We must have been crazy," Leslie said, shaking her head. "We'll never use all this."

"Let's take it up anyway."

She laughed at me. "But why?"

"Just a whim. Will you help me carry it?"

We took double armfuls up to the fourteenth floor. That still left a couple of bags in the trunk. "Never mind them," Leslie said. "We've got the rumaki and the bottles and the nuts. What more do we need?"

"The cheeses. The crackers. The foie gras."

"Forget 'em."

"No."

"You're out of your mind," she explained to me, slowly so that I would understand. "You could be steamed dead on the way down. We might not have more than a few minutes left, and you want food for a week! *Why?*"

"I'd rather not say."

"Go then!" She slammed the door with terrible force.

The elevator was an ordeal. I kept wondering if Leslie was right. The shrilling of the wind was muffled, here at the core of the building. Perhaps it was about to rip electrical cables somewhere, leave me stranded in a darkened box. But I made it down.

The upper level was knee-deep in water.

My second surprise was that it was lukewarm, like old bathwater, unpleasant to wade through. Steam curdled on the surface, then blew away on a wind that howled through the concrete echo chamber like the screaming of the damned.

Going up was another ordeal. If what I was thinking was wish fulfillment, if a roaring wind of live steam caught me now . . . I'd feel like such an idiot . . . But the doors opened, and the lights hadn't even flickered.

Leslie wouldn't let me in.

"Go away!" She shouted through the locked door. "Go eat your cheese and crackers somewhere else!"

"You got another date?"

That was a mistake. I got no answer at all.

I could almost see her viewpoint. The extra trip for the extra bags was no big thing to fight about; but why did it have to be? How long was our love affair going to last, anyway? An hour, with luck. Why back down on a perfectly good argument, to preserve so ephemeral a thing?

"I wasn't going to bring this up," I shouted, hoping she could hear me through the door. The wind must be three times as loud on the other side. "We may need food for a week! And a place to hide!"

Silence. I began to wonder if I could kick the door down. Would I be better off waiting in the hall? Eventually she'd have to—

The door opened. Leslie was pale. "That was cruel," she said quietly.

"I can't promise anything. I wanted to wait, but you forced it. I've been wondering if the sun really has exploded."

"That's cruel. I was just getting used to the idea." She turned her face to the doorjamb. Tired, she was tired. I'd kept her up too late . . .

"Listen to me. It was all wrong," I said. "There should have been an aurora borealis to light up the night sky from pole to pole. A shock wave of particles exploding out of the sun, traveling at an inch short of the speed of light, would rip into the atmosphere like—why, we'd have seen blue fire over every building!

"Then, the storm came too slow," I screamed, to be heard above the thunder. "A nova would rip away the sky over half the planet. The shock wave would move around the night side with a sound to break all the glass in the world, all at once! And crack concrete and marble—and, Leslie love, it just hasn't happened. So I started wondering."

She said it in a mumble. "Then what is it?"

"A flare. The worst—"

She shouted it at me like an accusation. "A flare! A solar flare! You think the sun could light up like that—"

"Easy, now—"

"—could turn the moon and planets into so many torches, then fade out as if nothing had happened! Oh, you idiot—"

"May I come in?"

She looked surprised. She stepped aside, and I bent and picked up the bags and walked in.

The glass doors rattled as if giants were trying to beat their way in. Rain had squeezed through cracks to make dark puddles on the rug.

I set the bags on the kitchen counter. I found bread in the refrigerator, dropped two slices in the toaster. While they were
toasting I opened the foie gras.

"My telescope's gone," she said. Sure enough, it was. The tripod was all by itself on the balcony, on its side.

I untwisted the wire on a champagne bottle. The toast popped
up, and Leslie found a knife and spread both slices with foie
gras. I held the bottle near her ear, figuring to trip conditioned
reflexes.

She did smile fleetingly as the cork popped. She said, "We
should set up our picnic grounds here. Behind the counter.
Sooner or later the wind is going to break those doors and
shower glass all over everything."

That was a good thought. I slid around the partition, swept all
the pillows off the floor and the couch and came back with them.
We set up a nest for ourselves.

It was kind of cosy. The kitchen counter was three and a half
feet high, just over our heads, and the kitchen alcove itself was
just wide enough to swing our elbows comfortably. Now the
floor was all pillows. Leslie poured the champagne into brandy
snifters, all the way to the lip.

I searched for a toast, but there were just too many possibilities, all depressing. We drank without toasting. And then
carefully set the snifters down and slid forward into each other's
arms. We could sit that way, face to face, leaning sideways
against each other.

"We're going to die," she said.

"Maybe not."

"Get used to the idea. I have," she said. "Look at you, you're
all nervous now. Afraid of dying. Hasn't it been a lovely night?"

"Unique. I wish I'd known in time to take you to dinner."

Thunder came in a string of six explosions. Like bombs in an
air raid. "Me too," she said when we could hear again.

"I wish I'd known this afternoon."

"Pecan pralines!"

"Farmer's Market. Double-roasted peanuts. Who would *you*
have murdered, if you'd had the time?"

"There was a girl in my sorority—"

—and she was guilty of sibling rivalry, so Leslie claimed. I named an editor who kept changing his mind. Leslie named one of my old girl friends, I named her only old boy friend that I knew about, and it got to be kind of fun before we ran out. My brother Mike had forgotten my birthday once. The fiend.

The lights flickered, then came on again.

Too casually, Leslie asked, "Do you really think the sun might go back to normal?"

"It better *be* back to normal. Otherwise we're dead anyway. I wish we could see Jupiter."

"Dammit, answer me! Do you think it was a flare?"

"Yes."

"Why?"

"Yellow dwarf stars don't go nova."

"What if ours did?"

"The astronomers know a lot about novas," I said. "More than you'd guess. They can see them coming months ahead. Sol is a gee-nought yellow dwarf. They don't go nova at all. They have to wander off the main sequence first, and that takes millions of years."

She pounded a fist softly on my back. We were cheek to cheek; I couldn't see her face. "I don't want to believe it. I don't dare. Stan, nothing like this has ever happened before. How can you know?"

"Something did."

"What? I don't believe it. We'd remember."

"Do you remember the first moon landing? Aldrin and Armstrong?"

"Of course. We watched it at Earl's Lunar Landing Party."

"They landed on the biggest, flattest place they could find on the moon. They sent back several hours of jumpy home movies, took a lot of very clear pictures, left corrugated footprints all over the place. And they came home with a bunch of rocks.

"Remember? People said it was a long way to go for rocks. But the first thing anyone noticed about those rocks was that they were half-melted."

"Sometime in the past—oh, say, the past hundred thousand years, there's no way of marking it closer than that—the sun flared up. It didn't stay hot enough long enough to leave any marks on the Earth. But the moon doesn't have an atmosphere to protect it. All the rocks melted on one side."

The air was warm and damp. I took off my coat, which was heavy with rainwater. I fished the cigarettes and matches out, lit a cigarette and exhaled past Leslie's ear.

"We'd remember. It *couldn't* have been this bad."

"I'm not so sure. Suppose it happened over the Pacific? It wouldn't do *that* much damage. Or over the American continents. It would have sterilized some plants and animals and burned down a lot of forests, and who'd know? The sun went back to normal, that time. It might again. The sun is a four percent variable star. Maybe it gets a touch more variable than that, every so often."

Something shattered in the bedroom. A window? A wet wind touched us, and the shriek of the storm was louder.

"Then we could live through this," Leslie said hesitantly.

"I believe you've put your finger on the crux of the matter. Skål!" I found my champagne and drank deep. It was past three in the morning, with a hurricane beating at our doors.

"Then shouldn't we be doing something about it?"

"We are."

"Something like trying to get up into the hills! Stan, there're going to be floods!"

"You bet your ass there are, but they won't rise this high. Fourteen stories. Listen, I've thought this through. We're in a building that was designed to be earthquake-proof. You told me so yourself. It'd take more than a hurricane to knock it over.

"As for heading for the hills, what hills? We won't get far tonight, not with the streets flooded already. Suppose we could get up into the Santa Monica Mountains; then what? Mudslides, that's what. That area won't stand up to what's coming. The flare must have boiled away enough water to make another ocean. It's going to rain for forty days and forty nights! Love, this is the safest place we could have reached tonight."

"Suppose the polar caps melt?"

"Yeah . . . well, we're pretty high, even for that. Hey, maybe that last flare was what started Noah's flood. Maybe it's happening again. Sure as hell, there's not a place on Earth that isn't the middle of a hurricane. Those two great counterrotating hurricanes, by now they must have broken up into hundreds of little storms—"

The glass doors exploded inward. We ducked, and the wind howled about us and dropped rain and glass on us.

"At least we've got food!" I shouted. "If the floods maroon us here, we can last it out!"

"But if the power goes, we can't cook it! And the refrigerator—"

"We'll cook everything we can. Hardboil all the eggs—"

The wind rose about us. I stopped trying to talk.

Warm rain sprayed us horizontally and left us soaked. Try to cook in a hurricane? I'd been stupid; I'd waited too long. The wind would tip boiling water on us if we tried it. Or hot grease—

Leslie screamed, "We'll have to use the oven!"

Of course. The oven couldn't possibly fall on us.

We set it for 400° and put the eggs in, in a pot of water. We took all the meat out of the meat drawer and shoved it in on a broiling pan. Two artichokes in another pot. The other vegetables we could eat raw.

What else? I tried to think.

Water. If the electricity went, probably the water and telephone lines would too. I turned on the faucet over the sink and started filling things: pots with lids, Leslie's thirty-cup percolator that she used for parties, her wash bucket. She clearly thought I was crazy, but I didn't trust the rain as a water source; I couldn't control it.

The sound. Already we'd stopped trying to shout through it. Forty days and nights of this and we'd be stone-deaf. Cotton? Too late to reach the bathroom. Paper towels! I tore and wadded and made four plugs for our ears.

Sanitary facilities? Another reason for picking Leslie's place over mine. When the plumbing stopped, there was always the balcony.

And if the flood rose higher than the fourteenth floor, there was the roof. Twenty stories up. If it went higher than that, there would be damn few people left when it was over.

And if it was a nova?

I held Leslie a bit more closely, and lit another cigarette one-handed. All the wasted planning, if it was a nova. But I'd have been doing it anyway. You don't stop planning just because there's no hope.

And when the hurricane turned to live steam, there was always the balcony. At a dead run, and over the railing, in preference to being boiled alive.

But now was not the time to mention it.

Anyway, she'd probably thought of it herself.

The lights went out about four. I turned off the oven, in case the power should come back. Give it an hour to cool down, then I'd put all the food in Baggies.

Leslie was asleep, sitting up in my arms. How could she sleep, not knowing? I piled pillows behind her and let her back easy.

For some time I lay on my back, smoking, watching the lightning make shadows on the ceiling. We had eaten all the foie gras and drunk one bottle of champagne. I thought of opening the brandy, but decided against it, with regret.

A long time passed. I'm not sure what I thought about. I didn't sleep, but certainly my mind was in idle. It only gradually came to me that the ceiling, between lightning flashes, had turned gray.

I rolled over, gingerly, soggily. Everything was wet.

My watch said it was nine-thirty.

I crawled around the partition into the living room. I'd been ignoring the storm sounds for so long that it took a faceful of warm whipping rain to remind me. There was a hurricane going on. But charcoal-gray light was filtering through the black clouds.

So. I was right to have saved the brandy. Flood, storms, intense radiation, fires lit by the flare—if the toll of destruction was as high as I expected, then money was about to become worthless. We would need trade goods.

I was hungry. I ate two eggs and some bacon—still warm— and started putting the rest of the food away. We had food for a week, maybe . . . but hardly a balanced diet. Maybe we could trade with other apartments. This was a big building. There must be empty apartments, too, that we could raid for canned soup and the like. And refugees from the lower floors to be taken care of, if the waters rose high enough . . .

Damn! I missed the nova. Life had been simplicity itself last night. Now . . . Did we have medicines? Were there doctors in the building? There would be dysentery and other plagues. And hunger. There was a supermarket near here; could we find a scuba rig in the building?

But I'd get some sleep first. Later we could start exploring the building. The day had become a lighter charcoal gray. Things could be worse, far worse. I thought of the radiation that must have sleeted over the far side of the world, and wondered if our children would colonize Europe, or Asia, or Africa.

1973
31st *CONVENTION*
TORONTO

Ursula K. Le Guin

The thirty-first convention was held in Toronto in 1973 and it was by far the most remarkable of the world conventions for reasons I'll get to later. (I have three more cracks at this one.)

For now, I'll just say that I attended the thirty-first convention with Janet, who was soon to become my wife. That in itself was a vast improvement on the twenty-ninth convention, which I attended alone.

You might think that attending a convention *alone* would insure the height of vice and revelry and perhaps you're right. I myself don't know about such things. Nor was I to be given a chance to find out. Lester del Rey and his new bride, Judy-Lynn, were in attendance too. They made sure that they had the room right next to me; they supervised my every breakfast and continually dogged my footsteps. All I was allowed to do was to wave at girls from a distance.

They said they were trying to save me from myself and to this day I don't know what they meant. I wasn't planning to do anything by myself. Anyway, by 1973, Janet was along and she was intent on saving me from myself too.

But to business. Here we have a Hugo-winning story that is written by a woman. As you all know (if you are old enough) there was once a time when science fiction was as masculine as testosterone. There were women writers and women readers but somehow they were ignored. Now things are different.

In Volume One, there were nine Hugo winners in the less-than-novel categories and not one, *not one*, was written by a woman. In Volume Two, there were fourteen stories and *one* was written by a woman, "Weyr Search" by the silver-throated Anne McCaffrey. Now, in Volume Three, we have fifteen stories of which two, count them, *two*, are written by women. At this rate, when *The Hugo Winners, Volume Fifteen* comes out in 2051 (with myself as editor, of course; who else?) we will have all the stories by women.

To be sure, there's the small complication that both stories by women in this volume were written by Ursula. If we continue to extrapolate, then, in sober scientific fashion, considering the undeniable fact that so far each volume has one more story by a woman than the volume before, but that each time a woman is represented, only *one* woman is (are you confused?), then all fifteen stories in *The Hugo Winners, Volume Fifteen* will have been written by the same woman.

You can't beat logic.

I've never met Ursula, by the way. I'm not sure I ought to. In the last few years, she has become just about the most highly regarded writer in science fiction and if I should, by sheer force of habit, greet her with the suavity which is usual to me in my approach to young women, she might be offended at the *lèse majesté* and slosh me one.

6

THE WORD FOR WORLD
IS FOREST

I

Two pieces of yesterday were in Captain Davidson's mind when he woke, and he lay looking at them in the darkness for a while. One up: the new shipload of women had arrived. Believe it or not. They were here, in Centralville, twenty-seven lightyears from Earth by NAFAL and four hours from Smith Camp by hopper, the second batch of breeding females for the New Tahiti Colony, all sound and clean, 212 head of prime human stock. Or prime enough, anyhow. One down: the report from Dump Island of crop failures, massive erosion, a wipe-out. The line of 212 buxom beddable breasty little figures faded from Davidson's mind as he saw rain pouring down onto ploughed dirt, churning it to mud, thinning the mud to a red broth that ran down rocks into the rainbeaten sea. The erosion had begun before he left Dump Island to run Smith Camp, and being gifted with an exceptional visual memory, the kind they called eidetic, he could recall it now all too clearly. It looked like that bigdome Kees was right and you had to leave a lot of trees standing where you planned to put farms. But he still couldn't see why a soybean farm needed to waste a lot of space on trees if the land was managed really scientifically. It wasn't like that in Ohio; if you wanted corn you grew corn, and no space wasted on trees and stuff. But then Earth was a tamed planet and New Tahiti wasn't. That's what he was here for: to tame it. If Dump Island was just rocks and gullies now, then scratch it; start over on a new island

and do better. Can't keep us down, we're Men. You'll learn what that means pretty soon, you godforsaken damn planet, Davidson thought, and he grinned a little in the darkness of the hut, for he liked challenges. Thinking Men, he thought Women, and again the line of little figures began to sway through his mind, smiling, jiggling.

"Ben!" he roared, sitting up and swinging his bare feet onto the bare floor. "Hot water get-ready, hurry-up-quick!" The roar woke him satisfyingly. He stretched and scratched his chest and pulled on his shorts and strode out of the hut into the sunlit clearing all in one easy series of motions. A big, hard-muscled man, he enjoyed using his well-trained body. Ben, his creechie, had the water ready and steaming over the fire, as usual, and was squatting staring at nothing, as usual. Creechies never slept, they just sat and stared. "Breakfast. Hurry-up-quick!" Davidson said, picking up his razor from the rough board table where the creechie had laid it out ready with a towel and a propped-up mirror.

There was a lot to be done today, since he'd decided, that last minute before getting up, to fly down to Central and see the new women for himself. They wouldn't last long, 212 among over two thousand men, and like the first batch probably most of them were Colony Brides, and only twenty or thirty had come as Recreation Staff; but those babies were real good greedy girls and he intended to be first in line with at least one of them this time. He grinned on the left, the right cheek remaining stiff to the whining razor.

The old creechie was moseying round taking an hour to bring his breakfast from the cookhouse. "Hurry-up-quick!" Davidson yelled, and Ben pushed his boneless saunter into a walk. Ben was about a meter high and his back fur was more white than green; he was old, and dumb even for a creechie, but Davidson knew how to handle him. A lot of men couldn't handle creechies worth a damn, but Davidson had never had trouble with them; he could tame any of them, if it was worth the effort. It wasn't, though. Get enough humans here, build machines and robots, make farms and cities, and nobody would need the creechies any more. And a good thing too. For this world, New Tahiti, was literally made for men. Cleaned up and cleaned out, the dark forests cut down for open fields of grain, the primeval murk and savagery and ignorance wiped out, it would be a paradise, a real Eden. A better world than worn-out Earth. And it would be his world. For that's what Don Davidson was, way down deep inside him: a world-tamer. He wasn't a boastful man, but he knew his own size. It just happened to be the way he was made. He knew what he wanted, and how to get it. And he always got it.

Breakfast landed warm in his belly. His good mood wasn't spoiled even by the sight of Kees Van Sten coming towards him, fat, white, and worried, his eyes sticking out like blue golf-balls.

"Don," Kees said without greeting, "the loggers have been hunting red deer in the Strips again. There are eighteen pair of antlers in the back room of the Lounge."

"Nobody ever stopped poachers from poaching, Kees."

"You can stop them. That's why we live under martial law, that's why the Army runs this colony. To keep the laws."

A frontal attack from Fatty Bigdome! It was almost funny. "All right," Davidson said reasonably, "I could stop 'em. But look, it's the men I'm looking after; that's my job, like you said. And it's the men that count. Not the animals. If a little extra-legal hunting helps the men get through this godforsaken life, then I intend to blink. They've got to have some recreation."

"They have games, sports, hobbies, films, teletapes of every major sporting event of the past century, liquor, marijuana, hallies, and a fresh batch of women at Central. For those unsatisfied by the Army's rather unimaginative arrangements for hygienic homosexuality. They are spoiled rotten, your frontier heroes, and they don't need to exterminate a rare native species 'for recreation.' If you don't act, I must record a major infraction of Ecological Protocols in my report to Captain Gosse."

"You can do that if you see fit, Kees," said Davidson, who never lost his temper. It was sort of pathetic the way a euro like Kees got all red in the face when he lost control of his emotions. "That's your job, after all. I won't hold it against you; they can do the arguing at Central and decide who's right. See, you want to keep this place just like it is, actually, Kees. Like one big National Forest. To look at, to study. Great, you're a spesh. But see we're just ordinary joes getting the work done. Earth needs wood, needs it bad. We find wood on New Tahiti. So—we're loggers. See, where we differ is that with you Earth doesn't come first, actually. With me it does."

Kees looked at him sideways out of those blue golf-ball eyes. "Does it? You want to make this world into Earth's image, eh? A desert of cement?"

"When I say Earth, Kees, I mean people. Men. You worry about deer and trees and fibreweed, fine, that's your thing. But I like to see things in perspective, from the top down, and the top, so far, is humans. We're here, now; and so this world's going to go our way. Like it or not, it's a fact you have to face; it happens to be the way things are. Listen, Kees, I'm going to hop down to Central and take a look at the new colonists. Want to come along?"

"No thanks, Captain Davidson," the spesh said, going on towards the Lab hut. He was really mad. All upset about those damn deer. They were great animals, all right. Davidson's vivid memory recalled the first one he had seen, here on Smith Land, a big red shadow, two meters at the shoulder, a crown of narrow golden antlers, a fleet, brave beast, the finest game-animal imaginable. Back on Earth they were using robodeer even in the High Rockies and Himalaya Parks now, the real ones were about gone. These things were a hunter's dream. So they'd be hunted. Hell, even the wild creechies hunted them, with their lousy little bows. The deer would be hunted because that's what they were there for. But poor old bleeding-heart Kees couldn't see it. He was actually a smart fellow, but not realistic, not tough-minded enough. He didn't see that you've got to play on the winning side or else you lose. And it's Man that wins, every time. The old Conquistador.

Davidson strode on through the settlement, morning sunlight in his eyes, the smell of sawn wood and woodsmoke sweet on the warm air. Things looked pretty neat, for a logging camp. The two hundred men here had tamed a fair patch of wilderness in just three E-months. Smith Camp: a couple of big corruplast geodesics, forty timber huts built by creechie-labor, the sawmill, the burner trailing a blue plume over acres of logs and cut lumber; uphill, the airfield and the big prefab hangar for helicopters and heavy machinery. That was all. But when they came here there had been nothing. Trees. A dark huddle and jumble and tangle of trees, endless, meaningless. A sluggish river overhung and choked by trees, a few creechie-warrens hidden among the trees, some red deer, hairy monkeys, birds. And trees. Roots, boles, branches, twigs, leaves, leaves overhead and underfoot and in your face and in your eyes, endless leaves on endless trees.

New Tahiti was mostly water, warm shallow seas broken here and there by reefs, islets, archipelagoes, and the five big Lands that lay in a 2,500-kilo arc across the Northwest Quartersphere. And all those flecks and blobs of land were covered with trees. Ocean: forest. That was your choice on New Tahiti. Water and sunlight, or darkness and leaves.

But men were here now to end the darkness, and turn the tree-jumble into clean sawn planks, more prized on Earth than gold. Literally, because gold could be got from seawater and from under the Antarctic ice, but wood could not; wood came only from trees. And it was a really necessary luxury on Earth. So the alien forests became wood. Two hundred men with robosaws and haulers had already cut eight mile-wide Strips on Smith Land, in three months. The stumps of the Strip nearest camp were already white and punky; chemically treated, they would have fallen into fertile ash by the time the permanent colonists, the farmers, came to settle Smith Land. All the farmers would have to do was plant seeds and let 'em sprout.

It had been done once before. That was a queer thing, and the proof, actually, that New Tahiti was intended for humans to take over. All the stuff here had come from Earth, about a million years ago, and the evolution had followed so close a path that you recognized things at once: pine, oak, walnut, chestnut, fir, holly, apple, ash; deer, bird, mouse, cat, squirrel, monkey. The humanoids on Hain-Davenant of course claimed they'd done it at the same time as they colonised Earth, but if you listened to those ETs you'd find they claimed to have settled every planet in the Galaxy and invented everything from sex to thumbtacks. The theories about Atlantis were a lot more realistic, and this might well be a lost Atlantean colony. But the humans had died out. And the nearest thing that had developed from the monkey line to replace them was the creechie—a meter tall and covered with green fur. As ETs they were about standard, but as men they were a bust, they just hadn't made it. Give 'em another million years, maybe. But the Conquistadors had arrived first. Evolution moved now not at the pace of a random mutation once a millennium, but with the speed of the starships of the Terran Fleet.

"Hey Captain!"

Davidson turned, only a microsecond late in his reaction, but that was late enough to annoy him. There was something about this damn planet, its gold sunlight and hazy sky, its mild winds smelling of leafmould and pollen, something that made you daydream. You mooched along thinking about conquistadors and destiny and stuff, till you were acting as thick and slow as a creechie. "Morning, Ok!" he said crisply to the logging foreman.

Black and tough as wire rope, Oknanawi Nabo was Kee's physical opposite, but he had the same worried look. "You got half a minute?"

"Sure. What's eating you, Ok?"

"The little bastards."

They leaned their backsides on a split rail fence. Davidson lit his first reefer of the day. Sunlight, smoke-blued, slanted warm across the air. The forest behind camp, a quarter-mile-wide uncut Strip, was full of the faint, ceaseless, cracking, chuckling, stirring, whirring, silvery noises that woods in the morning are full of. It might have been Idaho in 1950, this clearing. Or Kentucky in 1830. Or Gaul in 50 B.C. "Te-whet," said a distant bird.

"I'd like to get rid of 'em, Captain."

"The creechies? How d'you mean, Ok?"

"Just let 'em go. I can't get enough work out of 'em in the mill to make up for their keep. Or for their being such a damn headache. They just don't work."

"They do if you know how to make 'em. They built the camp."

Oknanawi's obsidian face was dour. "Well, you got the touch with 'em, I guess. I don't." He paused. "In that Applied History course I took in training for Far-out, it said that slavery never worked. It was uneconomical."

"Right, but this isn't slavery, Ok baby. Slaves are humans. When you raise cows, you call that slavery? No. And it works."

Impassive, the foreman nodded; but he said, "They're too little. I tried starving the sulky ones. They just sit and starve."

"They're little, all right, but don't let 'em fool you, Ok. They're tough; they've got terrific endurance; and they don't feel pain like humans. That's the part you forget, Ok. You think hitting one is like hitting a kid, sort of. Believe me, it's more like hitting a robot for all they feel it. Look, you've laid some of the females, you know how they don't seem to feel anything, no pleasure, no pain, they just lay there like mattresses no matter what you do. They're all like that. Probably they've got more primitive nerves than humans do. Like fish. I'll tell you a weird one about that. When I was in Central, before I came up here, one of the tame males jumped me once. I know they'll tell you they never fight, but this one went spla, right off his nut, and lucky he wasn't armed or he'd have killed me. I had to damn near kill him before he'd even let go. And he kept coming back. It was incredible the beating he took and never even felt it. Like some beetle you have to keep stepping on because it doesn't know it's been squashed already. Look at this." Davidson bent down his close-cropped head to show a gnarled lump behind one ear. "That was damn near a concussion. And he did it after I'd broken his arm and pounded his face into cranberry sauce. He just kept coming back and coming back. The thing is, Ok, the creechies are lazy, they're dumb, they're treacherous, and they don't feel pain. You've got to be tough with 'em and stay tough with 'em."

"They aren't worth the trouble, Captain. Damn sulky little green bastards, they won't fight, won't work, won't nothing. Except give me the pip." There was a geniality in Oknanawi's grumbling which did not conceal the stubbornness beneath. He wouldn't beat up creechies because they were so much smaller; that was clear in his mind, and clear now to Davidson, who at once accepted it. He knew how to handle his men. "Look, Ok. Try this. Pick out the ringleaders and tell 'em you're going to give them a shot of hallucinogen. Mesc, lice, any one, they don't know one from the other. But they're scared of them. Don't over-work it, and it'll work. I can guarantee."

"Why are they scared of hallies?" the foreman asked curiously.

"How do I know? Why are women scared of rats? Don't look for good sense from women or creechies, Ok! Speaking of which I'm on the way to Central this morning, shall I put the finger on a Collie Girl for you?"

"Just keep the finger off a few till I get my leave," Ok said grinning. A group of creechies passed, carrying a long 12×12 beam for the Rec Room being built down by the river. Slow, shambling little figures, they worried the big beam along like a lot of ants with a dead caterpillar, sullen and inept. Oknanawi watched them and said, "Fact is, Captain, they give me the creeps."

That was queer, coming from a tough, quiet guy like Ok.

"Well, I agree with you, actually, Ok, that they're not worth the trouble, or the risk. If that fart Lyubov wasn't around and the Colonel wasn't so stuck on following the Code, I think we might just clean out the areas we settle, instead of this Voluntary Labor routine. They're going to get rubbed out sooner or later, and it might as well be sooner. It's just how things happen to be. Primitive races always have to give way to civilised ones. Or be assimilated. But we sure as hell can't assimilate a lot of green monkeys. And like you say, they're just bright enough that they'll never be quite trustworthy. Like those big monkeys used to live in Africa, what were they called."

"Gorillas?"

"Right. We'll get on better without creechies here, just like we get on better without gorillas in Africa. They're in our way . . . But Daddy Ding-Dong he say use creechie-labor, so we use creechie-labor. For a while. Right? See you tonight, Ok."

"Right, Captain."

Davidson checked out the hopper from Smith Camp HQ: a pine-plank 4-meter cube, two desks, a watercooler, Lt. Birno repairing a walkytalky. "Don't let the camp burn down, Birno."

"Bring me back a Collie, Cap. Blonde. 34-22-36."

"Christ, is that all?"

"I like 'em neat, not floppy, see?" Birno expressively outlined his preference in the air. Grinning, Davidson went on up to the hangar. As he brought the helicopter back over camp he looked down at it: kid's blocks, sketch-lines of paths, long stump-stubbled clearings, all shrinking as the machine rose and he saw the green of the uncut forests of the great island, and beyond that dark green the pale green of the sea going on and on. Now Smith Camp looked like a yellow spot, a fleck on a vast green tapestry.

He crossed Smith Straits and the wooded, deep-folded ranges

of north Central Island, and came down by noon in Centralville. It looked like a city, at least after three months in the woods; there were real streets, real buildings, it had been there since the Colony began four years ago. You didn't see what a flimsy little frontier-town it really was, until you looked south of it a halfmile and saw glittering above the stumplands and the concrete pads a single golden tower, taller than anything in Centralville. The ship wasn't a big one but it looked so big, here. And it was only a launch, a lander, a ship's boat; the NAFAL ship of the line, *Shackleton,* was half a million kilos up, in orbit. The launch was just a hint, just a fingertip of the hugeness, the power, the golden precision and grandeur of the star-bridging technology of Earth.

That was why tears came to Davidson's eyes for a second at the sight of the ship from home. He wasn't ashamed of it. He was a patriotic man, it just happened to be the way he was made.

Soon enough, walking down those frontier-town streets with their wide vistas of nothing much at each end, he began to smile. For the women were there, all right, and you could tell they were fresh ones. They mostly had long tight skirts and big shoes like galoshes, red or purple or gold, and gold or silvery frilly shirts. No more nipplepeeps. Fashions had changed; too bad. They all wore their hair piled up high, it must be sprayed with that glue stuff they used. Ugly as hell, but it was the sort of thing only women would do to their hair, and so it was provocative. Davidson grinned at a chesty little euraf with more hair than head; he got no smile, but a wag of the retreating hips that said plainly, Follow follow follow me. But he didn't. Not yet. He went to Central HQ: quickstone and plastiplate Standard Issue, 40 offices 10 watercoolers and a basement arsenal, and checked in with New Tahiti Central Colonial Administration Command. He met a couple of the launch-crew, put in a request for a new semirobo bark-stripper at Forestry, and got his old pal Juju Sereng to meet him at the Luau Bar at fourteen hundred.

He got to the bar an hour early to stock up on a little food before the drinking began. Lyubov was there, sitting with a couple of guys in Fleet uniform, some kind of speshes that had come down on the *Shackleton*'s launch. Davidson didn't have a high regard for the Navy, a lot of fancy sunhoppers who left the dirty, muddy, dangerous on-planet work to the Army; but brass was brass, and anyhow it was funny to see Lyubov acting chummy with anybody in uniform. He was talking, waving his hands around the way he did. Just in passing Davidson tapped his shoulder and said, "Hi, Raj old pal, how's tricks?" He went on without waiting for the scowl, though he hated to miss it. It was really funny the way Lyubov hated him. Probably the guy was effeminate like a lot of intellectuals, and resented Davidson's virility. Anyhow Davidson wasn't going to waste any time hating Lyubov, he wasn't worth the trouble.

The Luau served a first-rate venison steak. What would they say on old Earth if they saw one man eating a kilogram of meat at one meal? Poor damn soybeansuckers! Then Juju arrived with —as Davidson had confidently expected—the pick of the new Collie Girls: two fruity beauties, not Brides, but Recreation Staff. Oh the old Colonial Administration sometimes came through! It was a long, hot afternoon.

Flying back to camp he crossed Smith Straits level with the sun that lay on top of a great gold bed of haze over the sea. He sang as he lolled in the pilot's seat. Smith Land came in sight hazy, and there was smoke over the camp, a dark smudge as if oil had got into the waste-burner. He couldn't even make out the buildings through it. It was only as he dropped down to the landing-field that he saw the charred jet, the wrecked hoppers, the burned-out hangar.

He pulled the hopper up again and flew back over the camp, so low that he might have hit the high cone of the burner, the only thing left sticking up. The rest was gone, mill, furnace, lumberyards, HQ, huts, barracks, creechie compound, everything. Black hulks and wrecks, still smoking. But it hadn't been a forest fire. The forest stood there, green, next to the ruins. Davidson swung back round to the field, set down and lit out looking for the motorbike, but it too was a black wreck along with the stinking, smouldering ruins of the hangar and the machinery. He loped down the path to camp. As he passed what had been the radio hut, his mind snapped back into gear. Without hesitating for even a stride he changed course, off the path, behind the gutted shack. There he stopped. He listened.

There was nobody. It was all silent. The fires had been out a long time; only the great lumber-piles still smouldered, showing a hot red under the ash and char. Worth more than gold, those oblong ash-heaps had been. But no smoke rose from the black skeletons of the barracks and huts; and there were bones among the ashes.

Davidson's brain was super-clear and active, now, as he crouched behind the radio shack. There were two possibilities. One: an attack from another camp. Some officer on King or New Java had gone spla and was trying a coup de planète. Two: an attack from off-planet. He saw the golden tower on the space-dock at Central. But if the *Shackleton* had gone privateer why would she start by rubbing out a small camp, instead of taking over Centralville? No, it must be invasion, aliens. Some unknown race, or maybe the Cetians or the Hainish had decided to move in on Earth's colonies. He'd never trusted those damned smart humanoids. This must have been done with a heatbomb. The invading force, with jets, air-cars, nukes, could easily be hidden on an island or reef anywhere in the SW Quartersphere. He must get back to his hopper and send out the alarm, then try a look around, reconnoiter, so he could tell HQ his assessment of the actual situation. He was just straightening up when he heard the voices.

Not human voices. High, soft, gabble-gobble. Aliens.

Ducking on hands and knees behind the shack's plastic roof, which lay on the ground deformed by heat into a batwing shape, he held still and listened.

Four creechies walked by a few yards from him, on the path. They were wild creechies, naked except for loose leather belts on which knives and pouches hung. None wore the shorts and leather collar supplied to tame creechies. The Volunteers in the compound must have been incinerated along with the humans.

They stopped a little way past his hiding-place, talking their slow gabble-gobble, and Davidson held his breath. He didn't want them to spot him. What the devil were creechies doing here? They could only be serving as spies and scouts for the invaders.

One pointed south as it talked, and turned, so that Davidson saw its face. And he recognised it. Creechies all looked alike, but this one was different. He had written his own signature all over that face, less than a year ago. It was the one that had gone spla and attacked him down in Central, the homicidal one, Lyubov's pet. What in the blue hell was it doing here?

Davidson's mind raced, clicked; reactions fast as always, he stood up, sudden, tall, easy, gun in hand. "You creechies. Stop. Stay-put. No moving!"

His voice cracked out like a whiplash. The four little green creatures did not move. The one with the smashed-in face looked at him across the black rubble with huge, blank eyes that had no light in them.

"Answer now. This fire, who start it?"

No answer.

"Answer now: hurry-up-quick! No answer, then I burn-up first one, then one, then one, see? This fire, who start it?"

"We burned the camp, Captain Davidson," said the one from Central, in a queer soft voice that reminded Davidson of some human. "The humans are all dead."

"You burned it, what do you mean?"

He could not recall Scarface's name for some reason.

"There were two hundred humans here. Ninety slaves of my people. Nine hundred of my people came out of the forest. First we killed the humans in the place in the forest where they were cutting trees, then we killed those in this place, while the houses were burning. I had thought you were killed. I am glad to see you, Captain Davidson."

It was all crazy, and of course a lie. They couldn't have killed all of them, Ok, Birno, Van Sten, all the rest, two hundred men, some of them would have got out. All the creechies had was bows and arrows. Anyway the creechies couldn't have done this. Creechies didn't fight, didn't kill, didn't have wars. They were intraspecies non-aggressive, that meant sitting ducks. They didn't fight back. They sure as hell didn't massacre two hundred men at a swipe. It was crazy. The silence, the faint stink of burning in the long, warm evening light, the pale-green faces with unmoving eyes that watched him, it all added up to nothing, to a crazy bad dream, a nightmare.

"Who did this for you?"

"Nine hundred of my people," Scarface said in that damned fake-human voice.

"No, not that. Who else? Who were you acting for? Who told you what to do?"

"My wife did."

Davidson saw then the telltale version of the creature's stance, yet it sprang at him so lithe and oblique that his shot missed, burning an arm or shoulder instead of smack between the eyes. And the creechie was on him, half his size and weight yet knocking him right off balance by its onslaught, for he had been relying on the gun and not expecting attack. The thing's arms were thin, tough, coarse-furred in his grip, and as he struggled with it, it sang.

He was down on his back, pinned down, disarmed. Four green muzzles looked down at him. The scarfaced one was still singing, a breathless gabble, but with a tune to it. The other three listened, their white teeth showing in grins. He had never seen a creechie smile. He had never looked up into a creechie's face from below. Always down, from above. From on top. He tried not to struggle, for at the moment it was wasted effort. Little as they were, they outnumbered him, and Scarface had his gun. He must wait. But there was a sickness in him, a nausea that made his body twitch and strain against his will. The small hands held him down effortlessly, the small green faces bobbed over him grinning.

Scarface ended his song. He knelt on Davidson's chest, a knife in one hand, Davidson's gun in the other.

"You can't sing, Captain Davidson, is that right? Well, then, you may run to your hopper, and fly away, and tell the Colonel in Central that this place is burned and the humans are killed."

Blood, the same startling red as human blood, clotted the fur of the creechie's right arm, and the knife shook in the green paw. The sharp, scarred face looked down into Davidson's from very close, and he could see now the queer light that burned way down in the charcoal-dark eyes. The voice was still soft and quiet.

They let him go.

He got up cautiously, still dizzy from the fall Scarface had given him. The creechies stood well away from him now, knowing his reach was twice theirs; but Scarface wasn't the only one armed, there was a second gun pointing at his guts. That was

Ben holding the gun. His own creechie Ben, the little grey mangy bastard, looking stupid as always but holding a gun.

It's hard to turn your back on two pointing guns, but Davidson did it and started walking towards the field.

A voice behind him said some creechie word, shrill and loud. Another said, "Hurry-up-quick!" and there was a queer noise like birds twittering that must be creechie laughter. A shot clapped and whined on the road right by him. Christ, it wasn't fair, they had the guns and he wasn't armed. He began to run. He could outrun any creechie. They didn't know how to shoot a gun.

"Run," said the quiet voice far behind him. That was Scarface —Selver, that was his name. Sam, they'd called him, till Lyubov stopped Davidson from giving him what he deserved and made a pet out of him, then they'd called him Selver. Christ, what was all this, it was a nightmare. He ran. The blood thundered in his ears. He ran through the golden, smoky evening. There was a body by the path, he hadn't even noticed it coming. It wasn't burned, it looked like a white balloon with the air gone out. It had staring blue eyes. They didn't dare kill him, Davidson. They hadn't shot at him again. It was impossible. They couldn't kill him. There was the hopper, safe and shining, and he lunged into the seat and had her up before the creechies could try anything. His hands shook, but not much, just shock. They couldn't kill him. He circled the hill and then came back fast and low, looking for the four creechies. But nothing moved in the streaky rubble of the camp.

There had been a camp there this morning. Two hundred men. There had been four creechies there just now. He hadn't dreamed all this. They couldn't just disappear. They were there, hiding. He opened up the machinegun in the hopper's nose and raked the burned ground, shot holes in the green leaves of the forest, strafed the burned bones and cold bodies of his men and the wrecked machinery and the rotting white stumps, returning again and again until the ammo was gone and the gun's spasms stopped short.

Davidson's hands were steady now, his body felt appeased, and he knew he wasn't caught in any dream. He headed back over the Straits, to take the news to Centralville. As he flew he could feel his face relax into its usual calm lines. They couldn't blame the disaster on him, for he hadn't even been there. Maybe they'd see that it was significant that the creechies had struck while he was gone, knowing they'd fail if he was there to organise the defense. And there was one good thing would come out of this. They'd do like they should have done to start with, and clean up the planet for human occupation. Not even Lyubov could stop them from rubbing out the creechies now, not when they heard it was Lyubov's pet creechie who'd led the massacre! They'd go in for rat-extermination for a while, now; and maybe, just maybe, they'd hand that little job over to him. At that thought he could have smiled. But he kept his face calm.

The sea under him was greyish with twilight, and ahead of him lay the island hills, the deep-folded, many-streamed, many-leaved forests in the dusk.

II

All the colors of rust and sunset, brown-reds and pale greens, changed ceaselessly in the long leaves as the wind blew. The roots of the copper willows, thick and ridged, were moss-green down by the running water, which like the wind moved slowly with many soft eddies and seeming pauses, held back by rocks, roots, hanging and fallen leaves. No way was clear, no light unbroken, in the forest. Into wind, water, sunlight, starlight, there always entered leaf and branch, bole and root, the shadowy, the complex. Little paths ran under the branches, around the boles, over the roots; they did not go straight, but yielded to every obstacle, devious as nerves. The ground was not dry and solid but damp and rather springy, product of the collaboration of living things with the long, elaborate death of leaves and trees; and from that rich graveyard grew ninety-foot trees, and tiny mushrooms that sprouted in circles half an inch across. The smell of the air was subtle, various, and sweet. The view was never long, unless looking up through the branches you caught sight of the stars. Nothing was pure, dry, arid, plain. Revelation was lacking. There was no seeing everything at once: no certainty. The colors of rust and sunset kept changing in the hanging leaves of the

copper willows, and you could not say even whether the leaves
of the willows were brownish-red, or reddish-green, or green.

Selver came up a path beside the water, going slowly and
often stumbling on the willow roots. He saw an old man dreaming, and stopped. The old man looked at him through the long
willow-leaves and saw him in his dreams.

"May I come to your Lodge, my Lord Dreamer? I've come a
long way."

The old man sat still. Presently Selver squatted down on his
heels just off the path, beside the stream. His head drooped
down, for he was worn out and had to sleep. He had been walking five days.

"Are you of the dream-time or of the world-time?" the old man
asked at last.

"Of the world-time."

"Come along with me then." The old man got up promptly
and led Selver up the wandering path out of the willow grove
into dryer, darker regions of oak and thorn. "I took you for a
god," he said, going a pace ahead. "And it seemed to me I had
seen you before, perhaps in a dream."

"Not in the world-time. I come from Sornol, I have never been
here before."

"This town is Cadast. I am Coro Mena. Of the Whitethorn."

"Selver is my name. Of the Ash."

"There are Ash people among us, both men and women. Also
your marriage-clans, Birch and Holly; we have no women of the
Apple. But you don't come looking for a wife, do you?"

"My wife is dead," Selver said.

They came to the Men's Lodge, on high ground in a stand of
young oaks. They stooped and crawled through the tunnel-en-
trance. Inside, in the firelight, the old man stood up, but Selver
stayed crouching on hands and knees, unable to rise. Now that
help and comfort was at hand his body, which he had forced too
far, would not go farther. It lay down and the eyes closed; and
Selver slipped, with relief and gratitude, into the great darkness.

The men of the Lodge of Cadast looked after him, and their
healer came to tend the wound in his right arm. In the night
Coro Mena and the healer Torber sat by the fire. Most of the
other men were with their wives that night; there were only a

couple of young prentice-dreamers over on the benches, and they had both gone fast asleep. "I don't know what would give a man such scars as he has on his face," said the healer, "and much less, such a wound as that in his arm. A very queer wound."

"It's a queer engine he wore on his belt," said Coro Mena.

"I saw it and didn't see it."

"I put it under his bench. It looks like polished iron, but not like the handiwork of men."

"He comes from Sornol, he said to you."

They were both silent a while. Coro Mena felt unreasoning fear press upon him, and slipped into dream to find the reason for the fear; for he was an old man, and long adept. In the dream the giants walked, heavy and dire. Their dry scaly limbs were swathed in cloths; their eyes were little and light, like tin beads. Behind them crawled huge moving things made of polished iron. The trees fell down in front of them.

Out from among the falling trees a man ran, crying aloud, with blood on his mouth. The path he ran on was the doorpath of the Lodge of Cadast.

"Well, there's little doubt of it," Coro Mena said, sliding out of the dream. "He came oversea straight from Sornol, or else came afoot from the coast of Kelme Deva on our own land. The giants are in both those places, travellers say."

"Will they follow him," said Torber; neither answered the question, which was no question but a statement of possibility.

"You saw the giants once, Coro?"

"Once," the old man said.

He dreamed; sometimes, being very old and not so strong as he had been, he slipped off to sleep for a while. Day broke, noon passed. Outside the Lodge a hunting-party went out, children chirped, women talked in voices like running water. A dryer voice called Coro Mena from the door. He crawled out into the evening sunlight. His sister stood outside, sniffing the aromatic wind with pleasure, but looking stern all the same. "Has the stranger waked up, Coro?"

"Not yet. Torber's looking after him."

"We must hear his story."

"No doubt he'll wake soon."

Ebor Dendep frowned. Headwoman of Cadast, she was anxious for her people; but she did not want to ask that a hurt man be disturbed, nor to offend the Dreamers by insisting on her right to enter their Lodge. "Can't you wake him, Coro?" she asked at last. "What if he is . . . being pursued?"

He could not run his sister's emotions on the same rein with his own, yet he felt them; her anxiety bit him. "If Torber permits, I will," he said.

"Try to learn his news, quickly. I wish he was a woman and would talk sense . . ."

The stranger had roused himself, and lay feverish in the half-dark of the Lodge. The unreined dreams of illness moved in his eyes. He sat up, however, and spoke with control. As he listened Coro Mena's bones seemed to shrink within him trying to hide from this terrible story, this new thing.

"I was Selver Thele, when I lived in Eshreth in Sornol. My city was destroyed by the yumens when they cut down the trees in that region. I was one of those made to serve them, with my wife Thele. She was raped by one of them and died. I attacked the yumen that killed her. He would have killed me then, but another of them saved me and set me free. I left Sornol, where no town is safe from the yumens now, and came here to the North Isle, and lived on the coast of Kelme Deva in the Red Groves. There presently the yumens came and began to cut down the world. They destroyed a city there, Penle. They caught a hundred of the men and women and made them serve them, and live in the pen. I was not caught. I lived with others who had escaped from Penle, in the bogland north of Kelme Deva. Sometimes at night I went among the people in the yumen's pens. They told me that that one was there. That one whom I had tried to kill. I thought at first to try again; or else to set the people in the pen free. But all the time I watched the trees fall and saw the world cut open and left to rot. The men might have escaped, but the women were locked in more safely and could not, and they were beginning to die. I talked with the people hiding in the boglands. We were all very frightened and very angry, and had no way to let our fear and anger free. So at last after long talking, and long dreaming, and the making of a plan, we went in daylight, and killed the yumens of Kelme Deva with arrows and hunting-lances, and burned their city and their engines. We left nothing. But that one had gone away. He came back alone. I sang over him, and let him go."

Selver fell silent.

"Then," Coro Mena whispered.

"Then a flying ship came from Sornol, and hunted us in the forest, but found nobody. So they set fire to the forest; but it rained, and they did little harm. Most of the people freed from the pens and the others have gone farther north and east, towards the Holle Hills, for we were afraid many yumens might come hunting us. I went alone. The yumens know me, you see, they know my face; and this frightens me, and those I stay with."

"What is your wound?" Torber asked.

"That one, he shot me with their kind of weapon; but I sang him down and let him go."

"Alone you downed a giant?" said Torber with a fierce grin, wishing to believe.

"Not alone. With three hunters, and with his weapon in my hand—this."

Torber drew back from the thing.

None of them spoke for a while. At last Coro Mena said, "What you tell us is very black, and the road goes down. Are you a Dreamer of your Lodge?"

"I was. There's no Lodge of Eshreth any more."

"That's all one; we speak the Old Tongue together. Among the willows of Asta you first spoke to me calling me Lord Dreamer. So I am. Do you dream, Selver?"

"Seldom now," Selver answered, obedient to the catechism, his scarred, feverish face bowed.

"Awake?"

"Awake."

"Do you dream well, Selver?"

"Not well."

"Do you hold the dream in your hands?"

"Yes."

"Do you weave and shape, direct and follow, start and cease at will?"

"Sometimes, not always."

"Can you walk the road your dream goes?"

"Sometimes. Sometimes I am afraid to."

"Who is not? It is not altogether bad with you, Selver."

"No, it is altogether bad," Selver said, "there's nothing good left," and he began to shake.

Torber gave him the willow-draught to drink and made him lie down. Coro Mena still had the headwoman's question to ask; reluctantly he did so, kneeling by the sick man. "Will the giants, the yumens you call them, will they follow your trail, Selver?"

"I left no trail. No one has seen me between Kelme Deva and this place, six days. That's not the danger." He struggled to sit up again. "Listen, listen. You don't see the danger. How can you see it? You haven't done what I did, you have never dreamed of it, making two hundred people die. They will not follow me, but they may follow us all. Hunt us, as hunters drive coneys. That is the danger. They may try to kill us. To kill us all, all men."

"Lie down—"

"No, I'm not raving, this is true fact and dream. There were two hundred yumens at Kelme Deva and they are dead. We killed them. We killed them as if they were not men. So will they not turn and do the same? They have killed us by ones, now they will kill us as they kill the trees, by hundreds, and hundreds, and hundreds."

"Be still," Torber said. "Such things happen in the fever-dream, Selver. They do not happen in the world."

"The world is always new," said Coro Mena, "however old its roots. Selver, how is it with these creatures, then? They look like men and talk like men, are they not men?"

"I don't know. Do men kill men, except in madness? Does any beast kill its own kind? Only the insects. These yumens kill us as lightly as we kill snakes. The one who taught me said that they kill one another, in quarrels, and also in groups, like ants fighting. I haven't seen that. But I know they don't spare one who asks life. They will strike a bowed neck, I have seen it! There is a wish to kill in them, and therefore I saw fit to put them to death."

"And all men's dreams," said Coro Mena, cross-legged in shadow, "will be changed. They will never be the same again. I shall never walk again that path I came with you yesterday, the way up from the willow grove that I've walked on all my life. It is changed. You have walked on it and it is utterly changed. Before this day the thing we had to do was the right thing to do; the way we had to go was the right way and led us home. Where is our home now? For you've done what you had to do, and it was not right. You have killed men. I saw them, five years ago, in the Lemgan Valley, where they came in a flying ship; I hid and watched the giants, six of them, and saw them speak, and look at rocks and plants, and cook food. They are men. But you have lived among them, tell me, Selver: do they dream?"

"As children do, in sleep."

"They have no training?"

"No. Sometimes they talk of their dreams, the healers try to use them in healing, but none of them are trained, or have any skill in dreaming. Lyubov, who taught me, understood me when I showed him how to dream, and yet even so he called the world-time 'real' and the dream-time 'unreal,' as if that were the difference between them."

"You have done what you had to do," Coro Mena repeated after a silence. His eyes met Selver's, across shadows. The desperate tension lessened in Selver's face; his scarred mouth relaxed, and he lay back without saying more. In a little while he was asleep.

"He's a god," Coro Mena said.

Torber nodded, accepting the old man's judgment almost with relief.

"But not like the others. Not like the Pursuer, nor the Friend who has no face, nor the Aspen-leaf Woman who walks in the forest of dreams. He is not the Gatekeeper, nor the Snake. Nor the Lyre-player nor the Carver nor the Hunter, though he comes in the world-time like them. We may have dreamed of Selver these last few years, but we shall no longer; he has left the dream-time. In the forest, through the forest he comes, where leaves fall, where trees fall, a god that knows death, a god that kills and is not himself reborn."

The headwoman listened to Coro Mena's reports and prophecies, and acted. She put the town of Cadast on alert, making sure that each family was ready to move out, with some food packed, and litters ready for the old and ill. She sent young women scouting south and east for news of the yumens. She kept one

armed hunting-group always around town, though the others
went out as usual every night. And when Selver grew stronger
she insisted that he come out of the Lodge and tell his story:
how the yumens killed and enslaved people in Sornol, and cut
down the forests; how the people of Kelme Deva had killed the
yumens. She forced women and undreaming men who did not
understand these things to listen again, until they understood,
and were frightened. For Ebor Dendep was a practical woman.
When a Great Dreamer, her brother, told her that Selver was a
god, a changer, a bridge between realities, she believed and
acted. It was the Dreamer's responsibility to be careful, to be
certain that his judgment was true. Her responsibility was then
to take that judgment and act upon it. He saw what must be
done; she saw that it was done.

"All the cities of the forest must hear," Coro Mena said. So the
headwoman sent out her young runners, and headwomen in
other towns listened, and sent out their runners. The killing at
Kelme Deva and the name of Selver went over North Island and
oversea to the other lands, from voice to voice, or in writing; not
very fast, for the Forest People had no quicker messengers than
footrunners; yet fast enough.

They were not all one people on the Forty Lands of the world.
There were more languages than lands, and each with a different
dialect for every town that spoke it; there were infinite ramifica-
tions of manners, morals, customs, crafts; physical types differed
on each of the five Great Lands. The people of Sornol were tall,
and pale, and great traders; the people of Rieshwel were short,
and many had black fur, and they ate monkeys; and so on and
on. But the climate varied little, and the forest little, and the sea
not at all. Curiosity, regular trade-routes, and the necessity of
finding a husband or wife of the proper Tree, kept up an easy
movement of people among the towns and between the lands,
and so there were certain likenesses among all but the remotest
extremes, the half-rumored barbarian isles of the Far East and
South. In all the Forty Lands, women ran the cities and towns,
and almost every town had a Men's Lodge. Within the Lodges
the Dreamers spoke an old tongue, and this varied little from
land to land. It was rarely learned by women or by men who
remained hunters, fishers, weavers, builders, those who dreamed
only small dreams outside the Lodge. As most writing was in this

Lodge-tongue, when headwomen sent fleet girls carrying messages, the letters went from Lodge to Lodge, and so were interpreted by the Dreamers to the Old Women, as were other docu-
ments, rumors, problems, myths, and dreams. But it was always
the Old Women's choice whether to believe or not.

Selver was in a small room at Eshsen. The door was not
locked, but he knew if he opened it something bad would come
in. So long as he kept it shut everything would be all right. The
trouble was that there were young trees, a sapling orchard,
planted out in front of the house; not fruit or nut trees but some
other kind, he could not remember what kind. He went out to
see what kind of trees they were. They all lay broken and
uprooted. He picked up the silvery branch of one and a little
blood ran out of the broken end. No, not here, not again, Thele,
he said: O Thele, come to me before your death! But she did not
come. Only her death was there, the broken birchtree, the
opened door. Selver turned and went quickly back into the
house, discovering that it was all built above ground like a
yumen house, very tall and full of light. Outside the other door,
across the tall room, was the long street of the yumen city Central. Selver had the gun in his belt. If Davidson came, he could
shoot him. He waited, just inside the open door, looking out into
the sunlight. Davidson came, huge, running so fast that Selver
could not keep him in the sights of the gun as he doubled crazily
back and forth across the wide street, very fast, always closer.
The gun was heavy. Selver fired it but no fire came out of it, and
in rage and terror he threw the gun and the dream away.

Disgusted and depressed, he spat, and sighed.

"A bad dream?" Ebor Dendep inquired.

"They're all bad, and all the same," he said, but the deep
unease and misery lessened a little as he answered. Cool morning
sunlight fell flecked and shafted through the fine leaves and
branches of the birch grove of Cadast. There the headwoman sat
weaving a basket of blackstem fern, for she liked to keep her
fingers busy, while Selver lay beside her in half-dream and
dream. He had been fifteen days at Cadast, and his wound was
healing well. He still slept much, but for the first time in many
months he had begun to dream waking again, regularly, not once

or twice in a day and night but in the true pulse and rhythm of dreaming which should rise and fall ten to fourteen times in the diurnal cycle. Bad as his dreams were, all terror and shame, yet he welcomed them. He had feared that he was cut off from his roots, that he had gone too far into the dead land of action ever to find his way back to the springs of reality. Now, though the water was very bitter, he drank again.

Briefly he had Davidson down again among the ashes of the burned camp, and instead of singing over him this time he hit him in the mouth with a rock. Davidson's teeth broke, and blood ran between the white splinters.

The dream was useful, a straight wish-fulfillment, but he stopped it there, having dreamed it many times, before he met Davidson in the ashes of Kelme Deva, and since. There was nothing to that dream but relief. A sip of bland water. It was the bitter he needed. He must go clear back, not to Kelme Deva but to the long dreadful street in the alien city called Central, where he had attacked Death, and had been defeated.

Ebor Dendep hummed as she worked. Her thin hands, their silky green down silvered with age, worked black fern-stems in and out, fast and neat. She sang a song about gathering ferns, a girl's song: I'm picking ferns, I wonder if he'll come back . . . Her faint old voice trilled like a cricket's. Sun trembled in birch leaves. Selver put his head down on his arms.

The birch grove was more or less in the center of the town of Cadast. Eight paths led away from it, winding narrowly off among trees. There was a whiff of woodsmoke in the air; where the branches were thin at the south edge of the grove you could see smoke rise from a house-chimney, like a bit of blue yarn unravelling among the leaves. If you looked closely among the live-oaks and other trees you would find houseroofs sticking up a couple of feet above ground, between a hundred and two hundred of them, it was very hard to count. The timber houses were three-quarters sunk, fitted in among tree-roots like badgers' setts. The beam roofs were mounded over with a thatch of small branches, pinestraw, reeds, earthmould. They were insulating, waterproof, almost invisible. The forest and the community of eight hundred people went about their business all around the birch grove where Ebor Dendep sat making a basket of fern. A bird among the branches over her head said, "Te-whet," sweetly. There was more people-noise than usual, for fifty or sixty strangers, young men and women mostly, had come drifting in these last few days, drawn by Selver's presence. Some were from other cities of the North, some were those who had done the killing at Kelme Deva with him; they had followed rumor here to follow him. Yet the voices calling here and there and the babble of women bathing or children playing down by the stream, were not so loud as the morning birdsong and insect-drone and under-noise of the living forest of which the town was one element.

A girl came quickly, a young huntress the color of the pale birch leaves. "Word of mouth from the southern coast, mother," she said. "The runner's at the Women's Lodge."

"Send her here when she's eaten," the headwoman said softly. "Sh, Tolbar, can't you see he's asleep?"

The girl stooped to pick a large leaf of wild tobacco, and laid it lightly over Selver's eyes, on which a shaft of the steepening, bright sunlight had fallen. He lay with his hands half open and his scarred, damaged face turned upward, vulnerable and foolish, a Great Dreamer gone to sleep like a child. But it was the girl's face that Ebor Dendep watched. It shone, in that uneasy shade, with pity and terror, with adoration.

Tolbar darted away. Presently two of the Old Women came with the messenger, moving silent in single file along the sun-flecked path. Ebor Dendep raised her hand, enjoining silence. The messenger promptly lay down flat, and rested; her brown-dappled green fur was dusty and sweaty, she had run far and fast. The Old Women sat down in patches of sun, and became still. Like two old grey-green stones they sat there, with bright living eyes.

Selver, struggling with a sleep-dream beyond his control, cried out as if in great fear, and woke.

He went to drink from the stream; when he came back he was followed by six or seven of those who always followed him. The headwoman put down her half-finished work and said, "Now be welcome, runner, and speak."

The runner stood up, bowed her head to Ebor Dendep, and spoke her message: "I come from Trethat. My words come from

Sorbron Deva, before that from sailors of the Strait, before that from Broter in Sornol. They are for the hearing of all Cadast but they are to be spoken to the man called Selver who was born of the Ash in Eshreth. Here are the words: There are new giants in the great city of the giants in Sornol, and many of these new ones are females. The yellow ship of fire goes up and down at the place that was called Peha. It is known in Sornol that Selver of Eshreth burned the city of the giants at Kelme Deva. The Great Dreamers of the Exiles in Broter have dreamed giants more numerous than the trees of the Forty Lands. These are all the words of the message I bear."

After the singsong recitation they were all silent. The bird, a little farther off, said, "Whet-whet?" experimentally.

"This is a very bad world-time," said one of the Old Women, rubbing a rheumatic knee.

A grey bird flew from a huge oak that marked the north edge of town, and went up in circles, riding the morning updraft on lazy wings. There was always a roosting-tree of these grey kites near a town; they were the garbage service.

A small, fat boy ran through the birch grove, pursued by a slightly larger sister, both shrieking in tiny voices like bats. The boy fell down and cried, the girl stood him up and scrubbed his tears off with a large leaf. They scuttled off into the forest hand in hand.

"There was one called Lyubov," Selver said to the head-woman. "I have spoken of him to Coro Mena, but not to you. When that one was killing me, it was Lyubov who saved me. It was Lyubov who healed me, and set me free. He wanted to know about us; so I would tell him what he asked, and he too would tell me what I asked. Once I asked how his race could survive, having so few women. He said that in the place where they come from, half the race is women; but the men would not bring women to the Forty Lands until they had made a place ready for them."

"Until the men made a fit place for the women? Well! they may have quite a wait," said Ebor Dendep. "They're like the people in the Elm Dream who come at you rump-first, with their heads put on front to back. They make the forest into a dry beach"—her language had no word for 'desert'—"and call that making things ready for the women? They should have sent the women first. Maybe with them the women do the Great Dreaming, who knows? They are backwards, Selver. They are insane."

"A people can't be insane."

"But they only dream in sleep, you said; if they want to dream waking they take poisons so that the dreams go out of control, you said! How can people be any madder? They don't know the dream-time from the world-time, any more than a baby does. Maybe when they kill a tree they think it will come alive again!"

Selver shook his head. He still spoke to the headwoman as if he and she were alone in the birch grove, in a quiet hesitant voice, almost drowsily. "No, they understand death very well . . . Certainly they don't see as we do, but they know more and understand more about certain things than we do. Lyubov mostly understood what I told him. Much of what he told me, I couldn't understand. It wasn't the language that kept me from understanding; I know his tongue, and he learned ours; we made a writing of the two languages together. Yet there were things he said I could never understand. He said the yumens are from outside the forest. That's quite clear. He said they want the forest: the trees for wood, the land to plant grass on." Selver's voice, though still soft, had taken on resonance; the people among the silver trees listened. "That too is clear, to those of us who've seen them cutting down the world. He said the yumens are men like us, that we're indeed related, as close kin maybe as the Red Deer to the Grey-buck. He said that they come from another place which is not the forest; the trees there are all cut down; it has a sun, not our sun, which is a star. All this, as you see, wasn't clear to me. I say his words but don't know what they mean. It does not matter much. It is clear that they want our forest for themselves. They are twice our stature, they have weapons that outshoot ours by far, and fire-throwers, and flying ships. Now they have brought more women, and will have children. There are maybe two thousand, maybe three thousand of them here now, mostly in Sornol. But if we wait a lifetime or two they will breed; their numbers will double and redouble. They kill men and women; they do not spare those who ask life. They cannot sing in contest. They have left their roots behind them, perhaps, in this other forest from which they came, this forest with no trees. So they take poison to let loose the dreams in them, but it only makes them drunk or sick. No one can say certainly whether they're men or not men, whether they're sane or insane, but that does not matter. They must be made to leave the forest, because they are dangerous. If they will not go they must be burned out of the Lands, as nests of stinging-ants must be burned out of the groves of cities. If we wait, it is we that will be smoked out and burned. They can step on us as we step on sting-ing-ants. Once I saw a woman, it was when they burned my city Eshreth, she lay down in the path before a yumen to ask him for life, and he stepped on her back and broke the spine, and then kicked her aside as if she was a dead snake. I saw that. If the yumens are men they are men unfit or untaught to dream and to act as men. Therefore they go about in torment killing and de-stroying, driven by the gods within, whom they will not set free but try to uproot and deny. If they are men they are evil men, having denied their own gods, afraid to see their own faces in the dark. Headwoman of Cadast, hear me." Selver stood up, tall and abrupt among the seated women. "It's time, I think, that I go back to my own land, to Sornol, to those that are in exile and those that are enslaved. Tell any people who dream of a city burning to come after me to Broter." He bowed to Ebor Dendep and left the birch grove, still walking lame, his arm bandaged; yet there was a quickness to his walk, a poise to his head, that made him seem more whole than other men. The young people followed quietly after him.

"Who is he?" asked the runner from Trethat, her eyes follow-ing him.

"The man to whom your message came, Selver of Eshreth, a god among us. Have you ever seen a god before, daughter?"

"When I was ten the Lyre-Player came to our town."

"Old Ertel, yes. He was of my Tree, and from the North Vales like me. Well, now you've seen a second god, and a greater. Tell your people in Trethat of him."

"Which god is he, mother?"

"A new one," Ebor Dendep said in her dry old voice. "The son of forest-fire, the brother of the murdered. He is the one who is not reborn. Now go on, all of you, go on to the Lodge. See who'll be going with Selver, see about food for them to carry. Let me

be a while. I'm as full of forebodings as a stupid old man, I must
dream . . ."

Coro Mena went with Selver that night as far as the place
where they first met, under the copper willows by the stream.
Many people were following Selver south, some sixty in all, as
great a troop as most people had ever seen on the move at once.
They would cause great stir and thus gather many more to them,
on their way to the sea-crossing to Sornol. Selver had claimed his
Dreamer's privilege of solitude for this one night. He was setting
off alone. His followers would catch him up in the morning; and
thenceforth, implicated in crowd and act, he would have little
time for the slow and deep running of the great dreams.

"Here we met," the old man said, stopping among the bowing
branches, the veils of dropping leaves, "and here part. This will
be called Selver's Grove, no doubt, by the people who walk our
paths hereafter."

Selver said nothing for a while, standing still as a tree, the restless leaves about him darkening from silver as clouds thickened
over the stars. "You are surer of me than I am," he said at last, a
voice in darkness.

"Yes, I'm sure, Selver . . . I was well taught in dreaming, and
then I'm old. I dream very little for myself any more. Why
should I? Little is new to me. And what I wanted from my life, I
have had, and more. I have had my whole life. Days like the
leaves of the forest. I'm an old hollow tree, only the roots live.
And so I dream only what all men dream. I have no visions and
no wishes. I see what is. I see the fruit ripening on the branch.
Four years it has been ripening, that fruit of the deep-planted
tree. We have all been afraid for four years, even we who live far
from the yumens' cities, and have only glimpsed them from hiding, or seen their ships fly over, or looked at the dead places
where they cut down the world, or heard mere tales of these
things. We are all afraid. Children wake from sleep crying of giants; women will not go far on their trading-journeys; men in the
Lodges cannot sing. The fruit of fear is ripening. And I see you
gather it. You are the harvester. All that we fear to know, you
have seen, you have known: exile, shame, pain, the roof and
walls of the world fallen, the mother dead in misery, the children

untaught, uncherished . . . This is a new time for the world: a
bad time. And you have suffered it all. You have gone farthest.
And at the farthest, at the end of the black path, there grows the
Tree; there the fruit ripens; now you reach up, Selver, now you
gather it. And the world changes wholly, when a man holds in
his hand the fruit of that tree, whose roots are deeper than the
forest. Men will know it. They will know you, as we did. It
doesn't take an old man or a Great Dreamer to recognise a god!
Where you go, fire burns; only the blind cannot see it. But listen,
Selver, this is what I see that perhaps others do not, this is why I
have loved you: I dreamed of you before we met here. You were
walking on a path, and behind you the young trees grew up, oak
and birch, willow and holly, fir and pine, alder, elm, white-
flowering ash, all the roof and walls of the world, forever
renewed. Now farewell, dear god and son, go safely."

The night darkened as Selver went, until even his night-seeing
eyes saw nothing but masses and planes of black. It began to
rain. He had gone only a few miles from Cadast when he must
either light a torch, or halt. He chose to halt, and groping found
a place among the roots of a great chestnut tree. There he sat,
his back against the broad, twisting bole that seemed to hold a
little sun-warmth in it still. The fine rain, falling unseen in darkness, pattered on the leaves overhead, on his arms and neck and
head protected by their thick silk-fine hair, on the earth and
ferns and undergrowth nearby, on all the leaves of the forest,
near and far. Selver sat as quiet as the grey owl on a branch
above him, unsleeping, his eyes wide open in the rainy dark.

III

Captain Raj Lyubov had a headache. It began softly in the
muscles of his right shoulder, and mounted crescendo to a
smashing drumbeat over his right ear. The speech centers are in
the left cerebral cortex, he thought, but he couldn't have said it;
couldn't speak, or read, or sleep, or think. Cortex, vortex. Migraine headache, margarine breadache, ow, ow, ow. Of course he
had been cured of migraine once at college and again during his
obligatory Army Prophylactic Psychotherapy Sessions, but he

had brought along some ergotamine pills when he left Earth, just in case. He had taken two, and a superhyperduper-analgesic, and a tranquillizer, and a digestive pill to counteract the caffeine which counteracted the ergotamine, but the awl still bored out from within, just over his right ear, to the beat of the big bass drum. Awl, drill, ill, pill, oh God. Lord deliver us. Liver sausage. What would the Athsheans do for a migraine? They wouldn't have one, they would have daydreamed the tensions away a week before they got them. Try it, try daydreaming. Begin as Selver taught you. Although knowing nothing of electricity he could not really grasp the principle of the EEG, as soon as he heard about alpha waves and when they appear he had said, "Oh yes, you mean this," and there appeared the unmistakable alpha-squiggles on the graph recording what went on inside his small green head; and he had taught Lyubov how to turn on and off the alpha-rhythms in one half-hour lesson. There really was nothing to it. But not now, the world is too much with us, ow, ow, ow above the right ear I always hear Time's winged chariot hurrying near, for the Athsheans had burned Smith Camp day before yesterday and killed two hundred men. Two hundred and seven to be precise. Every man alive except the Captain. No wonder pills couldn't get at the center of his migraine, for it was on an island two hundred miles away two days ago. Over the hills and far away. Ashes, ashes, all fall down. And amongst the ashes, all his knowledge of the High Intelligence Life Forms of World 41. Dust, rubbish, a mess of false data and fake hypotheses. Nearly five E-years here, and he had believed the Athsheans to be incapable of killing men, his kind or their kind. He had written long papers to explain how and why they couldn't kill men. All wrong. Dead wrong.

What had he failed to see?

It was nearly time to be going over to the meeting at HQ. Cautiously Lyubov stood up, moving all in one piece so that the right side of his head would not fall off; he approached his desk with the gait of a man underwater, poured out a shot of General Issue vodka, and drank it. It turned him inside out: it extraverted him: it normalized him. He felt better. He went out, and unable to stand the jouncing of his motorbike, started to walk down the long, dusty main street of Centralville to HQ.

Passing the Luau he thought with greed of another vodka; but
Captain Davidson was just going in the door, and Lyubov went
on.

The people from the *Shackleton* were already in the conference room. Commander Yung, whom he had met before, had
brought some new faces down from orbit this time. They were
not in Navy uniform; after a moment Lyubov recognised them,
with a slight shock, as non-Terran humans. He sought an introduction at once. One, Mr. Or, was a Hairy Cetian, dark grey,
stocky, and dour; the other, Mr. Lepennon, was tall, white, and
comely: a Hainishman. They greeted Lyubov with interest,
and Lepennon said, "I've just been reading your report on the
conscious control of paradoxical sleep among the Athsheans, Dr.
Lyubov," which was pleasant, and it was pleasant also to be
called by his own, earned title of doctor. Their conversation indicated that they had spent some years on Earth, and that they
might be hilfers, or something like it; but the Commander, introducing them, had not mentioned their status or position.

The room was filling up. Gosse, the colony ecologist, came in;
so did all the high brass; so did Captain Susun, head of Planet
Development—logging operations—whose captaincy like Lyubov's was an invention necessary to the peace of the military
mind. Captain Davidson came in alone, straight-backed and
handsome, his lean, rugged face calm and rather stern. Guards
stood at all the doors. The Army necks were all stiff as crowbars.
The conference was plainly an Investigation. *Whose fault?* My
fault, Lyubov thought despairingly; but out of his despair he
looked across the table at Captain Don Davidson with detesta-
tion and contempt.

Commander Yung had a very quiet voice. "As you know,
gentlemen, my ship stopped here at World 41 to drop you off a
new load of colonists, and nothing more; *Shackleton*'s mission is
to World 88, Prestno, one of the Hainish Group. However, this
attack on your outpost camp, since it chanced to occur during
our week here, can't be simply ignored; particularly in the light
of certain developments which you would have been informed of
a little later, in the normal course of events. The fact is that the
status of World 41 as an Earth Colony is now subject to revision,
and the massacre at your camp may precipitate the Adminis-

tration's decisions on it. Certainly the decisions *we* can make must be made quickly, for I can't keep my ship here long. Now first, we wish to make sure that the relevant facts are all in the possession of those present. Captain Davidson's report on the events at Smith Camp was taped and heard by all of us on ship; by all of you here also? Good. Now if there are questions any of you wish to ask Captain Davidson, go ahead. I have one myself. You returned to the site of the camp the following day, Captain Davidson, in a large hopper with eight soldiers; had you the permission of a senior officer here at Central for that flight?"

Davidson stood up. "I did, sir."

"Were you authorised to land and to set fires in the forest near the campsite?"

"No, sir."

"You did, however, set fires?"

"I did, sir. I was trying to smoke out the creechies that killed my men."

"Very well. Mr. Lepennon?"

The tall Hainishman cleared his throat. "Captain Davidson," he said, "do you think that the people under your command at Smith Camp were mostly content?"

"Yes, I do."

Davidson's manner was firm and forthright; he seemed indifferent to the fact that he was in trouble. Of course these Navy officers and foreigners had no authority over him; it was to his own Colonel that he must answer for losing two hundred men and making unauthorized reprisals. But his Colonel was right there, listening.

"They were well fed, well housed, not overworked, then, as well as can be managed in a frontier camp?"

"Yes."

"Was the discipline maintained very harsh?"

"No, it was not."

"What, then, do you think motivated the revolt?"

"I don't understand."

"If none of them were discontented, why did some of them massacre the rest and destroy the camp?"

There was a worried silence.

"May I put in a word," Lyubov said. "It was the native hilfs,

the Athsheans employed in the camp, who joined with an attack
by the forest people against the Terran humans. In his report
Captain Davidson referred to the Athsheans as 'creechies.'"

Lepennon looked embarrassed and anxious. "Thank you, Dr.
Lyubov. I misunderstood entirely. Actually I took the word
'creechie' to stand for a Terran caste that did rather menial work
in the logging camps. Believing, as we all did, that the Athsheans
were intraspecies non-aggressive, I never thought they might be
the group meant. In fact I didn't realise that they cooperated
with you in your camps.—However, I am more at a loss than
ever to understand what provoked the attack and mutiny."

"I don't know, sir."

"When he said the people under his command were content,
did the Captain include native people?" said the Cetian, Or, in a
dry mumble. The Hainishman picked it up at once, and asked
Davidson, in his concerned, courteous voice, "Were the Athsheans living at the camp content, do you think?"

"So far as I know."

"There was nothing unusual in their position there, or the
work they had to do?"

Lyubov felt the heightening of tension, one turn of the screw,
in Colonel Dongh and his staff, and also in the starship commander. Davidson remained calm and easy. "Nothing unusual."

Lyubov knew now that only his scientific studies had been
sent up to the *Shackleton;* his protests, even his annual assess-
ments of 'Native Adjustment to Colonial Presence' required by
the Administration, had been kept in some desk drawer deep in
HQ. These two N.-T.H.'s knew nothing about the exploitation of
the Athsheans. Commander Yung did, of course; he had been
down before today and had probably seen the creechie-pens. In
any case a Navy commander on Colony runs wouldn't have
much to learn about Terran-hilf relations. Whether or not he
approved of how the Colonial Administration ran its business,
not much would come as a shock to him. But a Cetian and a
Hainishman, how much would they know about Terran colonies,
unless chance brought them to one on the way to somewhere
else? Lepennon and Or had not intended to come on-planet
here at all. Or possibly they had not been intended to come on-
planet, but, hearing of trouble, had insisted. Why had the com-

mander brought them down: his will, or theirs? Whoever they
were they had about them a hint of authority, a whiff of the dry,
intoxicating odor of power. Lyubov's headache had gone, he felt
alert and excited, his face was rather hot. "Captain Davidson,"
he said, "I have a couple of questions, concerning your con-
frontation with the four natives, day before yesterday. You're
certain that one of them was Sam, or Selver Thele?"

"I believe so."

"You're aware that he has a personal grudge against you."

"I don't know."

"You don't? Since his wife died in your quarters immediately
subsequent to sexual intercourse with you, he holds you responsible for her death; you didn't know that? He attacked you once
before, here in Centralville; you had forgotten that? Well, the
point is, that Selver's personal hatred for Captain Davidson may
serve as a partial explanation or motivation for this unprecedented assault. The Athsheans aren't incapable of personal violence, that's never been asserted in any of my studies of them.
Adolescents who haven't mastered controlled dreaming or competitive singing do a lot of wrestling and fist-fighting, not all oᶠ it
good-tempered. But Selver is an adult and an adept; and his first,
personal attack on Captain Davidson, which I happened to witness part of, was pretty certainly an attempt to kill. As was the
Captain's retaliation, incidentally. At the time, I thought that attack an isolated psychotic incident, resulting from grief and
stress, not likely to be repeated. I was wrong.—Captain, when
the four Athsheans jumped you from ambush, as you describe in
your report, did you end up prone on the ground?"

"Yes."

"In what position?"

Davidson's calm face tensed and stiffened, and Lyubov felt a
pang of compunction. He wanted to corner Davidson in his lies,
to force him into speaking truth once, but not to humiliate him
before others. Accusations of rape and murder supported Davidson's image of himself as the totally virile man, but now that
image was endangered: Lyubov had called up a picture of him,
the soldier, the fighter, the cool tough man, being knocked down
by enemies the size of six-year-olds . . . . What did it cost David-

son, then, to recall that moment when he had lain looking up at the little green men, for once, not down at them?

"I was on my back."

"Was your head thrown back, or turned aside?"

"I don't know."

"I'm trying to establish a fact here, Captain, one that might help explain why Selver didn't kill you, although he had a grudge against you and had helped kill two hundred men a few hours earlier. I wondered if you might by chance have been in one of the positions which, when assumed by an Athshean, prevent his opponent from further physical aggression."

"I don't know."

Lyubov glanced round the conference table; all the faces showed curiosity and some tension. "These aggression-halting gestures and positions may have some innate basis, may rise from a surviving trigger-response, but they are socially developed and expanded, and of course learned. The strongest and completest of them is a prone position, on the back, eyes shut, head turned so the throat is fully exposed. I think an Athshean of the local cultures might find it impossible to hurt an enemy who took that position. He would have to do something else to release his anger or aggressive drive.—When they had all got you down, Captain, did Selver by any chance sing?"

"Did he what?"

"Sing."

"I don't know."

Block. No go. Lyubov was about to shrug and give it up when the Cetian said, "Why, Mr. Lyubov?" The most winning characteristic of the rather harsh Cetian temperament was curiosity, inopportune and inexhaustible curiosity; Cetians died eagerly, curious as to what came next.

"You see," Lyubov said, "the Athsheans use a kind of ritualised singing to replace physical combat. Again it's a universal social phenomenon that might have a physiological foundation, though it's very hard to establish anything as 'innate' in human beings. However the higher primates here all go in for vocal competing between two males, a lot of howling and whistling; the dominant male may finally give the other a cuff, but usually they just spend an hour or so trying to outbellow each other. The

Athsheans themselves see the similarity to their singing-matches, which are also only between males; but as they observe, theirs are not only aggression-releases, but an art-form. The better artist wins. I wondered if Selver sang over Captain Davidson, and if so, whether he did because he could not kill, or because he preferred the bloodless victory. These questions have suddenly become rather urgent."

"Dr. Lyubov," said Lepennon, "how effective are these aggression-channelling devices? Are they universal?"

"Among adults, yes. So my informants state, and all my observation supported them, until day before yesterday. Rape, violent assault, and murder virtually don't exist among them. There are accidents, of course. And there are psychotics. Not many of the latter."

"What do they do with dangerous psychotics?"

"Isolate them. Literally. On small islands."

"The Athsheans are carnivorous, they hunt animals?"

"Yes, meat is a staple."

"Wonderful," Lepennon said, and his white skin paled further with pure excitement. "A human society with an effective war-barrier! What's the cost, Dr. Lyubov?"

"I'm not sure, Mr. Lepennon. Perhaps change. They're a static, stable, uniform society. They have no history. Perfectly integrated, and wholly unprogressive. You might say that like the forest they live in, they've attained a climax state. But I don't mean to imply that they're incapable of adaptation."

"Gentlemen, this is very interesting but in a somewhat specialist frame of reference, and it may be somewhat out of the context which we're attempting to clarify here—"

"No, excuse me, Colonel Dongh, this may be the point. Yes, Dr. Lyubov?"

"Well, I wonder if they're not proving their adaptability, now. By adapting their behavior to us. To the Earth Colony. For four years they've behaved to us as they do to one another. Despite the physical differences, they recognised us as members of their species, as men. However, we have not responded as members of their species should respond. We have ignored the responses, the rights and obligations of non-violence. We have killed, raped, dispersed, and enslaved the native humans, destroyed their communities, and cut down their forests. It wouldn't be surprising if they'd decided that we are not human."

"And therefore can be killed, like animals, yes yes," said the Cetian, enjoying logic; but Lepennon's face now was stiff as white stone. "Enslaved?" he said.

"Captain Lyubov is expressing his personal opinions and theories," said Colonel Dongh, "which I should state I consider possibly to be erroneous, and he and I have discussed this type of thing previously, although the present context is unsuitable. We do not employ slaves, sir. Some of the natives serve a useful role in our community. The Voluntary Autochthonous Labor Corps is a part of all but the temporary camps here. We have very limited personnel to accomplish our tasks here and we need workers and use all we can get, but on any kind of basis that could be called a slavery basis, certainly not."

Lepennon was about to speak, but deferred to the Cetian, who said only, "How many of each race?"

Gosse replied: "2641 Terrans, now. Lyubov and I estimate the native hilf population very roughly at 3 million."

"You should have considered these statistics, gentlemen, before you altered the native traditions!" said Or, with a disagreeable but perfectly genuine laugh.

"We are adequately armed and equipped to resist any type of aggression these natives could offer," said the Colonel. "However there was a general consensus by both the first Exploratory Missions and our own research staff of specialists here headed by Captain Lyubov, giving us to understand that the New Tahitians are a primitive, harmless, peace-loving species. Now this information was obviously erroneous—"

Or interrupted the Colonel. "Obviously! You consider the human species to be primitive, harmless, and peace-loving, Colonel? No. But you knew that the hilfs of this planet are human? As human as you or I or Lepennon—since we all came from the same, original, Hainish stock?"

"That is the scientific theory, I am aware—"

"Colonel, it is the historic fact."

"I am not forced to accept it as a fact," the old Colonel said, getting hot, "and I don't like opinions stuffed into my own mouth. The fact is that these creechies are a meter tall, they're covered with green fur, they don't sleep, and they're not human beings in my frame of reference!"

"Captain Davidson," said the Cetian, "do you consider the native hilfs human, or not?"

"I don't know."

"But you had sexual intercourse with one—this Selver's wife. Would you have sexual intercourse with a female animal? What about the rest of you?" He looked about at the purple colonel, the glowering majors, the livid captains, the cringing specialists. Contempt came into his face. "You have not thought things through," he said. By his standards it was a brutal insult.

The Commander of the *Shackleton* at last salvaged words from the gulf of embarrassed silence. "Well, gentlemen, the tragedy at Smith Camp clearly is involved with the entire colony-native relationship, and is not by any means an insignificant or isolated episode. That's what we had to establish. And this being the case, we can make a certain contribution towards easing your problems here. The main purpose of our journey was not to drop off a couple of hundred girls here, though I know you've been waiting for 'em, but to get to Prestno, which has been having some difficulties, and give the government there an ansible. That is, an ICD transmitter."

"What?" said Sereng, an engineer. Stares became fixed, all round the table.

"The one we have aboard is an early model, and it cost a planetary annual revenue, roughly. That, of course, was twenty-seven years ago planetary time, when we left Earth. Nowadays they're making them relatively cheaply; they're SI on Navy ships; and in the normal course of things a robo or manned ship would be coming out here to give your colony one. As a matter of fact it's a manned Administration ship, and is on the way, due here in 9.4 E-years if I recall the figure."

"How do you know that?" somebody said, setting it up for Commander Yung, who replied smiling, "By the ansible: the one we have aboard. Mr. Or, your people invented the device, perhaps you'd explain it to those here who are unfamiliar with the terms?"

The Cetian did not unbend. "I shall not attempt to explain the principles of ansible operation to those present," he said. "Its effect can be stated simply: the instantaneous transmission of a message over any distance. One element must be on a large-mass body, the other can be anywhere in the cosmos. Since arrival in orbit the *Shackleton* has been in daily communication with Terra, now twenty-seven lightyears distant. The message does not take fifty-four years for delivery and response, as it does on an electromagnetic device. It takes no time. There is no more time-gap between worlds."

"As soon as we came out of NAFAL time-dilatation into planetary space-time, here, we rang up home, as you might say," the soft-voiced Commander went on. "And were told what had happened during the twenty-seven years we were travelling. The time-gap for bodies remains, but the information lag does not. As you can see, this is as important to us as an interstellar species, as speech itself was to us earlier in our evolution. It'll have the same effect: to make a society possible."

"Mr. Or and I left the Earth, twenty-seven years ago, as Legates for our respective governments, Tau II and Hain," said Lepennon. His voice was still gentle and civil, but the warmth had gone out of it. "When we left, people were talking about the possibility of forming some kind of league among the civilised worlds, now that communication was possible. The League of Worlds now exists. It has existed for eighteen years. Mr. Or and I are now Emissaries of the Council of the League, and so have certain powers and responsibilities we did not have when we left Earth."

The three of them from the ship kept saying these things: an instantaneous communicator exists, an interstellar supergovernment exists . . . Believe it or not. They were in league, and lying. This thought went through Lyubov's mind; he considered it, decided it was a reasonable but unwarranted suspicion, a defense-mechanism, and discarded it. Some of the military staff, however, trained to compartmentalize their thinking, specialists in self-defense, would accept it as unhesitatingly as he discarded it. They must believe that anyone claiming a sudden new authority was a liar or conspirator. They were no more constrained than Lyubov, who had been trained to keep his mind open whether he wanted to or not.

"Are we to take all—all this simply on your word, sir?" said

Colonel Dongh, with dignity and some pathos; for he, too muddleheaded to compartmentalize neatly, knew that he shouldn't believe Lepennon and Or and Yung, but did believe them, and was frightened.

"No," said the Cetian. "That's done with. A colony like this had to believe what passing ships and outdated radio-messages told them. Now you don't. You can verify. We are going to give you the ansible destined for Prestno. We have League authority to do so. Received, of course, by ansible. Your colony here is in a bad way. Worse than I thought from your reports. Your reports are very incomplete; censorship or stupidity have been at work. Now, however, you'll have the ansible, and can talk with your Terran Administration; you can ask for orders, so you'll know how to proceed. Given the profound changes that have been occurring in the organisation of the Terran Government since we left there, I should recommend that you do so at once. There is no longer any excuse for acting on outdated orders; for ignorance; for irresponsible autonomy."

Sour a Cetian and, like milk, he stayed sour. Mr. Or was being overbearing, and Commander Yung should shut him up. But could he? How did an "Emissary of the Council of the League of Worlds" rank? Who's in charge here, thought Lyubov, and he too felt a qualm of fear. His headache had returned as a sense of constriction, a sort of tight headband over the temples.

He looked across the table at Lepennon's white, long-fingered hands, lying left over right, quiet, on the bare polished wood of the table. The white skin was a defect to Lyubov's Earth-formed aesthetic taste, but the serenity and strength of those hands pleased him very much. To the Hainish, he thought, civilisation came naturally. They had been at it so long. They lived the social-intellectual life with the grace of a cat hunting in a garden, the certainty of a swallow following summer over the sea. They were experts. They never had to pose, to fake. They were what they were. Nobody seemed to fit the human skin so well. Except, perhaps, the little green men? the deviant, dwarfed, over-adapted, stagnated creechies, who were as absolutely, as honestly, as serenely what they were . . .

An officer, Benton, was asking Lepennon if he and Or were on this planet as observers for the (he hesitated) League of Worlds, or if they claimed any authority to . . . Lepennon took him up politely: "We are observers here, not empowered to command, only to report. You are still answerable only to your own government on Earth."

Colonel Dongh said with relief, "Then nothing has essentially changed—"

"You forget the ansible," Or interrupted. "I'll instruct you in its operation, Colonel, as soon as this discussion is over. You can then consult with your Colonial Administration."

"Since your problem here is rather urgent, and since Earth is now a League member and may have changed the Colonial Code somewhat during recent years, Mr. Or's advice is both proper and timely. We should be very grateful to Mr. Or and Mr. Lepennon for their decision to give this Terran colony the ansible destined for Prestno. It was their decision; I can only applaud it. Now, one more decision remains to be made, and this one I have to make, using your judgment as my guide. If you feel the colony is in imminent peril of further and more massive attacks from the natives, I can keep my ship here for a week or two as a defense arsenal; I can also evacuate the women. No children yet, right?"

"No, sir," said Gosse. "482 women now."

"Well, I have space for 380 passengers; we might crowd a hundred more in; the extra mass would add a year or so to the trip home, but it could be done. Unfortunately that's all I can do. We must proceed to Prestno; your nearest neighbor, as you know, 1.8 lightyears distant. We'll stop here on the way home to Terra, but that's going to be three and a half more E-years at least. Can you stick it out?"

"Yes," said the Colonel, and others echoed him. "We've had warning now and we won't be caught napping again."

"Equally," said the Cetian, "can the native inhabitants stick it out for three and a half Earth-years more?"

"Yes," said the Colonel. "No," said Lyubov. He had been watching Davidson's face, and a kind of panic had taken hold of him.

"Colonel?" said Lepennon, politely.

"We've been here four years now and the natives are flourishing. There's room enough and to spare for all of us, as you can see the planet's heavily underpopulated and the Administration wouldn't have cleared it for colonisation purposes if that hadn't been as it is. As for if this entered anyone's head, they won't catch us off guard again, we were erroneously briefed concerning the nature of these natives, but we're fully armed and able to defend ourselves, but we aren't planning any reprisals. That is expressly forbidden in the Colonial Code, though I don't know what new rules this new government may have added on, but we'll just stick to our own as we have been doing and they definitely negative mass reprisals or genocide. We won't be sending any messages for help out, after all a colony twenty-seven lightyears from home has come out expecting to be on its own and to in fact be completely self-sufficient, and I don't see that the ICD really changes that, due to ship and men and material still have to travel at near lightspeed. We'll just keep on shipping the lumber home, and look out for ourselves. The women are in no danger."

"Mr. Lyubov?" said Lepennon.

"We've been here four years. I don't know if the native human culture will survive four more. As for the total land ecology, I think Gosse will back me if I say that we've irrecoverably wrecked the native life-systems on one large island, have done great damage on this subcontinent Sornol, and if we go on logging at the present rate, may reduce the major habitable lands to desert within ten years. This isn't the fault of the colony's HQ or Forestry Bureau; they've simply been following a Development Plan drawn up on Earth without sufficient knowledge of the planet to be exploited, its life-systems, or its native human inhabitants."

"Mr. Gosse?" said the polite voice.

"Well, Raj, you're stretching things a bit. There's no denying that Dump Island, which was overlogged in direct contravention to my recommendations, is a dead loss. If more than a certain percentage of the forest is cut over a certain area, then the fibreweed doesn't reseed, you see, gentlemen, and the fibreweed root-system is the main soil-binder on clear land; without it the soil goes dusty and drifts off very fast under wind-erosion and the heavy rainfall. But I can't agree that our basic directives are at fault, so long as they're scrupulously followed. They were based on careful study of the planet. We've succeeded, here on Central, by following the Plan: erosion is minimal, and the cleared soil is highly arable. To log off a forest doesn't, after all, mean to make a desert—except perhaps from the point of view of a squirrel. We can't forecast precisely how the native forest life-systems will adapt to the new woodland-prairie-plowland ambiance foreseen in the Development Plan, but we know the chances are good for a large percentage of adaptation and survival."

"That's what the Bureau of Land Management said about Alaska during the First Famine," said Lyubov. His throat had tightened so that his voice came out high and husky. He had counted on Gosse for support. "How many Sitka spruce have you seen in your lifetime, Gosse? Or snowy owl? or wolf? or Eskimo? The survival percentage of native Alaskan species in habitat, after fifteen years of the Development Program, was .3 percent. It's now zero.—A forest ecology is a delicate one. If the forest perishes, its fauna may go with it. The Athshean word for *world* is also the word for *forest*. I submit, Commander Yung, that though the colony may not be in imminent danger, the planet is—"

"Captain Lyubov," said the old Colonel, "such submissions are not properly submitted by staff specialist officers to officers of other branches of the service but should rest on the judgment of the senior officers of the Colony, and I cannot tolerate any further such attempts as this to give advice without previous clearance."

Caught off guard by his own outburst, Lyubov apologised and tried to look calm. If only he didn't lose his temper, if his voice didn't go weak and husky, if he had poise . . .

The Colonel went on. "It appears to us that you made some serious erroneous judgments concerning the peacefulness and non-aggressiveness of the natives here, and because we counted on this specialist description of them as non-aggressive is why we left ourselves open to this terrible tragedy at Smith Camp, Captain Lyubov. So I think we have to wait until some other specialists in hilfs have had time to study them, because evidently your theories were basically erroneous to some extent."

Lyubov sat and took it. Let the men from the ship see them all passing the blame around like a hot brick: all the better. The more dissension they showed, the likelier were these Emissaries to have them checked and watched over. And he was to blame; he had been wrong. To hell with my self-respect so long as the forest people get a chance, Lyubov thought, and so strong a sense of his own humiliation and self-sacrifice came over him that tears rose to his eyes.

He was aware that Davidson was watching him.

He sat up stiff, the blood hot in his face, his temples drumming. He would not be sneered at by that bastard Davidson. Couldn't Or and Lepennon see what kind of man Davidson was, and how much power he had here, while Lyubov's powers, called "advisory," were simply derisory? If the colonists were left to go on with no check on them but a super-radio, the Smith Camp massacre would almost certainly become the excuse for systematic aggression against the natives. Bacteriological extermination, most likely. The *Shackleton* would come back in three and a half or four years to "New Tahiti," and find a thriving Terran colony, and no more Creechie Problem. None at all. Pity about the plague, we took all precautions required by the Code, but it must have been some kind of mutation, they had no natural resistance, but we did manage to save a group of them by transporting them to the New Falkland Isles in the southern hemisphere and they're doing fine there, all sixty-two of them . . .

The conference did not last much longer. When it ended he stood up and leaned across the table to Lepennon. "You must tell the League to do something to save the forests, the forest people," he said almost inaudibly, his throat constricted, "you must, please, you must."

The Hainishman met his eyes; his gaze was reserved, kindly, and deep as a well. He said nothing.

IV

It was unbelievable. They'd all gone insane. This damned alien world had sent them all right round the bend, into byebye dreamland, along with the creechies. He still wouldn't believe

what he'd seen at that "conference" and the briefing after it, if he
saw it all over again on film. A Starfleet ship's commander
bootlicking two humanoids. Engineers and techs cooing and
ooing over a fancy radio presented to them by a Hairy Cetian
with a lot of sneering and boasting, as if ICD's hadn't been
predicted by Terran science years ago! The humanoids had
stolen the idea, implemented it, and called it an "ansible" so
nobody would realise it was just an ICD. But the worst part of it
had been the conference, with that psycho Lyubov raving and
crying, and Colonel Dongh letting him do it, letting him insult
Davidson and HQ staff and the whole Colony; and all the time
the two aliens sitting and grinning, the little grey ape and the
big white fairy, sneering at humans.

It had been pretty bad. It hadn't got any better since the
Shackleton left. He didn't mind being sent down to New Java
Camp under Major Muhamed. The Colonel had to discipline
him; old Ding Dong might actually be very happy about that
fire-raid he'd pulled in reprisal on Smith Island, but the raid had
been a breach of discipline and he had to reprimand Davidson.
All right, rules of the game. But what wasn't in the rules was this
stuff coming over that overgrown TV set they called the ansible
—their new little tin god at HQ.

Orders from the Bureau of Colonial Administration in Kara-
chi: *Restrict Terran-Athshean contact to occasions arranged by
Athsheans.* In other words you couldn't go into a creechie warren
and round up a work-force any more. *Employment of volunteer
labor is not advised; employment of forced labor is forbidden.*
More of same. How the hell were they supposed to get the work
done? Did Earth want this wood or didn't it? They were still
sending the robot cargo ships to New Tahiti, weren't they, four a
year, each carrying about thirty million new-dollars worth of
prime lumber back to Mother Earth. Sure the Development people wanted those millions. They were businessmen. These messages weren't coming from them, any fool could see that.

The colonial status of World 41—why didn't they call it New
Tahiti any more?—*is under consideration. Until decision is
reached colonists should observe extreme caution in all dealings
with native inhabitants . . . The use of weapons of any kind except small side-arms carried in self-defense is absolutely forbid-*

den—just as on Earth, except 'that there a man couldn't even carry side-arms any more. But what the hell was the use coming twenty-seven lightyears to a frontier world and then get told No guns, no firejelly, no bugbombs, no no, just sit like nice little boys and let the creechies come spit in your faces and sing songs at you and then stick a knife in your guts and burn down your camp, but don't you hurt the cute little green fellers, no sir!

A policy of avoidance is strongly advised; a policy of aggression or retaliation is strictly forbidden.

That was the gist of all the messages actually, and any fool could tell that that wasn't the Colonial Administration talking. They couldn't have changed that much in thirty years. They were practical, realistic men who knew what life was like on frontier planets. It was clear, to anybody who hadn't gone spla from geoshock, that the "ansible" messages were phoneys. They might be planted right in the machine, a whole set of answers to high-probability questions, computer run. The engineers said they could have spotted that; maybe so. In that case the thing did communicate instantaneously with another world. But that world wasn't Earth. Not by a long long shot! There weren't any men typing the answers onto the other end of that little trick: they were aliens, humanoids. Probably Cetians, for the machine was Cetian-made, and they were a smart bunch of devils. They were the kind that might make a real bid for interstellar supremacy. The Hainish would be in the conspiracy with them, of course; all that bleeding-heart stuff in the so-called directives had a Hainish sound to it. What the long-term objective of the aliens was, was hard to guess from here; it probably involved weakening the Terran Government by tying it up in this "league of worlds" business, until the aliens were strong enough to make an armed takeover. But their plan for New Tahiti was easy to see. They'd let the creechies wipe out the humans for them. Just tie the humans' hands with a lot of fake "ansible" directives and let the slaughter begin. Humanoids help humanoids: rats help rats.

And Colonel Dongh had swallowed it. He intended to obey orders. He had actually said that to Davidson. "I intend to obey my orders from Terra-HQ, and by God, Don, you'll obey my orders the same way, and in New Java you'll obey Major Muhamed's orders there." He was stupid, old Ding Dong, but he liked Davidson, and Davidson liked him. If it meant betraying the human race to an alien conspiracy then he couldn't obey his orders, but he still felt sorry for the old soldier. A fool, but a loyal and brave one. Not a born traitor like that whining, tattling prig Lyubov. If there was one man he hoped the creechies did get, it was bigdome Raj Lyubov, the alien-lover.

Some men, especially the asiatiforms and hindi types, are actually born traitors. Not all, but some. Certain other men are born saviors. It just happened to be the way they were made, like being of euraf descent, or like having a good physique; it wasn't anything he claimed credit for. If he could save the men and women of New Tahiti, he would; if he couldn't, he'd make a damn good try; and that was all there was to it, actually.

The women, now, that rankled. They'd pulled out the ten Collies who'd been in New Java and none of the new ones were being sent out from Centralville. "Not safe yet," HQ bleated. Pretty rough on the three outpost camps. What did they expect the outposters to do when it was hands off the she-creechies, and all the she-humans were for the lucky bastards at Central? It was going to cause terrific resentment. But it couldn't last long, the whole situation was too crazy to be stable. If they didn't start easing back to normal now the *Shackleton* was gone, then Captain D. Davidson would just have to do a little extra work to get things headed back towards normalcy.

The morning of the day he left Central, they had let loose the whole creechie work-force. Made a big noble speech in pidgin, opened the compound gates, and let out every single tame creechie, carriers, diggers, cooks, dustmen, houseboys, maids, the lot. Not one had stayed. Some of them had been with their masters ever since the start of the colony, four E-years ago. But they had no loyalty. A dog, a chimp would have hung around. These things weren't even that highly developed, they were just about like snakes or rats, just smart enough to turn around and bite you as soon as you let 'em out of the cage. Ding Dong was spla, letting all those creechies loose right in the vicinity. Dumping them on Dump Island and letting them starve would have been actually the best final solution. But Dongh was still pan-

icked by that pair of humanoids and their talky-box. So if the
wild creechies on Central were planning to imitate the Smith
Camp atrocity, they now had lots of real handy new recruits,
who knew the layout of the whole town, the routines, where the
arsenal was, where guards were posted, and the rest. If Centralville got burned down, HQ could thank themselves. It would be
what they deserved, actually. For letting traitors dupe them, for
listening to humanoids and ignoring the advice of men who really knew what the creechies were like.

None of those guys at HQ had come back to camp and found
ashes and wreckage and burned bodies, like he had. And Ok's
body, out where they'd slaughtered the logging crew, it had had
an arrow sticking out of each eye like some sort of weird insect
with antennae sticking out feeling the air, Christ, he kept seeing
that.

One thing anyhow, whatever the phoney "directives" said, the
boys at Central wouldn't be stuck with trying to use "small side-
arms" for self-defense. They had fire-throwers and machine guns;
the 16 little hoppers had machine guns and were useful for dropping firejelly cans from; the five big hoppers had full armament.
But they wouldn't need the big stuff. Just take up a hopper over
one of the deforested areas and catch a mess of creechies there,
with their damned bows and arrows, and start dropping firejelly
cans and watch them run around and burn. It would be all right.
It made his belly churn a little to imagine it, just like when he
thought about making a woman, or whenever he remembered
about when that Sam creechie had attacked him and he had
smashed in his whole face with four blows one right after the
other. It was eidetic memory plus a more vivid imagination than
most men had, no credit due, just happened to be the way he
was made.

The fact is, the only time a man is really and entirely a man is
when he's just had a woman or just killed another man. That
wasn't original, he'd read it in some old books; but it was true.
That was why he liked to imagine scenes like that. Even if the
creechies weren't actually men.

New Java was the southernmost of the five big lands, just
north of the equator, and so was hotter than Central or Smith

which were just about perfect climate-wise. Hotter and a lot wetter. It rained all the time in the wet seasons anywhere on New Tahiti, but in the northern lands it was a kind of quiet fine rain that went on and on and never really got you wet or cold. Down here it came in buckets, and there was a monsoon-type storm that you couldn't even walk in, let alone work in. Only a solid roof kept that rain off you, or else the forest. The damn forest was so thick it kept out the storms. You'd get wet from all the drippings off the leaves, of course, but if you were really inside the forest during one of those monsoons you'd hardly notice the wind was blowing; then you came out in the open and wham! got knocked off your feet by the wind and slobbered all over with the red liquid mud that the rain turned the cleared ground into, and you couldn't duck back into the forest quick enough; and inside the forest it was dark, and hot, and easy to get lost.

Then the C.O., Major Muhamed, was a sticky bastard. Everything at N. J. was done by the book: the logging all in kilo-strips, the fibreweed crap planted in the logged strips, leave to Central granted in strict non-preferential rotation, hallucinogens rationed and their use on duty punished, and so on and so on. However, one good thing about Muhamed was he wasn't always radioing Central. New Java was his camp, and he ran it his way. He didn't like orders from HQ. He obeyed them all right, he'd let the creechies go, and locked up all the guns except little popgun pistols, as soon as the orders came. But he didn't go looking for orders, or for advice. Not from Central or anybody else. He was a self-righteous type: knew he was right. That was his big fault.

When he was on Dongh's staff at HQ Davidson had had occasion sometimes to see the officers' records. His unusual memory held on to such things, and he could recall for instance that Muhamed's IQ was 107. Whereas his own happened to be 118. There was a difference of 11 points; but of course he couldn't say that to old Moo, and Moo couldn't see it, and so there was no way to get him to listen. He thought he knew better than Davidson, and that was that.

They were all a bit sticky at first, actually. None of the men at N. J. knew anything about the Smith Camp atrocity, except that the camp C.O. had left for Central an hour before it happened, and so was the only human that escaped alive. Put like that, it did sound bad. You could see why at first they looked at him like a kind of Jonah, or worse, a kind of Judas even. But when they got to know him they'd know better. They'd begin to see that, far from being a deserter or traitor, he was dedicated to preventing the colony of New Tahiti from betrayal. And they'd realise that getting rid of the creechies was going to be the only way to make this world safe for the Terran way of life.

It wasn't too hard to start getting that message across to the loggers. They'd never liked the little green rats, having to drive them to work all day and guard them all night; but now they began to understand that the creechies were not only repulsive but dangerous. When Davidson told them what he'd found at Smith; when he explained how the two humanoids on the Fleet ship had brainwashed HQ; when he showed them that wiping out the Terrans on New Tahiti was just a small part of the whole alien conspiracy against Earth; when he reminded them of the cold hard figures, twenty-five *hundred* humans to three *million* creechies—then they began to really get behind him.

Even the Ecological Control Officer here was with him. Not like poor old Kees, mad because men shot Red Deer and then getting shot in the guts himself by the sneaking creechies. This fellow, Atranda, was a creechie-hater. Actually he was kind of spla about them, he had geoshock or something; he was so afraid the creechies were going to attack the camp that he acted like some woman afraid of getting raped. But it was useful to have the local spesh on his side anyhow.

No use trying to line up the C.O.; a good judge of men, Davidson had seen it was no use almost at once. Muhamed was rigid-minded. Also he had a prejudice against Davidson which he wouldn't drop; it had something to do with the Smith Camp affair. He as much as told Davidson he didn't consider him a trustworthy officer.

He was a self-righteous bastard, but his running N. J. camp on such rigid lines was an advantage. A tight organization, used to obeying orders, was easier to take over than a loose one full of independent characters, and easier to keep together as a unit for defensive and offensive military operations, once he was in command. He would have to take command. Moo was a good logging-camp boss, but no soldier.

Davidson kept busy getting some of the best loggers and junior officers really firmly with him. He didn't hurry. When he had enough of them he could really trust, a squad of ten lifted a few items from old Moo's locked-up room in the Rec House basement full of war toys, and then went off one Sunday into the woods to play.

Davidson had located the creechie town some weeks ago, and had saved up the treat for his men. He could have done it single-handed, but it was better this way. You got the sense of comradeship, of a real bond among men. They just walked into the place in broad open daylight, and coated all the creechies caught above-ground with firejelly and burned them, then poured kerosene over the warren-roofs and roasted the rest. Those that tried to get out got jellied; that was the artistic part, waiting at the rat-holes for the little rats to come out, letting them think they'd made it, and then just frying them from the feet up so they made torches. That green fur sizzled like crazy.

It actually wasn't much more exciting than hunting real rats, which were about the only wild animals left on Mother Earth, but there was more thrill to it; the creechies were a lot bigger than rats, and you knew they could fight back, though this time they didn't. In fact some of them even lay down instead of running away, just lay there on their backs with their eyes shut. It was sickening. The other fellows thought so too, and one of them actually got sick and vomited after he'd burned up one of the lying-down ones.

Hard up as the men were, they didn't leave even one of the females alive to rape. They had all agreed with Davidson beforehand that it was too damn near perversity. Homosexuality was with other humans, it was normal. These things might be built like human women but they weren't human, and it was better to get your kicks from killing them, and stay *clean*. That had made good sense to all of them, and they stuck to it.

Every one of them kept his trap shut back at camp, no boasting even to their buddies. They were sound men. Not a word of the expedition got to Muhamed's ears. So far as old Moo knew, all his men were good little boys just sawing up logs and keeping away from creechies, yes sir; and he could go on believing that until D-Day came.

For the creechies would attack. Somewhere. Here, or one of the camps on King Island, or Central. Davidson knew that. He was the only officer in the entire colony that did know it. No credit due, he just happened to know he was right. Nobody else had believed him, except these men here whom he'd had time to convince. But the others would all see, sooner or later, that he was right.

And he was right.

V

It had been a shock, meeting Selver face to face. As he flew back to Central from the foothill village, Lyubov tried to decide why it had been a shock, to analyse out the nerve that had jumped. For after all one isn't usually terrified by a chance meeting with a good friend.

It hadn't been easy to get the headwoman to invite him. Tuntar had been his main locus of study all summer; he had several excellent informants there and was on good terms with the Lodge and with the headwoman, who had let him observe and participate in the community freely. Wangling an actual invitation out of her, via some of the ex-serfs still in the area, had taken a long time, but at last she had complied, giving him, according to the new directives, a genuine "occasion arranged by the Athsheans." His own conscience, rather than the Colonel, had insisted on this. Dongh wanted him to go. He was worried about the Creechie Threat. He told Lyubov to size them up, to "see how they're reacting now that we're leaving them strictly alone." He hoped for reassurance. Lyubov couldn't decide whether the report he'd be turning in would reassure Colonel Dongh, or not.

For ten miles out of Central, the plain had been logged and the stumps had all rotted away; it was now a great dull flat of fibreweed, hairy grey in the rain. Under those hirsute leaves the seedling shrubs got their first growth, the sumacs, dwarf aspens, and salviforms which, grown, would in turn protect the seedling trees. Left alone, in this even, rainy climate, this area might reforest itself within thirty years and reattain the full climax forest within a hundred. Left alone.

Suddenly the forest began again, in space not time: under the helicopter the infinitely various green of leaves covered the slow swells and foldings of the hills of North Sornol.

Like most Terrans on Terra, Lyubov had never walked among wild trees at all, never seen a wood larger than a city block. At first on Athshe he had felt oppressed and uneasy in the forest, stifled by its endless crowd and incoherence of trunks, branches, leaves in the perpetual greenish or brownish twilight. The mass and jumble of various competitive lives all pushing and swelling outwards and upwards towards light, the silence made up of many little meaningless noises, the total vegetable indifference to the presence of mind, all this had troubled him, and like the others he had kept to clearings and to the beach. But little by little he had begun to like it. Gosse teased him, calling him Mr. Gibbon; in fact Lyubov looked rather like a gibbon, with a round, dark face, long arms, and hair greying early; but gibbons were extinct. Like it or not, as a hilfer he had to go into the forests to find the hilfs; and now after four years of it he was completely at home under the trees, more so perhaps than anywhere else.

He had also come to like the Athsheans' names for their own lands and places, sonorous two-syllabled words: Sornol, Tuntar, Eshreth, Eshsen—that was now Centralville—Endtor, Abtan, and above all Athshe, which meant the Forest, and the World. So earth, terra, tellus mean both the soil and the planet, two meanings and one. But to the Athsheans soil, ground, earth was not that to which the dead return and by which the living live: the substance of their world was not earth, but forest. Terran man was clay, red dust. Athshean man was branch and root. They did not carve figures of themselves in stone, only in wood.

He brought the hopper down in a small glade north of the town, and walked in past the Women's Lodge. The smell of an Athshean settlement hung pungent in the air, woodsmoke, dead fish, aromatic herbs, alien sweat. The atmosphere of an underground house, if a Terran could fit himself in at all, was a rare compound of CO_2 and stinks. Lyubov had spent many intellectually stimulating hours doubled up and suffocating in the reeking gloom of the Men's Lodge in Tuntar. But it didn't look as if he would be invited in this time.

Of course the townsfolk knew of the Smith Camp massacre, now six weeks ago. They would have known of it soon, for word got around fast among the islands, though not so fast as to constitute a "mysterious power of telepathy" as the loggers liked to believe. The townsfolk also knew that the twelve hundred slaves at Centralville had been freed soon after the Smith Camp massacre, and Lyubov agreed with the Colonel that the natives might take the second event to be a result of the first. That gave what Colonel Dongh would call "an erroneous impression," but it probably wasn't important. What was important was that the slaves had been freed. Wrongs done could not be righted, but at least they were not still being done. They could start over: the natives without that painful, unanswerable wonder as to why the "yumens" treated men like animals; and he without the burden of explanation and the gnawing of irremediable guilt.

Knowing how they valued candor and direct speech concerning frightening or troublous matters, he expected that people in Tuntar would talk about these things with him, in triumph, or apology, or rejoicing, or puzzlement. No one did. No one said much of anything to him.

He had come in late afternoon, which was like arriving in a Terran city just after dawn. Athsheans did sleep—the colonists' opinion, as often, ignored observable fact—but their physiological low was between noon and 4 P.M., whereas with Terrans it is usually between 2 and 5 A.M.; and they had a double-peak cycle of high temperature and high activity, coming in the two twilights, dawn and evening. Most adults slept five or six hours in twenty-four, in several catnaps; and adept men slept as little as two hours in twenty-four; so, if one discounted both their naps and their dreaming-states as "laziness," one might say they never slept. It was much easier to say that than to understand what they actually did do.—At this point, in Tuntar, things were just beginning to stir again after the late-day slump.

Lyubov noticed a good many strangers. They looked at him, but none approached; they were mere presences passing on other paths in the dusk of the great oaks. At last someone he knew came along his path, the headwoman's cousin Sherrar, an old woman of small importance and small understanding. She greeted him civilly, but did not or would not respond to his inquiries about the headwoman and his two best informants, Egath the orchard-keeper and Tubab the Dreamer. Oh, the headwoman was very busy, and who was Egath, did he mean Geban, and Tubab might be here or perhaps he was there, or not. She stuck to Lyubov, and nobody else spoke to him. He worked his way, accompanied by the hobbling, complaining, tiny, green crone, across the groves and glades to Tuntar to the Men's Lodge. "They're busy in there," said Sherrar.

"Dreaming?"

"However should I know? Come along now, Lyubov, come see . . ." She knew he always wanted to see things, but she couldn't think what to show him to draw him away. "Come see the fishing-nets," she said feebly.

A girl passing by, one of the Young Hunters, looked up at him: a black look, a stare of animosity such as he had never received from any Athshean, unless perhaps from a little child frightened into scowling by his height and his hairless face. But this girl was not frightened.

"All right," he said to Sherrar, feeling that his only course was docility. If the Athsheans had indeed developed—at last, and abruptly—the sense of group enmity, then he must accept this, and simply try to show them that he remained a reliable, unchanging friend.

But how could their way of feeling and thinking have changed so fast, after so long? And why? At Smith Camp, provocation had been immediate and intolerable: Davidson's cruelty would drive even Athsheans to violence. But this town, Tuntar, had never been attacked by the Terrans, had suffered no slave-raids, had not seen the local forest logged or burned. He, Lyubov himself, had been there—the anthropologist cannot always leave his own shadow out of the picture he draws—but not for over two months now. They had got the news from Smith, and there were among them now refugees, ex-slaves, who had suffered at the Terrans' hands and would talk about it. But would news and hearsay change the hearers, change them radically?—when their unaggressiveness ran so deep in them, right through their culture and society and on down into their subconscious, their "dream time," and perhaps into their very physiology? That an Athshean could be provoked, by atrocious cruelty, to attempt murder, he knew: he had seen it happen—once. That a disrupted community might be similarly provoked by similarly intolerable injuries, he had to believe: it had happened at Smith Camp. But that talk and hearsay, no matter how frightening and outrageous, could enrage a settled community of these people to the point where they acted against their customs and reason, broke entirely out of their whole style of living, this he couldn't believe. It was psychologically improbable. Some element was missing.

Old Tubab came out of the Lodge, just as Lyubov passed in front of it. Behind the old man came Selver.

Selver crawled out of the tunnel-door, stood upright, blinked at the rain-greyed, foliage-dimmed brightness of daylight. His dark eyes met Lyubov's, looking up. Neither spoke. Lyubov was badly frightened.

Flying home in the hopper, analysing out the shocked nerve, he thought, why fear? Why was I afraid of Selver? Unprovable intuition or mere false analogy? Irrational in any case.

Nothing between Selver and Lyubov had changed. What Selver had done at Smith Camp could be justified, even if it couldn't be justified, it made no difference. The friendship between them was too deep to be touched by moral doubt. They had worked very hard together; they had taught each other, in rather more than the literal sense, their languages. They had spoken without reserve. And Lyubov's love for his friend was deepened by that gratitude the savior feels towards the one whose life he has been privileged to save.

Indeed he had scarcely realised until that moment how deep his liking and loyalty to Selver were. Had his fear in fact been the personal fear that Selver might, having learned racial hatred, reject him, despise his loyalty, and treat him not as "you," but as "one of them"?

After that long first gaze Selver came forward slowly and greeted Lyubov, holding out his hands.

Touch was a main channel of communication among the forest people. Among Terrans touch is always likely to imply threat, aggression, and so for them there is often nothing between the formal handshake and the sexual caress. All that blank was filled

by the Athsheans with varied customs of touch. Caress as signal
and reassurance was as essential to them as it is to mother and
child or to lover and lover; but its significance was social, not
only maternal and sexual. It was part of their language. It was
therefore patterned, codified, yet infinitely modifiable. "They're
always pawing each other," some of the colonists sneered, unable
to see in these touch-exchanges anything but their own eroticism
which, forced to concentrate itself exclusively on sex and then repressed and frustrated, invades and poisons every sensual pleasure, every humane response: the victory of a blinded, furtive
Cupid over the great brooding mother of all the seas and stars,
all the leaves of trees, all the gestures of men, Venus Gene-
trix . . .

So Selver came forward with his hands held out, shook
Lyubov's hand Terran fashion, and then took both his arms with
a stroking motion just above the elbow. He was not much more
than half Lyubov's height, which made all gestures difficult and
ungainly for both of them, but there was nothing uncertain or
childlike in the touch of his small, thin boned green-furred hand
on Lyubov's arms. It was reassurance. Lyubov was very glad to
get it.

"Selver, what luck to meet you here. I want very much to talk
with you—"

"I can't, now, Lyubov."

He spoke gently, but when he spoke Lyubov's hope of an
unaltered friendship vanished. Selver had changed. He was
changed, radically: from the root.

"Can I come back," Lyubov said urgently, "another day, and
talk with you, Selver? It is important to me—"

"I leave here today," Selver said even more gently, but letting
go Lyubov's arms, and also looking away. He thus put himself
literally out of touch. Civility required that Lyubov do the same,
and let the conversation end. But then there would be no one to
talk to. Old Tubab had not even looked at him; the town had
turned its back on him. And this was Selver, who had been his
friend.

"Selver, this killing at Kelme Deva, maybe you think that lies
between us. But it does not. Maybe it brings us closer together.
And your people in the slave-pens, they've all been set free, so

that wrong no longer lies between us. And even if it does—it always did—all the same I . . . I am the same man I was, Selver."

At first the Athshean made no response. His strange face, the large deepset eyes, the strong features misshapen by scars and blurred by the short silken fur that followed and yet obscured all contours, this face turned from Lyubov, shut, obstinate. Then suddenly he looked round as if against his own intent. "Lyubov, you shouldn't have come here. You should leave Central two nights from now. I don't know what you are. It would be better if I had never known you."

And with that he was off, a light walk like a long-legged cat, a green flicker among the dark oaks of Tuntar, gone. Tubab followed slowly after him, still without a glance at Lyubov. A fine rain fell without sound on the oak-leaves and on the narrow pathways to the Lodge and the river. Only if you listened intently could you hear the rain, too multitudinous a music for one mind to grasp, a single endless chord played on the entire forest.

"Selver is a god," said old Sherrar. "Come and see the fishing-nets now."

Lyubov declined. It would be impolite and impolitic to stay; anyway he had no heart to.

He tried to tell himself that Selver had not been rejecting him, Lyubov, but him as a Terran. It made no difference. It never does.

He was always disagreeably surprised to find how vulnerable his feelings were, how much it hurt him to be hurt. This sort of adolescent sensitivity was shameful, he should have a tougher hide by now.

The little crone, her green fur all dusted and besilvered with raindrops, sighed with relief when he said goodbye. As he started the hopper he had to grin at the sight of her, hop-hobbling off into the trees as fast as she could go, like a little toad that has escaped a snake.

Quality is an important matter, but so is quantity: relative size. The normal adult reaction to a very much smaller person may be arrogant, or protective, or patronising, or affectionate, or bullying, but whatever it is it's liable to be better fitted to a child than to an adult. Then, when the child-sized person was furry, a further response got called upon, which Lyubov had labelled the

Teddybear Reaction. Since the Athsheans used caress so much, its manifestation was not inappropriate, but its motivation remained suspect. And finally there was the inevitable Freak Reaction, the flinching away from what is human but does not quite look so.

But quite outside all that was the fact that the Athsheans, like Terrans, were simply funny-looking at times. Some of them did look like little toads, owls, caterpillars. Sherrar was not the first little old lady who had struck Lyubov as looking funny from behind . . .

And that's one trouble with the colony, he thought as he lifted the hopper and Tuntar vanished beneath the oaks and the leafless orchards. We haven't got any old women. No old men either, except Dongh and he's only about sixty. But old women are different from everybody else, they say what they think. The Athsheans are governed, in so far as they have government, by old women. Intellect to the men, politics to the women, and ethics to the interaction of both: that's their arrangement. It has charm, and it works—for them. I wish the Administration had sent out a couple of grannies along with all those nubile fertile high-breasted young women. Now that girl I had over the other night, she's really very nice, and nice in bed, she has a kind heart, but my God it'll be forty years before she'll say anything to a man . . .

But all the time, beneath his thoughts concerning old women and young ones, the shock persisted, the intuition or recognition that would not let itself be recognised.

He must think this out before he reported to HQ.

Selver: what about Selver, then?

Selver was certainly a key figure to Lyubov. Why? Because he knew him well, or because of some actual power in his personality, which Lyubov had never consciously appreciated?

But he had appreciated it; he had picked Selver out very soon as an extraordinary person. "Sam," he had been then, bodyservant for three officers sharing a prefab. Lyubov remembered Benson boasting what a good creechie they'd got, they'd broke him in right.

Many Athsheans, especially Dreamers from the Lodges, could not change their polycyclic sleep-pattern to fit the Terran one. If they caught up with their normal sleep at night, that prevented them from catching up with the REM or paradoxical sleep, whose 120-minute cycle ruled their life both day and night, and could not be fitted in to the Terran workday. Once you have learned to do your dreaming wide awake, to balance your sanity not on the razor's edge of reason but on the double support, the fine balance, of reason and dream, once you have learned that, you cannot unlearn it any more than you can unlearn to think. So many of the men became groggy, confused, withdrawn, even cat- atonic. Women, bewildered and abased, behaved with the sul- len listlessness of the newly enslaved. Male non-adepts and some of the younger Dreamers did best; they adapted, working hard in the logging camps or becoming clever servants. Sam had been one of these, an efficient, characterless bodyservant, cook, laundry-boy, butler, backsoaper and scapegoat for his three masters. He had learned how to be invisible. Lyubov borrowed him as an ethnological informant, and had, by some affinity of mind and nature, won Sam's trust at once. He found Sam the ideal informant, trained in his people's customs, perceptive of their significances, and quick to translate them, to make them in- telligible to Lyubov, bridging the gap between two languages, two cultures, two species of the genus Man.

For two years Lyubov had been travelling, studying, inter- viewing, observing, and had failed to get at the key that would let him into the Athshean mind. He didn't even know where the lock was. He had studied the Athsheans' sleeping-habits and found that they apparently had no sleeping-habits. He had wired countless electrodes onto countless furry green skulls, and failed to make any sense at all out of the familiar patterns, the spindles and jags, the alphas and deltas and thetas, that appeared on the graph. It was Selver who had made him understand, at last, the Athshean significance of the word "dream," which was also the word for "root," and so hand him the key of the kingdom of the forest people. It was with Selver as EEG subject that he had first seen with comprehension the extraordinary impulse-patterns of a brain entering a dream-state neither sleeping nor awake: a condition which related to Terran dreaming-sleep as the Parthe- non to a mud hut: the same thing basically, but with the addi- tion of complexity, quality, and control.

What then, what more?

Selver might have escaped. He stayed, first as a valet, then (through one of Lyubov's few useful perquisites as a Spesh) as Scientific Aide, still locked up nightly with all other creechies in the pen (the Voluntary Autochthonous Labor Personnel Quarters). "I'll fly you up to Tuntar and work with you there," Lyubov had said, about the third time he talked with Selver, "for God's sake why stay here?"—"My wife Thele is in the pen," Selver had said. Lyubov had tried to get her released, but she was in the HQ kitchen, and the sergeants who managed the kitchen-gang resented any interference from "brass" and "speshes." Lyubov had to be very careful, lest they take out their resentment on the woman. She and Selver had both seemed willing to wait patiently until both could escape or be freed. Male and female creechies were strictly segregated in the pens— why, no one seemed to know—and husband and wife rarely saw each other. Lyubov managed to arrange meetings for them in his hut, which he had to himself at the north end of town. It was when Thele was returning to HQ from one such meeting that Davidson had seen her and apparently been struck by her frail, frightened grace. He had had her brought to his quarters that night, and had raped her.

He had killed her in the act, perhaps; this had happened before, a result of the physical disparity; or else she had stopped living. Like some Terrans the Athsheans had the knack of the authentic death-wish, and could cease to live. In either case it was Davidson who had killed her. Such murders had occurred before. What had not occurred before was what Selver did, the second day after her death.

Lyubov had got there only at the end. He could recall the sounds; himself running down Main Street in hot sunlight; the dust, the knot of men. The whole thing could have lasted only five minutes, a long time for a homicidal fight. When Lyubov got there Selver was blinded with blood, a sort of toy for Davidson to play with, and yet he had picked himself up and was coming back, not with berserk rage but with intelligent despair. He kept coming back. It was Davidson who was scared into rage at last by that terrible persistence; knocking Selver down with a side-blow he had moved forward lifting his booted foot to stamp on the skull. Even as he moved, Lyubov had broken into the circle. He stopped the fight (for whatever blood-thirst the ten or twelve men watching had had, was more than appeased, and they backed Lyubov when he told Davidson hands off); and thenceforth he hated Davidson, and was hated by him, having come between the killer and his death.

For if it's all the rest of us who are killed by the suicide, it's himself whom the murderer kills; only he has to do it over, and over, and over.

Lyubov had picked up Selver, a light weight in his arms. The mutilated face had pressed against his shirt so that the blood soaked through against his own skin. He had taken Selver to his own bungalow, splinted his broken wrist, done what he could for his face, kept him in his own bed, night after night tried to talk to him, to reach him in the desolation of his grief and shame. It was, of course, against regulations.

Nobody mentioned the regulations to him. They did not have to. He knew he was forfeiting most of what favor he had ever had with the officers of the colony.

He had been careful to keep on the right side of HQ, objecting only to extreme cases of brutality against the natives, using persuasion not defiance, and conserving what shred of power and influence he had. He could not prevent the exploitation of the Athsheans. It was much worse than his training had led him to expect, but he could do little about it here and now. His reports to the Administration and to the Committee on Rights might—after the roundtrip of fifty-four years—have some effect; Terra might even decide that the Open Colony policy for Athshe was a bad mistake. Better fifty-four years late than never. If he lost the tolerance of his superiors here they would censor or invalidate his reports, and there would be no hope at all.

But he was too angry now to keep up his strategy. To hell with the others, if they insisted on seeing his care of a friend as an insult to Mother Earth and a betrayal of the colony. If they labelled him "creechie-lover" his usefulness to the Athsheans would be impaired; but he could not set a possible, general good above Selver's imperative need. You can't save a people by selling your friend. Davidson, curiously infuriated by the minor injuries Selver had done him and by Lyubov's interference, had gone around saying he intended to finish off that rebel creechie; he certainly would do so if he got the chance. Lyubov stayed with Selver night and day for two weeks, and then flew him out of Central and put him down in a west coast town, Broter, where he had relatives.

There was no penalty for aiding slaves to escape, since the Athsheans were not slaves at all except in fact: they were Voluntary Autochthonous Labor Personnel. Lyubov was not even reprimanded. But the regular officers distrusted him totally, instead of partially, from then on; and even his colleagues in the Special Services, the exobiologist, the ag and forestry coordinators, the ecologists, variously let him know that he had been irrational, quixotic, or stupid. "Did you think you were coming on a picnic?" Gosse had demanded.

"No. I didn't think it would be any bloody picnic," Lyubov answered, morose.

"I can't see why any hilfer voluntarily ties himself up to an Open Colony. You know the people you're studying are going to get plowed under, and probably wiped out. It's the way things are. It's human nature, and you must know you can't change that. Then why come and watch the process? Masochism?"

"I don't know what 'human nature' is. Maybe leaving descriptions of what we wipe out is part of human nature.—Is it much pleasanter for an ecologist, really?"

Gosse ignored this. "All right then, write up your descriptions. But keep out of the carnage. A biologist studying a rat colony doesn't start reaching in and rescuing pet rats of his that get attacked, you know."

At this Lyubov had blown loose. He had taken too much. "No, of course not," he said. "A rat can be a pet, but not a friend. Selver is my friend. In fact he's the only man on this world whom I consider to be a friend." That had hurt poor old Gosse, who wanted to be a father-figure to Lyubov, and it had done nobody any good. Yet it had been true. And the truth shall make you free . . . I like Selver, respect him; saved him; suffered with him; fear him. Selver is my friend.

Selver is a god.

So the little green crone had said as if everybody knew it, as flatly as she might have said So-and-so is a hunter. "Selver sha'ab." What did *sha'ab* mean, though? Many words of the Women's Tongue, the everyday speech of the Athsheans, came from the Men's Tongue that was the same in all communities, and these words often were not only two-syllabled but two-sided. They were coins, obverse and reverse. *Sha'ab* meant god, or numinous entity, or powerful being; it also meant something quite different, but Lyubov could not remember what. By this stage in his thinking, he was home in his bungalow, and had only to look it up in the dictionary which he and Selver had compiled in four months of exhausting but harmonious work. Of course: *sha'ab*, translator.

It was almost too pat, too apposite.

Were the two meanings connected? Often they were, yet not so often as to constitute a rule. If a god was a translator, what did he translate? Selver was indeed a gifted interpreter, but that gift had found expression only through the fortuity of a truly foreign language having been brought into his world. Was a *sha'ab* one who translated the language of dream and philosophy, the Men's Tongue, into the everyday speech? But all Dreamers could do that. Might he then be one who could translate into waking life the central experience of vision: one serving as a link between the two realities, considered by the Athsheans as equal, the dream-time and the world-time, whose connections, though vital, are obscure. A link: one who could speak aloud the perceptions of the subconscious. To "speak" that tongue is to act. To do a new thing. To change or to be changed, radically, from the root. For the root is the dream.

And the translator is the god. Selver had brought a new word into the language of his people. He had done a new deed. The word, the deed, murder. Only a god could lead so great a newcomer as Death across the bridge between the worlds.

But had he learned to kill his fellowmen among his own dreams of outrage and bereavement, or from the undreamed-of actions of the strangers? Was he speaking his own language, or was he speaking Captain Davidson's? That which seemed to rise from the root of his own suffering and express his own changed being, might in fact be an infection, a foreign plague, which would not make a new people of his race, but would destroy them.

It was not in Raj Lyubov's nature to think, "What can I do?" Character and training disposed him not to interfere in other men's business. His job was to find out what they did, and his inclination was to let them go on doing it. He preferred to be enlightened, rather than to enlighten; to seek facts rather than the Truth. But even the most unmissionary soul, unless he pretend he has no emotions, is sometimes faced with a choice between commission and omission. "What are they doing?" abruptly becomes, "What are we doing?" and then, "What must I do?"

That he had reached such a point of choice now, he knew, and yet did not know clearly why, nor what alternatives were offered him.

He could do no more to improve the Athsheans' chance of survival at the moment; Lepennon, Or, and the ansible had done more than he had hoped to see done in his lifetime. The Administration on Terra was explicit in every ansible communication, and Colonel Dongh, though under pressure from some of his staff and the logging bosses to ignore the directives, was carrying out orders. He was a loyal officer; and besides, the *Shackleton* would be coming back to observe and report on how orders were being carried out. Reports home meant something, now that this ansible, this *machina ex machina*, functioned to prevent all the comfortable old colonial autonomy, and make you answerable within your own lifetime for what you did. There was no more fifty-four-year margin for error. Policy was no longer static. A decision by the League of Worlds might now lead overnight to the colony's being limited to one Land, or forbidden to cut trees, or encouraged to kill natives—no telling. How the League worked and what sort of policies it was developing could not yet be guessed from the flat directives of the Administration. Dongh was worried by these multiple-choice futures, but Lyubov enjoyed them. In diversity is life and where there's life there's hope, was the general sum of his creed, a modest one to be sure.

The colonists were letting the Athsheans alone and they were letting the colonists alone. A healthy situation, and one not to be disturbed unnecessarily. The only thing likely to disturb it was fear.

At the moment the Athsheans might be expected to be suspicious and still resentful, but not particularly afraid. As for the panic felt in Centralville at news of the Smith Camp massacre, nothing had happened to revive it. No Athshean anywhere had shown any violence since; and with the slaves gone, the creechies all vanished back into their forests, there was no more constant irritation of xenophobia. The colonists were at last beginning to relax.

If Lyubov reported that he had seen Selver at Tuntar, Dongh and the others would be alarmed. They might insist on trying to capture Selver and bring him in for trial. The Colonial Code forbade prosecution of a member of one planetary society under the laws of another, but the Court Martial over-rode such distinctions. They could try, convict, and shoot Selver. With Davidson brought back from New Java to give evidence. Oh no, Lyubov thought, shoving the dictionary onto an overcrowded shelf. Oh no, he thought, and thought no more about it. So he made his choice without even knowing he had made one.

He turned in a brief report next day. It said that Tuntar was going about its business as usual, and that he had not been turned away or threatened. It was a soothing report, and the most inaccurate one Lyubov ever wrote. It omitted everything of significance: the headwoman's non-appearance, Tubab's refusal to greet Lyubov, the large number of strangers in town, the young huntress' expression, Selver's presence . . . Of course that last was an intentional omission, but otherwise the report was quite factual, he thought; he had merely omitted subjective impressions, as a scientist should. He had a severe migraine whilst writing the report, and a worse one after submitting it.

He dreamed a lot that night, but could not remember his dreams in the morning. Late in the second night after his visit to Tuntar he woke, and in the hysterical whooping of the alarm-siren and the thudding of explosions he faced, at last, what he had refused. He was the only man in Centralville not taken by surprise. In that moment he knew what he was: a traitor.

And yet even now it was not clear in his mind that this was an Athshean raid. It was the terror in the night.

His own hut had been ignored, standing in its yard away from other houses; perhaps the trees around it protected it, he thought as he hurried out. The center of town was all on fire. Even the stone cube of HQ burned from within like a broken kiln. The ansible was in there: the precious link. There were fires also in the direction of the helicopter port and the Field. Where had they got explosives? How had the fires got going all at once? All the buildings along both sides of Main Street, built of wood, were burning; the sound of the burning was terrible. Lyubov ran towards the fires. Water flooded the way; he thought at first it was from a fire-hose, then realised the main from the river Menend was flooding uselessly over the ground while the houses burned with that hideous sucking roar. How had they done this? There were guards, there were always guards in jeeps at the Field . . . Shots: volleys, the yatter of a machinegun. All around Lyubov were small running figures, but he ran among them without giving them much thought. He was abreast of the Hostel now, and saw a girl standing in the doorway, fire flickering at her back and a clear escape before her. She did not move. He shouted at her, then ran across the yard to her and wrested her hands free of the doorjambs which she clung to in panic, pulling her away by force, saying gently, "Come on, honey, come on." She came then, but not quite soon enough. As they crossed the yard the front of the upper storey, blazing from within, fell slowly forward, pushed by the timbers of the collapsing roof. Shingles and beams shot out like shell-fragments; a blazing beam-end struck Lyubov and knocked him sprawling. He lay face down in the firelit lake of mud. He did not see a little green-furred huntress leap at the girl, drag her down backwards, and cut her throat. He did not see anything.

VI

No songs were sung that night. There was only shouting and silence. When the flying ships burned Selver exulted, and tears came into his eyes, but no words into his mouth. He turned away in silence, the fire thrower heavy in his arms, to lead his group back into the city.

Each group of people from the West and North was led by an ex-slave like himself, one who had served the yumens in Central and knew the buildings and ways of the city.

Most of the people who came to the attack that night had never seen the yumen city; many of them had never seen a yumen. They had come because they followed Selver, because they were driven by the evil dream and only Selver could teach them how to master it. There were hundreds and hundreds of them, men and women; they had waited in utter silence in the rainy darkness all around the edges of the city, while the ex-slaves, two or three at a time, did those things which they judged must be done first: break the water-pipe, cut the wires that carried light from Generator House, break into and rob the Arsenal. The first deaths, those of guards, had been silent, accomplished with hunting weapons, noose, knife, arrow, very quickly, in the dark. The dynamite, stolen earlier in the night from the logging camp ten miles south, was prepared in the Arsenal, the basement of HQ Building, while fires were set in other places; and then the alarm went off and the fires blazed and both night and silence fled. Most of the thunderclap and tree-fall crashing of gunfire came from the yumens defending themselves, for only ex-slaves had taken weapons from the Arsenal and used them; all the rest kept to their own lances, knives, and bows. But it was the dynamite, placed and ignited by Reswan and others who had worked in the loggers' slave-pen, that made the noise that conquered all other noises, and blew out the walls of the HQ Building and destroyed the hangars and the ships.

There were about seventeen hundred yumens in the city that night, above five hundred of them female; all the yumen females were said to be there now, that was why Selver and the others had decided to act, though not all the people who wished to come had yet gathered. Between four and five thousand men and women had come through the forests to the Meeting at Endtor, and from there to this place, to this night.

The fires burned huge, and the smell of burning and of butchering was foul.

Selver's mouth was dry and his throat sore, so that he could not speak, and longed for water to drink. As he led his group down the middle path of the city, a yumen came running towards him, looming huge in the black and dazzle of the smoky air. Selver lifted the fire-thrower and pulled back on the tongue of it, even as the yumen slipped in mud and fell scrambling to its knees. No hissing jet of flame sprang from the machine, it had all been spent on burning the airships that had not been in the hangar. Selver dropped the heavy machine. The yumen was not armed, and was male. Selver tried to say, "Let him run away," but his voice was weak, and two men, hunters of the Abtam Glades, had leapt past him even as he spoke, holding their long knives up. The big, naked hands clutched at air, and dropped limp. The big corpse lay in a heap on the path. There were many others lying dead, there in what had been the center of the city. There was not much noise any more except the noise of the fires.

Selver parted his lips and hoarsely sent up the home-call that ends the hunt; those with him took it up more clearly and loudly, in carrying falsetto; other voices answered it, near and far off in the mist and reek and flame-shot darkness of the night. Instead of leading his group at once from the city, he signalled them to go on, and himself went aside, onto the muddy ground between the path and a building which had burned and fallen. He stepped across a dead female yumen and bent over one that lay pinned down under a great, charred beam of wood. He could not see the features obliterated by mud and shadow.

It was not just; it was not necessary; he need not have looked at that one among so many dead. He need not have known him in the dark. He started to go after his group. Then he turned back; straining, lifted the beam off Lyubov's back; knelt down, slipping one hand under the heavy head so that Lyubov seemed to lie easier, his face clear of the earth; and so knelt there, motionless.

He had not slept for four days and had not been still to dream for longer than that—he did not know how long. He had acted, spoken, travelled, planned, night and day, ever since he left Broter with his followers from Cadast. He had gone from city to city speaking to the people of the forest, telling them the new thing, waking them from the dream into the world, arranging the thing done this night, talking, always talking and hearing others talk, never in silence and never alone. They had listened, they had heard and had come to follow him, to follow the new path. They had taken up the fire they feared into their own hands: taken up the mastery over the evil dream: and loosed the death they feared upon their enemy. All had been done as he said it should be done. All had gone as he said it would go. The lodges and many dwellings of the yumens were burnt, their airships burnt or broken, their weapons stolen or destroyed: and their females were dead. The fires were burning out, the night growing very dark, fouled with smoke. Selver could scarcely see; he looked up to the east, wondering if it were nearing dawn. Kneeling there in the mud among the dead he thought, This is the dream now, the evil dream. I thought to drive it, but it drives me.

In the dream, Lyubov's lips moved a little against the palm of his own hand; Selver looked down and saw the dead man's eyes open. The glare of dying fires shone on the surface of them. After a while he spoke Selver's name.

"Lyubov, why did you stay here? I told you to be out of the city this night." So Selver spoke in dream, harshly, as if he were angry at Lyubov.

"Are you the prisoner?" Lyubov said, faintly and not lifting his head, but in so commonplace a voice that Selver knew for a moment that this was not the dream-time but the world-time, the forest's night. "Or am I?"

"Neither, both, how do I know? All the engines and machines are burned. All the women are dead. We let the men run away if they would. I told them not to set fire to your house, the books will be all right. Lyubov, why aren't you like the others?"

"I am like them. A man. Like them. Like you."

"No. You are different—"

"I am like them. And so are you. Listen, Selver. Don't go on. You must not go on killing other men. You must go back . . . to your own . . . to your roots."

"When your people are gone, then the evil dream will stop."

"*Now*," Lyubov said, trying to lift his head, but his back was broken. He looked up at Selver and opened his mouth to speak. His gaze dropped away and looked into the other time, and his lips remained parted, unspeaking. His breath whistled a little in his throat.

They were calling Selver's name, many voices far away, calling over and over. "I can't stay with you, Lyubov!" Selver said in tears, and when there was no answer stood up and tried to run away. But in the dream-darkness he could go only very slowly, like one wading through deep water. The Ash Spirit walked in front of him, taller than Lyubov or any yumen, tall as a tree, not turning its white mask to him. As Selver went he spoke to Lyubov: "We'll go back," he said. "I will go back. Now. We will go back, now, I promise you, Lyubov!"

But his friend, the gentle one, who had saved his life and betrayed his dream, Lyubov did not reply. He walked somewhere in the night near Selver, unseen, and quiet as death.

A group of the people of Tuntar came on Selver wandering in the dark, weeping and speaking, overmastered by dream; they took him with them in their swift return to Endtor.

In the makeshift Lodge there, a tent on the river-bank, he lay helpless and insane for two days and nights, while the Old Men tended him. All that time people kept coming in to Endtor and going out again, returning to the Place of Eshsen which had been called Central, burying their dead there and the alien dead: of theirs more than three hundred, of the others more than seven hundred. There were about five hundred yumens locked into the compound, the creechie-pens, which, standing empty and apart, had not been burnt. As many more had escaped, some of whom had got to the logging camps farther south, which had not been attacked; those who were still hiding and wandering in the forest or the Cut Lands were hunted down. Some were killed, for many of the younger hunters and huntresses still heard only Selver's voice saying *Kill them*. Others had left the night of killing behind them as if it had been a nightmare, the evil dream that must be understood lest it be repeated; and these, faced with a thirsty, exhausted yumen cowering in a thicket, could not kill him. So maybe he killed them. There were groups of ten and twenty yumens, armed with logger's axes and hand-guns, though few had ammunition left; these groups were tracked until sufficient numbers were hidden in the forest about them, then

overpowered, bound, and led back to Eshsen. They were all captured within two or three days, for all that part of Sornol was
swarming with the people of the forest, there had never in the
knowledge of any man been half or a tenth so great a gathering
of people in one place; some still coming in from distant towns
and other Lands, others already going home again. The captured
yumens were put in among the others in the compound, though
it was overcrowded and the huts were too small for yumens.
They were watered, fed twice daily, and guarded by a couple of
hundred armed hunters at all times.

In the afternoon following the Night of Eshsen an airship
came rattling out of the east and flew low as if to land, then shot
upward like a bird of prey that misses its kill, and circled the
wrecked landing-place, the smouldering city, and the Cut Lands.
Reswan had seen to it that the radios were destroyed, and perhaps it was the silence of the radios that had brought the airship
from Kushil or Rieshwel, where there were three small towns of
yumens. The prisoners in the compound rushed out of the barracks and yelled at the machine whenever it came rattling overhead, and once it dropped an object on a small parachute into
the compound: at last it rattled off into the sky.

There were four such winged ships left on Athshe now, three
on Kushil and one on Rieshwel, all of the small kind that carried
four men; they also carried machineguns and flamethrowers,
and they weighed much on the minds of Reswan and the others,
while Selver lay lost to them, walking the cryptic ways of the
other time.

He woke into the world-time on the third day, thin, dazed,
hungry, silent. After he had bathed in the river and had eaten,
he listened to Reswan and the headwoman of Berre and the
others chosen as leaders. They told him how the world had gone
while he dreamed. When he had heard them all, he looked about
at them and they saw the god in him. In the sickness of disgust
and fear that followed the Night of Eshsen, some of them had
come to doubt. Their dreams were uneasy and full of blood and
fire; they were surrounded all day by strangers, people come
from all over the forests, hundreds of them, thousands, all
gathered here like kites to carrion, none knowing another: and it
seemed to them as if the end of things had come and nothing
would ever be the same, or be right, again. But in Selver's pres-

ence they remembered purpose; their distress was quietened, and they waited for him to speak.

"The killing is all done," he said. "Make sure that everyone knows that." He looked round at them. "I have to talk with the ones in the compound. Who is leading them in there?"

"Turkey, Flapfeet, Weteyes," said Reswan, the ex-slave.

"Turkey's alive? Good. Help me get up, Greda, I have eels for bones . . ."

When he had been afoot a while he was stronger, and within the hour he set off for Eshsen, two hours' walk from Endtor.

When they came Reswan mounted a ladder set against the compound wall and bawled in the pidgin-English taught the slaves, "Dong-a come to gate hurry-up-quick!"

Down in the alleys between the squat cement barracks, some of the yumens yelled and threw clods of dirt at him. He ducked, and waited.

The old Colonel did not come out, but Gosse, whom they called Weteyes, came limping out of a hut and called up to Reswan, "Colonel Dongh is ill, he cannot come out."

"Ill what kind?"

"Bowels, water-illness. What you want?"

"Talk-talk.—My lord god," Reswan said in his own language, looking down at Selver, "the Turkey's hiding, do you want to talk with Weteyes?"

"All right."

"Watch the gate there, you bowmen!—To gate, Mis-ter Goss-a, hurry-up-quick!"

The gate was opened just wide enough and long enough for Gosse to squeeze out. He stood in front of it alone, facing the group led by Selver. He favored one leg, injured on the Night of Eshsen. He was wearing torn pajamas, mudstained and rain-sodden. His greying hair hung in lank festoons around his ears and over his forehead. Twice the height of his captors, he held himself very stiff, and stared at them in courageous, angry misery.

"What you want?"

"We must talk, Mr. Gosse," said Selver, who had learned plain English from Lyubov. "I'm Selver of the Ash Tree of Eshreth. I'm Lyubov's friend."

"Yes, I know you. What have you to say?"

"I have to say that the killing is over, if that be made a promise kept by your people and my people. You may all go free, if you will gather in your people from the logging camps in South Sornol, Kushil, and Rieshwel, and make them all stay together here. You may live here where the forest is dead, where you grow your seed-grasses. There must not be any more cutting of trees."

Gosse's face had grown eager: "The camps weren't attacked?"

"No."

Gosse said nothing.

Selver watched his face, and presently spoke again: "There are less than two thousand of your people left living in the world, I think. Your women are all dead. In the other camps there are still weapons; you could kill many of us. But we have some of your weapons. And there are more of us than you could kill. I suppose you know that, and that's why you have not tried to have the flying ships bring you fire-throwers, and kill the guards, and escape. It would be not good; there really are so many of us. If you make the promise with us it will be much the best, and then you can wait without harm until one of your Great Ships comes, and you can leave the world. That will be in three years, I think."

"Yes, three local years—How do you know that?"

"Well, slaves have ears, Mr. Gosse."

Gosse looked straight at him at last. He looked away, fidgeted, tried to ease his leg. He looked back at Selver, and away again. "We had already 'promised' not to hurt any of your people. It's why the workers were sent home. It did no good, you didn't listen—"

"It was not a promise made to us."

"How can we make any sort of agreement or treaty with a people who have no government, no central authority?"

"I don't know. I'm not sure you know what a promise is. This one was soon broken."

"What do you mean? By whom, how?"

"In Rieshwel, New Java. Fourteen days ago. A town was burned and its people killed by yumens of the Camp in Rieshwel."

"What are you talking about?"

"About news brought us by messengers from Rieshwel."

"It's a lie. We were in radio contact with New Java right along, until the massacre. Nobody was killing natives there or anywhere else."

"You're speaking the truth you know," Selver said, "I the truth I know. I accept your ignorance of the killings on Rieshwel; but you must accept my telling you that they were done. This remains: the promise must be made to us and with us, and it must be kept. You'll wish to talk about these matters with Colonel Dongh and the others."

Gosse moved as if to re-enter the gate, then turned back and said in his deep, hoarse voice, "Who are you, Selver? Did you—was it you that organised the attack? Did you lead them?"

"Yes, I did."

"Then all this blood is on your head," Gosse said, and with sudden savagery, "Lyubov's too, you know. He's dead—your 'friend Lyubov.'"

Selver did not understand the idiom. He had learned murder, but of guilt he knew little beyond the name. As his gaze locked for a moment with Gosse's pale, resentful stare, he felt afraid. A sickness rose up in him, a mortal chill. He tried to put it away from him, shutting his eyes a moment. At last he said, "Lyubov is my friend, and so not dead."

"You're children," Gosse said with hatred. "Children, savages. You have no conception of reality. This is no dream, this is real! You killed Lyubov. He's dead. You killed the women—the *women*—you burned them alive, slaughtered them like animals!"

"Should we have let them live?" said Selver with vehemence equal to Gosse's, but softly, his voice singing a little. "To breed like insects in the carcase of the World? To overrun us? We killed them to sterilise you. I know what a realist is, Mr. Gosse. Lyubov and I have talked about these words. A realist is a man who knows both the world and his own dreams. You're not sane: there's not one man in a thousand of you who knows how to dream. Not even Lyubov and he was the best among you. You sleep, you wake and forget your dreams, you sleep again and wake again, and so you spend your whole lives, and you think that is being, life, reality! You are not children, you are grown men, but insane. And that's why we had to kill you, before you drove us mad. Now go back and talk about reality with the other insane men. Talk long, and well!"

The guards opened the gate, threatening the crowding yumens inside with their spears; Gosse re-entered the compound, his big shoulders hunched as if against the rain.

Selver was very tired. The headwoman of Berre and another woman came to him and walked with him, his arms over their shoulders so that if he stumbled he should not fall. The young hunter Greda, a cousin of his Tree, joked with him, and Selver answered light-headedly, laughing. The walk back to Endtor seemed to go on for days.

He was too weary to eat. He drank a little hot broth and lay down by the Men's Fire. Endtor was no town but a mere camp by the great river, a favorite fishing place for all the cities that had once been in the forest round about, before the yumens came. There was no Lodge. Two fire-rings of black stone and a long grassy bank over the river where tents of hide and plaited rush could be set up, that was Endtor. The river Menend, the master river of Sornol, spoke ceaselessly in the world and in the dream at Endtor.

There were many old men at the fire, some whom he knew from Broter and Tuntar and his own destroyed city Eshreth, some whom he did not know; he could see in their eyes and gestures, and hear in their voices, that they were Great Dreamers; more dreamers than had ever been gathered in one place before, perhaps. Lying stretched out full length, his head raised on his hands, gazing at the fire, he said, "I have called the yumens mad. Am I mad myself?"

"You don't know one time from the other," said old Tubab, laying a pine-knot on the fire, "because you did not dream either sleeping or waking for far too long. The price for that takes long to pay."

"The poisons the yumens take do much the same as does the lack of sleep and dream," said Heben, who had been a slave both at Central and Smith Camp. "The yumens poison themselves in order to dream. I saw the dreamer's look in them after they took the poisons. But they couldn't call the dreams, nor control them, nor weave nor shape nor cease to dream; they were driven, overpowered. They did not know what was within them at all. So it

is with a man who hasn't dreamed for many days. Though he be
the wisest of his Lodge, still he'll be mad, now and then, here
and there, for a long time after. He'll be driven, enslaved. He
will not understand himself."

A very old man with the accent of South Sornol laid his hand
on Selver's shoulder, caressing him, and said, "My dear young
god, you need to sing, that would do you good."

"I can't. Sing for me."

The old man sang; others joined in, their voices high and
reedy, almost tuneless, like the wind blowing in the water-reeds
of Endtor. They sang one of the songs of the ash-tree, about the
delicate parted leaves that turn yellow in autumn when the berries turn red, and one night the first frost silvers them.

While Selver was listening to the song of the Ash, Lyubov lay
down beside him. Lying down he did not seem so monstrously
tall and large-limbed. Behind him was the half-collapsed, fire-
gutted building, black against the stars. "I am like you," he said,
not looking at Selver, in that dream-voice which tries to reveal
its own untruth. Selver's heart was heavy with sorrow for his
friend. "I've got a headache," Lyubov said in his own voice, rubbing the back of his neck as he always did, and at that Selver
reached out to touch him, to console him. But he was shadow
and firelight in the world-time, and the old men were singing the
song of the Ash, about the small white flowers on the black
branches in spring among the parted leaves.

The next day the yumens imprisoned in the compound sent for
Selver. He came to Eshsen in the afternoon, and met with them
outside the compound, under the branches of an oak-tree, for all
Selver's people felt a little uneasy under the bare open sky. Eshsen had been an oak grove; this tree was the largest of the few
the colonists had left standing. It was on the long slope behind
Lyubov's bungalow, one of the six or eight houses that had come
through the night of the burning undamaged. With Selver under
the oak were Reswan, the headwoman of Berre, Greda of
Cadast, and others who wished to be in on the parley, a dozen or
so in all. Many bowmen kept guard, fearing the yumens might
have hidden weapons, but they sat behind bushes or bits of
wreckage left from the burning, so as not to dominate the scene
with the hint of threat. With Gosse and Colonel Dongh were

three of the yumens called officers and two from the logging
camp, at the sight of one of whom, Benton, the ex-slaves drew in
their breaths. Benton had used to punish "lazy creechies" by cas-
trating them in public.

The Colonel looked thin, his normally yellow-brown skin a
muddy yellow-grey; his illness had been no sham. "Now the first
thing is," he said when they were all settled, the yumens standing, Selver's people squatting or sitting on the damp, soft oak-
leafmould, "the first thing is that I want first to have a working
definition of just precisely what these terms of yours mean and
what they mean in terms of guaranteed safety of my personnel
under my command here."

There was a silence.

"You understand English, don't you, some of you?"

"Yes. I don't understand your question, Mr. Dongh."

"Colonel Dongh, if you please!"

"Then you'll call me Colonel Selver, if you please." A singing
note came into Selver's voice; he stood up, ready for the contest,
tunes running in his mind like rivers.

But the old yumen just stood there, huge and heavy, angry yet
not meeting the challenge. "I did not come here to be insulted by
you little humanoids," he said. But his lips trembled as he said it.
He was old, and bewildered, and humiliated. All anticipation of
triumph went out of Selver. There was no triumph in the world
any more, only death. He sat down again. "I didn't intend insult,
Colonel Dongh," he said resignedly. "Will you repeat your question, please?"

"I want to hear your terms, and then you'll hear ours, that's all
there is to it."

Selver repeated what he had said to Gosse.

Dongh listened with apparent impatience. "All right. Now you
don't realise that we've had a functioning radio in the prison
compound for three days now." Selver did know this, as Reswan
had at once checked on the object dropped by the helicopter,
lest it be a weapon; the guards reported it was a radio, and he
let the yumens keep it. Selver merely nodded. "So we've been in
contact with the three outlying camps, the two on King Land
and one on New Java, right along, and if we had decided to
make a break for it and escape from that prison compound then

it would have been very simple for us to do that, with the helicopters to drop us weapons and covering our movements with their mounted weapons, one flamethrower could have got us out of the compound and in case of need they also have the bombs that can blow up an entire area. You haven't seen those in action of course."

"If you'd left the compound, where would you have gone?"

"The point is, without introducing into this any beside the point or erroneous factors, now we are certainly greatly outnumbered by your forces, but we have the four helicopters at the camps, which there's no use you trying to disable as they are under fully armed guard at all times now, and also all the serious fire-power, so that the cold reality of the situation is we can pretty much call it a draw and speak in positions of mutual equality. This of course is a temporary situation. If necessary we are enabled to maintain a defensive police action to prevent all-out war. Moreover we have behind us the entire fire-power of the Terran Interstellar Fleet, which could blow your entire planet right out of the sky. But these ideas are pretty intangible to you, so let's just put it as plainly and simply as I can, that we're prepared to negotiate with you, for the present time, in terms of an equal frame of reference."

Selver's patience was short; he knew his ill-temper was a symptom of his deteriorated mental state, but he could no longer control it. "Go on, then!"

"Well, first I want it clearly understood that as soon as we got the radio we told the men at the other camps not to bring us weapons and not to try any airlift or rescue attempts, and reprisals were strictly out of order—"

"That was prudent. What next?"

Colonel Dongh began an angry retort, then stopped; he turned very pale. "Isn't there anything to sit down on," he said.

Selver went around the yumen group, up the slope, into the empty two-room bungalow, and took the folding desk-chair. Before he left the silent room he leaned down and laid his cheek on the scarred, raw wood of the desk, where Lyubov had always sat when he worked with Selver or alone; some of his papers were lying there now; Selver touched them lightly. He carried the chair out and set it in the rainwet dirt for Dongh. The old man sat down, biting his lips, his almond-shaped eyes narrow with pain.

"Mr. Gosse, perhaps you can speak for the Colonel," Selver said. "He isn't well."

"I'll do the talking," Benton said, stepping forward, but Dongh shook his head and muttered, "Gosse."

With the Colonel as auditor rather than speaker it went more easily. The yumens were accepting Selver's terms. With a mutual promise of peace, they would withdraw all their outposts and live in one area, the region they had forested in Middle Sornol: about seventeen hundred square miles of rolling land, well watered. They undertook not to enter the forest; the forest people undertook not to trespass on the Cut Lands.

The four remaining airships were the cause of some argument. The yumens insisted they needed them to bring their people from the other islands to Sornol. Since the machines carried only four men and would take several hours for each trip, it appeared to Selver that the yumens could get to Eshsen rather sooner by walking, and he offered them ferry service across the straits; but it appeared that yumens never walked far. Very well, they could keep the hoppers for what they called the "Airlift Operation." After that, they were to destroy them.—Refusal. Anger. They were more protective of their machines than of their bodies. Selver gave in, saying they could keep the hoppers if they flew them only over the Cut Lands and if the weapons in them were destroyed. Over this they argued, but with one another, while Selver waited, occasionally repeating the terms of his demand, for he was not giving in on this point.

"What's the difference, Benton," the old Colonel said at last, furious and shaky, "can't you see that we can't use the damned weapons? There's three million of these aliens all scattered out all over every damned island, all covered with trees and undergrowth, no cities, no vital network, no centralised control. You can't disable a guerrilla type structure with bombs, it's been proved, in fact my own part of the world where I was born proved it for about thirty years fighting off major super-powers one after the other in the twentieth century. And we're not in a position until a ship comes to prove our superiority. Let the big stuff go, if we can hold on to the side-arms for hunting and self-defense!"

He was their Old Man, and his opinion prevailed in the end, as it might have done in a Men's Lodge. Benton sulked. Gosse started to talk about what would happen if the truce was broken, but Selver stopped him. "These are possibilities, we aren't yet done with certainties. Your Great Ship is to return in three years, that is three and a half years of your count. Until that time you are free here. It will not be very hard for you. Nothing more will be taken away from Centralville, except some of Lyubov's work that I wish to keep. You still have most of your tools of tree-cutting and ground-moving; if you need more tools, the iron-mines of Peldel are in your territory. I think all this is clear. What remains to be known is this: When that ship comes, what will they seek to do with you, and with us?"

"We don't know," Gosse said. Dongh amplified: "If you hadn't destroyed the ansible communicator first thing off, we might be receiving some current information on these matters, and our reports would of course influence the decisions that may be made concerning a finalised decision on the status of this planet, which we might then expect to begin to implement before the ship returns from Prestno. But due to wanton destruction due to your ignorance of your own interests, we haven't even got a radio left that will transmit over a few hundred miles."

"What is the ansible?" The word had come up before in this talk; it was a new one to Selver.

"ICD," the Colonel said, morose.

"A kind of radio," Gosse said, arrogant. "It put us in instant touch with our home-world."

"Without the twenty-seven-year waiting?"

Gosse stared down at Selver. "Right. Quite right. You learned a great deal from Lyubov, didn't you?"

"Didn't he just," said Benton. "He was Lyubov's little green buddyboy. He picked up everything worth knowing and a bit more besides. Like all the vital points to sabotage, and where the guards would be posted, and how to get into the weapon stockpile. They must have been in touch right up to the moment the massacre started."

Gosse looked uneasy. "Raj is dead. All that's irrelevant now, Benton. We've got to establish—"

"Are you trying to infer in some way that Captain Lyubov was involved in some activity that could be called treachery to the Colony, Benton?" said Dongh, glaring and pressing his hands against his belly. "There were no spies or treachers on my staff, it was absolutely handpicked before we ever left Terra and I know the kind of men I have to deal with."

"I'm not inferring anything, Colonel. I'm saying straight out that it was Lyubov stirred up the creechies, and if orders hadn't been changed on us after that Fleet ship was here, it never would have happened."

Gosse and Dongh both started to speak at once. "You are all very ill," Selver observed, getting up and dusting himself off, for the damp brown oak-leaves clung to his short body-fur as to silk. "I'm sorry we've had to hold you in the creechie-pen, it is not a good place for the mind. Please send for your men from the camps. When all are here and the large weapons have been destroyed, and the promise has been spoken by all of us, then we shall leave you alone. The gates of the compound will be opened when I leave here today. Is there more to be said?"

None of them said anything. They looked down at him. Seven big men, with tan or brown hairless skin, cloth-covered, dark-eyed, grim-faced; twelve small men, green or brownish-green, fur-covered, with the large eyes of the seminocturnal creature, with dreamy faces; between the two groups, Selver, the translator, frail, disfigured, holding all their destinies in his empty hands. Rain fell softly on the brown earth about them.

"Farewell then," Selver said, and led his people away.

"They're not so stupid," said the headwoman of Berre as she accompanied Selver back to Endtor. "I thought such giants must be stupid, but they saw that you're a god, I saw it in their faces at the end of the talking. How well you talk that gobble-gubble. Ugly they are, do you think even their children are hairless?"

"That we shall never know, I hope."

"Ugh, think of nursing a child that wasn't furry. Like trying to suckle a fish."

"They are all insane," said old Tubab, looking deeply distressed. "Lyubov wasn't like that, when he used to come to

Tuntar. He was ignorant, but sensible. But these ones, they argue, and sneer at the old man, and hate each other, like this," and he contorted his grey-furred face to imitate the expressions of the Terrans, whose words of course he had not been able to follow. "Was that what you said to them, Selver, that they're mad?"

"I told them that they were ill. But then, they've been defeated, and hurt, and locked in that stone cage. After that anyone might be ill and need healing."

"Who's to heal them," said the headwoman of Berre, "their women are all dead. Too bad for them. Poor ugly things—great naked spiders they are, ugh!"

"They are men, men, like us, men," Selver said, his voice shrill and edged like a knife.

"Oh, my dear lord god, I know it, I only meant they *look* like spiders," said the old woman, caressing his cheek. "Look here, you people, Selver is worn out with this going back and forth between Endtor and Eshsen, let's sit down and rest a bit."

"Not here," Selver said. They were still in the Cut Lands, among stumps and grassy slopes, under the bare sky. "When we come under the trees . . ." He stumbled, and those who were not gods helped him to walk along the road.

VII

Davidson found a good use for Major Muhamed's tape recorder. Somebody had to make a record of events on New Tahiti, a history of the crucifixion of the Terran Colony. So that when the ships came from Mother Earth they could learn the truth. So that future generations could learn how much treachery and cowardice and folly humans were capable of, and how much courage against all odds. During his free moments—not much more than moments since he had assumed command—he recorded the whole story of the Smith Camp Massacre, and brought the record up to date for New Java, and for King and Central also, as well as he could with the garbled hysterical stuff that was all he got by way of news from Central HQ.

Exactly what had happened there nobody would ever know,

except the creechies, for the humans were trying to cover up their own betrayals and mistakes. The outlines were clear, though. An organised bunch of creechies, led by Selver, had been let into the Arsenal and the Hangars, and turned loose with dynamite, grenades, guns, and flamethrowers to totally destruct the city and slaughter the humans. It was an inside job, the fact that HQ was the first place blown up proved that. Lyubov of course had been in on it, and his little green buddies had proved just as grateful as you might expect, and cut his throat like the others. At least, Gosse and Benton claimed to have seen him dead the morning after the massacre. But could you believe any of them, actually? You could assume that any human left alive in Central after that night was more or less of a traitor. A traitor to his race.

The women were all dead, they claimed. That was bad enough, but what was worse, there was no reason to believe it. It was easy for the creechies to take prisoners in the woods, and nothing would be easier to catch than a terrified girl running out of a burning town. And wouldn't the little green devils like to get hold of a human girl and try experiments on her? God knows how many of the women were still alive in the creechie warrens, tied down underground in one of those stinking holes, being touched and felt and crawled over and defiled by the filthy, hairy little monkeymen. It was unthinkable. But by God sometimes you have to be able to think about the unthinkable.

A hopper from King had dropped the prisoners at Central a receiver-transmitter the day after the massacre, and Muhamed had taped all his exchanges with Central starting that day. The most incredible one was a conversation between him and Colonel Dongh. The first time he played it Davidson had torn the thing right off the reel and burned it. Now he wished he had kept it, for the records, as a perfect proof of the total incompetence of the C.O.'s at both Central and New Java. He had given in to his own hotbloodedness, destroying it. But how could he sit there and listen to the recording of the Colonel and the Major discussing total surrender to the creechies, agreeing not to try retaliation, not to defend themselves, to give up all their big weapons, to all squeeze together onto a bit of land picked out for them by the creechies, a reservation conceded to them by their generous conquerors, the little green beasts. It was incredible. Literally incredible.

Probably old Ding Dong and Moo were not actually traitors by intent. They had just gone spla, lost their nerve. It was this damned planet that did it to them. It took a very strong personality to withstand it. There was something in the air, maybe pollens from all those trees, acting as some kind of drug maybe, that made ordinary humans begin to get as stupid and out of touch with reality as the creechies were. Then, being so outnumbered, they were pushovers for the creechies to wipe out.

It was too bad Muhamed had had to be put out of the way, but he would never have agreed to accept Davidson's plans, that was clear; he'd been too far gone. Anyone who'd heard that incredible tape would agree. So it was better he got shot before he really knew what was going on, and now no shame would attach to his name, as it would to Dongh's and all the other officers left alive at Central.

Dongh hadn't come on the radio lately. Usually it was Juju Sereng, in Engineering. Davidson had used to pal around a lot with Juju and had thought of him as a friend, but now you couldn't trust anybody any more. And Juju was another asiatiform. It was really queer how many of them had survived the Centralville Massacre; of those he'd talked to, the only non-asio was Gosse. Here in Java the fifty-five loyal men remaining after the reorganization were most eurafs like himself, some afros and afrasians, not one pure asio. Blood tells, after all. You couldn't be fully human without some blood in your veins from the Cradle of Man. But that wouldn't stop him from saving those poor yellow bastards at Central, it just helped explain their moral collapse under stress.

"Can't you realise what kind of trouble you're making for us, Don?" Juju Sereng had demanded in his flat voice. "We've made a formal truce with the creechies. And we're under direct orders from Earth not to interfere with the hilfs and not to retaliate. Anyhow how the hell can we retaliate? Now all the fellows from King Land and South Central are here with us we're still less than two thousand, and what have you got there on Java, about sixty-five men isn't it? Do you really think two thousand men can take on three million intelligent enemies, Don?"

"Juju, fifty men can do it. It's a matter of will, skill, and weaponry."

"Batshit! But the point is, Don, a truce has been made. And if it's broken, we've had it. It's all that keep us afloat, now. Maybe when the ship gets back from Prestno and sees what happened, they'll decide to wipe out the creechies. We don't know. But it does look like the creechies intend to keep the truce, after all it was their idea, and we have got to. They can wipe us out by sheer numbers, any time, the way they did Centralville. There were thousands of them. Can't you understand that, Don?"

"Listen, Juju, sure I understand. If you're scared to use the three hoppers you've still got there, you could send 'em over here, with a few fellows who see things like we do here. If I'm going to liberate you fellows singlehanded, I sure could use some more hoppers for the job."

"You aren't going to liberate us, you're going to incinerate us, you damned fool. Get that last hopper over here to Central now: that's the Colonel's personal order to you as Acting C.O. Use it to fly your men here; twelve trips, you won't need more than four local dayperiods. Now act on those orders, and get to it." Ponk, off the air—afraid to argue with him any more.

At first he worried that they might send their three hoppers over and actually bomb or strafe New Java Camp; for he was, technically, disobeying orders, and old Dongh wasn't tolerant of independent elements. Look how he'd taken it out on Davidson already, for that tiny reprisal-raid on Smith. Initiative got punished. What Ding Dong liked was submission, like most officers. The danger with that is that it can make the officer get submissive himself. Davidson finally realized, with a real shock, that the hoppers were no threat to him, because Dongh, Sereng, Gosse, even Benton were *afraid* to send them. The creechies had ordered them to keep the hoppers inside the Human Reservation: and they were obeying orders.

Christ, it made him sick. It was time to act. They'd been waiting around nearly two weeks now. He had his camp well defended; they had strengthened the stockade fence and built it up so that no little green monkeymen could possibly get over it, and that clever kid Aabi had made lots of neat home-made land mines and sown 'em all around the stockade in a hundred-meter

belt. Now it was time to show the creechies that they might push
around those sheep on Central but on New Java it was men they
had to deal with. He took the hopper up and with it guided an
infantry squad of fifteen to a creechie-warren south of camp.
He'd learned how to spot the things from the air; the giveaway
was the orchards, concentrations of certain kinds of tree, though
not planted in rows like humans would. It was incredible how
many warrens there were once you learned to spot them. The
forest was crawling with the things. The raiding party burned up
that warren by hand, and then flying back with a couple of his
boys he spotted another, less than four kilos from camp. On that
one, just to write his signature real clear and plain for everybody
to read, he dropped a bomb. Just a firebomb, not a big one, but
baby did it make the green fur fly. It left a big hole in the forest,
and the edges of the hole were burning.

Of course that was his real weapon when it actually came to
setting up massive retaliation. Forest fire. He could set one of
these whole islands on fire, with bombs and firejelly dropped
from the hopper. Have to wait a month or two, till the rainy season was over. Should he burn King or Smith or Central? King
first, maybe, as a little warning, since there were no humans left
there. Then Central, if they didn't get in line.

"What are you trying to do?" said the voice on the radio, and
it made him grin, it was so agonised, like some old woman being
held up. "Do you know what you're doing, Davidson?"

"Yep."

"Do you think you're going to subdue the creechies?" It wasn't
Juju this time, it might be that bigdome Gosse, or any of them;
no difference; they all bleated baa.

"Yes, that's right," he said with ironic mildness.

"You think if you keep burning up villages they'll come to you
and surrender—three million of them. Right?"

"Maybe."

"Look, Davidson," the radio said after a while, whining and
buzzing; they were using some kind of emergency rig, having
lost the big transmitter, along with that phoney ansible which
was no loss. "Look, is there somebody else standing by there we
can talk to?"

"No; they're all pretty busy. Say, we're doing great here, but we're out of dessert stuff, you know, fruit cocktail, peaches, crap like that. Some of the fellows really miss it. And we were due for a load of maryjanes when you fellows got blown up. If I sent the hopper over, could you spare us a few crates of sweet stuff and grass?"

A pause. "Yes, send it on over."

"Great. Have the stuff in a net, and the boys can hook it without landing." He grinned.

There was some fussing around at the Central end, and all of a sudden old Dongh was on, the first time he'd talked to Davidson. He sounded feeble and out of breath on the whining shortwave. "Listen, Captain, I want to know if you fully realize what form of action your actions on New Java are going to be forcing me into taking. If you continue to disobey your orders. I am trying to reason with you as a reasonable and loyal soldier. In order to ensure the safety of my personnel here at Central I'm going to be put into the position of being forced to tell the natives here that we can't assume any responsibility at all for your actions.

"That's correct, sir."

"What I'm trying to make clear to you is that means that we are going to be put into the position of having to tell them that we can't stop you from breaking the truce there on Java. Your personnel there is sixty-six men, is that correct, well I want those men safe and sound here at Central with us to wait for the *Shackleton* and keep the Colony together. You're on a suicide course and I'm responsible for those men you have there with you."

"No, you're not, sir. I am. You just relax. Only when you see the jungle burning, pick up and get out into the middle of a Strip, because we don't want to roast you folks along with the creechies."

"Now listen, Davidson, I order you to hand your command over to Lt. Temba at once and report to me here," said the distant whining voice, and Davidson suddenly cut off the radio, sickened. They were all spla, playing at still being soldiers, in full retreat from reality. There were actually very few men who could face reality when the going got tough.

As he expected, the local creechies did absolutely nothing about his raids on the warrens. The only way to handle them, as

he'd known from the start, was to terrorise them and never let up
on them. If you did that, they knew who was boss, and knuckled
under. A lot of the villages within a thirty-kilo radius seemed to
be deserted now before he got to them, but he kept his men
going out to burn them up every few days.

The fellows were getting rather jumpy. He had kept them logging, since that's what forty-eight of the fifty-five loyal survivors
were, loggers. But they knew that the robo-freighters from Earth
wouldn't be called down to load up the lumber, but would just
keep coming in and circling in orbit waiting for the signal that
didn't come. No use cutting trees just for the hell of it; it was
hard work. Might as well burn them. He exercised the men in
teams, developing fire-setting techniques. It was still too rainy
for them to do much, but it kept their minds busy. If only he had
the other three hoppers, he'd really be able to hit and run. He
considered a raid on Central to liberate the hoppers, but did not
yet mention this idea even to Aabi and Temba, his best men.
Some of the boys would get cold feet at the idea of an armed
raid on their own HQ. They kept talking about "when we get
back with the others." They didn't know those others had abandoned them, betrayed them, sold their skins to the creechies. He
didn't tell them that, they couldn't take it.

One day he and Aabi and Temba and another good sound
man would just take the hopper over, then three of them jump
out with machineguns, take a hopper apiece, and so home again,
home again, jiggety jog. With four nice egg-beaters to beat eggs
with. Can't make an omelet without beating eggs. Davidson
laughed aloud, in the darkness of his bungalow. He kept that
plan hidden just a little longer, because it tickled him so much to
think about it.

After two more weeks they had pretty well closed out the
creechie-warrens within walking distance, and the forest was
neat and tidy. No vermin. No smoke-puffs over the trees.
Nobody hopping out of bushes and flopping down on the ground
with their eyes shut, waiting for you to stomp them. No little
green men. Just a mess of trees and some burned places. The
boys were getting really edgy and mean; it was time to make the
hopper-raid. He told his plan one night to Aabi, Temba, and
Post.

None of them said anything for a minute, then Aabi said, "What about fuel, Captain?"

"We got enough fuel."

"Not for four hoppers; wouldn't last a week."

"You mean there's only a month's supply left for this one?"

Aabi nodded.

"Well then, we pick up a little fuel too, looks like."

"How?"

"Put your minds to it."

They all sat there looking stupid. It annoyed him. They looked to him for everything. He was a natural leader, but he liked men who thought for themselves too. "Figure it out, it's your line of work, Aabi," he said, and went out for a smoke, sick of the way everybody acted, like they'd lost their nerve. They just couldn't face the cold hard facts.

They were low on maryjanes now and he hadn't had one for a couple of days. It didn't do anything for him. The night was overcast and black, damp, warm, smelling like spring. Ngenene went by walking like an ice-skater, or almost like a robot on treads; he turned slowly through a gliding step and gazed at Davidson, who stood on the bungalow porch in the dim light from the doorway. He was a power-saw operator, a huge man. "The source of my energy is connected to the Great Generator I cannot be switched off," he said in a level tone, gazing at Davidson.

"Get to your barracks and sleep it off!" Davidson said in the whipcrack voice that nobody ever disobeyed, and after a moment Ngenene skated carefully on, ponderous and graceful. Too many of the men were using hallies more and more heavily. There was plenty, but the stuff was for loggers relaxing on Sundays, not for soldiers of a tiny outpost marooned on a hostile world. They had no time for getting high, for dreaming. He'd have to lock the stuff up. Then some of the boys might crack. Well, let 'em crack. Can't make an omelet without cracking eggs. Maybe he could send them back to Central in exchange for some fuel. You give me two, three tanks of gas and I'll give you two, three warm bodies, loyal soldiers, good loggers, just your type, a little far gone in bye-bye dreamland . . .

He grinned, and was going back inside to try this one out on

Temba and the others, when the guard posted up on the lumber-yard smoke stack yelled. "They're coming!" he screeched out in a high voice, like a kid playing Blacks and Rhodesians. Somebody else over on the west side of the stockade began yelling too. A gun went off.

And they came. Christ, they came. It was incredible. There were thousands of them, thousands. No sound, no noise at all, until that screech from the guard; then one gunshot; then an explosion—a land mine going up—and another, one after another, and hundreds and hundreds of torches flaring up lit one from another and being thrown and soaring through the black wet air like rockets, and the walls of the stockade coming alive with creechies, pouring in, pouring over, pushing, swarming, thousands of them. It was like an army of rats Davidson had seen once when he was a little kid, in the last Famine, in the streets of Cleveland, Ohio, where he grew up. Something had driven the rats out of their holes and they had come up in day-light, seething up over the wall, a pulsing blanket of fur and eyes and little hands and teeth, and he had yelled for his mom and run like crazy, or was that only a dream he'd had when he was a kid? It was important to keep cool. The hopper was parked in the creechie-pen; it was still dark over on that side and he got there at once. The gate was locked, he always kept it locked in case one of the weak sisters got a notion of flying off to Papa Ding Dong some dark night. It seemed to take a long time to get the key out and fit it in the lock and turn it right, but it was just a matter of keeping cool, and then it took a long time to sprint to the hopper and unlock it. Post and Aabi were with him now. At last came the huge rattle of the rotors, beating eggs, covering up all the weird noises, the high voices yelling and screeching and singing. Up they went, and hell dropped away below them: a pen full of rats, burning.

"It takes a cool head to size up an emergency situation quickly," Davidson said. "You men thought fast and acted fast. Good work. Where's Temba?"

"Got a spear in his belly," Post said.

Aabi, the pilot, seemed to want to fly the hopper, so Davidson let him. He clambered into one of the rear seats and sat back, letting his muscles relax. The forest flowed beneath them, black under black.

"Where you heading, Aabi?"

"Central."

"No. We don't want to go to Central."

"Where do we want to go to?" Aabi said with a kind of womanish giggle. "New York? Peking?"

"Just keep her up a while, Aabi, and circle camp. Big circles. Out of earshot."

"Captain, there isn't any Java Camp any more by now," said Post, a logging-crew foreman, a stocky, steady man.

"When the creechies are through burning the camp, we'll come in and burn the creechies. There must be four thousand of them all in one place there. There's six flamethrowers in the back of this helicopter. Let's give 'em about twenty minutes. Start with the jelly bombs and then catch the ones that run with the flamethrowers."

"Christ," Aabi said violently, "some of our guys might be there, the creechies might take prisoners, we don't know. I'm not going back there and burn up humans, maybe." He had not turned the hopper.

Davidson put the nose of his revolver against the back of Aabi's skull and said, "Yes, we're going back; so pull yourself together, baby, and don't give me a lot of trouble."

"There's enough fuel in the tank to get us to Central, Captain," the pilot said. He kept trying to duck his head away from the touch of the gun, like it was a fly bothering him. "But that's all. That's all we got."

"Then we'll get a lot of mileage out of it. Turn her, Aabi."

"I think we better go on to Central, Captain," Post said in his stolid voice, and this ganging up against him enraged Davidson so much that reversing the gun in his hand he struck out fast as a snake and clipped Post over the ear with the gun-butt. The logger just folded over like a Christmas card, and sat there in the front seat with his head between his knees and his hands hanging to the floor. "Turn her, Aabi," Davidson said, the whiplash in his voice. The helicopter swung around in a wide arc. "Hell, where's camp, I never had this hopper up at night without any signal to follow," Aabi said, sounding dull and snuffly like he had a cold.

"Go east and look for the fire," Davidson said, cold and quiet. None of them had any real stamina, not even Temba. None of them had stood by him when the going got really tough. Sooner or later they all joined up against him, because they just couldn't take it the way he could. The weak conspire against the strong, the strong man has to stand alone and look out for himself. It just happened to be the way things are. Where was the camp?

They should have been able to see the burning buildings for miles in this blank dark, even in the rain. Nothing showed. Grey-black sky, black ground. The fires must have gone out. Been put out. Could the humans have driven off the creechies? After he'd escaped? The thought went like a spray of icewater through his mind. No, of course not, not fifty against thousands. But by God there must be a lot of pieces of blown-up creechie lying around on the minefields, anyway. It was just that they'd come so damned thick. Nothing could have stopped them. He couldn't have planned for that. Where had they come from? There hadn't been any creechies in the forest anywhere around for days and days. They must have poured in from somewhere, from all directions, sneaking along in the woods, coming up out of their holes like rats. There wasn't any way to stop thousands and thousands of them like that. Where the hell was camp? Aabi was tricking, faking course. "Find the camp, Aabi," he said softly.

"For Christ's sake I'm trying to," the boy said.

Post never moved, folded over there by the pilot.

"It couldn't just disappear, could it, Aabi? You got seven minutes to find it."

"Find it yourself," Aabi said, shrill and sullen.

"Not till you and Post get in line, baby. Take her down lower."

After a minute Aabi said, "That looks like the river."

There was a river, and a big clearing; but where was Java Camp? It didn't show up as they flew north over the clearing. "This must be it, there isn't any other big clearing in there," Aabi said, coming back over the treeless area. Their landing-lights glared but you couldn't see anything outside the tunnels of the lights; it would be better to have them off. Davidson reached over the pilot's shoulder and switched the lights off. Blank wet dark was like black towels slapped on their eyes. "For Christ's sake!" Aabi screamed, and flipping the lights back on slewed the hopper left and up, but not fast enough. Trees leaned hugely out of the night and caught the machine.

The vanes screamed, hurling leaves and twigs in a cyclone through the bright lanes of the lights, but the boles of the trees were very old and strong. The little winged machine plunged, seemed to lurch and tear itself free, and went down sideways into the trees. The lights went out. The noise stopped.

"I don't feel so good," Davidson said. He said it again. Then he stopped saying it, for there was nobody to say it to. Then he realised he hadn't said it anyway. He felt groggy. Must have hit his head. Aabi wasn't there. Where was he? This was the hopper. It was all slewed around, but he was still in his seat. It was so dark, like being blind. He felt around, and so found Post, inert, still doubled up, crammed in between the front seat and the control panel. The hopper trembled whenever Davidson moved, and he figured out at last that it wasn't on the ground but wedged in between trees, stuck like a kite. His head was feeling better, and he wanted more and more to get out of the black, tilted-over cabin. He squirmed over into the pilot's seat and got his legs out, hung by his hands, and could not feel ground, only branches scraping his dangling legs. Finally he let go, not knowing how far he'd fall, but he had to get out of that cabin. It was only a few feet down. It jolted his head, but he felt better standing up. If only it wasn't so dark, so black. He had a torch in his belt, he always carried one at night around camp. But it wasn't there. That was funny. It must have fallen out. He'd better get back into the hopper and get it. Maybe Aabi had taken it. Aabi had intentionally crashed the hopper, taken Davidson's torch, and made a break for it. The slimy little bastard, he was like all the rest of them. The air was black and full of moisture, and you couldn't tell where to put your feet, it was all roots and bushes and tangles. There were noises all around, water dripping, rustling, tiny noises, little things sneaking around in the darkness. He'd better get back up into the hopper, get his torch. But he couldn't see how to climb back up. The bottom edge of the doorway was just out of reach of his fingers.

There was a light, a faint gleam seen and gone away off in the trees. Aabi had taken the torch and gone off to reconnoiter, get orientated, smart boy. "Aabi!" he called in a piercing whisper. He stepped on something queer while he was trying to see the light among the trees again. He kicked at it with his boots, then put a hand down on it, cautiously, for it wasn't wise to go feeling things you couldn't see. A lot of wet stuff, slick, like a dead rat. He withdrew his hand quickly. He felt in another place after a while; it was a boot under his hand, he could feel the crossings of the laces. It must be Aabi lying there right under his feet. He'd got thrown out of the hopper when it came down. Well, he'd deserved it with his Judas trick, trying to run off to Central. Davidson did not like the wet feel of the unseen clothes and hair. He straightened up. There was the light again, black-barred by near and distant tree-trunks, a distant glow that moved.

Davidson put his hand to his holster. The revolver was not in it.

He'd had it in his hand, in case Post or Aabi acted up. It was not in his hand. It must be up in the helicopter with his torch.

He stood crouching, immobile; then abruptly began to run. He could not see where he was going. Tree-trunks jolted him from side to side as he knocked into them, and roots tripped up his feet. He fell full length, crashing down among bushes. Getting to hands and knees he tried to hide. Bare, wet twigs dragged and scraped over his face. He squirmed farther into the bushes. His brain was entirely occupied by the complex smells of rot and growth, dead leaves, decay, new shoots, fronds, flowers, the smells of night and spring and rain. The light shone full on him. He saw the creechies.

He remembered what they did when cornered, and what Lyubov had said about it. He turned over on his back and lay with his head tipped back, his eyes shut. His heart stuttered in his chest.

Nothing happened.

It was hard to open his eyes, but finally he managed it. They just stood there: a lot of them, ten or twenty. They carried those spears they had for hunting, little toy-looking things but the iron blades were sharp, they could cut right through your guts. He shut his eyes and just kept lying there.

And nothing happened.

His heart quieted down, and it seemed like he could think better. Something stirred down inside him, something almost like laughter. By God they couldn't get him down! If his own men betrayed him, and human intelligence couldn't do any more for him, then he used their own trick against them—played dead like this, and triggered this instinct reflex that kept them from killing anybody who took that position. They just stood around him, muttering at each other. *They couldn't hurt him.* It was as if he was a god.

"Davidson."

He had to open his eyes. Again. The resin-flare carried by one of the creechies still burned, but it had grown pale, and the forest was dim grey now, not pitch-black. How had that happened? Only five or ten minutes had gone by. It was still hard to see but it wasn't night any more. He could see the leaves and branches, the forest. He could see the face looking down at him. It had no color in this toneless twilight of dawn. The scarred features looked like a man's. The eyes were like dark holes.

"Let me get up," Davidson said suddenly in a loud, hoarse voice. He was shaking with cold from lying on the wet ground. He could not lie there with Selver looking down at him.

Selver was emptyhanded, but a lot of the little devils around him had not only spears but revolvers. Stolen from his stockpile at camp. He struggled to his feet. His clothes clung icy to his shoulders and the backs of his legs, and he could not stop shaking.

"Get it over with," he said. "Hurry-up-quick!"

Selver just looked at him. At least now he had to look up, way up, to meet Davidson's eyes.

"Do you wish me to kill you now?" he inquired. He had learned that way of talking from Lyubov, of course; even his voice, it could have been Lyubov talking. It was uncanny.

"It's my choice, is it?"

"Well, you have lain all night in the way that means you wished us to let you live; now do you want to die?"

The pain in his head and stomach, and his hatred for this horrible little freak that talked like Lyubov and that had got him at its mercy, the pain and the hatred combined and set his belly churning, so he retched and was nearly sick. He shook with cold and nausea. He tried to hold on to courage. He suddenly stepped forward a pace and spat in Selver's face.

There was a little pause, and then Selver, with a kind of dancing movement, spat back. And laughed. And made no move to kill Davidson. Davidson wiped the cold spittle off his lips.

"Look, Captain Davidson," the creechie said in that quiet little voice that made Davidson go dizzy and sick, "we're both gods, you and I. You're an insane one, and I'm not sure whether I'm sane or not. But we are gods. There will never be another meeting in the forest like this meeting now between us. We bring each other such gifts as gods bring. You gave me a gift, the killing of one's kind, murder. Now, as well as I can, I give you my people's gift, which is not killing. I think we each find each other's gift heavy to carry. However, you must carry it alone. Your people at Eshsen tell me that if I bring you there, they have to make a judgment on you and kill you, it's their law to do so. So, wishing to give you life, I can't take you with the other prisoners to Eshsen; and I can't leave you to wander in the forest, for you do too much harm. So you'll be treated like one of us when we go mad. You'll be taken to Rendlep where nobody lives any more, and left there."

Davidson stared at the creechie, could not take his eyes off it. It was as if it had some hypnotic power over him. He couldn't stand this. Nobody had any power over him. Nobody could hurt him. "I should have broken your neck right away, that day you tried to jump me," he said, his voice still hoarse and thick.

"It might have been best," Selver answered. "But Lyubov prevented you. As he now prevents me from killing you.—All the killing is done now. And the cutting of trees. There aren't trees to cut on Rendlep. That's the place you call Dump Island. Your people left no trees there, so you can't make a boat and sail from it. Nothing much grows there any more, so we shall have to bring you food and wood to burn. There's nothing to kill on Rendlep. No trees, no people. There were trees and people, but now there are only the dreams of them. It seems to me a fitting place for you to live, since you must live. You might learn how to dream there, but more likely you will follow your madness through to its proper end, at last."

"Kill me now and quit your damned gloating."

"Kill you?" Selver said, and his eyes looking up at Davidson seemed to shine, very clear and terrible, in the twilight of the forest. "I can't kill you, Davidson. You're a god. You must do it yourself."

He turned and walked away, light and quick, vanishing among the grey trees within a few steps.

A noose slipped over Davidson's head and tightened a little on his throat. Small spears approached his back and sides. They did not try to hurt him. He could run away, make a break for it, they didn't dare kill him. The blades were polished, leaf-shaped, sharp as razors. The noose tugged gently at his neck. He followed where they led him.

VIII

Selver had not seen Lyubov for a long time. That dream had gone with him to Rieshwel. It had been with him when he spoke the last time to Davidson. Then it had gone, and perhaps it slept now in the grave of Lyubov's death at Eshsen, for it never came to Selver in the town of Broter where he now lived.

But when the great ship returned, and he went to Eshsen, Lyubov met him there. He was silent and tenuous, very sad, so that the old carking grief awoke in Selver.

Lyubov stayed with him, a shadow in the mind, even when he met the yumens from the ship. These were people of power; they were very different from all yumens he had known, except his friend, but they were much stronger men than Lyubov had been.

His yumen speech had gone rusty, and at first he mostly let them talk. When he was fairly certain what kind of people they were, he brought forward the heavy box he had carried from Broter. "Inside this there is Lyubov's work," he said, groping for the words. "He knew more about us than the others do. He learned my language and the Men's Tongue; we wrote all that down. He understood somewhat how we live and dream. The others do not. I'll give you the work, if you'll take it to the place he wished."

The tall, white-skinned one, Lepennon, looked happy, and thanked Selver, telling him that the papers would indeed be taken where Lyubov wished, and would be highly valued. That pleased Selver. But it had been painful to him to speak his friend's name aloud, for Lyubov's face was still bitterly sad when he turned to it in his mind. He withdrew a little from the yumens, and watched them. Dongh and Gosse and others of Eshsen were there along with the five from the ship. The new ones looked clean and polished as new iron. The old ones had let the hair grow on their faces, so that they looked a little like huge, black-furred Athsheans. They still wore clothes, but the clothes were old and not kept clean. They were not thin, except for the Old Man, who had been ill ever since the Night of Eshsen; but they all looked a little like men who are lost or mad.

This meeting was at the edge of the forest, in that zone where by tacit agreement neither the forest people nor the yumens had built dwellings or camped for these past years. Selver and his companions settled down in the shade of a big ash-tree that stood out away from the forest eaves. Its berries were only small green knots against the twigs as yet, its leaves were long and soft, labile, summer-green. The light beneath the great tree was soft, complex with shadows.

The yumens consulted and came and went, and at last one came over to the ash-tree. It was the hard one from the ship, the Commander. He squatted down on his heels near Selver, not asking permission but not with any evident intention of rudeness. He said, "Can we talk a little?"

"Certainly."

"You know that we'll be taking all the Terrans away with us. We brought a second ship with us to carry them. Your world will no longer be used as a colony."

"This was the message I heard at Broter, when you came three days ago."

"I wanted to be sure that you understand that this is a permanent arrangement. We're not coming back. Your world has been placed under the League Ban. What that means in your terms is this: I can promise you that no one will come here to cut the trees or take your lands, so long as the League lasts."

"None of you will ever come back," Selver said, statement or question.

"Not for five generations. None. Then perhaps a few men, ten or twenty, no more than twenty, might come to talk to your people, and study your world, as some of the men here were doing."

"The scientists, the Speshes," Selver said. He brooded. "You decide matters all at once, your people," he said, again between statement and question.

"How do you mean?" The Commander looked wary.

"Well, you say that none of you shall cut the trees of Athshe: and all of you stop. And yet you live in many places. Now if a headwoman in Karach gave an order, it would not be obeyed by the people of the next village, and surely not by all the people in the world at once . . ."

"No, because you haven't one government over all. But we do —now—and I assure you its orders are obeyed. By all of us at once. But, as a matter of fact, it seems to me from the story we've been told by the colonists here, that when *you* gave an order, Selver, it was obeyed by everybody on every island here at once. How did you manage that?"

"At that time I was a god," Selver said, expressionless.

After the Commander had left him, the long white one came sauntering over and asked if he might sit down in the shade of the tree. He had tact, this one, and was extremely clever. Selver was uneasy with him. Like Lyubov, this one would be gentle; he would understand, and yet would himself be utterly beyond understanding. For the kindest of them was as far out of touch, as unreachable, as the cruellest. That was why the presence of Lyubov in his mind remained painful to him, while the dreams in which he saw and touched his dead wife Thele were precious and full of peace.

"When I was here before," Lepennon said, "I met this man, Raj Lyubov. I had very little chance to speak with him, but I remember what he said; and I've had time to read some of his studies of your people, since. His work, as you say. It's largely because of that work of his that Athshe is now free of the Terran Colony. This freedom had become the direction of Lyubov's life, I think. You, being his friend, will see that his death did not stop him from arriving at his goal, from finishing his journey."

Selver sat still. Uneasiness turned to fear in his mind. This one spoke like a Great Dreamer.

He made no response at all.

"Will you tell me one thing, Selver? If the question doesn't offend you. There will be no more questions after it . . . There were the killings: at Smith Camp, then at this place, Eshsen, then finally at New Java Camp where Davidson led the rebel group. That was all. No more since then . . . Is that true? Have there been no more killings?"

"I did not kill Davidson."

"That does not matter," Lepennon said, misunderstanding; Selver meant that Davidson was not dead, but Lepennon took him to mean that someone else had killed Davidson. Relieved to see that the yumen could err, Selver did not correct him.

"There has been no more killing, then?"

"None. They will tell you," Selver said, nodding towards the Colonel and Gosse.

"Among your own people, I mean. Athsheans killing Athsheans."

Selver was silent.

He looked up at Lepennon, at the strange face, white as the mask of the Ash Spirit, that changed as it met his gaze.

"Sometimes a god comes," Selver said. "He brings a new way to do a thing, or a new thing to be done. A new kind of singing, or a new kind of death. He brings this across the bridge between the dream-time and the world-time. When he has done this, it is done. You cannot take things that exist in the world and try to drive them back into the dream, to hold them inside the dream with walls and pretenses. That is insanity. What is, is. There is no use pretending, now, that we do not know how to kill one another."

Lepennon laid his long hand on Selver's hand, so quickly and gently that Selver accepted the touch as if the hand were not a stranger's. The green-gold shadows of the ash leaves flickered over them.

"But you must not pretend to have reasons to kill one another. Murder has no reason," Lepennon said, his face as anxious and sad as Lyubov's face. "We shall go. Within two days we shall be gone. All of us. Forever. Then the forests of Athshe will be as they were before."

Lyubov came out of the shadows of Selver's mind and said, "I shall be here."

"Lyubov will be here," Selver said. "And Davidson will be here. Both of them. Maybe after I die people will be as they were before I was born, and before you came. But I do not think they will."

Here's Poul again. Poul happens to be the only writer represented in all three *Hugo Winners* volumes. Here is the list of his stories:

VOLUME ONE	*"The Longest Voyage"*
VOLUME TWO	*"No Truce with Kings"*
	"The Sharing of Flesh"
VOLUME THREE	*"The Queen of Air and Darkness"*
	"Goat Song"

You see, he has five stories included altogether, which ties him with Harlan Ellison, whose five are to be found in Volumes Two and Three only.

Well, I have always believed in returning good for evil, so Poul's vicious behavior in this regard (for which, I am sure, he will be punished in the other world) shall elicit from me only a saintly smile and I will tell you another one of the jokes that I heard from him. (For heaven's sake, if you don't like these jokes, send nasty letters to Poul. If you *do* like them, on the other hand, you may write to me. I'm willing to share *part* of the burden.)

The scene is set in a nasty, cruel dictatorship—just about anywhere. A long line of people, four abreast, stretches out for many blocks in the queue for the daily ration of inferior hamburger meat.

Our hero, whom we shall call Smith, in order to make it impossible to guess to which nation we are referring, is working his way through a slow burn, and finally bubbles over. Turning to his companion, who is standing to his right, he says:

"I can endure this no longer. Since that scoundrel who rules us took over the government by his coup, he and his cronies live in the lap of luxury while we, the people, are slowly starving to death. My friend, I am dashing home for the rifle which I hid when they took away our arms. I will make my way to the Presidential Palace and, though it cost me my life, I shall assassinate that vicious criminal who lords it over us."

And he left at a run.

An hour later, the line had inched forward a block and a half, and our hero returned, silent and glum. He took his old place in the line and said nothing. His friend whispered to him out of the corner of his mouth, "Well?"

Our hero shook his head and said, with infinite bitterness, "You call *this* a line?"

7

GOAT SONG

Three women: one is dead; one is alive; One is both and neither, and will never live and never die, being immortal in SUM.

On a hill above that valley through which runs the highroad, I await Her passage. Frost came early this year, and the grasses have paled. Otherwise the slope is begrown and blackberry bushes that have been harvested by men and birds, leaving only briars, and with certain apple trees. They are very old, those trees, survivors of an orchard raised by generations which none but SUM now remembers (I can see a few fragments of wall thrusting above the brambles)—scattered crazily over the hillside and as crazily gnarled. A little fruit remains on them. Chill across my skin, a gust shakes loose an apple. I hear it knock on the earth, another stroke of some eternal clock. The shrubs whisper to the wind.

Elsewhere the ridges around me are wooded, afire with scarlets and brasses and bronzes. The sky is huge, the westering sun wan-bright. The valley is filling with a deeper blue, a haze whose slight smokiness touches my nostrils. This is Indian summer, the funeral pyre of the year.

There have been other seasons. There have been other lifetimes, before mine and hers; and in those days they had words to sing with. We still allow ourselves music, though, and I have spent much time planting melodies around my rediscovered words. *"In the greenest growth of the Maytime—"* I unsling the harp on my back, and tune it afresh, and sing to her, straight into autumn and the waning day.

> *"—You came, and the sun came after,*
> *And the green grew golden above;*

> *And the flag-flowers lightened with laughter,*
> *And the meadowsweet shook with love."*

A footfall stirs the grasses, quite gently, and the woman says, trying to chuckle, "Why, thank you."

Once, so soon after my one's death that I was still dazed by it, I stood in the home that had been ours. This was on the hundred and first floor of a most desirable building. After dark the city flamed for us, blinked, glittered, flung immense sheets of radiance forth like banners. Nothing but SUM could have controlled the firefly dance of a million aircars among the towers, or, for that matter, have maintained the entire city, from nuclear powerplants through automated factories, physical and economic distribution networks, sanitation, repair, services, education, culture, order, everything as one immune immortal organism. We had gloried in belonging to this as well as to each other.

But that night I told the kitchen to throw the dinner it had made for me down the waste chute, and ground under my heel the chemical consolations which the medicine cabinet extended to me, and kicked the cleaner as it picked up the mess, and ordered the lights not to go on, anywhere in our suite. I stood by the vieWall, looking out across megalopolis, and it was tawdry. In my hands I had a little clay figure she had fashioned herself. I turned it over and over and over.

But I had forgotten to forbid the door to admit visitors. It recognized this woman and opened for her. She had come with the kindly intention of teasing me out of a mood that seemed to her unnatural. I heard her enter, and looked around through the gloom. She had almost the same height as my girl did, and her hair chanced to be bound in a way that my girl often favored, and the figurine dropped from my grasp and shattered, because for an instant I thought she was my girl. Since then I have been hard put not to hate Thrakia.

This evening, even without so much sundown light, I would not make that mistake. Nothing but the silvery bracelet about her left wrist bespeaks the past we share. She is in wildcountry garb: boots, kilt of true fur and belt of true leather, knife at hip and rifle slung on shoulder. Her locks are matted and snarled, her skin brown from weeks of weather; scratches and smudges show beneath the fantastic zigzags she has painted in many colors on herself. She wears a necklace of bird skulls.

Now that one who is dead was, in her own way, more a child of trees and horizons than Thrakia's followers. She was so much at home in the open that she had no need to put off clothes or cleanliness, reason or gentleness, when we sickened of the cities and went forth beyond them. From this trait I got many of the names I bestowed on her, such as Wood's Colt or Fallow Hind or, from my prowlings among ancient books, Dryad and Elven. (She liked me to choose her names, and this pleasure had no end, because she was inexhaustible.)

I let my harpstring ring into silence. Turning about, I say to Thrakia, "I wasn't singing for you. Not for anyone. Leave me alone."

She draws a breath. The wind ruffles her hair and brings me an odor of her: not female sweetness, but fear. She clenches her fists and says, "You're crazy."

"Wherever did you find a meaningful word like that?" I gibe; for my own pain and—to be truthful—my own fear must strike out at something, and here she stands. "Aren't you content any longer with 'untranquil' or 'disequilibrated'?"

"I got it from you," she says defiantly, "you and your damned archaic songs. There's another word, 'damned.' And how it suits you! When are you going to stop this morbidity?"

"And commit myself to a clinic and have my brain laundered nice and sanitary? Not soon, darling." I use *that* last word aforethought, but she cannot know what scorn and sadness are in it for me, who know that once it could also have been a name for my girl. The official grammar and pronunciation of language is as frozen as every other aspect of our civilization, thanks to electronic recording and neuronic teaching; but meanings shift and glide about like subtle serpents. (O adder that stung my Foalfoot!)

I shrug and say in my driest, most city-technological voice, "Actually, I'm the practical, non-morbid one. Instead of running away from my emotions—via drugs, or neuroadjustment, or playing at savagery like you, for that matter—I'm about to implement a concrete plan for getting back the person who made me happy."

"By disturbing Her on Her way home?"

"Anyone has the right to petition the Dark Queen while She's abroad on earth."

"But this is past the proper time—"

"No law's involved, just custom. People are afraid to meet Her outside a crowd, a town, bright flat lights. They won't admit it, but they are. So I came here precisely not to be a part of a queue. I don't want to speak into a recorder for subsequent computer analysis of my words. How could I be sure She was listening? I want to meet Her as myself, a unique being, and look in Her eyes while I make my prayer."

Thrakia chokes a little. "She'll be angry."

"Is She able to be angry, any more?"

"I . . . I don't know. What you mean to ask for is so impossible, though. So absurd. That SUM should give you back your girl. You know It never makes exceptions."

"Isn't She Herself an exception?"

"That's different. You're being silly. SUM has to have a, well, a direct human liaison. Emotional and cultural feedback, as well as statistics. How else can It govern rationally? And She must have been chosen out of the whole world. Your girl, what was she? Nobody!"

"To me, she was everybody."

"You—" Thrakia catches her lip in her teeth. One hand reaches out and closes on my bare forearm, a hard hot touch, the grimy fingernails biting. When I make no response, she lets go and stares at the ground. A V of outbound geese passes overhead. Their cries come shrill through the wind, which is loudening in the forest.

"Well," she says, "you are special. You always were. You went to space and came back, with the Great Captain. You're maybe the only man alive who understands about the ancients. And your singing, yes, you don't really entertain, your songs trouble people and can't be forgotten. So maybe She will listen to you. But SUM won't. It can't give special resurrections. Once that was done, a single time, wouldn't it have to be done for everybody? The dead would overrun the living."

"Not necessarily," I say. "In any event, I mean to try."

"Why can't you wait for the promised time? Surely, then, SUM will re-create you two in the same generation."

"I'd have to live out this life, at least, without her," I say, looking away also, down to the highroad which shines through shadow like death's snake, the length of the valley. "Besides, how do you know there ever will be any resurrections? We have only a promise. No, less than that. An announced policy."

She gasps, steps back, raises her hands as if to fend me off. Her soul bracelet casts light into my eyes. I recognize an embryo exorcism. She lacks ritual; every "superstition" was patiently scrubbed out of our metal-and-energy world, long ago. But if she has no word for it, no concept, nevertheless she recoils from blasphemy.

So I say, wearily, not wanting an argument, wanting to wait here alone: "Never mind. There could be some natural catastrophe, like a giant asteroid striking, that wiped out the system before conditions had become right for resurrections to commence."

"That's impossible," she says, almost frantic. "The homeostats, the repair functions—"

"All right, call it a vanishingly unlikely theoretical contingency. Let's declare that I'm so selfish I want Swallow Wing back now, in this life of mine, and don't give a curse whether that'll be fair to the rest of you."

You won't care either, anyway, I think. None of you. You don't grieve. It is your own precious private consciousnesses that you wish to preserve; no one else is close enough to you to matter very much. Would you believe me if I told you I am quite prepared to offer SUM my own death in exchange for It releasing Blossom-in-the-Sun?

I don't speak that thought, which would be cruel, nor repeat what is crueller: my fear that SUM lies, that the dead never will be disgorged. For (I am not the All-Controller, I think not with vacuum and negative energy levels but with ordinary earth-begotten molecules; yet I can reason somewhat dispassionately, being disillusioned) consider—

The object of the game is to maintain a society stable, just, and sane. This requires satisfaction not only of somatic, but of symbolic and instinctual needs. Thus children must be allowed

to come into being. The minimum number per generation is
equal to the maximum: that number which will maintain a constant population.

It is also desirable to remove the fear of death from men.
Hence the promise: At such time as it is socially feasible, SUM
will begin to refashion us, with our complete memories but in
the pride of our youth. This can be done over and over, life after
life across the millennia. So death is, indeed, a sleep.

—in that sleep of death, what dreams may come— No. I myself dare not dwell on this. I ask merely, privately: Just when
and how does SUM expect conditions (in a stabilized society,
mind you) to have become so different from today's that the
reborn can, in their millions, safely be welcomed back?

I see no reason why SUM should not lie to us. We, too, are objects in the world that It manipulates.

"We've quarreled about this before, Thrakia," I sigh. "Often.
Why do you bother?"

"I wish I knew," she answers low. Half to herself, she goes on:
"Of course I want to copulate with you. You must be good, the
way that girl used to follow you about with her eyes, and smile
when she touched your hand, and— But you can't be better than
everyone else. That's unreasonable. There are only so many possible ways. So why do I care if you wrap yourself up in silence
and go off alone? Is it that that makes you a challenge?"

"You think too much," I say. "Even here. You're a pretend
primitive. You visit wildcountry to 'slake inborn atavistic im-
pulses' . . . but you can't dismantle that computer inside yourself and simply feel, simply be."

She bristles. I touched a nerve there. Looking past her, along
the ridge of fiery maple and sumac, brassy elm and great dun
oak, I see others emerge from beneath the trees. Women exclusively, her followers, as unkempt as she; one has a brace of ducks
lashed to her waist, and their blood has trickled down her thigh
and dried black. For this movement, this unadmitted mystique
has become Thrakia's by now: that not only men should forsake
the easy routine and the easy pleasure of the cities, and become
again, for a few weeks each year, the carnivores who begot our
species; women too should seek out starkness, the better to
appreciate civilization when they return.

I feel a moment's unease. We are in no park, with laid-out trails and campground services. We are in wildcountry. Not many men come here, ever, and still fewer women; for the region is, literally, beyond the law. No deed done here is punishable. We are told that this helps consolidate society, as the most violent among us may thus vent their passions. But I have spent much time in wildcountry since my Morning Star went out—myself in quest of nothing but solitude—and I have watched what happens through eyes that have also read anthropology and history. Institutions are developing; ceremonies, tribalisms, acts of blood and cruelty and acts elsewhere called unnatural are becoming more elaborate and more expected every year. Then the practitioners go home to their cities and honestly believe they have been enjoying fresh air, exercise, and good tension-releasing fun.

Let her get angry enough and Thrakia can call knives to her aid.

Wherefore I make myself lay both hands on her shoulders, and meet the tormented gaze, and say most gently, "I'm sorry. I know you mean well. You're afraid She will be annoyed and bring misfortune on your people."

Thrakia gulps. "No," she whispers. "That wouldn't be logical. But I'm afraid of what might happen to you. And then—" Suddenly she throws herself against me. I feel arms, breasts, belly press through my tunic, and smell meadows in her hair and musk in her mouth. "You'd be gone!" she wails. "Then who'd sing to us?"

"Why, the planet's crawling with entertainers," I stammer.

"You're more than that," she says. "So much more. I don't like what you sing, not really—and what you've sung since that stupid girl died, oh, meaningless, horrible!—but, I don't know why, I *want* you to trouble me."

Awkward, I pat her back. The sun now stands very little above the treetops. Its rays slant interminably through the booming, frosting air. I shiver in my tunic and buskins and wonder what to do.

A sound rescues me. It comes from one end of the valley below us, where further view is blocked off by two cliffs; it thunders deep in our ears and rolls through the earth into our bones. We have heard that sound in the cities, and been glad to have walls and lights and multitudes around us. Now we are alone with it, the noise of Her chariot.

The women shriek, I hear them faintly across wind and rumble and my own pulse, and they vanish into the woods. They will seek their camp, dress warmly, build enormous fires; presently they will eat their ecstatics, and rumors are uneasy about what they do after that.

Thrakia seizes my left wrist, above the soul bracelet, and hauls. "Harper, come with me!" she pleads. I break loose from her and stride down the hill toward the road. A scream follows me for a moment.

Light still dwells in the sky and on the ridges, but as I descend into that narrow valley I enter dusk, and it thickens. Indistinct bramblebushes whicker where I brush them, and claw back at me. I feel the occasional scratch on my legs, the tug as my garment is snagged, the chill that I breathe, but dimly. My perceived-outer-reality is overpowered by the rushing of Her chariot and my blood. My inner-universe is fear, yes, but exaltation, too, a drunkenness which sharpens instead of dulling the senses, a psychedelia which opens the reasoning mind as well as the emotions; I have gone beyond myself, I am embodied purpose. Not out of need for comfort, but to voice what Is, I return to words whose speaker rests centuries dust, and lend them my own music. I sing:

> "—Gold is my heart, and the world's golden,
>   And one peak tipped with light;
> And the air lies still about the hill
>   With the first fear of night;
>
> Till mystery down the soundless valley
>   Thunders, and dark is here;
> And the wind blows, and the light goes,
>   And the night is full of fear.
>
> And I know one night, on some far height,
>   In the tongue I never knew.
> I yet shall hear the tidings clear
>   From them that were friends of you.

> *They'll call the news from hill to hill,*
> *Dark and uncomforted,*
> *Earth and sky and the winds; and I*
> *Shall know that you are dead.—"*

But I have reached the valley floor, and She has come in sight.

Her chariot is unlit, for radar eyes and inertial guides need no lamps, nor sun nor stars. Wheelless, the steel tear rides on its own roar and thrust of air. The pace is not great, far less than any of our mortals' vehicles are wont to take. Men say the Dark Queen rides thus slowly in order that She may perceive with Her own senses and so be the better prepared to counsel SUM. But now Her annual round is finished; She is homeward bound; until spring She will dwell with It Which is our lord. Why does She not hasten tonight?

Because Death has never a need of haste? I wonder. And as I step into the middle of the road, certain lines from the yet more ancient past rise tremendous within me, and I strike my harp and chant them louder than the approaching car:

> *"I that in heill was and gladness*
> *Am trublit now with great sickness*
> *And feblit with infirmitie:—*
> *Timor mortis conturbat me."*

The car detects me and howls a warning. I hold my ground. The car could swing around, the road is wide and in any event a smooth surface is not absolutely necessary. But I hope, I believe that She will be aware of an obstacle in Her path, and tune in Her various amplifiers, and find me abnormal enough to stop for. Who, in SUM's world—who, even among the explorers that It has sent beyond in Its unappeasable hunger for data—would stand in a cold wildcountry dusk and shout while his harp snarls.

> *"Our plesance here is all vain glory,*
> *This fals world is but transitory,*
> *The flesh is bruckle, the Feynd is slee:—*
> *Timor mortis conturbat me.*
>
> *The state of man does change and vary,*
> *Now sound, now sick, now blyth, now sary,*
> *Now dansand mirry, now like to die:—*
> *Timor mortis conturbat me.*

> No state in Erd here standis sicker;
> As with the wynd wavis the wicker
> So wannis this world's vanitie:—
> Timor mortis conturbat me.—?"

The car draws alongside and sinks to the ground. I let my strings die away into the wind. The sky overhead and in the west is gray-purple; eastward it is quite dark and a few early stars peer forth. Here, down in the valley, shadows are heavy and I cannot see very well.

The canopy slides back. She stands erect in the chariot, thus looming over me. Her robe and cloak are black, fluttering like restless wings; beneath the cowl Her face is a white blur. I have seen it before, under full light, and in how many thousands of pictures; but at this hour I cannot call it back to my mind, not entirely. I list sharp-sculptured profile and pale lips, sable hair and long green eyes, but these are nothing more than words.

"What are you doing?" She has a lovely low voice; but is it, as oh, how rarely since SUM took Her to Itself, is it the least shaken? "What is that you were singing?"

My answer comes so strong that my skull resonates; for I am borne higher and higher on my tide. "Lady of Ours, I have a petition."

"Why did you not bring it before Me when I walked among men? Tonight I am homebound. You must wait till I ride forth with the new year."

"Lady of Ours, neither You nor I would wish living ears to hear what I have to say."

She regards me for a long while. Do I indeed sense fear also in Her? (Surely not of me. Her chariot is armed and armored, and would react with machine speed to protect Her should I offer violence. And should I somehow, incredibly, kill Her, or wound Her beyond chemosurgical repair, She of all beings has no need to doubt death. The ordinary bracelet cries with quite sufficient radio loudness to be heard by more than one thanatic station, when we die; and in that shielding the soul can scarcely be damaged before the Winged Heels arrive to bear it off to SUM. Surely the Dark Queen's circlet can call still farther, and is still better insulated, than any mortal's. And She will most absolutely be re-created. She has been, again and again; death and rebirth every seven years keep Her eternally young in the service of SUM. I have never been able to find out when She was first born.)

Fear, perhaps, of what I have sung and what I might speak?

At last She says—I can scarcely hear through the gusts and creakings in the trees—"Give me the Ring, then."

The dwarf robot which stands by Her throne when She sits among men appears beside Her and extends the massive dull-silver circle to me. I place my left arm within, so that my soul is enclosed. The tablet on the upper surface of the Ring, which looks so much like a jewel, slants away from me; I cannot read what flashes onto the bezel. But the faint glow picks Her features out of murk as She bends to look.

Of course, I tell myself, the actual soul is not scanned. That would take too long. Probably the bracelet which contains the soul has an identification code built in. The Ring sends this to an appropriate part of SUM, Which instantly sends back what is recorded under that code. I hope there is nothing more to it. SUM has not seen fit to tell us.

"What do you call yourself at the moment?" She asks.

A current of bitterness crosses my tide. "Lady of Ours, why should You care? Is not my real name the number I got when I was allowed to be born?"

Calm descends once more upon Her. "If I am to evaluate properly what you say, I must know more about you than these few official data. Name indicates mood."

I too feel unshaken again, my tide running so strong and smooth that I might not know I was moving did I not see time recede behind me. "Lady of Ours, I cannot give You a fair answer. In this past year I have not troubled with names, or with much of anything else. But some people who knew me from earlier days call me Harper."

"What do you do besides make that sinister music?"

"These days, nothing, Lady of Ours. I've money to live out my life, if I eat sparingly and keep no home. Often I am fed and housed for the sake of my songs."

"What you sang is unlike anything I have heard since—" Anew, briefly, that robot serenity is shaken. "Since before the world was stabilized. You should not wake dead symbols, Harper. They walk through men's dreams."

"Is that bad?"

"Yes. The dreams become nightmares. Remember: mankind, every man who ever lived, was insane before SUM brought order, reason, and peace."

"Well, then," I say, "I will cease and desist if I may have my own dead wakened for me."

She stiffens. The tablet goes out. I withdraw my arm and the Ring is stored away by Her servant. So again She is faceless, beneath flickering stars, here at the bottom of this shadowed valley. Her voice falls cold as the air: "No one can be brought back to life before Resurrection Time is ripe."

I do not say, "What about You?" for that would be vicious. What did She think, how did She weep, when SUM chose Her of all the young on earth? What does She endure in Her centuries? I dare not imagine.

Instead, I smite my harp and sing, quietly this time:

> *"Strew on her roses, roses,*
> *And never a spray of yew.*
> *In quiet she reposes:*
> *Ah! would that I did too."*

The Dark Queen cries, "What are you doing? Are you really insane?" I go straight to the last stanza.

> *"Her cabin'd, ample Spirit*
> *It flutter'd and fail'd for breath.*
> *To-night it doth inherit*
> *The vasty hall of Death."*

I know why my songs strike so hard: because they bear dreads and passions that no one is used to—that most of us hardly know could exist—in SUM's ordered universe. But I had not the courage to hope She would be as torn by them as I see. Has She not lived with more darkness and terror than the ancients themselves could conceive? She calls, "Who has died?"

"She had many names, Lady of Ours," I say. "None was beautiful enough. I can tell You her number, though."

"Your daughter? I . . . sometimes I am asked if a dead child cannot be brought back. Not often, any more, when they go so soon to the crèche. But sometimes. I tell the mother she may have a new one; but if ever We started re-creating dead infants, at what age level could We stop?"

"No, this was my woman."

"Impossible!" Her tone seeks to be not unkindly but is, instead, well-nigh frantic. "You will have no trouble finding others. You are handsome, and your psyche is, is, is extraordinary. It burns like Lucifer."

"Do You remember the name Lucifer, Lady of Ours?" I pounce. "Then You are old indeed. So old that You must also remember how a man might desire only one woman, but her above the whole world and heaven."

She tries to defend Herself with a jeer: "Was that mutual, Harper? I know more of mankind than you do, and surely I am the last chaste woman in existence?"

"Now that she is gone, Lady, yes, perhaps You are. But we—Do You know how she died? We had gone to a wildcountry area. A man saw her, alone, while I was off hunting gem rocks to make her a necklace. He approached her. She refused him. He threatened force. She fled. This was desert land, viper land, and she was barefoot. One of them bit her. I did not find her till hours later. By then the poison and the unshaded sun— She died quite soon after she told me what had happened and that she loved me. I could not get her body to chemosurgery in time for normal revival procedures. I had to let them cremate her and take her soul away to SUM."

"What right have you to demand her back, when no one else can be given their own?"

"The right that I love her, and she loves me. We are more necessary to each other than sun or moon. I do not think You could find another two people of whom this is so, Lady. And is not everyone entitled to claim what is necessary to his life? How else can society be kept whole?"

"You are being fantastic," She says thinly. "Let me go."

"No, Lady, I am speaking sober truth. But poor plain words won't serve me. I sing to You because then maybe You will understand." And I strike my harp anew; but it is more to her than Her that I sing.

"If I had thought thou couldst have died,
I might not weep for thee;
But I forgot, when by thy side,
That thou couldst mortal be:
It never through my mind had past
The time would e'er be o'er,
And I on thee should look my last,
And thou shouldst smile no more!"

"I cannot—" She falters. "I did not know—any such feelings—so strong—existed any longer."

"Now You do, Lady of Ours. And is that not an important datum for SUM?"

"Yes. If true." Abruptly She leans toward me. I see Her shudder in the murk, under the flapping cloak, and hear Her jaws clatter with cold. "I cannot linger here. But ride with Me. Sing to Me. I think I can bear it."

So much have I scarcely expected. But my destiny is upon me. I mount into the chariot. The canopy slides shut and we proceed.

The main cabin encloses us. Behind its rear door must be facilities for Her living on earth; this is a big vehicle. But here is little except curved panels. They are true wood of different comely grains: so She also needs periodic escape from our machine existence, does She? Furnishing is scant and austere. The only sound is our passage, muffled to a murmur for us; and, because their photomultipliers are not activated, the scanners show nothing outside but night. We huddle close to a glower, hands extended toward its fieriness. Our shoulders brush, our bare arms. Her skin is soft and Her hair falls loose over the thrown-back cowl, smelling of the summer which is dead. What, is She still human?

After a timeless time, She says, not yet looking at me: "The thing you sang, there on the highroad as I came near—I do not remember it. Not even from the years before I became what I am."

"It is older than SUM," I answer, "And its truth will outlive It."

"Truth?" I see Her tense Herself. "Sing Me the rest."

My fingers are no longer too numb to call forth chords.

> *"—Unto the Death gois all Estatis,*
> *Princis, Prelattis, and Potestatis,*
> *Baith rich and poor of all degree:—*
>   *Timor mortis conturbat me.*

> *He takis the knichtis in to the field*
> *Enarmit under helm and scheild:*
> *Victor he is at all mellie:—*
>   *Timor mortis conturbat me.*

> *That strong unmerciful tyrand*
> *Takis, on the mother's breast sowkand,*
> *The babe full of benignitio:—*
>   *Timor mortis conturbat me.*

> *He takis the campion in the stour,*
> *The captain closit in the tour,*
> *The ladie in bour full of bewtie:—"*

(There I must stop a moment.)

>   *"Timor mortis conturbat me.*

> *He sparis no lord for his piscence,*
> *Ha clerk for his intelligence;*
> *His awful straik may no man flee:—*
>   *Timor mortis conturbat me."*

She breaks me off, clapping hands to ears and half-shrieking, "No!"

I, grown unmerciful, pursue Her: "You understand now, do You not? You are not eternal either. SUM isn't. Not Earth, not sun, not stars. We hid from the truth. Every one of us. I too, until I lost the one thing which made everything make sense. Then I had nothing left to lose, and could look with clear eyes. And what I saw was Death."

"Get out! Let Me alone!"

"I will not let the whole world alone, Queen, until I get her back. Give me her again, and I'll believe in SUM again. I'll praise It till men dance for joy to hear Its name."

She challenges me with wildcat eyes. "Do you think such matters to It?"

"Well," I shrug, "songs could be useful. They could help

achieve the great objective sooner. Whatever that is. 'Optimiza-
tion of total human activity'—wasn't that the program? I don't
know if it still is. SUM has been adding to Itself so long. I doubt
if You Yourself understand Its purposes, Lady of Ours."

"Don't speak as if It were alive," She says harshly. "It is a com-
puter-effector complex. Nothing more."

"Are You certain?"

"I— Yes. It thinks, more widely and deeply than any human
ever did or could; but It is not alive, not aware. It has no consciousness. That is one reason why It decided It needed Me."

"Be that as it may, Lady," I tell Her, "the ultimate result,
whatever It finally does with us, lies far in the future. At present
I care about that; I worry; I resent our loss of self-determination.
But that's because only such abstractions are left to me. Give me
back my Lightfoot, and she, not the distant future, will be my
concern. I'll be grateful, honestly grateful, and You Two will
know it from the songs I then choose to sing. Which, as I said,
might be helpful to It."

"You are unbelievably insolent," She says without force.

"No, Lady, just desperate," I say.

The ghost of a smile touches Her lips. She leans back, eyes
hooded, and murmurs, "Well, I'll take you there. What happens
then, you realize, lies outside My power. My observations, My
recommendations, are nothing but a few items to take into account, among billions. However . . . we have a long way to
travel this night. Give me what data you think will help you,
Harper."

I do not finish the Lament. Nor do I dwell in any other fashion
on grief. Instead, as the hours pass, I call upon those who dealt
with the joy (not the fun, not the short delirium, but the joy)
that man and woman might once have of each other.

Knowing where we are bound, I too need such comfort.

And the night deepens, and the leagues fall behind us, and
finally we are beyond habitation, beyond wildcountry, in the
land where life never comes. By crooked moon and waning starlight I see the plain of concrete and iron, the missiles and energy
projectors crouched like beasts, the robot aircraft wheeling aloft:
and the lines, the relay towers, the scuttling beetle-shaped carriers, that whole transcendent nerve-blood-sinew by which SUM

knows and orders the world. For all the flitting about, for all the forces which seethe, here is altogether still. The wind itself seems to have frozen to death. Hoarfrost is gray on the steel shapes. Ahead of us, tiered and mountainous, begins to appear the castle of SUM.

She Who rides with me does not give sign of noticing that my songs have died in my throat. What humanness She showed is departing; Her face is cold and shut, Her voice bears a ring of metal. She looks straight ahead. But She does speak to me for a little while yet:

"Do you understand what is going to happen? For the next half year I will be linked with SUM, integral, another component of It. I suppose you will see Me, but that will merely be My flesh. What speaks to you will be SUM."

"I know." The words must be forced forth. My coming this far is more triumph than any man in creation before me has won; and I am here to do battle for my Dancer-on-Moonglades; but nonetheless my heart shakes me, and is loud in my skull, and my sweat stinks.

I manage, though, to add: "You *will* be a part of It, Lady of Ours. That gives me hope."

For an instant She turns to me, and lays Her hand across mine, and something makes Her again so young and untaken that I almost forget the girl who died; and she whispers, "If you knew how I hope!"

The instant is gone, and I am alone among machines.

We must stop before the castle gate. The wall looms sheer above, so high and high that it seems to be toppling upon me against the westward march of the stars, so black and black that it does not only drink down every light, it radiates blindness. Challenge and response quiver on electronic bands I cannot sense. The outer-guardian parts of It have perceived a mortal aboard this craft. A missile launcher swings about to aim its three serpents at me. But the Dark Queen answers—She does not trouble to be peremptory—and the castle opens its jaws for us.

We descend. Once, I think, we cross a river. I hear a rushing and hollow echoing and see droplets glitter where they are cast onto the viewports and outlined against dark. They vanish at once: liquid hydrogen, perhaps, to keep certain parts near absolute zero?

Much later we stop and the canopy slides back. I rise with Her. We are in a room, or cavern, of which I can see nothing, for there is no light except a dull bluish phosphorescence which streams from every solid object, also from Her flesh and mine. But I judge the chamber is enormous, for a sound of great machines at work comes very remotely, as if heard through dream, while our own voices are swallowed up by distance. Air is pumped through, neither warm nor cold, totally without odor, a dead wind.

We descend to the floor. She stands before me, hands crossed on breast, eyes half shut beneath the cowl and not looking at me nor away from me. "Do what you are told, Harper," She says in a voice that has never an overtone, "Precisely as you are told." She turns and departs at an even pace. I watch Her go until I can no longer tell Her luminosity from the formless swirlings within my own eyeballs.

A claw plucks my tunic. I look down and am surprised to see that the dwarf robot has been waiting for me this whole time. How long a time that was, I cannot tell.

Its squat form leads me in another direction. Weariness crawls upward through me, my feet stumble, my lips tingle, lids are weighted and muscles have each their separate aches. Now and then I feel a jag of fear, but dully. When the robot indicates *Lie down here,* I am grateful.

The box fits me well. I let various wires be attached to me, various needles be injected which lead into tubes. I pay little attention to the machines which cluster and murmur around me. The robot goes away. I sink into blessed darkness.

I wake renewed in body. A kind of shell seems to have grown between my forebrain and the old animal parts. Far away I can feel the horror and hear the screaming and thrashing of my instincts; but awareness is chill, calm, logical. I have also a feeling that I slept for weeks, months, while leaves blew loose and snow fell on the upper world. But this may be wrong, and in no case does it matter. I am about to be judged by SUM.

The little faceless robot leads me off, through murmurous black corridors where the dead wind blows. I unsling my harp and clutch it to me, my sole friend and weapon. So the tranquillity of the reasoning mind which has been decreed for me cannot be absolute. I decide that It simply does not want to be bothered by anguish. (No; wrong; nothing so humanlike; It has no desires; beneath that power to reason is nullity.)

At length a wall opens for us and we enter a room where She sits enthroned. The self-radiation of metal and flesh is not apparent here, for light is provided, a featureless white radiance with no apparent source. White, too, is the muted sound of the machines which encompass Her throne. White are Her robe and face. I look away from the multitudinous unwinking scanner eyes, into Hers, but She does not appear to recognize me. Does She even see me? SUM has reached out with invisible fingers of electromagnetic induction and taken Her back into Itself. I do not tremble or sweat—I cannot—but I square my shoulders, strike one plangent chord, and wait for It to speak.

It does, from some invisible place. I recognize the voice It has chosen to use: my own. The overtones, the inflections are true, normal, what I myself would use in talking as one reasonable man to another. Why not? In computing what to do about me, and in programming Itself accordingly, SUM must have used so many billion bits of information that adequate accent is a negligible sub-problem.

No . . . there I am mistaken again . . . SUM does not do things on the basis that It might as well do them as not. This talk with myself is intended to have some effect on me. I do not know what.

"Well," It says pleasantly, "you made quite a journey, didn't you? I'm glad. Welcome."

My instincts bare teeth to hear those words of humanity used by the unfeeling unalive. My logical mind considers replying with an ironic "Thank you," decides against it, and holds me silent.

"You see," SUM continues after a moment that whirrs, "you are unique. Pardon Me if I speak a little bluntly. Your sexual monomania is just one aspect of a generally atavistic, superstition-oriented personality. And yet, unlike the ordinary misfit, you're both strong and realistic enough to cope with the world. This chance to meet you, to analyze you while you rested, has opened new insights for Me on human psychophysiology. Which may lead to improved techniques for governing it and its evolution."

"That being so," I reply, "give me my reward."

"Now look here," SUM says in a mild tone, "you if anyone should know I'm not omnipotent. I was built originally to help govern a civilization grown too complex. Gradually, as My program of self-expansion progressed, I took over more and more decision-making functions. They were *given* to Me. People were happy to be relieved of responsibility, and they could see for themselves how much better I was running things than any mortal could. But to this day, My authority depends on a substantial consensus. If I started playing favorites, as by re-creating your girl, well, I'd have troubles."

"The consensus depends more on awe than on reason," I say. "You haven't abolished the gods, You've simply absorbed them into Yourself. If You choose to pass a miracle to me, your prophet singer—and I will be Your prophet if You do this—why, that strengthens the faith of the rest."

"So you think. But your opinions aren't based on any exact data. The historical and anthropological records from the past before Me are unquantitative. I've already phased them out of the curriculum. Eventually, when the culture's ready for such a move, I'll order them destroyed. They're too misleading. Look what they've done to you."

I grin into the scanner eyes. "Instead," I say, "people will be encouraged to think that before the world was, was SUM. All right. I don't care, as long as I get my girl back. Pass me a miracle, SUM, and I'll guarantee You a good payment."

"But I have no miracles. Not in your sense. You know how the soul works. The metal bracelet encloses a pseudo-virus, a set of giant protein molecules with tapes directly to the bloodstream and nervous system. They record the chromosome pattern, the synapse flash, the permanent changes, everything. At the owner's death, the bracelet is dissected out. The Winged Heels bring it here, and the information contained is transferred to one of My memory banks. I can use such a record to guide the growing of a new body in the vats: a young body, on which the former habits and recollections are imprinted. But you don't understand the complexity of the process, Harper. It takes Me weeks, every seven years, and every available biochemical facility, to re-create My human liaison. And the process isn't perfect, either. The pattern is affected by storage. You might say that this body and brain you see before you remembers each death. And those are short deaths. A longer one—man, use your sense. Imagine."

I can; and the shield between reason and feeling begins to crack. I had sung, of my darling dead:

> "No motion has she now, no force;
>   She neither hears nor sees;
> Roll'd round in earth's diurnal course,
>   With rocks, and stones, and trees."

Peace, at least. But if the memory-storage is not permanent but circulating; if, within those gloomy caverns of tubes and wire and outer-space cold, some remnant of her psyche must flit and flicker, alone, unremembering, aware of nothing but having lost life—No!

I smite the harp and shout so the room rings: "Give her back! Or I'll kill you!"

SUM finds it expedient to chuckle; and, horribly, the smile is reflected for a moment on the Dark Queen's lips, though otherwise She never stirs. "And how do you propose to do that?" It asks me.

It knows, I know, what I have in mind, so I counter: "How do You propose to stop me?"

"No need. You'll be considered a nuisance. Finally someone will decide you ought to have psychiatric treatment. They'll query My diagnostic outlet. I'll recommend certain excisions."

"On the other hand, since You've sifted my mind by now, and since You know how I've affected people with my songs—even the Lady yonder, even Her—wouldn't you rather have me working for You? With words like, 'O taste, and see, how gracious the Lord is; blessed is the man that trusteth in him. O fear the Lord, ye that are his saints: for they that fear him lack nothing.' I can make You into God."

"In a sense, I already am God."

"And in another sense not. Not yet." I can endure no more.

"Why are we arguing? You made Your decision before I woke. Tell me and let me go!"

With an odd carefulness, SUM responds: "I'm still studying you. No harm in admitting to you, My knowledge of the human psyche is as yet imperfect. Certain areas won't yield to computation. I don't know precisely what you'd do, Harper. If to that uncertainty I added a potentially dangerous precedent—"

"Kill me, then. Let my ghost wander forever with hers, down in Your cryogenic dreams."

"No, that's also inexpedient. You've made yourself too conspicuous and controversial. Too many people know by now that you went off with the Lady." Is it possible that, behind steel and energy, a nonexistent hand brushes across a shadow face in puzzlement? My heartbeat is thick in the silence.

Suddenly It shakes me with decision: "The calculated probabilities do favor your keeping your promises and making yourself useful. Therefore I shall grant your request. However—"

I am on my knees. My forehead knocks on the floor until blood runs into my eyes. I hear through stormwinds:

"—testing must continue. Your faith in Me is not absolute; in fact, you're very skeptical of what you call My goodness. Without additional proof of your willingness to trust Me, I can't let you have the kind of importance which your getting your dead back from Me would give you. Do you understand?"

The question does not sound rhetorical. "Yes," I sob.

"Well, then," says my civilized, almost amiable voice, "I computed that you'd react much as you have done, and prepared for the likelihood. Your woman's body was re-created while you lay under study. The data which make personality are now being fed back into her neurones. She'll be ready to leave this place by the time you do.

"I repeat, though, there has to be a testing. The procedure is also necessary for its effect on you. If you're to be My prophet, you'll have to work pretty closely with Me; you'll have to undergo a great deal of reconditioning; this night we begin the process. Are you willing?"

"Yes, yes, yes, what must I do?"

"Only this: follow the robot out. At some point, she, your woman, will join you. She'll be conditioned to walk so quietly you can't hear her. Don't look back. Not once, until you're in the upper world. A single glance behind you will be an act of rebellion against Me, and a datum indicating you can't really be trusted . . . and that ends everything. Do you understand?"

"Is that all?" I cry. "Nothing more?"

"It will prove more difficult than you think," SUM tells me. My voice fades, as if into illimitable distances: "Farewell, worshipper."

The robot raises me to my feet. I stretch out my arms to the Dark Queen. Half-blinded with tears, I nonetheless see that She does not see me. "Goodbye," I mumble, and let the robot lead me away.

Our walking is long through those mirk miles. At first I am in too much of a turmoil, and later too stunned, to know where or how we are bound. But later still, slowly, I become aware of my flesh and clothes and the robot's alloy, glimmering blue in blackness. Sounds and smells are muffled; rarely does another machine pass by, unheeding of us. (What work does SUM have for them?) I am so careful not to look behind me that my neck grows stiff.

Though it is not prohibited, is it, to lift my harp past my shoulder, in the course of strumming a few melodies to keep up my courage, and see if perchance a following illumination is reflected in this polished wood?

Nothing. Well, her second birth must take time—O SUM, be careful of her!—and then she must be led through many tunnels, no doubt, before she makes rendezvous with my back. Be patient, Harper.

Sing. Welcome her home. No, these hollow spaces swallow all music; and she is as yet in that trance of death from which only the sun and my kiss can wake her; if, indeed, she has joined me yet. I listen for other footfalls than my own.

Surely we haven't much farther to go. I ask the robot, but of course I get no reply. Make an estimate. I know about how fast the chariot traveled coming down . . . The trouble is, time does not exist here. I have no day, no stars, no clock but my heartbeat and I have lost the count of that. Nevertheless, we must come to the end soon. What purpose would be served by walking me through this labyrinth till I die?

Well, if I am totally exhausted at the outer gate, I won't make undue trouble when I find no Rose-in-Hand behind me.

No, now that's ridiculous. If SUM didn't want to heed my plea, It need merely say so. I have no power to inflict physical damage on Its parts.

Of course, It might have plans for me. It did speak of reconditioning. A series of shocks, culminating in that last one, could make me ready for whatever kind of gelding It intends to do.

Or It might have changed Its mind. Why not? It was quite frank about an uncertainty factor in the human psyche. It may have re-evaluated the probabilities and decided: better not to serve my desire.

Or It may have tried, and failed. It admitted the recording process is imperfect. I must not expect quite the Gladness I knew; she will always be a little haunted. At best. But suppose the tank spawned a body with no awareness behind the eyes? Or a monster? Suppose, at this instant, I am being followed by a half-rotten corpse?

No! Stop that! SUM would know, and take corrective measures.

"Would It? *Can It?*

I comprehend how this passage through night, where I never look to see what follows me, how this is an act of submission and confession. I am saying, with my whole existent being, that SUM is all-powerful, all-wise, all-good. To SUM I offer the love I came to win back. Oh, It looked more deeply into me than ever I did myself.

But I shall not fail.

Will SUM, though? If there has indeed been some grisly error . . . let me not find it out under the sky. Let her, my only, not. For what then shall we do? Could I lead her here again, knock on the iron gate, and cry, "Master, You have given me a thing unfit to exist. Destroy it and start over?" For what might the wrongness be? Something so subtle, so pervasive, that it does not show in any way save my slow, resisted discovery that I embrace a zombie? Doesn't it make better sense to look—make certain while she is yet drowsy with death—use the whole power of SUM to correct what may be awry?

No, SUM wants me to believe that It makes no mistakes. I

agreed to that price. And to much else . . . I don't know how
much else, I am daunted to imagine, but that word "recondition"
is ugly . . . Does not my woman have some rights in the matter
too? Shall we not at least ask her if she wants to be the wife of a
prophet; shall we not, hand in hand, ask SUM what the price of
her life is to her?

Was that a footfall? Almost, I whirl about. I check myself and
stand shaking; names of hers break from my lips. The robot
urges me on.

Imagination. It wasn't her step. I am alone. I will always be
alone.

The halls wind upward. Or so I think; I have grown too weary
for much kinesthetic sense. We cross the sounding river and I am
bitten to the bone by the cold which blows upward around the
bridge, and I may not turn about to offer the naked newborn
woman my garment. I lurch through endless chambers where
machines do meaningless things. She hasn't seen them before.
Into what nightmare has she risen; and why don't I, who wept
into her dying senses that I loved her, why don't I look at her,
why don't I speak?

Well, I could talk to her. I could assure the puzzled mute dead
that I have come to lead her back into sunlight. Could I not? I
ask the robot. It does not reply. I cannot remember if I may
speak to her. If indeed I was ever told. I stumble forward.

I crash into a wall and fall bruised. The robot's claw closes on
my shoulder. Another arm gestures. I see a passageway, very
long and narrow, through the stone. I will have to crawl through.
At the end, at the end, the door is swinging wide. The dear real
dusk of Earth pours through into this darkness. I am blinded and
deafened.

Do I hear her cry out? Was that the final testing; or was my
own sick, shaken mind betraying me; or is there a destiny which,
like SUM with us, makes tools of suns and SUM? I don't know. I
know only that I turned, and there she stood. Her hair flowed
long, loose, past the remembered face from which the trance was
just departing, on which the knowing and the love of me had just
awakened—flowed down over the body that reached forth arms,
that took one step to meet me and was halted.

The great grim robot at her own back takes her to it. I think it sends lightning through her brain. She falls. It bears her away.

My guide ignores my screaming. Irresistible, it thrusts me out through the tunnel. The door clangs in my face. I stand before the wall which is like a mountain. Dry snow hisses across concrete. The sky is bloody with dawn; stars still gleam in the west, and arc lights are scattered over the twilit plain of the machines.

Presently I go dumb. I become almost calm. What is there left to have feelings about? The door is iron, the wall is stone fused into one basaltic mass. I walk some distance off into the wind, turn around, lower my head and charge. Let my brains be smeared across Its gate; the pattern will be my hieroglyphic for hatred.

I am seized from behind. The force that stops me must needs be bruisingly great. Released, I crumple to the ground before a machine with talons and wings. My voice from it says, "Not here. I'll carry you to a safe place."

"What more can You do to me?" I croak.

"Release you. You won't be restrained or molested on any orders of Mine."

"Why not?"

"Obviously you're going to appoint yourself My enemy forever. This is an unprecedented situation, a valuable chance to collect data."

"You tell me this, You warn me, deliberately?"

"Of course. My computation is that these words will have the effect of provoking your utmost effort."

"You won't give her again? You don't want my love?"

"Not under the circumstances. Too uncontrollable. But your hatred should, as I say, be a useful experimental tool."

"I'll destroy You," I say.

It does not deign to speak further. Its machine picks me up and flies off with me. I am left on the fringes of a small town farther south. Then I go insane.

I do not much know what happens during that winter, nor care. The blizzards are too loud in my head. I walk the ways of Earth, among lordly towers, under neatly groomed trees, into careful gardens, over bland, bland campuses. I am unwashed, uncombed, unbarbered; my tatters flap about me and my bones are near thrusting through the skin; folk do not like to meet these eyes sunken so far into this skull, and perhaps for that reason they give me to eat. I sing to them.

> *"From the hag and hungry goblin*
> *That into rags would rend ye*
> *And the spirit that stan' by the naked man*
> *In the Book of Moons defend ye!*
> *That of your five sound senses*
> *You never be forsaken*
> *Nor travel from yourselves with Tom*
> *Abroad to beg your bacon."*

Such things perturb them, do not belong in their chrome-edged universe. So I am often driven away with curses, and sometimes I must flee those who would arrest me and scrub my brain smooth. An alley is a good hiding place, if I can find one in the oldest part of a city; I crouch there and yowl with the cats. A forest is also good. My pursuers dislike to enter any place where any wildness lingers.

But some feel otherwise. They have visited parklands, preserves, actual wildcountry. Their purpose was overconscious—measured, planned savagery, and a clock to tell them when they must go home—but at least they are not afraid of silences and unlighted nights. As spring returns, certain among them begin to follow me. They are merely curious, at first. But slowly, month by month, especially among the younger ones, my madness begins to call to something in them.

> *"With an host of furious fancies*
> *Whereof I am commander*
> *With a burning spear, and a horse of air,*
> *To the wilderness I wander.*
> *By a knight of ghosts and shadows*
> *I summoned am to tourney*
> *Ten leagues beyond the wide world's edge.*
> *Me thinks it is no journey."*

They sit at my feet and listen to me sing. They dance, crazily, to my harp. The girls bend close, tell me how I fascinate them, invite me to copulate. This I refuse, and when I tell them why they are puzzled, a little frightened maybe, but often they strive to understand.

For my rationality is renewed with the hawthorn blossoms. I bathe, have my hair and beard shorn, find clean raiment and take care to eat what my body needs. Less and less do I rave before anyone who will listen; more and more do I seek solitude, quietness, under the vast wheel of the stars, and think.

What is man? Why is man? We have buried such questions; we have sworn they are dead—that they never really existed, being devoid of empirical meaning—and we have dreaded that they might raise the stones we heaped on them, rise and walk the world again of nights. Alone, I summon them to me. They cannot hurt their fellow dead, among whom I now number myself.

I sing to her who is gone. The young people hear and wonder. Sometimes they weep.

> *"Fear no more the heat o' the sun,*
> *Nor the furious winter's rages;*
> *Thou thy worldly task hast done,*
> *Home art gone, and ta'en thy wages:*
> *Golden lads and girls all must*
> *As chimney-sweepers, come to dust."*

"But this is not so!" they protest. "We will die and sleep a while, and then we will live forever in SUM."

I answer as gently as may be: "No. Remember I went there. So I know you are wrong. And even if you were right, it would not be right that you should be right."

"What?"

"Don't you see, it is not right that a thing should be the lord of man. It is not right that we should huddle through our whole lives in fear of finally losing them. You are not parts in a machine, and you have better ends than helping the machine run smoothly."

I dismiss them and stride off, solitary again, into a canyon where a river clangs, or onto some gaunt mountain peak. No revelation is given me. I climb and creep toward the truth.

Which is that SUM must be destroyed, not in revenge, not in

hate, not in fear, simply because the human spirit cannot exist in
the same reality as It.

But what, then, is our proper reality? And how shall we attain
to it?

I return with my songs to the lowlands. Word about me has
gone widely. They are a large crowd who follow me down the
highroad until it has changed into a street.

"The Dark Queen will soon come to these parts," they tell me.
"Abide till She does. Let Her answer those questions you put to
us, which make us sleep so badly."

"Let me retire to prepare myself," I say. I go up a long flight
of steps. The people watch from below, dumb with awe, till I
vanish. Such few as were in the building depart. I walk down
vaulted halls, through hushed high-ceilinged rooms full of tables,
among shelves made massive by books. Sunlight slants dusty
through the windows.

The half memory has plagued me of late: once before, I know
not when, this year of mine also took place. Perhaps in this library I can find the tale that—casually, I suppose, in my abnormal childhood—I read. For man is older than SUM: wiser, I
swear; his myths hold more truth than Its mathematics. I spend
three days and most of three nights in my search. There is scant
sound but the rustling of leaves between my hands. Folk place
offerings of food and drink at the door. They tell themselves they
do so out of pity, or curiosity, or to avoid the nuisance of having
me die in an unconventional fashion. But I know better.

At the end of the three days I am little further along. I have
too much material; I keep going off on sidetracks of beauty and
fascination. (Which SUM means to eliminate.) My education
was like everyone else's, science, rationality, good sane adjustment. (SUM writes our curricula, and the teaching machines
have direct connections to It.) Well, I can make some of my lopsided training work for me. My reading has given me sufficient
clues to prepare a search program. I sit down before an information retrieval console and run my fingers across its keys. They
make a clattery music.

Electron beams are swift hounds. Within seconds the screen
lights up with words, and I read who I am.

It is fortunate that I am a fast reader. Before I can press the

Clear button, the unreeling words are wiped out. For an instant the screen quivers with formlessness, then appears

I HAD NOT CORRELATED THESE DATA WITH THE FACTS CONCERNING YOU. THIS INTRODUCES A NEW AND INDETERMINATE QUANTITY INTO THE COMPUTATIONS.

The nirvana which has come upon me (yes, I found that word among the old books, and how portentous it is) is not passiveness, it is a tide more full and strong than that which bore me down to the Dark Queen those ages apast in wildcountry. I say, as coolly as may be, "An interesting coincidence. If it is a coincidence." Surely sonic receptors are emplaced hereabouts.

EITHER THAT, OR A CERTAIN NECESSARY CONSEQUENCE OF THE LOGIC OF EVENTS.

The vision dawning within me is so blinding bright that I cannot refrain from answering, "Or a destiny, SUM?"

MEANINGLESS. MEANINGLESS. MEANINGLESS.

"Now why did You repeat Yourself in that way? Once would have sufficed. Thrice, though, makes an incantation. Are You by any chance hoping Your words will make me stop existing?"

I DO NOT HOPE. YOU ARE AN EXPERIMENT. IF I COMPUTE A SIGNIFICANT PROBABILITY OF YOUR CAUSING SERIOUS DISTURBANCE, I WILL HAVE YOU TERMINATED.

I smile. "SUM," I say, "I am going to terminate You." I lean over and switch off the screen. I walk out into the evening.

Not everything is clear to me yet, that I must say and do. But enough is that I can start preaching at once to those who have been waiting for me. As I talk, others come down the street, and hear, and stay to listen. Soon they number in the hundreds.

I have no immense new truth to offer them: nothing that I have not said before, although piecemeal and unsystematically; nothing they have not felt themselves, in the innermost darknesses of their beings. Today, however, knowing who I am and therefore why I am, I can put these things in words. Speaking quietly, now and then drawing on some forgotten song to show my meaning, I tell them how sick and starved their lives are; how they have made themselves slaves; how the enslavement is not even to a conscious mind, but to an insensate inanimate thing which their own ancestors began; how that thing is not the centrum of existence, but a few scraps of metal and bleats of energy, a few sad stupid patterns, adrift in unbounded space-time. Put not your faith in SUM, I tell them. SUM is doomed, even as you and I. Seek out mystery; what else is the whole cosmos but mystery? Live bravely, die and be done, and you will be more than any machine. You may perhaps be God.

They grow tumultuous. They shout replies, some of which are animal howls. A few are for me, most are opposed. That doesn't matter. I have reached into them, my music is being played on their nervestrings, and this is my entire purpose.

The sun goes down behind the buildings. Dusk gathers. The city remains unilluminated. I soon realize why. She is coming, the Dark Queen Whom they wanted me to debate with. From afar we hear Her chariot thunder. Folk wail in terror. They are not wont to do that either. They used to disguise their feelings from Her and themselves by receiving Her with grave sparse ceremony. Now they would flee if they dared. I have lifted the masks.

The chariot halts in the street. She dismounts, tall and shadowy cowled. The people make way before Her like water before a shark. She climbs the stairs to face me. I see for the least instant that Her lips are not quite firm and Her eyes abrim with tears. She whispers, too low for anyone else to hear, "Oh, Harper, I'm sorry."

"Come join me," I invite. "Help me set the world free."

"No. I cannot. I have been too long with It." She straightens. Imperium descends upon Her. Her voice rises for everyone to hear. The little television robots flit close, bat shapes in the twilight, that the whole planet may witness my defeat. "What is this freedom you rant about?" She demands.

"To feel," I say. "To venture. To wonder. To become men again."

"To become beasts, you mean. Would you demolish the machines that keep us alive?"

"Yes. We must. Once they were good and useful, but we let them grow upon us like a cancer, and now nothing but destruction and a new beginning can save us."

"Have you considered the chaos?"

"Yes. It too is necessary. We will not be men without the freedom to know suffering. In it is also enlightenment. Through it we travel beyond ourselves, beyond earth and stars, space and time, to Mystery."

"So you maintain that there is some undefined ultimate vagueness behind the measurable universe?" She smiles into the bat eyes. We have each been taught, as children, to laugh on hearing sarcasms of this kind. "Please offer me a little proof."

"No," I say. "Prove to me instead, beyond any doubt, that there is *not* something we cannot understand with words and equations. Prove to me likewise that I have no right to seek for it.

"The burden of proof is on You Two, so often have You lied to us. In the name of rationality, You resurrected myth. The better to control us! In the name of liberation, You chained our inner lives and castrated our souls. In the name of service, You bound and blinkered us. In the name of achievement, You held us to a narrower round than any swine in its pen. In the name of beneficence, You created pain, and horror, and darkness beyond darkness." I turn to the people. "I went there. I descended into the cellars. I know!"

"He found that SUM would not pander to his special wishes, at the expense of everyone else," cries the Dark Queen. Do I hear shrillness in Her voice? "Therefore he claims SUM is cruel."

"I saw my dead," I tell them. "She will not rise again. Nor yours, nor you. Not ever, SUM will not, cannot raise us. In Its house is death indeed. We must seek life and rebirth elsewhere, among the mysteries."

She laughs aloud and points to my soul bracelet, glimmering faintly in the gray-blue thickening twilight. Need She say anything?

"Will someone give me a knife and an ax?" I ask.

The crowd stirs and mumbles. I smell their fear. Street lamps go on, as if they could scatter more than this corner of the night which is rolling upon us. I fold my arms and wait. The Dark Queen says something to me. I ignore Her.

The tools pass from hand to hand. He who brings them up the stairs comes like a flame. He kneels at my feet and lifts what I have desired. The tools are good ones, a broad-bladed hunting knife and a long double-bitted ax.

Before the world, I take the knife in my right hand and slash beneath the bracelet on my left wrist. The connections to my inner body are cut. Blood flows, impossibly brilliant under the lamps. It does not hurt; I am too exalted.

The Dark Queen shrieks, "You meant it! Harper, Harper!"

"There is no life in SUM," I say. I pull my hand through the circle and cast the bracelet down so it rings.

A voice of brass: *"Arrest that maniac for correction. He is deadly dangerous."*

The monitors who have stood on the fringes of the crowd try to push through. They are resisted. Those who seek to help them encounter fists and fingernails.

I take the ax and smash downward. The bracelet crumples. The organic material within, starved of my secretions, exposed to the night air, withers.

I raise the tools, ax in right hand, knife in bleeding left. "I seek eternity where it is to be found," I call. "Who goes with me?"

A score or better break loose from the riot, which is already calling forth weapons and claiming lives. They surround me with their bodies. Their eyes are the eyes of prophets. We make haste to seek a hiding place, for one military robot has appeared and others will not be long in coming. The tall engine strides to stand guard over Our Lady, and this is my last glimpse of Her.

My followers do not reproach me for having cost them all they were. They are mine. In me is the godhead which can do no wrong.

And the war is open, between me and SUM. My friends are few, my enemies many and mighty. I go about the world as a fugitive. But always I sing. And always I find someone who will listen, will join us, embracing pain and death like a lover.

With the Knife and the Ax I take their souls. Afterward we hold for them the ritual of rebirth. Some go thence to become outlaw missionaries; most put on facsimile bracelets and return home, to whisper my word. It makes little difference to me. I have no haste, who own eternity.

For my word is of what lies beyond time. My enemies say I call forth ancient bestialities and lunacies; that I would bring civilization down in ruin; that it matters not a madman's giggle to me whether war, famine, and pestilence will again scour the earth. With these accusations I am satisfied. The language of them shows me that here, too, I have reawakened anger. And that emotion belongs to us as much as any other. More than the others, maybe, in the autumn of mankind. We need a gale, to strike down SUM and everything It stands for. Afterward will come the winter of barbarism.

And after that the springtime of a new and (perhaps) more human civilization. My friends seem to believe this will come in their very lifetimes: peace, brotherhood, enlightenment, sanctity. I know otherwise. I have been in the depths. The wholeness of mankind, which I am bringing back, has its horrors.

When one day

> *the Eater of the Gods returns*
> *the Wolf breaks his chain*
> *the Horsemen ride forth*
> *the Age ends*
> *the Beast is reborn*

then SUM will be destroyed; and you, strong and fair, may go back to earth and rain.

I shall await you.

My aloneness is nearly ended, Daybright. Just one task remains. The god must die, that his followers may believe he is raised from the dead and lives forever. Then they will go on to conquer the world.

There are those who say I have spurned and offended them. They too, borne on the tide which I raised, have torn out their machines souls and seek in music and ecstasy to find a meaning for existence. But their creed is a savage one, which has taken them into wildcountry, where they ambush the monitors sent against them and practice cruel rites. They believe that the final reality is female. Nevertheless, messengers of theirs have approached me with the suggestion of a mystic marriage. This I refused; my wedding was long ago, and will be celebrated again when this cycle of the world has closed.

Therefore they hate me. But I have said I will come and talk to them.

I leave the road at the bottom of the valley and walk singing up the hill. Those few I let come this far with me have been told to abide my return. They shiver in the sunset; the vernal equinox is three days away. I feel no cold myself. I stride exultant among briars and twisted ancient apple trees. If my bare feet leave a little blood in the snow, that is good. The ridges around are dark with forest, which waits like the skeleton dead for leaves to be breathed across it again. The eastern sky is purple, where stands the evening star. Overhead, against blue, cruises an early flight of homebound geese. Their calls drift faintly down to me. Westward, above me and before me, smolders redness. Etched black against it are the women.

Frederik Pohl and C. M. Kornbluth

Now it is time to tell you why the thirty-first was the most magnificent convention ever to meet anywhere, any time, and in any field. I had published my novel *The Gods Themselves* (Doubleday) in 1972, and it was up for consideration for a Hugo.

As you all know, I am dreadfully short on Hugos. After I had listed my justifiable complaints in that respect in Volume One, attempts were made to rectify it. I got a Hugo for my science articles in 1963 and a Hugo, in retrospect, for my Foundation novels in 1966, but I wanted to win something current, if you know what I mean. *The Gods Themselves* had already taken the Nebula award for that year, and an honest pride in my craft (as opposed to the simple greed with which others approach these awards) made me wish the Hugo as well.

Lester del Rey was toastmaster that year. He twisted and turned in his efforts to delay the inevitable but was finally forced, grudgingly, to announce that victory was mine. I got it—a beautiful Hugo, which is prominently displayed in my living room along with the other two.

I'm not yet *completely* satisfied but I'll get to that in the Afterword.

At the Torcon, there were seated along with myself and Janet, Barbara and Ben Bova, Carol and Fred Pohl, and Gordon Dickson. First I had won in the novel category and brought my Hugo gleefully back to the table. Then Fred won in the short story category and brought back two, one for himself and one in the name of Cyril Kornbluth. Then Ben won in the editor category and brought back his.

Four Hugos sat there resplendent on that one table and I felt revolted that we had not made a clean sweep. I turned to sweet, innocent Gordie and said, censoriously, "Your non-Hugo presence at this table disgraces us. Aren't you ashamed?"

He hung his head and pretended to wipe a tear from his eye but I know phoniness when I see it. He wasn't crying. He won in the short story category with "Soldier, Ask Not" at the twenty-third convention in London, in 1965—this is included in Volume Two—and of course, he's let it go to his head.

Personally, I can't stand people without humility. I'm surprised more people don't model themselves on me. I take great pride in the extent of my humility.

I was pleased, by the way, that Cyril was in this way recorded in the archives as a Hugo winner. He died on March 21, 1958, at the age of thirty-six. Had he lived a normal life-span, he would undoubtedly have won a number of Hugos on his own.

8

THE MEETING

Harry Vladek was too large a man for his Volkswagen, but he was too poor a man to trade it in, and as things were going he was going to stay that way a long time. He applied the brakes carefully ("master cylinder's leaking like a sieve, Mr. Vladek. What's the use of just fixing up the linings?"—but the estimate was a hundred and twenty-eight dollars, and where was it going to come from?) and parked in the neatly graveled lot. He squeezed out of the door, the upsetting telephone call from Dr. Nicholson on his mind, locked the car up, and went into the school building.

The Parent-Teachers Association of the Bingham County School for Exceptional Children was holding its first meeting of the term. Of the twenty people already there, Vladek knew only Mrs. Adler, the principal, or headmistress, or owner of the school. She was the one he needed to talk to most, he thought. Would there be any chance to see her privately? Right now she sat across the room at her scuffed golden-oak desk in a posture chair, talking in low, rapid tones with a gray-haired woman in a tan suit. A teacher? She seemed too old to be a parent, although his wife had told him some of the kids seemed to be twenty or more.

It was 8:30 and the parents were still driving up to the school, a converted building that had once been a big country house—almost a mansion. The living room was full of elegant reminders of that. *Two* chandeliers. Intricate vineleaf molding on the plaster above the dropped ceiling. The pink-veined, white-marble fireplace, unfortunately prominent because of the unsuitable andirons, too cheap and too small, that now stood in it. Golden-oak, sliding double doors to the hall. And visible through them a grim, fireproof staircase of concrete and steel. They must, Vladek thought, have had to rip out a beautiful wooden thing to install the fireproof stairs for compliance with the state school laws.

People kept coming in, single men, single women, and occasionally a couple. He wondered how the couples managed their baby-sitting problem. The subtitle on the school's letterhead was "an institution for emotionally disturbed and cerebrally damaged children capable of education." Harry's nine-year-old Thomas was one of the emotionally disturbed ones. With a taste of envy he wondered if cerebrally damaged children could be baby-sat by any reasonably competent grown-up. Thomas could not. The Vladeks had not had an evening out together since he was two, so that tonight Margaret was holding the fort at home, no doubt worrying herself sick about the call from Dr. Nicholson, while Harry was representing the family at the PTA.

As the room filled up, chairs were getting scarce. A young couple was standing at the end of the row near him, looking around for a pair of empty seats. "Here," he said to them. "I'll move over." The woman smiled politely and the man said thanks. Emboldened by an ashtray on the empty seat in front of him, Harry pulled out his pack of cigarettes and offered it to them, but it turned out they were nonsmokers. Harry lit up anyway, listening to what was going on around him.

Everybody was talking. One woman asked another, "How's the gall bladder? Are they going to take it out after all?" A heavy balding man said to a short man with bushy sideburns, "Well, my accountant says the tuition's medically deductible if the school is for psycho*somatic,* not just for psycho. That we've got to clear up." The short man told him positively, "Right, but all you need is a doctor's letter: he recommends the school, refers the child to the school." And a very young woman said intensely, "Dr. Shields was very optimistic, Mrs. Clerman. He says without a doubt the thyroid will make Georgie accessible. And then—" A light-coffee-colored black man in an aloha shirt told a plump woman, "He really pulled a wingding over the weekend, two stitches in his face, busted my fishing pole in three places." And the woman said, "They get so bored. My little girl has this thing about crayons, so that rules out coloring books altogether. You wonder what you can do."

Harry finally said to the young man next to him, "My name's Vladek. I'm Tommy's father. He's in the beginners group."

"That's where ours is," said the young man. "He's Vern. Six years old. Blond like me. Maybe you've seen him."

Harry did not try very hard to remember. The two or three times he had picked Tommy up after class he had not been able to tell one child from another in the great bustle of departure. Coats, handkerchiefs, hats, one little girl who always hid in the supply closet and a little boy who never wanted to go home and hung onto the teacher. "Oh, yes," he said politely.

The young man introduced himself and his wife; they were named Murray and Celia Logan. Harry leaned over the man to shake the wife's hand, and she said, "Aren't you new here?"

"Yes. Tommy's been in the school a month. We moved in from Elmira to be near it." He hesitated, then added, "Tommy's nine, but the reason he's in the beginners group is that Mrs. Adler thought it would make the adjustment easier."

Logan pointed to a suntanned man in the first row. "See that fellow with the glasses? He moved here from *Texas*. Of course, he's got money."

"It must be a good place," Harry said questioningly.

Logan grinned, his expression a little nervous.

"How's your son?" Harry asked.

"That little rascal," said Logan. "Last week I got him another copy of the *My Fair Lady* album, I guess he's used up four or five of them, and he goes around singing 'luv-er-ly, luv-er-ly.' But *look* at you? No."

"Mine doesn't talk," said Harry.

Mrs. Logan said judiciously, "Ours talks. Not *to* anybody, though. It's like a wall."

"I know," said Harry, and pressed. "Has, ah, has Vern shown much improvement with the school?"

Murray Logan pursed his lips. "I would say, yes. The bedwetting's not too good, but life's a great deal smoother in some ways. You know, you don't hope for a dramatic breakthrough. But in little things, day by day, it goes smoother. Mostly smoother. Of course there are setbacks."

Harry nodded, thinking of seven years of setbacks, and two years of growing worry and puzzlement before that. He said,

"Mrs. Adler told me that, for instance, a special outbreak of destructiveness might mean something like a plateau in speech therapy. So the child fights it and breaks out in some other direction."

"That too," said Logan, "but what I meant—Oh, they're starting."

Vladek nodded, stubbing out his cigarette and absent-mindedly lighting another. His stomach was knotting up again. He wondered at these other parents, who seemed so safe and well, untouched. Wasn't it the same with them as with Margaret and himself? And it had been a long time since either of them had felt the world comfortable around them, even without Dr. Nicholson pressing for a decision. He forced himself to lean back and look as tranquil as the others.

Mrs. Adler was tapping her desk with a ruler. "I think everybody who is coming is here," she said. She leaned against the desk and waited for the room to quiet down. She was short, dark, plump, and surprisingly pretty. She did not look at all like a competent professional. She looked so unlike her role that, in fact, Harry's heart had sunk three months ago when their correspondence about admitting Tommy had been climaxed by the long trip from Elmira for the interview. He had expected a steel-gray lady with rimless glasses, a Valkyrie in a white smock like the nurse who had held wriggling, screaming Tommy while waiting for the suppository to quiet him down for his first EEG, a disheveled old fraud, he didn't know what. Anything except this pretty young woman. Another blind alley, he had thought in despair. Another, after a hundred too many already. First, "Wait for him to outgrow it." He doesn't. Then, "We must reconcile ourselves to God's will." But you don't want to. Then give him the prescription three times a day for three months. And it doesn't work. Then chase around for six months with the Child Guidance Clinic to find out it's only letterheads and one circuit-riding doctor who doesn't have time for anything. Then, after four dreary, weepy weeks of soul-searching, the State Training School, and find out it has an eight-year waiting list. Then the private custodial school, and find they're fifty-five hundred dollars a year—without medical treatment!—and where do you get fifty-five hundred dollars a year? And all the time everybody warns you, as if you didn't know it: "Hurry! Do something! Catch it early! This is the critical stage! Delay is fatal!" And then this soft-looking little woman; how could she do anything?

She had rapidly shown him how. She had questioned Margaret and Harry incisively, turned to Tommy, rampaging through the same room like a rogue bull, and turned his rampage into a game. In three minutes he was happily experimenting with an indestructible old windup cabinet Victrola, and Mrs. Adler was saying to the Vladeks, "Don't count on a miracle cure. There isn't any. But improvements, yes, and I think we can help Tommy."

Perhaps she had, thought Vladek bleakly. Perhaps she was helping as much as anyone ever could.

Meanwhile, Mrs. Adler had quickly and pleasantly welcomed the parents, suggested they remain for coffee and get to know each other, and introduced the PTA president, a Mrs. Rose, tall, prematurely gray and very executive. "This being the first meeting of the term," she said, "there are no minutes to be read, so we'll get to the committee work reports. What about the transportation problem, Mr. Baer?"

The man who got up was old. More than sixty; Harry wondered what it was like to have your life crowned with a late retarded child. He wore all the trappings of success—a four hundred dollar suit, an electronic wristwatch, a large gold fraternal ring. In a slight German accent he said, "I was to the district school board and they are not cooperating. My lawyer looked it up and the trouble is all one word. What the law says, the school board may, that is the word, may, reimburse parents of handicapped children for transportation to private schools. Not shall, you understand, but may. They were very frank with me. They said they just didn't want to spend the money. They have the impression we're all rich people here."

Slight sour laughter around the room.

"So my lawyer made an appointment, and we appeared before the full board and presented the case—we don't care, reimbursement, a school bus, anything so we can relieve the transportation burden a little. The answer was no." He shrugged and remained standing, looking at Mrs. Rose, who said:

"Thank you, Mr. Baer. Does anybody have any suggestions?"

A woman said angrily, "Put some heat on them. We're all voters!"

A man said, "Publicity, that's right. The principle is perfectly clear in the law, one taxpayer's child is supposed to get the same service as another taxpayer's child. We should write letters to the papers."

Mr. Baer said, "Wait a minute. Letters, I don't think mean anything, but I've got a public relations firm. I'll tell them to take a little time off my food specialties and use it for the school. They can use their own know-how, how to do it. They're the experts."

This was moved, seconded, and passed, while Murray Logan whispered to Vladek, "He's Marijane Garlic Mayonnaise. He had a twelve-year-old girl in very bad shape that Mrs. Adler helped in her old private class. He bought this building for her, along with a couple of other parents."

Harry Vladek was musing over how it felt to be a parent who could buy a building for a school that would help your child, while the committee reports continued. Some time later, to Harry's dismay, the business turned to financing, and there was a vote to hold a fund-raising theater party for which each couple with a child in the school would have to sell "at least" five pairs of orchestra seats at sixty dollars a pair. Let's get this straightened out now, he thought, and put up his hand.

"My name is Harry Vladek," he said when he was recognized, "and I'm brand new here. In the school and in the county. I work for a big insurance company, and I was lucky enough to get a transfer here so my boy can go to the school. But I just don't know anybody yet that I can sell tickets to for sixty dollars. That's an awful lot of money for my kind of people."

Mrs. Rose said, "It's an awful lot of money for most of us. You can get rid of your tickets, though. We've got to. It doesn't matter if you try a hundred people and ninety-five say no just as long as the others say yes."

He sat down, already calculating. Well, Mr. Crine at the office. He was a bachelor and he did go to the theater. Maybe work up an officer raffle for another pair. Or two pairs. Then there was, let's see, the real estate dealer who had sold them the house, the lawyer they'd used for the closing . . .

Well. It had been explained to him that the tuition, while decidedly not nominal, eighteen hundred dollars a year in fact, did not cover the cost per child. Somebody had to pay for the speech therapist, the dance therapist, the full-time psychologist, and the part-time psychiatrist, and all the others, and it might as well be Mr. Crine at the office. And the lawyer.

And half an hour later Mrs. Rose looked at the agenda, checked off an item and said, "That seems to be all for tonight. Mr. and Mrs. Perry brought us some very nice cookies, and we all know that Mrs. Howe's coffee is out of this world. They're in the beginners room, and we hope you'll all stay to get acquainted. The meeting is adjourned."

Harry and the Logans joined the polite surge to the beginners room, where Tommy spent his mornings. "There's Miss Hackett," said Celia Logan. That was the beginners' teacher. She saw them and came over, smiling. Harry had seen her only in a tentlike smock, her armor against chocolate milk, finger paints, and sudden jets from the "water play" corner of the room. Without it she was handsomely middle-aged in a green pants suit.

"I'm glad you parents have met," she said. "I wanted to tell you that your little boys are getting along nicely. They're forming a sort of conspiracy against the others in the class. Vern swipes their toys and gives them to Tommy."

"He *does*?" cried Logan.

"Yes, indeed. I think he's beginning to relate. And, Mr. Vladek, Tommy's taken his thumb out of his mouth for minutes at a time. At least half a dozen times this morning, without my saying a word."

Harry said excitedly, "You know, I thought I noticed he was tapering off. I couldn't be sure. You're positive about that?"

"Absolutely," she said. "And I bluffed him into drawing a face. He gave me that glare of his when the others were drawing, so I started to take the paper away. He grabbed it back and scribbled a kind of Picasso-ish face in one second flat. I wanted to save it for Mrs. Vladek and you, but Tommy got it and shredded it in that methodical way he has."

"I wish I could have seen it," said Vladek.

"There'll be others. I can see the prospect of real improvement in your boys," she said, including the Logans in her smile. "I have a private case afternoons that's really tricky. A nine-year-old boy, like Tommy. He's not bad except for one thing. He thinks Donald Duck is out to get him. His parents somehow managed to convince themselves for two years that he was kidding them, in spite of three broken TV picture tubes. Then they went to a psychiatrist and learned the score. Excuse me, I want to talk to Mrs. Adler."

Logan shook his head and said, "I guess we could be worse off, Vladek. Vern giving something to another boy! How do you like that?"

"I like it," his wife said radiantly.

"And did you hear about that other boy? Poor kid. When I hear about something like that . . . And then there was the Baer girl. I always think it's worse when it's a little girl because, you know, you worry with little girls that somebody will take advantage, but our boys'll make out, Vladek. You heard what Miss Hackett said."

Harry was suddenly impatient to get home to his wife. "I don't think I'll stay for coffee, or do they expect you to?"

"No, no, leave when you like."

"I have a half-hour drive," he said apologetically and went through the golden-oak doors, past the ugly but fireproof staircase, out onto the graveled parking lot. His real reason was that he wanted very much to get home before Margaret fell asleep so he could tell her about the thumb-sucking. Things were happening, definite things, after only a month. And Tommy drew a face. And Miss Hackett said . . .

He stopped in the middle of the lot. He had remembered about Dr. Nicholson, and besides, what was it, exactly, that Miss Hackett had said? Anything about a normal life? Not anything about a cure? "Real improvement," she said, but improvement how far?

He lit a cigarette, turned, and plowed his way back through the parents to Mrs. Adler. "Mrs. Adler," he said, "may I see you just for a moment?"

She came with him immediately out of earshot of the others. "Did you enjoy the meeting, Mr. Vladek?"

"Oh, sure. What I wanted to see you about is that I have to make a decision. I don't know what to do. I don't know who to go to. It would help a lot if you could tell me, well, what are Tommy's chances?"

She waited a moment before she responded. "Are you considering committing him, Mr. Vladek?" she demanded.

"No; it's not exactly that. It's—well, what can you tell me, Mrs. Adler? I know a month isn't much. But is he ever going to be like everybody else?"

He could see from her face that she had done this before and had hated it. She said patiently, "'Everybody else,' Mr. Vladek, includes some terrible people who just don't happen, technically, to be handicapped. Our objective isn't to make Tommy like 'everybody else.' It's just to help him to become the best and most rewarding Tommy Vladek he can."

"Yes, but what's going to happen later on? I mean, if Margaret and I—if anything happens to us?"

She was suffering. "There is simply no way to know, Mr. Vladek," she said gently. "I wouldn't give up hope. But I can't tell you to expect miracles."

Margaret wasn't asleep; she was waiting up for him, in the small living room of the small new house. "How was he?" Vladek asked, as each of them had asked the other on returning home for seven years.

She looked as though she had been crying, but she was calm enough. "Not too bad. I had to lie down with him to get him to go to bed. He took his gland gunk well, though. He licked the spoon."

"That's good," he said and told her about the drawing of the face, about the conspiracy with little Vern Logan, about the thumb-sucking. He could see how pleased she was, but she only said, "Dr. Nicholson called again."

"I told him not to bother you!"

"He didn't bother me, Harry. He was very nice. I promised him you'd call him back."

"It's eleven o'clock, Margaret. I'll call him in the morning."

"No, I said tonight, no matter what time. He's waiting, and he said to be sure and reverse the charges."

"I wish I'd never answered the son of a bitch's letter," he burst out and then, apologetically, "Is there any coffee? I didn't stay for it at the school."

She had put the water on to boil when she heard the car whine into the driveway, and the instant coffee was already in the cup. She poured it and said, "You have to talk to him, Harry. He has to know tonight."

"Know tonight! Know tonight," he mimicked savagely. He scalded his lips on the coffee cup and said, "What do you want me to do, Margaret? How do I make a decision like this? Today I picked up the phone and called the company psychologist, and when his secretary answered, I said I had the wrong number. I didn't know what to say to him."

"I'm not trying to pressure you, Harry. But he has to know."

Vladek put down the cup and lit his fiftieth cigarette of the day. The little dining room—it wasn't that, it was a half break-fast alcove off the tiny kitchen, but they called it a dining room even to each other—was full of Tommy. The new paint on the wall where Tommy had peeled off the cups-and-spoons wallpa-per. The Tommy-proof latch on the stove. The one odd aqua seat that didn't match the others on the kitchen chairs, where Tommy had methodically gouged it with the handle of his spoon. He said, "I know what my mother would tell me, talk to the priest. Maybe I should. But we've never even been to Mass here."

Margaret sat down and helped herself to one of his cigarettes. She was still a good-looking woman. She hadn't gained a pound since Tommy was born, although she usually looked tired. She said, carefully and straightforwardly, "We agreed, Harry. You said you would talk to Mrs. Adler, and you've done that. We said if she didn't think Tommy would ever straighten out we'd talk to Dr. Nicholson. I know it's hard on you, and I know I'm not much help. But I don't know what to do, and I have to let you decide."

Harry looked at his wife, lovingly and hopelessly, and at that moment the phone rang. It was, of course, Dr. Nicholson.

"I haven't made a decision," said Harry Vladek at once. "You're rushing me, Dr. Nicholson."

The distant voice was calm and assured. "No, Mr. Vladek, it's not me that's rushing you. The other boy's heart gave out an hour ago. That's what's rushing you."

"You mean he's dead?" cried Vladek.

"He's on the heart-lung machine, Mr. Vladek. We can hold him for at least eighteen hours, maybe twenty-four. The brain is all right. We're getting very good waves on the oscilloscope. The tissue match with your boy is satisfactory. Better than satisfactory. There's a flight out of JFK at six fifteen in the morning, and I've reserved space for yourself, your wife, and Tommy. You'll be met at the airport. You can be here by noon, so we have time. Only just time, Mr. Vladek. It's up to you now."

Vladek said furiously, "I can't decide that! Don't you understand? I don't know how."

"I do understand, Mr. Vladek," said the distant voice and, strangely, Vladek thought, it seemed he did. "I have a suggestion. Would you like to come down anyhow? I think it might help you to see the other boy, and you can talk to his parents. They feel they owe you something even for going this far, and they want to thank you."

"Oh, no!" cried Vladek.

The doctor went on, "All they want is for their boy to have a life. They don't expect anything but that. They'll give you custody of the child—your child, yours and theirs. He's a very fine little boy, Mr. Vladek. Eight years old. Reads beautifully. Makes model airplanes. They let him ride his bike because he was sensible and reliable, and the accident wasn't his fault. The truck came right up on the sidewalk and hit him."

Harry was trembling. "That's like giving me a bribe," he said harshly. "That's telling me I can trade Tommy in for somebody smarter and nicer."

"I didn't mean it that way, Mr. Vladek. I only wanted you to know the kind of a boy you can save."

"You don't even know the operation's going to work!"

"No," agreed the doctor. "Not positively. I can tell you that we've transplanted animals, including primates, and human cadavers, and one pair of terminal cases, but you're right, we've never had a transplant into a well body. I've shown you all the records, Mr. Vladek. We went over them with your own doctor when we first talked about this possibility, five months ago. This is the first case since then when the match was close and there was a real hope for success, but you're right, it's still unproved.

Unless you help us prove it. For what it's worth, I think it will work. But no one can be sure."

Margaret had left the kitchen, but Vladek knew where she was from the scratchy click in the earpiece: in the bedroom, listening on the extension phone. He said at last, "I can't say now, Dr. Nicholson. I'll call you back in—in half an hour. I can't do any more than that right now."

"That's a great deal, Mr. Vladek. I'll be waiting right here for your call."

Harry sat down and drank the rest of his coffee. You had to be an expert in a lot of things to get along, he was thinking. What did he know about brain transplants? In one way, a lot. He knew that the surgery part was supposed to be straightforward, but the tissue rejection was the problem, but Dr. Nicholson thought he had that licked. He knew that every doctor he had talked to, and he had now talked to seven of them, had agreed that medically it was probably sound enough, and that every one of them had carefully clammed up when he got the conversation around to whether it was right. It was his decision, not theirs, they all said, sometimes just by their silence. But who was he to decide?

Margaret appeared in the doorway. "Harry. Let's go upstairs and look at Tommy."

He said harshly, "Is that supposed to make it easier for me to murder my son?"

She said, "We talked that out, Harry, and we agreed it isn't murder. Whatever it is. I only think that Tommy ought to be with us when we decide, even if he doesn't know what we're deciding."

The two of them stood next to the outsize crib that held their son, looking in the night light at the long fair lashes against the chubby cheeks and the pouted lips around the thumb. Reading. Model airplanes. Riding a bike. Against a quick sketch of a face and the occasional, cherished, tempestuous, bruising flurry of kisses.

Vladek stayed there the full half hour and then, as he had promised, went back to the kitchen, picked up the phone and began to dial.

R. A. Lafferty

Science fiction writers are born, not made. That, at least, is the way I feel about it. My ambition to write science fiction stretches almost as far back as I can remember, and so it must be with lots of other people.

Many times I get letters in crayon on large sheets of widely ruled paper that say:

Dear Dr. Asimov:

I am in the first grade and I would like to write science fiction. Can you tell me how to copyright my manuscripts? Also give me the name of five editors who will discuss my stories with me and guarantee, under bond, that they will not steal my ideas. Please write back. I am five years old.

Incidentally, I have noticed that everyone under the age of twenty says "Please write back." I have had to look up the word "reply" in the dictionary to make sure that it hasn't been lost or misplaced and, by heaven, it's still there.

As another proof of my contention, I remember little Bobby Silverberg in the days when he was still unbearded and publishing no more than two or three science fiction stories a month, and little Harlan Ellison in the days when he was still biting unwary passers-by on the knee (or on the lower thigh if he stood on tiptoe).

Naturally, then, every time a new name comes up in science fiction, I sigh and think: Another young snot-nose kid coming up to take the bread out of my mouth.

Consequently, when I was at the thirty-first convention and someone offered to introduce me to that new sensation, R. A. Lafferty, I was all prepared to meet some downy-cheeked grade-

school youngster and was all set to pat his head and say,
graciously, that I hoped he would continue to write successful
science fiction after he had grown up.

Imagine, then, my horror when I was introduced to a fine gentleman, well-stricken in years.

That really puts the cherry on it—when middle-aged people,
who should be playing golf or something, enter the field and also
try to take the bread out of my mouth.

9

EUREMA'S DAM

He was about the last of them.

What? The last of the great individualists? The last of the true creative geniuses of the century? The last of the sheer precursors?

No. No. He was the last of the dolts.

Kids were being born smarter all the time when he came along, and they would be so forever more. He was about the last dumb kid ever born.

Even his mother had to admit that Albert was a slow child. What else can you call a boy who doesn't begin to talk till he is four years old, who won't learn to handle a spoon till he is six, who can't operate a doorknob till he is eight? What else can you say about one who put his shoes on the wrong feet and walked in pain? And who had to be told to close his mouth after yawning?

Some things would always be beyond him—like whether it was the big hand or the little hand of the clock that told the hours. But this wasn't something serious. He never did care what time it was.

When, about the middle of his ninth year, Albert made a breakthrough at telling his right hand from his left, he did it by the most ridiculous set of mnemonics ever put together. It had to do with the way a dog turns around before lying down, the direction of whirlpools and whirlwinds, the side a cow is milked from and a horse is mounted from, the direction of twist of oak and sycamore leaves, the maze patterns of rock moss and of tree moss, the cleavage of limestone, the direction of a hawk's wheeling, of a shrike's hunting, and of a snake's coiling (remembering that the mountain boomer is an exception, and that it isn't a true snake), the lay of cedar fronds and of balsam fronds, the twist of a hole dug by a skunk and by a badger (remembering pungently that skunks sometimes use old badger holes). Well, Albert finally learned to remember which was right and which was left, but an observant boy would have learned his right hand from his left without all that nonsense.

Albert never learned to write a readable hand. To get by in school he cheated. From a bicycle speedometer, a midget motor, tiny eccentric cams, and batteries stolen from his grandfather's hearing aid, Albert made a machine to write for him. It was small as a doodlebug and fitted onto a pen or pencil so that Albert could conceal it with his fingers. It formed the letters beautifully as Albert had set the cams to follow a copybook model. He triggered the different letters with keys no bigger than whiskers. Sure it was crooked, but what else can you do when you're too dumb to learn how to write passably?

Albert couldn't figure at all. He had to make another machine to figure for him. It was a palm-of-the-hand thing that would add and subtract and multiply and divide. The next year when he was in the ninth grade they gave him algebra, and he had to devise a flipper to go on the end of his gadget to work quadratic and simultaneous equations. If it weren't for such cheating Albert wouldn't have gotten any marks at all in school.

He had another difficulty when he came to his fifteenth year. People, that is an understatement. There should be a stronger word than "difficulty" for it. Albert was afraid of girls.

What to do?

"I will build me a machine that is not afraid of girls," Albert said. He set to work on it. He had it nearly finished when a thought came to him: "But no machine is afraid of girls. How will this help me?"

His logic was at fault and analogy broke down. He did what he always did. He cheated.

He took the programming rollers out of an old player piano in the attic, found a gear case that would serve, used magnetized sheets instead of perforated music rolls, fed a copy of *Worm-*

wood's Logic into the matrix, and he had a logic machine that would answer questions.

"What's the matter with me that I'm afraid of girls?" Albert asked his logic machine.

"Nothing the matter with you," the logic mahine told him. "It's logical to be afraid of girls. They seem pretty spooky to me too."

"But what can I do about it?"

"Wait for time and circumstances. They sure are slow. Unless you want to cheat—"

"Yes, yes, what then?"

"Build a machine that looks just like you, Albert, and talks just like you. Only make it smarter than you are, and not bashful. And, ah, Albert, there's a special thing you'd better put into it in case things go wrong. I'll whisper it to you. It's dangerous."

So Albert made Little Danny, a dummy who looked like him and talked like him, only he was smarter and not bashful. He filled Little Danny with quips from *Mad Magazine* and from *Quip*, and then they were set.

Albert and Little Danny went to call on Alice.

"Why, he's wonderful," Alice said. "Why can't you be like that, Albert? Aren't you wonderful, Little Danny. Why do you have to be so stupid, Albert, when Little Danny is so wonderful?"

"I, uh, uh, I don't know," Albert said. "Uh, uh, uh."

"He sounds like a fish with the hiccups," Little Danny said.

"You do, Albert, really you do!" Alice screamed. "Why can't you say smart things like Little Danny does, Albert? Why are you so stupid?"

This wasn't working out very well, but Albert kept on with it. He programmed Little Danny to play the ukulele and to sing. He wished that he could program himself to do it. Alice loved everything about Little Danny, but she paid no attention to Albert. And one day Albert had had enough.

"Wha-wha-what do we need with this dummy?" Albert asked. "I just made him to am- to amu- to make you laugh. Let's go off and leave him."

"Go off with you, Albert?" Alice asked. "But you're so stupid. I tell you what. Let's you and me go off and leave Albert, Little Danny. We can have more fun without him."

"Who needs him?" Little Danny asked. "Get lost, buster."

Albert walked away from them. He was glad that he'd taken
his logic machine's advice as to the special thing to be built into
Little Danny. Albert walked fifty steps. A hundred.

"Far enough," Albert said, and he pushed a button in his
pocket.

Nobody but Albert and his logic machine ever did know what
that explosion was. Tiny wheels out of Little Danny and small
pieces of Alice rained down a little later, but there weren't
enough fragments for anyone to identify.

Albert had learned one lesson from his logic machine: never
make anything that you can't unmake.

Well, Albert finally grew to be a man, in years at least. He
would always have something about him of a very awkward
teen-ager. And yet he fought his own war against those who
were teen-agers in years, and he defeated them completely.
There was enmity between them forever. Albert hadn't been a
very well-adjusted adolescent, and he hated the memory of it.
And nobody ever mistook him for an adjusted man.

Albert was too awkward to earn a living at an honest trade.
He was reduced to peddling his little tricks and contrivances to
shysters and promoters. But he did back into a sort of fame, and
he did become burdened with wealth.

He was too stupid to handle his own monetary affairs, but he
built an actuary machine to do his investing and he became rich
by accident. He built the damned thing too good and he regret-
ted it.

Albert became one of that furtive group that has saddled us
with all the mean things in our history. There was that Punic
who couldn't learn the rich variety of hieroglyphic characters
and who devised the crippled short alphabet for wan-wits. There
was the nameless Arab who couldn't count beyond ten and who
set up the ten-number system for babies and idiots. There was
the double-Dutchman with his movable type who drove fine
copy out of the world. Albert was of their miserable company.

Albert himself wasn't much good for anything. But he had
in himself the low knack for making machines that were good at
everything.

His machines did a few things. You remember that anciently
there was smog in the cities. Oh, it could be drawn out of the air

easily enough. All it took was a tickler. Albert made a tickler machine. He would set it fresh every morning. It would clear the air in a circle three hundred yards around his hovel and gather a little over a ton of residue every twenty-four hours. This residue was rich in large polysyllabic molecules which one of his chemical machines could use.

"Why can't you clear all the air?" the people asked him.

"This is as much of the stuff as Clarence Deoxyribonucleiconibus needs every day," Albert said. That was the name of this particular chemical machine.

"But we die of the smog," the people said. "Have mercy on us."

"Oh, all right," Albert said. He turned it over to one of his reduplicating machines to make as many copies as were necessary.

You remember that once there was a teen-ager problem? You remember when those little buggers used to be mean? Albert got enough of them. There was something ungainly about them that reminded him too much of himself. He made a teen-ager of his own. It was rough. To the others it looked like one of themselves, the ring in the left ear, the dangling side-locks, the brass knucks and the long knife, the guitar pluck to jab in an eye. But it was incomparably rougher than the human teen-agers. It terrorized all in the neighborhood and made them behave, and dress like real people. And there was one thing about the teen-age machine that Albert made: it was made of such polarized metal and glass that it was invisible except to teen-ager eyes.

"Why is your neighborhood different?" the people asked Albert. "Why are there such good and polite teen-agers in your neighborhood and such mean ones everywhere else? It's as though something had spooked all those right around here."

"Oh, I thought I was the only one who didn't like the regular kind," Albert said.

"Oh, no, no," the people answered him. "If there is anything at all you can do about them—"

So Albert turned his mostly invisible teen-ager machine over to one of his reduplicating machines to make as many copies as were necessary, and set one up in every neighborhood. From that day till this the teen-agers have all been good and polite and a little bit frightened. But there is no evidence of what keeps them that way except an occasional eye dangling from the jab of an invisible guitar pluck.

So the two most pressing problems of the latter part of the twentieth century were solved, but accidentally, and to the credit of no one.

As the years went by, Albert felt his inferiority most when in the presence of his own machines, particularly those in the form of men. Albert just hadn't their urbanity or sparkle or wit. He was a clod beside them, and they made him feel it.

Why not? One of Albert's devices sat in the President's Cabinet. One of them was on the High Council of World-Watchers that kept the peace everywhere. One of them presided at Riches Unlimited, that private-public-international instrument that guaranteed reasonable riches to everyone in the world. One of them was the guiding hand in the Health and Longevity Foundation which provided those things to everyone. Why should not such splendid and successful machines look down on their shabby uncle who had made them?

"I'm rich by a curious twist," Albert said to himself one day, "and honored through a mistake in circumstance. But there isn't a man or a machine in the world who is really my friend. A book here tells how to make friends, but I can't do it that way. I'll make one my own way."

So Albert set out to make a friend.

He made Poor Charles, a machine as stupid and awkward and inept as himself.

"Now I will have a companion," Albert said, but it didn't work. Add two zeros together and you still have zero. Poor Charles was too much like Albert to be good for anything.

Poor Charles! Unable to think, he made a—(but wait a moleskin-gloved minute here, Colonel, this isn't going to work at all)—he made a machi—(but isn't this the same blamed thing all over again?)—he made a machine to think for him and to—

Hold it, hold it! That's enough. Poor Charles was the only machine that Albert ever made that was dumb enough to do a thing like that.

Well, whatever it was, the machine that Poor Charles made was in control of the situation and of Poor Charles when Albert came onto them accidentally. The machine's machine, the device that Poor Charles had constructed to think for him, was lecturing Poor Charles in a humiliating way.

"Only the inept and deficient will invent," that damned machine's machine was droning. "The Greeks in their high period did not invent. They used neither adjunct power nor instrumentation. They used, as intelligent men or machines will always use, slaves. They did not descend to gadgets. They, who did the difficult with ease, did not seek the easier way.

"But the incompetent will invent. The insufficient will invent. The depraved will invent. And knaves will invent."

Albert, in a seldom fit of anger, killed them both. But he knew that the machine of his machine had spoken the truth.

Albert was very much cast down. A more intelligent man would have had a hunch as to what was wrong. Albert had only a hunch that he was not very good at hunches and would never be. Seeing no way out, he fabricated a machine and named it Hunchy.

In most ways this was the worst machine he ever made. In building it he tried to express something of his unease for the future. It was an awkward thing in mind and mechanism, a misfit.

Albert's more intelligent machines gathered around and hooted at him while he put it together.

"Boy! Are you lost!" they taunted. "That thing is a primitive! To draw its power from the ambient! We talked you into throwing that away twenty years ago and setting up coded power for all of us."

"Uh—someday there may be social disturbances and all centers of power seized," Albert stammered. "But Hunchy would be able to operate if the whole world were wiped smooth."

"It isn't even tuned to our information matrix," they jibed. "It's worse than Poor Charles. That stupid thing practically starts from scratch."

"Maybe there'll be a new kind of itch for it," said Albert.

"It's not even housebroken!" the urbane machines shouted their indignation. "Look at that! Some sort of primitive lubrication all over the floor."

"Remembering my childhood, I sympathize," Albert said.

"What's it good for?" they demanded.

"Ah—it gets hunches," Albert mumbled.

"Duplication!" they shouted. "That's all you're good for your-self, and not very good at that. We suggest an election to replace you as—pardon our laughter—the head of these enterprises."

"Boss, I've got a hunch how we can block them there," the unfinished Hunchy whispered.

"They're bluffing." Albert whispered back. "My first logic machine taught me never to make anything that I can't unmake. I've got them there and they know it. I wish I could think up things like that myself."

"Maybe there will come an awkward time and I will be good for something," Hunchy said.

Only once, and that rather late in life, did a sort of honesty flare up in Albert. He did one thing (and it was a dismal failure) on his own. That was the night of the year of the double millennium when Albert was presented with the Finnerty-Hochmann Trophy, the highest award that the intellectual world could give. Albert was certainly an odd choice for it, but it had been noticed that almost every basic invention for thirty years could be traced back to him or to the devices with which he had surrounded himself.

You know the trophy. Atop it was Eurema, the synthetic Greek goddess of invention, with arms spread as if she would take flight. Below this was a stylized brain cut away to show the convoluted cortex. And below this was the coat of arms of the Academicians: Ancient Scholar rampant (argent); the Anderson Analyzer sinister (gules); the Mondeman Space-Drive dexter (vair). It was a fine work by Groben, his ninth period.

Albert had a speech composed for him by his speech-writing machine, but for some reason he did not use it. He went on his own, and that was disaster. He got to his feet when he was introduced, and he stuttered and spoke nonsense!

"Ah—only the sick oyster produces nacre," he said, and they all gaped at him. What sort of beginning for a speech was that? "Or do I have the wrong creature?" Albert asked weakly.

"Eurema doesn't look like that!" Albert gawked out and

pointed suddenly at the trophy. "No, no, that isn't her at all. Eurema walks backward and is blind. And her mother is a brainless hulk."

Everybody was watching him with pained expression.

"Nothing rises without a leaven," Albert tried to explain, "but the yeast is itself a fungus and a disease. You be regularizers all, splendid and supreme! But you cannot live without the irregulars. You will die, and who will tell you that you are dead? When there are no longer any deprived or insufficient, *who will invent?* What will you do when there is none of us defectives left? Who will leaven your lump then?"

"Are you unwell?" the master of ceremonies asked him quietly. "Should you not make an end to it? People will understand."

"Of course I'm unwell. Always have been," Albert said. "What good would I be otherwise? You set the ideal that all should be healthy and well adjusted. No! No! Were we all well adjusted, we would ossify and die. The world is kept healthy only by some of the unhealthy minds lurking in it. The first implement made by man was not a scraper or celt or stone knife. It was a crutch, and it wasn't devised by a hale man."

"Perhaps you should rest," a functionary said in a low voice, for this sort of rambling nonsense talk had never been heard at an awards dinner before.

"Know you," said Albert, "that it is not the fine bulls and wonderful cattle who make the new paths. Only a crippled calf makes a new path. In everything that survives there must be an element of the incongruous. Hey, you know the woman who said, 'My husband is incongruous, but I never liked Washington in the summertime.'"

Everybody gazed at him in stupor.

"That's the first joke I ever made," Albert said lamely. "My joke-making machine makes them a lot better than I do." He paused and gaped, and gulped a big breath.

"Dolts!" he croaked out fiercely then. "What will you do for dolts when the last of us is gone? How will you survive without us?"

Albert had finished. He gaped and forgot to close his mouth. They led him back to his seat. His publicity machine explained that Albert was tired from overwork, and then that machine passed around copies of the speech that Albert was supposed to have given.

It had been an unfortunate episode. How noisome it is that the innovators are never great men, and that the great men are never good for anything but just being great men.

In that year a decree went forth from Caesar that a census of the whole country should be taken. The decree was from Cesare Panebianco, the President of the country. It was the decimal year proper for the census, and there was nothing unusual about the decree. Certain provisions, however, were made for taking a census of the drifters and decrepits who were usually missed, to examine them and to see why they were so. It was in the course of this that Albert was picked up. If any man ever looked like a drifter and decrepit, it was Albert.

Albert was herded in with other derelicts, set down at a table, and asked tortuous questions. As:

"What is your name?"

He almost muffed that one, but he rallied and answered, "Albert."

"What time is it by that clock?"

They had him in his old weak spot. Which hand was which? He gaped and didn't answer.

"Can you read?" they asked him.

"Not without my—" Albert began. "I don't have with me my— No, I can't read very well by myself."

"Try."

They gave him a paper to mark up with true and false questions. Albert marked them all true, believing that he would have half of them right. But they were all false. The regularized people are partial to falsehood. Then they gave him a supply-the-word test on proverbs.

"——— is the best policy" didn't mean a thing to him. He couldn't remember the names of the companies that he had his own policies with.

"A ——— in time saves nine" contained more mathematics than Albert could handle.

"There appear to be six unknowns," he told himself, "and only one positive value, nine. The equating verb 'saves' is a vague one. I cannot solve this equation. I am not even sure that it is an equation. If only I had with me my—"

But he hadn't any of his gadgets or machines with him. He was on his own. He left half a dozen other proverb fill-ins blank. Then he saw a chance to recoup. Nobody is so dumb as not to know one answer if enough questions are asked.

"——— is the mother of invention," it said.

"Stupidity," Albert wrote in his weird ragged hand. Then he sat back in triumph. "I know that Eurema and her mother," he snickered. "Man, how I do know them!"

But they marked him wrong on that one too. He had missed every answer to every test. They began to fix him a ticket to a progressive booby hatch where he might learn to do something with his hands, his head being hopeless.

A couple of Albert's urbane machines came down and got him out of it. They explained that, while he was a drifter and a derelict, yet he was a rich drifter and derelict, and that he was even a man of some note.

"He doesn't look it, but he really is—pardon our laughter—a man of some importance," one of the fine machines explained. "He has to be told to close his mouth after he has yawned, but for all that he is the winner of the Finnerty-Hochmann Trophy. We will be responsible for him."

Albert was miserable as his fine machines took him out, especially when they asked that he walk three or four steps behind them and not seem to be with them. They gave him some pretty rough banter and turned him into a squirming worm of a man. Albert left them and went to a little hide-out he kept.

"I'll blow my crawfishing brains out," he swore. "The humiliation is more than I can bear. Can't do it myself, though. I'll have to have it done."

He set to work building a device in his hide-out.

"What you doing, boss?" Hunchy asked him. "I had a hunch you'd come here and start building something."

"I'm building a machine to blow my pumpkin-picking brains out," Albert shouted. "I'm too yellow to do it myself."

"Boss, I got a hunch there's something better to do. Let's have some fun."

"Don't believe I know how to," Albert said thoughtfully. "I built a fun machine once to do it for me. He had a real revel till he flew apart, but he never seemed to do anything for me."

"This fun will be for you and me, boss. Consider the world spread out. What is it?"

"It's a world too fine for me to live in any longer," Albert said. "Everything and all the people are perfect, and all alike. They're at the top of the heap. They've won it all and arranged it all neatly. There's no place for a clutter-up like me in the world. So I get out."

"Boss, I've got a hunch that you're seeing it wrong. You've got better eyes than that. Look again, real canny, at it. Now what do you see?"

"Hunchy, Hunchy, is that possible? Is that really what it is? I wonder why I never noticed it before. That's the way of it, though, now that I look closer.

"Six billion patsies waiting to be took! Six billion patsies without a defense of any kind! A couple of guys out for some fun, man, they could mow them down like fields of Albert-Improved Concho Wheat!"

"Boss, I've got a hunch that this is what I was made for. The world sure had been getting stuffy. Let's tie into it and eat off the top layer. Man, we can cut a swath."

"We'll inaugurate a new era!" Albert gloated. "We'll call it the Turning of the Worm. We'll have fun, Hunchy. We'll gobble them up like goobers. How come I never saw it like that before? Six billion patsies!"

The twenty-first century began on this rather odd note.

1974
32nd CONVENTION
WASHINGTON

James Tiptree, Jr.

And this bring us to the thirty-second convention at Washington in 1974.

Pleasant memories! It was at the twenty-first convention at Washington in 1963 that I got my first Hugo, and it was also then that I absented myself long enough to take a tour through the White House, while it was still Camelot.

The thirty-second convention was a monster, though. There were some four thousand people in attendance, and I'm not sure that's entirely a good thing. It was almost impossible to see old friends because between any two of the true conventioneers there were a thousand strangers. Now back at the thirteenth convention at Cleveland in 1955, when I was guest of honor, the total attendance was three hundred. (Lester del Rey says it's because I was guest of honor that the attendance was that low, but, as we all know, Lester will say anything—and constantly does.)

The thirty-second convention was so enormous that I can't honestly tell you whether Tiptree was there, and if he was there, whether I met him. All I can remember clearly is the banquet at which Andy Offutt (I think he spells his name in lower case but I can't bring myself to do that) labored manfully under considerable difficulties to keep things going.

Tip and I have, however, corresponded, and on the basis of that correspondence, I can tell you Tip's a very nice person. Not only does he praise my science articles (sterling evidence of good taste on his part) but he invariably urges me not to answer, being fully aware of how incredibly busy I am. Of *course* I answer. He's not going to be politer than I am.

Incidentally, the thirty-second convention may be the most populous world science fiction convention I ever attended, but there were others that were even more spectacular, if that's the word I want.

In February 1976 there was a "Star Trek" convention (well, a variety of science fiction convention at that) at the New York Hilton in which the number of tickets sold far outweighed the space available. The entire population of New York City, I believe, bought tickets and all came to the convention. I walked in on the particular day they all came, gazed in horror at the crystallization of humanity (believe me, everyone was wedged in), and when I turned to leave found that thousands had crystallized behind me. It took me half an hour to diffuse out into the street again.

10

THE GIRL
WHO WAS PLUGGED IN

Listen, zombie. Believe me. What I could tell you—you with your silly hands leaking sweat on your growth-stocks portfolio. One-ten lousy hacks of AT&T on twenty-point margin and you think you're Evel Knievel. AT&T? You doubleknit dummy, how I'd love to show you something.

Look, dead daddy, I'd say. See for instance that rotten girl?

In the crowd over there, that one gaping at her gods. One rotten girl in the city of the future. (That's what I said.) Watch.

She's jammed among bodies, craning and peering with her soul yearning out of her eyeballs. Love! Oo-ooh, love them! Her gods are coming out of a store called Body East. Three youngbloods, larking along loverly. Dressed like simple streetpeople but . . . smashing. See their great eyes swivel above their nosefilters, their hands lift shyly, their inhumanly tender lips melt? The crowd moans. Love! This whole boiling megacity, this whole fun future world loves its gods.

You don't believe gods, dad? Wait. Whatever turns you on, there's a god in the future for you, custom-made. Listen to this mob. "I touched his foot. Ow-oow, I TOUCHED Him!"

Even the people in the GTX tower up there love the gods—in their own way and for their own reasons.

The funky girl on the street, she just loves. Grooving on their beautiful lives, their mysterioso problems. No one ever told her about mortals who love a god and end up as a tree or a sighing sound. In a million years it'd never occur to her that her gods might love her back.

She's squashed against the wall now as the godlings come by.

They move in a clear space. A holocam bobs above but its shadow never falls on them. The store display screens are magically clear of bodies as the gods glance in and a beggar underfoot is suddenly alone. They give him a token. "Aaaaah!" goes the crowd.

Now one of them flashes some wild new kind of timer and they all trot to catch a shuttle, just like people. The shuttle stops for them—more magic. The crowd sighs, closing back. The gods are gone.

(In a room far from—but not unconnected to—the GTX tower a molecular flipflop closes too, and three account tapes spin.)

Our girl is still stuck by the wall while guards and holocam equipment pull away. The adoration's fading from her face. That's good, because now you can see she's the ugly of the world. A tall monument to pituitary dystrophy. No surgeon would touch her. When she smiles, her jaw—it's half purple— almost bites her left eye out. She's also quite young, but who could care?

The crowd is pushing her along now, treating you to glimpses of her jumbled torso, her mismatched legs. At the corner she strains to send one last fond spasm after the godlings' shuttle. Then her face reverts to its usual expression of dim pain and she lurches onto the moving walkway, stumbling into people. The walkway junctions with another. She crosses, trips and collides with the casualty rail. Finally she comes out into a little place called a park. The sportshow is working, a basketball game in 3-di is going on right overhead. But all she does is squeeze onto a bench and huddle there while a ghostly free-throw goes by her ear.

After that nothing at all happens except a few furtive hand-mouth gestures which don't even interest her benchmates.

But you're curious about the city? So ordinary after all, in the FUTURE?

Ah, there's plenty to swing with here—and it's not all that *far* in the future, dad. But pass up the sci-fi stuff for now, like for instance the holovision technology that's put TV and radio in museums. Or the worldwide carrier field bouncing down from satellites, controlling communication and transport systems all over the globe. That was a spin-off from asteroid mining, pass it by. We're watching that girl.

I'll give you just one goodie. Maybe you noticed on the sportshow or the streets? No commercials. No ads.

That's right. NO ADS. An eyeballer for you.

Look around. Not a billboard, sign, slogan, jingle, skywrite, blurb, sublimflash, in this whole fun world. Brand names? Only in those ticky little peep-screens on the stores and you could hardly call that advertising. How does that finger you?

Think about it. That girl is still sitting there.

She's parked right under the base of the GTX tower as a matter of fact. Look way up and you can see the sparkles from the bubble on top, up there among the domes of godland. Inside that bubble is a boardroom. Neat bronze shield on the door: Global Transmissions Corporation—not that that means anything.

I happen to know there's six people in that room. Five of them technically male, and the sixth isn't easily thought of as a mother. They are absolutely unremarkable. Those faces were seen once at their nuptials and will show again in their obituaries and impress nobody either time. If you're looking for the secret Big Blue Meanies of the world, forget it. I know. Zen, do I know! Flesh? Power? Glory? You'd horrify them.

What they do like up there is to have things orderly, especially their communications. You could say they've dedicated their lives to that, to freeing the world from garble. Their nightmares are about hemorrhages of information: channels screwed up, plans misimplemented, garble creeping in. Their gigantic wealth only worries them, it keeps opening new vistas of disorder. Luxury? They wear what their tailors put on them, eat what their cooks serve them. See that old boy there—his name is Isham—he's sipping water and frowning as he listens to a databall. The water was prescribed by his medistaff. It tastes awful. The databall also contains a disquieting message about his son, Paul.

But it's time to go back down, far below to our girl. Look!

She's toppled over sprawling on the ground.

A tepid commotion ensues among the bystanders. The consensus is she's dead, which she disproves by bubbling a little. And presently she's taken away by one of the superb ambulances of the future, which are a real improvement over ours when one happens to be around.

At the local bellevue the usual things are done by the usual team of clowns aided by a saintly mop-pusher. Our girl revives enough to answer the questionnaire without which you can't die, even in the future. Finally she's cast up, a pumped-out hulk on a cot in the long, dim ward.

Again nothing happens for a while except that her eyes leak a little from the understandable disappointment of finding herself still alive.

But somewhere one GTX computer has been tickling another, and toward midnight something does happen. First comes an attendant who pulls screens around her. Then a man in a business doublet comes daintily down the ward. He motions the attendant to strip off the sheet and go.

The groggy girl-brute heaves up, big hands clutching at bodyparts you'd pay not to see.

"Burke? P. Burke, is that your name?"

"Y-yes." Croak. "Are you . . . policeman?"

"No. They'll be along shortly, I expect. Public suicide's a felony."

". . . I'm sorry."

He has a 'corder in his hand. "No family, right?"

"No."

"You're seventeen. One year city college. What did you study?"

"La-languages."

"H'm. Say something."

Unintelligible rasp.

He studies her. Seen close, he's not so elegant. Errand-boy type.

"Why did you try to kill yourself?"

She stares at him with dead-rat dignity, hauling up the gray sheet. Give him a point, he doesn't ask twice.

"Tell me, did you see Breath this afternoon?"

Dead as she nearly is, that ghastly love-look wells up. Breath is the three young gods, a loser's cult. Give the man another point, he interprets her expression.

"How would you like to meet them?"

The girl's eyes bug out grotesquely.

"I have a job for someone like you. It's hard work. If you did well you'd be meeting Breath and stars like that all the time."

Is he insane? She's deciding she really did die.

"But it means you never see anybody you know again. Never, *ever*. You will be legally dead. Even the police won't know. Do you want to try?"

It all has to be repeated while her great jaw slowly sets. *Show me the fire I walk through.* Finally P. Burke's prints are in his 'corder, the man holding up the rancid girl-body without a sign of distaste. It makes you wonder what else he does.

And then—THE MAGIC. Sudden silent trot of litterbearers tucking P. Burke into something quite different from a bellevue stretcher, the oiled slide into the daddy of all luxury ambulances —real flowers in that holder!—and the long jarless rush to nowhere. Nowhere is warm and gleaming and kind with nurses. (Where did you hear that money can't buy genuine kindness?) And clean clouds folding P. Burke into bewildered sleep.

. . . Sleep which merges into feedings and washings and more sleeps, into drowsy moments of afternoon where midnight should be, and gentle businesslike voices and friendly (but very few) faces, and endless painless hyposprays and peculiar numbnesses. And later comes the steadying rhythm of days and nights, and a quickening which P. Burke doesn't identify as health, but only knows that the fungus place in her armpit is gone. And then she's up and following those few new faces with growing trust, first tottering, then walking strongly, all better now, clumping down the short hall to the tests, tests, tests, and the other things.

And here is our girl, looking—

If possible, worse than before. (You thought this was Cinderella transistorized?)

The disimprovement in her looks comes from the electrode jacks peeping out of her sparse hair, and there are other meldings of flesh and metal. On the other hand, that collar and spinal plate are really an asset; you won't miss seeing that neck.

P. Burke is ready for training in her new job.

The training takes place in her suite, and is exactly what you'd call a charm course. How to walk, sit, eat, speak, blow her nose, how to stumble, to urinate, to hiccup—DELICIOUSLY. How to make each nose-blow or shrug delightfully, subtly different from any ever spooled before. As the man said, it's hard work.

But P. Burke proves apt. Somewhere in that horrible body is a gazelle, a houri who would have been buried forever without this crazy chance. See the ugly duckling go!

Only it isn't precisely P. Burke who's stepping, laughing, shaking out her shining hair. How could it be? P. Burke is doing it all right, but she's doing it through something. The something is to all appearances a live girl. (You were warned, this is the FUTURE.)

When they first open the big cryocase and show her her new body she says just one word. Staring, gulping, "How?"

Simple, really. Watch P. Burke in her sack and scuffs stump down the hall beside Joe, the man who supervises the technical part of her training. Joe doesn't mind P. Burke's looks, he hasn't noticed them. To Joe, system matrices are beautiful.

They go into a dim room containing a huge cabinet like a one-man sauna and a console for Joe. The room has a glass wall that's all dark now. And just for your information, the whole shebang is five hundred feet underground near what used to be Carbondale, Pa.

Joe opens the sauna-cabinet like a big clamshell standing on end with a lot of funny business inside. Our girl shucks her shift and walks into it bare, totally unembarrassed. *Eager.* She settles in face-forward, butting jacks into sockets. Joe closes it carefully onto her humpback. Clunk. She can't see in there or hear or move. She hates this minute. But how she loves what comes next!

Joe's at his console and the lights on the other side of the glass wall come up. A room is on the other side, all fluff and kicky bits, a girly bedroom. In the bed is a small mound of silk with a rope of yellow hair hanging out.

The sheets stirs and gets whammed back flat.

Sitting up in the bed is the darlingest girl child you've EVER seen. She quivers—porno for angels. She sticks both her little arms straight up, flips her hair, looks around full of sleepy pazazz. Then she can't resist rubbing her hands down over her minibreasts and belly. Because, you see, it's the godawful P.

Burke who is sitting there hugging her perfect girl-body, looking at you out of delighted eyes.

Then the kitten hops out of bed and crashes flat on the floor.

From the sauna in the dim room comes a strangled noise. P. Burke, trying to rub her wired-up elbow is suddenly smothered in *two* bodies, electrodes jerking in her flesh. Joe juggles inputs, crooning into his mike. The flurry passes; it's all right.

In the lighted room the elf gets up, casts a cute glare at the glass wall and goes into a transparent cubicle. A bathroom, what else? She's a live girl, and live girls have to go to the bathroom after a night's sleep even if their brains are in a sauna cabinet in the next room. And P. Burke isn't in that cabinet, she's in the bathroom. Perfectly simple, if you have the glue for that closed training circuit that's letting her run her neural system by remote control.

Now let's get one thing clear. P. Burke does not *feel* her brain is in the sauna room, she feels she's in that sweet little body. When you wash your hands, do you feel the water is running on your brain? Of course not. You feel the water on your hand, although the "feeling" is actually a potential-pattern flickering over the electrochemical jelly between your ears. And it's delivered there via the long circuits from your hands. Just so, P. Burke's brain in the cabinet feels the water on her hands in the bathroom. The fact that the signals have jumped across space on the way in makes no difference at all. If you want the jargon, it's known as eccentric projection or sensory reference and you've done it all your life. Clear?

Time to leave the honey-pot to her toilet training—she's made a booboo with the toothbrush, because P. Burke can't get used to what she sees in the mirror—

But wait, you say. Where did that girl-body come from?

P. Burke asks that too, dragging out the words.

"They grow 'em," Joe tells her. He couldn't care less about the flesh department. "PDs. Placental decanters. Modified embryos, see? Fit the control implants in later. Without a Remote Operator it's just a vegetable. Look at the feet—no callus at all." (He knows because they told him.)

"Oh . . . oh, she's incredible . . ."

"Yeah, a neat job. Want to try walking-talking mode today? You're coming on fast."

And she is. Joe's reports and the reports from the nurse and the doctor and style man go to a bushy man upstairs who is some kind of medical cybertech but mostly a project administrator. His reports in turn go—to the GTX boardroom? Certainly not, did you think this is a *big* thing? His reports just go up. The point is, they're green, very green. P. Burke promises well.

So the bushy man—Doctor Tesla—has procedures to initiate. The little kitten's dossier in the Central Data Bank, for instance. Purely routine. And the phase-in schedule which will put her on the scene. This is simple: a small exposure in an off-network holoshow.

Next he has to line out the event which will fund and target her. That takes budget meetings, clearances, coordinations. The Burke project begins to recruit and grow. And there's the messy business of the name, which always gives Doctor Tesla an acute pain in the bush.

The name comes out weird, when it's suddenly discovered that Burke's "P." stands for "Philadelphia," Philadelphia? The astrologer grooves on it. Joe thinks it would help identification. The semantics girl references *brotherly love, Liberty-Bell, main-line, low teratogenesis,* blah-blah. Nicknames Philly? Pala? Pooty? Delphi? Is it good, bad? Finally "Delphi" is gingerly declared goodo. ("Burke" is replaced by something nobody remembers.)

Coming along now. We're at the official checkout down in the underground suite, which is as far as the training circuits reach. The bushy Doctor Tesla is there, braced by two budgetary types and a quiet fatherly man whom he handles like hot plasma.

Joe swings the door wide and she steps shyly in.

Their little Delphi, fifteen and flawless.

Tesla introduces her around. She's child-solemn, a beautiful baby to whom something so wonderful has happened you can feel the tingles. She doesn't smile, she . . . brims. That brimming joy is all that shows of P. Burke, the forgotten hulk in the sauna next door. But P. Burke doesn't know she's alive—it's Delphi who lives, every warm inch of her.

One of the budget types lets go a libidinous snuffle and

freezes. The fatherly man, whose name is Mr. Cantle, clears his throat.

"Well, young lady, are you ready to go to work?"

"Yes sir," gravely from the elf.

"We'll see. Has anybody told you what you're going to do for us?"

"No, sir." Joe and Tesla exhale quietly.

"Good." He eyes her, probing for the blind brain in the room next door.

"Do you know what *advertising* is?"

He's talking dirty, hitting to shock. Delphi's eyes widen and her little chin goes up. Joe is in ecstasy at the complex expressions P. Burke is getting through. Mr. Cantle waits.

"It's, well, it's when they used to tell people to buy things." She swallows. "It's not allowed."

"That's right." Mr. Cantle leans back, grave. "Advertising as it used to be is against the law. *A display other than the legitimate use of the product, intended to promote its sale.* In former times every manufacturer was free to tout his wares any way, place or time he could afford. All the media and most of the landscape was taken up with extravagant competing displays. The thing became uneconomic. The public rebelled. Since the so-called Huckster Act, sellers have been restrained to, I quote, displays in or on the product itself, visible during its legitimate use or in on-premise sales." Mr. Cantle leans forward. "Now tell me, Delphi, why do people buy one product rather than another?"

"Well . . ." Enchanting puzzlement from Delphi. "They, um, they see them and like them, or they hear about them from somebody?" (Touch of P. Burke there; she didn't say, from a friend.)

"Partly. Why did *you* buy your particular body-lift?"

"I never had a body-lift, sir."

Mr. Cantle frowns; what gutters do they drag for these Remotes?

"Well, what brand of water do you drink?"

"Just what was in the faucet, sir," says Delphi humbly. "I—I did try to boil it—"

"Good God." He scowls; Tesla stiffens. "Well, what did you boil it in? A cooker?"

The shining yellow head nods.

"What *brand* of cooker did you buy?"

"I didn't buy it, sir," says frightened P. Burke through Delphi's lips. "But—I know the best kind! Ananga has a Burnbabi, I saw the name when she—"

"Exactly!" Cantle's fatherly beam comes back strong; the Burnbabi account is a strong one, too. "You saw Ananga using one so you thought it must be good, eh? And it is good or a great human being like Ananga wouldn't be using it. Absolutely right. And now, Delphi, you know what you're going to be doing for us. You're going to show some products. Doesn't sound very hard, does it?"

"Oh, no, sir . . ." Baffled child's stare; Joe gloats.

"And you must never, *never* tell anyone what you're doing." Cantle's eyes bore for the brain behind this seductive child.

"You're wondering why we ask you to do this, naturally. There's a very serious reason. All those products people use, foods and healthaids and cookers and cleaners and clothes and car—they're all made by *people*. Somebody put in years of hard work designing and making them. A man comes up with a fine new idea for a better product. He has to get a factory and machinery, and hire workmen. Now. What happens if people have no way of hearing about his product? Word-of-mouth is far too slow and unreliable. Nobody might ever stumble onto his new product or find out how good it was, right? And then he and all the people who worked for him—they'd go bankrupt, right? So, Delphi, there has to be *some way* that large numbers of people can get a look at a good new product, right? How? By letting people see you using it. You're giving that man a chance."

Delphi's little head is nodding in happy relief.

"Yes, sir, I do see now—but sir, it seems so sensible, why don't they let you—"

Cantle smiles sadly.

"It's an overreaction, my dear. History goes by swings. People overreact and pass harsh unrealistic laws which attempt to stamp out an essential social process. When this happens, the people who understand have to carry on as best they can until the pendulum swings back. He sighs. "The Huckster Laws are bad, inhuman laws, Delphi, despite their good intent. If they were strictly observed they would wreak havoc. Our economy, our society would be cruelly destroyed. We'd be back in caves!" His inner fire is showing; if the Huckster Laws were strictly enforced he'd be back punching a databank.

"It's our duty, Delphi. Our solemn social duty. We are not breaking the law. You will be using the product. But people wouldn't understand, if they knew. They would become upset, just as you did. So you must be very, very careful not to mention any of this to anybody."

(And somebody will be very, very carefully monitoring Delphi's speech circuits.)

"Now we're all straight, aren't we? Little Delphi here"— He is speaking to the invisible creature next door— "Little Delphi is going to live a wonderful, exciting life. She's going to be a girl people watch. And she's going to be using fine products people will be glad to know about and helping the good people who make them. Yours will be a genuine social contribution." He keys up his pitch; the creature in there must be older.

Delphi digests this with ravishing gravity.

"But sir, how do I—?"

"Don't worry about a thing. You'll have people behind you whose job it is to select the most worthy products for you to use. Your job is just to do as they say. They'll show you what outfits to wear to parties, what suncars and viewers to buy and so on. That's all you have to do."

Parties—clothes—suncars! Delphi's pink mouth opens. In P. Burke's starved seventeen-year-old head the ethics of product sponsorship float far away.

"Now tell me in your own words what your job is, Delphi."

"Yes sir. I—I'm to go to parties and buy things and use them as they tell me, to help the people who work in factories."

"And what did I say was so important?"

"Oh—I shouldn't let anybody know, about the things."

"Right." Mr. Cantle has another paragraph he uses when the subject shows, well, immaturity. But he can sense only eagerness here. Good. He doesn't really enjoy the other speech.

"It's a lucky girl who can have all the fun she wants while doing good for others, isn't it?" He beams around. There's a prompt shuffling of chairs. Clearly this one is go.

Joe leads her out, grinning. The poor fool thinks they're admiring her coordination.

It's out into the world for Delphi now, and at this point the up-channels get used. On the administrative side account schedules are opened, subprojects activated. On the technical side the reserved bandwidth is cleared. (That carrier field, remember?) A new name is waiting for Delphi, a name she'll never hear. It's a long string of binaries which have been quietly cycling in a GTX tank ever since a certain Beautiful Person didn't wake up.

The name winks out of cycle, dances from pulses into modulations of modulations, whizzes through phasing, and shoots into a giga-band beam racing up to a synchronous satellite poised over Guatemala. From there the beam pours twenty thousand miles back to earth again, forming an all-pervasive field of structured energics supplying tuned demand-points all over the CanAm quadrant.

With that field, if you have the right credit rating you can sit at a GTX console and operate a tuned ore-extractor in Brazil. Or —if you have some simple credentials like being able to walk on water—you could shoot a spool into the network holocam shows running day and night in every home and dorm and rec. site. *Or* you could create a continentwide traffic jam. Is it any wonder GTX guards those inputs like a sacred trust?

Delphi's "name" appears as a tiny analyzable nonredundancy in the flux, and she'd be very proud if she knew about it. It would strike P. Burke as magic; P. Burke never even understood robotcars. But Delphi is in no sense a robot. Call her a waldo if you must. The fact is she's just a girl, a real live girl with her brain in an unusual place. A simple real-time on-line system with plenty of bit-rate—even as you and you.

The point of all this hardware, which isn't very much hardware in this society, is so Delphi can walk out of that underground suite, a mobile demand-point draining an omnipresent fieldform. And she does—eighty-nine pounds of tender girl flesh and blood with a few metallic components, stepping out into the sunlight to be taken to her new life. A girl with everything going for her including a meditech escort. Walking lovely, stopping to widen her eyes at the big antennae system overhead.

The mere fact that something called P. Burke is left behind

down underground has no bearing at all. P. Burke is totally un-self aware and happy as a clam in its shell. (Her bed has been moved into the waldo cabinet room now.) And P. Burke isn't in the cabinet; P. Burke is climbing out of an airvan in a fabulous Colorado beef preserve and her name is Delphi. Delphi is look-ing at live Charolais steers and live cottonwoods and aspens gold against the blue smog and stepping over live grass to be wel-comed by the reserve super's wife.

The super's wife is looking forward to a visit from Delphi and her friends and by a happy coincidence there's a holocam outfit here doing a piece for the nature nuts.

You could write the script yourself now, while Delphi learns a few rules about structural interferences and how to handle the tiny time lag which results from the new forty-thousand-mile pa-renthesis in her nervous system. That's right—the people with the leased holocam rig naturally find the gold aspen shadows look a lot better on Delphi's flank than they do on a steer. And Delphi's face improves the mountains too, when you can see them. But the nature freaks aren't quite as joyful as you'd expect.

"See you in Barcelona, kitten," the head man says sourly as they pack up.

"Barcelona?" echoes Delphi with that charming little sublimi-nal lag. She sees where his hand is and steps back.

"Cool, it's not her fault," another man says wearily. He knocks back his grizzled hair. "Maybe they'll leave in some of the gut."

Delphi watches them go off to load the spools on the GTX transport for processing. Her hand roves over the breast the man had touched. Back under Carbondale, P. Burke has discovered something new about her Delphi-body.

About the difference between Delphi and her own grim car-cass.

She's always known Delphi has almost no sense of taste or smell. They explained about that: only so much bandwidth. You don't have to taste a suncar, do you? And the slight overall dim-ness of Delphi's sense of touch—she's familiar with that, too. Fabrics that would prickle P. Burke's own hide feel like a cool plastic film to Delphi.

But the blank spots. It took her a while to notice them. Delphi doesn't have much privacy; investments of her size don't. So she's slow about discovering there's certain definite places where her beastly P. Burke body *feels* things that Delphi's dainty flesh does not. H'mm! Channel space again, she thinks—and forgets it in the pure bliss of being Delphi.

You ask how a girl could forget a thing like that? Look. P. Burke is about as far as you can get from the concept *girl*. She's a female, yes—but for her, sex is a four-letter word spelled P-A-I-N. She isn't quite a virgin. You don't want the details; she'd been about twelve and the freak-lovers were bombed blind. When they came down they threw her out with a small hole in her anatomy and a mortal one elsewhere. She dragged off to buy her first and last shot and she can still hear the clerk's incredulous guffaws.

Do you see why Delphi grins, stretching her delicious little numb body in the sun she faintly feels? Beams, saying, "Please, I'm ready now."

Ready for what? For Barcelona like the sour man said, where his nature-thing is now making it strong in the amateur section of the Festival. A winner! Like he also said, a lot of strip-mines and dead fish have been scrubbed but who cares with Delphi's darling face so visible?

So it's time for Delphi's face and her other delectabilities to show on Barcelona's Playa Neuva. Which means switching her channel to the EurAf synchsat.

They ship her at night so the nanosecond transfer isn't even noticed by that insignificant part of Delphi that lives five hundred feet under Carbondale, so excited the nurse has to make sure she eats. The circuit switches while Delphi "sleeps," that is, while P. Burke is out of the waldo cabinet. The next time she plugs in to open Delphi's eyes it's no different—do you notice which relay boards your phone calls go through?

And now for the event that turns the sugarcube from Colorado into the PRINCESS.

Literally true, he's a prince, or rather an Infante of an old Spanish line that got shined up in the Neomonarchy. He's also eighty-one, with a passion for birds—the kind you see in zoos. Now it suddenly turns out that he isn't poor at all. Quite the reverse; his old sister laughs in their tax lawyer's face and starts restoring the family hacienda while the Infante totters out to court Delphi. And little Delphi begins to live the life of the gods.

What do gods do? Well, everything beautiful. But (remember Mr. Cantle?) the main point is Things. Ever see a god empty-handed? You can't be a god without at least a magic girdle or an eight-legged horse. But in the old days some stone tablets or winged sandals or a chariot drawn by virgins would do a god for life. No more! Gods make it on novelty now. By Delphi's time the hunt for new god-gear is turning the earth and seas inside-out and sending frantic fingers to the stars. And what gods have, mortals desire.

So Delphi starts on a Euromarket shopping spree squired by her old Infante, thereby doing her bit to stave off social collapse.

Social what? Didn't you get it, when Mr. Cantle talked about a world where advertising is banned and fifteen billion consumers are glued to their holocam shows? One capricious self-powered god can wreck you.

Take the nose-filter massacre. Years, the industry sweated years to achieve an almost invisible enzymatic filter. So one day a couple of pop-gods show up wearing nose-filters like *big purple bats*. By the end of the week the world market is screaming for purple bats. Then it switched to bird-heads and skulls, but by the time the industry retooled the crazies had dropped bird-heads and gone to injection globes. Blood!

Multiply that by a million consumer industries and you can see why it's economic to have a few controllable goods. Especially with the beautiful hunk of space R&D the Peace Department laid out for, and which the taxpayers are only too glad to have taken off their hands by an outfit like GTX which everybody knows is almost a public trust.

And so you—or rather, GTX—find a creature like P. Burke and give her Delphi. And Delphi helps keep things *orderly*, she does what you tell her to. Why? That's right, Mr. Cantle never finished his speech.

But here come the tests of Delphi's button-nose twinkling in the torrent of news and entertainment. And she's noticed. The feedback shows a flock of viewers turning up the amps when this country baby gets tangled in her new colloidal body-jewels. She registers at a couple of major scenes, too, and when the Infante

gives her a suncar, little Delphi trying out suncars is a tiger.
There's a solid response in high-credit country. Mr. Cantle is
humming his happy tune as he cancels a Benelux subnet option
to guest her on a nude cook-show called Work Venus.

And now for the superposh old-world wedding! The hacienda
has Moorish baths and six-foot silver candelabra and real black
horses and the Spanish Vatican blesses them. The final event is a
grand gaucho ball with the old prince and his little Infanta on a
bowered balcony. She's a spectacular doll of silver lace, wildly
launching toy doves at her new friends whirling by below.

The Infante beams, twitches his old nose to the scent of her
sweet excitement. His doctor has been very helpful. Surely now,
after he has been so patient with the suncars and all the nonsense—

The child looks up at him, saying something incomprehensible
about "breath." He makes out that she's complaining about the
three singers she had begged for.

"They've changed!" she marvels. "Haven't they changed?
They're so dreary. I'm so happy now!"

And Delphi falls fainting against a gothic vargueno.

Her American duenna rushes up, calls help. Delphi's eyes are
open, but Delphi isn't there. The duenna pokes among Delphi's
hair, slaps her. The old prince grimaces. He has no idea what she
is beyond an excellent solution to his tax problems, but he had
been a falconer in his youth. There comes to his mind the small
pinioned birds which were flung up to stimulate the hawks. He
pockets the veined claw to which he had promised certain indul-
gences and departs to design his new aviary.

And Delphi also departs with her retinue to the Infante's
newly discovered yacht. The trouble isn't serious. It's only that
five thousand miles away and five hundred feet down P. Burke
has been doing it too well.

They've always known she has terrific aptitude. Joe says he
never saw a Remote take over so fast. No disorientations, no re-
jections. The psychomed talks about self-alienation. She's going
into Delphi like a salmon to the sea.

She isn't eating or sleeping, they can't keep her out of the
body-cabinet to get her blood moving, there are necroses under
her grisly sit-down. Crisis!

So Delphi gets a long "sleep" on the yacht and P. Burke gets it pounded through her perforated head that she's endangering Delphi. (Nurse Fleming thinks of that, thus alienating the psychomed.)

They rig a pool down there (Nurse Fleming again) and chase P. Burke back and forth. And she loves it. So naturally when they let her plug in again Delphi loves it too. Every noon beside the yacht's hydrofoils darling Delphi clips along in the blue sea they've warned her not to drink. And every night around the shoulder of the world an ill-shaped thing in a dark burrow beats its way across a sterile pool.

So presently the yacht stands up on its foils and carries Delphi to the program Mr. Cantle has waiting. It's long-range; she's scheduled for at least two decades' product life. Phase One calls for her to connect with a flock of young ultra-riches who are romping loose between Brioni and Djakarta where a competitor named PEV could pick them off.

A routine luxgear op, see; no politics, no policy angles, and the main budget items are the title and the yacht which was idle anyway. The storyline is that Delphi goes to accept some rare birds for her prince—who cares? The *point* is that the Haiti area is no longer radioactive and look!—the gods are there. And so are several new Carib West Happy Isles which can afford GTX rates, in fact two of them are GTX subsids.

But you don't want to get the idea that all these newsworthy people are wired-up robbies, for pity's sake. You don't need many if they're placed right. Delphi asks Joe about that when he comes down to Baranquilla to check her over. (P. Burke's own mouth hasn't said much for a while.)

"Are there many like me?"

"Nobody's like you, buttons. Look, are you still getting that Van Allen warble?"

"I mean, like Davy. Is he a Remote?"

(Davy is the lad who is helping her collect the birds. A sincere redhead who needs a little more exposure.)

"Davy? He's one of Matt's boys, some psychojob. They haven't any channel."

"What about the real ones? Djuma van O, or Ali, or Jim Ten?"

"Djuma was born with a pile of GTX basic where her brain

should be, she's nothing but a pain. Jimsy does what his astrologer tells him. Look, peanut, where do you get the idea you aren't real? You're the reallest. Aren't you having joy?"

"Oh, Joe!" Flinging her little arms around him and his analyzer grids. "Oh, *me gusto mucho, muchissimo!*"

"Hey, hey." He pets her yellow head, folding the analyzer.

Three thousand miles north and five hundred feet down a forgotten hulk in a body-waldo glows.

And is she having joy. To waken out of the nightmare of being P. Burke and find herself a peri, a star-girl? On a yacht in paradise with no more to do than adorn herself and play with toys and attend revels and greet her friends—her, P. Burke, having friends!—and turn the right way for the holocams? Joy!

And it shows. One look at Delphi and the viewers know: DREAMS CAN COME TRUE.

Look at her riding pillions on Davy's sea-bike, carrying an apoplectic macaw in a silver hoop. *Oh, Morton, let's go there this winter!* Or learning the Japanese chinchona from that Kobe group, in a dress that looks like a blowtorch rising from one knee, and which should sell big in Texas. *Morton, is that real fire?* Happy, happy little girl!

And Davy. He's her pet and her baby and she loves to help him fix his red-gold hair. (P. Burke marveling, running Delphi's fingers through the curls.) Of course Davy is one of Matt's boys —not impotent exactly, but very *very* low drive. (Nobody knows exactly what Matt does with his bitty budget but the boys are useful and one or two have made names.) He's perfect for Delphi; in fact the psychomed lets her take him to bed, two kittens in a basket. Davy doesn't mind the fact that Delphi "sleeps" like the dead. That's when P. Burke is out of the body-waldo up at Carbondale, attending to her own depressing needs.

A funny thing about that. Most of her sleepy-time Delphi's just a gently ticking lush little vegetable waiting for P. Burke to get back on the controls. But now and again Delphi all by herself smiles a bit or stirs in her "sleep." Once she breathed a sound: "Yes."

Under Carbondale P. Burke knows nothing. She's asleep too, dreaming of Delphi, what else? But if the bushy Dr. Tesla had heard that single syllable his bush would have turned snow-white. Because Delphi is TURNED OFF.

He doesn't. Davy is too dim to notice and Delphi's staff boss, Hopkins, wasn't monitoring.

And they've all got something else to think about now, be-cause the cold-fire dress sells half a million copies, and not only in Texas. The GTX computers already know it. When they corre-late a minor demand for macaws in Alaska the problem comes to human attention: Delphi is something special.

It's a problem, see, because Delphi is targeted on a limited consumer bracket. Now it turns out she has mass-pop potential—those macaws in *Fairbanks,* man!—it's like trying to shoot mice with an ABM. A whole new ball game. Dr. Tesla and the fa-therly Mr. Cantle start going around in headquarters circles and buddy-lunching together when they can get away from a sev-enth-level weasel boy who scares them both.

In the end it's decided to ship Delphi down to the GTX holocam enclave in Chile to try a spot on one of the mainstream shows. (Never mind why an Infanta takes up acting.) The holocam complex occupies a couple of mountains where an ob-servatory once used the clear air. Holocam total-environment shells are very expensive and electronically super-stable. Inside them actors can move freely without going off-register and the whole scene or any selected part will show up in the viewer's home in complete 3-di, so real you can look up their noses and much denser than you get from mobile rigs. You can blow a tit ten feet tall when there's no molecular skiffle around.

The enclave looks—well, take everything you know about Hollywood-Burbank and throw it away. What Delphi sees com-ing down is a neat giant mushroom-farm, domes of all sizes up to monsters for the big games and stuff. It's orderly. The idea that art thrives on creative flamboyance has long been torpedoed by proof that what art needs is computers. Because this showbiz has something TV and Hollywood never had—*automated inbuilt viewer feedback.* Samples, ratings, critics, polls? Forget it. With that carrier field you can get real-time response-sensor readouts from every receiver in the world, served up at your console. That started as a thingie to give the public more influence on content.

Yes.

Try it, man. You're at the console. Slice to the sex-age-educ-econ-ethno-cetera audience of your choice and start. You can't miss. Where the feedback warms up, give 'em more of that. Warm—warmer—*hot!* You've hit it—the secret itch under those hides, the dream in those hearts. You don't need to know its name. With your hand controlling all the input and your eye reading all the response you can make them a god . . . and somebody'll do the same for you.

But Delphi just sees rainbows, when she gets through the degaussing ports and the field relay and takes her first look at the insides of those shells. The next thing she sees is a team of shapers and technicians descending on her, and millisecond timers everywhere. The tropical leisure is finished. She's in gigabuck mainstream now, at the funnel maw of the unceasing hose that's pumping the sight and sound and flesh and blood and sobs and laughs and dreams of *reality* into the world's happy head. Little Delphi is going plonk into a zillion homes in prime time and nothing is left to chance. Work!

And again Delphi proves apt. Of course it's really P. Burke down under Carbondale who's doing it, but who remembers that carcass? Certainly not P. Burke, she hasn't spoken through her own mouth for months. Delphi doesn't even recall dreaming of her when she wakes up.

As for the show itself, don't bother. It's gone on so long no living soul could unscramble the plotline. Delphi's trial spot has something to do with a widow and her dead husband's brother's amnesia.

The flap comes after Delphi's spots begin to flash out along the world-hose and the feedback appears. You've guessed it, of course. Sensational! As you'd say, they IDENTIFY.

The report actually says something like InskinEmp with a string of percentages meaning that Delphi not only has it for anybody with a Y-chromosome, but also for women and every thing in between. It's the sweet supernatural jackpot, the million-to-one.

Remember your Harlow? A sexpot, sure. But why did bitter hausfraus in Gary and Memphis know that the vanilla-ice-cream goddess with the white hair and crazy eyebrows was *their baby girl?* And write loving letters to Jean warning her that their husbands weren't good enough for her? Why? The GTX analysts don't know either, but they know what to do with it when it happens.

(Back in his bird sanctuary the old Infante spots it without benefit of computers and gazes thoughtfully at his bride in widow's weeds. It might, he feels, be well to accelerate the completion of his studies.)

The excitement reaches down to the burrow under Carbondale where P. Burke gets two medical exams in a week and a chronically inflamed electrode is replaced. Nurse Fleming also gets an assistant who doesn't do much nursing but is very interested in access doors and identity tabs.

And in Chile little Delphi is promoted to a new home up among the stars' residential spreads and a private jitney to carry her to work. For Hopkins there's a new computer terminal and a full-time schedule man. What is the schedule crowded with?

Things.

And here begins the trouble. You probably saw that coming too.

"What does she think she is, a goddam *consumer rep?*" Mr. Cantle's fatherly face in Carbondale contorts.

"The girl's upset," Miss Fleming says stubbornly. "She *believes* that, what you told her about helping people and good new products."

"They are good products," Mr. Cantle snaps automatically, but his anger is under control. He hasn't got where he is by irrelevant reactions.

"She says the plastic gave her a rash and the glo-pills made her dizzy."

"Good god, she shouldn't swallow them," Doctor Tesla puts in agitatedly.

"You told her she'd use them," persists Miss Fleming. Mr. Cantle is busy figuring how to ease this problem to the weasel-faced young man. What, was it a goose that lays golden eggs?

Whatever he says to level Seven, down in Chile the offending products vanish. And a symbol goes into Delphi's tank matrix, one that means roughly *Balance unit resistance against PR index.* This means that Delphi's complaints will be endured as long as her Pop Response stays above a certain level. (What happens when it sinks need not concern us.) And to compensate, the price of her exposure-time rises again. She's a regular on the show now and response is still climbing.

See her under the sizzling lasers, in a holocam shell set up as a walkway accident. (The show is guesting an acupuncture school expert.)

"I don't think this new body-lift is safe," Delphi's saying. "It's made a funny blue spot on me—look, Mr. Vere."

She wiggles to show where the mini-grav pak that imparts a delicious sense of weightlessness is attached.

"So don't leave it *on*, Dee. With your meat—watch that deck-spot, it's starting to synch."

"But if I don't wear it it isn't honest. They should insulate it more or something, don't you see?"

The show's beloved old father, who is the casualty, gives a senile snigger.

"I'll tell them," Mr. Vere mutters. "Look now, as you step back bend like this so it just shows, see? And hold two beats."

Obediently Delphi turns, and through the dazzle her eyes connect with a pair of strange dark ones. She squints. A quite young man is lounging alone by the port, apparently waiting to use the chamber.

Delphi's used by now to young men looking at her with many peculiar expressions, but she isn't used to what she gets here. A jolt of something somber and knowing. *Secrets.*

"Eyes! Eyes, Dee!"

She moves through the routine, stealing peeks at the stranger. He stares back. He knows something.

When they let her go she comes shyly to him.

"Living wild, kitten." Cool voice, hot underneath.

"What do you mean?"

"Dumping on the product. You trying to get dead?"

"But it isn't right," she tells him. "They don't know, but I do, I've been wearing it."

His cool is jolted.

"You're out of your head."

"Oh, they'll see I'm right when they check it," she explains. "They're just so busy. When I tell them—"

He is staring down at little flower-face. His mouth opens,

closes. "What are you doing in this sewer anyway? Who are you?"

Bewilderedly she says, "I'm Delphi."

"Holy Zen."

"What's wrong. Who are you, please?"

Her people are moving her out now, nodding at him.

"Sorry we ran over, Mister Uhunh," the script girl says.

He mutters something but it's lost as her convoy bustles her toward the flower-decked jitney.

(Hear the click of an invisible ignition-train being armed?)

"Who was he?" Delphi asks her hair man.

The hair man is bending up and down from his knees as he works.

"Paul. Isham. Three," he says and puts a comb in his mouth.

"Who's that? I can't see."

He mumbles around the comb, meaning "Are you jiving?" Because she has to be, in the middle of the GTX enclave.

Next day there's a darkly smoldering face under a turban-towel when Delphi and the show's paraplegic go to use the carbonated pool.

She looks.

He looks.

And the next day, too.

(Hear that automatic sequencer cutting in? The system couples, the fuels begin to travel.)

Poor old Isham senior. You have to feel sorry for a man who values order: when he begets young, genetic information is still transmitted in the old ape way. One minute it's a happy midget with a rubber duck—look around and here's this huge healthy stranger, opaquely emotional, running with God knows who. Questions are heard where there's nothing to question, and eruptions claiming to be moral outrage. When this is called to Papa's attention—it may take time, in that boardroom—Papa does what he can, but without immortality-juice the problem is worrisome.

And young Paul Isham is a bear. He's bright and articulate and tender-souled and incessantly active and he and his friends are choking with appallment at the world their fathers made. And it hasn't taken Paul long to discover that *his* father's house has many mansions and even the GTX computers can't relate everything to everything else. He noses out a decaying project which adds up to something like Sponsoring Marginal Creativity (the free-lance team that "discovered" Delphi was one such grantee). And from there it turns out that an agile lad named Isham can get his hands on a viable packet of GTX holocam facilities.

So here he is with his little band, way down the mushroomfarm mountain, busily spooling a show which has no relation to Delphi's. It's built on bizarre techniques and unsettling distortions pregnant with social protest. An *underground* expression to you.

All this isn't unknown to his father, of course, but so far it has done nothing more than deepen Isham senior's apprehensive frown.

Until Paul connects with Delphi.

And by the time Papa learns this, those invisible hypergolics have exploded, the energy-shells are rushing out. For Paul, you see, is the genuine article. He's serious. He dreams. He even reads—for example, *Green Mansions*—and he wept fiercely when those fiends burned Rima alive.

When he hears that some new GTX pussy is making it big he sneers and forgets it. He's busy. He never connects the name with this little girl making her idiotic, doomed protest in the holocam chamber. This strangely simple little girl.

And she comes and looks up at him and he sees Rima, lost Rima the enchanted bird girl, and his unwired human heart goes twang.

And Rima turns out to be Delphi.

Do you need a map? The angry puzzlement. The rejection of the dissonance Rima-hustling-for-GTX-My-Father. Garbage, cannot be. The loitering around the pool to confirm the swindle . . . dark eyes hitting on blue wonder, jerky words exchanged in a peculiar stillness . . . the dreadful reorganization of the image into Rima-Delphi *in my Father's tentacles*—

You don't need a map.

Nor for Delphi either, the girl who loved her gods. She's seen their divine flesh close now, heard their unamplified voices call her name. She's played their god-games, worn their garlands. She's even become a goddess herself, though she doesn't believe it. She's not disenchanted, don't think that. She's still full of love. It's just that some crazy kind of *hope* hasn't—

Really you can skip all this, when the loving little girl on the yellow-brick road meets a Man. A real human male burning with angry compassion and grandly concerned with human justice, who reaches for her with real male arms and—boom! She loves him back with all her heart.

A happy trip, see?

Except.

Except that it's really P. Burke five thousand miles away who loves Paul. P. Burke the monster, down in a dungeon, smelling of electrode-paste. A caricature of a woman burning, melting, obsessed with true love. Trying over twenty-double-thousand miles of hard vacuum to reach her beloved through the girl-flesh numbed by an invisible film. Feeling his arms around the body he thinks is hers, fighting through shadows to give herself to him. Trying to taste and smell him through beautiful dead nostrils, to love him back with a body that goes dead in the heart of the fire.

Perhaps you get P. Burke's state of mind?

She has phases. The trying, first. And the shame. The SHAME. *I am not what thou lovest.* And the fiercer trying. And the realization that there is no, no way, none. Never. *Never.* . . . A bit delayed, isn't it, her understanding that the bargain she made was forever? P. Burke should have noticed those stories about mortals who end up as grasshoppers.

You see the outcome—the funneling of all this agony into one dumb protoplasmic drive to fuse with Delphi. To leave, to close out the beast she is chained to. *To become Delphi.*

Of course it's impossible.

However her torments have an effect on Paul. Delphi-as Rima is a potent enough love object, and liberating Delphi's mind requires hours of deeply satisfying instruction in the rottenness of it all. Add in Delphi's body worshipping his flesh, burning in the fire of P. Burke's savage heart—do you wonder Paul is involved?

That's not all.

By now they're spending every spare moment together and some that aren't so spare.

"Mister Isham, would you mind staying out of this sports sequence? The script calls for Davy here."

(Davy's still around, the exposure did him good.)

"What's the difference?" Paul yawns. "It's just an ad. I'm not
blocking that thing."

Shocked silence at his two-letter word. The script girl swallows bravely.

"I'm sorry, sir, our directive is to do the *social sequence* exactly
as scripted. We're having to respool the segments we did last
week, Mister Hopkins is very angry with me."

"Who the hell is Hopkins? Where is he?"

"Oh, please, Paul. *Please*."

Paul unwraps himself, saunters back. The holocam crew nervously check their angles. The GTX boardroom has a foible about
having things *pointed* at them and theirs. Cold shivers, when the
image of an Isham nearly went onto the world beam beside that
Dialadinner.

Worse yet. Paul has no respect for the sacred schedules which
are now a full-time job for ferret boy up at headquarters. Paul
keeps forgetting to bring her back on time and poor Hopkins
can't cope.

So pretty soon the boardroom data-ball has an urgent personal
action-tab for Mr. Isham senior. They do it the gentle way, at
first.

"I can't today, Paul."

"Why not?"

"They say I have to, it's *very* important."

He strokes the faint gold down on her narrow back. Under
Carbondale, Pa., a blind mole-woman shivers.

"Important. Their importance. Making more gold. Can't you
see? To them you're just a thing to get scratch with. A *huckster*.
Are you going to let them screw you, Dee? Are you?"

"Oh, Paul—"

He doesn't know it but he's seeing a weirdie; Remotes aren't
hooked up to flow tears.

"Just say no, Dee. No. Integrity. You have to."

"But they say, it's my job—"

"You won't believe I can take care of you, Dee, baby, baby,
you're letting them rip us. You have to choose. Tell them, no."

"Paul . . . I w-will . . ."

And she does. Brave little Delphi (insane P. Burke). Saying "No, please, I promised, Paul."

They try some more, still gently.

"Paul, Mr. Hopkins told me the reason they don't want us to be together so much. It's because of who you are, your father."

She thinks her father is like Mr. Cantle, maybe.

"Oh great. Hopkins. I'll fix him. Listen, I can't think about Hopkins now. Ken came back today, he found out something."

They are lying on the high Andes meadow watching his friends dive their singing kites.

"Would you believe, on the coast the police have *electrodes in their heads?*"

She stiffens in his arms.

"Yeah, weird. I thought they only used PPs on criminals and the army. Don't you see, Dee—something has to be going on. Some movement. Maybe somebody's organizing. How can we find out?" He pounds the ground behind her. "We should make *contact!* If we could only find out."

"The, the news?" she asks distractedly.

"The news." He laughs. "There's nothing in the news except what they want people to know. Half the country could burn up and nobody would know it if they didn't want. Dee, can't you take what I'm explaining to you? They've got the whole world programmed! Total control of communication. They've got everybody's minds wired in to think what they show them and want what they give them and they give them what they're programmed to want—you can't break in or out of it, you can't get *hold* of it anywhere. I don't think they even have a plan except to keep things going round and round—and God knows what's happening to the people or the earth or the other planets, maybe. One great big vortex of lies and garbage pouring round and round getting bigger and bigger and nothing can ever change. If people don't wake up soon we're through!"

He pounds her stomach, softly.

"You have to break out, Dee."

"I'll try, Paul, I will—"

"You're mine. They can't have you."

And he goes to see Hopkins, who is indeed cowed.

But that night up under Carbondale the fatherly Mr. Cantle goes to see P. Burke.

P. Burke? On a cot in a utility robe like a dead camel in a tent, she cannot at first comprehend that he is telling *her* to break it off with Paul. P. Burke has never seen Paul. *Delphi* sees Paul. The fact is, P. Burke can no longer clearly recall that she exists apart from Delphi.

Mr. Cantle can scarcely believe it either but he tries.

He points out the futility, the potential embarrassment for Paul. That gets a dim stare from the bulk on the bed. Then he goes into her duty to GTX, her job, isn't she grateful for the opportunity, etcetera. He's very persuasive.

The cobwebby mouth of P. Burke opens and croaks.

"No."

Nothing more seems to be forthcoming.

Mr. Cantle isn't dense, he knows an immovable obstacle when he bumps one. He also knows an irresistible force: GTX. The simple solution is to lock the waldo-cabinet until Paul gets tired of waiting for Delphi to wake up. But the cost, the schedules! And there's something odd here . . . he eyes the corporate asset hulking on the bed and his hunch-sense prickles.

You see, Remotes don't love. They don't have real sex, the circuits designed that out from the start. So it's been assumed that it's *Paul* who is diverting himself or something with the pretty little body in Chile. P. Burke can only be doing what comes natural to any ambitious gutter-meat. It hasn't occurred to anyone that they're dealing with the real hairy thing whose shadow is blasting out of every holoshow on earth.

Love?

Mr. Cantle frowns. The idea is grotesque. But his instinct for the fuzzy line is strong; he will recommend flexibility.

And so, in Chile:

"Darling, I don't have to work tonight! And Friday too—isn't that right, Mr. Hopkins?"

"Oh, great. When does she come up for parole?"

"Mr. Isham, please be reasonable. Our schedule—surely your own production people must be needing you?"

This happens to be true. Paul goes away. Hopkins stares after him wondering distastefully why an Isham wants to ball a waldo. (How sound are those boardroom belly-fears—garble creeps, creeps in!) It never occurs to Hopkins that an Isham might not know what Delphi is.

Especially with Davy crying because Paul has kicked him out of Delphi's bed.

Delphi's bed is under a real window.

"Stars," Paul says sleepily. He rolls over, pulling Delphi on top. "Are you aware that this is one of the last places on earth where people can see the stars? Tibet, too, maybe."

"Paul . . ."

"Go to sleep. I want to see you sleep."

"Paul, I . . . I sleep so *hard,* I mean, it's a joke how hard I am to wake up. Do you mind?"

"Yes."

But finally, fearfully, she must let go. So that five thousand miles north a crazy spent creature can crawl out to gulp concentrates and fall on her cot. But not for long. It's pink dawn when Delphi's eyes open to find Paul's arms around her, his voice saying rude, tender things. He's been kept awake. The nerveless little statue that was her Delphi-body nuzzled him in the night.

Insane hope rises, is fed a couple of nights later when he tells her she called his name in her sleep.

And that day Paul's arms keep her from work and Hopkins' wails go up to headquarters where the sharp-faced lad is working his sharp tailbone off packing Delphi's program. Mr. Cantle defuses that one. But next week it happens again, to a major client. And ferret-face has connections on the technical side.

Now you can see that when you have a field of complexly heterodyned energy modulations tuned to a demand-point like Delphi there are many problems of standwaves and lashback and skiffle of all sorts which are normally balanced out with ease by the technology of the future. By the same token they can be delicately unbalanced too, in ways that feed back into the waldo operator with striking results.

"Darling—what the hell! What's wrong? DELPHI!"

Helpless shrieks, writhings. Then the Rima-bird is lying wet and limp in his arms, her eyes enormous.

"I . . . I wasn't supposed to . . ." she gasps faintly. "They told me not to . . ."

"Oh my god—*Delphi*."

And his hard fingers are digging in her thick yellow hair. Electronically knowledgeable fingers. They freeze.

"You're a *doll!* You're one of those. PP implants. They control you. I should have known. Oh God, I should have known."

"No, Paul," she's sobbing. "No, no, no—"

"Damn them. Damn them, what they've done—you're not *you*—"

He's shaking her, crouching over her in the bed and jerking her back and forth, glaring at the pitiful beauty.

"No!" She pleads (it's not true, that dark bad dream back there). "I'm Delphi!"

"My father. Filth, pigs—damn them, damn them, damn them."

"No, no," she babbles. "They were good to me—" P. Burke underground mouthing, "They were good to me—AAH-AAAAH!"

Another agony skewers her. Up north the sharp young man wants to make sure this so-tiny interference works. Paul can scarcely hang onto her, he's crying too. "I'll kill them."

His Dephi, a wired-up slave! Spikes in her brain, electronic shackles in his bird's heart. Remember when those savages burned Rima alive?

"I'll *kill* the man that's doing this to you."

He's still saying it afterward but she doesn't hear. She's sure he hates her now, all she wants is to die. When she finally understands that the fierceness is tenderness she thinks it's a miracle. *He knows—and he still loves!*

How can she guess that he's got it a little bit wrong?

You can't blame Paul. Give him credit that he's even heard about pleasure-pain implants and snoops, which by their nature aren't mentioned much by those who know them most intimately. That's what he thinks is being used on Delphi, something to *control* her. And to listen—he burns at the unknown ears in their bed.

Of waldo-bodies and objects like P. Burke he has heard nothing.

So it never crosses his mind as he looks down at his violated bird, sick with fury and love, that he isn't holding *all* of her. Do you need to be told the mad resolve jelling in him now?

To free Delphi.

How? Well, he is after all Paul Isham III. And he even has an idea where the GTX neurolab is. In Carbondale.

But first things have to be done for Delphi, and for his own stomach. So he gives her back to Hopkins and departs in a restrained and discreet way. And the Chile staff is grateful and do not understand that his teeth don't normally show so much.

And a week passes in which Delphi is a very good, docile little ghost. They let her have the load of wildflowers Paul sends and the bland loving notes. (He's playing it coony.) And up in headquarters weasel boy feels that *his* destiny has clicked a notch onward and floats the word up that he's handy with little problems.

And no one knows what P. Burke thinks in any way whatever, except that Miss Fleming catches her flushing her food down the can and next night she faints in the pool. They haul her out and stick her with IVs. Miss Fleming frets, she's seen expressions like that before. But she wasn't around when crazies who called themselves Followers of the Fish looked through flames to life everlasting. P. Burke is seeing Heaven on the far side of death, too. Heaven is spelled P-a-u-l, but the idea's the same. *I will die and be born again in Delphi.*

Garbage, electronically speaking. No way.

Another week and Paul's madness has become a plan. (Remember, he does have friends.) He smolders, watching his love paraded by her masters. He turns out a scorching sequence for his own show. And finally, politely, he requests from Hopkins a morsel of his bird's free time, which duly arrives.

"I thought you didn't *want* me any more," she's repeating as they wing over mountain flanks in Paul's suncar. "Now you *know—*"

"Look at me!"

His hand covers her mouth and he's showing her a lettered card.

DON'T TALK THEY CAN HEAR EVERYTHING WE SAY.
I'M TAKING YOU AWAY NOW.

She kisses his hand. He nods urgently, flipping the card.

DON'T BE AFRAID. I CAN STOP THE PAIN IF THEY TRY TO HURT YOU.

With his free hand he shakes out a silvery scrambler-mesh on a power pack. She is dumfounded.

THIS WILL CUT THE SIGNALS AND PROTECT YOU
DARLING.

She's staring at him, her head going vaguely from side to side,
No.

"Yes!" He grins triumphantly. "Yes!"

For a moment she wonders. That powered mesh will cut
off the field, all right. It will also cut off Delphi. But he is *Paul*.
Paul is kissing her, she can only seek him hungrily as he sweeps
the suncar through a pass.

Ahead is an old jet ramp with a shiny bullet waiting to go.
(Paul also has credits and a Name.) The little GTX patrol
courier is built for nothing but speed. Paul and Delphi wedge in
behind the pilot's extra fuel tank and there's no more talking
when the torches start to scream.

They're screaming high over Quito before Hopkins starts to
worry. He wastes another hour tracking the beeper on Paul's
suncar. The suncar is sailing a pattern out to sea. By the time
they're sure it's empty and Hopkins gets on the hot flue to headquarters the fugitives are a sourceless howl about Carib West.

Up at headquarters weasel boy gets the squeal. His first impulse is to repeat his previous play but then his brain snaps to.
This one is too hot. Because, see, although in the long run they
can make P. Burke do anything at all except maybe *live*, instant
emergencies can be tricky. And—Paul Isham III.

"Can't you order her back?"

They're all in the GTX tower monitor station, Mr. Cantle and
ferret-face and Joe and a very neat man who is Mr. Isham senior's personal eyes and ears.

"No sir," Joe says doggedly. "We can read channels, particularly speech, but we can't interpolate organized patterns. It takes
the waldo op to send one-to-one—"

"What are they saying?"

"Nothing at the moment, sir." The console jockey's eyes are
closed. "I believe they are, ah, embracing."

"They're not answering," a traffic monitor says. "Still heading
zero zero three zero—due north, sir."

"You're certain Kennedy is alerted not to fire on them?" the
neat man asks anxiously.

"Yes sir."

"Can't you just turn her off?" The sharp-faced lad is angry. "Pull that pig out of the controls!"

"If you cut the transmission cold you'll kill the Remote," Joe explains for the third time. "Withdrawal has to be phased right, you have to fade over to the Remote's own autonomics. Heart, breathing, cerebellum would go blooey. If you pull Burke out you'll probably finish her too. It's a fantastic cybersystem, you don't want to do that."

"The investment." Mr. Cantle shudders.

Weasel boy puts his hand on the console jock's shoulder, it's the contact who arranged the No-no effect for him.

"We can at least give them a warning signal, sir." He licks his lips, gives the neat man his sweet ferret smile. "We know that does no damage."

Joe frowns, Mr. Cantle sighs. The neat man is murmuring into his wrist. He looks up. "I am authorized," he says reverently, "I am authorized to, ah, direct a signal. If this is the only course. But minimal, minimal."

Sharp-face squeezes his man's shoulder.

In the silver bullet shrieking over Charleston Paul feels Delphi arch in his arms. He reaches for the mesh, hot for action. She thrashes, pushing at his hands, her eyes roll. She's afraid of that mesh despite the agony. (And she's right.) Frantically Paul fights her in the cramped space, gets it over her head. As he turns the power up she burrows free under his arm and the spasm fades.

"They're calling you again, Mister Isham!" the pilot yells.

"Don't answer. Darling, keep this over your head damn it how can I—"

An AX90 barrels over their nose, there's a flash.

"Mister Isham! Those are Air Force jets!"

"Forget it," Paul shouts back. "They won't fire. Darling, don't be afraid."

Another AX90 rocks them.

"Would you mind pointing your pistol at my head where they can see it, sir?" the pilot howls.

Paul does so. The AX90s take up escort formation around them. The pilot goes back to figuring how he can collect from GTX too, and after Goldsboro AB the escort peels away.

"Holding the same course," Traffic is reporting to the group around the monitor. "Apparently they've taken on enough fuel to bring them to towerport here."

"In that case it's just a question of waiting for them to dock." Mr. Cantle's fatherly manner revives a bit.

"Why can't they cut off that damn freak's life-support," the sharp young man fumes. "It's ridiculous."

"They're working on it," Cantle assures him.

What they're doing, down under Carbondale, is arguing.

Miss Fleming's watchdog has summoned the bushy man to the waldo room.

"Miss Fleming, you will obey orders."

"You'll kill her if you try that, sir. I can't believe you meant it, that's why I didn't. We've already fed her enough sedative to affect heart action; if you cut any more oxygen she'll die in there."

The bushy man grimaces. "Get Doctor Quine here fast."

They wait, staring at the cabinet in which a drugged, ugly madwoman fights for consciousness, fights to hold Delphi's eyes open.

High over Richmond the silver pod starts a turn. Delphi is sagged into Paul's arm, her eyes swim up to him.

"Starting down now, baby. It'll be over soon, all you have to do is stay alive, Dee."

". . . Stay alive . . ."

The traffic monitor has caught them. "Sir! They've turned off for Carbondale—Control has contact—"

"Let's go."

But the headquarters posse is too late to intercept the courier wailing into Carbondale. And Paul's friends have come through again. The fugitives are out through the freight dock and into the neurolab admin port before the guard gets organized. At the elevator Paul's face plus his handgun get them in.

"I want Doctor—what's his name, Dee? Dee!"

". . . Tesla . . ." She's reeling on her feet.

"Doctor Tesla. Take me down to Tesla, fast."

Intercoms are squalling around them as they whoosh down, Paul's pistol in the guard's back. When the door slides open the bushy man is there.

"I'm Tesla."

"I'm Paul Isham. *Isham.* You're going to take your flaming implants out of this girl—now. Move!"

"What?"

"You heard me. Where's your operating room? Go!"

"But—"

"Move! Do I have to burn somebody?"

Paul waves the weapon at Dr. Quine, who has just appeared.

"No, no," says Tesla hurriedly. "But I can't, you know. It's impossible, there'll be nothing left."

"You screaming well can, right now. You mess up and I'll kill you," says Paul murderously. "Where is it, there? And wipe the feke that's on her circuits now."

He's backing them down the hall, Delphi heavy on his arm.

"Is this the place, baby? Where they did it to you?"

"Yes," she whispers, blinking at a door. "Yes . . ."

Because it is, see. Behind that door is the very suite where she was born.

Paul herds them through it into a gleaming hall. An inner door opens and a nurse and a gray man rush out. And freeze.

Paul sees there's something special about that inner door. He crowds them past it and pushes it open and looks in.

Inside is a big mean-looking cabinet with its front door panels ajar.

And inside that cabinet is a poisoned carcass to whom something wonderful, unspeakable, is happening. Inside is P. Burke the real living woman who knows that HE is there, coming closer —Paul whom she had fought to reach through forty thousand miles of ice—PAUL is here!—is yanking at the waldo doors—

The doors tear open and a monster rises up.

"Paul darling!" croaks the voice of love and the arms of love reach for him.

And he responds.

Wouldn't you, if a gaunt she-golem flab-naked and spouting wires and blood came at you clawing with metal studded paws—

"Get away!" He knocks wires.

It doesn't much matter which wires, P. Burke has so to speak her nervous system hanging out. Imagine somebody jerking a handful of your medulla—

She crashes onto the floor at his feet, flopping and roaring "*PAUL-PAUL-PAUL*" in rictus.

It's doubtful he recognizes his name or sees her life coming out of her eyes at him. And at the last it doesn't go to him. The eyes find Delphi, fainting by the doorway, and die.

Now of course Delphi is dead, too.

There's total silence as Paul steps away from the thing by his foot.

"You killed her," Tesla says. "That was her."

"Your control." Paul is furious, the thought of that monster fastened into little Delphi's brain nauseates him. He sees her crumpling and holds out his arms. Not knowing she is dead.

And Delphi comes to him.

One foot before the other, not moving very well—but moving. Her darling face turns up. Paul is distracted by the terrible quiet, and when he looks down he sees only her tender little neck.

"Now you get the implants out," he warns them. Nobody moves.

"But, she's dead," Miss Fleming whispers wildly.

Paul feels Delphi's life under his hand, they're talking about their monster. He aims his pistol at the gray man.

"You. If we aren't in your surgery when I count three I'm burning off this man's leg."

"Mr. Isham," Tesla says desperately, "you have just killed the person who animated the body you call Delphi. Delphi herself is dead. If you release your arm you'll see what I say is true."

The tone gets through. Slowly Paul opens his arm, looks down.

"Delphi?"

She totters, sways, stays upright. Her face comes slowly up.

"Paul . . ." Tiny voice.

"Your crotty tricks," Paul snarls at them. "*Move!*"

"Look at her eyes," Dr. Quine croaks.

They look. One of Delphi's pupils fills the iris, her lips writhe weirdly.

"Shock." Paul grabs her to him. "*Fix* her!" He yells at them, aiming at Tesla.

"For God's sake . . . bring it in the lab." Tesla quavers.

"Goodbye-bye," says Delphi clearly. They lurch down the hall, Paul carrying her, and meet a wave of people.

Headquarters has arrived.

Joe takes one look and dives for the waldo room, running into Paul's gun.

"Oh no, you don't."

Everybody is yelling. The little thing in his arm stirs, says plaintively, "I'm Delphi."

And all through the ensuing jabber and ranting she hangs on, keeps it up, the ghost of P. Burke or whatever whispering crazily, "Paul . . . Paul . . . Please, I'm Delphi . . . Paul?"

"I'm here, darling, I'm here." He's holding her in the nursing bed. Tesla talks, talks, talks unheard.

"Paul . . . don't sleep . . ." the ghost-voice whispers. Paul is in agony, he will not accept, WILL NOT believe.

Tesla runs down.

And then near midnight Delphi says roughly, "Ag-ag-ag—" and slips onto the floor, making a rough noise like a seal.

Paul screams. There's more of the *ag-ag* business and more gruesome convulsive disintegrations, until by two in the morning Delphi is nothing but a warm little bundle of vegetative functions hitched to some expensive hardware—the same that sustained her before her life began. Joe has finally persuaded Paul to let him at the waldo-cabinet. Paul stays by her long enough to see her face change in a dreadfully alien and coldly convincing way, and then he stumbles out bleakly through the group in Tesla's office.

Behind him Joe is working wet-faced, sweating to reintegrate the fantastic complex of circulation, respiration, endocrines, midbrain homeostases, the patterned flux that was a human being— it's like saving an orchestra abandoned in midair. Joe is also crying a little; he alone had truly loved P. Burke. P. Burke, now a dead pile on a table, was the greatest cybersystem he has ever known, and he never forgets her.

The end, really.

You're curious?

Sure, Delphi lives again. Next year she's back on the yacht getting sympathy for her tragic breakdown. But there's a different chick in Chile, because while Delphi's new operator is competent, you don't get two P. Burkes in a row—for which GTX is duly grateful.

The real belly-bomb of course is Paul. He was *young*, see. Fighting abstract wrong. Now life has clawed into him and he goes through gut rage and grief and grows in human wisdom and resolve. So much so that you won't be surprised, some time later, to find him—where?

In the GTX boardroom, dummy. Using the advantage of his birth to radicalize the system. You'd call it "boring from within."

That's how he put it, and his friends couldn't agree more. It gives them a warm, confident feeling to know that Paul is up there. Sometimes one of them who's still around runs into him and gets a big hello.

And the sharp-faced lad?

Oh, he matures too. He learns fast, believe it. For instance, he's the first to learn that an obscure GTX research unit is actually getting something with their loopy temporal anomalizer project. True, he doesn't have a physics background, and he's bugged quite a few people. But he doesn't really learn about that until the day he stands where somebody points him during a test run—and wakes up lying on a newspaper headlined NIXON UNVEILS PHASE TWO.

Lucky he's a fast learner.

Believe it, zombie. When I say growth I mean *growth*. Capital appreciation. You can stop sweating. There's a great future there.

Harlan Ellison

Here's Harlan. We can't have a Hugo winners volume without Harlan, can we?

There seems to be an odd feeling about Harlan and me. A lot of the readers think we are annoyed with each other. Nothing can be further from the truth. We love each other.

It's just that neither can resist the other's physiognomy. I can't resist short and he can't resist plump. So we each talk about our irresistibles in the other's presence. It's a harmless little hobby we have, and we both laugh very heartily about it.

For instance, earlier this year I introduced Harlan at a Manhattan hall where he was going to read a couple of his stories (and if you haven't heard him read his stories, you're missing something great—good as he is as a writer, he's even better as a reader). As I stood up to perform the introduction, with a smile of Judeo-Christian benevolence on my face, I heard him mutter behind me, "Here comes a short joke."

How could he think that of me? Nothing like that had ever entered my mind. It was my every intention to comment on his rangy build and his loose-limbed lankiness. Of course, however, he set me off. I couldn't help it. I told of the festivities at Harlan's birth and how every fairy in the land had been invited, all except the wicked fairy, Diabola, who had been overlooked by accident. At the height of the celebration she appeared in a swirl of sulfur fumes, stood over the crib of Baby Harlan, and said, "All right, you rotten creep, you have a choice—talent or tall."

Would I have said that if he hadn't put short jokes into my head? Of course not.

But we have to end our little game. It's gotten away from us. You see, no one can go fifteen rounds of insult with Harlan, except me. (He goes easy on me out of love.) One of the games at conventions is to have us get up on the stage and give each other the Don Rickles treatment. And we did that at the thirty-second convention at Washington. Each of us was on a separate platform with four thousand people in between us and we proceeded to make unflattering comments about each other.

No, I guess it wasn't a dignified and conservative thing to do. Worse yet, the sulfur fumes of the wicked fairy, Diabola, got into Harlan in his crib, and he is very apt to use sulfurous language, and he did on this occasion.

What we didn't know was that there was a newspaperman on the scene, and he was horrified. He had never *heard* language like that. He had a little girl who sat next to him translate some of the expressions and he blushed furiously. Well, it got written up in the paper, and Harlan and I agreed that the conventions just weren't private enough any more and we quit.

Too bad. The world is getting old.

THE DEATHBIRD

1

This is a test. Take notes. This will count as three fourths of your final grade. Hints: remember, in chess, kings cancel each other out and cannot occupy adjacent squares, are therefore all-powful and totally powerless, cannot affect one another, produce stalemate. Hinduism is a polytheistic religion; the sect of Atman worships the divine spark of life within Man; in effect saying, "Thou art God." Provisos of equal time are not served by one viewpoint having media access to two hundred million people in prime time while opposing viewpoints are provided with a soapbox on the corner. Not everyone tells the truth. Operational note: these sections may be taken out of numerical sequence: rearrange to suit yourself for optimum clarity. Turn over your test papers and begin.

2

Uncounted layers of rock pressed down on the magma pool. White-hot with the bubbling ferocity of the molten nickel-iron core, the pool spat and shuddered, yet did not pit or char or smoke or damage in the slightest the smooth and reflective surfaces of the strange crypt.

Nathan Stack lay in the crypt—silent, sleeping.

A shadow passed through rock. Through shale, through coal, through marble, through mica schist, through quartzite; through miles-thick deposits of phosphates, through diatomaceous earth, through feldspars, though diorite; through faults and folds, through anticlines and monoclines, through dips and synclines;

through hellfire; and came to the ceiling of the great cavern and passed through; and saw the magma pool and dropped down; and came to the crypt. The shadow.

A triangular face with a single eye peered into the crypt, saw Stack, and laid four-fingered hands on the crypt's cool surface. Nathan Stack woke at the touch, and the crypt became transparent; he woke though the touch had not been upon his body. His soul felt the shadowy pressure and he opened his eyes to see the leaping brilliance of the world-core around him, to see the shadow with its single eye staring in at him.

The serpentine shadow enfolded the crypt; its darkness flowed upward again, through the Earth's mantle, toward the crust, toward the surface of the cinder, the broken toy that was the Earth.

When they reached the surface, the shadow bore the crypt to a place where the poison winds did not reach, and caused it to open.

Nathan Stack tried to move, and moved only with difficulty. Memories rushed through his head of other lives, many other lives, as many other men; then the memories slowed and melted into a background tone that could be ignored.

The shadow thing reached down a hand and touched Stack's naked flesh. Gently, but firmly, the thing helped him to stand, and gave him garments, and a neck-pouch that contained a short knife and a warming-stone and other things. He offered his hand, and Stack took it, and after two hundred and fifty thousand years sleeping in the crypt, Nathan Stack stepped out on the face of the sick planet Earth.

Then the thing bent low against the poison winds and began walking away. Nathan Stack, having no other choice, bent forward and followed the shadow creature.

3

A messenger had been sent for Dira and he had come as quickly as the meditations would permit. When he reached the Summit, he found the fathers waiting, and they took him gently into their cove, where they immersed themselves and began to speak.

"We've lost the arbitration," the coil-father said. "It will be necessary for us to go and leave it to him."

Dira could not believe it. "But didn't they listen to our arguments, to our logic?"

The fang-father shook his head sadly and touched Dira's shoulder. "There were . . . accommodations to be made. It was their time. So we must leave."

The coil-father said, "We've decided you will remain. One was permitted, in caretakership. Will you accept our commission?"

It was a very great honor but Dira began to feel the loneliness even as they told him they would leave. Yet he accepted. Wondering why they had selected *him*, of all their people. There were reasons, there were always reasons, but he could not ask. And so he accepted the honor, with all its attendant sadness, and remained behind when they left.

The limits of his caretakership were harsh, for they insured he could not defend himself against whatever slurs or legends would be spread, nor could he take action unless it became clear the trust was being breached by the other—who now held possession. And he had no threat save the Deathbird. A final threat that could be used only when final measures were needed; and therefore too late.

But he was patient. Perhaps the most patient of all his people.

Thousands of years later, when he saw how it was destined to go, when there was no doubt left how it would end, he understood *that* was the reason he had been chosen to stay behind.

But it did not help the loneliness.

Nor could it save the Earth. Only Stack could do that.

4

1 *Now the serpent was more subtil than any beast of the field which the LORD God had made. And he said unto the woman, Yea, hath God said, Ye shall not eat of every tree of the garden?*

2 *And the woman said unto the serpent, We may eat of the fruit of the trees of the garden:*

3 *But of the fruit of the tree which is in the midst of the garden, God hath said, Ye shall not eat of it, neither shall ye touch it, lest ye die.*

4 *And the serpent said unto the woman, Ye shall not surely die:*

5 *(Omitted)*

6 *And when the woman saw that the tree was good for food, and that it was pleasant to the eyes, and a tree to be desired to make one wise, she took of the fruit thereof, and did eat, and gave also unto her husband with her; and he did eat.*

7 *(Omitted)*

8 *(Omitted)*

9 *And the LORD God called unto Adam, and said unto him, Where art thou?*

10 *(Omitted)*

11 *And he said, Who told thee that thou wast naked? Hast thou eaten of the tree, whereof I commanded thee that thou shouldst not eat?*

12 *And the man said, The woman whom thou gavest to be with me, she gave me of the tree, and I did eat.*

13 *And the LORD God said unto the woman, What is this that thou hast done? And the woman said, The serpent beguiled me, and I did eat.*

14 *And the LORD God said unto the serpent, Because thou hast done this, thou art cursed above all cattle, and above every beast of the field; upon thy belly shalt thou go, and dust shalt thou eat all the days of thy life:*

15 *And I will put enmity between thee and the woman, and between thy seed and her seed; it shall bruise thy head, and thou shalt bruise his heel.*

GENESIS——3:1–15

TOPICS FOR DISCUSSION

(Give 5 points per right answer.)

1. Melville's *Moby Dick* begins, "Call me Ishmael." We say it is told in the *first* person. In what person is Genesis told? From whose viewpoint?

2. Who is the "good guy" in this story? Who is the "bad guy"? Can you make a strong case for reversal of the roles?

3. Traditionally, the apple is considered to be the fruit the serpent offered to Eve. But apples are not endemic to the Near East. Select one of the following, more logical substitutes, and discuss how myths come into being and are corrupted over long periods of time: olive, fig, date, pomegranate.

4. Why is the word LORD always in capitals and the name God always capitalized? Shouldn't the serpent's name be capitalized, as well? If no, why?

5. If God created everything (see *Genesis*, Chap. I), why did he create problems for himself by creating a serpent who would lead his creations astray? Why did God create a tree he did not want Adam and Eve to know about, and then go out of his way to warn them against it?

6. Compare and contrast Michelangelo's Sistine Chapel ceiling panel of the *Expulsion from Paradise* with Bosch's *Garden of Earthly Delights*.

7. Was Adam being a gentleman when he placed blame on Eve? Who was Quisling? Discuss "narking" as a character flaw.

8. God grew angry when he found out he had been defied. If God is omnipotent and omniscient, didn't he know? Why couldn't he find Adam and Eve when they hid?

9. If God had not wanted Adam and Eve to taste the fruit of the forbidden tree, why didn't he warn the serpent? Could God have prevented the serpent from tempting Adam and Eve? If yes, why didn't he? If no, discuss the possibility the serpent was as powerful as God.

10. Using examples from two different media journals, demonstrate the concept of "slanted news."

5

The poison winds howled and tore at the powder covering the land. Nothing lived there. The winds, green and deadly, dived out of the sky and raked the carcass of the Earth, seeking, seeking: anything moving, anything still living. But there was nothing. Powder. Talc. Pumice.

And the onyx spire of the mountain toward which Nathan Stack and the shadow thing had moved, all that first day. When night fell they dug a pit in the tundra and the shadow thing coated it with a substance thick as glue that had been in Stack's neck-pouch. Stack had slept the night fitfully, clutching the warming-stone to his chest and breathing through a filter tube from the pouch.

Once he had awakened, at the sound of great batlike creatures flying overhead; he had seen them swooping low, coming in flat trajectories across the wasteland toward his pit in the earth. But they seemed unaware that he—and the shadow thing—lay in the hole. They defecated thin, phosphorescent stringers that fell glowing through the night and were lost on the plains; then the creatures swooped upward and were whirled away on the winds. Stack resumed sleeping with difficulty.

In the morning, frosted with an icy light that gave everything a blue tinge, the shadow thing scrabbled its way out of the choking powder and crawled along the ground, then lay flat, fingers clawing for purchase in the whiskaway surface. Behind it, from the powder, Stack bore toward the surface, reached up a hand and trembled for help.

The shadow creature slid across the ground, fighting the winds that had grown stronger in the night, back to the soft place that had been their pit, to the hand thrust up through the powder. It grasped the hand, and Stack's fingers tightened convulsively. Then the crawling shadow exerted pressure and pulled the man from the treacherous pumice.

Together they lay against the earth, fighting to see, fighting to draw breath without filling their lungs with suffocating death.

"Why is it like this . . . what *happened?*" Stack screamed against the wind. The shadow creature did not answer, but it looked at Stack for a long moment and then, with very careful movements, raised its hand, held it up before Stack's eyes and slowly, making claws of the fingers, closed the four fingers into a cage, into a fist, into a painfully tight ball that said more eloquently than words: *destruction.*

Then they began to crawl toward the mountain.

6

The onyx spire of the mountain rose out of hell and struggled toward the shredded sky. It was monstrous arrogance. Nothing should have tried that climb out of desolation. But the black mountain had tried, and succeeded.

It was like an old man. Seamed, ancient, dirt caked in striated lines, autumnal, lonely; black and desolate, piled strength upon strength. It would *not* give in to gravity and pressure and death. It struggled for the sky. Ferociously alone, it was the only feature that broke the desolate line of the horizon.

In another twenty-five million years the mountain might be worn as smooth and featureless as a tiny onyx offering to the deity night. But though the powder plains swirled and the poison winds drove the pumice against the flanks of the pinnacle, thus far their scouring had only served to soften the edges of the mountain's profile, as though divine intervention had protected the spire.

Lights moved near the summit.

7

Stack learned the nature of the phosphorescent strings excreted onto the plain the night before by the batlike creatures. They were spores that became, in the wan light of day, strange bleeder plants.

All around them as they crawled through the dawn, the little live things sensed their warmth and began thrusting shoots up through the talc. As the fading red ember of the dying sun climbed painfully into the sky, the bleeding plants were already reaching maturity.

Stack cried out as one of the vine tentacles fastened around his ankle, holding him. A second looped itself around his neck.

Thin films of berry-black blood coated the vines, leaving rings on Stack's flesh. The rings burned terribly.

The shadow creature slid on its belly and pulled itself back to the man. Its triangular head came close to Stack's neck, and it bit into the vine. Thick black blood spurted as the vine parted, and the shadow creature rasped its razor-edged teeth back and forth till Stack was able to breathe again. With a violent movement Stack folded himself down and around, pulling the short knife from the neck-pouch. He sawed through the vine tightening inexorably around his ankle. It screamed as it was severed, in the same voice Stack had heard from the skies the night before. The severed vine writhed away, withdrawing into the talc.

Stack and the shadow thing crawled forward once again, low, flat, holding onto the dying earth: toward the mountain. High in the bloody sky, the Deathbird circled.

8

On their own world, they had lived in luminous, oily-walled caverns for millions of years, evolving and spreading their race through the universe. When they had had enough of empire-building, they turned inward, and much of their time was spent in the intricate construction of songs of wisdom, and the designing of fine worlds for many races.

There were other races that designed, however. And when there was a conflict over jurisdiction, an arbitration was called, adjudicated by a race whose *raison d'être* was impartiality and cleverness in unraveling knotted threads of claim and counter-claim. Their racial honor, in fact, depended on the flawless application of these qualities. Through the centuries they had refined their talents in more and more sophisticated arenas of arbitration until the time came when they were the final authority. The litigants were compelled to abide by the judgments, not merely because the decisions were always wise and creatively fair, but because the judges' race would, if its decisions were questioned as suspect, destroy itself. In the holiest place on their world they had erected a religious machine. It could be activated to emit a tone that would shatter their crystal carapaces. They were a race of exquisite cricket-like creatures, no larger than the thumb of a man. They were treasured throughout the civilized worlds, and their loss would have been catastrophic. Their honor and their value were never questioned. All races abided by their decisions.

So Dira's people gave over jurisdiction to that certain world, and went away, leaving Dira with only the Deathbird, a special caretakership the adjudicators had creatively woven into their judgment.

There is recorded one last meeting between Dira and those who had given him his commission. There were readings that could not be ignored—had, in fact, been urgently brought to the attention of the fathers of Dira's race by the adjudicators—and the Great Coiled One came to Dira at the last possible moment to tell him of the mad thing into whose hands this world had been given, to tell Dira of what the mad thing could do.

The Great Coiled One—whose rings were loops of wisdom acquired through centuries of gentleness and perception and immersed meditations that had brought forth lovely designs for many worlds—he who was the holiest of Dira's race, honored Dira by coming to *him*, rather than commanding Dira to appear.

We have only one gift to leave them, he said. *Wisdom. This mad one will come, and he will lie to them, and he will tell them: created he them. And we will be gone, and there will be nothing between them and the mad one but you. Only you can give them the wisdom to defeat him in their own good time.* Then the Great Coiled One stroked the skin of Dira with ritual affection, and Dira was deeply moved and could not reply. Then he was left alone.

The mad one came, and interposed himself, and Dira gave them wisdom, and time passed. His name became other than Dira, it became Snake, and the new name was despised: but Dira could see the Great Coiled One had been correct in his readings. So Dira made his selection. A man, one of them, and gifted him with the spark.

All of this is recorded somewhere. It is history.

9

The man was not Jesus of Nazareth. He may have been Simon. Not Genghis Khan, but perhaps a foot soldier in his horde. Not

Aristotle, but possibly one who sat and listened to Socrates in the
agora. Neither the shambler who discovered the wheel nor the
link who first ceased painting himself blue and applied the colors
to the walls of the cave. But one near them, somewhere near at
hand. The man was not Richard *Coeur de Lion,* Rembrandt,
Richelieu, Rasputin, Robert Fulton or the Mahdi. Just a man.
With the spark.

10

Once, Dira came to the man. Very early on. The spark was
there, but the light needed to be converted to energy. So Dira
came to the man, and did what had to be done before the mad
one knew of it, and when the mad one discovered that Dira,
the Snake, had made contact, he quickly made explanations.

This legend has come down to us as the fable of *Faust.*

TRUE or FALSE?

11

Light converted to energy, thus:

In the fortieth year of his five hundredth incarnation, all-un-
knowing of the eons of which he had been part, the man found
himself wandering in a terrible dry place under a thin, flat burning disc of sun. He was a Berber tribesman who had never considered shadows save to relish them when they provided shade.
The shadow came to him, sweeping down across the sands like
the *khamsin* of Egypt, the *simoom* of Asia Minor, the *harmattan,*
all of which he had known in his various lives, none of which he
remembered. The shadow came over him like the *sirocco.*

The shadow stole the breath from his lungs and the man's eyes
rolled up in his head. He fell to the ground and the shadow took
him down and down, through the sands, into the Earth.

Mother Earth.

She lived, this world of trees and rivers and rocks with deep
stone thoughts. She breathed, had feelings, dreamed dreams,

gave birth, laughed and grew contemplative for millennia. This great creature swimming in the sea of space.

What a wonder, thought the man, for he had never understood that the Earth was his mother, before this. He had never understood, before this, that the Earth had a life of its own, at once a part of mankind and quite separate from mankind. A mother with a life of her own.

Dira, Snake, shadow . . . took the man down and let the spark of light change itself to energy as the man became one with the Earth. His flesh melted, and became quiet, cool soil. His eyes glowed with the light that shines in the darkest centers of the planet and he saw the way the mother cared for her young: the worms, the roots of plants, the rivers that cascaded for miles over great cliffs in enormous caverns, the bark of trees. He was taken once more to the bosom of that great Earth mother, and understood the joy of her life.

Remember this, Dira said to the man.

What a wonder, the man thought . . .

. . . and was returned to the sands of the desert, with no remembrance of having slept with, loved, enjoyed the body of his natural mother.

12

They camped at the base of the mountain, in a greenglass cave; not deep but angled sharply so the blown pumice could not reach them. They put Nathan Stack's stone in a fault in the cave's floor, and the heat spread quickly, warming them. The shadow thing with its triangular head sank back in shadow and closed its eye and sent its hunting instinct out for food. A shriek came back on the wind.

Much later, when Nathan Stack had eaten, when he was reasonably content and well-fed, he stared into the shadows and spoke to the creature sitting there.

"How long was I down there . . . how long was the sleep?"

The shadow thing spoke in whispers. *A quarter of a million years.*

Stack did not reply. The figure was beyond belief. The shadow creature seemed to understand.

In the life of a world no time at all.

Nathan Stack was a man who could make accommodations. He smiled quickly and said, "I must have been tired."

The shadow did not respond.

"I don't understand very much of this. It's pretty damned frightening. To die, then to wake up . . . here. Like this."

You did not die. You were taken, put down there. By the end you will understand everything, I promise you.

"Who put me down there?"

I did. I came and found you when the time was right, and I put you down there.

"Am I still Nathan Stack?"

If you wish.

"But *am* I Nathan Stack?"

You always were. You had many other names, many other bodies, but the spark was always yours. Stack seemed about to speak, and the shadow creature added, *You were always on your way to being who you are.*

"But what *am* I? Am I still Nathan Stack, dammit?"

If you wish.

"Listen: you don't seem too sure about that. You came and got me, I mean I woke up and there you were; now who should know better than you what my name is?"

You have had many names in many times. Nathan Stack is merely the one you remember. You had a very different name long ago, at the start, when I first came to you.

Stack was afraid of the answer, but he asked, "What was my name then?"

Ish-lilith. Husband of Lilith. Do you remember her?

Stack thought, tried to open himself to the past, but it was as unfathomable as the quarter of a million years through which he had slept in the crypt.

"No. But there were other women, in other times."

Many. There was one who replaced Lilith.

"I don't remember."

Her name . . . does not matter. But when the mad one took

her from you and replaced her with the other . . . then I knew it would end like this. The Deathbird.

"I don't mean to be stupid, but I haven't the faintest idea what you're talking about."

Before it ends, you will understand everything.

"You said that before." Stack paused, stared at the shadow creature for a long time only moments long, then, "What was your name?"

Before I met you my name was Dira.

He said it in his native tongue. Stack could not pronounce it.

"Before you met me. What is it now?"

Snake.

Something slithered past the mouth of the cave. It did not stop, but it called out with the voice of moist mud sucking down into a quagmire.

"Why did you put *me* down there? Why did you come to me in the first place? What spark? Why can't I remember these other lives or who I was? What do you want from me?"

You should sleep. It will be a long climb. And cold.

"I slept for two hundred and fifty thousand years, I'm hardly tired," Stack said. "Why did you pick me?"

Later. Now sleep. Sleep has other uses.

Darkness deepened around Snake, seeped out around the cave, and Nathan Stack lay down near the warming-stone, and the darkness took him.

13

SUPPLEMENTARY READING

This is an essay by a writer. It is clearly an appeal to the emotions. As you read it ask yourself how it applies to the subject under discussion. What is the writer trying to say? Does he succeed in making his point? Does this essay cast light on the point of the subject under discussion? After you have read this essay, using the reverse side of your test paper, write your own essay (500 words or less) on the loss of a loved one. If you have never lost a loved one, fake it.

AHBHU

Yesterday my dog died. For eleven years Ahbhu was my closest friend. He was responsible for my writing a story about a boy and his dog that many people have read. He was not a pet, he was a person. It was impossible to anthropomorphize him, he wouldn't stand for it. But he was so much his own kind of creature, he had such a strongly formed personality, he was so determined to share his life with only those *he* chose, that it was also impossible to think of him as simply a dog. Apart from those canine characteristics into which he was locked by his species, he comported himself like one of a kind.

We met when I came to him at the West Los Angeles Animal Shelter. I'd wanted a dog because I was lonely and I'd remembered when I was a little boy how my dog had been a friend when I had no other friends. One summer I went away to camp and when I returned I found a rotten old neighbor lady from up the street had had my dog picked up and gassed while my father was at work. I crept into the woman's back yard that night and found a rug hanging on the clothesline. The rug beater was hanging from a post. I stole it and buried it.

At the Animal Shelter there was a man in line ahead of me. He had brought in a puppy only a week or so old. A Puli, a Hungarian sheep dog; it was a sad-looking little thing. He had too many in the litter and had brought in this one to either be taken by someone else, or to be put to sleep. They took the dog inside and the man behind the counter called my turn. I told him I wanted a dog and he took me back inside to walk down the line of cages.

In one of the cages the little Puli that had just been brought in was being assaulted by three larger dogs who had been earlier tenants. He was a little thing, and he was on the bottom, getting the stuffing knocked out of him. But he was struggling mightily. The runt of the litter.

"Get him out of there!" I yelled. "I'll take him, I'll take him, get him out of there!"

He cost two dollars. It was the best two bucks I ever spent.

Driving home with him, he was lying on the other side of the front seat, staring at me. I had had a vague idea what I'd name a pet, but as I stared at him, and he stared back at me, I suddenly was put in mind of the scene in Alexander Korda's 1939 film *The Thief of Bagdad*, where the evil vizier, played by Conrad Veidt, had changed Ahbhu, the little thief, played by Sabu, into a dog. The film had superimposed the human over the canine face for a moment so there was an extraordinary look of intelligence in the face of the dog. The little Puli was looking at me with that same expression. "Ahbhu," I said.

He didn't react to the name, but then he couldn't have cared less. But that was his name, from that time on.

No one who ever came into my house was unaffected by him. When he sensed someone with good vibrations, he was right there, lying at their feet. He loved to be scratched, and despite years of admonitions he refused to stop begging for scraps at table, because he found most of the people who had come to dinner at my house were patsies, unable to escape his woebegone Jackie-Coogan-as-the-Kid look.

But he was a certain barometer of bums, as well. On any number of occasions when I found someone I liked, and Ahbhu would have nothing to do with him or her, it always turned out the person was a wrongo. I took to noting his attitude toward newcomers, and I must admit it influenced my own reactions. I was always wary of someone Ahbhu shunned.

Women with whom I had had unsatisfactory affairs would nonetheless return to the house from time to time—to visit the dog. He had an intimate circle of friends, many of whom had nothing to do with me, and numbering among their company some of the most beautiful actresses in Hollywood. One exquisite lady used to send her driver to pick him up for Sunday afternoon romps at the beach.

I never asked him what happened on those occasions. He didn't talk.

Last year he started going downhill, though I didn't realize it because he maintained the manner of a puppy almost to the end. But he began sleeping too much, and he couldn't hold down his food—not even the Hungarian meals prepared for him by the Magyars who lived up the street. And it became apparent to me something was wrong with him when he got scared during the big Los Angeles earthquake last year. Ahbhu wasn't afraid of anything. He attacked the Pacific Ocean and walked tall around vicious cats. But the

quake terrified him and he jumped up in my bed and threw his forelegs around my neck. I was very nearly the only victim of the earthquake to die from animal strangulation.

He was in and out of the veterinarian's shop all through the
early part of this year, and the idiot always said it was his diet.

Then one Sunday when he was out in the backyard, I found him
lying at the foot of the porch stairs, covered with mud, vomiting so
heavily all he could bring up was bile. He was matted with his own
refuse and he was trying desperately to dig his nose into the earth
for coolness. He was barely breathing, I took him to a different vet.

At first they thought it was just old age . . . that they could pull
him through. But finally they took X-rays and saw the cancer had
taken hold in his stomach and liver.

I put off the day as much as I could. Somehow I just couldn't
conceive of a world that didn't have him in it. But yesterday I went
to the vet's office and signed the euthanasia papers.

"I'd like to spend a little time with him, before," I said.

They brought him in and put him on the stainless steel examination
table. He had grown so thin. He'd always had a pot-belly and it
was gone. The muscles in his hind legs were weak, flaccid. He came
to me and put his head into the hollow of my armpit. He was trembling violently. I lifted his head and he looked at me with that comic
face I'd always thought made him look like Lawrence Talbot, the
Wolf Man. He knew. Sharp as hell right up to the end, hey old
friend? He knew, and he was scared. He trembled all the way down
to his spiderweb legs. This bouncing ball of hair that, when lying on
a dark carpet, could be taken for a sheepskin rug, with no way to
tell at which end head and which end tail. So thin. Shaking, knowing what was going to happen to him. But still a puppy.

I cried and my eyes closed as my nose swelled with the crying,
and he buried his head in my arms because we hadn't done much
crying at one another. I was ashamed of myself not to be taking it
as well as he was.

"I got to, pup, because you're in pain and you can't eat. I got
to." But he didn't want to know that.

The vet came in, then. He was a nice guy and he asked me if I
wanted to go away and just let it be done.

Then Ahbhu came up out of there and looked at me.

There is a scene in Kazan's Viva Zapata where a close friend of

Zapata's, Brando's, has been condemned for conspiring with the *Federales*. A friend that had been with Zapata since the mountains, since the *revolución* had begun. And they come to the hut to take him to the firing squad, and Brando starts out, and his friend stops him with a hand on his arm, and he says to him with great friendship, "Emiliano, do it yourself."

Ahbhu looked at me and I know he was just a dog, but if he could have spoken with human tongue he could not have said more eloquently than he did with a look, *don't leave me with strangers.*

So I held him as they laid him down and the vet slipped the lanyard up around his right foreleg and drew it tight to bulge the vein, and I held his head and he turned it away from me as the needle went in. It was impossible to tell the moment he passed over from life to death. He simply laid his head on my hand, his eyes fluttered shut and he was gone.

I wrapped him in a sheet with the help of the vet, and I drove home with Ahbhu on the seat beside me, just the way we had come home eleven years before. I took him out in the backyard and began digging his grave. I dug for hours, crying and mumbling to myself, talking to him in the sheet. It was a very neat, rectangular grave with smooth sides and all the loose dirt scooped out by hand.

I laid him down in the hole and he was so tiny in there for a dog who had seemed to be so big in life, so furry, so funny. And I covered him over and when the hole was packed full of dirt I replaced the neat divot of grass I'd scalped off at the start. And that was all.

But I couldn't send him to strangers.

THE END

QUESTIONS FOR DISCUSSION

1. Is there any significance to the reversal of the word *god* being *dog*? If so, what?

2. Does the writer try to impart human qualities to a non-human creature? *Why?* Discuss anthropomorphism in the light of the phrase, "Thou art God."

3. Discuss the love the writer shows in this essay. Compare and contrast it with other forms of love: the love of a man for a woman, a mother for a child, a son for a mother, a botanist for plants, an ecologist for the Earth.

14

In his sleep, Nathan Stack talked.
"Why did you pick me? Why me . . ."

15

Like the Earth, the Mother was in pain.

The great house was very quiet. The doctor had left, and the relatives had gone into town for dinner. He sat by the side of her bed and stared down at her. She looked gray and old and crumpled; her skin was a soft ashy hue of moth-dust. He was crying softly.

He felt her hand on his knee, and looked up to see her staring at him. "You weren't supposed to catch me," he said.

"I'd be disappointed if I hadn't," she said. Her voice was very thin, very smooth.

"How is it?"

"It hurts. Ben didn't dope me too well."

He bit his lower lip. The doctor had used massive doses, but the pain was more massive. She gave little starts as tremors of sudden agony hit her. Impacts. He watched the life leaking out of her eyes.

"How is your sister taking it?"

He shrugged. "You know Charlene. She's sorry, but it's all pretty intellectual to her."

His mother let a tiny ripple of a smile move her lips. "It's a terrible thing to say, Nathan, but your sister isn't the most likeable woman in the world. I'm glad you're here." She paused, thinking, then added, "It's just possible your father and I missed something from the gene pool. Charlene isn't whole."

"Can I get you something? A drink of water?"

"No. I'm fine."

He looked at the ampoule of narcotic pain killer. The syringe lay mechanical and still on a clean towel beside it. He felt her eyes on him. She knew what he was thinking. He looked away.

"I would kill for a cigarette," she said.

He laughed. At sixty-five, both legs gone, what remained of her left side paralyzed, the cancer spreading like deadly jelly toward her heart, she was still the matriarch. "You can't have a cigarette, so forget it."

"Then why don't you use that hypo and let me out of here."

"Shut up, Mother."

"Oh, for Christ's sake, Nathan. It's hours if I'm lucky. Months if I'm not. We've had this conversation before. You know I always win."

"Did I ever tell you you were a bitchy old lady?"

"Many times, but I love you anyhow."

He got up and walked to the wall. He could not walk through it, so he went around the inside of the room.

"You can't get away from it."

"Mother, Jesus! Please!"

"All right. Let's talk about the business."

"I couldn't care less about the business right now."

"Then what should we talk about? The lofty uses to which an old lady can put her last moments?"

"You know, you're really ghoulish. I think you're enjoying this in some sick way."

"What other way is there to enjoy it."

"An adventure."

"The biggest. A pity your father never had the chance to savor it."

"I hardly think he'd have savored the feeling of being stamped to death in a hydraulic press."

Then he thought about it, because that little smile was on her lips again. "Okay, he probably would have. The two of you were so unreal, you'd have sat there and discussed it and analyzed the pulp."

"And you're our son."

He was, and he was. And he could not deny it, nor had he ever. He was hard and gentle and wild just like them, and he remembered the days in the jungle beyond Brasilia, and the hunt in the Cayman Trench, and the other days working in the mills alongside his father, and he knew when his moment came he would savor death as she did.

"Tell me something. I've always wanted to know. Did Dad kill Tom Golden?"

"Use the needle and I'll tell you."

"I'm a Stack. I don't bribe."

"I'm a Stack, and know what a killing curiosity you've got. Use the needle and I'll tell you."

He walked widdershins, around the room. She watched him, eyes bright as the mill vats.

"You old bitch."

"Shame, Nathan. You know you're not the son of a bitch. Which is more than your sister can say. Did I ever tell you she wasn't your father's child?"

"No, but I knew."

"You'd have liked her father. He was Swedish. Your father liked him."

"Is that why Dad broke both his arms?"

"Probably. But I never heard the Swede complain. One night in bed with me in those days was worth a couple of broken arms. Use the needle."

Finally, while the family was between the entree and the dessert, he filled the syringe and injected her. Her eyes widened as the stuff smacked her heart, and just before she died she rallied all her strength and said, "A deal's a deal. Your father didn't kill Tom Golden, I did. You're a hell of a man, Nathan, and you fought us the way we wanted, and we both loved you more than you could know. Except, dammit, you cunning s.o.b., you do know, don't you?"

"I know," he said, and she died; and he cried; and that was the extent of the poetry in it.

16

He knows we are coming.

They were climbing the northern face of the onyx mountain. Snake had coated Nathan Stack's feet with the thick glue and, though it was hardly a country walk, he was able to keep a foothold and pull himself up. Now they had paused to rest on a spiral ledge, and Snake had spoken for the first time of what waited for them where they were going.

"He?"

Snake did not answer. Stack slumped against the wall of the ledge. At the lower slopes of the mountain they had encountered slug-like creatures that had tried to attach themselves to Stack's flesh, but when Snake had driven them off they had returned to sucking the rocks. They had not come near the shadow creature. Farther up, Stack could see the lights that flickered at the summit; he had felt fear that crawled up from his stomach. A short time before they had come to this ledge they had stumbled past a cave in the mountain where the bat creatures slept. They had gone mad at the presence of the man and the Snake and the sounds they had made sent waves of nausea through Stack. Snake had helped him and they had gotten past. Now they had stopped and Snake would not answer Stack's questions.

We must keep climbing.

"Because he knows we're here." There was a sarcastic rise in Stack's voice.

Snake started moving. Stack closed his eyes. Snake stopped and came back to him. Stack looked up at the one-eyed shadow.

"Not another step."

There is no reason why you should not know.

"Except, friend, I have the feeling you aren't going to tell me anything."

It is not yet time for you to know.

"Look: just because I haven't asked, doesn't mean I don't want to know. You've told me things I shouldn't be able to handle . . . all kinds of crazy things . . . I'm as old as, as . . . I don't know *how* old, but I get the feeling you've been trying to tell me I'm Adam . . ."

That is so.

". . . uh." He stopped rattling and stared back at the shadow creature. Then, very softly, accepting even more than he had thought possible, he said, "Snake." He was silent again. After a time he asked, "Give me another dream and let me know the rest of it?"

You must be patient. The one who lives at the top knows we are coming but I have been able to keep him from perceiving your danger to him only because you do not know yourself.

"Tell me this, then: does he *want* us to come up . . . the one on the top?"

He allows it. Because he doesn't know.

Stack nodded, resigned to following Snake's lead. He got to his feet and performed an elaborate butler's motion, after you, Snake.

And Snake turned, his flat hands sticking to the wall of the ledge, and they climbed higher, spiraling upward toward the summit.

The Deathbird swooped, then rose toward the Moon. There was still time.

17

Dira came to Nathan Stack near sunset, appearing in the board room of the industrial consortium Stack had built from the empire bequeathed him by his family.

Stack sat in the pneumatic chair that dominated the conversation pit where top-level decisions were made. He was alone. The others had left hours before and the room was dim with only the barest glow of light from hidden banks that shone through the soft walls.

The shadow creature passed through the walls—and at his passage they became rose quartz, then returned to what they had been. He stood staring at Nathan Stack, and for long moments the man was unaware of any other presence in the room.

You have to go now, Snake said.

Stack looked up, his eyes widened in horror, and through his mind flitted the unmistakable image of Satan, fanged mouth smiling, horns gleaming with scintillas of light as though seen through crosstar filters, rope tail with its spade-shaped pointed tip thrashing, large cloven hoofs leaving burning imprints in the carpet, eyes as deep as pools of oil, the pitchfork, the satin-lined cape, the hairy legs of a goat, talons. He tried to scream but the sound dammed up in his throat.

No, Snake said, *that is not so. Come with me, and you will understand.*

There was a tone of sadness in the voice. As though Satan had been sorely wronged. Stack shook his head violently.

There was no time for argument. The moment had come, and Dira could not hesitate. He gestured and Nathan Stack rose from the pneumatic chair, leaving behind something that looked like Nathan Stack asleep, and he walked to Dira and Snake took him by the hand and they passed through rose quartz and went away from there.

Down and down Snake took him.

The Mother was in pain. She had been sick for eons, but it had reached the point where Snake knew it would be terminal, and the Mother knew it, too. But she would hide her child, she would intercede in her own behalf and hide him away deep in her bosom where no one, not even the mad one, could find him.

Dira took Stack to Hell.

It was a fine place.

Warm and safe and far from the probing of mad ones.

And the sickness raged on unchecked. Nations crumbled, the oceans boiled and then grew cold and filmed over with scum, the air became thick with dust and killing vapors, flesh ran like oil, the skies grew dark, the sun blurred and became dull. The Earth moaned.

The planets suffered and consumed themselves, beasts became crippled and went mad, trees burst into flame and from their ashes rose glass shapes that shattered in the wind. The Earth was dying; a long, slow, painful death.

In the center of the Earth, in the fine place, Nathan Stack slept. *Don't leave me with strangers.*

Overhead, far away against the stars, the Deathbird circled and circled, waiting for the word.

18

When they reached the highest peak, Nathan Stack looked across through the terrible burning cold and the ferocious grittiness of the demon wind and saw the sanctuary of always, the

cathedral of forever, the pillar of remembrance, the haven of
perfection, the pyramid of blessings, the toyshop of creation, the
vault of deliverance, the monument of longing, the receptacle of
thoughts, the maze of wonder, the catafalque of despair, the po-
dium of pronouncements and the kiln of last attempts.

On a slope that rose to a star pinnacle, he saw the home of the
one who dwelled here—lights flashing and flickering, lights that
could be seen far off across the deserted face of the planet—and
he began to suspect the name of the resident.

Suddenly everything went red for Nathan Stack. As though a
filter had been dropped over his eyes, the black sky, the flickering lights, the rocks that formed the great plateau on which they
stood, even Snake became red, and with the color came pain.
Terrible pain that burned through every channel of Stack's body,
as though his blood had been set afire. He screamed and fell to
his knees, the pain crackling through his brain, following every
nerve and blood vessel and ganglion and neural track. His skull
flamed.

Fight him, Snake said. *Fight him!*

I can't, screamed silently through Stack's mind, the pain too
great even to speak. Fire licked and leaped and he felt the delicate tissues of thought shriveling. He tried to focus his thoughts
on ice. He clutched for salvation at ice, chunks of ice, mountains of ice, swimming icebergs of ice half-buried in frozen
water, even as his soul smoked and smoldered. *Ice!* He thought
of millions of particles of hail rushing, falling, thundering against
the firestorm eating his mind, and there was a spit of steam, a
flame that went out, a corner that grew cool . . . and he took his
stand in that corner, thinking ice, thinking blocks and chunks
and monuments of ice, edging them out to widen the circle of
coolness and safety. Then the flames began to retreat, to slide
back down the channels, and he sent ice after them, snuffing
them, burying them in ice and chill waters that raced after the
flames and drove them out.

When he opened his eyes, he was still on his knees, but he
could think again, and the red surfaces had become normal
again.

He will try again. You must be ready.

"Tell me *everything!* I can't go through this without knowing,
I need help! Tell me, Snake, tell me now!"

*You can help yourself. You have the strength. I gave you the
spark.*

. . . and the second derangement struck!

The air turned shaverasse and he held dripping chunks of
unclean rova in his jowls, the taste making him weak with nausea. His pods withered and drew up into his shell and as the
bones cracked he howled with strings of pain that came so fast
they were almost one. He tried to scuttle away, but his eyes
magnified the shatter of light that beat against him. Facets of his
eyes cracked and the juice began to bubble out. The pain was
unbelievable.

Fight him!

Stack rolled onto his back, sending out cilia to touch the earth,
and for an instant he realized he was seeing through the eyes of
another creature, another form of life he could not even describe.
But he was under an open sky and that produced fear, he was
surrounded by air that had become deadly and *that* produced
fear, he was going blind and *that* produced fear, he was . . . he
was a man . . . he fought back against the feeling of being some
other thing . . . he was a *man* and he would not feel fear, he
would stand.

He rolled over, withdrew his cilia, and struggled to lower his
pods. Broken bones grated and pain thundered though his body.
He forced himself to ignore it, and finally the pods were down
and he was breathing and he felt his head reeling . . .

And when he opened his eyes he was Nathan Stack again.

. . . and the third derangement struck:

Hopelessness.

Out of unending misery he came back to be Stack.

. . . and the fourth derangement struck:

Madness.

Out of raging lunacy he fought his way to be Stack.

. . . and the fifth derangement, and the sixth, and the seventh,
and the plagues, and the whirlwinds, and the pools of evil, and
the reduction in size and accompanying fall forever through submicroscopic hells, and the things that fed on him from inside,
and the twentieth, and the fortieth, and the sound of his voice
screaming for release, and the voice of Snake always beside him,
whispering *Fight him!*

Finally it stopped.

Quickly, now.

Snake took Stack by the hand and half-dragging him they raced to the great palace of light and glass on the slope, shining brightly under the star pinnacle, and they passed under an arch of shining metal into the ascension hall. The portal sealed behind them.

There were tremors in the walls. The inlaid floors of jewels began to rumble and tremble. Bits of high and faraway ceilings began to drop. Quaking, the palace gave one hideous shudder and collapsed around them.

Now, Snake said. *Now you will know everything!*

And everything forgot to fall. Frozen in mid-air, the wreckage of the palace hung suspended above them. Even the air ceased to swirl. Time stood still. The movement of the Earth was halted. Everything held utterly immobile as Nathan Stack was permitted to understand all.

19

MULTIPLE CHOICE (Counts for ½ your final grade.)

1. God is:

    A. An invisible spirit with a long beard.

    B. A small dog dead in a hole.

    C. Everyman.

    D. The Wizard of Oz.

2. Nietzsche wrote "God is dead." By this did he mean:

    A. Life is pointless.

    B. Belief in supreme deities has waned.

    C. There never was a God to begin with.

    D. Thou art God.

3. Ecology is another name for:

    A. Mother love.

B. Enlightened self-interest.

C. A good health salad with Granola.

D. God.

4. Which of these phrases most typifies the profoundest love:

A. Don't leave me with strangers.

B. I love you.

C. God is love.

D. Use the needle.

5. Which of these powers do we usually associate with God:

A. Power.

B. Love.

C. Humanity.

D. Docility.

20

None of the above.

Starlight shone in the eyes of the Deathbird and its passage through the night cast a shadow on the Moon.

21

Nathan Stack raised his hands and around them the air was still as the palace fell crashing. They were untouched. *Now you know all there is to know,* Snake said, sinking to one knee as though worshipping. There was no one there to worship but Nathan Stack.

"Was he always mad?"

From the first.

"Then those who gave our world to him were mad, and your race was mad to allow it."

Snake had no answer.

"Perhaps it was supposed to be like this," Stack said.

He reached down and lifted Snake to his feet, and he touched the shadow creature's sleek triangular head. "Friend," he said.

Snake's race was incapable of tears. He said, *I have waited longer than you can know for that word.*

"I'm sorry it comes at the end."

Perhaps it was supposed to be like this.

Then there was a swirling of air, a scintillation in the ruined palace, and the owner of the mountain, the owner of the ruined Earth came to them in a burning bush.

AGAIN, SNAKE? AGAIN YOU ANNOY ME?

The time for toys is ended.

NATHAN STACK YOU BRING TO STOP ME? *I* SAY WHEN THE TIME IS ENDED. *I* SAY, AS I'VE ALWAYS SAID.

Then, to Nathan Stack:

GO AWAY. FIND A PLACE TO HIDE UNTIL I COME FOR YOU.

Stack ignored the burning bush. He waved his hand and the cone of safety in which they stood vanished. "Let's find him, first, then I know what to do."

The Deathbird sharpened its talons on the night wind and sailed down through emptiness toward the cinder of the Earth.

22

Nathan Stack had once contracted pneumonia. He had lain on the operating table as the surgeon made the small incision in the chest wall. Had he not been stubborn, had he not continued working around the clock while the infection developed into empyema, he would never have had to go under the knife, even for an operation as safe as a thoracotomy. But he was a Stack, and so he lay on the operating table as the rubber tube was inserted into the chest cavity to drain off the pus in the pleural cavity, and heard someone speak his name.

NATHAN STACK.

He heard it, from far off, across an Arctic vastness; heard it echoing over and over, down an endless corridor; as the knife sliced.

NATHAN STACK.

He remembered Lilith, with hair the color of dark wine. He remembered taking hours to die beneath a rock slide as his hunting companions in the pack ripped apart the remains of the bear and ignored his grunted moans for help. He remembered the impact of the crossbow bolt as it ripped through his hauberk and split his chest and he died at Agincourt. He remembered the icy water of the Ohio as it closed over his head and the flatboat disappearing without his mates noticing his loss. He remembered the mustard gas that ate his lungs as he tried to crawl toward a farmhouse near Verdun. He remembered looking directly into the flash of the bomb and feeling the flesh of his face melt away. He remembered Snake coming to him in the board room and husking him like corn from his body. He remembered sleeping in the molten core of the Earth for a quarter of a million years.

Across the dead centuries he heard his mother pleading with him to set her free, to end her pain. *Use the needle.* Her voice mingled with the voice of the Earth crying out in endless pain at her flesh that had been ripped away, at her rivers turned to arteries of dust, at her rolling hills and green fields slagged to greenglass and ashes. The voices of his mother and the mother that was Earth became one, and mingled to become Snake's voice telling him he was the one man in the world—the last man in the world—who could end the terminal case the Earth had become.

Use the needle. Put the suffering Earth out of its misery. *It belongs to you now.*

Nathan Stack was secure in the power he contained. A power that far outstripped that of gods or Snakes or mad creators who stuck pins in their creations, who broke their toys.

YOU CAN'T. I WON'T LET YOU.

Nathan Stack walked around the burning bush as it crackled impotently in rage. He looked at it almost pityingly, remembering the Wizard of Oz with his great and ominous disembodied head floating in mist and lightning, and the poor little man behind the curtain turning the dials to create the effects. Stack walked around the effect, knowing he had more power than this sad, poor thing that had held his race in thrall since before Lilith had been taken from him.

He went in search of the mad one who capitalized his name.

23

Zarathustra descended alone from the mountains, encountering no one. But when he came into the forest, all at once there stood before him an old man who had left his holy cottage to look for roots in the woods. And thus spoke the old man to Zarathustra.

"No stranger to me is this wanderer: many years ago he passed this way. Zarathustra he was called, but he has changed. At that time you carried your ashes to the mountains; would you now carry your fire into the valleys? Do you not fear to be punished as an arsonist?

"Zarathustra has changed, Zarathustra has become a child, Zarathustra is an awakened one; what do you now want among the sleepers? You lived in your solitude as in the sea, and the sea carried you. Alas, would you now climb ashore? Alas, would you again drag your own body?"

Zarathustra answered: "I love man."

"Why," asked the saint, "did I go into the forest and the desert? Was it not because I loved man all-too-much? Now I love God; man I love not. Man is for me too imperfect a thing. Love of man would kill me."

"And what is the saint doing in the forest?" asked Zarathustra.

The saint answered: "I make songs and sing them; and when I make songs, I laugh, cry, and hum: thus I praise God. With singing, crying, laughing, and humming, I praise the god who is my god. But what do you bring us as a gift?"

When Zarathustra had heard these words he bade the saint farewell and said: "What could I have to give you? But let me go quickly lest I take something from you!" And thus they separated, the old one and the man, laughing as two boys laugh.

But when Zarathustra was alone he spoke thus to his heart:

"Could it be possible? This old saint in the forest had not yet heard anything of this, that *God is dead!*"

24

Stack found the mad one wandering in the forest of final moments. He was an old, tired man, and Stack knew with a wave of his hand he could end it for this god in a moment. But what was the reason for it? It was even too late for revenge. It had been too late from the start. So he let the old one go his way, wandering in the forest, mumbling to himself, I WON'T LET YOU DO IT, in the voice of a cranky child; mumbling pathetically, OH, PLEASE, I DON'T WANT TO GO TO BED YET, I'M NOT YET DONE PLAYING.

And Stack came back to Snake, who had served his function and protected Stack until Stack had learned that he was more powerful than the God he'd worshipped all through the history of Men. He came back to Snake and their hands touched and the bond of friendship was sealed at last, at the end.

Then they worked together and Nathan Stack used the needle with a wave of his hands, and the Earth could not sigh with relief as its endless pain was ended . . . but it did sigh, and it settled in upon itself, and the molten core went out, and the winds died, and from high above them Stack heard the fulfillment of Snake's final act; he heard the descent of the Deathbird.

"What was your name?" Stack asked his friend.

Dira.

And the Deathbird settled down across the tired shape of the Earth, and it spread its wings wide, and brought them over and down, and enfolded the Earth as a mother enfolds her weary child. Dira settled down on the amethyst floor of the dark-shrouded palace, and closed his single eye with gratitude. To sleep at last, at the end.

All this, as Nathan Stack stood watching. He was the last, at the end, and because he had come to own—if even for a few moments—that which could have been his from the start, had he but known, he did not sleep but stood and watched. Knowing at last, at the end, that he had loved and done no wrong.

25

The Deathbird closed its wings over the Earth until at last, at the end, there was only the great bird crouched over the dead cinder. Then the Deathbird raised its head to the star-filled sky and repeated the sigh of loss the Earth had felt at the end. Then its eyes closed, it tucked its head carefully under its wing, and all was night.

Far away, the stars waited for the cry of the Deathbird to reach them so final moments could be observed at last, at the end, for the race of Men.

26

THIS IS FOR MARK TWAIN

Ursula K. Le Guin

Here's the other story by Ursula. She wasn't at Toronto for her novella award and she wasn't at Washington for her short story award and I still haven't met her.

I did see her picture once.

It came about this way . . . Every once in a while, some newspaper or magazine decides that a feature article on science fiction should be prepared. This generally strikes us old pros with consternation. We would *like* to see science fiction dealt with appropriately, but our notion of the appropriate and that of the various members of the news media rarely match. Too many of the non-science-fiction people of the press have some vague memory of wrist-radios in a Dick Tracy comic strip or once saw a Flash Gordon episode and that's all.

To be sure, this is not always so. Once at a local convention in New York, a reporter from the New York *Post* approached me and asked if he could interview me in connection with a story he was writing on the convention.

"Why?" I said. "Can't you make fun of us without interviewing me?"

He said, quite seriously, "Why don't you read my story tomorrow and see if that's my intention."

So I thought: Yes, I'm prejudging him, and I shouldn't.

I answered his questions straightforwardly and he wrote a nice article that treated us well.

That's the exception that keeps us hoping—and then hurting. A weekly newsmagazine did a feature article on science fiction and lots of us co-operated, out of hope. I was interviewed for an hour and a half. So was Ben Bova. So was Judy-Lynn del Rey. So were lots of good and honest people.

But nothing of it showed in the final article, which hung us up for laughs and let us twist slowly, slowly in the wind. The general impression was that science fiction was essentially a twelve-year-old boy wearing Spock ears.

In this article there was a picture of Ursula smoking a pipe.

I understand that Ursula does smoke a pipe, and why not? I hate tobacco and I think anyone who smokes is a dolt, but I'm a feminist and I will maintain to my dying breath that women have, and what's more *should* have, fully as much capacity for dolthood as men do.

I do not believe, however, that the picture was run for the sake of supporting feminism. Rather, I suspect it was included because the magazine thought it would help demonstrate how nutty science fiction people were.

Alas!

THE ONES WHO WALK AWAY FROM OMELAS

(Variations on a Theme by William James)

With a clamor of bells that set the swallows soaring, the Festival of Summer came to the city Omelas, bright-towered by the sea. The rigging of the boats in harbor sparkled with flags. In the streets between houses with red roofs and painted walls, between old moss-grown gardens and under avenues of trees, past great parks and public buildings, processions moved. Some were decorous: old people in long stiff robes of mauve and gray, grave master workmen, quiet, merry women carrying their babies and chatting as they walked. In other streets the music beat faster, a shimmering of gong and tambourine, and the people went dancing, the procession was a dance. Children dodged in and out, their high calls rising like the swallows' crossing flights over the music and the singing. All the processions wound toward the north side of the city, where on the great watermeadow called the Green Fields boys and girls, naked in the bright air, with mudstained feet and ankles and long, lithe arms, exercised their restive horses before the race. The horses wore no gear at all but a halter without bit. Their manes were braided with streamers of silver, gold, and green. They blew out their nostrils and pranced and boasted to one another; they were vastly excited, the horse being the only animal who has adopted our ceremonies as his own. Far off to the north and west the mountains stood up half-encircling Omelas on her bay. The air of morning was so clear that the snow still crowning the Eighteen Peaks burned with white-gold fire across the miles of sunlit air, under the dark blue of the sky. There was just enough wind to make the banners that marked the race course snap and flutter now and then. In the silence of the broad green meadows one could hear the music winding through the city streets, farther and nearer and ever approaching, a cheerful faint sweetness of the air that from time to time trembled and gathered together and broke out into the great joyous clanging of the bells.

Joyous! How is one to tell about joy? How describe the citizens of Omelas?

They were not simple folk, you see, though they were happy. But we do not say the words of cheer much any more. All smiles have become archaic. Given a description such as this one tends to make certain assumptions. Given a description such as this one tends to look next for the King, mounted on a splendid stallion and surrounded by his noble knights, or perhaps in a golden litter borne by great-muscled slaves. But there was no king. They did not use swords, or keep slaves. They were not barbarians. I do not know the rules and laws of their society, but I suspect that they were singularly few. As they did without monarchy and slavery, so they also got on without the stock exchange, the advertisement, the secret police, and the bomb. Yet I repeat that these were not simple folk, not dulcet shepherds, noble savages, bland utopians. They were not less complex than we. The trouble is that we have a bad habit, encouraged by pedants and sophisticates, of considering happiness as something rather stupid. Only pain is intellectual, only evil interesting. This is the treason of the artist: a refusal to admit the banality of evil and the terrible boredom of pain. If you can't lick 'em, join 'em. If it hurts, repeat it. But to praise despair is to condemn delight, to embrace violence is to lose hold of everything else. We have almost lost hold; we can no longer describe a happy man, nor make any celebration of joy. How can I tell you about the people of Omelas? They were not naive and happy children—though their children were, in fact, happy. They were mature, intelligent, passionate adults whose lives were not wretched. O miracle! But I wish I could describe it better. I wish I could convince you. Omelas sounds in my words like a city in a fairytale, long ago and far away, once upon a time. Perhaps it would be best if you imagined it as your own fancy bids, assuming it will rise to the occasion, for certainly I cannot suit you all. For instance, how about technology? I think that there would be no cars or helicopters in and above the streets; this follows from the fact that the people of Omelas are happy people. Happiness is based on a just discrimination of what is necessary, what is neither necessary nor destructive, and what is destructive. In the middle category, however—that of the unnecessary but undestructive, that of comfort, luxury, exuberance, etc.—they could perfectly well have central heating, subway trains, washing machines, and all kinds of marvelous devices not yet invented here, floating lightsources, fuelless power, a cure for the common cold. Or they could have none of that: it doesn't matter. As you like it. I incline to think that people from towns up and down the coast have been coming in to Omelas during the last days before the Festival on very fast little trains and doubledecked trams, and that the train station of Omelas is actually the handsomest building in town, though plainer than the magnificent Farmers Market. But even granted trains, I fear that Omelas so far strikes some of you as goody-goody. Smiles, bells, parades, horses, bleh. If so, please add an orgy. If an orgy would help, don't hesitate. Let us not, however, have temples from which issue beautiful nude priests and priestesses already half in ecstasy and ready to copulate with whosoever, man or woman, lover or stranger, desires union with the deep godhead of the blood, although that was my first idea. But really it would be better not to have any temples in Omelas—at least, not manned temples. Religion yes, clergy no. Surely the beautiful nudes can just wander about, offering themselves like divine soufflés to the hunger of the needy and the rapture of the flesh. Let them join the processions. Let tambourines be struck above the copulations, and the glory of desire be proclaimed upon the gongs, and (a not unimportant point) let the offspring of these delightful rituals be beloved and looked after by all. One thing I know there is none of in Omelas is guilt. But what else should there be? I thought at first there were no drugs, but that is puritanical. For those who like it, the faint insistent sweetness of *drooz* may perfume the ways of the city, *drooz* which first brings a great lightness and brilliance to the mind and limbs, and then after some hours a dreamy languor, and wonderful visions at last of the very arcana and inmost secrets of the Universe, as well as exciting the pleasure of sex beyond all belief; and it is not habit-forming. For more modest tastes I think there ought to be beer. What else, what else belongs in the joyous city? The sense of victory, surely, the celebration of courage. But as we did without clergy, let us do without soldiers. The joy built upon successful slaughter is not the right kind of joy; it will not do; it is fearful and it is trivial. A boundless and generous contentment, a magnanimous triumph felt not against some outer enemy but in communion with the finest and fairest in the souls of all men everywhere and the splendor of the world's summer: this is what swells the hearts of the people of Omelas, and the victory they celebrate is that of life. I really don't think many of them need to take *drooz*.

Most of the processions have reached the Green Fields by now. A marvelous smell of cooking goes forth from the red and blue tents of the provisioners. The faces of small children are amiably sticky; in the benign gray beard of a man a couple of crumbs of rich pastry are entangled. The youths and girls have mounted their horses and are beginning to group around the starting line of the course. An old woman, small, fat, and laughing, is passing out flowers from a basket, and tall young men wear her flowers in their shining hair. A child of nine or ten sits at the edge of the crowd, alone, playing on a wooden flute. People pause to listen, and they smile, but they do not speak to him, for he never ceases playing and never sees them, his dark eyes wholly rapt in the sweet, thin magic of the tune.

He finishes, and slowly lowers his hands holding the wooden flute.

As if that little private silence were the signal, all at once a trumpet sounds from the pavilion near the starting line: imperious, melancholy, piercing. The horses rear on their slender legs, and some of them neigh in answer. Sober-faced, the young riders stroke the horses' necks and soothe them, whispering, "Quiet, quiet, there my beauty, my hope . . ." They begin to form in rank along the starting line. The crowds along the race course are like a field of grass and flowers in the wind. The Festival of Summer has begun.

Do you believe? Do you accept the festival, the city, the joy? No? Then let me describe one more thing.

In a basement under one of the beautiful buildings of Omelas, or perhaps in the cellar of one of its spacious private homes, there is a room. It has one locked door, and no window. A little light seeps in dustily between cracks in the boards, secondhand from a cobwebbed window somewhere across the cellar. In one corner of the little room a couple of mops, with stiff, clotted, foul-smelling heads, stand near a rusty bucket. The floor is dirt, a little damp to the touch, as cellar dirt usually is. The room is about three paces long and two wide: a mere broom closet or disused toolroom. In the room a child is sitting. It might be a boy or a girl. It looks about six, but actually is nearly ten. It is feebleminded. Perhaps it was born defective, or perhaps it has become imbecile through fear, malnutrition, and neglect. It picks its nose and occasionally fumbles vaguely with its toes or genitals, as it sits hunched in the corner farthest from the bucket and the two mops. It is afraid of the mops. It finds them horrible. It shuts its eyes, but it knows the mops are still standing there; and the door is locked; and nobody will come. The door is always locked, and nobody ever comes, except that sometimes—the child has no understanding of time or interval—sometimes the door rattles terribly and opens, and a person, or several people, are there. One of them may come in and kick the child to make it stand up. The others never come close, but peer in at it with frightened, disgusted eyes. The food bowl and the water jug are hastily filled, the door is locked, the eyes disappear. The people at the door never say anything, but the child, who has not always lived in the toolroom, and can remember sunlight and its mother's voice, sometimes speaks. "I will be good," it says. "Please let me out. I will be good!" They never answer. The child used to scream for help at night, and cry a good deal, but now it only makes a kind of whining, "eh-haa, eh-haa," and it speaks less and less often. It is so thin there are no calves to its legs; its belly protrudes; it lives on a half-bowl of cornmeal and grease a day. It is naked. Its buttocks and thighs are a mass of festered sores, as it sits in its own excrement continually.

They all know it is there, all the people of Omelas. Some of them have come to see it, others are content merely to know it is there. They all know that it has to be there. Some of them understand why, and some do not, but they all understand that their happiness, the beauty of their city, the tenderness of their friendships, the health of their children, the wisdom of their scholars, the skill of their makers, even the abundance of their harvest and the kindly weathers of their skies, depend wholly on this child's abominable misery.

This is usually explained to children when they are between eight and twelve, whenever they seem capable of understanding; and most of those who come to see the child are young people, though often enough an adult comes, or comes back, to see the child. No matter how well the matter has been explained to them, these young spectators are always shocked and sickened at the sight. They feel disgust, which they had thought themselves superior to. They feel anger, outrage, impotence, despite all the explanations. They would like to do something for the child. But there is nothing they can do. If the child were brought up into the sunlight out of that vile place, if it were cleaned and fed and comforted, that would be a good thing, indeed; but if it were done, in that day and hour all the prosperity and beauty and delight of Omelas would wither and be destroyed. Those are the terms. To exchange all the goodness and grace of every life in Omelas for that single, small improvement: to throw away the happiness of thousands for the chance of the happiness of one: that would be to let guilt within the walls indeed.

The terms are strict and absolute; there may not even be a kind word spoken to the child.

Often the young people go home in tears, or in a tearless rage, when they have seen the child and faced this terrible paradox. They may brood over it for weeks or years. But as time goes on they begin to realize that even if the child could be released, it would not get much good of its freedom: a vague pleasure of warmth and food, no doubt, but little more. It is too degraded and imbecile to know any real joy. It has been afraid too long ever to be free of fear. Its habits are too uncouth for it to respond to humane treatment. Indeed after so long it would probably be wretched without walls about it to protect it, and darkness for its eyes, and its own excrement to sit in. Their tears at the bitter injustice dry when they begin to perceive the terrible justice of reality, and to accept it. Yet it is their tears and anger, the trying of their generosity and the acceptance of their helplessness, which are perhaps the true source of the splendor of their lives. Theirs is no vapid, irresponsible happiness. They know that they, like the child, are not free. They know compassion. It is the existence of the child, and their knowledge of its existence, that makes possible the nobility of their architecture, the poignancy of their music, the profundity of their science. It is because of the child that they are so gentle with children. They know that if the wretched one were not there sniveling in the dark, the other one, the flute player, could make no joyful music as the young riders line up in their beauty for the race in the sunlight of the first morning of summer.

Now do you believe in them? Are they not more credible? But there is one more thing to tell, and this is quite incredible.

At times one of the adolescent girls or boys who go to see the child does not go home to weep or rage, does not, in fact, go home at all. Sometimes also a man or woman much older falls silent for a day or two, and then leaves home. These people go out into the street, and walk down the street alone. They keep walking, and walk straight out of the city of Omelas, through the beautiful gates. They keep walking across the farmlands of Omelas. Each one goes alone, youth or girl, man or woman. Night falls; the traveler must pass down village streets, between the houses with yellow-lit windows, and on out into the darkness of the fields. Each alone, they go west or north, toward the mountains. They go on. They leave Omelas, they walk ahead into the darkness, and they do not come back. The place they go toward is a place even less imaginable to most of us than the city of happiness. I cannot describe it at all. It is possible that it does not exist. But they seem to know where they are going, the ones who walk away from Omelas.

1975
33rd *CONVENTION*
MELBOURNE

George R. R. Martin

The first convention was held in New York in 1939 (and I was there, by the way). It was the brainchild of Sam Moskowitz, who gets very little credit for having originated this grand and fruitful concept, and who is for this and for many other reasons one of my favorite science fiction people. It was Sam who placed the adjective "World" on the convention, though there were few people who attended who came from a distance of more than a hundred miles from New York. (Forrest J. Ackerman came from Los Angeles, but Forrie would have come from Mars, if he'd had to.)

The first twenty-two world conventions were held in the United States (well, one of them was in Canada), and it was not till the twenty-third, in 1965, that a world convention was held overseas, in London. The twenty-eighth convention was in Heidelberg in 1970, the first one in a non-English-speaking country. And the thirty-third was in Melbourne in 1975, for the first time in the Southern Hemisphere.

We're getting there. Someday there's got to be a World Science Fiction Convention on the moon—except that will raise a problem with the familiar names usually given the conventions. Thus, conventions in Toronto are "Torcons," those in Washington are "Discons," those in New York are "Nycons" and so on. A convention on the moon should be a "Lunacon" but that is the title given the annual science fiction convention held in New York at Easter time. We'll have to call the moon convention the Selenocon.

But I'll never be at these far-out conventions. I wonder if George R. R. Martin was at the thirty-third. If I had been there I might have met him—if he had been there. As it is, I haven't met him anywhere. The only thing I know about him is that Ben Bova calls him George Railroad Martin.

Which brings up the importance of names. A memorable name is usually thought to be useful to a writer, who, after all, depends on instant recognition to help sales. George Martin is a very bland name; add the R.R. and it gains flavor. Change Ed Smith to E. E. Smith, Ph.D., and you have the best-known science fiction name of the 1930s. Or think how dull Jack Campbell would be in comparison with John W. Campbell, Jr.

Yet is that so? Jack Williamson got along. So did Jack Vance. In the last analysis it's the stories that count. You can call yourself Abdul Alhazred, if you want to, or even Fyodor Dostoevski, but if your stories consistently stink, so will your name.

And if your stories are good, your name will glow, however dull it might be intrinsically—even if it be something as ordinary and commonplace as Isaac Asimov.

13

A SONG FOR LYA

The cities of the Shkeen are old, older far than man's, and the great rust-red metropolis that rose from their sacred hill country had proved to be the oldest of them all. The Shkeen city had no name. It needed none. Though they built cities and towns by the hundreds and the thousands, the hill city had no rivals. It was the largest in size and population, and it was alone in the sacred hills. It was their Rome, Mecca, Jerusalem; all in one. It was *the* city, and all Shkeen came to it at last, in the final days before Union.

That city had been ancient in the days before Rome fell, had been huge and sprawling when Babylon was still a dream. But there was no feel of age to it. The human eye saw only miles and miles of low, red-brick domes; small hummocks of dried mud that covered the rolling hills like a rash. Inside they were dim and nearly airless. The rooms were small and the furniture crude.

Yet it was not a grim city. Day after day it squatted in those scrubby hills, broiling under a hot sun that sat in the sky like a weary orange melon; but the city teemed with life: smells of cooking, the sounds of laughter and talk and children running, the bustle and sweat of brickmen repairing the domes, the bells of the Joined ringing in the streets. The Shkeen were a lusty and exuberant people, almost childlike. Certainly there was nothing about them that told of great age or ancient wisdom. This is a young race, said the signs, this is a culture in its infancy.

But that infancy had lasted more than fourteen thousand years.

The human city was the real infant, less than ten Earth years old. It was built on the edge of the hills, between the Shkeen metropolis and the dusty brown plains where the spaceport had gone up. In human terms, it was a beautiful city: open and airy, full of graceful archways and glistening fountains and wide boulevards lined by trees. The buildings were wrought of metal and colored plastic and native woods, and most of them were low in deference to Shkeen architecture. Most of them . . . the Administration Tower was the exception, a polished blue steel needle that split a crystal sky.

You could see it for miles in all directions. Lyanna spied it even before we landed, and we admired it from the air. The gaunt skyscrapers of Old Earth and Baldur were taller, and the fantastic webbed cities of Arachne were far more beautiful—but that slim blue Tower was still imposing enough as it rose unrivaled to its lonely dominance above the sacred hills.

The spaceport was in the shadow of the Tower, easy walking distance. But they met us anyway. A low-slung scarlet aircar sat purring at the base of the ramp as we disembarked, with a driver lounging against the stick. Dino Valcarenghi stood next to it, leaning on the door and talking to an aide.

Valcarenghi was the planetary administrator, the boy wonder of the sector. Young, of course, but I'd known that. Short, and good-looking, in a dark, intense way, with black hair that curled thickly against his head and an easy, genial smile.

He flashed us that smile then, when we stepped off the ramp, and reached to shake hands. "Hi," he began, "I'm glad to see you." There was no nonsense with formal introductions. He knew who we were, and we knew who he was, and Valcarenghi wasn't the kind of man who put much stock in ritual.

Lyanna took his hand lightly in hers, and gave him her vampire look: big, dark eyes opened wide and staring, thin mouth lifted in a tiny faint smile. She's a small girl, almost waiflike, with short brown hair and a child's figure. She can look very fragile, very helpless. When she wants to. But she rattles people with that look. If they know Lya's a telepath, they figure she's poking around amid their innermost secrets. Actually she's playing with them. When Lyanna is *really* reading, her whole body goes stiff and you can almost see her tremble. And those big, soul-sucking eyes get narrow and hard and opaque.

But not many people know that, so they squirm under her vampire eyes and look the other way and hurry to release her hand. Not Valcarenghi, though. He just smiled and stared back, then moved on to me.

I *was* reading when I took his hand—my standard operating procedure. Also a bad habit, I guess, since it's put some promising friendships into an early grave. My talent isn't equal to Lya's. But it's not as demanding, either. I read emotions. Valcarenghi's geniality came through strong and genuine. With nothing behind it, or at least nothing that was close enough to the surface for me to catch.

We also shook hands with the aide, a middle-aged blond stork named Nelson Gourlay. Then Valcarenghi ushered everybody into the aircar and we took off. "I imagine you're tired," he said after we were airborne, "so we'll save the tour of the city and head straight for the Tower. Nelse will show you your quarters, then you can join us for a drink, and we'll talk over the problem. You've read the materials I sent?"

"Yes," I said. Lya nodded. "Interesting background, but I'm not sure why we're here."

"We'll get to that soon enough," Valcarenghi replied. "I ought to be letting you enjoy the scenery." He gestured toward the window, smiled, and fell silent.

So Lya and I enjoyed the scenery, or as much as we could enjoy during the five-minute flight from spaceport to tower. The aircar was whisking down the main street at treetop level, stirring up a breeze that whipped the thin branches as we went by. It was cool and dark in the interior of the car, but outside the Shkeen sun was riding toward noon, and you could see the heat waves shimmering from the pavement. The population must have been inside huddled around their air-conditioners, because we saw very little traffic.

We got out near the main entrance to the Tower and walked through a huge, sparkling-clean lobby. Valcarenghi left us then to talk to some underlings. Gourlay led us into one of the tubes and we shot up fifty floors. Then we waltzed past a secretary into another, private tube, and climbed some more.

Our rooms were lovely, carpeted in cool green, and paneled with wood. There was a complete library there, mostly Earth classics bound in synthaleather, with a few novels from Baldur, our home world. Somebody had been researching our tastes. One of the walls of the bedroom was tinted glass, giving a panoramic view of the city far below us, with a control that could darken it for sleeping.

Gourlay showed it to us dutifully, like a dour bellhop. I read him briefly though, and found no resentment. He was nervous, but only slightly. There was honest affection there for someone. Us? Valcarenghi?

Lya sat down on one of the twin beds. "Is someone bringing our luggage?" she asked.

Gourlay nodded. "You'll be well taken care of," he said. "Anything you want, ask."

"Don't worry, we will," I said. I dropped to the second bed, and gestured Gourlay to a chair. "How long you been here?"

"Six years," he said, taking the chair gratefully and sprawling out all over it. "I'm one of the veterans. I've worked under four administrators now. Dino, and Stuart before him, and Gustaffson before *him*. I was even under Rockwood a few months."

Lya perked up, crossing her legs under her and leaning forward. "That was all Rockwood lasted, wasn't it?"

"Right," Gourlay said. "He didn't like the planet, took a quick demotion to assistant administrator someplace else. I didn't care much, to tell the truth. He was the nervous type, always giving orders to prove who was boss."

"And Valcarenghi?" I asked.

Gourlay made a smile look like a yawn. "Dino? Dino's OK, the best of the lot. He's good, knows he's good. He's only been here two months, but he's gotten a lot done, and he's made a lot of friends. He treats the staff like people, calls everybody by his first name, all that stuff. People like that."

I was reading, and I read sincerity. It was Valcarenghi that Gourlay was affectionate toward, then. He believed what he was saying.

I had more questions, but I didn't get to ask them. Gourlay got up suddenly. "I really shouldn't stay," he said. "You want to rest, right? Come up to the top in about two hours and we'll go over things with you. You know where the tube is?"

We nodded, and Gourlay left. I turned to Lyanna. "What do you think?"

She lay back on the bed and considered the ceiling. "I don't know," she said. "I wasn't reading. I wonder why they've had so many administrators. And why they wanted us."

"We're Talented," I said, smiling. With the capital, yes. Lyanna and I have been tested and registered as psi Talents, and we have the licenses to prove it.

"Uh-huh," she said, turning on her side and smiling back at me. Not her vampire half-smile this time. Her sexy little girl smile.

"Valcarenghi wants us to get some rest," I said. "It's probably not a bad idea."

Lya bounced out of bed. "OK," she said, "but these twins have got to go."

"We could push them together."

She smiled again. We pushed them together.

And we *did* get some sleep. Eventually.

Our luggage was outside the door when we woke. We changed into fresh clothes, old casual stuff, counting on Valcarenghi's notorious lack of pomp. The tube took us to the top of the Tower.

The office of the planetary administrator was hardly an office. There was no desk, none of the usual trappings. Just a bar and lush blue carpets that swallowed us ankle high, and six or seven scattered chairs. Plus lots of space and sunlight, with Shkea laid out at our feet beyond the tinted glass. All four walls this time.

Valcarenghi and Gourlay were waiting for us, and Valcarenghi did the bartending chores personally. I didn't recognize the beverage, but it was cool and spicy and aromatic, with a real sting to it. I sipped it gratefully. For some reason I felt I needed a lift.

"Shkeen wine," Valcarenghi said, smiling, in answer to an unasked question. "They've got a name for it, but I can't pronounce it yet. But give me time. I've only been here two months, and the language is rough."

"You're learning Shkeen?" Lya asked, surprised. I knew why. Shkeen is rough on human tongues, but the natives learned Terran with stunning ease. Most people accepted that happily, and just forgot about the difficulties of cracking the alien language.

"It gives me an insight into the way they think," Valcarenghi said. "At least that's the theory." He smiled.

I read him again, although it was more difficult. Physical contact makes things sharper. Again, I got a simple emotion, close to the surface—pride this time. With pleasure mixed in. I chalked that up to the wine. Nothing beneath.

"However you pronounce the drink, I like it," I said.

"The Shkeen produce a wide variety of liquors and foodstuffs," Gourlay put in. "We've cleared many for export already, and we're checking others. Market should be good."

"You'll have a chance to sample more of the local produce this evening," Valcarenghi said. "I've set up a tour of the city, with a stop or two in Shkeentown. For a settlement of our size, our night life is fairly interesting. I'll be your guide."

"Sounds good," I said. Lya was smiling too. A tour was unusually considerate. Most Normals feel uneasy around Talents, so they rush us in to do whatever they want done, then rush us out again as quickly as possible. They certainly don't socialize with us.

"Now—the problem," Valcarenghi said, lowering his drink and leaning forward in the chair. "You read about the Cult of the Union?"

"A Shkeen religion," Lya said.

"*The* Shkeen religion," corrected Valcarenghi. "Every one of them is a believer. This is a planet without heretics."

"We read the materials you sent on it," Lya said. "Along with everything else."

"What do you think?"

I shrugged. "Grim. Primitive. But no more than any number of others I've read about. The Shkeen aren't very advanced, after all. There were religions on Old Earth that included human sacrifice."

Valcarenghi shook his head, and looked toward Gourlay.

"No, you don't understand," Gourlay started, putting his drink down on the carpet. "I've been studying their religion for six years. It's like no other in history. Nothing on Old Earth like it, no sir. Nor in any other race we've encountered.

"And Union, well, it's wrong to compare it to human sacrifice, just wrong. The Old Earth religions sacrificed one or two unwilling victims to appease their gods. Killed a handful to get mercy for the millions. And the handful generally protested. The Shkeen don't work it that way. The Greeshka takes *everyone*. And they go willingly. Like lemmings they march off to the caves to be eaten alive by those parasites. *Every* Shkeen is Joined at forty, and goes to Final Union before he's fifty."

I was confused. "All right," I said. "I see the distinction, I guess. But so what? Is this the problem? I imagine that Union is rough on the Shkeen, but that's their business. Their religion is no worse than the ritual cannibalism of the Hrangans, is it?"

Valcarenghi finished his drink and got up, heading for the bar. As he poured himself a refill, he said, almost casually, "As far as I know, Hrangan cannibalism has claimed no human converts."

Lya looked startled. I felt startled. I sat up and stared. "What?"

Valcarenghi headed back to his seat, glass in hand. "Human converts have been joining the Cult of the Union. Dozens of them are already Joined. None of them have achieved full Union yet, but that's only a question of time." He sat down, and looked at Gourlay. So did we.

The gangling blond aide picked up the narrative. "The first convert was about seven years ago. Nearly a year before I got here, two and a half after Shkea was discovered and the settlement built. Guy named Magly. Psi-psych, worked closely with the Shkeen. He was it for two years. Then another in '08, more than next year. And the rate's been climbing every since. There was one big one. Phil Gustaffson."

Lya blinked. "The planetary administrator?"

"The same," said Gourlay. "We've had a lot of administrators. Gustaffson came in after Rockwood couldn't stand it. He was a big, gruff old guy. Everybody loved him. He'd lost his wife and kids on his last assignment, but you'd never have known it. He was always hearty, full of fun. Well, he got interested in the Shkeen religion, started talking to them. Talked to Magly and some of the other converts too. Even went to see a Greeshka. That shook him up real bad for a while. But finally he got over it, went back to his researches. I worked with him, but I never guessed what he had in mind. A little over a year ago, he converted. He's Joined now. Nobody's ever been accepted that fast.

I hear talk in Shkeentown that he may even be admitted to Final Union, rushed right in. Well, Phil was administrator here longer than anybody else. People liked him, and when he went over, a lot of his friends followed. The rate's way up now."

"Not quite one percent, and rising," Valcarenghi said. "That seems low, but remember what it means. One percent of the people in my settlement are choosing a religion that includes a very unpleasant form of suicide."

Lya looked from him to Gourlay and back again. "Why hasn't this been reported?"

"It should have been," Valcarenghi said. "But Stuart succeeded Gustaffson, and he was scared stiff of a scandal. There's no law against humans adopting an alien religion, so Stuart defined it as a nonproblem. He reported the conversion rate routinely, and nobody higher up ever bothered to make the correlation and remember just what all these people were converting *to*."

I finished my drink, set it down. "Go on," I said to Valcarenghi.

"I define the situation as a problem," he said. "I don't care how few people are involved, the idea that human beings would allow the Greeshka to consume them alarms me. I've had a team of psychs on it since I took over, but they're getting nowhere. I needed Talent. I want you two to find out *why* these people are converting. Then I'll be able to deal with the situation."

The problem was strange, but the assignment seemed straightforward enough. I read Valcarenghi to be sure. His emotions were a bit more complex this time, but not much. Confidence above all: he was sure we could handle the problem. There was honest concern there, but no fear, and not even a hint of deception. Again, I couldn't catch anything below the surface. Valcarenghi kept his hidden turmoil well hidden, if he had any.

I glanced at Lyanna. She was sitting awkwardly in her chair, and her fingers were wrapped very tightly around her wine glass. Reading. Then she loosened up and looked my way and nodded.

"All right," I said. "I think we can do it."

Valcarenghi smiled. "That I never doubted," he said. "It was only a question of whether you *would*. But enough of business for tonight. I've promised you a night on the town, and I always try to deliver on my promises. I'll meet you downstairs in the lobby in a half-hour."

Lya and I changed into something more formal back in our room. I picked a dark blue tunic, with white slacks and a matching mesh scarf. Not the height of fashion, but I was hoping that Shkea would be several months behind the times. Lya slipped into a silky white skintight with a tracery of thin blue lines that flowed over her in sensuous patterns in response to her body heat. The lines were definitely lecherous, accentuating her thin figure with a singleminded determination. A blue raincape completed the outfit.

"Valcarenghi's funny," she said as she fastened it.

"Oh?" I was struggling with the sealseam on my tunic, which refused to seal. "You catch something when you read him?"

"No," she said. She finished attaching the cape and admired herself in the mirror. Then she spun toward me, the cape swirling behind her. "That's it. He was thinking what he was saying. Oh, variations in the wording, of course, but nothing important. His mind was on what we were discussing, and behind that there was only a wall." She smiled. "Didn't get a single one of his deep dark secrets."

I finally conquered the sealseam. "Tsk," I said. "Well, you get another chance tonight."

That got me a grimace. "The hell I do. I don't read people on off-time. It isn't fair. Besides, it's such a strain. I wish I could catch thoughts as easily as you do feelings."

"The price of Talent," I said. "You're more Talented, your price is higher." I rummaged in our luggage for a raincape, but I didn't find anything that went well, so I decided not to wear one. Capes were out, anyway. "I didn't get much on Valcarenghi either. You could have told as much by watching his face. He must be a very disciplined mind. But I'll forgive him. He serves good wine."

Lya nodded. "Right! That stuff did me good. Got rid of the headache I woke up with."

"The altitude," I suggested. We headed for the door.

The lobby was deserted, but Valcarenghi didn't keep us waiting long. This time he drove his own aircar, a battered black job that had evidently been with him for a while. Gourlay wasn't the sociable type, but Valcarenghi had a woman with him, a stunning auburn-haired vision named Laurie Blackburn. She was even younger than Valcarenghi—mid-twenties, by the look of her.

It was sunset when we took off. The whole far horizon was a gorgeous tapestry in red and orange, and a cool breeze was blowing in from the plains. Valcarenghi left the coolers off and opened the car windows, and we watched the city darken into twilight as we drove.

Dinner was at a plush restaurant with Baldurian decor—to make us feel comfortable, I guessed. The food, however, was very cosmopolitan. The spices, the herbs, the *style* of cooking were all Baldur. The meats and vegetables were native. It made for an interesting combination. Valcarenghi ordered for all four of us, and we wound up sampling about a dozen different dishes. My favorite was a tiny Shkeen bird that they cooked in sourtang sauce. There wasn't very much of it, but what there was tasted great. We also polished off three bottles of wine during the meal: more of the Shkeen stuff we'd sampled that afternoon, a flask of chilled Veltaar from Baldur, and some real Old Earth Burgundy.

The talk warmed up quickly; Valcarenghi was a born storyteller and an equally good listener. Eventually, of course, the conversation got around to Shkea and the Shkeen. Laurie led it there. She'd been on Shkea for about six months, working toward an advanced degree in extee anthropology. She was trying to discover why the Shkeen civilization had remained frozen for so many millennia.

"They're older than we are, you know," she told us. "They had cities before men were using tools. It should have been space-traveling Shkeen that stumbled on primitive men, not the other way around."

"Aren't there theories on that already?" I asked.

"Yes, but none of them is universally accepted," she said. "Cullen cites a lack of heavy metals, for example. A factor, but is it the *whole* answer? Von Hamrin claims the Shkeen didn't get enough competition. No big carnivores on the planet, so there was nothing to breed aggressiveness into the race. But he's come

under a lot of fire. Shkea isn't all *that* idyllic; if it were, the
Shkeen never would have reached their present level. Besides,
what's the Greeshka if not a carnivore? It *eats* them, doesn't it?"

"What do you think?" Lya asked.

"I think it had something to do with the religion, but I haven't
worked it all out yet. Dino's helping me talk to people and the
Shkeen are open enough, but research isn't easy." She stopped
suddenly and looked at Lya hard. "For me, anyway. I imagine
it'd be easier for you."

We'd heard that before. Normals often figure that Talents
have unfair advantages, which is perfectly understandable. We
do. But Laurie wasn't resentful. She delivered her statement in a
wistful, speculative tone, instead of etching it in verbal acid.

Valcarenghi leaned over and put an arm around her. "Hey," he
said. "Enough shop talk. Robb and Lya shouldn't be worrying
about the Shkeen until tomorrow."

Laurie looked at him, and smiled tentatively. "OK," she said
lightly. "I get carried away. Sorry."

"That's OK," I told her. "It's an interesting subject. Give us a
day and we'll probably be getting enthusiastic too."

Lya nodded agreement, and added that Laurie would be the
first to know if our work turned up anything that would support
her theory. I was hardly listening. I know it's not polite to read
Normals when you're out with them socially, but there are times
I can't resist. Valcarenghi had his arm around Laurie and had
pulled her toward him gently. I was curious.

So I took a quick, guilty reading. He was very high—slightly
drunk, I guess, and feeling very confident and protective. The
master of the situation. But Laurie was a jumble—uncertainty,
repressed anger, a vague fading hint of fright. And love, confused but very strong. I doubted that it was for me or Lya. She
loved Valcarenghi.

I reached under the table, searching for Lya's hand, and found
her knee. I squeezed it gently and she looked at me and smiled.
She wasn't reading, which was good. It bothered me that Laurie
loved Valcarenghi, though I didn't know why, and I was just as
glad that Lya didn't see my discontent.

We finished off the last of the wine in short order, and Valcarenghi took care of the whole bill. Then he rose. "Onward!" he announced. "The night is fresh, and we've got visits to make."

So we made visits. No holoshows or anything that drab, although the city had its share of theaters. A casino was next on the list. Gambling was legal on Shkea, of course, and Valcarenghi would have legalized it if it weren't. He supplied the chips and I lost some for him, as did Laurie. Lya was barred from playing; her Talent was too strong. Valcarenghi won big; he was a superb mindspin player, and pretty good at the traditional games too.

Then came a bar. More drinks, plus local entertainment which was better than I would have expected.

It was pitch black when we got out, and I assumed that the expedition was nearing its end. Valcarenghi surprised us. When we got back to the car, he reached under the controls, pulled out a box of sober-ups, and passed them around.

"Hey," I said. "You're driving. Why do I need this? I just barely got up here."

"I'm about to take you to a genuine Shkeen cultural event, Robb," he said. "I don't want you making rude comments or throwing up on the natives. Take your pill."

I took my pill, and the buzz in my head began to fade. Valcarenghi already had the car airborne. I leaned back and put my arm around Lya, and she rested her head on my shoulder. "Where are we going?" I asked.

"Shkeentown," he replied, never looking back, "to their Great Hall. There's a Gathering tonight, and I figured you'd be interested."

"It will be in Shkeen, of course," Laurie said, "but Dino can translate for you. I know a little of the language too, and I'll fill in whatever he misses."

Lya looked excited. We'd read about Gatherings, of course, but we hardly expected to go see one on our first day of Shkea. The Gatherings were a species of religious rite; a mass confessional of sorts for pilgrims who were about to be admitted to the ranks of the Joined. Pilgrims swelled the hill city daily, but Gatherings were conducted only three or four times a year when the numbers of those-about-to-be-Joined climbed high enough.

The aircar streaked almost soundlessly through the brightly lit settlement, passing huge fountains that danced with a dozen colors and pretty ornamental arches that flowed like liquid fire. A few other cars were airborne, and here and there we flew above pedestrians strolling the city's broad malls. But most people were inside, and light and music flooded from many of the homes we passed.

Then, abruptly, the character of the city began to change. The level ground began to roll and heave, hills rose before us and then behind us, and the lights vanished. Below, the malls gave way to unlit roads of crushed stone and dust, and the domes of glass and metal done in fashionable mock-Shkeen yielded to their older brick brothers. The Shkeen city was quieter than its human counterpart; most of the houses were darkly silent.

Then, ahead of us, a hummock appeared that was larger than the others—almost a hill in itself, with a big arched door and a series of slitlike windows. And light leaked from this one, and noise, and there were Shkeen outside.

I suddenly realized that, although I'd been on Shkea for nearly a day, this was the first sight I'd caught of the Shkeen. Not that I could see them all that clearly from an aircar at night. But I did see them. They were smaller than men—the tallest was around five feet—with big eyes and long arms. That was all I could tell from above.

Valcarenghi put the car down alongside the Great Hall, and we piled out. Shkeen were trickling through the arch from several directions, but most of them were already inside. We joined the trickle, and nobody even looked twice at us, except for one character who hailed Valcarenghi in a thin, squeaky voice and called him Dino. He had friends even here.

The interior was one huge room, with a great crude platform built in the center and an immense crowd of Shkeen circling it. The only light was from torches that were stuck in grooves along the walls, and on high poles surrounding the platform. Someone was speaking, and every one of those great, bulging eyes was turned his way. We four were the only humans in the Hall.

The speaker, outlined brightly by the torches, was a fat, middle-aged Shkeen who moved his arms slowly, almost hypnotically, as he talked. His speech was a series of whistles, wheezes, and grunts, so I didn't listen very closely. He was much too far away to read. I was reduced to studying his appearance, and that of other Shkeen near me. All of them were hairless, as far as I could see, with softish-looking orange skin that was creased by a thousand tiny wrinkles. They wore simple shifts of crude, multicolored cloth, and I had difficulty telling male from female.

Valcarenghi leaned over toward me and whispered, careful to keep his voice low. "The speaker is a farmer," he said. "He's telling the crowd how far he's come, and some of the hardships of his life."

I looked around. Valcarenghi's whisper was the only sound in the place. Everyone else was dead quiet, eyes riveted on the platform, scarcely breathing. "He's saying that he has four brothers," Valcarenghi told me. "Two have gone on to Final Union, one is among the Joined. The other is younger than himself, and now owns the farm." He frowned. "The speaker will never see his farm again," he said, more loudly, "but he's happy about it."

"Bad crops?" asked Lya, smiling irreverently. She'd been listening to the same whisper. I gave her a stern look.

The Shkeen went on. Valcarenghi stumbled after him. "Now he's telling his crimes, all the things he's done that he's ashamed of, his blackest soul-secrets. He's had a sharp tongue at times, he's vain, once he actually struck his younger brother. Now he speaks of his wife, and the other women he has known. He has betrayed her many times, copulating with others. As a boy, he mated with animals for he feared females. In recent years he has grown incapable, and his brother has serviced his wife."

On and on and on it went, in incredible detail, detail that was both startling and frightening. No intimacy went untold, no secret was left undisturbed. I stood and listened to Valcarenghi's whispers, shocked at first, finally growing bored with the squalor of it all. I began to get restless. I wondered briefly if I knew any human half so well as I now knew this great fat Shkeen. Then I wondered whether Lyanna, with her Talent, knew anyone half so well. It was almost as if the speaker wanted all of us to live through his life right here and now.

His speech lasted for what seemed hours, but finally it began to wind up. "He speaks now of Union," Valcarenghi whispered. "He will be Joined, he is joyful about it, he has craved it for so long. His misery is at an end, his aloneness will cease, soon he shall walk the streets of the sacred city and peal his joy with the bells. And then Final Union, in the years to come. He will be with his brothers in the afterlife."

"No, Dino." This whisper was Laurie. "Quit wrapping human phrases around what he says. He will be his brothers, he says. The phrase also implies they will be him."

Valcarenghi smiled. "OK, Laurie. If you say so . . ."

Suddenly the fat farmer was gone from the platform. The crowd rustled, and another figure took his place: much shorter, wrinkled excessively, one eye a great gaping hole. He began to speak, haltingly at first, then with greater skill.

"This one is a brickman, he has worked many domes, he lives in the sacred city. His eye was lost many years ago, when he fell from a dome and a sharp stick poked into him. The pain was very great, but he returned to work within a year, he did not beg for premature Union, he was very brave, he is proud of his courage. He has a wife, but they never had offspring, he is sad of that, he cannot talk to his wife easily, they are apart even when together and she weeps at night, he is sad of that too, but he has never hurt her and . . ."

It went on for hours again. My restlessness stirred again, but I cracked down on it—this was too important. I let myself get lost in Valcarenghi's narration, and the story of the one-eyed Shkeen. Before long, I was riveted as closely to the tale as the aliens around me. It was hot and stuffy and all but airless in the dome, and my tunic was getting sooty and soaked by sweat, some of it from the creatures who pressed around me. But I hardly noticed.

The second speaker ended as had the first, with a long praise of the joy of being Joined and the coming of Final Union. Toward the end, I hardly even needed Valcarenghi's translation—I could hear the happiness in the voice of the Shkeen, and see it in his trembling figure. Or maybe I was reading, unconsciously. But I can't read at that distance—unless the target is emoting very hard.

A third speaker ascended the platform, and spoke in a voice louder than the others. Valcarenghi kept pace. "A woman this time," he said. "She has carried eight children for her man, she has four sisters and three brothers, she has farmed all her life, she . . ."

Suddenly her speech seemed to peak, and she ended a long sequence with several sharp, high whistles. Then she fell silent. The crowd, as one, began to respond with whistles of their own. An eerie, echoing music filled the Great Hall, and the Shkeen around us all began to sway and whistle. The woman looked out at the scene from a bent and broken position.

Valcarenghi started to translate, but he stumbled over something. Laurie cut in before he could backtrack. "She has now told them of great tragedy," she whispered. "They whistle to show their grief, their oneness with her pain."

"Sympathy, yes," said Valcarenghi, taking over again. "When she was young, her brother grew ill, and seemed to be dying. Her parents told her to take him to the sacred hills, for they could not leave the younger children. But she shattered a wheel on her cart through careless driving, and her brother died upon the plains. He perished without Union. She blames herself."

The Shkeen had begun again. Laurie began to translate, leaning close to us and using a soft whisper. "Her brother died, she is saying again. She faulted him, denied him Union, now he is sundered and alone and gone without . . . without . . ."

"Afterlife," said Valcarenghi. "Without afterlife."

"I'm not sure that's entirely right," Laurie said. "That concept is . . ."

Valcarenghi waved her silent. "Listen," he said. He continued to translate.

We listened to her story, told in Valcarenghi's increasingly hoarse whisper. She spoke longest of all, and her story was the grimmest of the three. When she finished, she too was replaced. But Valcarenghi put a hand on my shoulder and beckoned toward the exit.

The cool night air hit like ice water, and I suddenly realized that I was drenched with sweat. Valcarenghi walked quickly toward the car. Behind us, the speaking was still in progress, and the Shkeen showed no signs of tiring.

"Gatherings go on for days, sometimes weeks," Laurie told us as we climbed inside the aircar. "The Shkeen listen in shifts, more or less—they try terribly to hear every word, but exhaustion gets to them sooner or later and they retire for brief rests, then return for more. It is a great honor to last through an entire Gathering without sleep."

Valcarenghi shot us aloft. "I'm going to try that someday," he said. "I've never attended for more than a couple of hours, but I think I could make it if I fortified myself with drugs. We'll get more understanding between human and Shkeen if we participate more fully in their rituals."

"Oh," I said. "Maybe Gustaffson felt the same way."

Valcarenghi laughed lightly. "Yes, well, I don't intend to participate *that* fully."

The trip home was a tired silence. I'd lost track of time but my body insisted that it was almost dawn. Lya, curled up under my arm, looked drained and empty and only half-awake. I felt the same way.

We left the aircar in front of the Tower, and took the tubes up. I was past thinking. Sleep came very, very quickly.

I dreamed that night. A good dream, I think, but it faded with the coming of the light, leaving me empty and feeling cheated. I lay there, after waking, with my arm around Lya and my eyes on the ceiling, trying to recall what the dream had been about. But nothing came.

Instead, I found myself thinking about the Gathering, running it through again in my head. Finally I disentangled myself and climbed out of bed. We'd darkened the glass, so the room was still pitch black. But I found the controls easily enough, and let through a trickle of late morning light.

Lya mumbed some sort of sleepy protest and rolled over, but made no effort to get up. I left her alone in the bedroom and went out to our library, looking for a book on the Shkeen—something with a little more detail than the material we'd been sent. No luck. The library was meant for recreation, not research.

I found a viewscreen and punched up to Valcarenghi's office. Gourlay answered. "Hello," he said. "Dino figured you'd be calling. He's not here right now. He's out arbitrating a trade contract. What do you need?"

"Books," I said, my voice still a little sleepy. "Something on the Shkeen."

"That I can't do," Gourlay said. "Are none, really. Lots of

papers and studies and monographs, but no full-fledged books. I'm going to write one, but I haven't gotten to it yet. Dino figured I could be your resource, I guess."

"Oh."

"Got any questions?"

I searched for a question, found none. "Not really," I said, shrugging. "I just wanted general background, maybe some more information on Gatherings."

"I can talk to you about that later," Gourlay said. "Dino figured you'd want to get to work today. We can bring people to the Tower, if you'd like, or you can get out to them."

"We'll go out," I said quickly. Bringing subjects in for interviews fouls up everything. They get all anxious, and that covers up any emotions I might want to read, and they *think* on different things, too, so Lyanna has trouble.

"Fine," said Gourlay. "Dino put an aircar at your disposal. Pick it up down in the lobby. Also, they'll have some keys for you, so you can come straight up here to the office without bothering with the secretaries and all."

"Thanks," I said. "Talk to you later." I flicked off the viewscreen and walked back to the bedroom.

Lya was sitting up, the covers around her waist. I sat down next to her and kissed her. She smiled, but didn't respond. "Hey," I said. "What's wrong?"

"Headache," she replied. "I thought sober-ups were supposed to get rid of hangovers."

"That's the theory. Mine worked pretty well." I went to the closet and began looking for something to wear. "We should have headache pills around here someplace. I'm sure Dino wouldn't forget anything that obvious."

"Umpf. Yes. Throw me some clothes."

I grabbed one of her coveralls and tossed it across the room. Lya stood up and slipped into it while I dressed, then went off to the washroom.

"Better," she said. "You're right, he didn't forget medicines."

"He's the thorough sort."

She smiled. "I guess. Laurie knows the language better, though. I read her. Dino made a couple of mistakes in that translation last night."

I'd guessed at something like that. No discredit to Valcarenghi; he was working on a four-month handicap, from what they'd said. I nodded. "Read anything else?"

"No. I tried to get those speakers, but the distance was too much." She came up and took my hand. "Where are we going today?"

"Shkeentown," I said. "Let's try to find some of these Joined. I didn't notice any at the Gathering."

"No. Those things are for Shkeen about-to-be-Joined."

"So I hear. Let's go."

We went. We stopped at the fourth level for a late breakfast in the Tower cafeteria, then got our aircar pointed out to us by a man in the lobby. A sporty green four-seater, very common, very inconspicuous.

I didn't take the aircar all the way into the Shkeen city, figuring we'd get more of the feel of the place if we went through on foot. So I dropped down just beyond the first range of hills, and we walked.

The human city had seemed almost empty, but Shkeentown lived. The crushed-rock streets were full of aliens, hustling back and forth busily, carrying loads of bricks and baskets of fruit and clothing. There were children everywhere, most of them naked: fat balls of orange energy that ran around us in circles, whistling and grunting and grinning, tugging at us every once in a while. The kids looked different from the adults. They had a few patches of reddish hair, for one thing, and their skins were still smooth and unwrinkled. They were the only ones who really paid any attention to us. The adult Shkeen just went about their business, and gave us an occasional friendly smile. Humans were obviously not all that uncommon in the streets of Shkeentown.

Most of the traffic was on foot, but small wooden carts were also common. The Shkeen draft animal looked like a big green dog that was about to be sick. They were strapped to the carts in pairs, and they whined constantly as they pulled. So, naturally, men called them whiners. In addition to whining, they also defecated constantly. That, with odors from the food peddled in baskets and the Shkeen themselves, gave the city a definite pungency.

There was noise too, a constant clamor. Kids whistling, Shkeen talking loudly with grunts and whimpers and squeaks, whiners whining and their carts rattling over the rocks. Lya and I walked through it all silently, hand in hand, watching and listening and smelling and . . . reading.

I was wide open when I entered Shkeentown, letting everything wash over me as I walked, unfocused but receptive. I was the center of a small bubble of emotion—feelings rushed up at me as Shkeen approached, faded as they walked away, circled around and around with the dancing children. I swam in a sea of impressions. And it startled me.

It startled me because it was all so familiar. I'd read aliens before. Sometimes it was difficult, sometimes it was easy, but it was never pleasant. The Hrangans have sour minds, rank with hate and bitterness, and I feel unclean when I come out. The Fyndii feel emotions so palely that I can scarcely read them at all. The Damoosh are . . . *different*. I read them strongly, but I can't find names for the feelings I read.

But the Shkeen—it was like walking down a street on Baldur. No wait—more like one of the Lost Colonies, when a human settlement has fallen back into barbarism and forgotten its origins. Human emotions rage there, primal and strong and real, but less sophisticated than on Old Earth or Baldur. The Shkeen were like that: primitive, maybe, but very understandable. I read joy and sorrow, envy, anger, whimsy, bitterness, yearning, pain. The same heady mixture that engulfs me everywhere, when I open myself to it.

Lya was reading, too. I felt her hand tense in mine. After a while, it softened again. I turned to her, and she saw the question in my eyes.

"They're people," she said. "They're like us."

I nodded. "Parallel evolution, maybe. Shkea might be an older Earth, with a few minor differences. But you're right. They're more human than any other race we've encountered in space." I considered that. "Does that answer Dino's question? If they're like us, it follows that their religion would be more appealing than a *really* alien one."

"No, Robb," Lya said. "I don't think so. Just the reverse. If they're like us, it doesn't make sense that *they'd* go off so willingly to die. See?"

She was right, of course. There was nothing suicidal in the emotions I'd read, nothing unstable, nothing really abnormal. Yet every one of the Shkeen went off to Final Union in the end.

"We should focus on somebody," I said. "This blend of thought isn't getting us anywhere." I looked around to find a subject, but just then I heard the bells begin.

They were off to the left somewhere, nearly lost in the city's gentle roar. I tugged Lya by the hand, and we ran down the street to find them, turning left at the first gap in the orderly row of domes.

The bells were still ahead, and we kept running, cutting through what must have been somebody's yard, and climbing over a low bush fence that bristled with sweethorns. Beyond that was another yard, a dung pit, more domes, and finally a street. It was there we found the bell-ringers.

There were four of them, all Joined, wearing long gowns of bright red fabric that trailed in the dust, with great bronze bells in either hand. They rang the bells constantly, their long arms swinging back and forth, the sharp, clanging notes filling the street. All four were elderly, as Shkeen go—hairless and pinched up with a million tiny wrinkles. But they smiled very widely, and the younger Shkeen that passed smiled at them.

On their heads rode the Greeshka.

I'd expected to find the sight hideous. I didn't. It was faintly disquieting, but only because I knew what it meant. The parasites were bright blobs of crimson goo, ranging in size from a pulsing wart on the back of one Shkeen skull to a great sheet of dripping, moving red that covered the head and shoulders of the smallest like a living cowl. The Greeshka lived by sharing the nutrients in the Shkeen bloodstream, I knew.

And also by slowly—oh so slowly—consuming its host.

Lya and I stopped a few yards from them, and watched them ring. Her face was solemn, and I think mine was. All of the others were smiling, and the songs that the bells sang were songs of joy. I squeezed Lyanna's hand tightly. "Read," I whispered.

We read.

Me: I read bells. Not the sound of bells, no, no, but the *feel* of bells, the *emotion* of bells, the bright clanging joy, the hooting-shouting-ringing loudness, the song of the Joined, the togeth-

erness and the sharing of it all. I read what the Joined felt as
they pealed their bells, their happiness and anticipation, their ecstasy in telling others of their clamorous contentment. And I
read love, coming from them in great hot waves, passionate possessive love of a man and woman together, not the weak watery
affection of the human who "loves" his brothers. This was real
and fervent and it burned almost as it washed over me and surrounded me. They loved themselves, and they loved all Shkeen,
and they loved the Greeshka, and they loved each other, and
they loved us. They loved us. They loved *me*, as hotly and wildly
as Lya loved me. And with love I read belonging, and sharing.
They four were all apart, all distinct, but they thought as one almost, and they belonged to the Greeshka, and they were all *together* and linked although each was still himself and none could
read the others as I read them.

And Lyanna? I reeled back from them, and shut myself off,
and looked at Lya. She was white-faced, but smiling. "They're
beautiful," she said, her voice very small and soft and wondering. Drenched in love, I still remembered how much I loved *her*,
and how I was part of her and her of me.

"What—what did you read?" I asked, my voice fighting the
continued clangor of the bells.

She shook her head, as if to clear it. "They love us," she said.
"You must know that, but oh, I felt it, they *do* love us. And it's so
deep. Below that love there's more love, and below that more,
and on and on forever. Their minds are so deep, so open. I don't
think I've ever read a human that deeply. Everything is right at
the surface, right there, their whole lives and all their dreams
and feelings and memories and oh—I just took it in, swept it up
with a reading, a glance. With men, with humans, it's so much
work. I have to dig, I have to fight, and even then I don't get
down very far. You know, Robb, you know. Oh, *Robb!*" And she
came to me and pressed tight against me, and I held her in my
arms. The torrent of feeling that had washed over me must have
been a tidal wave for her. Her Talent was broader and deeper
than mine, and now she was shaken. I read her as she clutched
me, and I read love, great love, and wonder and happiness, but
also fear, nervous fear swirling through it all.

Around us, the ringing suddenly stopped. The bells, one by

one, ceased to swing, and the four Joined stood in silence for a brief second. One of the other Shkeen nearby came up to them with a huge, cloth-covered basket. The smallest of the Joined threw back the cloth, and the aroma of hot meatrolls rose in the street. Each of the Joined took several from the basket, and before long they were all crunching away happily, and the owner of the rolls was grinning at them. Another Shkeen, a small nude girl, ran up and offered them a flask of water, and they passed it around without comment.

"What's going on?" I asked Lya. Then, even before she told me, I remembered. Something from the literature that Valcarenghi had sent. The Joined did no work. Forty Earth-years they lived and toiled, but from First Joining to Final Union there was only joy and music, and they wandered the streets and rang their bells and talked and sang, and other Shkeen gave them food and drink. It was an honor to feed a Joined, and the Shkeen who had given up his meatrolls was radiating pride and pleasure.

"Lya," I whispered, "can you read them now?"

She nodded against my chest and pulled away and stared at the Joined, her eyes going hard and then softening again. She looked back at me. "It's different," she said, curious.

"How?"

She squinted in puzzlement. "I don't know. I mean, they still love us, and all. But now their thoughts are, well, sort of more human. There are levels, you know, and digging isn't easy, and there are hidden things, things they hide even from themselves. It's not all open like it was. They're thinking about the food now and how good it tastes. It's all very vivid. I could taste the rolls myself. But it's not the same."

I had an inspiration. "How many minds are there?"

"Four," she said. "Linked somehow, I think. But not really." She stopped, confused, and shook her head. "I mean, they sort of feel each other's emotions, like you do, I guess. But not thoughts, not the detail. I can read them, but they don't read each other. Each one is distinct. They were closer before, when they were ringing, but they were always individuals."

I was slightly disappointed. "Four minds then, not one?"

"Umpf, yes. Four."

"And the Greeshka?" My other bright idea. If the Greeshka had minds of their own . . .

"Nothing," Lya said. "Like reading a plant, or a piece of clothing. Not even yes-I-live."

That was disturbing. Even lower animals had some vague consciousness of life—the feeling Talents called yes-I-live—usually only a dim spark that it took a major Talent to see. But Lya *was* a major Talent.

"Let's talk to them," I said. She nodded, and we walked up to where the Joined were munching their meatrolls. "Hello," I said awkwardly, wondering how to address them. "Can you speak Terran?"

Three of them looked at me without comprehension. But the fourth one, the little one whose Greeshka was a rippling red cape, bobbed his head up and down. "Yesh," he said, in a piping-thin voice.

I suddenly forgot what I was going to ask, but Lyanna came to my rescue. "Do you know of human Joined?" she said.

He grinned. "All Joined are one," he said.

"Oh," I said. "Well, yes, but do you know any who look like us? Tall, you know, with hair and skin that's pink or brown or something?" I came to another awkward halt, wondering just how *much* Terran the old Shkeen knew, and eyeing his Greeshka a little apprehensively.

His head bobbed from side to side. "Joined are all different, but all are one, all are shame. Shome look ash you. Would you Join?"

"No, thanks," I said. "Where can I find a human Joined?"

He bobbled his head some more. "Joined shing and ring and walk the shacred city."

Lya had been reading. "He doesn't know," she told me. "The Joined just wander and play their bells. There's no pattern to it, nobody keeps track. It's all random. Some travel in groups, some alone, and new groups form every time two bunches meet."

"We'll have to search," I said.

"Eat," the Shkeen told us. He reached into the basket on the ground and his hands came out with two steaming meatrolls. He pressed one into my hand, one in Lya's.

I looked at it dubiously. "Thank you," I told him. I pulled at

Lya with my free hand and we walked off together. The Joined grinned at us as we left, and started ringing once more before we were halfway down the street.

The meatroll was still in my hand, its crust burning my fingers. "Should I eat this?" I asked Lya.

She took a bite out of hers. "Why not? We had them last night in the restaurant, right? And I'm sure Valcarenghi would've warned us if the native food was poisonous."

That made sense, so I lifted the roll to my mouth and took a bite as I walked. It was hot, and also *hot,* and it wasn't a bit like the meatrolls we'd sampled the previous night. Those had been golden, flaky things, seasoned gently with orangespice from Baldur. The Shkeen version was crunchy, and the meat inside dripped grease and burned my mouth. But it was good, and I was hungry, and the roll didn't last long.

"Get anything else when you read the small guy?" I asked Lya around a mouthful of hot roll.

She swallowed, and nodded. "Yes, I did. He was happy, even more than the rest. He's older. He's near Final Union, and he's very thrilled about it." She spoke with her old easy manner; the after effects of reading the Joined seemed to have faded.

"Why?" I was musing out loud. "He's going to *die*. Why is he so happy about it?"

Lya shrugged. "He wasn't thinking in any great analytical detail, I'm afraid."

I licked my fingers to get rid of the last of the grease. We were at a crossroads, with Shkeen bustling by us in all directions, and now we could hear more bells on the wind. "More Joined," I said. "Want to look them up?"

"What would we find out? That we don't already know? We need a *human* Joined."

"Maybe one of this batch *will* be human."

I got Lya's withering look. "Ha. What are the odds?"

"All right," I conceded. It was now late afternoon. "Maybe we'd better head back. Get an earlier start tomorrow. Besides, Dino is probably expecting us for dinner."

Dinner, this time, was served in Valcarenghi's office, after a little additional furniture had been dragged in. His quarters, it turned out, were on the level below, but he preferred to entertain upstairs where his guests could enjoy the spectacular Tower view.

There were five of us, all told: me and Lya, Valcarenghi and Laurie, plus Gourlay. Laurie did the cooking, supervised by master chef Valcarenghi. We had beefsteaks, bred on Shkea from Old Earth stock, plus a fascinating blend of vegetables that included mushrooms from Old Earth, groundpips from Baldur, and Shkeen sweethorns. Dino liked to experiment and the dish was one of his inventions.

Lya and I gave a full report on the day's adventures, interrupted only by Valcarenghi's sharp, perceptive questioning. After dinner, we got rid of tables and dishes and sat around drinking Veltaar and talking. This time Lya and I asked the questions, with Gourlay supplying the biggest chunk of the answers. Valcarenghi listened from a cushion on the floor, one arm around Laurie, the other holding his wine glass. We were not the first Talents to visit Shkea, he told us. Nor the first to claim the Shkeen were manlike.

"Suppose that means something," he said. "But I don't know. They're *not* men, you know. No, sir. They're much more social, for one thing. Great little city builders from way back, always in towns, always surrounding themselves with others. And they're more communal than man, too. Cooperate in all sorts of things, and they're big on sharing. Trade, for instance—they see that as mutual sharing."

Valcarenghi laughed. "You can say that again. I just spent the whole day trying to work out a trade contract with a group of farmers who hadn't dealt with us before. It's not easy, believe me. They give us as much of their stuff as we ask for, if they don't need it themselves and no one else has asked for it earlier. But then they want to get whatever *they* ask for in the future. They expect it, in fact. So every time we deal we've got a choice; hand them a blank check, or go through an incredible round of talks that ends with them convinced that we're totally selfish."

Lya wasn't satisfied. "What about sex?" she demanded. "From the stuff you were translating last night, I got the impression they're monogamous."

"They're confused about sex relationships," Gourlay said. "It's very strange. Sex is sharing, you see, and it's good to share with everyone. But the sharing has to be real and meaningful. That creates problems."

Laurie sat up, attentive. "I've studied the point," she said quickly. "Shkeen morality insists they love *everybody*. But they can't do it, they're too human, too possessive. They wind up in monogamous relationships, because a really deep sex-sharing with one person is better than a million shallow physical things, in their culture. The ideal Shkeen would sex-share with everyone, with each of the unions being just as deep, but they can't achieve that ideal."

I frowned. "Wasn't somebody guilty last night over betraying his wife?"

Laurie nodded eagerly. "Yes, but the guilt was because his other relationships caused his sharing with his wife to diminish. *That* was the betrayal. If he'd been able to manage it without hurting his older relationship, the sex would have been meaningless. And, if all of the relationships have been real love-sharing, it would have been a plus. His wife would have been proud of him. It's quite an achievement for a Shkeen to be in a multiple union that works."

"And one of the greatest Shkeen crimes is to leave another alone," Gourlay said. "Emotionally alone. Without sharing."

I mulled over that, while Gourlay went on. The Shkeen had little crime, he told us. Especially no violent crime. No murders, no beatings, no prisons, no wars in their long, empty history.

"They're a race without murderers," Valcarenghi said. "Which may explain something. On Old Earth, the same cultures that had the highest suicide rates often had the lowest murder rates, too. And the Shkeen suicide rate is one hundred percent."

"They kill animals," I said.

"Not part of the Union," Gourlay replied. "The Union embraces all that thinks, and its creatures may not be killed. They do not kill Shkeen, or humans, or Greeshka."

Lya looked at me, then at Gourlay. "The Greeshka don't think," she said. "I tried to read them this morning and got nothing but the minds of the Shkeen they rode. Not even a yes-I-live."

"We've known that, but the point's always puzzled me," Valcarenghi said, climbing to his feet. He went to the bar for more wine, brought out a bottle, and filled our glasses. "A truly mind-less parasite, but an intelligent race like the Shkeen are enslaved by it. Why?"

The new wine was good and chilled, a cold trail down my throat. I drank it, and nodded, remembering the flood of eupho-ria that had swept over us earlier that day. "Drugs," I said, specu-latively. "The Greeshka must produce an organic pleasure drug. The Shkeen submit to it willingly and die happy. The joy is real, believe me. We felt it."

Lyanna looked doubtful, though, and Gourlay shook his head adamantly. "No, Robb. Not so. We've experimented on the Greeshka, and . . ."

He must have noticed my raised eyebrows. He stopped.

"How did the Shkeen feel about that?" I asked.

"Didn't tell them. They wouldn't have liked it, not at all. Greeshka's just an animal, but it's their God. Don't fool around with God, you know. We refrained for a long time, but when Gustaffson went over, old Stuart had to know. His orders. We didn't get anywhere, though. No extracts that might be a drug, no secretions, nothing. In fact, the Shkeen are the *only* native life that submits so easily. We caught a whiner, you see, and strapped it down, and let a Greeshka link up. Then, couple hours later, we yanked the straps. Damn whiner was furious, screech-ing and yelping, attacking the thing on its head. Nearly clawed its own skull to ribbons before it got it off."

"Maybe only the Shkeen are susceptible?" I said. A feeble res-cue attempt.

"Not quite," said Valcarenghi, with a small, thin smile. "There's us."

Lya was strangely silent in the tube, almost withdrawn. I as-sumed she was thinking about the conversation. But the door to our suite had barely slid shut behind us when she turned toward me and wrapped her arms around me.

I reached up and stroked her soft brown hair, slightly startled by the hug. "Hey," I muttered, "what's wrong?"

She gave me her vampire look, big-eyed and fragile. "Make love to me, Robb," she said with a soft sudden urgency. "Please. Make love to me now."

I smiled, but it was a puzzled smile, not my usual lecherous bedroom grin. Lya generally comes on impish and wicked when she's horny, but now she was all troubled and vulnerable. I didn't quite get it.

But it wasn't a time for questions, and I didn't ask any. I just pulled her to me wordlessly and kissed her hard, and we walked together to the bedroom.

And we made love, *really* made love, more than poor Normals can do. We joined our bodies as one, and I felt Lya stiffen as her mind reached out to mine. And as we moved together I was opening myself to her, drowning myself in the flood of love and need and fear that was pouring from her.

Then, quickly as it had begun, it ended. Her pleasure washed over me in a raw red wave. And I joined her on the crest, and Lya clutched me tightly, her eyes shrunk up small as she drank it all in.

Afterwards, we lay there in the darkness and let the stars of Shkea pour their radiance through the window. Lya huddled against me, her head on my chest, while I stroked her.

"That was good," I said in a drowsy-dreamy voice, smiling in the star-filled darkness.

"Yes," she replied. Her voice was soft and small, so small I barely heard it. "I love you, Robb," she whispered.

"Uh-huh," I said. "And I love you."

She pulled loose of my arm and rolled over, propping her head on a hand to stare at me and smile. "You do," she said. "I read it. I know it. And you know how much I love you, too, don't you?"

I nodded, smiling. "Sure."

"We're lucky, you know. The Normals have only words. Poor little Normals. How can they *tell*, with just words? How can they *know*? They're always apart from each other, trying to reach each other and failing. Even when they make love, even when they come, they're always apart. They must be very lonely."

There was something . . . disturbing . . . in that. I looked at Lya, into her bright happy eyes, and thought about it. "Maybe," I said, finally. "But it's not that bad for them. They don't know any other way. And they try, they love too. They bridge the gap sometimes."

"Only a look and a voice, then darkness again and a silence,"

Lya quoted, her voice sad and tender. "We're luckier, aren't we? We have so much more."

"We're luckier," I echoed. And I reached out to read her too. Her mind was a haze of satisfaction, with a gentle scent of wistful, lonely longing. But there was something else, way down, almost gone now, but still faintly detectable.

I sat up slowly. "Hey," I said. "You're worried about something. And before, when we came in, you were scared. What's the matter?"

"I don't know, really," she said. She sounded puzzled and she *was* puzzled; I read it there. "I *was* scared, but I don't know why. The Joined, I think. I kept thinking about how much they loved me. They didn't even *know* me, but they loved me so much, and they understood—it was almost like what we have. It —I don't know. It bothered me. I mean, I didn't think I could ever be loved that way, except by you. And they were so *close,* so together. I felt kind of lonely, just holding hands and talking. I wanted to be close to *you* that way. After the way they were all sharing and everything, being alone just seemed empty. And frightening. You know?"

"I know," I said, touching her lightly again, with hand and mind. "I understand. We do understand each other. We're together almost as they are, as Normals can't ever be."

Lya nodded, and smiled, and hugged me. We went to sleep in each other's arms.

Dreams again. But again, at dawn, the memory stole away from me. It was all very annoying. The dream had been pleasant, comfortable. I wanted it back, and I couldn't even remember what it was. Our bedroom, washed by harsh daylight, seemed drab compared to the splendors of my lost vision.

Lya woke after me, with another headache. This time she had the pills on hand, by the bedstand. She grimaced and took one.

"It must be the Shkeen wine," I told her. "Something about it takes a dim view of your metabolism."

She pulled on a fresh coverall and scowled at me. "Ha. We were drinking Veltaar last night, remember? My father gave me my first glass of Veltaar when I was nine. It never gave me headaches before."

"A first!" I said, smiling.

"It's not funny," she said. "It hurts."

I quit kidding, and tried to read her. She was right. It *did* hurt. Her whole forehead throbbed with pain. I withdrew quickly before I caught it too.

"All right," I said. "I'm sorry. The pills will take care of it, though. Meanwhile, we've got work to do."

Lya nodded. She'd never let anything interfere with work yet.

The second day was a day of manhunt. We got off to a much earlier start, had a quick breakfast with Gourlay, then picked up our aircar outside the Tower. This time we didn't drop down when we hit Shkeentown. We wanted a human Joined, which meant we had to cover a lot of ground. The city was the biggest I'd ever seen, in area at any rate, and the thousand-odd human cultists were lost among millions of Shkeen. And, of those humans, only about half were actually Joined yet.

So we kept the aircar low, and buzzed up and down the dome-dotted hills like a floating rollercoaster, causing quite a stir in the streets below us. The Shkeen had seen aircars before, of course, but it still had some novelty value, particularly to the kids, who tried to run after us whenever we flashed by. We also panicked a whiner, causing him to upset the cart full of fruit he was dragging. I felt guilty about that, so I kept the car higher afterwards.

We spotted Joined all over the city, singing, eating, walking—and ringing those bells, those eternal bronze bells. But for the first three hours, all we found were Shkeen Joined. Lya and I took turns driving and watching. After the excitement of the previous day, the search was tedious and tiring.

Finally, however, we found something: a large group of Joined, ten of them, clustered around a bread cart behind one of the steeper hills. Two were taller than the rest.

We landed on the other side of the hill and walked around to meet them, leaving our aircar surrounded by a crowd of Shkeen children. The Joined were still eating when we arrived. Eight of them were Shkeen of various sizes and hues, Greeshka pulsing atop their skulls. The other two were human.

They wore the same long red gowns as the Shkeen, and they carried the same bells. One of them was a big man, with loose skin that hung in flaps, as if he'd lost a lot of weight recently. His hair was white and curly, his face marked by a broad smile and laugh wrinkles around his eyes. The other was a thin, dark weasel of a man with a big hooked nose.

Both of them had Greeshka sucking at their skulls. The parasite riding the weasel was barely a pimple, but the older man had a lordly specimen that dripped down beyond his shoulders and into the back of the gown.

Somehow, this time, it *did* look hideous.

Lyanna and I walked up to them, trying hard to smile, not reading—at least at first. They smiled at us as we approached. Then they waved.

"Hello," the weasel said cheerily when we got there. "I've never seen you. Are you new on Shkea?"

That took me slightly by surprise. I'd been expecting some sort of garbled mystic greeting, or maybe no greeting at all. I was assuming that somehow the human converts would have abandoned their humanity to become mock-Shkeen. I was wrong.

"More or less," I replied. And I read the weasel. He was genuinely pleased to see us, and just bubbled with contentment and good cheer. "We've been hired to talk to people like you." I'd decided to be honest about it.

The weasel stretched his grin farther than I thought it would go. "I am Joined, and happy," he said. "I'll be glad to talk to you. My name is Lester Kamenz. What do you want to know, brother?"

Lya, next to me, was going tense. I decided I'd let her read in depth while I asked questions. "When did you convert to the Cult?"

"Cult?" Kamenz said.

"The Union."

He nodded, and I was struck by the grotesque similarity of his bobbing head and that of the elderly Shkeen we'd seen yesterday. "I have always been in the Union. You are in the Union. All that thinks is in the Union."

"Some of us weren't told," I said. "How about you? When did you realize you were in the Union?"

"A year ago, Old Earth time. I was admitted to the ranks of the Joined only a few weeks ago. The First Joining is a joyful time. I am joyful. Now I will walk the streets and ring my bells until the Final Union."

"What did you do before?"

"Before?" A short vague look. "I ran machines once. I ran computers, in the Tower. But my life was empty, brother. I did not know I was in the Union, and I was alone. I had only machines, cold machines. Now I am Joined. Now I am"—again he searched —"not alone."

I reached into him, and found the happiness still there, with love. But now there was an ache too, a vague recollection of past pain, the stink of unwelcome memories. Did these fade? Maybe the gift the Greeshka gave its victims was oblivion, sweet mindless rest and end of struggle. Maybe.

I decided to try something. "That thing on your head," I said, sharply. "It's a parasite. It's drinking your blood right now, feeding on it. As it grows, it will take more and more of the things *you* need to live. Finally it will start to eat your tissue. Understand? It will *eat* you. I don't know how painful it will be, but however it feels, at the end you'll be *dead*. Unless you come back to the Tower now, and have the surgeons remove it. Or maybe you could remove it yourself. Why don't you try? Just reach up and pull it off. Go ahead."

I'd expected—what? Rage? Horror? Disgust? I got none of these. Kamenz just stuffed bread in his mouth and smiled at me, and all I read was his love and joy and a little pity.

"The Greeshka does not kill," he said finally. "The Greeshka gives joy and happy Union. Only those who have no Greeshka die. They are . . . alone. Oh, forever alone." Something in his mind trembled with sudden fear, but it faded quickly.

I glanced at Lya. She was stiff and hard-eyed, still reading. I looked back and began to phrase another question. But suddenly the Joined began to ring. One of the Shkeen started it off, swinging his bell up and down to produce a single sharp clang. Then his other hand swung, then the first again, then the second, then another Joined began to ring, then still another, and then they were all swinging and clanging and the noise of their bells was smashing against my ears as the joy and the love and the feel of the bells assaulted my mind once again.

I lingered to savor it. The love there was breathtaking, awesome, almost frightening in its heat and intensity, and there was so much sharing to frolic in and wonder at, such a soothing-calming-exhilarating tapestry of good feelings. Something happened to the Joined when they rang, something touched them and lifted them and gave them a glow, something strange and glorious that mere Normals could not hear in their harsh clanging music. I was no Normal, though. I could hear it.

I withdrew reluctantly, slowly. Kamenz and the other human were both ringing vigorously now, with broad smiles and glowing twinkling eyes that transfigured their faces. Lyanna was still tense, still reading. Her mouth was slightly open, and she trembled where she stood.

I put an arm around her and waited, listening to the music, patient. Lya continued to read. Finally, after minutes, I shook her gently. She turned and studied me with hard, distant eyes. Then blinked. And her eyes widened and she came back, shaking her head and frowning.

Puzzled, I looked into her head. Strange and stranger. It was a swirling fog of emotion, a dense moving blend of more feelings than I'd care to put a name to. No sooner had I entered than I was lost, lost and uneasy. Somewhere in the fog there was a bottomless abyss lurking to engulf me. At least it felt that way.

"Lya," I said. "What's wrong?"

She shook her head again, and looked at the Joined with a look that was equal parts fear and longing. I repeated my question.

"I—I don't know," she said. "Robb, let's not talk now. Let's go. I want time to think."

"OK," I said. What was going on here? I took her hand and we walked slowly around the hill to the slope where we'd left the car. Shkeen kids were climbing all over it. I chased them, laughing. Lya just stood there, her eyes gone all faraway on me. I wanted to read her again, but somehow I felt it would be an invasion of privacy.

Airborne, we streaked back toward the Tower, riding higher and faster this time. I drove, while Lya sat beside me and stared out into the distance.

"Did you get anything useful?" I asked her, trying to get her mind back on the assignment.

"Yes. No. Maybe." Her voice sounded distracted, as if only part of her was talking to me. "I read their lives, both of them.

Kamenz was a computer programmer, as he said. But he wasn't very good. An ugly little man with an ugly little personality, no friends, no sex, no nothing. Lived by himself, avoided the Shkeen, didn't like them at all. Didn't even like people, really. But Gustaffson got through to him, somehow. He ignored Kamenz' coldness, his bitter little cuts, his cruel jokes. He didn't retaliate, you know? After a while, Kamenz came to like Gustaffson, to admire him. They were never really friends in any normal sense, but still Gustaffson was the nearest thing to a friend that Kamenz had."

She stopped suddenly. "So he went over with Gustaffson?" I prompted, glancing at her quickly. Her eyes still wandered.

"No, not at first. He was still afraid, still scared of the Shkeen and terrified of the Greeshka. But later, with Gustaffson gone, he began to realize how empty his life was. He worked all day with people who despised him and machines that didn't care, then sat alone at night reading and watching holoshows. Not life, really. He hardly touched the people around him. Finally he went to find Gustaffson, and wound up converted. Now . . ."

"Now . . . ?"

She hesitated. "He's happy, Robb," she said. "He really is. For the first time in his life, he's happy. He'd never known love before. Now it fills him."

"You got a lot," I said.

"Yes." Still the distracted voice, the lost eyes. "He was open, sort of. There were levels, but digging wasn't as hard as it usually is—as if his barriers were weakening, coming down almost . . ."

"How about the other guy?"

She stroked the instrument panel, staring only at her hand. "Him? That was Gustaffson . . ."

And that, suddenly, seemed to wake her, to restore her to the Lya I knew and loved. She shook her head and looked at me, and the aimless voice became an animated torrent of words. "Robb, listen, that was *Gustaffson*, he's been Joined over a year now, and he's going on to Final Union within a week. The Greeshka has accepted him, and he wants it, you know? He really does, and—and—oh Robb, he's *dying!*"

"Within a week, according to what you just said."

"No. I mean yes, but that's not what I mean. Final Union isn't death, to him. He believes it, all of it, the whole religion. The Greeshka is his god, and he's going to join it. But before, and now, he was dying. He's got the Slow Plague, Robb. A terminal case. It's been eating at him from inside for fifteen years now. He got it back on Nightmare, in the swamps, when his family died. That's no world for people, but he was there, the administrator over a research base, a short-term thing. They lived on Thor; it was only a visit, but the ship crashed. Gustaffson got all wild and tried to reach them before the end, but he grabbed a faulty pair of skinthins, and the spores got through. And they were all dead when he got there. He had an awful lot of pain, Robb. From the Slow Plague, but more from the loss. He really loved them, and it was never the same after. They gave him Shkea as a reward, kind of, to take his mind off the crash, but he still thought of it all the time. I could see the picture, Robb. It was vivid. He couldn't forget it. The kids were inside the ship, safe behind the walls, but the life system failed and choked them to death. But his wife—oh, Robb—she took some skinthins and tried to go for help, and outside those *things*, those big wrigglers they have on Nightmare—?"

I swallowed hard, feeling a little sick. "The eater-worms," I said, dully. I'd read about them, and seen holos. I could imagine the picture that Lya'd seen in Gustaffson's memory, and it wasn't at all pretty. I was glad I didn't have her Talent.

"They were still—still—when Gustaffson got there. You know. He killed them all with a screech gun."

I shook my head. "I didn't think things like that really went on."

"No," Lya said. "Neither did Gustaffson. They'd been so—so *happy* before that, before the thing on Nightmare. He loved her, and they were really close, and his career had been almost charmed. He didn't have to go to Nightmare, you know. He took it because it was a challenge, because nobody else could handle it. That gnaws at him, too. And he remembers all the time. He—they—" Her voice faltered. "They thought they were *lucky*," she said, before falling into silence.

There was nothing to say to that. I just kept quiet and drove, thinking, feeling a blurred, watered-down version of what

Gustaffson's pain must have been like. After a while, Lya began to speak again.

"It was all there, Robb," she said, her voice softer and slower and more thoughtful once again. "But he was at peace. He still remembered it all, and the way it had hurt, but it didn't bother him as it had. Only now he was sorry they weren't with him. He was sorry that they died without Final Union. Almost like the Shkeen woman, remember? The one at the Gathering? With her brother?"

"I remember," I said.

"Like that. And his mind was open, too. More than Kamenz, much more. When he rang, the levels all vanished, and everything was right at the surface, all the love and pain and everything. His whole life, Robb. I shared his whole life with him, in an instant. And all his thoughts, too . . . he's seen the caves of Union . . . he went down once, before he converted. I . . ."

More silence, settling over us and darkening the car. We were close to the end of Shkeentown. The Tower slashed the sky ahead of us, shining in the sun. And the lower domes and archways of the glittering human city were coming into view.

"Robb," Lya said. "Land here. I have to think a while, you know? Go back without me. I want to walk among the Shkeen a little."

I glanced at her, frowning. "Walk? It's a long way back to the Tower, Lya."

"I'll be all right. Please. Just let me think a bit."

I read her. The thought fog had returned, denser than ever, laced through with the colors of fear. "Are you sure?" I said. "You're scared, Lyanna. Why? What's wrong? The eater-worms are a long way off."

She just looked at me, troubled. "Please, Robb," she repeated.

I didn't know what else to do, so I landed.

And I, too, thought, as I guided the aircar home. Of what Lyanna had said, and read—of Kamenz and Gustaffson. I kept my mind on the problem we'd been assigned to crack. I tried to keep it off Lya, and whatever was bothering her. That would solve itself, I thought.

Back at the Tower, I wasted no time. I went straight up to

Valcarenghi's office. He was there, alone, dictating into a machine. He shut it off when I entered.

"Hi, Robb," he began. "Where's Lya?"

"Out walking. She wanted to think. I've been thinking, too. And I believe I've got your answer."

He raised his eyebrows, waiting.

I sat down. "We found Gustaffson this afternoon, and Lya read him. I think it's clear why he went over. He was a broken man, inside, however much he smiled. The Greeshka gave him an end to his pain. And there was another convert with him, a Lester Kamenz. He'd been miserable, too, a pathetic lonely man with nothing to live for. Why *shouldn't* he convert? Check out the other converts, and I bet you'll find a pattern. The most lost and vulnerable, the failures, the isolated—those will be the ones that turned to Union."

Valcarenghi nodded. "OK, I'll buy that," he said. "But our psychs guessed that long ago, Robb. Only it's no answer, not really. Sure, the converts on the whole have been a messed-up crew, I won't dispute that. But why turn to the Cult of the Union? The psychs can't answer that. Take Gustaffson now. He was a strong man, believe me. I never knew him personally, but I knew his career. He took some rough assignments, generally for the hell of it, and beat them. He could have had the cushy jobs, but he wasn't interested. I've heard about the incident on Nightmare. It's famous, in a warped sort of way. But Phil Gustaffson wasn't the sort of man to be beaten, even by something like that. He snapped out of it very quickly, from what Nelse tells me. He came to Shkea and really set the place in order, cleaning up the mess that Rockwood had left. He pushed through the first real trade contract we ever got, *and* he made the Shkeen understand what it meant, which isn't easy.

"So here he is, this competent, talented man, who's made a career of beating tough jobs and handling men. He's gone through a personal nightmare, but it hasn't destroyed him. He's as tough as ever. And suddenly he turns to the Cult of the Union, signs up for a grotesque suicide. Why? For an end to his pain, you say? An interesting theory, but there are other ways to end pain. Gustaffson had years between Nightmare and the Greeshka. He never ran away from pain then. He didn't turn to drink, or drugs, or any of the usual outs. He didn't head back to Old Earth to have a psi-psych clean up his memories—and believe me, he could've gotten it paid for, if he'd wanted it. The colonial office would have done anything for him, after Nightmare. He went on, swallowed his pain, rebuilt. Until suddenly he converts.

"His pain made him more vulnerable, yes, no doubt of it. But something else brought him over—something that Union offered, something he couldn't get from wine or memory wipe. The same's true of Kamenz, and the others. They had other outs, other ways to vote no on life. They passed them up. But they chose Union. You see what I'm getting at?"

I did, of course. My answer was no answer at all, and I realized it. But Valcarenghi was wrong too, in parts.

"Yes," I said. "I guess we've still got some reading to do." I smiled wanly. "One thing, though. Gustaffson hadn't really beaten his pain, not ever. Lya was very clear on that. It was inside him all the time, tormenting him. He just never let it come out."

"That's victory, isn't it?" Valcarenghi said. "If you bury your hurts so deep that no one can tell you have them?"

"I don't know. I don't think so. But . . . anyway, there was more. Gustaffson has the Slow Plague. He's dying. He's been dying for years."

Valcarenghi's expression flickered briefly. "That I didn't know, but it just bolsters my point. I've read that some eighty percent of Slow Plague victims opt for euthanasia, if they happen to be on a planet where it's legal. Gustaffson was a planetary administrator. He could have *made* it legal. If he passed up suicide for all those years, why choose it now?"

I didn't have an answer for that. Lyanna hadn't given me one, if she had one. I didn't know where we could find one, either unless . . .

"The caves," I said suddenly. "The caves of Union. We've got to witness a Final Union. There must be something about it, something that accounts for the conversions. Give us a chance to find out what it is."

Valcarenghi smiled. "All right," he said. "I can arrange it. I expected it would come to that. It's not pleasant, though, I'll warn you. I've gone down myself, so I know what I'm talking about."

"That's OK," I told him. "If you think reading Gustaffson was any fun, you should have seen Lya when she was through. She's out now trying to walk it off." That, I'd decided, must have been what was bothering her. "Final Union won't be any worse than those memories of Nightmare, I'm sure."

"Fine, then. I'll set it up for tomorrow. I'm going with you, of course. I don't want to take any chances on anything happening to you."

I nodded. Valcarenghi rose. "Good enough," he said. "Meanwhile, let's think about more interesting things. You have any plans for dinner?"

We wound up eating at a mock-Shkeen restaurant run by humans, in the company of Gourlay and Laurie Blackburn. The talk was mostly social noises—sports, politics, art, old jokes, that sort of thing. I don't think there was a mention of the Shkeen or the Greeshka all evening.

Afterwards, when I got back to our suite, I found Lyanna waiting for me. She was in bed, reading one of the handsome volumes from our library, a book of Old Earth poetry. She looked up when I entered.

"Hi," I said. "How was your walk?"

"Long." A smile creased her pale, small face, then faded. "But I had time to think. About this afternoon, and yesterday, and about the Joined. And us."

"Us?"

"Robb, do you love me?" The question was delivered almost matter-of-factly, in a voice full of question. As if she didn't know. As if she really didn't know.

I sat down on the bed and took her hand and tried to smile. "Sure," I said. "You know that, Lya."

"I did. I do. You love me, Robb, really you do. As much as a human can love. But . . ." She stopped. She shook her head and closed her book and sighed. "But we're still apart, Robb. We're still apart."

"What *are* you talking about?"

"This afternoon. I was so confused afterwards, and scared. I wasn't sure why, but I've thought about it. When I was reading, Robb—I was in there, with the Joined, sharing them and their love. I really was. And I didn't want to come out. I didn't want to leave them, Robb. When I did, I felt so isolated, so cut off."

"That's your fault," I said. "I tried to talk to you. You were too busy thinking."

"Talking? What good is talking? It's communication, I guess, but is it *really?* I used to think so, before they trained my Talent. After that, reading seemed to be the real communication, the real way to reach somebody else, somebody like you. But now I don't know. The Joined—when they ring—they're so *together*, Robb. All linked. Like us when we make love, almost. And they love each other, too. And they love us, so intensely. I felt—I don't know. But Gustaffson loves me as much as you do. No. He loves me more."

Her face was white as she said that, her eyes wide, lost, lonely. And me, I felt a sudden chill, like a cold wind blowing through my soul. I didn't say anything. I only looked at her, and wet my lips. And bled.

She saw the hurt in my eyes, I guess. Or read it. Her hand pulled at mine, caressed it. "Oh, Robb. Please. I don't mean to hurt you. It's not you. It's all of us. What do *we* have, compared to *them?*"

"I don't know what you're talking about, Lya." Half of me suddenly wanted to cry. The other half wanted to shout. I stifled both halves, and kept my voice steady. But inside I wasn't steady, I wasn't steady at all.

"Do you love me, Robb?" Again. Wondering.

"Yes!" Fiercely. A challenge.

"What does that mean?" she said.

"You know what it means," I said. "Dammit, Lya, *think!* Remember all we've had, all we've shared together. *That's* love, Lya. It is. We're the lucky ones, remember? You said that yourself. The Normals have only a touch and a voice, then back to their darkness. They can barely find each other. They're alone. Always. Groping. Trying, over and over, to climb out of their isolation booths, and failing, over and over. But not us, we found the way, we know each other as much as any human beings ever can. There's nothing I wouldn't tell you, or share with you. I've said that before, and you know it's true, you can read it in me. *That's love*, dammit. *Isn't it?*"

"I don't know," she said, in a voice so sadly baffled. Soundlessly, without even a sob, she began to cry. And while the tears ran in lonely paths down her cheeks, she talked. "Maybe that's love. I always thought it was. But now I don't know. If what we have is love, what was it I felt this afternoon, what was it I touched and shared in? Oh, Robb, I love you too. You know that. I try to share with you. I want to share what I read, what it was like. But I can't. We're cut off. I can't make you understand. I'm here and you're there and we can touch and make love and talk, but we're still apart. You see? You see? I'm alone. And this afternoon, I *wasn't*."

"You're not alone, dammit," I said suddenly. "I'm here." I clutched her hand tightly. "Feel? Hear? You're not alone!"

She shook her head, and the tears flowed on. "You don't understand, see? And there's no way I can make you. You said we know each other as much as any human beings ever can. You're right. But how much can human beings know each other? Aren't all of them cut off, really? Each alone in a big, dark, empty universe? We only trick ourselves when we think that someone else is there. In the end, in the cold lonely end, it's only us, by ourselves, in the blackness. Are you there, Robb? How do I know? Will you die with me, Robb? Will we be together then? Are we together *now*? You say we're luckier than the Normals. I've said it too. They have only a touch and voice, right? How many times have I quoted that? But what do *we* have? A touch and two voices, maybe. It's not enough anymore. I'm scared. Suddenly I'm scared."

She began to sob. Instinctively I reached out to her, wrapped her in my arms, stroked her. We lay back together, and she wept against my chest. I read her, briefly, and I read her pain, her sudden loneliness, her hunger, all aswirl in a darkening mindstorm of fear. And, though I touched her and caressed her and whispered—over and over—that it would be all right, that I was here, that she wasn't alone, I knew that it would not be enough. Suddenly there was a gulf between us, a great dark yawning thing that grew and grew, and I didn't know how to bridge it. And Lya, my Lya, was crying, and she needed me. And I needed her, but I couldn't get to her.

Then I realized that I was crying too.

We held each other, in silent tears, for what must have been an hour. But finally the tears ran out. Lya clutched her body to me so tightly I could hardly breathe, and I held her just as tightly.

"Robb," she whispered. "You said—you said we really know each other. All those times you've said it. And you say, sometimes, that I'm *right* for you, that I'm perfect."

I nodded, wanting to believe. "Yes. You are."

"No," she said, choking out the word, forcing it into the air, fighting herself to say it. "It's not *so*. I read you, yes. I can hear the words rattling around in your head as you fit a sentence together before saying it. And I listen to you scold yourself when you've done something stupid. And I see memories, some memories, and live through them with you. But it's all on the surface, Robb, all on the top. Below it, there's more, more of *you*. Drifting half-thoughts I don't quite catch. Feelings I can't put a name to. Passions you suppress, and memories even you don't know you have. Sometimes I can get to that level. Sometimes. If I really fight, if I drain myself to exhaustion. But when I get there, I know—I *know*—that there's another level below *that*. And more and more, on and on, down and down. I can't reach them, Robb, though they're part of you. I don't know you. I can't know you. You don't even know yourself, see? And me, do you know me? No. Even less. You know what I tell you, and I tell you the truth, but maybe not all. And you read my feelings, my surface feelings —the pain of a stubbed toe, a quick flash of annoyance, the pleasure I get when you're in me. Does that mean you know me? What of *my* levels, and levels? What about the things I don't even know myself? Do *you* know them? How, Robb, how?"

She shook her head again, with that funny little gesture she had whenever she was confused. "And you say I'm perfect, and that you love me. I'm so right for you. But *am* I? Robb, *I read your thoughts*. I know when you want me to be sexy, so I'm sexy. I see what turns you on, so I do it. I know when you want me to be serious, and when you want me to joke. I know what kind of jokes to tell, too. Never the cutting kind, you don't like that, to hurt or see people hurt. You laugh *with* people not *at* them, and I laugh with you, and love you for your tastes. I know when you want me to talk, and when to keep quiet. I know when you want me to be your proud tigress, your tawny telepath, and when you want a little girl to shelter in your arms. And I *am* those things, Robb, because you want me to be, because I love you, because I can feel joy in your mind at every *right* thing that I do. I never set out to do it that way, but it happened. I didn't mind, I don't mind. Most of the time it wasn't even conscious. You do the same thing, too. I read it in you. You can't read as I do, so sometimes you guess wrong—you come on witty when I want silent understanding, or you act the strong man when I need a boy to mother. But you get it right sometimes, too. And you *try*, you always try.

"But is it really *you*? Is it really *me*? What if I wasn't perfect, you see, if I was just myself, with all my faults and the things you don't like out in the open? Would you love me *then*? I don't know. But Gustaffson would, and Kamenz. I know that, Robb. I saw it. I know *them*. Their levels . . . vanished. I *KNOW* them, and if I went back I could share with them, more than with you. And they know me, the real me, all of me, I think. And they love me. You see? *You see?*"

Did I see? I don't know. I was confused. Would I love Lya if she was "herself"? But what was "herself"? How was it different from the Lya I knew? I thought I loved Lya and would always love Lya—but what if the real Lya wasn't like my Lya? *What* did I love? The strange abstract concept of a human being, or the flesh and voice and personality that I thought of as Lya? I didn't know. I didn't know who Lya was, or who I was, or what the hell it all meant. And I was scared. Maybe I couldn't feel what she had felt that afternoon. But I knew what she was feeling then. I was alone, and I needed someone.

"Lya," I called. "Lya, let's try. We don't have to give up. We can reach each other. There's a way, our way. We've done it before. Come, Lya, come with me, come to me."

As I spoke, I undressed her, and she responded and her hands joined mine. When we were nude, I began to stroke her, slowly, and she me. Our minds reached out to each other. Reached and probed as never before. I could feel her, inside my head, digging. Deeper and deeper. Down. And I opened myself to her, I surrendered, all the petty little secrets I had kept even from her, or tried to, now I yielded up to her everything I could remember, my triumphs and shames, the good moments and the pain, the times I'd hurt someone, the times I'd been hurt, the long crying sessions by myself, the fears I wouldn't admit, the prejudices I fought, the vanities I battled when the time struck, the silly boyish sins. All. Everything. I buried nothing. I hid nothing. I gave myself to her, to Lya, to *my* Lya. She had to know me.

And so, too, she yielded. Her mind was a forest through which I roamed, hunting down wisps of emotion, the fear and the need and the love at the top, the fainter things beneath, the half-formed whims and passions still deeper into the woods. I don't have Lya's Talent, I read only feelings, never thoughts. But I read thoughts then, for the first and only time, thoughts she threw at me because I'd never seen them before. I couldn't reach much, but some I got.

And as her mind opened to mine, so did her body. I entered her, and we moved together, bodies one, minds entwined, as close as human beings can join. I felt pleasure washing over me in great glorious waves, my pleasure, her pleasure, both together building on each other, and I rode the crest for an eternity as it approached a far distant shore. And finally as it smashed into that beach, we came together, and for a second—for a tiny, fleeting second—I could not tell which orgasm was mine, and which was hers.

But then it passed. We lay, bodies locked together, on the bed. In the starlight. But it was not a bed. It was the beach, the flat black beach, and there were no stars above. A thought touched me, a vagrant thought that was not mine. Lya's thought. We were on a plain, she was thinking, and I saw that she was right. The waters that had carried us here were gone, receded. There was only a vast flat blackness stretching away in all directions, with dim ominous shapes moving on either horizon. *We are here as on a darkling plain*, Lya thought. And suddenly I knew what those shapes were, and what poem she had been reading.

We slept.

I woke, alone.

The room was dark. Lya lay on the other side of the bed, curled up, still asleep. It was late, near dawn I thought. But I wasn't sure. I was restless.

I got up and dressed in silence. I needed to walk somewhere, to think, to work things out. Where, though?

There was a key in my pocket. I touched it when I pulled on my tunic, and remembered. Valcarenghi's office. It would be locked and deserted at this time of night. And the view might help me think.

I left, found the tubes, and shot up, up, up to the apex of the Tower, the top of man's steel challenge to the Shkeen. The office was unlit, the furniture dark shapes in the shadows. There was only the starlight. Shkea is closer to the galactic center than Old Earth, or Baldur. The stars are a fiery canopy across the night sky. Some of them are very close, and they burn like red and blue-white fires in the awesome blackness above. In Valcarenghi's office, all the walls are glass. I went to one, and looked out. I wasn't thinking. Just feeling. And I felt cold and lost and little.

Then there was a soft voice behind me saying hello. I barely heard it.

I turned away from the window, but other stars leaped at me from the far walls. Laurie Blackburn sat in one of the low chairs, concealed by the darkness.

"Hello," I said. "I didn't mean to intrude. I thought no one would be here."

She smiled. A radiant smile in a radiant face, but there was no humor in it. Her hair fell in sweeping auburn waves past her shoulders, and she was dressed in something long and gauzy. I could see her gentle curves through its folds, and she made no effort to hide herself.

"I come up here a lot," she said. "At night, usually. When Dino's asleep. It's a good place to think."

"Yes," I said, smiling. "My thoughts, too."

"The stars are pretty, aren't they?"

"Yes."

"I think so. I—" Hesitation. Then she rose and came to me. "Do you love Lya?" she said.

A hammer of a question. Timed terribly. But I handled it well, I think. My mind was still on my talk with Lya. "Yes," I said. "Very much. Why?"

She was standing close to me, looking at my face, and past me, out to the stars. "I don't know. I wonder about love, sometimes. I love Dino, you know. He came here two months ago, so we haven't known each other long. But I love him already. I've never known anybody like him. He's kind, and considerate, and he does everything well. I've never seen him fail at anything he tried. Yet he doesn't seem driven, like some men. He wins so easily. He believes in himself a lot, and that's attractive. He's given me anything I could ask for, everything."

I read her, caught her love and worry and guessed. "Except himself," I said.

She looked at me, startled. Then she smiled. "I forgot. You're a Talent. Of course you know. You're right. I don't know what I worry about, but I do worry. Dino is so perfect, you know. I've told him—well, everything. All about me and my life. And he listens and understands. He's always receptive, he's there when I need him. But—"

"It's all one way," I said. It was a statement. I knew.

She nodded. "It's not that he keeps secrets. He doesn't. He'll answer any question I ask. But the answers mean nothing. I ask him what he fears, and he says nothing, and makes me believe it. He's very rational, very calm. He never gets angry, he never has. I asked him. He doesn't hate people, he thinks hate is bad. He's never felt pain, either, or he *says* he hasn't. Emotional pain, I mean. Yet he understands me when I talk about my life. Once he said his biggest fault was laziness. But he's not lazy at all, I know that. Is he really that perfect? He tells me he's always sure of himself, because he *knows* he's good, but he smiles when he says it, so I can't even accuse him of being vain. He says he believes in God, but he never talks about it. If you try to talk seriously, he'll listen patiently, or joke with you, or lead the conversation away. He says he loves me, but—"

I nodded. I knew what was coming.

It came. She looked at me, eyes begging. "You're a Talent," she said. "You've read him, haven't you? You know him? Tell me. Please tell me."

I was reading her. I could see how much she needed to know, how much she worried and feared, how much she loved. I couldn't lie to her. Yet it was hard to give her the answer I had to.

"I've read him," I said. Slowly. Carefully. Measuring out my words like precious fluids. "And you, you too. I saw your love, on that first night, when we ate together."

"And Dino?"

My words caught in my throat. "He's—funny, Lya said once. I can read his surface emotions easily enough. Below that, nothing. He's very self-contained, walled off. Almost as if his only emotions are the ones he—*allows* himself to feel. I've felt his confidence, his pleasure. I've felt worry too, but never real fear. He's very affectionate toward you, very protective. He enjoys feeling protective."

"Is that all?" So hopeful. It hurt.

"I'm afraid it is. He's walled off, Laurie. He needs himself, only himself. If there's love in him, it's behind that wall, hidden. I can't read it. He thinks a lot of you, Laurie. But love—well, it's different. It's stronger and more unreasoning and it comes in crashing floods. And Dino's not like that, at least not out where I can read."

"Closed," she said. "He's closed to me. I opened myself to him, totally. But he didn't. I was always afraid—even when he was with me, I felt sometimes that he wasn't there at all—"

She sighed. I read her despair, her welling loneliness. I didn't know what to do. "Cry if you like," I told her, inanely. "Sometimes it helps. I know. I've cried enough in my time."

She didn't cry. She looked up, and laughed lightly. "No," she said. "I can't. Dino taught me never to cry. He said tears never solve anything."

A sad philosophy. Tears don't solve anything, maybe, but they're part of being human. I wanted to tell her so, but instead I just smiled at her.

She smiled back, and cocked her head. "You cry," she said suddenly, in a voice strangely delighted. "That's funny. That's more of an admission than I ever heard from Dino, in a way. Thank you, Robb. Thank you."

And Laurie stood on her toes and looked up, expectant. And I could read what she expected. So I took her and kissed her, and she pressed her body hard against mine. And all the while I thought of Lya, telling myself that she wouldn't mind, that she'd be proud of me, that she'd understand.

Afterwards, I stayed up in the office alone to watch the dawn come up. I was drained, but somehow content. The light that crept over the horizon was chasing the shadows before it, and suddenly all the fears that had seemed so threatening in the night were silly, unreasoning. We'd bridged it, I thought—Lya and I. Whatever it was, we'd handled it, and today we'd handle the Greeshka with the same ease, together.

When I got back to our room, Lya was gone.

"We found the aircar in the middle of Shkeentown," Valcarenghi was saying. He was cool, precise, reassuring. His voice told me, without words, that there was nothing to worry about. "I've got men out looking for her. But Shkeentown's a big place. Do you have any idea where she might have gone?"

"No," I said, dully. "Not really. Maybe to see some more Joined. She seemed—well, almost obsessed by them. I don't know."

"Well, we've got a good police force. We'll find her, I'm certain of that. But it may take a while. Did you two have a fight?"

"Yes. No. Sort of, but it wasn't a real fight. It was strange."

"I see," he said. But he didn't. "Laurie tells me you came up here last night, alone."

"Yes. I needed to think."

"All right," said Valcarenghi. "So let's say Lya woke up, decided she wanted to think too. You came up here. She took a ride. Maybe she just wants a day off to wander around Shkeentown. She did something like that yesterday, didn't she?"

"Yes."

"So she's doing it again. No problem. She'll probably be back well before dinner." He smiled.

"Why did she go without telling me, then? Or leaving a note, or *something?*"

"I don't know. It's not important."

Wasn't it, though? *Wasn't it?* I sat in the chair, head in my hands and a scowl on my face, and I was sweating. Suddenly I was very much afraid, of what I didn't know. I should never have left her alone, I was telling myself. While I was up here with Laurie, Lyanna woke alone in a darkened room, and—and—and *what?* And left.

"Meanwhile, though," Valcarenghi said, "we've got work to do. The trip to the caves is all set."

I looked up, disbelieving. "The caves? I can't go there, not now, not alone."

He gave a sigh of exasperation, exaggerated for effect. "Oh, come now, Robb. It's not the end of the world. Lya will be all right. She seemed to be a perfectly sensible girl, and I'm sure she can take care of herself. Right?"

I nodded.

"Meanwhile, we'll cover the caves. I still want to get to the bottom of this."

"It won't do any good," I protested. "Not without Lya. She's the major Talent. I—I just read emotions. I can't get down deep, as she can. I won't solve anything for you."

He shrugged. "Maybe not. But the trip is on, and we've got nothing to lose. We can always make a second run after Lya comes back. Besides, this should do you good, get your mind off this other business. There's nothing you can do for Lya now. I've got every available man out searching for her, and if they don't find her you certainly won't. So there's no sense dwelling on it. Just get back into action, keep busy." He turned, headed for the tube. "Come. There's an aircar waiting for us. Nelse will go too."

Reluctantly, I stood. I was in no mood to consider the problems of the Shkeen, but Valcarenghi's arguments made a certain amount of sense. Besides which, he'd hired Lyanna and me, and we still had obligations to him. I could try anyway, I thought.

On the ride out, Valcarenghi sat in the front with the driver, a hulking police sergeant with a face chiseled out of granite. He'd selected a police car this time so we could keep posted on the search for Lya. Gourlay and I were in the back seat together. Gourlay had covered our laps with a big map, and he was telling me about the caves of Final Union.

"Theory is the caves are the original home of the Greeshka," he said. "Probably true, makes sense. Greeshka are a lot bigger there. You'll see. The caves are all through the hills, away from our part of Shkeentown, where the country gets wilder. A regular little honeycomb. Greeshka in every one, too. Or so I've heard. Been in a few myself, Greeshka in all of *them*. So I believe what they say about the rest. The city, the sacred city, well, it was probably built *because* of the caves. Shkeen come here from all over the continent, you know, for Final Union. Here, this is the cave region." He took out a pen, and made a big circle in red near the center of the map. It was meaningless to me. The map was getting me down. I hadn't realized that the Shkeen city was so *huge*. How the hell could they find anyone who didn't want to be found?

Valcarenghi looked back from the front seat. "The cave we're going to is a big one, as these places go. I've been there before. There's no formality about Final Union, you understand. The Shkeen just pick a cave, and walk in, and lie down on top of the Greeshka. They'll use whatever entrance is most convenient. Some of them are no bigger than sewer pipes, but if you went in far enough, theory says you'd run into a Greeshka, setting back in the dark and pulsing away. The biggest caves are lighted with torches, like the Great Hall, but that's just a frill. It doesn't play any real part in the Union."

"I take it we're going to one of them?" I said.

Valcarenghi nodded. "Right. I figured you'd want to see what a mature Greeshka is like. It's not pretty, but it's educational. So we need lighting."

Gourlay resumed his narrative then, but I tuned him out. I felt I knew quite enough about the Shkeen and the Greeshka, and I was still worried about Lyanna. After a while he wound down, and the rest of the trip was in silence. We covered more ground than we ever had before. Even the Tower—our shining steel landmark—had been swallowed by the hills behind us.

The terrain got rougher, rockier, and more overgrown, and the hills rose higher and wilder. But the domes went on and on and on, and there were Shkeen everywhere. Lya could be down there. I thought, lost among those teeming millions. Looking for what? Thinking what?

Finally we landed, in a wooded valley between two massive, rock-studded hills. Even here there were Shkeen, the red-brick domes rising from the undergrowth among the stubby trees. I had no trouble spotting the cave. It was halfway up one of the slopes, a dark yawn in the rock face, with a dusty road winding up to it.

We set down in the valley and climbed that road. Gourlay ate up the distance with long, gawky strides, while Valcarenghi moved with an easy, untiring grace, and the policeman plodded on stolidly. I was the straggler. I dragged myself up, and I was half-winded by the time we got to the cave mouth.

If I'd expected cave paintings, or an altar, or some kind of nature temple, I was sadly disappointed. It was an ordinary cave, with damp stone walls and low ceilings and cold, wet air. Cooler than most of Shkea, and less dusty, but that was about it. There was one long, winding passage through the rock, wide enough for the four of us to walk abreast yet low enough so Gourlay had to stoop. Torches were set along the walls at regular intervals, but only every fourth one or so was lit. They burned with an oily smoke that seemed to cling to the top of the cave and drift down into the depths before us. I wondered what was sucking it in.

After about ten minutes of walking, most of it down a barely perceptible incline, the passage led us out into a high, brightly lit room, with a vaulting stone roof that was stained sooty by torch smoke. In the room, the Greeshka.

Its color was a dull brownish red, like old blood, not the bright near-translucent crimson of the small creatures that clung to the skulls of the Joined. There were spots of black, too, like burns or soot stains on the vasty body. I could barely see the far side of the cave; the Greeshka was too huge, it towered above us so that there was only a thin crack between it and the roof. But it sloped down abruptly halfway across the chamber, like an immense jellied hill, and ended a good twenty feet from where we stood. Between us and the great bulk of the Greeshka was a forest of hanging, dangling red strands, a living cobweb of Greeshka tissue that came almost to our faces.

And it pulsed. As one organism. Even the strands kept time, widening and then contracting again, moving to a silent beat that was one with the great Greeshka behind them.

My stomach churned, but my companions seemed unmoved. They'd seen this before. "Come," Valcarenghi said, switching on a flashlight he'd brought to augment the torchlight. The light, twisting around the pulsing web, gave the illusion of some weird haunted forest. Valcarenghi stepped into that forest. Lightly. Swinging the light and brushing aside the Greeshka.

Gourlay followed him, but I recoiled. Valcarenghi looked back and smiled. "Don't worry," he said. "The Greeshka takes hours to attach itself, and it's easily removed. It won't grab you if you stumble against it."

I screwed up my courage, reached out, and touched one of the living strands. It was soft and wet, and there was a slimy feel to it. But that was all. It broke easily enough. I walked through it, reaching before me and bending and breaking the web to clear my path. The policeman walked silently behind me.

Then we stood on the far side of the web, at the foot of the great Greeshka. Valcarenghi studied it for a second, then pointed with his flashlight. "Look," he said. "Final Union."

I looked. His beam had thrown a pool of light around one of the dark spots, a blemish on the reddish hulk. I looked closer. There was a head in the blemish. Centered in the dark spot, with just the face showing, and even that covered by a thin reddish film. But the features were unmistakable. An elderly Shkeen, wrinkled and big-eyed, his eyes closed now. But smiling. Smiling.

I moved closer. A little lower and to the right, a few fingertips hung out of the mass. But that was all. Most of the body was already gone, sunken into the Greeshka, dissolved or dissolving. The old Shkeen was dead, and the parasite was digesting his corpse.

"Every one of the dark spots is a recent Union," Valcarenghi was saying, moving his light around like a pointer. "The spots fade in time, of course. The Greeshka is growing steadily. In another hundred years it will fill this chamber, and start up the passageway."

Then there was a rustle of movement behind us. I looked back. Someone else was coming through the web.

She reached us soon, and smiled. A Shkeen woman, old, naked, breasts hanging past her waist. Joined, of course. Her Greeshka covered most of her head and hung lower than her breasts. It was still bright and translucent from its time in the sun. You could see through it, to where it was eating the skin off her back.

"A candidate for Final Union," Gourlay said.

"This is a popular cave," Valcarenghi added in a low, sardonic voice.

The woman did not speak to us, nor we to her. Smiling, she walked past us. And lay down on the Greeshka.

The little Greeshka, the one that rode her back, seemed almost to dissolve on contact, melting away into the great cave creature, so the Shkeen woman and the great Greeshka were joined as one. After that, nothing. She just closed her eyes, and lay peacefully, seemingly asleep.

"What's happening?" I asked.

"Union," said Valcarenghi. "It'll be an hour before you'd notice anything, but the Greeshka is closing over her even now, swallowing her. A response to her body heat, I'm told. In a day she'll be buried in it. In two, like him—" The flash found the half-dissolved face above us.

"Can you read her?" Gourlay suggested. "Maybe that'd tell us something."

"All right," I said, repelled but curious. I opened myself. And the mindstorm hit.

But it's wrong to call it a mindstorm. It was immense and awesome and intense, searing and blinding and choking. But it was peaceful too, and gentle with a gentleness that was more violent than human hate. It shrieked soft shrieks and siren calls and pulled at me seductively, and it washed over me in crimson waves of passion, and drew me to it. It filled me and emptied me all at once. And I heard the bells somewhere, clanging a harsh bronze song, a song of love and surrender and togetherness, of joining and union and never being alone.

Storm, mindstorm, yes, it was that. But it was to an ordinary mindstorm as a supernova is to a hurricane, and its violence was the violence of love. It loved me, that mindstorm, and it wanted me, and its bells called to me, and sang its love, and I reached to it and touched, wanting to be with it, wanting to link, wanting never to be alone again. And suddenly I was on the crest of a great wave once again, a wave of fire that washed across the stars forever, and this time I knew the wave would never end, this time I would not be alone afterwards upon my darkling plain.

But with that phrase I thought of Lya.

And suddenly I was struggling, fighting it, battling back against the sea of sucking love. I ran, ran, *ran, RAN* . . . and closed my minddoor and hammered shut the latch and let the storm flail and howl against it while I held it with all my strength, resisting. Yet the door began to buckle and crack.

I screamed. The door smashed open, and the storm whipped in and clutched at me, whirled me out and around and around. I sailed up to the cold stars but they were cold no longer, and I grew bigger and bigger until I *was* the stars and they were me, and I was Union, and for a single solitary glittering instant I was the universe.

Then nothing.

I woke up back in my room, with a headache that was trying to tear my skull apart. Gourlay was sitting on a chair reading one of our books. He looked up when I groaned.

Lya's headache pills were still on the bedstand. I took one hastily, then struggled to sit up in bed.

"You all right?" Gourlay asked.

"Headache," I said, rubbing my forehead. It *throbbed,* as if it was about to burst. Worse than the time I'd peered into Lya's pain. "What happened?"

He stood up. "You scared the hell out of us. After you began to read, all of a sudden you started trembling. Then you walked right into the goddamn Greeshka. And you screamed. Dino and the sergeant had to drag you out. You were stepping right in the thing, and it was up to your knees. Twitching, too. Weird. Dino hit you, knocked you out."

He shook his head, started for the door. "Where are you going?" I said.

"To sleep," he said. "You've been out for eight hours or so. Dino asked me to watch you till you came to. OK, you came to. Now get some rest, and I will too. We'll talk about it tomorrow."

"I want to talk about it now."

"It's late," he said, as he closed the bedroom door. I listened to his footsteps on the way out. And I'm sure I heard the outer door lock. Somebody was clearly afraid of Talents who steal away into the night. I wasn't going anywhere.

I got up and went out for a drink. There was Veltaar chilling. I put away a couple of glasses quick, and ate a light snack. The headache began to fade. Then I went back to the bedroom, turned off the light and cleared the glass, so the stars would all shine through. Then back to sleep.

But I didn't sleep, not right away. Too much had happened. I had to think about it. The headache first, the incredible headache that ripped at my skull. Like Lya's. But Lya hadn't been through what I had. Or had she? Lya was a major Talent, much more sensitive than I was, with a greater range. Could that mindstorm have reached *this* far, over miles and miles? Late at night, when humans and Shkeen were sleeping and their thoughts dim? Maybe. And maybe my half-remembered dreams were pale reflections of whatever she had felt the same nights. But my dreams had been pleasant. It was waking that bothered me, waking and not remembering.

But again, had I had this headache when I slept? Or when I woke?

What the hell had happened? What was that thing, that reached me there in the cave, and pulled me to it? The Greeshka? It had to be. I hadn't even time to focus on the Shkeen woman, it *had* to be the Greeshka. But Lyanna had said that Greeshka had no minds, not even a yes-I-live . . .

It all swirled around me, questions on questions on questions, and I had no answers. I began to think of Lya then, to wonder where she was and why she'd left me. Was this what she had been going through? Why hadn't I understood? I missed her then. I needed her beside me, and she wasn't there. I was alone, and very aware of it.

I slept.

Long darkness then, but finally a dream, and finally I remembered. I was back on the plain again, the infinite darkling plain with its starless sky and black shapes in the distance, the plain Lya had spoken of so often. It was from one of her favorite poems. I was alone, forever alone, and I knew it. That was the nature of things. I was the only reality in the universe, and I was cold and hungry and frightened, and the shapes were moving toward me, inhuman and inexorable. And there was no one to call to, no one to turn to, no one to hear my cries. There never had been anyone. There never would be anyone.

Then Lya came to me.

She floated down from the starless sky, pale and thin and fragile, and stood beside me on the plain. She brushed her hair back with her hand, and looked at me with glowing wide eyes, and smiled. And I knew it was no dream. She was with me, somehow. We talked.

Hi, Robb.

Lya? Hi, Lya. Where are you? You left me.

I'm sorry. I had to. You understand, Robb. You have to. I didn't want to be here anymore, ever, in this place, this awful place. I would have been, Robb. Men are always here, but for brief moments.

A touch and a voice?

Yes, Robb. Then darkness again, and a silence. And the darkling plain.

You're mixing two poems, Lya. But it's OK. You know them better than I do. But aren't you leaving out something? The earlier part. "Ah love, let us be true . . ."

Oh, Robb.

Where are you?

I'm—everywhere. But mostly in a cave. I was ready, Robb. I was already more open than the rest. I could skip the Gathering, and the Joining. My Talent made me used to sharing. It took me.

Final Union?

Yes.

Oh, Lya.

Robb. Please. Join us, join me. It's happiness, you know? Forever and forever, and belonging and sharing and being together. I'm in love, Robb, I'm in love with a billion billion people, and I know all of them better than I ever knew you, and they know me, all of me, and they love me. And it will last forever. Me. Us. The Union. I'm still me, but I'm them too, you see? And they're me. The Joined, the reading, opened me, and the Union called to me every night, because it loved me, you see? Oh, Robb, join us, join us. I love you.

The Union. The Greeshka, you mean. I love you, Lya. Please come back. It can't have absorbed you already. Tell me where you are. I'll come to you.

Yes, come to me. Come anywhere, Robb. The Greeshka is all one, the caves all connect under the hills, the little Greeshka are all part of the Union. Come to me and join me. Love me as you said you did. Join me. You're so far away, I can hardly reach you, even with the Union. Come and be one with us.

No. I will not be eaten. Please, Lya, tell me where you are.

Poor Robb. Don't worry, love. The body isn't important. The Greeshka needs it for nourishment, and we need the Greeshka. But, oh Robb, the Union isn't just the Greeshka, you see? The Greeshka isn't important, it doesn't even have a mind, it's just the link, the medium, the Union is the Shkeen. A million billion billion Shkeen, all the Shkeen that have lived and Joined in fourteen thousand years, all together and loving and belonging, immortal. It's beautiful, Robb, it's more than we had, much more, and we were the lucky ones, remember? We were! But this is better.

Lya. My Lya. I loved you. This isn't for you, this isn't for humans. Come back to me.

This isn't for humans? Oh, it IS! It's what humans have always been looking for, searching for, crying for on lonely nights. It's love, Robb, real love, and human love is only a pale imitation. You see?

No.

Come, Robb. Join. Or you'll be alone forever, alone on the plain, with only a voice and a touch to keep you going. And in the end when your body dies, you won't even have that. Just an eternity of empty blackness. The plain, Robb, forever and ever. And I won't be able to reach you, not ever. But it doesn't have to be . . .

No.

Oh, Robb. I'm fading. Please come.

No. Lya, don't go. I love you, Lya. Don't leave me.

I love you, Robb. I did. I really did . . .

And then she was gone. I was alone on the plain again. A wind was blowing from somewhere, and it whipped her fading words away from me, out into the cold vastness of infinity.

In the cheerless morning, the outer door was unlocked. I ascended the tower and found Valcarenghi alone in his office. "Do you believe in God?" I asked him.

He looked up, smiled. "Sure." Said lightly. I was reading him. It was a subject he'd never thought about.

"I don't," I said. "Neither did Lya. Most Talents are atheists, you know. There was an experiment tried back on Old Earth fifty years ago. It was organized by a major Talent named Linnel, who was also devoutly religious. He thought that by using drugs, and linking together the minds of the world's most potent Talents, he could reach something he called the Universal Yes-I-Live. Also known as God. The experiment was a dismal failure, but *something* happened. Linnel went mad, and the others came away with only a vision of a vast, dark, uncaring nothingness, a void without reason or form or meaning. Other Talents have felt the same way, and Normals too. Centuries ago there was a poet named Arnold, who wrote of a darkling plain. The poem's in one of the old languages, but it's worth reading. It shows—fear, I think. Something basic in man, some dread of being alone in the cosmos. Maybe it's just fear of death, maybe it's more. I don't know. But it's primal. All men are forever alone, but they don't want to be. They're always searching, trying to make contact, trying to reach others across the void. Some people never succeed, some break through occasionally. Lya and I were lucky. But it's never permanent. In the end you're alone again, back on the darkling plain. You see, Dino? *Do you see?*"

He smiled an amused little smile. Not derisive—that wasn't his style—just surprised and disbelieving. "No," he said.

"Look again, then. Always people are reaching for something, for somone, searching. Talk, Talent, love, sex, it's all part of the same thing, the same search. And gods, too. Man invents gods because he's afraid of being alone, scared of an empty universe, scared of the darkling plain. That's why your men are converting, Dino, that's why people are going over. They've found God, or as much of a God as they're ever likely to find. The Union is a mass-mind, an immortal mass-mind, many in one, all love. The Shkeen don't die, dammit. No wonder they don't have the concept of an afterlife. They *know* there's a God. Maybe it didn't create the universe, but it's love, pure love, and they say that God is love, don't they? Or maybe what we call love is a tiny piece of God. I don't care, whatever it is, the Union is it. The end of the search for the Shkeen, and for Man too. We're alike after all, we're so alike it hurts."

Valcarenghi gave his exaggerated sigh. "Robb, you're overwrought. You sound like one of the Joined."

"Maybe that's just what I should be. Lya is. She's part of the Union now."

He blinked. "How do you know that?"

"She came to me last night in a dream."

"Oh. A dream."

"It was *true,* dammit. It's all true."

Valcarenghi stood, and smiled. "I believe you," he said. "That is, I believe that the Greeshka uses a psi-lure, a love lure if you will, to draw in its prey, something so powerful that it convinces men—even you—that it's God. Dangerous, of course. I'll have to think about this before taking action. We could guard the caves to keep humans out, but there are too many caves. And sealing off the Greeshka wouldn't help our relations with the Shkeen. But now it's my problem. You've done your job."

I waited until he was through. "You're wrong, Dino. This is real, no trick, no illusion. I *felt* it, and Lya too. The Greeshka hasn't even a yes-I-live, let alone a psi-lure strong enough to bring in Shkeen and men."

"You expect me to believe that God is an animal who lives in the caves of Shkea?"

"Yes."

"Robb, that's absurd, and you know it. You think the Shkeen have found the answer to the mysteries of creation. But look at them. The oldest civilized race in known space, but they've been stuck in the Bronze Age for fourteen thousand years. We came to *them*. Where are their spaceships? Where are their towers?"

"Where are our bells?" I said. "And our joy? They're happy, Dino. Are we? Maybe they've found what we're still looking for. Why the hell is man so driven, anyway? Why is he out to conquer the galaxy, the universe, whatever? Looking for God, maybe . . . ? Maybe. He can't find him anywhere, though, so on he goes, on and on, always looking. But always back to the same darkling plain in the end."

"Compare the accomplishments. I'll take humanity's record."

"Is it worth it?"

"I think so." He went to the window, and looked out. "We've got the only Tower on their world," he said, smiling, as he looked down through the clouds.

"They've got the only God in our universe," I told him. But he only smiled.

"All right, Robb," he said, when he finally turned from the window. "I'll keep all this in mind. And we'll find Lyanna for you."

My voice softened. "Lya is lost," I said. "I know that now. I will be too, if I wait. I'm leaving tonight. I'll book passage on the first ship out to Baldur."

He nodded. "If you like. I'll have your money ready." He grinned. "And we'll send Lya after you, when we find her. I imagine she'll be a little miffed, but that's your worry."

I didn't answer. Instead I shrugged, and headed for the tube. I was almost there when he stopped me.

"Wait," he said. "How about dinner tonight? You've done a good job for us. We're having a farewell party anyway, Laurie and me. She's leaving too."

"I'm sorry," I said.

His turn to shrug. "What for? Laurie's a beautiful person, and I'll miss her. But it's no tragedy. There are other beautiful people. I think she was getting restless with Shkea, anyway."

I'd almost forgotten my Talent, in my heat and the pain of my loss. I remembered it now. I read him. There was no sorrow, no pain, just a vague disappointment. And below that, his wall. Always the wall, keeping him apart, this man who was a first-name friend to everyone and an intimate to none. And on it, it was almost of if there were a sign that read, THIS FAR YOU GO, AND NO FARTHER.

"Come up," he said. "It should be fun." I nodded.

I asked myself, when my ship lifted off, why I was leaving.

Maybe to return home. We have a house on Baldur, away from the cities, on one of the undeveloped continents with only wilderness for a neighbor. It stands on a cliff, above a high waterfall that tumbles endlessly down into a shaded green pool. Lya and I swam there often, in the sunlit days between assignments. And afterwards we'd lie down nude in the shade of the orangespice trees, and make love on a carpet of silver moss. Maybe I'm returning to that. But it won't be the same without Lya, lost Lya . . .

Lya whom I could still have. Whom I could have now. It would be easy, so easy. A slow stroll into a darkened cave, a short sleep. Then Lya with me for eternity, in me, sharing me, being me, and I her. Loving and knowing more of each other than men can ever do. Union and joy, and no darkness again, ever. God. If I believed that, what I told Valcarenghi, then why did I tell Lya no?

Maybe because I'm not sure. Maybe I still hope, for something still greater and more loving than the Union, for the God they told me of so long ago. Maybe I'm taking a risk, because part of me still believes. But if I'm wrong . . . then the darkness, and the plain . . .

But maybe it's something else, something I saw in Valcarenghi, something that made me doubt what I had said. For man is more than Shkeen, somehow; there are men like Dino and Gourlay as well as Lya and Gustaffson, men who fear love and Union as much as they crave it. A dichotomy, then. Man has two primal urges, and the Shkeen only one? If so, perhaps there is a human answer, to reach and join and not be alone, and yet to still be men.

I do not envy Valcarenghi. He cries behind his wall, I think, and no one knows, not even he. And no one will ever know, and in the end he'll always be alone in smiling pain. No, I do not envy Dino.

Yet there is something of him in me, Lya, as well as much of you. And that is why I ran, though I loved you.

Laurie Blackburn was on the ship with me. I ate with her after liftoff, and we spent the evening talking over wine. Not a happy conversation, maybe, but a human one. Both of us needed someone, and we reached out.

Afterwards, I took her back to my cabin, and made love to her as fiercely as I could. Then, the darkness softened, we held each other and talked away the night.

"Adrift Just Off the Islets of Langerhans: Latitude 38° 54′ N, Longitude 77° 00′ 13″ W"

What a story title!

John Campbell, when he was in his prime, liked short titles, preferably one-word titles, because they fit on the cover very nicely.

I liked short titles, too, preferably one-word titles, because that made it easier for readers to discuss the story, and helped in that word-of-mouth advertising which is the only kind I'm ever likely to get.

Now look at Harlan's mistake—

One reader says enthusiastically to another, "I just read a great story. You've got to read it."

"Oh boy, what's the name?"

"It's 'Adrift Off the—' I mean 'Adrift Just Off the Islands—uh —'Islets of Something or Other' with some figures— Listen, this other story I read is called 'Nightfall,' you've got to read it."

But don't get Harlan wrong. He's playing for other stakes. He won the Hugo with it, didn't he? Well, the reason he won this Hugo was that by the time they got through printing up the title of this story there was no room to include the rest of the nominees.*

Anyway, I had occasion to use Harlan recently. I was doing a murder mystery (*Murder at the ABA*, Doubleday, 1976) and I needed a hero. Since ABA stands for "American Booksellers Association," I wanted someone who would naturally attend such a

---

* One of which was a story of my very own entitled "That Thou Art Mindful of Him." My fault. I should have called it "Mindful," then they might just barely have squeezed it in.

meeting, and I chose a writer. I wanted him to be fearfully intelligent so that he could solve the murder, and fearfully courageous so he could beat off the bad guys, and fearfully charming so he could get the girl, and fearfully nice so he could interest the reader. And it couldn't be me (my first thought) because I'm a character—an innocent bystander—in the book, so it had to be a friend of mine.

"Well," thought I to myself, "who do I know who is a writer, and who is fearfully intelligent, courageous, charming, and nice, and who is a friend of mine?"

That was easy. So I made my hero five feet two inches tall.†

Then I wrote to Harlan and asked if it would be all right. Harlan, who, underneath that assiduously cultivated outer armor composed exclusively of porcupine quills and crocodile scales, is the world's nicest pussycat, sent me a letter of permission and blessed the enterprise. I promptly stapled the letter to my contract.

My hero is named Darius Just and I love him—but not as much as I love Harlan.

---

† Height note from Ellison proofing the galleys: All the rest about me is dead on the button true; I am a terrific person. Only the height is wrong. As I have pointed out to Isaac, both in person and in print, I am not 5′ 2″; I am 5′ 5″. This makes the tenth such correction. And I wuv you, too, Ike.
—H.E.

14

ADRIFT JUST OFF THE ISLETS OF LANGERHANS: LATITUDE 38° 54′ N, LONGITUDE 77° 00′ 13″ W

As Moby Dick awoke one morning from uneasy dreams, he found himself changed in his bed of kelp into a monstrous Ahab.

Crawling in stages from the soggy womb of sheets, he stumbled into the kitchen and ran water into the teapot. There was lye in the corner of each eye. He put his head under the spigot and let the cold water rush around his cheeks.

Dead bottles littered the living room. One hundred and eleven empty bottles that had contained Robitussin and Romilar-CF. He padded through the debris to the front door and opened it a crack. Daylight assaulted him. "Oh, God," he murmured, and closed his eyes to pick up the folded newspaper from the stoop.

Once more in dusk, he opened the paper. The headline read: BOLIVIAN AMBASSADOR FOUND MURDERED, and the feature story heading column one detailed the discovery of the ambassador's body, badly decomposed, in an abandoned refrigerator in an empty lot in Secaucus, New Jersey.

The teapot whistled.

Naked, he padded toward the kitchen; as he passed the aquarium he saw that terrible fish was still alive, and this morning whistling like a bluejay, making tiny streams of bubbles that rose to burst on the scummy surface of the water. He paused be-

side the tank, turned on the light and looked in through the
drifting eddies of stringered algae. The fish simply would not
die. It had killed off every other fish in the tank—prettier fish,
friendlier fish, livelier fish, even larger and more dangerous fish
—had killed them all one by one, and eaten out the eyes. Now it
swam the tank alone, ruler of its worthless domain.

He had tried to let the fish kill itself, trying every form of neglect short of outright murder by not feeding it; but the pale,
worm-pink devil even thrived in the dark and filth-laden waters.

Now it sang like a bluejay. He hated the fish with a passion he
could barely contain.

He sprinkled flakes from a plastic container, grinding them between thumb and forefinger as experts had advised him to do it,
and watched the multi-colored granules of fish meal, roe, milt,
brine shrimp, day-fly eggs, oatflour and egg yolk ride on the surface for a moment before the detestable fish-face came snapping
to the top to suck them down. He turned away, cursing and hating the fish. It would not die. Like him, it would not die.

In the kitchen, bent over the boiling water, he understood for
the first time the true status of his situation. Though he was
probably nowhere near the rotting outer edge of sanity, he could
smell its foulness on the wind, coming in from the horizon; and
like some wild animal rolling its eyes at the scent of carrion and
the feeders thereon, he was being driven closer to lunacy every
day, just from the smell.

He carried the teapot, a cup and two tea bags to the kitchen
table and sat down. Propped open in a plastic stand used for
keeping cookbooks handy while mixing ingredients, the Mayan
Codex translations remained unread from the evening before. He
poured the water, dangled the tea bags in the cup, and tried to
focus his attention. The references to Itzamna, the chief divinity
of the Maya pantheon, and medicine, his chief sphere of
influence, blurred. Ixtab, the goddess of suicide, seemed more
apropos for this morning, this deadly terrible morning. He tried
reading, but the words only went in, nothing happened to them,
they didn't sing. He sipped tea and found himself thinking of the
chill, full circle of the Moon. He glanced over his shoulder at the
kitchen clock. Seven forty-four.

He shoved away from the table, taking the half-full cup of tea, and went into the bedroom. The impression of his body, where it had lain in tortured sleep, still indented the bed. There were clumps of blood-matted hair clinging to the manacles that he had riveted to metal plates in the headboard. He rubbed his wrists where they had been scored raw, slopping a little tea on his left forearm. He wondered if the Bolivian ambassador had been a piece of work he had tended to the month before.

His wrist watch lay on the bureau. He checked it. Seven forty-six. Slightly less than an hour and a quarter to make the meeting with the consultation service. He went into the bathroom, reached inside the shower stall and turned the handle till a fine needle-spray of icy water smashed the tiled wall of the stall. Letting the water run, he turned to the medicine cabinet for his shampoo. Taped to the mirror was an Ouchless Telfa finger bandage on which three lines had been neatly typed, in capitals:

THE WAY YOU WALK IS
THORNY, MY SON, THROUGH
NO FAULT OF YOUR OWN.

Then, opening the cabinet, removing a plastic bottle of herbal shampoo that smelled like friendly, deep forests, Lawrence Talbot resigned himself to the situation, turned and stepped into the shower, the merciless ice-laden waters of the Arctic pounding against his tortured flesh.

Suite 1544 of the Tishman Airport Center Building was a men's toilet. He stood against the wall opposite the door labeled MEN and drew the envelope from the inner breast pocket of his jacket. The paper was of good quality, the envelope crackled as he thumbed up the flap and withdrew the single sheet letter inside. It was the correct address, the correct floor, the correct suite. Suite 1544 was a men's toilet, nonetheless. Talbot started to turn away. It was a vicious joke; he found no humor in the situation; not in his present circumstances.

He took one step toward the elevators.

The door to the men's room shimmered, fogged over like a windshield in winter, and re-formed. The legend on the door had changed. It now read:

INFORMATION ASSOCIATES

Suite 1544 was the consultation service that had written the invitational letter on paper of good quality in response to Talbot's mail inquiry responding to a noncommittal but judiciously-phrased advertisement in *Forbes*.

He opened the door and stepped inside. The woman behind the teak reception desk smiled at him, and his glance was split between the dimples that formed and her legs, very nice, smooth legs, crossed and framed by the kneehole of the desk. "Mr. Talbot?"

He nodded. "Lawrence Talbot."

She smiled again. "Mr. Demeter will see you at once, sir. Would you like something to drink? Coffee? A soft drink?"

Talbot found himself touching his jacket where the envelope lay in an inner pocket. "No. Thank you."

She stood up, moving toward an inner office door, as Talbot said, "What do you do when someone tries to flush your desk?" He was not trying to be cute. He was annoyed. She turned and stared at him. There was silence in her appraisal, nothing more.

"Mr. Demeter is right through here, sir."

She opened the door and stood aside. Talbot walked past her, catching a scent of mimosa.

The inner office was furnished like the reading room of an exclusive men's club. Old money. Deep quiet. Dark, heavy woods. A lowered ceiling of acoustical tile on tracks, concealing a crawl space and probably electrical conduits. The pile rug of oranges and burnt umbers swallowed his feet to the ankles. Through a wall-sized window could be seen not the city that lay outside the building, but a panoramic view of Hanauma Bay, on the Koko Head side of Oahu. The pure aquamarine waves came in like undulant snakes, rose like cobras, crested out white, tunneled, and struck like asps at the blazing yellow beach. It was not a window; there were no windows in the office. It was a photograph. A deep, real photograph that was neither a projection nor a hologram. It was a wall looking out on another place entirely. Talbot knew nothing about exotic flora, but he was certain that the tall, razor-edged-leafed trees growing right down to beach's boundary were identical to those pictured in books depicting the Carboniferous period of the Earth before even the saurians had walked the land. What he was seeing had been gone for a very long time.

"Mr. Talbot. Good of you to come. John Demeter."

He came up from a wingback chair, extended his hand. Talbot took it. The grip was firm and cool. "Won't you sit down," Demeter said. "Something to drink? Coffee, perhaps, or a soft drink?" Talbot shook his head; Demeter nodded dismissal to the receptionist; she closed the door behind her, firmly, smoothly, silently.

Talbot studied Demeter in one long appraisal as he took the chair opposite the wingback. Demeter was in his early fifties, had retained a full and rich mop of hair that fell across his forehead in gray waves that clearly had not been touched up. His eyes were clear and blue, his features regular and jovial, his mouth wide and sincere. He was trim. The dark brown business suit was hand-tailored and hung well. He sat easily and crossed his legs, revealing black hose that went above the shins. His shoes were highly polished.

"That's a fascinating door, the one to your outer office," Talbot said.

"Do we talk about my door?" Demeter asked.

"Not if you don't want to. That isn't why I came here."

"I don't want to. So let's discuss your particular problem."

"Your advertisement. I was intrigued."

Demeter smiled reassuringly. "Four copywriters worked very diligently at the proper phraseology."

"It brings in business."

"The right kind of business."

"You slanted it toward smart money. Very reserved. Conservative portfolios, few glamors, steady climbers. Wise old owls."

Demeter steepled his fingers and nodded; an understanding uncle. "Directly to the core, Mr. Talbot: wise old owls."

"I need some information. Some special, certain information. How confidential is your service, Mr. Demeter?"

The friendly uncle, the wise old owl, the reassuring businessman understood all the edited spaces behind the question. He nodded several times. Then he smiled and said, "That *is* a clever door I have, isn't it? You're absolutely right, Mr. Talbot."

"A certain understated eloquence."

"One hopes it answers more questions for our clients than it poses."

Talbot sat back in the chair for the first time since he had entered Demeter's office. "I think I can accept that."

"Fine. Then why don't we get to specifics. Mr. Talbot, you're having some difficulty dying. Am I stating the situation succinctly?"

"Gently, Mr. Demeter."

"Always."

"Yes. You're on the target."

"But you have some problems, some rather unusual problems."

"Inner ring."

Demeter stood up and walked around the room, touching an astrolabe on a bookshelf, a cut glass decanter on a sideboard, a sheaf of *London Times*es held together by a wooden pole. "We are only information specialists, Mr. Talbot. We can put you on to what you need, but the effectation is your problem."

"If I have the *modus operandi,* I'll have no trouble taking care of getting it done."

"You've put a little aside."

"A little."

"Conservative portfolio? A few glamors, mostly steady climbers?"

"Bullseye, Mr. Demeter."

Demeter came back and sat down again. "All right, then. If you'll take the time to very carefully write out *precisely* what you want—I know generally, from your letter, but I want this *precise,* for the contract—I think I can undertake to supply the data necessary to solving your problem."

"At what cost?"

"Let's decide what it is you want, first, shall we?"

Talbot nodded. Demeter reached over and pressed a call button on the smoking stand beside the wingback. The door opened. "Susan, would you show Mr. Talbot to the sanctum and provide him with writing materials." She smiled and stood aside, waiting for Talbot to follow her. "And bring Mr. Talbot something to drink if he'd like it . . . some coffee? A soft drink, perhaps?" Talbot did not respond to the offer.

"I might need some time to get the phraseology down just right. I might have to work as diligently as your copywriters. It might take me a while. I'll go home and bring it in tomorrow."

Demeter looked troubled. "That might be inconvenient. That's why we provide a quiet place where you can think."

"You'd prefer I do it now."

"Inner ring, Mr. Talbot."

"You might be a toilet if I came back tomorrow."

"Bullseye."

"Let's go, Susan. Bring me a glass of orange juice if you have it." He preceded her through the door.

He followed her down the corridor at the far side of the reception room. He had not seen it before. She stopped at a door and opened it for him. There was an escritoire and a comfortable chair inside the small room. He could hear Muzak. "I'll bring you your orange juice," she said.

He went in and sat down. After a long time he wrote seven words on a sheet of paper.

Two months later, long after the series of visitations from silent messengers who brought rough drafts of the contract to be examined, who came again to take them away revised, who came again with counter-proposals, who came again to take away further revised versions, who came again—finally—with Demeter-signed finals, and who waited while he examined and initialed and signed the finals—two months later, the map came via the last, mute messenger. He arranged for the final installment of the payment to Information Associates that same day: he had ceased wondering where fifteen boxcars of maize—grown specifically as the Zuni nation had grown it—was of value.

Two days later, a small item on an inside page of the New York *Times* noted that fifteen boxcars of farm produce had somehow vanished off a railroad spur near Albuquerque. An official investigation had been initiated.

The map was very specific, very detailed; it looked accurate.

He spent several days with Grey's *Anatomy* and, when he was satisfied that Demeter and his organization had been worth the staggering fee, he made a phone call. The long distance operator turned him over to Inboard and he waited for the static-laden connection to be made. He insisted the Budapest operator on the other end let it ring twenty times, twice the number the phone company permitted per call. On the twenty-first ring it was picked up. Miraculously, the background noise-level dropped and he heard Victor's voice as though it was across the room.

"Yes! Hello!" Impatient, surly as always.

"Victor . . . Larry Talbot."

"Where are you calling from?"

"The States. How are you?"

"Busy. What do you want?"

"I have a project. I want to hire you and your lab."

"Forget it. I'm coming down to final moments on a project and I can't be bothered now."

The imminence of hangup was in his voice. Talbot cut in quickly. "How long do you anticipate?"

"Till what?"

"Till you're clear."

"Another six months inside, eight to ten if it gets muddy. I said: forget it, Larry. I'm *not* available."

"At least let's talk."

"No."

"Am I wrong, Victor, or do you owe me a little?"

"After all this time you're calling in debts?"

"They only ripen with age."

There was a long silence in which Talbot heard dead space being pirated off their line. At one point he thought the other man had racked the receiver. Then, finally, "Okay, Larry. We'll *talk*. But you'll have to come to me; I'm too involved to be hopping any jets."

"That's fine. I have free time." A slow beat, then he added, "Nothing but free time."

"*After* the full moon, Larry." It was said with great specificity.

"Of course. I'll meet you at the last place we met, at the same time, on the thirtieth of this month. Do you remember?"

"I remember. That'll be fine."

"Thank you, Victor. I appreciate this."

There was no response.

Talbot's voice softened: "How is your father?"

"Goodbye, Larry," he answered, and hung up.

They met on the thirtieth of that month, at moonless midnight, on the corpse barge that plied between Buda and Pesht. It was the correct sort of night: chill fog moved in a pulsing curtain up the Danube from Belgrade.

They shook hands in the lee of a stack of cheap wooden coffins and, after hesitating awkwardly for a moment, they embraced like brothers. Talbot's smile was tight and barely discernible by the withered illumination of the lantern and the barge's running light as he said, "All right, get it said so I don't have to wait for the other shoe to drop."

Victor grinned and murmured ominously.

> *"Even a man who is pure in heart*
> *"And says his prayers by night,*
> *"May become a wolf when the wolfbane blooms*
> *"And the Autumn moon shines bright."*

Talbot made a face. "And other songs from the same album."

"Still saying your prayers at night?"

"I stopped that when I realized the damned thing didn't scan."

"Hey. We aren't here getting pneumonia just to discuss forced rhyme."

The lines of weariness in Talbot's face settled into a joyless pattern. "Victor, I need your help."

"I'll listen, Larry. Further than that it's doubtful."

Talbot weighed the warning and said, "Three months ago I answered an advertisement in *Forbes,* the business magazine. Information Associates. It was cleverly-phrased, very reserved, small box, inconspicuously placed. Except to those who knew how to read it. I won't waste your time on details but the sequence went like this: I answered the ad, hinting at my problem as circuitously as possible without being completely impenetrable. Vague words about important money. I had hopes. Well, I hit with this one. They sent back a letter calling a meet. Perhaps another false trail, was what I thought . . . God knows there've been enough of those."

Victor lit a Sobranie Black & Gold and let the pungent scent of the smoke drift away on the fog. "But you went."

"I went. Peculiar outfit, sophisticated security system; I had a strong feeling they came from, well, I'm not sure where . . . or when."

Victor's glance was abruptly kilowatts heavier with interest. "*When,* you say? Temporal travelers?"

"I don't know."

"I've been waiting for something like that, you know. It's inevitable. And they'd certainly make themselves known eventually."

He lapsed into silence, thinking. Talbot brought him back sharply. "I don't know, Victor. I really don't. But that's not my concern at the moment.

"Oh. Right. Sorry, Larry. Go on. You met with them . . ."

"Man named Demeter. I thought there might be some clue there. The name. I didn't think of it at the time. The name Demeter, there was a florist in Cleveland, many years ago. But later, when I looked it up, Demeter, the Earth goddess, Greek mythology . . . no connection. At least, I don't think so.

"We talked. He understood my problem and said he'd undertake the commission. But he wanted it specific, what I required of him, wanted it specific for the contract—God knows how he would have enforced the contract, but I'm sure he could have— he had a *window,* Victor, it looked out on—"

Victor spun the cigarette off his thumb and middle finger, snapping it straight down into the blood-black Danube. "Larry, you're maundering."

Talbot's words caught in his throat. It was true. "I'm counting on you, Victor. I'm afraid it's putting my usual aplomb out of phase."

"All right, take it easy. Let me hear the rest of this and we'll see. Relax."

Talbot nodded and felt grateful. "I wrote out the nature of the commission. It was only seven words." He reached into his topcoat pocket and brought out a folded slip of paper. Victor unfolded the paper and read:

GEOGRAPHICAL COORDINATES
FOR LOCATION OF MY SOUL

Victor looked at the line of type long after he had absorbed its message. When he handed it back to Talbot, he wore a new, fresher expression. "You'll never give up, will you, Larry?"

"Did your father?"

"No." Great sadness flickered across the face of the man Talbot called Victor. "And," he added, tightly, after a beat, "he's been lying in a catatonia sling for sixteen years *because* he wouldn't give up." He lapsed into silence. Finally, softly, "It never hurts to know when to give up, Larry. Never hurts. Sometimes you've just got to leave it alone."

Talbot snorted softly with bemusement. "Easy enough for you to say, old chum. You're going to die."

"That wasn't fair, Larry."

"Then help me, dammit! I've gone further toward getting myself out of all this than I ever have. Now I need *you*. You've got the expertise."

"Have you sounded out 3M or Rand or even General Dynamics? They've got good people there."

"Damn you."

"Okay. Sorry. Let me think a minute."

The corpse barge cut through the invisible water, silent, fog-shrouded, without Charon, without Styx, merely a public service, a garbage scow of unfinished sentences, uncompleted errands, unrealized dreams. With the exception of these two, talking, the barge's supercargo had left decisions and desertions behind.

Then, Victor said, softly, talking as much to himself as to Talbot, "We could do it with microtelemetry. Either through direct microminiaturizing techniques or by shrinking a servomechanism package containing sensing, remote control, and guidance/manipulative/propulsion hardware. Use a saline solution to inject it into the bloodstream. Knock you out with 'Russian sleep' and/or tap into the sensory nerves so you'd perceive or control the device as if you were there . . . conscious transfer of point of view."

Talbot looked at him expectantly.

"No. Forget it," said Victor. "It won't do."

He continued to think. Talbot reached into the other's jacket pocket and brought out the Sobranies. He lit one and stood silently, waiting. It was always thus with Victor. He had to worm his way through the analytical labyrinth.

"Maybe the biotechnic equivalent: a tailored microorganism or slug . . . injected . . . telepathic link established. No. Too many flaws: possible ego/control conflict. Impaired perceptions. Maybe it could be a hive creature injected for multiple p.o.v." A pause, then, "No. No good."

Talbot drew on the cigarette, letting the mysterious Eastern smoke curl through his lungs. "How about . . . say, just for the sake of discussion, Victor said, "say the ego-id exists to some extent in each sperm. It's been ventured. Raise the consciousness in one cell and send it on a mission to . . . forget it, that's metaphysical bullshit. Oh, damn damn damn . . . this will take time and thought, Larry. Go away, let me think on it. I'll get back to you."

Talbot butted the Sobranie on the railing, and exhaled the final stream of smoke. "Okay, Victor. I take it you're interested sufficiently to work at it."

"I'm a scientist, Larry. That means I'm hooked. I'd have to be an idiot not to be . . . this speaks directly to what . . . to what my father . . ."

"I understand. I'll let you alone. I'll wait."

They rode across in silence, the one thinking of solutions, the other considering the problems. When they parted, it was with an embrace.

Talbot flew back the next morning, and waited through the nights of the full moon, knowing better than to pray. It only muddied the waters. And angered the gods.

When the phone rang, and Talbot lifted the receiver, he knew what it would be. He had known *every* time the phone had rung, for over two months. "Mr. Talbot? Western Union. We have a cablegram for you, from Moldava, Czechoslovakia."

"Please read it."

"It's very short, sir. It says, 'Come immediately. The trail has been marked.' It's signed, 'Victor.'"

He departed less than an hour later. The Learjet had been on the ready line since he had returned from Budapest, fuel tanks regularly topped-off and flight-plan logged. His suitcase had been packed for seventy-two days, waiting beside the door, visas and passport current, and handily stored in an inner pocket. When he departed, the apartment continued to tremble for some time with the echoes of his leaving.

The flight seemed endless, interminable; he *knew* it was taking longer than necessary.

Customs, even with high government clearances (all masterpieces of forgery) and bribes, seemed to be drawn out sadistically by the mustached trio of petty officials; secure, and reveling in their momentary power.

The overland facilities could not merely be called slow. They were reminiscent of the Molasses Man who cannot run till he's warmed-up and who, when he's warmed-up, grows too soft to run.

Expectedly, like the most suspenseful chapter of a cheap gothic novel, a fierce electrical storm suddenly erupted out of the mountains when the ancient touring car was within a few miles of Talbot's destination. It rose up through the steep mountain pass, hurtling out of the sky, black as a grave, and swept across the road obscuring everything.

The driver, a taciturn man whose accent had marked him as a Serbian, held the big saloon to the center of the road with the tenacity of a rodeo rider, hands at ten till and ten after midnight on the wheel.

"Mister Talbot."

"Yes?"

"It grow worse. Will I turn back?"

"How much farther?"

"Perhaps seven kilometer."

Headlights caught the moment of uprootment as a small tree by the roadside toppled toward them. The driver spun the wheel and accelerated. They rushed past as naked branches scraped across the boot of the touring car with the sound of fingernails on a blackboard. Talbot found he had been holding his breath. Death was beyond him, yet the menace of the moment denied that knowledge.

"I have to get there."

"Then I go on. Be at ease."

Talbot settled back. He could see the Serb smiling in the rearview mirror. Secure, he stared out the window. Branches of lightning shattered the darkness, causing the surrounding landscape to assume ominous, unsettling shapes.

Finally, he arrived.

The laboratory, an incongruous modernistic cube—bone white '

against the—again—ominous basalt of the looming prominences
—sat high above the rutted road. They had been climbing steadily for hours and now, like carnivores waiting for the most op-
portune moment, the Carpathians loomed all around them.

The driver negotiated the final mile and a half up the access
road to the laboratory with difficulty: tides of dark, topsoil-and-
twig-laden water rushed past them.

Victor was waiting for him. Without extended greetings he
had an associate take the suitcase, and he hurried Talbot to the
sub-ground floor theater where a half dozen technicians moved
quickly at their tasks, plying between enormous banks of controls and a huge glass plate hanging suspended from guy-wires
beneath the track-laden ceiling.

The mood was one of highly-charged expectancy; Talbot
could feel it in the sharp, short glances the technicians threw
him, in the way Victor steered him by the arm, in the uncanny
racehorse readiness of the peculiar-looking machines around
which the men and women swarmed. And he sensed in Victor's
manner that something new and wonderful was about to be born
in this laboratory. That perhaps . . . at last . . . after so terribly,
lightlessly long . . . peace waited for him in this white-tiled
room. Victor was fairly bursting to talk.

"Final adjustments," he said, indicating two female technicians
working at a pair of similar machines mounted opposite each
other on the walls facing the glass plate. To Talbot, they looked
like laser projectors of a highly complex design. The women
were tracking them slowly left and right on their gimbals, accompanied by soft electrical humming. Victor let Talbot study
them for a long moment, then said, "Not lasers. *Grasers*. Gamma
Ray Amplification by Stimulated Emission of Radiation. Pay attention to them, they're at least half the heart of the answer to
your problem."

The technicians took sightings across the room, through the
glass, and nodded at each another. Then the older of the two, a
woman in her fifties, called to Victor.

"On line, Doctor."

Victor waved acknowledgment, and turned back to Talbot.
"We'd have been ready sooner, but this damned storm. It's been

going on for a week. It wouldn't have hampered us but we had a freak lightning strike on our main transformer. The power supply was on emergency for several days and it's taken a while to get everything up to peak strength again."

A door opened in the wall of the gallery to Talbot's right. It opened slowly, as though it was heavy and the strength needed to force it was lacking. The yellow baked enamel plate on the door said, in heavy black letters, in French, PERSONNEL MONITORING DEVICES ARE REQUIRED BEYOND THIS ENTRANCE. The door swung fully open, at last, and Talbot saw the warning plate on the other side:

CAUTION

RADIATION

AREA

There was a three-armed, triangular-shaped design beneath the words. He thought of the Father, the Son, and the Holy Ghost. For no rational reason.

Then he saw the sign beneath, and had his rational reason: OPENING THIS DOOR FOR MORE THAN 30 SECONDS WILL REQUIRE A SEARCH AND SECURE.

Talbot's attention was divided between the doorway and what Victor had said. "You seem worried about the storm."

"Not worried," Victor said, "just cautious. There's no conceivable way it could interfere with the experiment, unless we had another direct hit, which I doubt—we've taken special precautions—but I wouldn't want to risk the power going out in the middle of the shot."

"The shot?"

"I'll explain all that. In fact, I *have* to explain it, so your mite will have the knowledge." Victor smiled at Talbot's confusion. "Don't worry about it." An old woman in a lab smock had come through the door and now stood just behind and to the right of Talbot, waiting, clearly, for their conversation to end so she could speak to Victor.

Victor turned his eyes to her. "Yes, Nadja?"

Talbot looked at her. An acid rain began falling in his stomach.

"Yesterday considerable effort was directed toward finding the cause of a high field horizontal instability," she said, speaking softly, tonelessly, a page of some specific status report. "The attendant beam blowup prevented efficient extraction." Eighty, if a day. Gray eyes sunk deep in folds of crinkled flesh the color of liver paste. "During the afternoon the accelerator was shut down to effect several repairs." Withered, weary, bent, too many bones for the sack. "The super pinger at C48 was replaced with a section of vacuum chamber; it had a vacuum leak." Talbot was in extreme pain. Memories came at him in ravening hordes, a dark wave of ant bodies gnawing at everything soft and folded and vulnerable in his brain. "Two hours of beam time were lost during the owl shift because a solenoid failed on a new vacuum valve in the transfer hall."

"Mother . . . ?" Talbot said, whispering hoarsely.

The old woman started violently, her head coming around and her eyes of settled ashes widening. "Victor," she said, terror in the word.

Talbot barely moved, and Victor took him by the arm and held him. "Thank you, Nadja; go down to target station B and log the secondary beams. Go right now."

She moved past them, hobbling, and quickly vanished through another door in the far wall, held open for her by one of the younger women.

Talbot watched her go, tears in his eyes.

"Oh my God, Victor. It was . . ."

"No, Larry, it wasn't."

"It was. So help me God it *was!* But *how,* Victor, tell me *how?*"

Victor turned him and lifted his chin with his free hand. "Look at me, Larry. *Damn it,* I said *look at me:* it wasn't. You're wrong."

The last time Lawrence Talbot had cried had been the morning he had awakened from sleep, lying under hydrangea shrubs in the botanical garden next to the Minneapolis Museum of Art, lying beside something bloody and still. Under his fingernails had been caked flesh and dirt and blood. That had been the time he learned about manacles and releasing oneself from them when in one state of consciousness, but not in another. Now he felt like crying. Again. With cause.

"Wait here a moment," Victor said. "Larry? Will you wait right here for me? I'll be back in a moment."

He nodded, averting his face, and Victor went away. While he stood there, waves of painful memory thundering through him, a door slid open into the wall at the far side of the chamber, and another white-smocked technician stuck his head into the room. Through the opening, Talbot could see massive machinery in an enormous chamber beyond. Titanium electrodes. Stainless steel cones. He thought he recognized it: a Cockroft-Walton pre-accelerator.

Victor came back with a glass of milky liquid. He handed it to Talbot.

"Victor—" the male technician called from the far doorway.

"Drink it," Victor said to Talbot, then turned to the technician.

"Ready to run."

Victor waved to him. "Give me about ten minutes, Karl, then take it up to the first phase shift and signal us." The technician nodded understanding and vanished through the doorway; the door slid out of the wall and closed, hiding the imposing chamberfull of equipment. "And that was part of the other half of the mystical, magical solution to your problem," the physicist said, smiling now like a proud father.

"What was that I drank?"

"Something to stabilize you. I can't have you hallucinating."

"I wasn't hallucinating. What was her name?"

"Nadja. You're wrong; you've never seen her before in your life. Have I ever lied to you? How far back do we know each other? I need your trust if this is going to be all the way."

"I'll be all right." The milky liquid had already begun to work. Talbot's face lost its flush, his hands ceased trembling.

Victor was very stern suddenly, a scientist without the time for sidetracks; there was information to be imparted. "Good; for a moment I thought I'd spent a great deal of time preparing . . . well," and he smiled again, quickly. "Let me put it this way: I thought for a moment no one was coming to my party."

Talbot gave a strained, tiny chuckle, and followed Victor to a bank of television monitors set into rolling frame-stacks in a corner. "Okay. Let's get you briefed." He turned on sets, one after another, till all twelve were glowing, each one holding a scene of dull-finished and massive installations.

Monitor #1 showed an endlessly long underground tunnel painted eggshell white. Talbot had spent much of his two-month wait reading; he recognized the tunnel as a view down the "straightaway" of the main ring. Gigantic bending magnets in their shockproof concrete cradles glowed faintly in the dim light of the tunnel.

Monitor #2 showed the linac tunnel.

Monitor #3 showed the rectifier stack of the Cockroft-Walton pre-accelerator.

Monitor #4 was a view of the booster. Monitor #5 showed the interior of the transfer hall. Monitors #6 through #9 revealed three experimental target areas and, smaller in scope and size, an internal target area supporting the meson, neutrino and proton areas.

The remaining three monitors showed research areas in the underground lab complex, the final one of which was the main hall itself, where Talbot stood looking into twelve monitors, in the twelfth screen of which could be seen Talbot standing looking into twelve . . .

Victor turned off the sets.

All Talbot could think of was the old woman called Nadja. It *couldn't* be. "Larry! What did you see?"

"From what I could see," Talbot said, "that looked to be a particle accelerator. And it looked as big as CERN's proton synchrotron in Geneva."

Victor was impressed. "You've been doing some reading."

"It behooved me."

"Well, well. Let's see if I can impress *you*. CERN's accelerator reaches energies up to 33 BeV; the ring underneath this room reaches energies of 15 GeV."

"Giga meaning trillion."

"You *have* been reading up, haven't you! Fifteen *trillion* electron volts. There's simply no keeping secrets from you, is there, Larry?"

"Only one."

Victor waited expectantly.

"Can you do it?"

"Yes. Meteorology says the eye is almost passing over us. We'll have better than an hour, more than enough time for the dangerous parts of the experiment."

"But you *can* do it."

"Yes, Larry. I don't like having to say it twice." There was no hesitancy in his voice, none of the "yes but" equivocations he'd always heard before. Victor had found the trail.

"I'm sorry, Victor. Anxiety. But if we're ready, why do I have to go through an indoctrination?"

Victor grinned wryly and began reciting, "As your Wizard, I am about to embark on a hazardous and technically unexplainable journey to the upper stratosphere. To confer, converse, and otherwise hobnob with my fellow wizards."

Talbot threw up his hands. "No more."

"Okay, then. Pay attention. If I didn't have to, I wouldn't; believe me, nothing is more boring than listening to the sound of my own lectures. But your mite has to have all the data *you* have. So listen. Now comes the boring—but incredibly informative—explanation."

Western Europe's CERN—*Conseil Européen pour la Recherche Nucléaire*—had settled on Geneva as the site for their Big Machine. Holland lost out on the rich plum because it was common knowledge the food was lousy in the Lowlands. A small matter, but a significant one.

The Eastern Bloc's CEERN—*Conseil de l'Europe de l'Est pour la Recherche Nucléaire*—had been forced into selecting this isolated location high in the White Carpathians (over such likelier and more hospitable sites as Cluj in Rumania, Budapest in Hungary and Gdańsk in Poland) because Talbot's friend Victor had selected this site. CERN had had Dahl and Wideroë and Goward and Adams and Reich; CEERN had Victor. It balanced. He could call the tune.

So the laboratory had been painstakingly built to his specifications, and the particle accelerator dwarfed the CERN Machine. It dwarfed the four-mile ring at the National Accelerator Lab in Batavia, Illinois. It was, in fact, the world's largest, most advanced "synchrophasotron."

Only seventy per cent of the experiments conducted in the underground laboratory were devoted to projects sponsored by CEERN. One hundred per cent of the staff of Victor's complex were personally committed to him, not to CEERN, not to the Eastern Bloc, not to philosophies or dogmas . . . to the man. So thirty per cent of the experiments run on the sixteen-mile-diameter accelerator ring were Victor's own. If CEERN knew—and it would have been difficult for them to find out—it said nothing. Seventy per cent of the fruits of genius was better than no per cent.

Had Talbot known earlier that Victor's research was thrust in the direction of actualizing advanced theoretical breakthroughs in the nature of the structure of fundamental particles, he would never have wasted his time with the pseudos and deadenders who had spent years on his problem, who had promised everything and delivered nothing but dust. But then, until Information Associates had marked the trail—a trail he had previously followed in every direction but the unexpected one that merged shadow with substance, reality with fantasy—until then, he had had no need for Victor's exotic talents.

While CEERN basked in the warmth of secure knowledge that their resident genius was keeping them in front in the Super Accelerator Sweepstakes, Victor was briefing his oldest friend on the manner in which he would gift him with the peace of death; the manner in which Lawrence Talbot would find his soul; the manner in which he would precisely and exactly go inside his own body.

"The answer to your problem is in two parts. First, we have to create a perfect simulacrum of you, a hundred thousand or a million times smaller than you, the original. Then, second, we have to *actualize* it, turn an image into something corporeal, material, something that exists. A miniature *you* with all the reality you possess, all the memories, all the knowledge."

Talbot felt very mellow. The milky liquid had smoothed out the churning waters of his memory. He smiled. "I'm glad it wasn't a difficult problem."

Victor looked rueful. "Next week I invent the steam engine. Get serious, Larry."

"It's that Lethe cocktail you fed me."

Victor's mouth tightened and Talbot knew he had to get hold of himself. "Go on, I'm sorry."

Victor hesitated a moment, securing his position of seriousness with a touch of free-floating guilt, then went on, "The first part of the problem is solved by using the Grasers we've developed. We'll shoot a hologram of you, using a wave generated not from the electrons of the atom, but from the nucleus . . . a wave a million times shorter, greater in resolution than that from a Laser." He walked toward the large glass plate hanging in the middle of the lab, Grasers trained on its center. "Come here."

Talbot followed him.

"Is this the holographic plate," he said, "it's just a sheet of photographic glass, isn't it?"

"Not this," Victor said, touching the ten-foot square plate, "*This!*" He put his finger on a spot in the center of the glass and Talbot leaned in to look. He saw nothing at first, then detected a faint ripple; and when he put his face as close as possible to the imperfection he perceived a light *moiré* pattern, like the surface of a fine silk scarf. He looked back at Victor.

"Microholographic plate," Victor said. "Smaller than an integrated chip. That's where we capture your spirit, white-eyes, a million times reduced. About the size of a single cell, maybe a red corpuscle."

Talbot giggled.

"Come on," Victor said wearily. "You've had too much to drink, and it's my fault. Let's get this show on the road. You'll be straight by the time we're ready . . . I just hope to God your mite isn't cockeyed."

They stood him, naked, in front of the ground photographic plate. The older of the female technicians aimed the Graser at him, there was a soft sound Talbot took to be some mechanism locking into position, and then Victor said, "All right, Larry, that's it."

He stared at them, expecting more.

"That's it?"

The technicians seemed very pleased, and amused at his reaction. "All done," said Victor. It had been that quick. He hadn't even seen the Graser wave hit and lock-in his image. "That's *it?*" he said again. Victor began to laugh. It spread through the lab. The technicians were clinging to their equipment; tears rolled down Victor's cheeks; everyone gasped for breath; and Talbot stood in front of the minute imperfection in the glass and felt like a retard.

"That's it?" he said again, helplessly.

After a long time, they dried their eyes and Victor moved him away from the huge plate of glass. "All done, Larry, and ready to go. Are you cold?"

Talbot's naked flesh was evenly polka dotted with goose-bumps. One of the technicians brought him a smock to wear, then ignored him. Talbot stood and watched. Clearly, he was no longer the center of attention.

Now the alternate Graser and the holographic plate ripple in the glass were the focuses of attention. Now the mood of released tension was past and the lines of serious attention were back in the faces of the lab staff. Now Victor was wearing an intercom headset, and Talbot heard him say, "All right, Karl. Bring it up to full power."

Almost instantly the lab was filled with the sound of generators phasing up. It became painful and Talbot felt his teeth begin to ache. It went up and up, a whine that climbed till it was beyond his hearing.

Victor made a hand signal to the younger female technician at the Graser behind the glass plate. She bent to the projector's sighting mechanism once, quickly, then cut it in. Talbot saw no light beam, but there was the same locking sound he had heard earlier, and then a soft humming, and a life-size hologram of himself, standing naked as he had been a few moments before, trembled in the air where he had stood. He looked at Victor questioningly. Victor nodded, and Talbot walked to the phantasm, passed his hand through it, stood close and looked into the clear brown eyes, noted the wide pore patterns in the flesh covering his nose, studied himself more closely than he had ever been able to do in a mirror. He felt: as if someone had walked over his grave.

Victor was talking to three male technicians, and a moment later they came to examine the hologram. They moved in with light meters and sensitive instruments that apparently were capable of gauging the sophistication and clarity of the ghost image. Talbot watched, fascinated and terrified. It seemed he was about to embark on the great journey of his life; a journey with a much-desired destination: surcease.

One of the technicians signaled Victor.

"It's pure," Victor said to Talbot. Then, to the younger female technician on the second Graser projector, "All right, Jana, move it out of there." She started up an engine and the entire projector apparatus turned on heavy rubber wheels and rolled out of the way. The image of Talbot, naked and vulnerable, a little sad to Talbot as he watched it fade and vanish like morning mist, had disappeared when the technician turned off the projector.

"All right, Karl," Victor was saying, "we're moving the pedestal in now. Narrow the aperture, and wait for my signal." Then, to Talbot, "Here comes your mite, old friend."

Talbot felt a sense of resurrection.

The older female technician rolled a four foot high stainless steel pedestal to the center of the lab, positioned it so the tiny, high-polished spindle atop the pedestal touched the very bottom of the faint ripple in the glass. It looked like, and was, an actualizing stage for the real test. The full-sized hologram had been a gross test to insure the image's perfection. Now came the creation of a living entity, a Lawrence Talbot, naked and the size of a single cell, possessing a consciousness and intelligence and memories and desires identical to Talbot's own.

"Ready, Karl?" Victor was saying.

Talbot heard no reply, but Victor nodded his head as if listening. Then he said, "All right, extract the beam!"

It happened so fast, Talbot missed most of it.

The micropion beam was composed of particles a million times smaller than the proton, smaller than the quark, smaller than the muon or the pion. Victor had termed them micropions. The slit opened in the wall, the beam was diverted, passed through the holographic ripple and was cut off as the slit closed again.

It had all taken a billionth of a second.

"Done," Victor said.

"I don't see anything," Talbot said, and realized how silly he must sound to these people. Of *course* he didn't see anything. There was nothing to see . . . with the naked eye. "Is he . . . is it there?"

"You're there," Victor said. He waved to one of the male technicians standing at a wall hutch of instruments in protective bays, and the man hurried over with the slim, reflective barrel of a microscope. He clipped it onto the tiny needle-pointed stand atop the pedestal in a fashion Talbot could not quite follow.

Then he stepped away, and Victor said, "Part two of your problem solved, Larry. Go look and see yourself."

Lawrence Talbot went to the microscope, adjusted the knob till he could see the reflective surface of the spindle, and saw himself in infinitely reduced perfection

staring up at himself. He recognized himself, though all he could see was a cyclopean brown eye staring down from the smooth glass satellite that dominated his sky.

He waved. The eye blinked.

Now it begins, he thought.

Lawrence Talbot stood at the lip of the huge crater that formed Lawrence Talbot's navel. He looked down into the bottomless pit with its atrophied remnants of umbilicus forming loops and protuberances, smooth and undulant and vanishing into utter darkness. He stood poised to descend and smelled the smells of his own body. First, sweat. Then the smells that wafted up from within. The smell of penicillin like biting down on tin foil with a bad tooth. The smell of aspirin, chalky and tickling the hairs of his nose like cleaning blackboard erasers by banging them together. The smells of rotted food, digested and turning to waste. All the odors rising up out of himself like a wild symphony of dark colors.

He sat down on the rounded rim of the navel and let himself slip forward.

He slid down, rode over an outcropping, dropped a few feet and slid again, tobogganing into darkness. He fell for only a short time, then brought up against the soft and yielding, faintly springy tissue plane where the umbilicus had been ligated. The darkness at the bottom of the hole suddenly shattered as blinding light filled the navel. Shielding his eyes, Talbot looked up the shaft toward the sky. A sun glowed there, brighter than a thousand novae. Victor had moved a surgical lamp over the hole to assist him. For as long as he could.

Talbot saw the umbra of something large moving behind the light; he strained to discern what it was: it seemed important to know what it was. And for an instant, before his eyes closed

against the glare, he thought he knew what it had been. Someone watching him, staring down past the surgical lamp that hung
above the naked, anesthetized body of Lawrence Talbot, asleep
on an operating table.

It had been the old woman, Nadja.

He stood unmoving for a long time, thinking of her.

Then he went to his knees and felt the tissue plane that
formed the floor of the navel shaft.

He thought he could see something moving beneath the surface, like water flowing under a film of ice. He went down onto
his stomach and cupped his hands around his eyes, putting his
face against the dead flesh. It was like looking through a pane of
isinglass. A trembling membrane through which he could see the
collapsed lumen of the atretic umbilical vein. There was no
opening. He pressed his palms against the rubbery surface and it
gave, but only slightly. Before he could find the treasure, he had
to follow the route of Demeter's map—now firmly and forever
consigned to memory—and before he could set foot upon that
route, he had to gain access to his own body.

But he had nothing with which to force that entrance.

Excluded, standing at the portal to his own body, Lawrence
Talbot felt anger rising within him. His life had been anguish
and guilt and horror, had been the wasted result of events over
which he had had no control. Pentagrams and full moons and
blood and never putting on even an ounce of fat because of a
diet high in protein, blood steroids healthier than any normal
adult male's, triglycerol and cholesterol levels balanced and
humming. And death forever a stranger. Anger flooded through
him. He heard an inarticulate little moan of pain, and fell forward, began tearing at the atrophied cord with teeth that had
been used for similar activity many times before. Through a
blood haze he knew he was savaging his own body, and it
seemed exactly the appropriate act of self-flagellation.

An outsider; he had been an outsider all his adult life, and
fury would permit him to be shut out no longer. With demonic
purpose he ripped away at the clumps of flesh until the membrane gave, at last, and a gap was torn through opening him to
himself . . .

And he was blinded by the explosion of light, by the rush of wind, by the passage of something that had been just beneath the surface writhing to be set free, and in the instant before he plummeted into unconsciousness he knew Castañeda's Don Juan had told the truth: a thick bundle of white cobwebby filaments, tinged with gold, fibers of light, shot free from the collapsed vein, rose up through the shaft and trembled toward the antiseptic sky.

A metaphysical, otherwise invisible beanstalk that trailed away above him, rising up and up and up as his eyes closed and he sank away into oblivion.

He was on his stomach, crawling through the collapsed lumen, the center, of the path the veins had taken back from the amniotic sac to the fetus. Propelling himself forward the way an infantry scout would through dangerous terrain, using elbows and knees, frog-crawling, he opened the flattened tunnel with his head just enough to get through. It was quite light, the interior of the world called Lawrence Talbot suffused with a golden luminescence.

The map had routed him out of this pressed tunnel through the inferior vena cava to the right atrium and thence through the right ventricle, the pulmonary arteries, through the valves, to the lungs, the pulmonary veins, crossover to the left side of the heart (left atrium, left ventricle), the aorta—bypassing the three coronary arteries above the aortic valves—and down over the arch of the aorta—bypassing the carotid and other arteries—to the celiac trunk where the arteries split in a confusing array: the gastro-duodenal to the stomach, the hepatic to the liver, the splenic to the spleen. And there, dorsal to the body of the diaphragm, he would drop down past the greater pancreatic duct to the pancreas itself. And there, among the islets of Langerhans, he would find, at the coordinates Information Associates had given him, he would find that which had been stolen from him one full-mooned night of horror so very long ago. And having found it, having assured himself of eternal sleep, not merely physical death from a silver bullet, he would stop his heart—how, he did not know, but he would—and it would all be ended for Lawrence Talbot, who had become what he had beheld. There, in the tail of the pancreas, supplied with blood by the splenic artery, lay the greatest treasure of all. More than doubloons, more than spices and silks, more than oil lamps used as djinn prisons by Solomon, lay final and sweet eternal peace, a release from monsterdom.

He pushed the final few feet of dead vein apart, and his head emerged into open space. He was hanging upside-down in a cave of deep orange rock.

Talbot wriggled his arms loose, braced them against what was clearly the ceiling of the cave, and wrenched his body out of the tunnel. He fell heavily, trying to twist at the last moment to catch the impact on his shoulders, and received a nasty blow on the side of the neck for his trouble.

He lay there for a moment, clearing his head. Then he stood and walked forward. The cave opened onto a ledge, and he walked out and stared at the landscape before him. The skeleton of something only faintly human lay tortuously crumpled against the wall of the cliff. He was afraid to look at it very closely.

He stared off across the world of dead orange rock, folded and rippled like a topographical view across the frontal lobe of a brain removed from its cranial casing.

The sky was a light yellow, bright and pleasant.

The grand canyon of his body was a seemingly horizonless tumble of atrophied rock, dead for millennia. He sought out and found a descent from the ledge, and began the trek.

There was water, and it kept him alive. Apparently, it rained more frequently here in this parched and stunned wasteland than appearance indicated. There was no keeping track of days or months, for there was no night and no day—always the same even, wonderful golden luminescence—but Talbot felt his passage down the central spine of orange mountains had taken him almost six months. And in that time it had rained forty-eight times, or roughly twice a week. Baptismal founts of water were filled at every downpour, and he found if he kept the soles of his naked feet moist, he could walk without his energy flagging. If he ate, he did not remember how often, nor what form the food had taken.

He saw no other signs of life.

Save an occasional skeleton lying against a shadowed wall of orange rock. Often, they had no skulls.

He found a pass through the mountains, finally, and crossed. He went up through foothills into lower, gentle slopes, and then up again, into cruel and narrow passages that wound higher and higher toward the heat of the sky. When he reached the summit, he found the path down the opposite side was straight and wide and easy. He descended quickly; only a matter of days, it seemed.

Descending into the valley, he heard the song of a bird. He followed the sound. It led him to a crater of igneous rock, quite large, set low among the grassy swells of the valley. He came upon it without warning, and trudged up its short incline, to stand at the volcanic lip looking down.

The crater had become a lake. The smell rose up to assault him. Vile, and somehow terribly sad. The song of the bird continued; he could see no bird anywhere in the golden sky. The smell of the lake made him ill.

Then as he sat on the edge of the crater, staring down, he realized the lake was filled with dead things, floating belly-up; purple and blue as a strangled baby, rotting white, turning slowly in the faintly rippled gray water; without features or limbs. He went down to the lowest outthrust of volcanic rock and stared at the dead things.

Something swam toward him. He moved back. It came on faster, and as it neared the wall of the crater, it surfaced, singing its bluejay song, swerved to rip a chunk of rotting flesh from the corpse of a floating dead thing, and paused only a moment as if to remind him that this was not his, Talbot's domain, but its own.

Like Talbot, the fish would not die.

Talbot sat at the lip of the crater for a long time, looking down into the bowl that held the lake, and he watched the corpses of dead dreams as they bobbed and revolved like maggoty pork in a gray soup.

After a time, he rose, walked back down from the mouth of the crater, and resumed his journey. He was crying.

When at last he reached the shore of the pancreatic sea, he found a great many things he had lost or given away when he was a child. He found a wooden machine gun on a tripod, painted olive drab, that made a rat-tat-tatting sound when a wooden handle was cranked. He found a set of toy soldiers, two companies, one Prussian and the other French, with a miniature Napoleon Bonaparte among them. He found a microscope kit with slides and petri dishes and racks of chemicals in nice little bottles, all of which bore uniform labels. He found a milk bottle filled with Indian head pennies. He found a hand puppet with the head of a monkey and the name *Roscoe* painted on the fabric glove with nail polish. He found a pedometer. He found a beautiful painting of a jungle bird that had been done with real feathers. He found a corncob pipe. He found a box of radio premiums: a cardboard detective kit with fingerprint dusting powder, invisible ink and a list of police band call codes; a ring with what seemed to be a plastic bomb attached, and when he pulled the red-finned rear section off the bomb, and cupped his hands around it in his palms, he could see little scintillae of light, deep inside the payload section; a china mug with a little girl and a dog running across one side; a decoding badge with a burning glass in the center of the red plastic dial.

But something was missing.

He could not remember what it was, but he knew it was important. As he had known it was important to recognize the shadowy figure who had moved past the surgical lamp at the top of the navel shaft, he knew whatever item was missing from this cache . . . was very important.

He took the boat anchored beside the pancreatic sea, and put all the items from the cache in the bottom of the watertight box under one of the seats. He kept out the large, cathedral-shaped radio, and put it on the bench seat in front of the oarlocks.

Then he unbeached the boat, and ran it out into the crimson water, staining his ankles and calves and thighs, and climbed aboard, and started rowing across toward the islets. Whatever was missing, was very important.

The wind died when the islets were barely in sight on the horizon. Looking out across the blood-red sea, Talbot sat becalmed at latitude 38° 54′ N, longitude 77° 00′ 13″ W.

He drank from the sea and was nauseated. He played with the toys in the watertight box. And he listened to the radio.

He listened to a program about a very fat man who solved murders, to an adaptation of *The Woman in the Window* with Edward G. Robinson and Joan Bennett, to a story that began in a great railroad station, to a mystery about a wealthy man who could make himself invisible by clouding the minds of others so they could not see him, and he enjoyed a suspense drama narrated by a man named Ernest Chapell in which a group of people descended in a bathyscaphe through the bottom of a mine shaft where, five miles down, they were attacked by pterodactyls. Then he listened to the news, broadcast by Graham MacNamee. Among the human interest items at the close of the program, Talbot heard the unforgettable MacNamee voice say:

"Datelined Columbus, Ohio; September 24th, 1973. Martha Nelson has been in an institution for the mentally retarded for 98 years. She is 102 years old and was first sent to Orient State Institute near Orient, Ohio, on June 25th, 1875. Her records were destroyed in a fire in the institution some time in 1882, and no one knows for certain why she is at the institute. At the time she was committed, it was known as the Columbus State Institute for the Feeble-Minded. 'She never had a chance,' said Dr. A. Z. Soforenko, appointed two months ago as superintendent of the institution. He said she was probably a victim of 'eugenic alarm,' which he said was common in the late 1800s. At that time some felt that because humans were made 'in God's image' the retarded must be evil or children of the devil, because they were not whole human beings. 'During that time,' Dr. Soforenko said, 'it was believed if you moved feeble-minded people out of a community and into an institution, the taint would never return to the community.' He went on to add, 'She was apparently trapped in that system of thought. No one can ever be sure if she actually *was* feeble-minded; it is a wasted life. She is quite coherent for her age. She has no known relatives and has had no contact with anybody but Institution staff for the last 78 or 80 years.'"

Talbot sat silently in the small boat, the sail hanging like a forlorn ornament from its single centerpole.

"I've cried more since I got inside you, Talbot, than I have in my whole life," he said, but could not stop. Thoughts of Martha Nelson, a woman of whom he had never before heard, of whom he would *never* have heard had it not been by chance by chance by chance he had heard by chance, by chance thoughts of her skirled through his mind like cold winds.

And the cold winds rose, and the sail filled, and he was no longer adrift, but was driven straight to the shore of the nearest islet. By chance.

He stood over the spot where Demeter's map had indicated he would find his soul. For a wild moment he chuckled, at the realization he had been expecting an enormous Maltese Cross or Capt. Kidd's "X" to mark the location. But it was only soft green sand, gentle as talc, blowing in dust-devils toward the blood-red pancreatic sea. The spot was midway between the low tide line and the enormous Bedlam-like structure that dominated the islet.

He looked once more, uneasily, at the fortress rising in the center of the tiny blemish of land. It was built square, seemingly carved from a single monstrous black rock . . . perhaps from a cliff that had been thrust up during some natural disaster. It had no windows, no opening he could see, though two sides of its bulk were exposed to his view. It troubled him. It was a dark god presiding over an empty kingdom. He thought of the fish that would not die, and remembered Nietzsche's contention that gods die when they lose their supplicants.

He dropped to his knees and, recalling the moment months before when he had dropped to his knees to tear at the flesh of his atrophied umbilical cord, he began digging in the green and powdery sand.

The more he dug, the faster the sand ran back into the shallow bowl. As in a nightmare, it ran back ceaselessly. He stepped into the middle of the depression and began slinging dirt back between his legs with both hands, a human dog excavating for a bone.

When his fingertips encountered the edge of the box, he yelped with pain as his nails broke.

He dug around the outline of the box, and then forced his bleeding fingers down through the sand to gain purchase under the buried shape. He wrenched at it, and it came loose. Heaving with tensed muscles, he freed it.

He took it to the edge of the beach and sat down.

It was just a box. A plain old wooden box, very much like an old cigar box, but larger. He turned it over and over and was not at all surprised to find it bore no arcane hieroglyphics or occult symbols. It wasn't that kind of treasure. Then he turned it right side up and pried open the lid. His soul was inside. It was not what he had expected to find, not at all. But it *was* what had been missing from the cache.

Holding it tightly in his fist, he walked up past the fast-filling hole in the green sand, toward the bastion on the high ground.

> *We shall not cease from exploration*
> *And the end of all our exploring*
> *Will be to arrive where we started*
> *And know the place for the first time.*
>   ——T. S. Eliot

Once inside the brooding darkness of the fortress—and finding the entrance had been disturbingly easier than he had expected—there was no way to go but down. The wet, black stones of the switchback stairways led inexorably downward into the bowels of the structure, clearly far beneath the level of the pancreatic sea. The stairs were steep, and each step had been worn into smooth curves by the pressure of feet that had descended this way since the dawn of memory. It was dark, but not so dark that Talbot could not see his way. There was no light, however. He did not care to think about how that could be.

When he came to the deepest part of the structure, having passed no rooms or chambers or openings along the way, he saw a doorway across an enormous hall, set into the far wall. He stepped off the last of the stairs, and walked to the door. It was built of crossed iron bars, as black and moist as the stones of the bastion. Through the interstices he saw something pale and still in a far corner of what could have been a cell.

There was no lock on the door.

It swung open at his touch.

Whoever lived in this cell had never tried to open the door; or having tried, and succeeded, had decided not to leave.

He moved into deeper darkness.

A long time of silence passed, and finally he stooped to help her to her feet. It was like lifting a sack of dead flowers, brittle and surrounded by dead air incapable of holding even the memory of fragrance.

He took her in his arms and carried her.

"Close your eyes against the light, Martha," he said, and started back up the long stairway to the golden sky.

Lawrence Talbot sat up on the operating table. He opened his eyes and looked at Victor. He smiled a peculiarly gentle smile. For the first time since they had been friends, Victor saw all torment cleansed from Talbot's face.

"It went well," he said. Talbot nodded.

They grinned at each other.

"How're your cryogenic facilities?" Talbot asked.

Victor's brows drew down in bemusement. "You want me to freeze you? I thought you'd want something more permanent . . . say, in silver."

"Not necessary."

Talbot looked around. He saw her standing against the far wall by one of the Grasers. She looked back at him with open fear. He slid off the table, wrapping the sheet upon which he had rested around himself, a makeshift toga. It gave him a patrician look.

He went to her and looked down into her ancient face. "Nadja," he said softly. After a long moment she looked up at him. He smiled and for an instant she was a girl again. She averted her gaze. He took her hand, and she came with him, to the table, to Victor.

"I'd be deeply grateful for a running account, Larry," the physicist said. So Talbot told him; all of it.

"My mother, Nadja, Martha Nelson, they're all the same," Talbot said, when he came to the end, "all wasted lives."

"And what was in the box?" Victor said.

"How well do you do with symbolism and cosmic irony, old friend?"

"Thus far I'm doing well enough with Jung and Freud," Victor said. He could not help but smile.

Talbot held tightly to the old technician's hand as he said, "It was an old, rusted Howdy Doody button."

Victor turned around.

When he turned back, Talbot was grinning. "That's not cosmic irony, Larry . . . it's slapstick," Victor said. He was angry. It showed clearly.

Talbot said nothing, simply let him work it out.

Finally Victor said, "What the hell's *that* supposed to signify? Innocence?"

Talbot shrugged. "I suppose if I'd known, I wouldn't have lost it in the first place. That's what it was, and that's what it is. A little metal pinback about an inch and a half in diameter, with that cockeyed face on it, the orange hair, the toothy grin, the pug nose, the freckles, all of it, just the way he always was." He fell silent, then after a moment added. "It seems right."

"And now that you have it back, you don't *want* to die."

"I don't *need* to die."

"And you want me to freeze you."

"Both of us."

Victor stared at him with disbelief. "For God's sake, Larry!"

Nadja stood quietly, as if she could not hear them.

"Victor, listen: Martha Nelson is in there. A wasted life. Nadja is out here. I don't know why or how or what did it . . . but . . . a wasted life. Another wasted life. I want you to create her mite, the same way you created mine, and send her inside. He's waiting for her, and he can make it right, Victor. All right, at last. He can be with her as she regains the years that were stolen from her. He can be—*I* can be—her father when she's a baby, her playmate when she's a child, her buddy when she's maturing, her boy friend when she's a young girl, her suitor when she's a young woman, her lover, her husband, her companion as she grows old. Let her be all the women she was never permitted to be, Victor. Don't steal from her a second time. And when it's over, it will start again . . ."

"*How,* for Christ sake, how the hell *how?* Talk sense, Larry! What is all this metaphysical crap?"

"I don't *know* how; it just is! I've been there, Victor, I was there for months, maybe years, and I never changed, never went to the wolf; there's no Moon there . . . no night and no day, just golden light and warmth, and I can try to make restitution. I can give back two lives. *Please,* Victor!"

The physicist looked at him without speaking. Then he looked at the old woman. She smiled up at him, and then, with arthritic fingers, removed her clothing.

When she came through the collapsed lumen, Talbot was waiting for her. She looked very tired, and he knew she would have to rest before they attempted to cross the orange mountains. He helped her free herself from the ceiling of the cave, and laid her down on soft, pale yellow moss he had carried back from the islets of Langerhans during the long trek with Martha Nelson. Side-by-side, the two old women lay on the moss, and Nadja fell asleep almost immediately. He stood over them, looking at their faces.

They were identical.

Then he went out on the ledge and stood looking toward the spine of the orange mountains. The skeleton held no fear for him now. He felt a sudden sharp chill in the air and knew Victor had begun the cryogenic preservation.

He stood that way for a long time, the little metal button with the sly, innocent face of a mythical creature painted on its surface in four brilliant colors held tightly in his left hand.

After a while, he heard the crying of a baby, just one baby, from inside the cave, and turned to return for the start of the easiest journey he had ever made.

Somewhere, a terrible devil-fish suddenly flattened its gills, turned slowly belly-up, and sank into darkness.

Remember I said in the general introduction that I don't say anything about the stories in these story introductions because I didn't select them and it was therefore inappropriate for me to make comments?

But I'm only human and I would like to make a comment on *classes* of stories. There are, after all, all kinds and varieties of science fiction (which is good, for the more kinds and varieties, the more flourishing and healthy the field). The trouble is that I don't like them all equally. Nobody does. Everyone has his preferences.

There are the funny or grisly science-fantasies, and the heroic or bloody sword-and-sorceries, and the artistic or puzzling new-waves, and the clever or satiric social-futures, and so on. All have their points; each pleases some of the readers most of the time and all of the readers some of the time.

But then there is something which is called, for want of any other title, "hard science fiction." That is the kind of science fiction that deals with science. The authors know science and use part of the story wordage to explain some interesting scientific point that manages to drive the story, set up the catastrophe, or resolve the problem.

That's the kind of stuff I like to write and that's the kind of stuff I like to read. Most of the writers who do it, like myself and Arthur Clarke and Hal Clement, are old-timers dating back to the early days of the Campbell era, and that would ordinarily make me feel as though we are part of a vanishing breed. I would be sad because all the soft science fiction in the world wouldn't compensate me (and the others who think like me, if any) for the loss of the hard.

But then I realize that there are new hard science fiction writers, too, entering the field all the time. There's Larry Niven, for instance, who had one story in Volume Two and two stories in Volume Three and who has won Hugos in the novel category as well. And when I think of that, I'm glad, and I feel that the world may survive after all.

15

THE HOLE MAN

One day Mars will be gone.

Andrew Lear says that it will start with violent quakes, and end hours or days later, very suddenly. He ought to know. It's all his fault.

Lear also says that it won't happen for from years to centuries. So we stay, Lear and the rest of us. We study the alien base for what it can tell us, while the center of the world we stand on is slowly eaten away. It's enough to give a man nightmares.

It was Lear who found the alien base.

We had reached Mars: fourteen of us, in the cramped bulbous life-support system of the *Percival Lowell*. We were circling in orbit, taking our time, correcting our maps and looking for anything that thirty years of Mariner probes might have missed.

We were mapping mascons, among other things. Those mass concentrations under the lunar maria were almost certainly left by good-sized asteroids, mountains of rock falling silently out of the sky until they struck with the energies of thousands of fusion bombs. Mars has been cruising through the asteroid belt for four billion years. Mars would show bigger and better mascons. They would affect our orbits.

So Andrew Lear was hard at work, watching pens twitch on graph paper as we circled Mars. A bit of machinery fell along-side the *Percival Lowell*, rotating. Within its thin shell was a weighted double lever system, deceptively simple: a Forward Mass Detector. The pens mapped its twitchings.

Over Sirbonis Palus, they began mapping strange curves.

Another man might have cursed and tried to fix it. Andrew

Lear thought it out, then sent the signal that would stop the free-falling widget from rotating.

It had to be rotating to map a stationary mass.

But now it was mapping simple sine waves.

Lear went running to Captain Childrey.

Running? It was more like trapeze artistry. Lear pulled himself along by handholds, kicked off from walls, braked with a hard push of hands or feet. Moving in free fall is hard work when you're in a hurry, and Lear was a forty-year-old astrophysicist, not an athlete. He was blowing hard when he reached the control bubble.

Childrey—who *was* an athlete—waited with a patient, slightly contemptuous smile while Lear caught his breath.

He already thought Lear was crazy. Lear's words only confirmed it. "Gravity for sending signals? Dr. Lear, will you please quit bothering me with your weird ideas. I'm busy. We all are."

This was not entirely unfair. Some of Lear's enthusiasms were peculiar. Gravity generators. Black holes. He thought we should be searching for Dyson spheres: stars completely enclosed by an artificial shell. He believed that mass and inertia were two separate things: that it should be possible to suck the inertia out of a spacecraft, say, so that it could accelerate to near lightspeed in a few minutes. He was a wide-eyed dreamer, and when he was flustered he tended to wander from the point.

"You don't understand," he told Childrey. "Gravity radiation is harder to block than electromagnetic waves. Patterned gravity waves would be easy to detect. The advanced civilizations in the galaxy may all be communicating by gravity. Some of them may even be modulating pulsars—rotating neutron stars. That's where Project Ozma went wrong: they were only looking for signals in the electromagnetic spectrum."

Childrey laughed. "Sure. Your little friends are using neutron stars to send you messages. What's that got to do with us?"

"Well, look!" Lear held up the strip of flimsy, nearly weightless paper he'd torn from the machine. "I got this over Sirbonis Palus. I think we ought to land there."

"We're landing in Mare Cimmerium, as you perfectly well know. The lander is already deployed and ready to board. Dr.

Lear, we've spent four days mapping this area. It's flat. It's in a green-brown area. When spring comes next month, we'll find out whether there's life there! And everybody wants it that way except you!"

Lear was still holding the graph paper before him like a shield. "Please. Take one more circuit over Sirbonis Palus."

Childrey opted for the extra orbit. Maybe the sine waves convinced him. Maybe not. He would have liked inconveniencing the rest of us in Lear's name, to show him for a fool.

But the next pass showed a tiny circular feature in Sirbonis Palus. And Lear's mass indicator was making sine waves again.

The aliens had gone. During our first few months we always expected them back any minute. The machinery in the base was running smoothly and perfectly, as if the owners had only just stepped out.

The base was an inverted pie plate two stories high, and windowless. The air inside was breathable, like Earth's air three miles up, but with a bit more oxygen. Mars's air is far thinner, and poisonous. Clearly they were not of Mars.

The walls were thick and deeply eroded. They leaned inward against the internal pressure. The roof was somewhat thinner, just heavy enough for the pressure to support it. Both walls and roof were of fused Martian dust.

The heating system still worked—and it was also the lighting system: grids in the ceiling glowing brick red. The base was always ten degrees too warm. We didn't find the off switches for almost a week: they were behind locked panels. The air system blew gusty winds through the base until we fiddled with the fans.

We could guess a lot about them from what they'd left behind. They must have come from a world smaller than Earth, circling a red dwarf star in close orbit. To be close enough to be warm enough, the planet would have to be locked in by tides, turning one face always to its star. The aliens must have evolved on the lighted side, in a permanent red day, with winds constantly howling over the border from the night side.

And they had no sense of privacy. The only doorways that had doors in them were airlocks. The second floor was a hexagonal metal gridwork. It would not block you off from your friends on the floor below. The bunk room was an impressive expanse of mercury-filled waterbed, wall to wall. The rooms were too small and cluttered, the furniture and machinery too close to the doorways, so that at first we were constantly bumping elbows and knees. The ceilings were an inch short of six feet high on both floors, so that we tended to walk stooped even if we were short enough to stand upright. Habit. But Lear was just tall enough to knock his head if he stood up fast, anywhere in the base.

We thought they must have been smaller than human. But their padded benches seemed human-designed in size and shape. Maybe it was their minds that were different: they didn't need psychic elbow room.

The ship had been bad enough. Now this. Within the base was instant claustrophobia. It put all of our tempers on hair triggers.

Two of us couldn't take it.

Lear and Childrey did not belong on the same planet.

With Childrey, neatness was a compulsion. He had enough for all of us. During those long months aboard *Percival Lowell*, it was Childrey who led us in calisthenics. He flatly would not let anyone skip an exercise period. We eventually gave up trying.

Well and good. The exercise kept us alive. We weren't getting the healthy daily exercise anyone gets walking around the living room in a one-gravity field.

But after a month on Mars, Childrey was the only man who still appeared fully dressed in the heat of the alien base. Some of us took it as a reproof, and maybe it was, because Lear had been the first to doff his shirt for keeps. In the mess Childrey would inspect his silverware for water spots, then line it up perfectly parallel.

On Earth, Andrew Lear's habits would have been no more than a character trait. In a hurry, he might choose mismatched socks. He might put off using the dishwasher for a day or two if he were involved in something interesting. He would prefer a house that looked "lived in." God help the maid who tried to clean up his study. He'd never be able to find anything afterward.

He was a brilliant but one-sided man. Backpacking or skin

diving might have changed his habits—in such pursuits you learn not to forget any least trivial thing—but they would never have tempted him. An expedition to Mars was something he simply could not turn down. A pity, because neatness is worth your life in space.

You don't leave your fly open in a pressure suit.

A month after the landing, Childrey caught Lear doing just that.

The "fly" on a pressure suit is a soft rubber tube over your male member. It leads to a bladder, and there's a spring clamp on it. You open the clamp to use it. Then you close the clamp and open an outside spigot to evacuate the bladder into vacuum.

Similar designs for women involve a catheter, which is hideously uncomfortable. I presume the designers will keep trying. It seems wrong to bar half the human race from our ultimate destiny.

Lear was addicted to long walks. He loved the Martian desert scene: the hard violet sky and the soft blur of whirling orange dust, the sharp close horizon, the endless emptiness. More: he needed the room. He was spending all his working time on the alien communicator, with the ceiling too close over his head and everything else too close to his bony elbows.

He was coming back from a walk, and he met Childrey coming out. Childrey noticed that the waste spigot on Lear's suit was open, the spring broken. Lear had been out for hours. If he'd had to go, he might have bled to death through flesh ruptured by vacuum.

We never learned all that Childrey said to him out there. But Lear came in very red about the ears, muttering under his breath. He wouldn't talk to anyone.

The NASA psychologists should not have put them both on that small a planet. Hindsight is wonderful, right? But Lear and Childrey were each the best choice for competence coupled to the kind of health they would need to survive the trip. There were astrophysicists as competent and as famous as Lear, but they were decades older. And Childrey had a thousand spaceflight hours to his credit. He had been one of the last men on the moon.

Individually, each of us was the best possible man. It was a damn shame.

The aliens had left the communicator going, like everything else in the base. It must have been hellishly massive, to judge by the thick support pillars slanting outward beneath it. It was a bulky tank of a thing, big enough that the roof had to bulge slightly to give it room. That gave Lear about a square meter of the only head room in the base.

Even Lear had no idea why they'd put it on the second floor. It would send through the first floor, or through the bulk of a planet. Lear learned that by trying it, once he knew enough. He beamed a dot-dash message through Mars itself to the Forward Mass Detector aboard *Lowell*.

Lear had set up a Mass Detector next to the communicator, on an extremely complex platform designed to protect it from vibration. The Detector produced waves so sharply pointed that some of us thought they could *feel* the gravity radiation coming from the communicator.

Lear was in love with the thing.

He skipped meals. When he ate he ate like a starved wolf. "There's a heavy point-mass in there," he told us, talking around a mouthful of food, two months after the landing. "The machine uses electromagnetic fields to vibrate it at high speed. Look—" He picked up a toothpaste tube of tuna spread and held it in front of him. He vibrated it rapidly. Heads turned to watch him around the zigzagged communal table in the alien mess. "I'm making gravity waves now. But they're too mushy because the tube's too big, and their amplitude is virtually zero. There's something very dense and massive in that machine, and it takes a hell of a lot of field strength to keep it there."

"What is it?" someone asked. "Neutronium? Like at the heart of a neutron star?"

Lear shook his head and took another mouthful. "That size, neutronium wouldn't be stable. I think it's a quantum black hole. I don't know how to measure its mass yet."

I said, "A *quantum* black hole?"

Lear nodded happily. "Luck for me. You know, I was against

the Mars expedition. We could get a lot more for our money by exploring the asteroids. Among other things, we might have found if there are really quantum black holes out there. But this one's already captured!" He stood up, being careful of his head. He turned in his tray and went back to work.

I remember we stared at each other along the zigzag mess table. Then we drew lots . . . and I lost.

The day Lear left his waste spigot open, Childrey had put a restriction on him. Lear was not to leave the base without an escort.

Lear had treasured the aloneness of those walks. But it was worse than that. Childrey had given him a list of possible escorts: half a dozen men Childrey could trust to see to it that Lear did nothing dangerous to himself or others. Inevitably they were the men most thoroughly trained in space survival routines, most addicted to Childrey's own compulsive neatness, least likely to sympathize with Lear's way of living. Lear was as likely to ask Childrey himself to go walking with him.

He almost never went out any more. I knew exactly where to find him.

I stood beneath him, looking up through the gridwork floor.

He'd almost finished dismantling the protective panels around the gravity communicator. What showed inside looked like parts of a computer in one spot, electromagnetic coils in most places, and a square array of pushbuttons that might have been the aliens' idea of a typewriter. Lear was using a magnetic induction sensor to try to trace wiring without actually tearing off the insulation.

I called, "How you making out?"

"No good," he said. "The insulation seems to be one hundred per cent perfect. Now I'm afraid to open it up. No telling how much power is running through there, if it needs shielding that good." He smiled down at me. "Let me show you something."

"What?"

He flipped a toggle above a dull gray circular plate. "This thing is a microphone. It took me a while to find it. I am Andrew Lear, speaking to whoever may be listening." He switched it off, then ripped paper from the Mass Indicator and showed me squiggles interrupting smooth sine waves. "There. The sound of my voice in gravity radiation. It won't disappear until it's reached the edges of the universe."

"Lear, you mentioned quantum black holes there. What's a quantum black hole?"

"Um. You know what a black hole is."

"I ought to." Lear had educated us on the subject, at length, during the months aboard *Lowell*.

When a not too massive star has used up its nuclear fuel, it collapses into a white dwarf. A heavier star—say, 1.44 times the mass of the sun and larger—can burn out its fuel, then collapse into itself until it is ten kilometers across and composed solely of neutrons packed edge to edge: the densest matter in this universe.

But a big star goes further than that. When a really massive star runs its course . . . when the radiation pressure within is no longer strong enough to hold the outer layers against the star's own ferocious gravity . . . then it can fall into itself entirely, until gravity is stronger than any other force, until it is compressed past the Swartzchild radius and effectively leaves the universe. What happens to it then is problematical. The Swartzchild radius is the boundary beyond which nothing can climb out of the gravity well, not even light.

The star is gone then, but the mass remains: a lightless hole in space, perhaps a hole into another universe.

"A collapsing star can leave a black hole," said Lear. "There may be bigger black holes, whole galaxies that have fallen into themselves. But there's no other way a black hole can form, *now*."

"So?"

"There was a time when black holes of all sizes could form. That was during the Big Bang, the explosion that started the expanding universe. The forces in that blast could have compressed little local vortices of matter past the Swartzchild radius. What that left behind—the smallest ones, anyway—we call quantum black holes."

I heard a distinctive laugh behind me as Captain Childrey walked into view. The bulk of the communicator would have hidden him from Lear, and I hadn't heard him come up. He called, "Just how big a thing are you talking about? Could I pick one up and throw it at you?"

"You'd disappear into one that size," Lear said seriously. "A black hole the mass of the Earth would only be a centimeter across. No, I'm talking about things from ten-to-the-minus-fifth grams on up. There could be one at the center of the sun—"

"Eek!"

Lear was trying. He didn't like being kidded, but he didn't know how to stop it. Keeping it serious wasn't the way, but he didn't know that either. "Say, ten-to-the-seventeenth grams in mass and ten-to-the-minus-eleven centimeters across. It would be swallowing a few atoms a day."

"Well, at least you know where to find it," said Childrey. "Now all you have to do is go after it."

Lear nodded, still serious. "There could be quantum black holes in asteroids. A small asteroid could capture a quantum black hole easily enough, especially if it was charged; a black hole can hold a charge, you know—"

"Ri-ight."

"All we'd have to do is check out a small asteroid with the Mass Detector. If it masses more than it should, we push it aside and see if it leaves a black hole behind."

"You'd need little teeny eyes to see something that small. Anyway, what would you do with it?"

"You put a charge on it, if it hasn't got one already, and electromagnetic fields. You can vibrate it to make gravity; then you manipulate it with radiation. I think I've got one in here," he said, patting the alien communicator.

"Ri-ight," said Childrey, and he went away laughing.

Within a week the whole base was referring to Lear as the Hole Man, the man with the black hole between his ears.

It hadn't sounded funny when Lear was telling me about it. The rich variety of the universe . . . But when Childrey talked about the black hole in Lear's Anything Box, it sounded hilarious.

Please note: Childrey did not misunderstand anything Lear had said. Childrey wasn't stupid. He merely thought Lear was crazy. He could not have gotten away with making fun of Lear, not among educated men, without knowing exactly what he was doing.

Meanwhile the work went on.

There were pools of Marsdust, fascinating stuff, fine enough to behave like viscous oil, and knee-deep. Wading through it wasn't dangerous, but it was very hard work, and we avoided it. One day Brace waded out into the nearest of the pools and started feeling around under the dust. Hunch, he said. He came up with some eroded plastic-like containers. The aliens had used the pool as a garbage dump.

We were having little luck with chemical analysis of the base materials. They were virtually indestructible. We learned more about the chemistry of the alien visitors themselves. They had left traces of themselves on the benches and on the communal waterbed. The traces had most of the chemical components of protoplasm, but Arsvey found no sign of DNA. Not surprising, he said. There must be other giant organic molecules suitable for gene coding.

The aliens had left volumes of notes behind. The script was a mystery, of course, but we studied the photographs and diagrams. A lot of them were notes on anthropology!

The aliens had been studying Earth during the first Ice Age.

None of us were anthropologists, and that was a damn shame. We never learned if we'd found anything new. All we could do was photograph the stuff and beam it up to *Lowell*. One thing was sure: the aliens had left very long ago, and they had left the lighting and air systems running and the communicator sending a carrier wave.

For us? Who else?

The alternative was that the base had been switched off for some six hundred thousand years, then come back on when something detected *Lowell* approaching Mars. Lear didn't believe it. "If the power had been off in the communicator," he said, "the mass wouldn't be in there any more. The fields have to be going to hold it in place. It's smaller than an atom; it'd fall through anything solid."

So the base power system had been running for all that time. What the hell could it be? And where? We traced some cables

and found that it was under the base, under several yards of
Marsdust fused to lava. We didn't try to dig through that.

The source was probably geophysical: a hole deep into the
core of the planet. The aliens might have wanted to dig such a
hole to take core samples. Afterward they would have set up a
generator to use the temperature difference between the core
and the surface.

Meanwhile, Lear spent some time tracing down the power
sources in the communicator. He found a way to shut off the carrier wave. Now the mass, if there was a mass, was at rest in
there. It was strange to see the Forward Mass Detector pouring
out straight lines instead of drastically peaked sine waves.

We were ill-equipped to take advantage of these riches. We
had been fitted out to explore Mars, not a bit of civilization from
another star. Lear was the exception. He was in his element,
with but one thing to mar his happiness.

I don't know what the final argument was about. I was engaged on another project.

The Mars lander still had fuel in it. NASA had given us plenty
of fuel to hover while we looked for a landing spot. After some
heated discussion, we had agreed to take the vehicle up and
hover it next to the nearby dust pool on low thrust.

It worked fine. The dust rose up in a great soft cloud and went
away toward the horizon, leaving the pond bottom covered with
otherworldly junk. And more! Arsvey started screaming at Brace
to back off. Fortunately Brace kept his head. He tilted us over to
one side and took us away on a gentle curve. The backblast
never touched the skeletons.

We worked out there for hours, being very finicky indeed.
Here was another skill none of us would own to, but we'd read
about how careful an archaeologist has to be, and we did our
best. Traces of water had had time to turn some of the dust to
natural cement, so that some of the skeletons were fixed to the
rock. But we got a couple free. We put them on stretchers and
brought them back. One crumbled the instant the air came hissing into the lock. We left the other outside.

The aliens had not had the habit of taking baths. We'd set up
a bathtub with very tall sides, in a room the aliens had reserved

for some incomprehensible ritual. I had stripped off my pressure suit and was heading for the bathtub, very tired, hoping that nobody would be in it.

I heard the voices before I saw them.

Lear was shouting.

Childrey wasn't, but his voice was a carrying one. It carried mockery. He was standing between the supporting pillars. His hands were on his hips, his teeth gleamed white, his head was thrown back to look up at Lear.

He finished talking. For a time neither of them moved. Then Lear made a sound of disgust. He turned away and pushed one of the buttons on what might have been an alien typewriter keyboard.

Childrey looked startled. He slapped at his right thigh and brought the hand away bloody. He stared at it, then looked up at Lear. He started to ask a question.

He crumpled slowly in the low gravity. I got to him before he hit the ground. I cut his pants open and tied a handkerchief over the blood spot. It was a small puncture, but the flesh was puckered above it on a line with his groin.

Childrey tried to speak. His eyes were wide. He coughed, and there was blood in his mouth.

I guess I froze. How could I help if I couldn't tell what had happened? I saw a blood spot on his right shoulder, and I tore the shirt open and found another tiny puncture wound.

The doctor arrived.

It took Childrey an hour to die, but the doctor had given up much earlier. Between the wound in his shoulder and the wound in his thigh, Childrey's flesh had been ruptured in a narrow line that ran through one lung and his stomach and part of his intestinal tract. The autopsy showed a tiny, very neat hole drilled through the hipbones.

We looked for, and found, a hole in the floor beneath the communicator. It was the size of a pencil lead, and packed with dust.

"I made a mistake," Lear told the rest of us at the inquest. "I should never have touched that particular button. It must have switched off the fields that held the mass in place. It just dropped. Captain Childrey was underneath."

And it had gone straight through him, eating the mass of him as it went.

"No, not quite," said Lear. "I'd guessed it massed about ten-to-the-fourteenth grams. That only makes it ten-to-the-minus-sixth Angstrom across, much smaller than an atom. It wouldn't have absorbed much. The damage was done to Childrey by tidal effects as it passed through him. You saw how it pulverized the material of the floor."

Not surprisingly, the subject of murder did come up.

Lear shrugged it off. "Murder with what? Childrey didn't believe there was a black hole in there at all. Neither did many of you." He smiled suddenly. "Can you imagine what the trial would be like? Imagine the prosecuting attorney trying to tell a jury what he thinks happened. First he's got to tell them what a black hole is. Then a quantum black hole. Then he's got to explain why he doesn't have the murder weapon, and where he left it, freely falling through Mars! And if he gets that far without being laughed out of court, he's still got to explain how a thing smaller than an atom could hurt anyone!"

But didn't Dr. Lear know the thing was dangerous? Could he not have guessed its enormous mass from the way it behaved?

Lear spread his hands. "Gentlemen, we're dealing with more variables than just mass. Field strength, for instance. I might have guessed its mass from the force it took to keep it there, but did any of us expect the aliens to calibrate their dials in the metric system?"

Surely there must have been safeties to keep the fields from being shut off accidentally. Lear must have bypassed them.

"Yes, I probably did, accidentally. I did quite a lot of fiddling to find out how things worked."

It got dropped there. Obviously there would be no trial. No ordinary judge or jury could be expected to understand what the attorneys would be talking about. A couple of things never did get mentioned.

For instance: Childrey's last words. I might or might not have repeated them if I'd been asked to. They were: "All right, show me! Show it to me or admit it isn't there!"

As the court was breaking up I spoke to Lear with my voice

lowered. "That was probably the most unique murder weapon in history."

He whispered, "If you said that in company I could sue for slander."

"Yeah? Really? Are *you* going to explain to a jury what you think I implied happened?"

"No, I'll let you get away with it this time."

"Hell, you didn't get away scot-free yourself. What are you going to study now? The only known black hole in the universe, and you let it drop through your fingers."

Lear frowned. "You're right. Partly right, anyway. But I knew as much about it as I was going to, the way I was going. Now . . . I stopped it vibrating in there, then took the mass of the entire setup with the Forward Mass Sensor. Now the black hole isn't in there any more. I can get the mass of the black hole by taking the mass of the communicator alone."

"Oh."

"And I can cut the machine open, see what's inside. How they controlled it. Damn it, I wish I were six years old."

"What? Why?"

"Well . . . I don't have the times straightened out. The math is chancy. Either a few years from now, or a few centuries, there's going to be a black hole between Earth and Jupiter. It'll be big enough to study. I think about forty years."

When I realized what he was implying, I didn't know whether to laugh or scream. "Lear, you can't think that something that small could absorb Mars!"

"Well, remember that it absorbs everything it comes near. A nucleus here, an electron there . . . and it's not just waiting for atoms to fall into it. Its gravity is ferocious, and it's falling back and forth through the center of the planet, sweeping up matter. The more it eats, the bigger it gets, with its volume going up as the cube of the mass. Sooner or later, yes, it'll absorb Mars. By then it'll be just less than a millimeter across—big enough to see."

"Could it happen within thirteen months?"

"Before we leave? Hmm." Lear's eyes took on a faraway look. "I don't think so. I'll have to work it out. The math is chancy . . ."

AFTERWORD

I started these volumes by making a fuss over the fact I had never won a Hugo. Winning three since then leaves me unsatisfied.

No, I'm not greedy. I'm logical. As I explained, one of the Hugos was for a non-fiction science column, one for a novel series, one for an individual novel.

Not one of them was for any of the shorter categories—novellas, novelettes, or short stories—which are included in the various volumes of the Hugo winners. So though twenty-five different authors have been included in the three volumes so far, with anywhere from one to five stories apiece, I myself am not represented.

Well, in 1976, I published a novelette which *may* finally make it. If it is nominated, it will come up for a vote in the thirty-fifth convention, to be held in Miami, Florida, in 1977. That's a little far for me, but I'm thinking of taking a train or something and going there.

After all, if I win, taking the train will be worth it.

If I don't win, of course, I will just give the train back.

APPENDIX

The Hugo Awards

1953–1961 inclusive—See Volume One
1962–1970 inclusive—See Volume Two

1971: 29th Convention—Boston

NOVEL—RINGWORLD by Larry Niven
NOVELLA—"Ill Met in Lankhmar" by Fritz Leiber
SHORT STORY—"Slow Sculpture" by Theodore Sturgeon
PROFESSIONAL MAGAZINE—*The Magazine of Fantasy and Science Fiction*
PROFESSIONAL ARTIST—Leo & Diane Dillon
FAN MAGAZINE—*Locus*, Charles & Dena Brown, eds.
FAN ARTIST—Alicia Austin
FAN WRITER—Richard Geis

1972: 30th Convention—Los Angeles

NOVEL—TO YOUR SCATTERED BODIES GO by Philip Jose Farmer
NOVELLA—"The Queen of Air and Darkness" by Poul Anderson
SHORT STORY—"Inconstant Moon" by Larry Niven
PROFESSIONAL MAGAZINE—*The Magazine of Fantasy and Science Fiction*
PROFESSIONAL ARTIST—Frank Kelly Freas
DRAMATIC PRESENTATION—"A Clockwork Orange"
FAN MAGAZINE—*Locus*, Charles & Dena Brown, eds.
FAN ARTIST—Tim Kirk
FAN WRITER—Harry Warner, Jr.

1973: 31st Convention—Toronto

NOVEL—THE GODS THEMSELVES by Isaac Asimov

NOVELLA—"The Word for World Is Forest" by Ursula K. Le Guin

NOVELETTE—"Goat Song" by Poul Anderson

SHORT STORY—"The Meeting" by Frederik Pohl & C. M. Kornbluth

"Eurema's Dam" by R. A. Lafferty

PROFESSIONAL EDITOR—Ben Bova

PROFESSIONAL ARTIST—Frank Kelly Freas

DRAMATIC PRESENTATION—"Slaughterhouse Five"

FAN MAGAZINE—*Energumen*, Michael & Susan Glicksohn, eds.

FAN ARTIST—Tim Kirk

FAN WRITER—Terry Carr

1974: 32nd Convention—Washington

NOVEL—RENDEZVOUS WITH RAMA by Arthur C. Clarke

NOVELLA—"The Girl Who Was Plugged In" by James Tiptree, Jr.

NOVELETTE—"The Deathbird" by Harlan Ellison

SHORT STORY—"The Ones Who Walk Away from Omelas" by Ursula K. Le Guin

PROFESSIONAL EDITOR—Ben Bova

DRAMATIC PRESENTATION—"Sleeper"

PROFESSIONAL ARTIST—Frank Kelly Freas

FAN MAGAZINE—*Algol*, Andy Porter, ed.

The Alien Critic by Richard E. Geis, ed.

FAN ARTIST—Tim Kirk

FAN WRITER—Susan Wood

SPECIAL HUGO AWARD—Chesley Bonestell

1975: 33rd Convention—Melbourne

NOVEL—THE DISPOSSESSED by Ursula K. Le Guin

NOVELLA—"A Song for Lya" by George R. R. Martin

NOVELETTE—"Adrift Just Off the Islets of Langerhans: Latitude 38° 54′ N, Longitude 77° 00′ 13″ W" by Harlan Ellison

SHORT STORY—"The Hole Man" by Larry Niven

DRAMATIC PRESENTATION—"Young Frankenstein"

PROFESSIONAL EDITOR—Ben Bova
PROFESSIONAL ARTIST—Frank Kelly Freas
FAN MAGAZINE—*The Alien Critic* by Richard Geis, ed.
FAN WRITER—Richard Geis
FAN ARTIST—Bill Rotsler
SPECIAL HUGO AWARDS—Donald A. Wollheim
Walt Lee